No Tombstones in the Sea

A Voyage Back to Hell

by

Dan Keough

RoseDog Books

PITTSBURGH, PENNSYLVANIA 15222

ISBN # 0-8059-9827-6
Printed in the United States of America

First Printing

For additional information or to order additional books,
please write:
RoseDog Publishing
701 Smithfield Street
Pittsburgh, Pennsylvania 15222
U.S.A.
1-800-834-1803
Or visit our web site and on-line bookstore at
www.rosedogbookstore.com

To all the veterans of
America's forgotten war

Memorandum to returning service personnel is reprinted through the courtesy of the Public Affairs Office, COMNAVFE, Yokosuka Naval Base. Pages 457-459.

Author's Note:
It is not necessary to refer to the glossary at the rear of this book to understand the narrative. It is included only as a service to the reader.

Cover Design by:
C.L. Mohn

Table of Contents

There is a port of no return, where ships
May ride at anchor for a little space
And then, some starless night, the cable slips,
Leaving an eddy at the mooring place...
Gulls, veer no longer. Sailor, rest your oar.
No tangled wreckage will be washed ashore.

Leslie Nelson Jennings
"Lost Harbor"

Chapter I - "Tin Can"

Commander Owen Garrett Royal, USN, smiled as he returned the exaggerated salute of the marine sentry. He presented his identification and walked on through the turnstile at the entrance to the fleet landing. Moored to the left of the pier was a small warship. The commander recognized her as a seaplane tender. Probably the *Floyds Bay* back from another Far East tour, he observed casually, not bothering to look at the bow number to confirm his supposition. Two crewmen in dungarees were playing a hose upon the single 5-inch gun mounted on the squat little vessel's foc'sle. The water hissed and splashed off the long gray gun barrel elevated against the flawless California sky causing Royal to quicken his pace to dodge the dirt and spray now raining down from the tender. He continued on toward the boat pool at the far end of the pier, his easy stride broken once more as he stepped aside to avoid a collision with a bouncing football followed closely by a hatless apprentice seaman who had just missed a forward pass.

"Sorry, sir!" the young man blurted out nervously, his line of sight zeroing-in on the officer's three gold cuff stripes. He started to raise his hand in salute forgetting for an instant that his head was uncovered.

With an easy underarm motion, Royal flipped the ball to the sailor and resumed his pace, walking with a military bearing that would draw the envy of a Coldstream Guard. Tall and spare, Royal prided himself on maintaining the same weight at 36 as he had on the day he graduated from the Naval Academy. In line with his modest nature, however, he attributed the credit to genetics, admitting to himself that he was never one to pass up an opportunity to sample the culinary specialties of the countless foreign ports he had visited during his 16 years of naval service.

The ladder leading to the boat-pool landing creaked each time the water brushed the pilings. A husky voiced chief bo'sun on the small platform below was shouting orders to the coxswains of the numerous launches and personnel boats circling to approach the landing. A patch of yellow-brown smoke wafted up from the stern exhaust of an open forty-footer.

"Got any boats for the *Prairie*, chief?"

The chief glanced at his clipboard. "One due in about ten minutes, Commander."

Royal scanned his watch, it was almost noon. From the North Island landing, he could see the business district of San Diego spread out across the bay and the submarine piers below Harbor Drive. The harbor was clustered with naval vessels of every type and size. There were carriers and "LST's", transports and repair ships, and huge tenders with their destroyer divisions nested alongside. The commander's interest was focused on one of the tenders, the *Prairie*, for it was among her brood that his new command was waiting.

The large white number on the bow of the *Prairie's* most outboard destroyer appeared to be "503." Royal was disappointed, he had hoped to see the "505" that would identify her as the *Charles P. Field*. He wondered which of the remaining three destroyers was his...his, he liked the word, especially since he had just about abandoned hope of ever getting a sea command. Like a true professional, Royal had reconciled himself to being a good exec...a good exec for other captains. Now things would be different he thought confidently as he watched a motor whaleboat pull out from the far side of the *Prairie* and point its nose toward the fleet landing.

Commander Royal was a confirmed sentimentalist so it was natural that his thoughts should skip back to a June morning in '37 when as a newly commissioned ensign he had waited on this same creaking pier for the launch that would ferry him to the *Arizona*. He could almost see the old 'wagon' sitting out there in the bay, her two fighting towers gray against the hilly smudge of green that formed Point Loma; her wooden planking, bleached and gleaming from the morning holystone as if diamonds had been haphazardly spewed about her decks. *Arizona* was a happy ship even for a buck ensign. He looked back on those formative years as his most rewarding in the navy, for they introduced him to a world of travel and adventure far beyond any he had marveled at during the Saturday matinee as a boy growing up in Boise, Idaho.

Owen Garrett Royal had detached from the *Arizona* just three weeks before Chuichi Nagumo led his *Kido Butai* against Pearl Harbor. He had left for assignment to the gunnery department of heavy cruiser *Indianapolis*, then flagship of Scouting Force Pacific Fleet. This was considered a choice billet for any young officer in the pre-war regular navy, and Royal was not so naïve that he didn't recognize so obvious a signal from the Bureau of Personnel that his star was on the rise. However, on that most infamous of Sundays, Lieutenant (Jg.) Royal was far too busy to be thinking about future admiral's stripes. Perched high up in the cruiser's main battery director, he was engaged in a simulated bombardment of Johnston Island, unaware that back at Oahu, 1,100 of his former shipmates were fighting what was to be their first and final battle. And while he had not requested transfer to the cruiser, he would always retain a feeling of guilt for not being at 'battleship row' on that December morning manning his old post as gun captain for *Arizona's* Mount 51.

Eight months later, he would leave the equally ill-fated *Indianapolis* to venture in harm's way aboard another cruiser and two successive destroyers. The string of gold battle stars almost obscuring his Pacific Campaign ribbon testified to his presence at Tassafaronga, Kolombangara, Vella Gulf, Cape St. George, Surigao Strait and a long roster of other lethal encounters that climaxed with the fiery onslaught of the "Divine Wind" off Iwo Jima and Okinawa.

It seemed odd, he thought, to be dredging up the war on such a significant day, and his thoughts immediately focused on Candace. She was the most beautiful and gifted woman he had ever known, and he had no doubt that marrying her had been the high point in his life. She'd be joining him here soon in Southern California. He had to be the luckiest guy in the whole damn navy…taking command of a battle proven man-of-war and having a wife like Candace to share his good fortune. With the *Field* assigned to training reservists, he knew that he would have plenty of time ashore to spend with her, not like the last few years when he was only able to see her infrequently between seven-month tours in the Mediterranean. He wondered how she'd adjust to La Jolla's rather quaint life style after five years on Madison Avenue. Coming out here to join him meant a big promotion but he was certain that this was purely a secondary consideration. The essential thing was that they would now be together.

Royal doubted that Candace would ever adapt to the life of the traditional navy wife, but that really didn't matter…he knew how much her work and career meant to her. Anyway, they could now start making plans to raise a family. She loved kids as much as he did so it was certainly time they got serious about having some of their own.

Candace should be in seventh heaven out here, he reassured himself. After all, she'd been runner-up for the title of "Miss Connecticut," and he'd never known anyone who could fill out a bathing suit the way she could. He'd last had the pleasure of observing that fact two summers ago at the Hamptons when even the lifeguards couldn't keep their eyes off her. He didn't mind though, and actually enjoyed watching the attention his beautiful blonde wife received from males wherever they went. It didn't bother him since he knew she'd never be unfaithful. Royal loved her more than life itself and he had no doubt that her feelings for him were the same.

As much as he adored Candace, he found it hard to understand how she could find career satisfaction in the phrenetic atmosphere of an ad agency. Besides, Candace was so forthright and honest, she seemed completely out of place in a world of half-truths and hard sell. Yet she managed to reach the upper echelons of her organization while still shy of thirty. Royal hated to admit, even to himself, that he resented his wife's achievements, but he was still traditional enough to believe that the husband should be the principal breadwinner. He tried not to dwell on the fact that although he was eight years older than Candace, her annual paycheck nearly tripled his. He dismissed the thought, telling himself this certainly wasn't the time or place for negative thinking. High noon in San Diego, a crisp March breeze blowing in from the sea, and a twenty-one hundred-ton destroyer awaiting him out there in the harbor…the world lay at his feet.

The commander paid scant attention to the second-class petty officer passing near the ladder. He returned the sailor's salute automatically, his mind still savoring the things that were and the things that would be. Royal didn't hear the sailor ask the chief bo'sun about the *Field*.

"She's out in the bay, moored with those 'cans' alongside the *Prairie*. That's her boat coming in now," the burly bo'sun grunted as he bit the end off his cigar and spat it into the water almost hitting a nearby personnel boat. Soon the motor whaleboat from the destroyer tender came gliding up to the landing.

The petty officer placed his sea bag on the concrete platform, shaking it forcefully until its bulkier contents had fallen smoothly in place. Then tightening the mouth of the bag, he slung it up over his shoulder. Conscious of the age long regulation about juniors entering a boat first, the sailor lowered his gear into the stern quarter and jumped in behind the boat's engineer. Commander Royal quickly followed, and the chief immediately ordered the coxswain to, "cast off and return to the *Prairie*." The engine sputtered and began to turn; the 26-footer cleared the confines of the boat pool and headed out into the bay.

Commander Royal sat forward, his face meeting the noon breeze from the open channel fresh with the smell of sea moss. A Martin Mariner flying boat sluggishly taxied past whipping up a heavy spray. Gradually gaining speed the patrol bomber lifted off the water with the ungainliness, Royal thought, of a drunken pterodactyl. The gull-winged aircraft circled the harbor once, then faded in the talcum clouds now forming over Coronado.

The whaleboat teetered, then dipped abruptly as it crossed the choppy wake left by the big seaplane. As Royal bent low to avoid the sudden spray, his glance inadvertently fell upon the sailor's sea bag and for the first time he became aware of his fellow passenger. LOGAN K.F. 384-68-92 USNR was stenciled on the bag in half-worn black lettering.

The sailor showed little interest in the panoramic view of the Pacific Fleet at rest in San Diego Harbor. Occasionally the wind would lift the broad collar of his dress blue jumper flapping it hard against the back of his head and neck. His chest bore no service ribbons but the left sleeve of his obviously new and well pressed uniform carried the emblem that identified him as a radarman-second class.

Royal was quick to notice the contrast between the crisp white piping on the sailor's collar and cuffs, and the faded, almost yellow canvas of the much used sea bag nearby. Reservist, recently recalled to active duty, the commander concluded even before he had read the entire stencil.

The radarman was in his late twenties and handsome with curly brown hair and clean-cut Celtic features. His face was boyish with bright blue eyes, but Royal could clearly detect an expression of bold assurance if not outright impudence. A possible troublemaker for some unsuspecting skipper, the commander decided, then chastised himself for making such a prejudgment. He certainly should be given the benefit of the doubt, Royal thought. After all, he is wearing a second class petty officer's "crow," and a radarman's at that. Having recently taken leave of the Sixth Fleet, Royal was keenly aware that the shortage of experienced radar and sonar operators had become a fleet wide problem by March of 1952.

"Are you reporting for duty on the *Prairie?*" Royal asked in a friendly tone.

"No, sir. I'm assigned to the *Field,*" the petty officer answered with noticeable lack of enthusiasm.

Royal smiled, recalling the sympathy he had so recently expended on that unsuspecting skipper. "I see by the stencil on your sea bag that you're a reservist. Have you been reactivated long?"

"Two weeks tomorrow, commander."

"The navy certainly didn't lose any time assigning you to a ship, did…"

"No, sir, they sure as hell didn't!" Logan cut in angrily.

Appreciative of the circumstances, Royal chose to ignore the sailor's bad manners and breach of naval courtesy. "Where are you from?" he asked, more to tactfully change the subject than out of genuine interest.

"Connecticut, just north of Bridgeport, but I've been living and working in Manhattan since '48."

Logan's words never registered. At that instant the whaleboat passed close to the nest of destroyers and the *Field's* bow came clearly into view.

"There she is! five-o-five!" Royal half shouted unable to restrain his fervor as he pointed to the large white bow number blatant and bold against the subdued gray of the hull.

The *Field* was third in line outboard of the tender and she had the dubious distinction of being the only destroyer in the nest still retaining her original pole mast.

While all four ships were *Fletcher* class, each of her three sister ships was sporting the newer tripod foremast devised to better support the weight of the latest electronic equipment. An old "Sugar Charlie" air-search antenna topped the *Field's* foremast, giving the destroyer an antiquated, almost malformed appearance alongside her now trimmer sisters. Probably original 1943 issue, Royal thought fearfully. Then he noticed that she was still carrying two banks of torpedo tubes, a clear indication that the ship could not have received more than a limited modernization, and possibly not even that. Royal was painfully aware that the forward torpedo tubes mounted between the two smokestacks of *Fletcher* class, as well as all other active U.S. destroyers, had long been removed in favor of increased anti-aircraft armament.

Now the commander wondered if the entire ship was little more than a leftover relic of the Second World War. He was particularly concerned about the condition of her engines. What if they haven't been fully overhauled? Royal frowned. He knew that the *Field* had been reactivated from the "mothball fleet" at Charleston, but so too had her three sisters, and all had recommissioned at approximately the same time. Why did he have to get the lemon?... why after waiting so long for a sea command must it start off with a handicap? His thoughts were muted by the loud clang of the coxswain's bell which signaled the whale-boat's engineer to cut the motor, allowing the 26-footer to coast the remaining distance around the *Prairie's* bow to the midships ladder on the tender's unob-structed side.

The warrant gunner assigned to the *Prairie's* quarterdeck watch saluted smartly and assigned his messenger-of-the-watch to escort Royal to the *Charles P. Field*. The radarman presented his orders and after a cursory examination, was per-mitted to continue on to the *Field* as best he could and with a stern reminder not to step on any of the tender's fresh paint-work during his long and circuitous jour-ney around the mother ship's fantail. Enjoying the privileges of rank, Commander Royal's route via the *Prairie's* thwartships passageway was decidedly more direct.

The quarterdeck of each destroyer was linked to the next by a length of planking. Royal noted the freshly painted, almost immaculate appearance of each warship as he made his way out to the *Field*. He was relieved to see that *DD-505* appeared to be as clean and sparkling as her three sisters. Unfortunately, the paint seemed to be the only new thing the ship had received since her first commis-sioning in 1943.

The *Field's* quarterdeck watch on this momentous day had been entrusted to the pride of Georgia, Ashton Bites, bo'sun mate-third. Newly rated, the twenty-two-year old was one of the few relatively conscientious petty officers assigned to the *Field's* ship's company. As fate would have it, however, Bites had chosen this untimely moment to duck down to the galley for a quick cup of "Joe." At the same time, McAlleney, the duty messenger, a not too ambitious apprentice sea-man from Northern Florida's Okefenokee Swamp region, was sleeping soundly in the nearby torpedo shed. It would have taken far more than the mere visit by a three striper to disturb his noonday nap.

Royal waited patiently at the quarterdeck for several minutes hoping to detect some evidence that at least one living creature still inhabited the *Field*. The quarterdeck roster indicated that all of *DD-505's* officers except the officer-of-the-deck, an Ensign Coates, had gone ashore. Royal had no way of knowing that Mister Coates was three ships away in the *Prairie's* wardroom totally engrossed in the doings of the "*Gary Moore Show.*"

A squeak of straining wood broke the silence. The commander turned to see Logan crossing over from the closest destroyer. Stepping off the tarry plank con-necting the two warships, Logan tossed a half-hearted salute in the direction of the slightly ragged ensign flapping lazily at the *Field's* stern. Dropping his sea bag to the deck, he once more extracted the large yellow envelope that contained both his orders and service record.

"We seem to be the only people on board," Royal greeted in a tone calculat-ed to mask his displeasure at discovering that he may very well have been given command of a ghost ship. He glanced forward to the rear of the bridge structure, hoping to spot a signalman or quartermaster tending the flag-bags. He doubted that he'd find this kind of laxity even on a merchant ship, much less aboard a man-of-war.

Logan eyed the flagless halyards hanging listlessly from the foremast. "I don't see the captain's absentee pennant so he must be aboard," he volunteered.

"I doubt this ship even has an absentee pennant," Royal snapped.

"Maybe they're all at chow or attending a lecture below." Logan said, knowing full well that it was past time for the noonday meal, and that there was no single compartment on a *Fletcher* class destroyer that was large enough to accommodate more than 35 men at the same time.

"I'm going to have a look around," Royal advised. "You wait here until the quarterdeck watch shows up...that is if there is one. You can inform him that the *Field's* new commanding officer is aboard."

Royal climbed the ladder at the base of the bridge precisely as Bites returned from the galley clutching a cup of black coffee and a fat piece of cornbread which he was dunking in lieu of a donut. Amply supplied with that air of self importance typical of the minor functionary, Bites scrutinized the radarman from head to toe, then without a word, took Logan's orders and entered the pertinent data into the quarterdeck log. "You reserve?" he snarled, handing back the envelope.

"That's what it says on those papers you just copied?"

"Well there's nobody in ship's office right now," Bites drawled in a tone of well-practiced arrogance. "Hang on to your papers till Gordy gets back."

"Who's Gordy?"

"That's Gordon, yeoman-first. He takes care o' things like signin' you to the Ops division. He'll see that you get squared away with berthin' 'n all o' that."

"When's he due back?"

"Now that's kinda' hard to figure. Ole' Gordy's a real liberty hound. If I know him, he's over on the beach right now chasin' up some tail for tonight. Chances are that ole' boy won't be showin' his lecherous face on this bucket till tomorrow mornin's muster."

"More power to him. All I care about right now is getting a bunk for tonight and getting my gear stowed away. How do I do that?" Logan asked with sudden fury in his eyes.

"That's your problem. I'm not a chaplain."

"Maybe so but you are the watch P.O. and you're wearing a third-class crow. In case you haven't noticed, mine is second-class so get your ass moving in high gear and get me squared away with everything I need or I'll boot your butt all the way back to the fantail!"

"Now hold your water," Bites replied in a friendlier but still condescending tone. "There should be somebody down in the Ops berthin' space. Go aft to the fantail hatch 'n go down one deck. By the way, you ever been on a tin can before?"

"Yeah, back in the big war, sonny." Logan smiled smugly as he hoisted his sea bag back on to his shoulder. He started aft for the fantail, then turned and casually announced, "I almost forgot to tell you, your new C.O. is aboard. He's scouting out the bridge right now."

Bites coughed into his coffee as Logan walked off. "Fuckin' feather merchant!" the bo'sun mumbled, hurriedly attempting to bring some semblance of order to the quarterdeck area. He tried jamming the half-full cup of coffee into the desk drawer but it was crammed with faded charts, lensless binoculars, broken pencils and a twisted checkerboard.

"That fool McAlleney," Bites muttered incoherently, wedging the cup out of sight behind a mounted length of fire hose. "I told that dumb swamp boy t' straighten out this desk draw over a week ago. He's just about as useless as tits on a fly!"

Commander Royal tried the door to the wheelhouse but found it locked as were the doors to the radio-shack, combat-information-center, and chart house which occupied most of the base of the bridge structure. Royal stopped before a brightly polished brass plaque mounted on the bulkhead. The words read:

> U.S.S CHARLES P. FIELD, DD-505 NAMED FOR ENSIGN CHARLES P. FIELD, USNR KILLED IN ACTION WHILE SERVING ABOARD THE U.S.S NEW ORLEANS, NOVEMBER 30, 1942.

> LAID DOWN   26 AUGUST 1942
> LAUNCHED   16 FEBRUARY 1943
> COMMISSIONED   13 AUGUST 1943

> THIS SHIP BUILT BY BATH IRON WORKS CORPORATION, BATH, MAINE

Tassafaronga, Royal mused, as he read the brass memorial, remembering how the "Tokyo Express" had clobbered his force that night. He had seen it all from his G.Q. station high up in *Honolulu's* searchlight control tower. He remembered watching a spread of "Long Lance" torpedoes simultaneously slam into the sides of four heavy cruisers. *Honolulu* had zigzagged out of the cruiser column just in time to evade the murderous torpedo barrage launched by "Tenacious Tanaka's" vaunted tin can sailors as they salvaged victory out of what should have been an overwhelming defeat. Excepting Savo Island, he always felt it was the worst licking the Nips had given the Navy in the entire Pacific War.

But Royal had been lucky again. His cruiser had been the only large ship in the force to escape unscathed. A few days later at Tulagi, he'd seen the wounded *New Orleans* with her bow and over 120 feet of hull missing. That morning, as his eyes scanned the cruiser's drastically altered profile, he had no way of knowing that a decade later he'd be taking command of a ship named for some poor bastard who'd been blown to hell-and-back aboard her that gory night in the Solomons.

Royal knew he should be the last one to bitch about anything, even about being given a gray "dinosaur." He'd come through the bloodiest war in history without getting a scratch. He had survived everything the Japs could throw at him from battleships off Leyte to suicide planes off Kyushu. He'd survived, he'd gone on to serve his country in the peacetime navy, and he'd managed to meet and marry a fantastic woman who could make him feel as young and vibrant as when he was a midshipman at the Academy.

It was even luck the way he had met Candace, Royal reflected. It was 1949 and he was serving aboard the aircraft carrier *Coral Sea* in the Mediterranean. He had gone ashore at Nice to buy a gift for a stewardess he had been seeing back in Virginia Beach. Registered as man and wife, they'd spent two weekends at the plush Cavalier Hotel. Royal was certain that a suitable gift for this young lady was in order.

His hunt for the gift had not been working out well since his French was practically non-existent. Then he learned of a shop in Cannes which specialized in serving American and British tourists. Never having been to Cannes, he saw this as a chance to kill two birds with that proverbial one stone. The shop was on the Quai St. Pierre which ran alongside the part of the harbor that served as home port for many of the world's biggest and most luxurious yachts. Upon viewing this armada, he had second thoughts about entering a shop which obviously catered to so rich a clientele. After a brief hesitation, he entered the posh establishment and was immediately confronted by a young and very pretty sales girl.

For its modest size, the shop accommodated a sizeable number of female customers. To Royal's embarrassment, he quickly discerned that he was the only male present, and as such, had become the center of attraction. He decided to make his purchase as quickly as possible, then beat a hasty retreat. The fact that he was all decked out in dress whites magnified his uneasiness, and he was convinced that every woman in the shop was secretly giggling at his discomfort.

As an added cross, the sales girl's English was far from flawless. He had asked her if she could recommend a new perfume that was popular in France but had not yet "hit the States." He discerned that the second part of his request had totally confused the petite mademoiselle, and prudently decided to rephrase his request in less colloquial style. Before he could do so, however, a wonderfully feminine voice, decidedly American, volunteered, "Why don't you try *J'Attendrai*? It means I will wait. It's very big over here right now, and I happen to know that it won't be marketed in the United States for at least six months."

Now, standing outside the doorway to *Field's* wardroom, he could vividly remember each minute detail of that special moment. The young lady was tall and blonde and very beautiful. He had never seen anyone with quite so perfect a face. She had to be a model, he surmised, probably a cover girl for those fashion magazines...the kind he occasionally sneaked a look at on the news stands. Royal thanked her for coming to his rescue, then studied her closely while she politely explained his request to the blushing sales girl. Her mastery of French

9

was impressive as was everything else about her. Spectacular, he thought, as his eyes probed each detail from well-curved calves and buttocks, to an incredibly small waist and sensuous upswept breasts. Her hair, long but pulled back neatly in a bun, rivaled the color of new grown wheat.

Royal purchased the suggested scent, thanked the young American once more, then started to leave. Almost to the rose colored door, he decided to "go for broke" and ask the young lady to lunch. Fully expecting a turn-down, he was happily surprised when she cheerfully accepted his invitation.

They dined at one of Cannes' most elegant harbor-side restaurants. The lunch tab cost him approximately five day's pay; a matter of little consequence, however, for at thirty-three, Royal at last had been swept off his feet…totally, completely and irrevocably.

Her name was Candace Moffet and she told him she was an account executive for the New York-based advertising agency that had won the contract to market and promote *J'Attendrai* in America. This was the first account that had been placed under her complete charge, and at twenty-five, she was the youngest senior account executive, not only in her agency, but on all of Madison Avenue.

She was in France to pick up as much information as possible about the new perfume and to touch base with its manufacturer who was headquartered just outside of Nice. Determined to make it as popular and well known in the States as *Chanel Number Five*, she had visited the shop in Cannes to observe how customers, especially American tourists, were reacting to *J'Attendrai*.

That evening Candace allowed him to call for her at her hotel, the Metropole, in Cannes, and they soon found that they had many of the same preferences in entertainment and the arts. They even liked the same food.

She said he looked very much like Cary Grant. Royal had been told that many times in the past by a wide variety of people but this was the first time he gave the suggestion any credence. He was particularly encouraged when Candace confessed a schoolgirl's crush for the dashing actor.

What followed was a whirlwind courtship to humble all whirlwind courtships. Fortunately for Royal, the *Coral Sea* had just completed extensive exercises in the Eastern Mediterranean with the British carrier *Indomitable*. Important new tactics for joint operations between the two navies had been successfully formulated, and as a reward, the American flattop was allowed to bask in the sunny waters off Nice for an unprecedented two weeks.

Being a Lt. Commander, Owen Garrett Royal managed to get ashore and see Candace almost every afternoon. Even on the two bleak days he had the quarterdeck watch, he managed to talk to her briefly on the ship-to-shore telephone. By the second week he knew the situation had become quite serious, at least on his part. He was not certain if she shared his feelings, however, since after six dates, she was still adroitly sidestepping each of his progressively more frequent sexual advances.

By now, Royal recognized that it was no longer merely an infatuation spurred on by the lady's exceptional looks, and he began to doubt his own hitherto unyielding preference for the bachelor's life.

On the next to last evening before the *Coral Sea* was slated to weigh anchor for her next series of inter-allied exercises, Royal took her out to his flattop for dinner in the officers mess. Candace had never seen a warship up close before, much less a mammoth aircraft carrier, and she was completely awed by this great floating city. Equally awed were the many officers and enlisted on board that evening who had occasion to visually inspect the fetching young advertising executive while she was inspecting the intricacies of the *Coral Sea*.

A few days after Royal and *Coral Sea* bid reluctant adieus to the French Riviera, Candace wrapped up her research project and flew back to the 10-foot by 10-foot cubicle she called her office at Baker, Barlow, Yaeger and Sigsbee. By early summer, *Coral Sea* was in a Portsmouth, Virginia dry dock undergoing a routine overhaul, and *J'Attendrai* was on the lips of every woman in America who could afford to trade a twenty-dollar bill for a four-ounce bottle of this magical Gallic liquid which was guaranteed to bring the strongest male trembling to his knees. Soon, Candace was B.B.Y. and S.'s undisputed *wunderkind*. Sales based on her campaign continued to soar throughout the summer. By September Candace was able to trade in her humble cubicle for a spacious office with real walls and three big windows, two of which actually faced on Madison Avenue.

During *Coral Sea's* four-month overhaul, Owen Royal and Candace managed to spend several weekends together in New York. Royal's roommate for his plebe year at the Academy was now assigned to Operations at Norfolk's Breezy Point Naval Air Station, a fortuitous circumstance, for it afforded Owen easy access to the weekend shuttle flights between Norfolk and Floyd Bennett Field in Brooklyn. This in turn not only reduced his travel time but also saved him a considerable amount of airfare.

By early fall, Candace, in keeping with her new executive status, purchased a gleaming red Alfa Romeo sports car. This, she and Owen used for long drives through the New York and Connecticut countrysides.

Royal had entered *Field's* wardroom now and it was here that he finally encountered one other living being aboard the *Field* besides himself and Logan. The stranger was a steward's mate first class, a Filipino named Manual San Jose Romulo Valencia. Brown as a bean, small and round, the petty officer had been brewing a fresh pot of coffee in the adjacent galley. Welcoming Royal with a toothy grin, he asked the commander if he had had anything to eat. If not, the steward would be happy to prepare something for the visiting officer.

Royal thanked his host but declined the invitation, deciding to wait in the wardroom for about ten minutes, certain that one of the ships' officers would show his face by then. Sitting there, his thoughts again skipped back to Candace and the "Christmas card" church in her hometown of Kent Falls, Connecticut, where they were married.

Royal returned to sea in the fall, and Candace, still working under her maiden name, continued to gain attention along Madison Avenue. Now, as he departed the wardroom, Royal glanced at his watch, noting that it was about 10:15 in the morning back in New York. He hoped Candace was clearing up all the loose ends back there. He'd been fearful for the past week that something would go wrong with the ad accounts she supervised and at the last moment delay her arrival in La Jolla in two weeks. As of now, everything was still on schedule, he reassured himself as he approached the quarterdeck which was now manned by both Bites and McAlleney.

"I'm Commander Royal," he said in a firm but friendly tone, deciding not to raise the subject of the empty quarterdeck he had found earlier, since he was not officially taking command of the destroyer for another twelve days. "Where's the O.D.?" Royal asked, glancing back in the direction of the bridge area.

"Mr. Coates, Sir?" Bites questioned after rendering the most regulation salute he had executed in the three years since he left boot camp. "I believe he's over on the *Prairie*."

"What's he doing over there? That's three ships away."

"I don't rightly know, Cap'n, I mean Commander," he stuttered nervously, realizing that the officer was not yet officially the *Field's* C.O. "I expect that Mr. Coates will be coming back soon, Sir," he added meekly.

"Well, when he does get back, please be certain to tell him that I was aboard," Royal instructed, saluting the colors flying aft. He then took leave of *DD-505*, knowing that the next time he departed the ship, he would be doing so as her commanding officer.

Waiting until Royal had crossed over to the next destroyer and was beyond hearing range, Bites spun around towards McAlleney who had already slumped down to a sitting position, a posture the watch messenger usually favored.

"Get your ass up off the deck, boy!" Bites fumed. "Suppose the new C.O. gets it in his mind to pay us another visit, I'm not goin' to lose this crow just 'cause you're too lazy to stand a watch the right way!"

"Oh, he ain't coming back till the day he takes command, 'n now that he's had a good look at this olé bucket, I wouldn't be t'all surprised t'see him go 'n tell BuPers that he wants no part o' the Charlie P. I know if I was him, I wouldn't want to be a skipper o' a beat-up ole' scow like this one, wet nursing a different batch o' damn reserves every couple o' weeks."

"That's not up to you," Bites cut in. "When you're assigned t' my watch, I don't want you crappin' out!" I told you fifteen minutes ago to get Coates. If you had, he'd made it back before the new C.O. left. That three striper was really pissed. Ole' Coatsie's gonna' find his ass in the sling, and it'll be partly your fault."

"How come you're so shook up over what happens to a dumb-ass ensign, 'n a damn Yankee ensign at that?" McAlleneny asked, scratching his neck.

"Coates ain't so bad."

"He ain't? Why just 'fore the exec took off on leave, I heard him chewin' out Coates real good. Told him he was 'n accident just lookin' fer' a place t' happen."

"Well, Cobb ain't nothin' t' cheer about himself. At least ole' Coatsie is harmless. Suppose they kick his ass off this ship and send us another gung-ho prick like Mr. MacKinlay. That ex-gyrene is one o' the meanest bastards I ever had for a department head. Those damn jarheads are lucky he didn't take a second lieutenant's commission 'n gone back in the marines when he graduated from Annapolis. They deserve a shit like him much more than we do."

McAlleney started to sit down.

"Damn you, swamp boy! You git your butt over t' the *Prairie* 'n tell Mr. Coates what happened! You'll probably find him in officers' country!"

"I know where t' find him, right in front of that 'telly' they got in their wardroom." McAlleney placed the frayed white cap a'top his head at a salty angle; it's leading edge balanced gingerly across the bridge of his nose. As he stepped on the tarry plank linking the adjoining destroyer, it would have been impossible for anyone watching to discern whether the messenger had actually saluted the colors or merely wiped some sleep from his right eye.

While Commander Royal was reading the *Field's* commissioning plate, Radarman Second-Class Kevin Francis Logan was standing on the fantail, his sea bag propped against an empty depth-charge rack. Logan looked around for the large deck hatch that would serve as gateway to what he sullenly acknowledged would be his home-away-from-home for the next year-and-a-half. Puffing on a badly crushed Chesterfield, he glanced around at the other destroyers sharing the nest. Outboard to port, wearing the number "503", was *Halsey Wayne*. The two inboard "cans" nestled tightly between the *Field* and the tender were "504," the *John Morgan*, and "506," the *Abner Ward*. Logan watched the stars and stripes at the stern of each vessel flap in almost perfect unison with the next in line. The flags danced to an afternoon breeze that was steadily gaining in momentum.

The radarman took a long drag on the cigarette as he studied the antennas mounted on the masts and stacks of the *Field* and the two closest destroyers. These ships should have been old friends, instead they were just so many tons of gray steel and cable. There was a time Logan would have viewed them differently, a time a million years ago …in 1943.

That was a big year for Kevin, he had turned eighteen and no longer required his parents' consent to enlist and get back at the Japs for Pearl Harbor and Bataan. His older brothers were already in uniform, even Brian, a Vincentian, was serving as a chaplain with the Eighth Air Force in England. And Neal, only two years his senior, was jockeying a Sherman tank across North Africa. Neal had survived the Kasserine Pass the previous February, and the last the family had heard, he was at some place called El Guettar in Tunisia. But his brothers could have the army; it would be the navy, especially destroyers, for Kevin Francis Logan.

When he was six years old, his father had taken him out on a fishing boat to the waters off Groton, Connecticut. It was there he was first introduced to the navy's "greyhounds of the sea," in this case a squadron of twelve "four-pipers" eagerly heading back to their home port of Newport, Rhode Island. Young Kevin was awestruck. The ships were flush-deckers built during the war to end all wars, and each flew a long thin pennant that streamed out from her mainmast far beyond the vessel's stern. One of the fishermen, an ex-bluejacket, told Kevin and his father that these strange looking flags were called "home coming pennants," and their length depended on the length of time the ship had been steaming on an overseas station, as well as the number of men in her crew.

From that day on, Logan lived only for the day he could go to sea with the "tin can" navy. He read every book and periodical that spotlighted destroyer development, and never missed a movie about the navy's jack-of-all-trades.

Enlisting in Bridgeport on his eighteenth birthday, Logan soon found himself at the Great Lakes Naval Training Station. Each day, during his three-month ordeal at boot camp, he continually tried to convince his company commander and instructors that he was ideal destroyerman material. During the final week of training, each recruit was handed a chit of paper on which they were to inscribe their first, second, and third choices of ship or shore duty. Of the ninety chits handed in, Logan's was the only one with the word "destroyer-Pacific" written three times.

Logan's orders were among the last to be posted. They went up on the board almost a week after he had completed the basic training that had so miraculously transformed him from civilian to bluejacket.

He was to proceed to Bath, Maine, immediately, where he would report to the *U.S.S. Laffey, DD-724*, which was slated to commission within a few days. As a member of her first crew, Logan would be a "plank owner," which by navy tradition, was a very special honor.

Laffey was one of the new 22 hundred-ton *Allen M. Sumner* class destroyers that were just joining the fleet. These ships had to be the most powerful destroyers ever built, Logan thought, knowing that they had been developed from the hard working, combat proven *Fletcher* class that were then bearing the full brunt of the Pacific fighting.

By May, *Laffey's* shakedown period was over and Logan knew he was bound for war and glory. It was the greatest sensation in life, possibly even better than sex, he decided, as his dark gray steed carried him through the U-boat's Atlantic playground. *Laffey* and Logan arrived at Greenock, Scotland just in time to participate in General Eisenhower's "Great Crusade."

On June 3rd, *Laffey* headed for France, escorting tugs, landing craft, and two Dutch gunboats. Logan was now convinced this was the ultimate adventure. It was great fun on the 12th when *Laffey* intercepted and pursued a group of "E" boats that had torpedoed another American destroyer. The fun stopped abruptly off Normandy on the 25th when a German shore battery looped a 240 mm shell on to *Laffey's* foc'sle. Logan's craving for adventure ceased completely eleven months later when four Jap bombs and six Kamikazes crashed into his beloved destroyer within a fateful 80 minutes. He passed his twentieth birthday sorting out arms and legs from charred, grotesquely twisted metal that had once been *Laffey's* superstructure. Now, seven years later, standing on *Field's* fantail, he remembered thinking that April day, how if there is such a thing as sculpture in hell, it must look like this.

The sleeping compartment for the Operations Department was located between frames 179 and 183 near the stern of the ship, and one deck beneath the fantail. The steering gear room, which housed the complex machinery necessary to operate the rudder, was directly aft. The ammunition handling room, which serviced Number "5" 5-inch gun-mount, was one space forward. A 2-inch by 4-inch aluminum plate screwed to the inside of the open fantail hatch-cover identified the compartment below as the berthing quarters for the Operations Department. Aboard the *Field*, this group was made up of those who practiced the three arts —- navigation, detection and communication. As a radarman, Logan would have to concern himself with all three.

Now Logan was certain that the *Field* was all screwed up. She must be the only can in the whole damn navy that doesn't berth her personnel within close proximity of their daily watch stations, he thought, thoroughly convinced that lack of logic was the order of the day on *DD-505*.

A steel rimmed, semi-vertical ladder set in the hatchway, linked the fantail to the sleeping compartment. Logan eased the heavy sea bag down the ladder, his free hand gripping the white canvas-coated line that served as a banister. He descended slowly, carefully lowering the bag so that its weight rested on each rim; preventing it from dragging him to the deck below.

The Ops berthing compartment was dimly lighted, and, like that of most warships, was very cramped. A strong odor of fresh paint was evident, and most of the bunks were without mattresses, indicating to Logan that the Operations Department was extremely undermanned. There were about fifty bunks, all grouped in triple tiers. The bedding consisted of very thin mattresses resting upon even thinner sheets of canvas. Each canvas, stretched inside a rectangular steel frame, was held to the frame by a piece of line. Some of the empty bunks were folded back at a 45-degree angle in an unsuccessful attempt to create tolerable living space.

A few of the bunks on the far side of the compartment were occupied. The overhead bulb in that section had been unscrewed for easier sleeping. Logan noticed a "scuttlebutt" near the ladder. The convenience of having such a drinking fountain nearby was of paramount importance, and the division possessing this luxury was always highly envied.

"Welcome to the good ship Charlie P!"

Logan turned toward the greeting. A sailor clad in shorts, t-shirt, and black socks, was seated on a footlocker, busily polishing a pair of shoes.

"I'm Howie Murray," he volunteered in a friendly voice, "I'm a pip-jockey too," he said eyeing the radarman's insignia on Logan's sleeve. The sailor appeared hardly past adolescence. His round baby face, slightly protruding upper front teeth, and a crew cut the color of sandpaper, reminded Logan of the stereotype teenager from an old Henry Aldrich movie. Introductions completed, the sailor held out one of the black shoes, catching the reflection from the overhead bulb. "Got to keep these shoes in top shape. I don't plan to buy another pair until I get out."

"How much time still left on your sentence?" Logan smiled.

"When I got the word from the warden…Harry Truman, that is, I was told that since I'm a vet, I'd only have to do sixteen months. I've already put two months in on this tub so I guess that leaves about fourteen more to go."

"You don't sound too enthusiastic," Logan said.

"Enthusiastic!" Murray shot back. "I was as inactive as an inactive reserve could be, in fact, I'd completely forgotten that I was even in the reserve! The extra discharge points that I got for signing that damn reserve agreement got me out of the navy a week early in 1945. Some deal, heh? I get a lousy seven days from the navy back then, and now, seven years later, I have to pay them back a year-and-a-half. Even a loan shark can't get away with charging that kind of interest."

"Well, at least I was in a drill unit drawing pay," Logan interjected, "the little dough they paid me for teaching radar came in handy while I was going through college on the G.I. bill."

Murray shrugged and said, "Being in the inactive reserve, they never paid me anything. I never even received any mail from them for seven years. Then those damn mobilization papers popped up one morning in my mailbox. The only obligation I had all those years was just to notify the navy if I had a change of address," Murray shook his head in disgust. "Stupidest thing I ever did," he moaned, "but after two combat tours in the Pacific, getting out even a day early, much less a whole week, sounded awfully good. Besides, who'd ever figure on another war after Hiroshima and Nagasaki? The Japs and Krauts were completely smashed, and those smart asses on the armed forces radio kept telling us how terrific our Russian allies were. Now with this Korean thing, I guess those Red bastards weren't so terrific after all."

"You had two tours in the Pacific?" Logan asked with marked incredulity in his tone.

"Yeah, one on the 'Big E' and the second on 'Big Ben'," Murray answered proudly. "In spite of the clobbering we took on both those ships, I'd take another 'bird farm' over a 'tin can' like this 'bum boat' any day."

"Say, just how old are you?" Logan queried. "What did you do, join the navy when you were nine?"

"I'm thirty-one. My age fools everyone. Guess it's a good thing I don't drink much. It would be embarrassing having to prove my age every time I ordered a brew."

"You sure fooled me," Kevin said, rubbing his hand across the back of his neck. "If I had to guess, I'd have said you couldn't be more than nineteen, and even that would be stretching it."

Murray laughed good-naturedly. "Except for inspections, I've even stopped wearing my 'glory bars'. Last time I wore them ashore, the jarheads at the gate wanted to write me up for wearing unauthorized decorations. I've been stopped by the shore patrol a couple of times, too. Anyway, I'm glad you're reserve," Murray said, abruptly changing the subject. "Most of the *Field's* ships company are regular navy, confirmed thirty year men. They don't' have much love for us 'reserves'."

"I noticed that when I came aboard."

"Oh, guess you mean Bites. Believe it or not, he's one of the friendlier types on this backwater bilge barge."

"Yeah, he's real congenial, alright," Logan snickered.

"Well, you've got to remember that to them, we're just a bunch of civilians playing at being sailors. They think we're coming on board just to takeover their jobs. It's even worse when we outrank them. Taking orders from weekend warriors really burns out their batteries," Murray grinned, extracting a neatly folded set of dress blues from an upright locker. "Most of the regulars assigned to the *Field* were too young for the war, and they've got no idea what it was like. They see us wearing our ribbons and battle stars but they never stop to think about how we got them. For all they know, or care, we could have found them in a box of Cracker Jacks. They probably don't know that the sea-going navy was over eighty percent reserve during the war. Just about the time they were starting high school, us amateur sailors were learning how to ride out typhoons, and stand up to anything the Nips could throw at us." Murray suddenly realized that he was beginning to sound like a recruiting film for the reserve program which, under the circumstances, was the last thing he wanted to champion. Changing the subject once more, he asked, "Where are you from?"

"New York, at least for the last four years. I'm originally from Trumbull, that's in Connecticut."

"I'm from Warren, Ohio," Murray announced, almost apologetically. "Sorry I can't match it against New York for excitement."

"Yeah, New York's got to be the greatest place in the world for making out."

That wasn't what Murray meant by excitement but his eyes lit up at Logan's remark.

"I had this really posh apartment on Seventy-third off Lex," Logan continued..." stocked with wall to wall models. Of course, there were a few stewardesses thrown in from time to time just to add a little spice. But that's all up in smoke now thanks to the U.S. Navy. Damn!" he pondered aloud. "I really had it made in the shade until I opened that telegram."

"Did you really date models?"

"Sure, why not? I harbor no prejudices against beautiful women."

Murray's eyes glowed. "The kind of models in magazines or the ones on T.V.?"

"Both," Logan frowned.

"How'd you get to meet so many models?" Murray probed, wondering if the newly arrived radarman might be putting him on.

"I use models in my work, I'm a copy writer...at least I was until a couple of weeks ago. I was with Brice and Gwyn. That's one of the top ad agencies on Madison Avenue. Models float in and out of our offices all day long. Even a ride on one of our elevators usually turns out to be a memorable experience."

"Looks like Uncle Sam really threw you a curve."

"More like a spitball. The navy's timing couldn't have been worse if they deliberately tried. I was just starting to score with a chorus girl from the Roxy," Logan smiled, recalling the lurid details of his latest conquest. "And if that wasn't enough," he said, swinging his sea bag up on to an empty bunk, "the navy also torpedoed my career at B and G. I was only three weeks away from moving into a juicy slot as an account exec. The job was in the bag."

"I guess my work was pretty dull compared to yours," Murray said, "but the navy did a first class job of screwing that up, too. I've been out in the field selling office stationery for the last six years. Next July, the company was going to move me into its home office in Cleveland and make me sales manager for a three state area. My salary would have doubled."

"Maybe they'll hold it open for you," Logan advised.

"Fat chance. Under the law they have to give me my old job back when I get out, but there's nothing in the law that says they have to give me the job they were planning to give me," Murray murmured, the smile now completely gone from his face.

"Don't give up the ship, maybe they'll be patriotic and give it to you anyway," Logan counseled, knowing only too well that in the cold cruel world of business, out of sight invariably meant out of mind. "Working in Ohio," Logan added, "I don't see how you could call your job dull, especially with all those beautiful girls the Buckeye state is famous for."

"I wouldn't know anything about beautiful girls, I'm married," Murray sighed, then realizing the negative tone of his words, quickly added, "My wife Mary Alice is all the woman I'll ever need. We've been sweethearts since back in high school," Murray explained as he slipped into his blue bell-bottoms. "We wrote each other all through the war and I'm firmly convinced that it was her letters that pulled me through, especially during those really bad days on the *Franklin*. And another thing," Murray's smile returned, "you can't experience the pleasure of having a family when you're out there jumping around from bed to bed, hoping you'll duck the clap." Murray finished buttoning the thirteen buttons on the front flap of his pants, then reached into his locker for his wallet.

Observing rosary beads that dangled on the inside of the aluminum locker door, Logan told himself that his new shipmate would really hit it off with his 'holy Joe' brother, Father Brian. Kevin was also more than certain that the good priest had long given up hope that his younger brother would change his lustful ways and once again adhere to the teachings of Holy Mother the Church. Kevin always reasoned that as long as he didn't try to corrupt his big brother, there was no reason why Brian should try to keep him on the straight and narrow.

Murray's face beamed as he produced a small snapshot from his wallet. Logan was convinced that his companion had waited until his pants front was completely buttoned before producing the photo.

"Most fathers probably feel this way but as far as I'm concerned, I'm not at all ashamed to say that I've got the two most beautiful daughters in the world," Murray announced, his face glowing as he impatiently waited for an immediate affirmation from the *Field's* newest crew member. "The littler one is Jenny, she's three, the other little sweetheart is Deirdre, she's almost six, and that of course is Mary Alice."

The girls were both towheads with rosy cheeks that looked like they'd been pasted on to their fat little faces with airplane glue. Both girls appeared to have inherited their father's upper front teeth.

"You're right," Logan smiled, "they sure are beautiful kids." His eyes focused next on Mary Alice, the *femme fatale* of the Murray household. A high cheekboned redhead, Mary Alice was plump but not pleasingly so. Perceiving her nononsense expression, Kevin had little doubt as to who issued the orders-of-the-day, and probably, of the night, back in Warren, Ohio.

"You're right, your wife's a real knockout," he tried to say it convincingly. "You really are a lucky guy."

"Boy, don't I know it," Murray smiled affectionately at the snapshot as he carefully slipped it back into his wallet. "I guess even a picture like this can't convince a guy like you that the real pleasure in life comes with meeting a girl you're certain you want to grow old with…and raising a family, and watching your kids grow up and have kids of their own."

"Well, I'm not knocking married life," he said, "I'm sure it's great for a lot of guys, fortunately, I'm not one of them."

"I suppose you're too much of a lady killer to ever settle down."

Logan wasn't certain if he had detected sarcasm or envy in Murray's remark, so he decided to pour it on. "I don't like to brag, but there's every chance the female suicide rate back in Manhattan is going to take a sharp rise once word gets around that old Kev's left town."

"Sounds like we'll have to start calling you Studs Logan," Murray quipped

"Hell no. That guy died in the gutter. When I kick off, I'll be in the saddle with a blonde. The death certificate will read, heart attack induced by too much ass. Besides the guy you're talking about was named Lonigan, not Logan."

"You mentioned that you were in college, did you get your degree?"

"I have a B.A. in English from U-Conn."

"How come there's no gold stripes on your cuffs?" Murray asked.

"I'd been thinking of applying for a commission until I found out that I'd have to go active navy for three years. The hell with that! Then last month when I got my call-up, I checked into it again. I even shot a lunch hour going down to

Officer Procurement on Spring Street. That's in Lower Manhattan, nowhere near where I worked up in Midtown. The recruiter told me that if I got the commission I'd do at least a year beyond the sixteen months they'd already nailed me for," Logan shrugged. "Hell, I'd rather ride it out as an RD-two for a year-and-a-half than as an ensign for twenty-eight months. My job at B and G is pretty cutthroat. As it is, sixteen months is going to be a real set-back, twenty-eight would be a total disaster." Logan leaned back against a stanchion. "Say who's the leading pip-jockey on this tub?"

"I am," Murray smiled, pointing to the sleeve insignia on the dress blue jumper that he was unfolding.

Logan eyed the three red chevrons of a first-class petty officer.

Still smiling, Murray said, "Guess you'll be my assistant. Besides you, we've got four third-class, plus some radar strikers, but they're not much good at plotting or working out maneuvering board problems. I use them mostly on the status boards and as telephone talkers. Once in awhile, if we're steaming in a quiet area without much traffic, I let them sit on the scopes and get some practice. By the way, do you know that the *Field's* assigned to training naval reservists?"

"No, I didn't, but that explains why she looks like a ghost ship. I should have guessed she was a training ship as soon as I saw all those empty bunks. I've made a few two-week cruises out of Brooklyn on destroyer escorts assigned to training reserves. I never thought I'd be on the other side of the fence."

"I hope you got better training on those DEs than the reserves get on this ship. We don't get many rated reservists aboard for training. Most of them have been called up like us. We've been getting mostly kids. Most of them are still in high school. They're practically all seamen deuce. They come aboard all eager and anxious to man the guns and fire the depth charges just like they've seen in the war movies," Murray laughed. "instead they get handed a paint brush and a chipping hammer. Good thing 'cans' don't have wooden decks or those kids would spend the whole two weeks pushing a holystone." He gulped some water from the scuttlebutt. "If they don't learn anything else in two weeks, they certainly become expert at removing rust from metal surfaces," he said wiping his lips with the back of his hand. "The only problem is all the kids in the world, with all the gray paint in the world, can't prevent this old bucket from rusting away at the hinges. Anyway, you're pretty damn lucky getting sent to the *Field* just now."

"Lucky? Why am I lucky?"

"Well, coming aboard just before we go in for an extended yard period. We're scheduled to go into dry dock at the destroyer base for at least four or five months."

"Hey that's great. I wonder why they didn't mention anything about that this morning when I checked in at the receiving station."

"We just got the word ourselves at this morning's muster." Murray's voice was barely audible during the few seconds it took him to slip the blue jumper over his head.

"I noticed the three souped-up cans' berthed alongside," Logan said. "Is the *Field* getting a face-lifting too?"

"Yep, complete modernization from stem to stern. New radars and sonar, a thorough engine overhaul; they're even going to replace our 40- and 20- millimeter gun mounts with new 3-inch-50's. That's a break for us. It will mean a complete new Mark-56 gun director system and an overhaul for the Mark-37 director. Then maybe those damn fire-controlmen will stop bugging us in C.I.C. for all their target solutions. That Mark 37 they've got is so old, Drake probably used it to sink the Spanish Armada. Its computer is all shot and the circuits burned out on the last cruise."

"Hey, don't go saying anything nasty about the Mark 37," Logan said affably. "I literally lived inside one of those metal boxes for days at a time at Iwo and Okinawa. It's still a damn good gun director system."

"What were you doing in a Mark 37? Weren't you a radarman during the war?"

"No, I started out as a fire-controlman. The reserve unit I joined in Connecticut in '46 didn't train FC's but they did train radarmen. As a fire-controlman, I had to know damn near as much about radar as any of you pip-jockey's did, so it was an easy thing to switch my rate. The reserve sent me to some C.I.C. team training courses at Norfolk and Newport and let me take a crack at the RD-two exam which I passed with flying colors. So, here I am," he grinned. "But enough about the Mark 37, How's the gear in C.I.C?"

"Not much better than the gun director. All the radars are original issue. I'm really glad we're only going to be training reserves. I'd sure hate to get into a shooting war on this tin coffin," Murray said, strolling over to the large mirror hanging on the side of an upright locker.

"The first class began to tie his neckerchief and Logan asked, "What's your C.O. like?"

"What C.O.? If you mean the clown we've got on this ship, he spends all his time trying to qualify for the playboy of the year award. Every time we hit port, Commander Carver's over on the beach making out before we can even get the whaleboat over the side. He's so hot to trot, he usually rides in on the pilot boat while we're still out in the stream. He always comes back to the ship about thirty seconds before we're scheduled to get underway. When that happens, he doesn't even bother to change into uniform. I've got to tell you, it is one weird sight to see the skipper of a U.S. destroyer running around the bridge in a canary yellow sports jacket shouting orders to the bridge-watch and line handlers."

"And I thought I was going to be the number one lady killer on this 'can'," Logan laughed.

"You'll have to settle for second place. Half the time we're tied up at the base, he's got this little Mexican chippy coming in and out of his cabin, all day and night, acting like she owns the ship. And I heard that the bastard's got a wife and a couple of kids back in Louisiana. "Fortunately, I don't think you and the 'old man will' have much time to compare notches, Carver gets relieved in twelve days."

"How come?"

"Oh, he screwed up royally on the cruise we made last month up to Avalon. That's on Catalina," Murray said, tightening the knot in his black silk neckerchief. "The way I heard it, the old man went on a grunion hunt, only the grunion he tried to grab turned out to be Admiral Whitlock's nineteen-year old daughter. I always knew that when Carver got his frequencies crossed, he'd do a first rate job of it. I'm only surprised he didn't get caught earlier. He may have been an officer but he sure as hell wasn't a gentlemen. And he wasn't very discreet, either."

"What do you mean?"

"Well, one night while they were having a dinner party in the wardroom for the officers and their ladies, I decided to take a run up to C.I.C. to make sure all the classified pubs had been put back in the safe. I snapped on the lights and there was old Carver with his hand up under the skirt of Ensign Ritter's wife. He had her panties down around her ankles, too."

"What'd you do?"

"I almost shit a brick! I was pretty scared, and Mr. Ritter's wife, she turned milk white. I thought for sure she was going to faint dead away…but old Carver, he never even changed his expression. I flew out of there faster than a cat in a dog kennel. Funny thing though, I saw Carver five or six times the next day and it was just as if nothing had ever happened. I'm sure he recognized me but if he did, he never let on. I don't think Ensign Ritter ever found out. I sure as hell wasn't going to be the one to tell him." Murray shook his head. "Too bad we can't blame the regular navy for Carver. He's U.S.N.R. on active duty. Anyway, he's past history now. Sorry I can't provide very much dope on the new C.O. His name is Owen Royal and he's U.S.N., and Annapolis at that."

"Annapolis? Why would the navy sentence one of its elite to a worn-out tub like the *Field*? As a reserve training ship, we probably won't be operating with the fleet very much. Royal must have screwed up somewhere along the way. Commanding a ship like the *Field* isn't what the navy would call a career enhancing billet."

"Think they're getting ready to dump him?" Murray asked.

"That's the only thing I can figure."

"That's too bad in a way," Murray intoned. "Ensign Coates, our C.I.C. officer, told me that he heard that this Commander Royal spent the last four years with the Sixth Fleet in the Med, including some time on a carrier. At least that's got to be a point in his favor," Murray quipped, recalling his days of glory on flattops *Enterprise* and *Franklin*. "I wonder what he's like," Murray mused aloud.

"As C.O.'s go, he seemed to be a pretty decent type," Logan answered casually.

"How do you know?" Murray snapped.

"I just rode out in the launch with him. I'm willing to bet that this is his first command."

"Why do you say that?"

"You should have seen him when he first spotted the *Field*. I thought he'd jump out of the whaleboat and kiss her. He was really pissed-off though when we came aboard and he couldn't find anyone at the quarter deck," Logan grinned.

"Coates had the deck. Wasn't he up there?"

"No, and your buddy Bites didn't show his ugly face until the commander had gone up to the bridge."

"Poor Coates, it looks like he's messed things up again," Murray commiserated with apparent sincerity. "Our ensigns are all U.S.N.R., typical ninety-day wonders. Coates is the exception, he's more of a ninety-day blunder. To make matters worse, he's number one on the exec's shit list. If he ever finds out that Coates took off while he was standing O.D., the wardroom will be serving chopped chuck ala Coates."

"If this Coates is such a meatball, how come he's C.I.C. officer? That's a job that requires some brains." Logan shot back.

"He's been bounced all over the ship. So far he's been in Deck, Gunnery and Engineering. He's only been in Ops three weeks. Funny though, he's not doing too bad a job. He's even become halfway competent on the maneuvering board. He surprised me the other day when he worked out a real bitch of a torpedo problem and came up with all the answers right on the money."

"Why's the exec on his ass?"

"Mostly because he hates reserves, which is kind of funny because I heard that he was reserve himself up to a few years ago. He graduated from one of those merchant marine academies back East and he thinks he's a real salt. I bet he's going to hate taking orders from the new C.O.," Murray seemed amused by the prospect.

"Why, because he's Annapolis?"

"Partly, but mostly because Cobb is use to being chief honcho around here. Carver was so busy trying to make out with every female that came into range, that he couldn't' find any spare time left over to run the ship. He gave Cobb a free hand, let him do anything he wanted to. But that's all going to change now. Hope the new C.O. squares Cobb away mucho quick."

"How are the rest of the officers?"

"Most of them are okay, except for Lieutenant (jg.) MacKinlay, the first lieutenant. He's a former marine and a real shithead. You can't miss him. He wears a big brass belt buckle with the Marine Corps insignia on it. Naturally, he's always blowing steam about how he use to do things in the Corps."

"Was he a gyrene during the war?"

"Yes, but you can tell from his ribbons that he never left the States. All he's got is the Victory Medal and American Theatre of Operations. Listen to him talk though, and you'd think he had made every landing from Guadalcanal to Iwo." Murray checked the mirror one final time, then satisfied that his hat was squared according to navy regs, he invited Logan to pick out any unoccupied bunk and footlocker that met his fancy.

Logan opted for an upper bunk with a nearby fan. "Are you off to San Diego or Coronado?" Kevin asked, more out of courtesy than interest.

"I'm just going over to the petty officer's club at the destroyer base. I can call Mary Alice and the girls from there. I call them almost every night when we're in port."

"You call Ohio every night?"

"Just about. I guess I keep the telephone company's stock holders pretty happy."

"I'd say you probably keep them ecstatic."

"Well, I guess a good portion of the few shekels the navy pays me these days does go for long distance, but Mary Alice and the girls are worth it. When you settle down some day, you'll know what I mean," he counseled solemnly as he ascended the ladder and cleared the fantail hatch.

Ensign Donald Coates arrived back at the *Field's* quarterdeck just in time to see a canvas-covered forty-footer pull away from the *Prairie* and sputter off toward the North Island landing. "You say our new C.O. just left in that boat, Bites?" he asked the young bo'sun's mate.

"Yes, sir," the watch petty officer announced. "He left just a few minutes ago. You probably missed colliding with him in the *Prairie's* thwartships passageway by just a few seconds."

Ensign Coates scratched the back of his head nervously as he wondered if he still had time to catch the closing moments of "*Dick Powell's Zane Grey Theatre*," back on the *Prairie*.

The harbor breeze surged and an uncomfortable chill gripped San Diego. Ashore, jukeboxes were playing Kay Starr's "*Wheel of Fortune*," Leroy Anderson's "*Blue Tango*," and Johnny Ray's "*Little White Cloud that Cried*." Across the nation, Americans were flocking to bookstores to pick up two stirring new novels about the Second World War. One dealt with a mutiny aboard a destroyer-minesweeper during a Pacific typhoon; the other, set in Hawaii, told of an ill-fated romance between an army bugler and a prostitute.

Tucked away on the more remote pages of American newspapers, an A.P. dispatch reported that North Korean infantry with armor support had launched a two-and-a-half-mile wide frontal assault against the U.S. Army's 25th Division in the "Punch Bowl" area…a second dispatch almost casually announced another stalemate at the Panmunjom armistice conference.

Chapter II - Change of Command

Homes shaded by palms and pepper trees, plush country clubs garnished with green satin lawns and rambler roses ———, Coronado, immediately adjacent to the North Island Naval Station, includes some of the most luxurious real estate in Southern California. Popular as a place of residence for retired flag officers, it is regarded throughout the Pacific Fleet as as much a part of "officers' country" as the wardroom of any battlewagon.

At the end of a long patch of white sand, the hotel Del Coronado stood watch on the Pacific. For a Wednesday night its swank dining room entertained an unusually large number of guests. Owen Royal arrived a little past seven-thirty wearing the gray Harris tweeds he had purchased in Italy the year before. From his table on the enclosed porch just off the main dining area, he could see the carrier *Princeton* clearing the channel near Zuniga Point. He watched the big flattop slip past Point Loma, then slowly merge with the blue expanse Magellan had named Pacific. To Royal, there was always something pathetically lonely about a ship leaving port. It seemed especially so at this time when the destination of so many ships like *Princeton* was Korea. His thoughts were interrupted by the entrance of a tall naval officer wearing the four gold stripes of a captain. The officer was looking around the dining room anxiously.

The commander motioned and a waiter ushered the captain to the table.

"Hey, Owen," the new arrival greeted excitedly, "how is it you always manage to get the best seat in the house?"

"It's probably these English tweeds," Royal said. "I picked them up in Rome. They seem to work some magic wherever I wear them."

Captain Tim Barrett was a big man with a red leathery face that bordered on pudginess and contrasted with the lean, finely defined features of Commander Royal.

"Tell me, Tim, how are Carolyn and the kids?" Royal asked, handing the captain the cocktail menu.

"Fine, talked to Carolyn long distance. She said to give you her best. You know, young Lee finishes up at the academy this June. Then he's off to Pensacola

25

for flight training. I tried to talk him into the black shoe navy, but he's determined to go brown shoe," Tim sighed. "As for Joanne, she's going through what I understand is called that difficult age. She's seventeen now and her latest passion seems to be ensigns. Can you imagine any young girl in her right mind seeing anything attractive about an ensign?" he asked with a broad grin, as he and Owen Royal reflected briefly on their own hectic days as junior officers. "We're packing her off to college in September," the captain continued. "We hope it will cool her down, but knowing Joanne, she'll quickly tire of ensigns and start in on jg's. Enough about my family, how's Candace?"

"Great, she'll be out here next week. You might say she's also getting her first command. She's going to run her agency's West Coast operations. She'll be right nearby in La Jolla, so things couldn't' be any better."

"That's terrific. I knew things would work out just right for you two. After all, didn't you have the good sense to let me be your best man?"

"Well, you being a happily married man, I figured you were just about the only one on the ship I could trust."

"That's the price you have to pay when you marry a beautiful woman."

"I can't argue that, Tim. I've sure been lucky alright. Say, let's get a look at that menu, I'm really starving."

After dinner, the two men walked along Ocean Boulevard. The sun had long retreated and the hiss of the breaking surf seemed to Royal more seductive than usual.

"What's on your mind, Owen?" the captain asked. "Isn't tomorrow that big day you've been waiting for since you graduated from the academy? I haven't been able to get a word out of you since we left the hotel."

"Sorry, Tim. Guess I'm a bit jumpy about tomorrow."

"Is that all. Hell, it's the crew that gets jumpy when a new skipper comes aboard. They stand there all through the change-of-command ceremony not hearing a single word. They're too damn nervous about what your policy will be on extra duty, or how many seventy-two hour passes you'll allow on a weekend. So cheer up, this is the only time in your life that you're going to enjoy hearing people refer to you as the old man." Lighting his cigar, Barrett asked, "Been out to see the *Field* yet?"

"Yes, I paid her an unofficial visit last week but nobody was aboard. The exec is acting C.O. but he's in New York on leave. He's supposed to get back some time today. I'll be relieving a reserve named Carver. He's flying in from the Great Lakes just for the ceremony."

"Great Lakes? Think I heard something about him before I left Washington. Seems he incurred the unremitting wrath of the great white father in BuPers...something about his making an unwelcome proposal to Admiral Whitlock's daughter. Apparently the young lady lost no time in telling daddy. I hear this Carver thought she was just another tourist until the bricks fell down on him. Now he's going to find himself in charge of pencil sharpeners for the next six months until the Bureau passes him over for promotion again and dumps him out on his ass."

"Seems to me I'm inheriting the *Field* by default," Royal said pensively.

"Don't be ridiculous. You know the navy wouldn't have assigned you to the ship if they didn't think you were the best man qualified to command her. Speaking of the *Field*, is she everything you expected? You know, your first command is like your first woman…she's the one you'll always remember. What class is she?"

"*Fletcher*."

"A *Fletcher*…you ought to feel right at home. Didn't you serve on one or two *Fletcher* class during the war?"

"Yes, the *O'Bannon* and the *Remey*." Royal reached into his pocket and extracted a folded piece of paper. Here's a brief synopsis of the Field's history. BuPers sent it along with the letter telling me I would be taking command."

They stopped beneath a lamp post and Barrett glanced at the paper.

U.S.S. Charles P. Field DD-505 (Fletcher Class)

Standard Displacement	2,050 tons
Overall Length	376'6"
Maximum Beam	39'4"
Maximum Draft	19'0"
Shaft Horsepower	60,000
Rated Speed	35.0 kts.
Main Battery	5 - 5"/38
Secondary Battery	5 - 40 mm. twin + 20 mm.
Torpedo Tubes	10 - 21" Quint.
Complement	300

The U.S.S. Charles P. Field was constructed by the Bath Iron Works Corporation, Bath, Maine. Commissioned 13 August, 1943. Bombarded Buka-Bonis area of Bougainville on 25 October, 1943. Shelled Shortland Islands 1 November, 1943. Took part in the Battle of Empress Augusta Bay on 2 November, 1943. Fought off air attack at Empress Augusta Bay on 3 November, 1943. Participated in the Battle of St. George Channel, 25 November, 1943. A unit of the Third Fleet during events leading up to the invasion of the Palau Islands and Morotai on 15 September, 1944. Part of Task Force 58 during invasion of Leyte, 20 October, and the Battle of Leyte Gulf, 23-26 October, 1944. Slightly damaged by a kamikaze near-miss off Okinawa on 12 April, 1945. Took part in attacks on Japan, July 10 - August 15, 1945. Entered Sagami Bay with occupation force 27 August, 1945. Returned to the United States where she was decommissioned and assigned to Atlantic Reserve Fleet in state of preservation, 14 September, 1946.

Recommissioned at Charleston, South Carolina, 31 January, 1951. Rejoined the Pacific Fleet 4 June, 1951.

Presently employed as training ship for Naval Reserve operating out of San Diego, California.

"You're taking over a proud ship, Owen. She's certainly seen her share of action. I was at Palau and Okinawa. I probably operated with her and didn't know it. We had so many 'cans' out there, it was impossible to keep track of them all. Has she received her modernization yet?"

"No, I take her into drydock a week from Monday. She's getting a complete modification. It'll probably take anywhere from four to six months. Then I assume she'll resume her training itinerary with the reserves."

"Well, whatever duty she pulls, the important thing to remember is she's your ship as long as the navy says she's your ship. For all of that time, as long or as short as it might be, you're the guy with his head on the block. If you make just one mistake, BuPers will chop it off...swish," Barrett made a karate motion with his hand.

"I've got to say, you're a real bundle of encouragement, Tim. Why the Dutch uncle routine?"

"Sorry, I'm not trying to rain on your big day. I'm just trying to make sure you know what you're getting into. You were the best exec I ever had, but you've got one failing, and as a C.O., it can kill you. You're just too nice a guy. I remember when you were my exec on the *Buffalo*. If I hadn't stepped in, two-thirds of the crew would have been over on the beach laughing at both of us. You're too soft a touch," Barrett said shaking his head in despair, "any con artist on that ship could get you to okay his emergency-leave chit. You've got to be a real hardass to run a navy ship. I just want you to wake up to that fact. You know there's a lot of truth in that old expression that says nice guys finish last."

"Okay, I promise you, next to me, Captain Bligh will seem like father Christmas," Owen smiled.

"And you'll check out all those Red Cross telegrams requesting emergency leave?"

"Every single telegram. One thing, though, if a sailor tells me his wife's giving birth and he'd like to get leave to be at her side, I flatly refuse to recite that old navy bromide, the one where I tell him that just because he was there for the laying of the keel, he's not automatically entitled to be there for the launching."

"That's too bad. I've always found that answer to be quite effective."

"Yes, you and ten thousand C.O.'s before you," Royal laughed, "but tell me, Tim, what do you think of this reserve training I seem to be stuck with?"

"Personally, I think it's pretty soft. Here I have to fly all the way to Japan while you live it up in sunny California, joy-riding with a bunch of civilians."

"Japan? I thought you were on your way to Guam."

"So did I, but my orders were changed en route. They're giving me a fleet tanker, the *Chickamagua*. I'll be picking her up in Sasebo."

"Does that mean Korea?"

"Probably. The way 77's been chewing up Korea's east coast, those flattops must need one hell of a lot of fuel."

"This probably sounds ridiculous, but I've been showing the flag around Southern Europe so long with the Sixth Fleet, I almost forgot that there is a shooting war going on over there. Guess I should have given it a little thought that morning I learned I'd be coming out here for the *Field*, not that there's any chance that she'll ever deploy with the Seventh Fleet. By the time our yard period is over, not to mention the weeks it will take to shake down all the new gear, that armistice conference going on at Panmunjom should have the war well wrapped up."

"Did they tell you the *Field* would continue training reserves after her overhaul?" Captain Barrett asked.

"No, but there's little chance we'll get any other assignment. Enough about me, how do you think you'll like tanker duty in Korean waters after commanding a cruiser?"

"I haven't given it very much thought. I know there's a lot of duty tours I'd like better, but we both know that that's not up to me."

The two continued their walk along Ocean Boulevard.

"It's funny," Royal said, gazing out at the blackness beyond the sand, "the first time I gave Korea any serious thought was tonight, just a few minutes before you showed up at the Del Coronado. I was watching the *Princeton* moving out. She looked the same as any other *Essex* class I've ever seen, except just as she cleared Point Loma and made that last turn towards the horizon, I suddenly felt like I was back in the war. It was the strangest sensation. I'm not certain I can put it into words, but suddenly I started remembering how it was coming back to Pearl after a tour in the Solomons or later in the Western Pacific. We'd all be counting our arms and legs and feeling pretty lucky. Then we'd pass some cruiser or 'pig boat' heading out to what we'd just left. For a few minutes, all those thoughts about hula skirts and a wild fling in Honolulu would vanish. Somehow, I'd find myself on the bridge of that other ship and it would be the most desolate spot in the world. I haven't had that feeling in seven years...until tonight. It's eerie, Tim, I'd really thought I'd shaken it when the war ended."

"I doubt you ever will," the captain answered softly. "I know I'll never forget those final days at Kerama Retto when I was on the *Duxbury Bay*. We were still playing mother hen for a flock of PBMs and Catalinas. Each day, usually late in the afternoon, I'd watch the cans slip out and head for the Okinawa picket line. They'd move out quietly in column, never more than three or four at a time. I made it a point never to look at their bow numbers. It seemed less personal that way when the casualty lists were posted. They say there are no tombstones in the sea, but who could ever count the memories?"

The taxi ride to the North Island Naval Air Station took less than ten minutes. Royal waited and watched the lights on his friend's plane join a thousand stars winking from the blackness. After the last soft hum of the engines had faded, he walked across the field to the base theatre where he hoped to head off the station bus on the return leg of its final shuttle run. The lights on the theatre marquee had been turned off but he could still make out the words proclaiming "The Greatest Show on Earth," starring Betty Hutton and Cornell Wilde.

After a brief wait, the commander boarded the bus to the B.O.Q., unaware that he and the *Charles P. Field* would soon be starring in a far greater show.

•   •   •

The small maroon curtains drawn tightly across the inside of the portholes in the wardroom failed to brighten the atmosphere or hide the fact that a heavy rain was falling on San Diego; nor could Commander Carver's red plaid sports jacket dispel the bleak cold morning which would initiate a new chapter in the *Field's* modest saga. Royal, neatly dressed in his best blues and a starched white collar, appeared the antithesis of the man he was about to relieve, whose clothing, neither neat nor starched, looked recently slept in. By 09:30, all registered pubs, logs and cipher manuals had been officially transferred to the custody of the new commanding officer. The annoying but necessary paper-work completed, Carver showed Royal to his new quarters where the latter checked the combination of the safe and acknowledged by written receipt, the correctness of its contents.

"Won't take me more than a minute to change, Commander," Carver said, reaching for the single uniform still hanging in the closet. "Had the rest of my gear moved out last week. Left these blues here for today's big event."

"I understand you have only seven officers on your roster," Royal said in a pleasant but probing tone. "Have you found that sufficient for this type of duty?"

"Seven's more than enough for the Mickey Mouse assignment they've given this ship. Every couple of weeks the district will be sending you more damn weekend warriors than you'll know what to do with. On our last run to Catilina, we had six lieutenants, four lieutenant commanders, and a doctor who was a full commander. That bastard didn't bother to attend a single morning sick call. I only got to see him at meals. All he cared about was getting ashore to play golf. He thought the *Field* was a miniature Matson liner. Far as I'm concerned, the navy can take this whole program and shove it. Well, Commander Royal, ready for the ceremony?"

The rain necessitated that the formal act of transferring command be held below decks. The crew's mess area was far from suitable for such a lofty and solemn ritual, but it was the only compartment large enough to accommodate the sizeable group of involuntary participants. Collapsible tables and benches had been stacked against the bulkhead. The men, minus twelve still on leave, were lined up in two groups of four ranks each, officers out front, the chiefs to the rear.

Commander Carver read the orders instructing him to report "aboard" U.S. Naval Testing Center, Great Lakes, Illinois, "for further assignment to appropriate duties as directed by the commandant of that station." Recognizing that naval orders, no matter how negative, are always worded in a most positive guise, Carver nevertheless, read his with all the outward enthusiasm of an officer about to assume command of the battleship *Missouri*. His show of bravado, however, failed to deceive even "Turk," the *Field's* dim-witted cook.

Flanked by a giant coffee urn closely resembling an over-sized kettle drum, and by a large, cage-like structure that served as a scullery closet, Royal read the brief lines that would place a U.S. man-of-war and her officers and men under his charge. As the traditional handshake terminated the ceremony, Royal knew he would no longer be referred to only as commander...from that second on, it would be "captain," "skipper," the "old man."

The steward's mates, supervised by Manuel San Jose Romulo, busily went about the work of serving pastry and fresh coffee to each of the officers seated around the huge wardroom table. Carver, dressed once more in civies, introduced the new captain to the seven officers who would assist him in the management and operation of the *Charles P. Field.*

Although this was his first meeting with the *Field's* "junior executives," Royal was already thoroughly familiar with the background of each officer from his service record, and had formed a clear mental image of each man prior to this first meeting. As executive officer on his last ship, the heavy cruiser *Buffalo*, he had played this little game each time a service jacket preceded the arrival of an officer reporting for duty. Royal would remember the details in the officer's record, then paint a mental picture of what the man looked like. He prided himself on the overall accuracy of his predictions.

The executive officer, Lieutenant Commander Aubrey Cobb was stocky, and to the eye, appeared shorter than he actually was. His brick red hair could more accurately be described as kinky rather than curly. A pleasant smile and seemingly casual manner caused the new C.O. to take an immediate liking to this man who would serve as his chief administrator and second-in-command. Cobb had been aboard the destroyer during the entire fourteen months since her resurrection from the "mothball fleet" and was thoroughly familiar with all her operational quirks and eccentricities. Aware of this, Royal considered his executive officer a most valuable asset.

As a Naval Academy graduate, Lieutenant (jg.) Alan MacKinlay was the only fellow alumnus of Commander Royal assigned to the *Field*. The destroyer's first lieutenant and gunnery officer, MacKinlay in no way bore any physical resemblance to the image Royal had fashioned in his mind after studying the Floridian's service jacket. Royal had pictured a rather robust, red cheeked Scot. Instead, MacKinlay was wiry and had a swarthy complexion that looked in dire need of a shave. His dark eyes and skin, and general facial features seemed far more akin to the hills and olive groves of Southern Europe than the crags and glens of the Scottish Highlands. As a former marine and a product of Annapolis, MacKinlay's grooming left much to be desired, Royal thought, passing it off without a comment, but filing it away as an item to receive special attention at a later

31

and more appropriate time. Of more immediate concern was MacKinlay's potential as the *Field's* "gun boss," and Deck Department honcho.

Lieutenant Donald Stockwell, the Operations Department head, greeted Royal with a deep drawl nurtured in the environs of Macon. A former tackle for Georgia Tech, Stockwell wore a perpetual smile and appeared to be fully content with his billet aboard *DD-505*. Royal hoped his complacency wouldn't affect the quality of his future performance or that of the Operations Department.

The *Field's* ensigns, Messrs. Warden, Daly, Ritter and Coates, were all fairly new arrivals aboard the destroyer. Products of either the O.C.S. or N.R.O.T.C. programs, they had far less sea duty than most of the reserves the destroyer had been assigned to train. Royal was always quick to make allowances for ensigns and these four seemed no worse nor any better than other one-stripers he had groomed into competent officers in the past.

After some light conversation, the captain outlined what he expected to be accomplished during the up-coming yard period. "White hats" were to be encouraged to utilize this time by taking maximum leave. This conformed with standard navy policy of getting crew members off the ship and out of the way of the small army of civilian workers who would flock aboard each morning armed with welding irons and acetylene torches. "Personnel not taking leave should be sent to school for further training in their specialties," Royal directed.

By early afternoon the rain stopped and crewmen appeared topside to carry out various tasks of ships maintenance. Such a sight was unprecedented aboard *DD-505* where manual labor was always the exclusive domain of the young reservists assigned to two-week training cruises. No one was more surprised by this sudden assiduity on the part of the *Field's* tars than Commander Carver who had lunched aboard the *Prairie*, then returned to *DD-505* to pick up the civilian clothes he had worn earlier. As Carver departed the *Field's* quarterdeck for the last time, even the shrill blast of the bo'sun's pipe was muted by clanging chipping hammers and squeaking wire brushes. Somehow, the sound of the *Field* at work had never seemed so loud or annoying before, Carver thought as he crossed the tarry plank to the *John Morgan*. Certain that this was the crew's not too subtle way of committing one final indignity, he noted that with the exception of Owen Royal, not a single member of the *Field's* company had bothered to wish him good luck in his next assignment. He was especially aware that Aubrey Cobb, his good friend and most trusted executive officer, had been conspicuously absent from the quarterdeck during his departure.

As Commander Royal made his way toward the bridge and his cabin, he glanced skyward to see the *Field's* big "Sugar-Charlie" radar antenna lazily spinning above the foremast. The commander stood there for a few seconds, studying the rectangular bedspring-like screen as it slowly made each 360-degree revolution. Pleased that at last something seemed to be functioning aboard the *Field*, he continued on.

Two more days and he'd be with Candace, Owen smiled, wishing there had been some way she could have witnessed the change of command ceremony. Then remembering its ungracious setting, he decided it was just as well that she'd missed it. His thoughts rambled through the busy itinerary of plays, scenic views and gourmet restaurants he would take her to while introducing her to the pleasures of Southern California. Maybe they'd even drive down to Tijuana and take in a bullfight, he thought, dismissing the idea a second later when the prospect of "Montezuma's Revenge" reared its ugly head. He'd waited eight months to see Candace...eight months to get that gorgeous body in the sack again. He'd be damned if polluted water and a dead Aztec's curse would screw up this weekend, he vowed.

His thoughts shifted to Tim Barrett. Tim's plane was just about taking off from Midway on its final leg to Japan, Royal reckoned. He wondered if the *Chickamagua* would run afoul of any Migs while on her refueling chores with Task Force 77. He visualized his portly friend up on the open wing of the tanker's bridge, booming out orders to his gunners as Chinese and North Korean jets zoomed in from all sides. Royal pondered what combat would feel like after seven years. As he entered his cabin and began unpacking his luggage, he suddenly realized that he had been whistling, a habit frowned upon by superstitious sailors. Stranger yet, the tune he was whistling was "*Shoo-Shoo Baby*," a song straight out of World War II.

Murray stood at the base of the gun-director atop the wheelhouse. He stared up at the antenna, studying carefully its uneven motion each time it came around to 045-degrees relative. Amplidyne-drive must be off, he decided after a few more minutes of deliberation, then scampered down four deck levels to the combat-information-center which was tucked away at the base of the bridge, a deck below the main weather deck. This location especially annoyed the *Field's* senior radarman since it permitted him no easy access to the outside world, which, in turn, made it more difficult for Murray to practice his own special "system" of radar navigation.

For a radarman, Howie Murray was guilty of the gravest heresy by professing more confidence in seamen's eye and good binoculars than in the myriad of electronic wonders, science and the Bureau of Ships had provided the *Field*. When radar navigating into a harbor, Murray's favorite tactic was to dart up from C.I.C. to the 0-1 level just below the bridge wing where he couldn't be observed from the wheelhouse. He would then take visual fixes from the various buoys and harbor markers, then "force" them to coincide with the most compatible ranges and bearings his inept radar operators had plotted. Ensign Coates, the C.I.C. officer, was party to this skulduggery and even abetted it by passing the information via the "squawk-box" to the wheelhouse just as if it had been culled from the radar scopes. Murray convinced himself that his "system" was merely a means of checking the accuracy of the equipment in C.I.C. By degrees, the "tail began to wag the dog" and Murray found himself using his radars only as a means of checking the accuracy of his visual sightings. Of course, such efforts only duplicated those of the various lookouts stationed above in the bridge. As a reserve training ship, the *Field* hadn't made it a practice to enter or depart a port at night. Murray's biggest worry was fog which so far had not been encountered.

DD-505's combat-information-center was cramped. Because the ship was not operating, most of the overhead lights were turned on. The *Field's* four RD-3's, Nugent, Holiday, Bacelli and Gardiner, were engaged in either updating the various equipment maintenance logs or were hunched over the plotting board, vainly attempting to show two of the radar-strikers how to solve a simple course and speed problem.

At the opposite end of the plotting table, Kevin Logan was busy honing re-discovered skills as he adjusted the dead-reckoning tracer, a complex device used to maintain a continuous up-to-the-minute geographic plot of the *Field's* position as well as that of all surface contacts within range of her radars.

"How's the antenna look?" Logan asked as Murray entered the combat-information-center.

"You can see it make a little jump each time it gets to 045, I guess you were right, it's probably that damn amplidyne again! We had the same trouble on the cruise to Catalina except we'd get the distortion at 265 instead of 045. Nugent and Holiday were calibrating the Sugar-Charlie yesterday," Murray added, turning to face the two third-class. "I'd bet my left tit that you two forgot to stop the antenna before you de-energized," he snickered.

"Hell no, we didn't forget. We followed the procedure just like the maintenance manual said," Nugent shrugged.

"Yeah, Murray, how come you always blame us whenever something gets fucked up around here?" Holiday chimed in.

"Because every time there's been a snafu, you two meatballs are usually the cause of it!"

"Want me to call the ET's?" Logan grinned.

"Yeah, give it a try," Murray replied. "You won't get Baubeck though. He's the only sharp electronics tech on this bucket. When I was topside a few minutes ago, I saw him going over to the beach with the guard mail. He was in the boat with our former skipper. The *Prairie's* launch passed right near our bow. I could see Carver looking up at the bridge. Boy, did he look pissed," Murray smiled broadly.

"*Sic transit Gloria mundi,*" Logan mumbled, not looking up from the DRT.

The remark passed over the heads of his fellow radarmen.

"Well, let's get one of the ET's hot on this gear right away," Murray snapped. "I want to get over to the beach as soon as I can. Mary Alice told me last night that she expected to have some important news for me tonight when I call. I think it's got something to do with that promotion my company promised."

An hour later, on their way to the Ops Department living space, Bacelli and Gardiner stopped by the galley to find out whether or not it was worth waiting for chow before catching the liberty boat. While there, they briefed Turk on their escapades of the night before which involved a lady cab driver and a one-legged hooker. Listening attentively, Turk looked up from his oven and asked, "How do you two lover boys think you'll make out with them slant-eyed broads?"

"What slant-eyed broads?" both radarmen asked in unison.

The cook extracted a large tray of oven-baked biscuits from the oven.

"Ain't you two got the word yet? I got it from the cook on the *Halsey Wayne*. It's been floatin' all over this tub all afternoon."

"What's been floating all over this tub?" Bacelli asked impatiently.

"That we're going to Korea," Turk slurred the words as he bit into one of the biscuits.

•   •   •

At 19:30, approximately six hours after the yeoman on the *Abner Ward* told three members of the I.C. gang on the *Halsey Wayne* who passed it on to the messenger-of-the-watch aboard the *John Morgan*, who in turn told his counterpart on the *Field*, Owen Garrett Royal received his first hint that his new command would be called upon to perform duty other than the training of reserves. The hint came in the form of a coded message from ComCruDesPac marked urgent. Delivered to Royal just seconds before he would have left to go ashore, the message directed him to prepare a complete inventory of missing title "B" equipment, rid the ship of all unnecessary articles that might prove inflammable, and take any other action required to make the *Field* ready for a sustained period at sea. A few moments later he received a second message, one originating from Captain W.A. Price, USN, commanding Destroyer Division 291. This dispatch had been routed simultaneously to all four ships in the division and it requested that each of the four commanding officers, along with his executive officer, report aboard division flagship *Abner Ward* at 09:30 the following morning.

Royal checked at the quarterdeck and learned that Aubrey Cobb could be reached at the Cortez Hotel.

Lt. Commander Cobb was back aboard the *Field* within an hour-and-a-half of the call which the O.D., Mr. Ritter, dispatched via the *Prairie*.

"Sit down, Aub," the captain said motioning Cobb over to the black leather armchair. "I've just received these two messages."

Cobb reached for them smiling and started to read the ComCruDesPac dispatch. Suddenly his eyes widened, his face turned milky white. "This is ridiculous!" he bawled. "We can't go to Korea! We've got no guns!"

"What do you mean no guns?" Royal asked in a confused tone.

"Didn't LeRoy, I mean Commander Carver tell you that only one of our 5-inch guns was fully activated when the *Field* was taken out of mothballs? There was no reason to fool around with the other mounts. We've only needed the number "2" gun to train the reserves. We never had enough gunners mates to

35

maintain all the mounts so activating only one of the guns was the most practical thing to do. The other four 5-inch guns won't revolve or elevate much less fire. We figured that they'd be activated with the rest of the gear when we go into the yard next week. That's what they did with the other three 'cans' in the division when they went in for refits."

"What do you mean by the rest of the gear?" Royal asked trying hard to keep his composure.

"Well, half the 40 millimeters, almost all the 20's, both banks of torpedo tubes, starboard depth-charge racks, I could give you a list a mile long. And besides Captain, we've only got sixty men aboard. The war-time complement for this ship is three hundred officers and men," he said, his voice rising sharply.

Commander Royal discerned Cobb's near state of panic. "I don't think we have too much to worry about, Aub. There's certainly no possibility that the *Field* will sail out to 'Indian country' in her present condition," he counseled in a calm, almost fatherly tone. "Let's hold back on the panic button until we've looked at this thing logically. DesPac must be aware of the *Field's* current state of readiness, and I'm certain they've made the necessary allowances. I've received no cancellation of our yard period so I don't see that there's much to worry about. The earliest they can complete our modernization is four months, and who knows, maybe the work will take a full half year. By then the war in Korea could be over. Besides, there's nothing in that dispatch that says we're going to deploy with the Seventh Fleet. I can think of at least twenty other assignments DesPac could have us slated for. For instance, it's quite possible they're planning to use us as plane guard for carrier qualifications."

"I don't know, Captain, when I read the dispatch, I only see one thing, and that's Korea...especially this part here about sustained periods at sea," he said pointing. "They wouldn't say that if they intended to send us on plane duty."

"You know the Navy, Aub," Royal said, forcing a smile. "They consider it regulation to put a tone of urgency in all their dispatches no matter how routine they might be. Besides the Seventh Fleet's got all the new *Sumners* and *Gearings*. I don't think they really need these tired old *Fletchers* over there." As Royal spoke, his thoughts belied the optimism of his words. Cobb's news about the *Field's* condition of readiness was unexpected and more than disheartening. His brief inspection prior to taking command revealed no indication that nine-tenths of her ordinance was inoperative. These things he could only have learned on the short cruise a new C.O. customarily takes prior to assuming command. Royal had not been afforded this preview of the *Field* in action because her captain and executive officer, as well as a large portion of a pitiful small ships' company, were away on leave when he arrived in California. And although he could understand Carver's bitterness at losing command, Royal could find no possible excuse for his failing to make known the *Field's* numerous deficiencies during their first meeting.

"This meeting tomorrow morning," Cobb said staring at the deck, "do you expect any clarification of our itinerary?"

"It's a safe guess the commodore has been informed of the order, but he may not know any more about it then we do. Will you be sure and get cracking on that title 'B' inventory as soon as possible. I'd like to review it and submit it to Captain Price sometime tomorrow. And Aub, please try and get somebody to type up that mile-long list you mentioned before we go over to the *Ward*."

"Alright, Captain, I'll get on it immediately," the exec frowned.

"Cheer up, Aub," Royal said rising from his chair, "I'm certain things will look a lot better tomorrow after the conference with the commodore."

"Do you know Captain Price, Sir?" Cobb asked as the two left the stateroom.

"Yes, unfortunately I do," Royal answered with a broad smile. "He was a couple of years ahead of me at the academy. I don't think he has too much love for me, but then, maybe he's forgotten. Afterall, that was eighteen years ago."

"What was?" Cobb inquired anxiously.

"Well it seems we were both interested in a certain young lady from Chevy Chase, and I was a bit more successful in winning her affections. As I remember, he was pretty sore at the time. Luckily, our career paths never crossed...until now that is. Anyway, Price is the least of my worries. I've got a wife flying in from New York in two days, and I have to make sure the furniture I ordered has been delivered to our apartment. I've rented a rather nice flat in La Jolla on Terryhill Drive. But I don't want to bother you with my personal problems. Try to get some sleep, Aub. I think we're both going to have to be at our best tomorrow morning."

The executive officer left, and Owen Royal walked out to the foc's'le where he sat on the small stool-like bitt just aft the port anchor. The rain which had fallen earlier flavored the air with a tang of kelp that bit at the nostrils. Royal watched the lights ashore in downtown San Diego and the small blinking lights of the buoys out in the channel. A few hundred yards ahead lay a cluster of mast-high red aircraft warning lights that indicated another nest of destroyers berthed alongside their tender. A little further on, the well lighted Coronado ferry was clearly visible inching her way across the harbor. Three ships away on the *Prairie*, the men were watching a movie; the canvas screen rigged to one of the tender's forward gun mounts. Royal could hear the soundtrack, it was an MGM musical called "*Three Little Words*." He recalled seeing it the year before in Naples Harbor aboard the *Buffalo*. He especially remembered a song and dance number, one that featured Arlene Dahl. Fantastic legs, almost the equal of Candace's, he reflected. He sat there for another hour thinking about his wife, sniffing the cool Pacific breeze, and listening to the gulls as they tried to compete with the music drifting over from the *Prairie*.

The meeting in the *Abner Ward's* wardroom kicked off promptly at 09:30. Commodore Price held the rank of captain, but his duties as commanding officer of Destroyer Division 291, entitled him to be called commodore. Price was tall and had the well-maintained body of an athlete. His blond haircut crew style and a light blond beard gave him an adventurous look and made him appear much younger than his forty years.

Each of the four destroyer captains, along with his executive officer, listened attentively for any hint Commodore Price might drop regarding their up-coming deployment. For the first half hour, the rather self-assured four-striper seemed only concerned with introductions and socialities. When it became Royal's turn to be introduced, the commodore displayed a noticeable coolness, his way of letting Owen know that like the proverbial elephant, Captain Price would never forget.

Price cleared his throat, then said, "Now the first serious business at hand, gentlemen,"...the wardroom fell suddenly silent..."is the selection of an appropriate insignia for our division. I'm certain you all have noticed that several of the other divisions in DesPac are now permitting their officers and men to wear a distinctive device on the upper left sleeve of their foul weather jackets and other working gear."

Was Price actually playing games, Royal wondered...or was this trivial matter really of major importance to this man who now controlled the fortunes of four American destroyers and their crews?

"The Bureau of Personnel," Price continued, "has authorized our contacting the Disney organization, or any other private art studio of our choosing. However, I think we can use this opportunity much more advantageously by announcing a contest among our own personnel." His face beamed with excitement. "This will be a real moral booster. I'm certain we can come up with some suitable prize for the sailor or officer who submits the winning design. Perhaps an extended weekend pass, or better yet," he smiled, "a letter of commendation in the enlisted man's service jacket which I will personally sign. If an officer should win, I'm certain we can decide upon some appropriate reward," he smiled.

The captive audience sat blank faced as Price rambled on, offering numerous suggestions as to what he considered an acceptable design. After a lengthy discourse on good taste, he instructed each C.O. to appoint one junior officer to a panel of judges. Then, as the officers prepared for the meeting's adjournment, Price suddenly announced, "Gentlemen, I assume that you all know that within a very short time we will be getting our tea wholesale. This division has been ordered to depart San Diego on May 26th for assignment with the Seventh Fleet. Of course, we all know that will mean Korea," he said softly, adding, "I've expected this for over a year...ever since the *Ward* went into the yard for modernization. When the *Wayne* and *Morgan* followed, I was certain. From what I was able to learn at DesPac yesterday, our primary duty will be screening the fast carriers in Task Force 77. However, there's always an outside chance that we will be called upon to perform limited bombardment missions and to support United Nations and South Korean forces ashore. As you probably know, our main opposition will be in the nature of mines and shore batteries. That doesn't mean that you can slack off on air defense training. Thus far, air attacks against our surface units off Korea have been fairly limited. Even so they have caused us, and the British, some damage and casualties. However, we've learned that the Chinese have massed a large striking force of aircraft just within the Manchurian border.

Intelligence believes this force of aircraft includes some hot new IL-28's they've just gotten from the Russians. And speaking of the Russians, another threat we must consider is the fleet of subs based at Vladivostok along with a larger force of aircraft than that of the Chinese and North Koreans combined. When we operate up north with Task Force 77, we will be within a relatively short distance of that area. The way Stalin's been rattling the swords in the Kremlin lately, we just might find ourselves occupying a front row seat for World War Three." Price hesitated, observing his audience for a few well measured seconds. "Gentlemen," he said grimly, "I'm not trying to sound like a crepe hanger but I suspect most of you look upon Korea as strictly a land war. Some of you probably think that you're going to get a free ride over there," his voice rose sharply. "To date, over seventy of our ships and those of allied forces operating with us have been damaged by enemy action. Five American warships have been sunk with considerable loss of life." He paused once more, then said, "One thing I won't stand for in this division is complacency. Therefore, from the moment you step out of this wardroom, you are to consider DesDiv 291 as being on a wartime footing. And another thing, I want every officer and man in this division trained and primed for any eventuality. Remember, you only have two short months to get this lashup combat ready!"

A few of the officers glanced nervously around the wardroom, trying to discern the reaction of their peers. Then Price said, almost compassionately, "Because the nature of our previous duty has fostered come understandable laxity on the part of the men, I know you will agree with me when I say you will need every possible moment to snap them back into shape. Finally, there is the matter of security. I must insist that our upcoming deployment not be discussed beyond this wardroom. The men will undoubtedly speculate as to our assignment when they learn that our training cruises have been cancelled. I suggest that you counter the scuttlebutt by spreading the word among your officers that our destination will be the Marshall Islands where we will participate in the nuclear tests scheduled to take place at Eniwetok Atoll. Now, gentlemen, are there any questions?"

Royal decided to wait until someone else broke the ice before asking about the *Field's* yard period. If they were leaving in May, what would happen to the four month overhaul he was promised? And,...how would he break the news to Candace? What would happen to the plans they made? How would she accept the fact that after being apart for almost a year, the navy was sending him to the other side of the world? He'd have to use every moment of the next two months to make this up to her, especially after she'd given up her apartment and job in New York to come to California to be near him.

Captain Boland's executive officer asked the first question. "Sir, we've only got sixty-three men aboard the *Wayne*, our wartime allowance calls for almost 350. When can we expect to receive the additional men?"

"DesPac has assured me that the drafts for your ship, as well as those for the *Ward* and *Morgan*, are already standing by at Treasure Island. Most of the men will be reservists called to active duty. There will be a few regular navy. We'll try to allot them evenly between each ships' company."

"Will that include officers, Sir?" Gil Hedling, the captain of the *Abner Ward* inquired in a flat, impersonal tone.

"Yes, they'll be mostly reserves...two stripers and probably rusty, so put them to work the second they report aboard."

"Will we be carrying torpedoes in Korea, Commodore?" Archie Fenchurch, *John Morgan's* C.O. asked. "I assume we won't be engaging any surface targets. With all that nitro in there, I'd sure hate to unnecessarily expose them to shore fire."

"That's a good point. Commander, but as far as I know, each ship in the division will be carrying her full load of fish."

As Commodore Price spoke, Royal was uncomfortably aware that his ship carried twice the number of tubes as any other destroyer in the division and most likely in the entire Pacific Fleet. Finally he asked, "Sir, I understand from what you've said that the *Field's* yard period will be drastically reduced. Can you tell me how much of a refit I can expect?"

"I'm sorry, Commander Royal, but our schedule will not permit even a limited refit of your ship. The *Field's* yard period has been modified to allow for a little more than the activation of ordinance and any other equipment still in a state of preservation. Of course, any missing items in your "B" inventory will be replaced while you're in the yard. DesPac has cut your time to four weeks, but they have made a dry-dock available so you'll have ample opportunity to check your shafts and screws."

"When can I expect my new draft?" Royal asked.

"They'll report aboard in San Francisco shortly after you leave the yard. Rather than encouraging your present personnel to take leave during the *Field's* overhaul, I strongly recommend that you make arrangements to get at least two-thirds of your men enrolled in courses at the Fleet Training Center. Be certain that your C.I.C. team and fire-control technicians get maximum training ashore. Your signalmen, radio operators and some of your radarmen should also take the course they're giving at Point Loma for ships operating off Korea. There's emphasis on the special signals, both visual and radio telephone that are in use only in the combat zone."

"Won't such training conflict with the rumor we'll be circulating about Eniwetok?" Royal asked.

"Yes, to some extent, but that can't be helped," Price answered in an annoyed tone that closely matched his expression.

"Commodore, I'd like to get back to the subject of torpedoes, if I may," Royal said impatiently.

"I didn't know there was anything to get back to," Price hunched his shoulders in exasperation. "I thought I covered that subject thoroughly a few minutes ago."

"Yes, Sir, but I'd like to call attention to the fact that my ship still has two full banks of tubes. I'm sure this is a unique situation. Will it be possible to have one of the banks removed? That will still leave the *Field* with five tubes. I share Commander Fenchurch's concern about the danger of the torpedoes being ignited by shore batteries, especially since there's little chance that we'll ever have occasion to use them off Korea."

"It's not our place to speculate whether we will or will not, Commander," Price shot back angrily. "As far as having half your tubes removed, that would require a major modification since the torpedo bank would have to be replaced with anti-aircraft mounts. There is no possibility that such a refit could be carried out in the short period of time your ship will be in the yard."

Commander Hedling started to ask a question but stopped as Price abruptly announced the termination of the meeting. "Remember, Gentlemen," he cautioned, "we can't afford to waste a single moment during the next two months. Training will be our top priority! I say again...training. You must put it above every personal consideration!"

Commander Royal and his executive officer returned to the *Field* shortly after 10:45 and went directly to the ships' office. There were several items that needed immediate attention, and the first was a revised duty roster to coincide with *DD-505's* newly abbreviated yard period.

"They've given us the dirty end of the stick this time," Cobb mumbled, attracting a curious glance from Gordon, the leading yeoman.

"I expect we'll survive," Royal said in a calm voice.

"Commodore Price seems to have it in for you," Cobb said feebly.

"Yes, I guess I did him an injustice earlier," Royal smiled. "His memory was much better than I anticipated."

"Captain," Gordon interjected, "is there anything to the scuttlebutt floatin' around the division about us goin' to Korea?"

"There's no truth in it!" Cobb cut in sharply. "Now how about taking whatever it is you're typing and finishing it in the log-yeoman's office. The captain and I have some confidential matters to discuss."

Cobb waited until the yeoman was out of hearing, then turning to the captain said, "Old Henderson will be working overtime when we hitch up with the Seventh Fleet."

"Henderson?" Royal looked puzzled.

"You mean you haven't heard about our private ghost, Captain?"

"No, but it's not surprising. There's quite a few things I wasn't told about the *Field*. Maybe you'd better fill me in on this ghost of yours." Royal tried to smile but didn't quite make it. "Maybe we can break him in as an extra watch stander. I imagine he'd be especially valuable on the mid-watch."

"Yes, Sir," Cobb grinned, "only Henderson's not just a ghost. He's also sort of a hex. Whenever anything goes wrong on this ship, the men blame it on Henderson. I guess it's something like those little green creatures the Airedales always blamed for sabotaging their planes during the war. I think they call them banshees."

"You mean gremlins," Royal chuckled.

"Gremlins, yes, that's it. Anyway, a lot of the men on this ship really believe this Henderson character haunts the Charlie P."

"Has anybody ever seen him? Who's he supposed to be?"

"The way the story goes, he's a chief petty officer. I really don't know any of the details, just that he's supposed to have put some kind of curse on the *Field*. I guess I've heard about six different versions of the story. I don't know which one to believe. There's one thing I do know, though," Cobb grimaced. "This ship's had more breakdowns, accidents and general screw-ups in the last eight months than any other ten 'cans' in the entire navy."

"Well, Aub, I think we better discount this ghost theory and start taking a closer look at the individual performance of each crew member. With the commodore breathing down my neck, we'd better make damn sure that each man on this ship knows what the hell he's doing. If the *Field's* been having breakdowns, it's not because of any damn ghost! It's due to the officers and the 'white hats' who can't cut the mustard. It's our job to make sure this ships' company becomes the equal of any 'can' in DesPac. After our meeting this morning, I don't think I have to tell you where I stand with the commodore. Price sent me a clear signal that he's out to nail my tail to the bulkhead. Well, I'm not going to let anyone on this ship hand him the hammer to do it with...and that includes this ghost of yours."

•　　•　　•

Owen Garrett Royal was at San Diego's Lindbergh Field at 8:30 a.m., a full hour-and-a-half earlier than the posted time of arrival for Candace's flight. Hoping that his wife's plane had picked up a tail wind and would arrive ahead of schedule, he grew increasingly impatient as he watched each incoming aircraft. At 10 o'clock, there was still no hint of Flight 23. He decided to check with the information desk for the third time when he detected the hum of another plane. It appeared first as a silver speck in the eastern sky; then it grew in size and started to descend, coming low over the Marine Corps boot camp that was spread out directly across the field from the airport's terminal building. By 10:15, the American Airlines' DC-6 had disembarked all it's passengers and by 10:21, Royal was embracing his wife, her blonde hair soft against his face.

Candace was as beautiful as ever. Even the very business-like tweed suit she was wearing failed to lessen her femininity or hide the fabulous curves that attracted appreciative glances from every man in the waiting room. Royal noticed that she was wearing the flesh colored nylons she knew he always preferred.

Loading her luggage into the rented Chevy, they headed off for La Jolla and their new apartment. During the drive which took them past Ocean, Mission and Pacific Beaches, Candace brought him up to date on the new accounts she would be handling in California. She mentioned her company's plans to move the office to Los Angeles but that was at least three years away, she said.

Then Garrett, she preferred his middle name to Owen, briefed her on the change-of-command ceremony and the sorry condition of the *Field's* hardware. He had intended to tell her about his up-coming deployment but then remembered the emphasis Price had placed on security. Deep down, however, Owen knew that Price's pronouncement had little bearing on his decision to postpone the news for a later date.

Candace was pleased with the spaciousness of the rooms and the general layout of the apartment. She was also happy to learn that she would have a relatively short commute to her new office on Bonair Drive. Unfortunately, her husband would not enjoy the same luxury. In these pre-freeway days of 1952, his drive to the fleet landing at the foot of Broadway in downtown San Diego would take close to an hour-and-a-half.

Royal had made certain that the bedroom set received priority in the delivery sequence. His wife rewarded him for his prudence by allowing herself to be quickly maneuvered under the sheets. She totally threw herself into the love making which took most of the afternoon.

It was ironic that getting command of a ship, the goal he had set his sights on since the day he'd entered the Academy, must now be the cause of separating him and Candace, he thought as he lay there next to her, and he found himself wondering how well he might adjust to civilian life after so many years in the navy. Maybe, he'd cash it in after this Korea tour even though he'd fall just short of qualifying for his twenty-year pension. It was bloody unfair...he'd had his war...damn bloody unfair...Owen told himself over and over again.

•   •   •

Addenda to the Plan of the Day   28 March, 1952

> The ship will get underway at approximately 07:00 and proceed to drydock No. 5, U.S. Naval Base, San Diego. Uniform for special sea detail will be: Officers — khakis with tie; Enlisted —undress blues with white hats. It is anticipated that the ship will remain in the yard for approximately three weeks.
>
> Signed:
> A.L. Cobb
> Executive Officer

The gray March dawn was dissolving behind the mossy green crest of Point Loma as more and more of the sky became suffused with the pinkish glow of a classic California sunrise. There was an undeniable scent of spring in the air and the chimes of the bell buoys seemed to Royal particularly serene. Special sea detail had been called away at 06:15, and from his vantage point on the open starboard wing of the bridge, he could easily observe the forward line handlers at their stations on the foc'sle of each of the four destroyers.

"The *Wayne* seems to be ready to single up, Captain," Ensign Warden, the J.O.D., said, glancing toward the outboard destroyer. Lt. Stockwell, the O.O.D., was back by the flag-bags, checking to see that the *Field's* line handling stations were sufficiently manned.

Captain Royal could see Sandy Boland on *Halsey Wayne's* open bridge, pointing the megaphone or "bullhorn" in the direction of the outboard ship's foc'sle.

"All stations report manned and ready, Sir," the *Field's* bridge talker interrupted.

"Very well," Royal said, glancing back at the now frantic activity aboard the *Wayne*. "Inform Mister Cobb in after-steering that the *Wayne* is preparing to single up," the captain instructed without turning his head.

A moment later he heard Commander Boland shout the order to *Wayne's* foc'sle detail to "single up!" His chief bo'sun passed the word across to the line handlers on the *Field* and the beige Manila ropes slithered through the round steel chocks back to their home aboard the *Wayne*. At the same time, the crewmen of the *Prairie* released the long bow and stern hawsers which had stretched through the *Halsey Wayne's* forward and after bull-nose. Royal was pleased at the snappy response of his line handlers. Then came the order to "cast off all lines" and the *Wayne*, sounding three piercing blasts on her klaxon, began to backdown, slipping smartly astern.

Now it was Royal's turn. He had only a few seconds to appraise the current as the outboard ship had obscured any possibility of an earlier observation. The current was as yet negligible, but the wind now began to press the ship against the *John Morgan* with some force. Royal was cognizant that as the newest commanding officer in DesDiv 291, this first demonstration of his ability as a ship handler would be of special interest to Commodore Price, the captains of the other three ships, and most important at this point, the crew of the *Field*. He was fully aware that this was the moment he would win or lose their confidence.

The sudden surge in wind velocity did not intimidate Royal. He had conned both the *O'Bannon* and *Remey* many times during the Pacific war, and only recently had received a commendation from the skipper of the *Buffalo* for skillfully maneuvering the big cruiser between two capsized freighters at Bizerte.

"Single up all lines!" Royal commanded.

"Single up all lines," the bridge talker repeated into the head-set connecting him with the foc'sle talker.

"Let go all lines aft! Hold lines two and three!"

"Let go all lines aft, hold lines two and three," the bridge talker barked into the sound-powered telephone.

Because the wind was still pressing his ship toward the inbound destroyer, Royal chose to use his two forward spring lines to swing the stern out and clear his screws.

44

His next command was to the helmsman. "Left full rudder!" he shouted toward the wheelhouse.

"Left full rudder, aye!" the helmsman responded, turning the wheel which put the rudder hard towards the nest.

"Starboard engine ahead one-third! Port engine back one-third!"

"Starboard engine ahead one-third, port engine back one-third," repeated the sailor on the engine-order telegraph. A second later the sailor reported the engine room's compliance with the order.

Royal leaned over the bulwark. Facing aft, he watched the water below the stern become a churning white mass, indicating that the *Field's* twin screws had come to life. The captain was careful not to permit the *Field* to make either head or sternway, but allowing her to slowly slip out sideways; the discharge flow from the inboard engine breasting the *Field* away from the *John Morgan*. The stern began to swing out neatly and when it had achieved the desired angle, Royal released his forward lines and backed down on both engines, keeping his rudder toward the nest. The *Field* slid aft and away from her sister ships.

Royal observed that Boland had already maneuvered *Halsey Wayne* to a position on the far side of the *Prairie* where she would wait to take her place in column behind the *Morgan* and division flagship *Abner Ward*, the latter carrying the harbor pilot. When the *Field* had moved a few hundred yards aft, Royal shifted his rudder, reversed his engines, and put the destroyer on course for her two-mile journey down channel to the repair base and dry dock Number "5".

It was a good feeling, the vibration of her engines, the wind whipping up over the foc'sle and across the roof of Number "2" gun. He looked aft toward the torpedo tubes and the Number "3" gun, then beyond at the deserted fantail and the empty flagstaff at the stern. Next his glance fell upon a small launch seesawing across *Field's* wake, it's deck crammed with gobs and marines on their way back to the North Island landing before their overnight liberty expired at 07:45. Royal remembered that the sailors always referred to this busy little craft as the "nickel snatcher," and found himself wondering how a similar launch which charged a quarter for the exact service, and as might be expected was called a "quarter snatcher," managed to survive against such formidable competition.

His thoughts were interrupted by a request from Ensign Warden for permission to sound "attention to port" as is the naval custom when passing another man-of-war. The object of this traditional courtesy was one of the *Prairie's* sister tenders, moored with her destroyer division just ahead. The rest of the *Field's* short cruise through the harbor was taken up with the routine of exchanging similar salutes with the various warships anchored or moored along her route.

As the *Field* approached the naval base, Royal felt a strong surge of disappointment that his first voyage in command of a man-of-war had to be of such short duration. He wished he could have at least taken her out of the harbor for a day's run with the division before going into the yard. The captain's rough calculations placed the other three destroyers just parallel to the Cabrillo National

Monument at the tip of old Point Loma. He knew that in another few moments the trio would be pointing their noses toward the open sea.

The recent thoughts he'd had about resigning his commission were now on the back burner. Owen was certain he could work things out with Candace. After all, he was already well overdue for a tour of shore duty. As short as this morning's cruise had been, it had rekindled an old yearning for a new adventure. Maybe he hadn't become jaded after all, he mused, then the whistle blast of a passing LST snapped him back to reality and to the immediate business at hand.

Soon, *Charles P. Field* slowed her engines awaiting the approach of the yard tug which would assist the destroyer into dry dock. Royal was suddenly proud of the old bucket as he paced her open wing, longing for the opportunity to put blue water under her keel.

· · ·

Near another harbor entrance, over 5,000 miles away, a Russian in a baggy suit stood on a rocky ledge and carefully studied the movements of the surface below. The Russian watched for several moments, timing the intervals between each wave that crashed against the base of the cliff. Scribbling some numbers on a pad, he scratched them out, then scribbled new ones. Finally satisfied that the spray could not penetrate the three large caves below him or the two jagged openings in the wall of the hill nearby, he tucked the pad in his hip pocket and started down the craggy path that led to a small fishing village. The Russian's name was Mychenko, and he was a graduate surveyor. He was also a major in the Leningrad Corps of Artillery.

The village was called Maksan, and it was very old. Strangers seldom ever came to Maksan for the place was bleak even in summer and it's few inhabitants seemed as old and depressing as the village itself. Mychenko worried almost excessively about his sinuses. He missed the warm hills near Baku on the Caspian where he had passed much of his military apprenticeship, and he tried not to dwell on the many months he would spend among these strange Orientals in this forgotten little village that smelled of urine and decaying fish.

Chapter IIII - "Candy Bar"

Two weeks before Royal took command of the *Charles P. Field*, the type commander at DesPac forwarded *DD-505's* docking plan to the docking officer at the repair facility of the San Diego Naval Base. This plan contained all the information necessary for proper docking accommodation with special emphasis on the underwater hull, its contours, extensions and peculiarities. As a unit of the *Fletcher* class, Royal's destroyer was not fitted with a docking keel, hence the use of special bilge blocks and struts called whale shores were required to keep the ship from toppling over when the water was pumped from the graving dock.

By early afternoon, the *Field* was fully secured and cradled within the gray concrete walls of the man-made canyon as the horde of tin-helmeted yard workers began their daily invasion. For three weeks, responsibility for the care and safety of the *Field* would rest in the well experienced hands of the dock master. In addition to the essential requirement of activating her equipment, arrangements were made to carry out the routine overhaul. repainting and caulking of the destroyer's underside.

In line with the commodore's instructions, most of *DD-505's* officers and enlisted were dispatched to various gunnery, fire-fighting, damage-control and electronics schools scattered throughout the 11th Naval Division. Logan, Murray, Bacelli and Gardiner were assigned to a highly classified course at Point Loma geared to familiarize radarmen with electronic identification equipment, radio-telephone procedures, and tactical formations employed exclusively by U.N. naval forces operating within the Korean combat zone. At the same time, Nugent, Holiday and the four radar strikers were shipped off to the C.I.C. team-training course at the San Diego destroyer base.

Kevin Logan was pleased with his Point Loma assignment especially since the class finished up each afternoon at 14:45 (2:45), and did not reconvene until 8:15 the following morning. Because Navy regs of the Korean War period specified that only officers and chief petty officers could keep civilian clothes aboard ship, Logan quickly joined a locker club ashore where, for a moderate fee, he was able to store a small portion of his cherished Brooks Brothers wardrobe. It also afforded him a convenient place to shower and change in and out of uniform.

Howie Murray also welcomed his temporary shore duty at Point Loma but for a much different reason; it gave him easy access to a telephone almost any time of day. Unfortunately, monetary considerations still limited his long distance phone calls to no more than one within each 24-hour time span.

Murray was still beaming from Mary Alice's big news...the announcement that a new addition would be joining the Murray clan in approximately seven months. Confident that it would be a boy, the *Field's* leading "pip-jockey" immediately purchased a pocket dictionary of male given names which he now carried with him everywhere he went, even to class.

"Find an appropriate name yet, Howie?" Kevin asked as the two sat down for lunch at a small but attractive mess hall at Point Loma.

"No, but I'm narrowing it down to eight or nine. How's Lyle sound?"

"Like the guy who didn't win the girl in one of those 1930's B movies," Logan snickered as he glanced at the menu.

"This place is great, no tin trays or chow lines. We've even got civilian waiters," Bacelli said sitting up eagerly.

"Boy, I hope this catches on," Gardiner chimed in. "This is the way officers get fed."

"My cousin's in the air force," Bacelli volunteered. "They've been feeding their enlisted like this for over a year now."

"Well, don't get your hopes up," Logan said, mashing his cigarette against the ash tray. "This is probably the only mess hall in the navy that's set up like this, and you're only going to have two weeks to enjoy it."

"You know, it might even be worth sticking around here for evening chow," Gardiner beamed, slicing into a slab of fatty beef.

"You've got to be operating two quarts low," Logan interjected. "You can get out of this place by three o'clock and you're going to hang around for a couple of hours just for some chow. Besides, what's going to happen to your legless lady of the evening? If you're not careful, your buddies Nugent and Holiday will find out about her and beat your time."

"Who do you think introduced us to her in the first place?" Gardiner retorted brusquely. "Besides, she's not legless; she's got one leg."

"Yeah," Bacelli agreed, "and she makes more dough than any other three whores in that cat house. She's such a fantastic lay, you've got to make reservations in advance."

"I'll bet," Logan chuckled.

"If you haven't tried it, don't knock it," Bacelli said peevishly. "Any time you want us to fix you up with her, just let us know. We've got a special in with Hatchet Sally. She's the madame."

"No thanks, I'm not into the bizarre," Logan said, still laughing. "Besides, you see this magazine?" Logan held up a tabloid-sized publication that looked more like a newspaper than a magazine.

"*Advertising Age*," Bacelli read aloud, eyeing the large blue letters on the masthead. "So what?"

"Yeah, what's the big deal about some lousy advertising magazine?" Gardiner piped-in sourly.

"Watch your language," Logan shot back with a sly smile. "This esteemed periodical happens to be my ticket to paradise."

"What are you talking about?" Murray frowned.

"Sorry boys, I don't kiss and tell. All I can say is that thanks to a little news item I just read in here, my brief stay in California is going to be a memorable one." And with that departing remark, Logan rose from the table and cut a course directly to the nearest exit.

"That's a guy with pussy on his mind if I ever saw one," Bacelli proclaimed in a loud voice. "How's he getting out of the classes we've got scheduled this afternoon?" he asked, turning to Murray.

"I don't know. I saw him talking to the school's training officer earlier. Knowing Logan, he probably fed him a real snow job."

"Well, I'd sure like to know what he found in that magazine," Gardiner said as he tried to pry a nugget of corned beef from a troublesome upper molar.

"How's Andrew for a name?" Murray grunted, his pug nose buried once more in the little reference book.

●   ●   ●

Commander Royal wondered why he had been so abruptly summoned away from the *Field* for a meeting with the commodore in his stateroom aboard *Abner Ward*. Knowing that a general meeting would have necessitated use of the flagship's wardroom, Royal quickly concluded that this powwow was to be just between him and Price.

He wondered what he had done to warrant a special audience, certain that Price had been looking for any excuse to put him on the carpet. Royal looked at his watch, it was almost three. He hoped the meeting wouldn't run into the evening; Price had a reputation for delivering long winded sermons. Royal was especially looking forward to this evening with Candace. They had dinner reservations at the Cortez, and after that, it would be sixth row center at San Diego's Russ Auditorium where Janet Blair had just opened in the road company of "*South Pacific*."

It was a brisk twenty minute walk from the dry-docked *Field* to *Abner Ward* and the other two destroyers berthed bow to stern along the quay at the destroyer base.

The messenger-of-the-watch dutifully ushered Commander Royal from *Ward's* quarterdeck to the commodore's cabin.

"Come in, Owen, sit down," Price beckoned in a surprisingly warm manner. Royal thought of "Greeks bearing gifts" as he eased down into a squeaky leather chair opposite the commodore.

"Owen, I'd like you to temporarily turn over supervision of the *Field's* refit to your executive officer," Price said in a solemn tone.

"Yes, sir, but may I ask why?" Royal's expression was one of complete puzzlement.

"I'd like you to spend time as an observer aboard the *Halsey Wayne*. While the *Field's* immobilized, I don't want you just spinning your wheels on the beach. Commander Boland has assured me that he's got ample room for you. I learned just a few minutes ago that the work on your ship might take an additional week. Therefore, I'd much prefer that you utilize this time at sea. This way, you'll be able to participate in all the division's exercises."

"Yes, sir. When will I be reporting aboard the *Wayne?*"

"I'd like you to get your gear over to the ship this afternoon. The division will be getting underway for San Francisco tomorrow morning at 07:45."

"Tomorrow morning?"

"Yes, we'll be gone a little over two weeks. Doesn't that fit into your schedule?" Price asked with sudden sharpness.

"No. I mean, yes, of course it does, Commodore. It's just that I've hardly seen my wife since we got married. She's just arrived in California, and frankly, I was looking forward to spending a little time with her before we shove off for Korea."

"I understand how you feel, but we're all in the same boat, excuse the pun," he said choking a burgeoning smile. "My wife's not out here. She's back in Yorktown. I'm certain you must remember her," Price's eyes glowed with sinister relish, "Carolyn Pinckney?"

"Yes, of course I remember Carolyn, how is she?" Royal tried not to grin, recalling the time she'd stood Price up to sit with him at the Army-Navy game.

"She's very well, thanks. We've got twin boys. In a few more years I hope to see them both enter the academy."

"That's terrific. You must be very proud," Royal answered.

"Yes, I am...Well, I'd better not keep you any longer. I know you will want to use the rest of the afternoon to brief your executive officer on his responsibilities while you're at sea on the *Wayne*. Then, of course, you'll need some time to get your things transferred over. So, unless you have any questions, I won't hold you up any more."

A few minutes later, Royal was on his way back to the *Field*. He'd have to move fast, he thought, if he was going to pick up Candace and reach the Cortez in time for dinner. How would he break this latest piece of news to her, he pondered, as he sighted the *Field's* masts and upper works protruding above the dry dock up ahead.

About the time Royal was aboard *Abner Ward* learning about his new assignment Kevin Logan, in his best Brooks Brothers pin stripe, was standing before an attractive young receptionist in the small but tastefully furnished reception area of Baker, Barlow, Yeager and Sigsbee's West Coast office.

"I'd like to see Miss Moffet," he asked politely.

"Do you have an appointment?" the brunette stared up at him wide-eyed.

"No, just tell her it's an old friend from New York. I'd like to surprise her."

"Well, I'm sorry but I don't think you'll be able to surprise her today. Miss Moffet just left. I don't believe she'll be coming back this afternoon."

"Do you know where she went?" Logan asked glumly.

"No, I really don't. I did hear her say something about an early dinner reservation so she could make the opening curtain of a play."

"A play? Do you remember which play she was talking about?"

"No, I didn't hear that but it's probably the one at the La Jolla Play House. That's the only theatre I know of around here except for a couple of movie houses."

"Thank you very much," he winked.

"That's okay, if you don't find her, you can always come back," the brunette smiled coyly.

Logan was sorry the receptionist worked at B.B.Y. and S. He recognized the vibrations. However, he was out after much bigger game, so regrettably he would have to pass in this instance.

Logan lost no time in purchasing a ticket for the evening's performance at the La Jolla Play House. An inspection of La Jolla's scenic beach with its intriguing rock formations took a little more than an hour. Logan killed the next two hours in a luncheonette. At eight o'clock, he was ushered to his seat in the last row of the small theatre. The play, a comedy called "*Season in the Sun,*" dealt with the assorted eccentrics that inhabited a boarding house on New York's Fire Island. Logan's interest, however, was focused entirely on the audience. If his quarry was present, he was unable to spot her.

Breakfast the following morning at Point Loma was the best he'd had since leaving Ohio, Murray remarked as he and Logan walked towards Building Number "2". Their first class of the morning was an analysis of radar jamming and counter-measure techniques employed by enemy forces in Korea. Howie sighted the three destroyers first, the *Ward, Wayne* and *Morgan,* steaming out to sea in a tight column.

"You know," Murray said, looking down on the gray trio, "they don't look half bad from up here."

"Navy ships always look good when you're not on them," Kevin answered sardonically, his thoughts still centered on La Jolla and the elusive Miss Moffet.

• • •

Halsey Wayne was steaming in the number two slot directly behind division flagship *Abner Ward*, while 500 yards astern, *John Morgan* followed in the wake of her two sisters. A steady wind was blowing from the east as Commander Owen Royal and Sandy Boland stepped out of the wheelhouse and on to the sun drenched wing of the bridge.

Turning to Royal, Boland asked, "How did your wife take the news about our deployment?"

"Much better than I had anticipated. It didn't seem to bother Candace very much at all. Well, I guess after almost three years of hardly seeing each other, she's learned to adjust. It's really a good thing she's so completely wrapped up in that advertising job of hers. It keeps her mind occupied. I was hoping she'd quit the Madison Avenue rat race, but now I'm glad she didn't."

"I'm only sorry my wife can't find something to help her pass the time while I'm overseas," Boland frowned. "Every time I ship out, Pam goes running back to Dayton to stay with her parents." Boland picked up the stadimeter. Peering through its small lens he measured the distance to *Abner Ward*, which, as lead ship in the column, was serving as the formation guide. "Mister Conte," he called into the wheelhouse, "we seem to be inching up on the guide. Better check your r.p.m.'s."

"Aye, aye, Sir," *Wayne's* officer-of-the-deck replied.

Boland turned to his companion on the bridge wing. "I bet you wish you were riding your own ship this morning."

"Yes, it will feel good taking the *Field* out here to maneuver with the division. I'm anxious to see how she handles, especially in a fast running sea like we've got this morning."

"I think you may find she's a bit slow answering her port helm. Outside of that, she can hold her own with the best of them."

"Did Commander Carver tell you that?"

"No, I really didn't know Carver."

"Don't keep me in suspense, Sandy. How do you know about the *Field's* handling characteristics?" Royal's expression revealed his complete bewilderment.

"Didn't Price tell you that I served on the Charlie P. during the war? I'm certain I mentioned it to him more than once. Actually, I rode the old girl for almost eighteen months. I was still serving as her gun boss when we brought her in for deactivation in forty-six."

"This is a lucky break for me. Is there anything else I should know about how she handles?" Royal asked eagerly.

"No, just that little sluggishness when she came left. Certainly, that was more than compensated for by the way she could get up speed. She accelerated like a rocket. I remember when we were running with Task Force 58, we'd always get on station way out in front of the carriers before any other 'can' in our screen."

"As gun boss, what do you think of her ordinance?"

"No better, no worse than any other *Fletcher* out there. That is, until Okinawa," Boland frowned.

"What happened at Okinawa?" Royal's body stiffened nervously as he asked the question.

"It's hard to put into words. It's nothing I can even explain logically," Boland hesitated, then said, "Guess it all started that day one of the Bushido boys almost crashed us. I swear that little Jappy missed us by inches. The two after gun mounts took a few splinters and wound up with some shrapnel holes but the damage was purely cosmetic, nothing that should have effected the performance of the guns. Nevertheless, from that day on, we couldn't hit a blimp at twenty yards. Even the midships and forward mounts that took no damage at all suddenly started missing every target they shot at. But it wasn't only the guns, all of a sudden we started having all kinds of electrical failures, breakdowns and steering casualties. But I don't think you've got anything to worry about. I'm sure they straightened out all those problems at Charleston when they took her out of 'mothballs' last year."

"Not according to my exec," Royal sighed. "According to him, the *Field* holds the navy record for breakdowns since she recommissioned. Which reminds me...since you were on the *Field* during the war, did you ever come across a C.P.O. named Henderson?"

"Henderson, where'd you hear about him?" Boland groaned.

"My exec. He says the crew is convinced that he's jinxed the ship. They think he's some kind of ghost who's haunting the *Field*."

A rueful expression crossed Boland's face. "Poor old Henderson, still up to his nasty tricks."

"Come on, Sandy. Don't tell me you believe in this ghost nonsense," Royal scowled, then tried to force back a smile. "You don't believe in ghosts, do you?"

"In this case, maybe I do."

"Now I know you're putting me on. I'm aware that sailors are supposed to be a superstitious lot. It comes with reading too much Conrad and Melville, but you've got to be kidding about this Henderson. You couldn't possibly be giving any credence to something as silly as a ghost."

"No, I guess not. It's just that I was thinking about Henderson a few minutes ago when I was telling you about all the trouble we had after Okinawa. I had no intention of mentioning anything about him to you. I didn't want to give you any extra things to worry about."

"Thanks for your consideration, Sandy, but since this Henderson character seems to be effecting the performance of my crew, I'd really appreciate it if you would fill me in on the details."

"Okay, Owen, as a fellow alumnus I guess I'm honor bound to tell you about Henderson. But let's go below and grab some coffee. It's not a tale I'd like to tell on an empty stomach," he smiled, "nor would I care to be overheard."

Halsey Wayne's wardroom was almost identical to that of the *Field* except the bulkheads were white rather than pale green. As the two officers sat down, a steward promptly placed a pot of steaming coffee and a platter of corn bread on the table. An ensign, sitting at the far end of the table, made a discreet but hasty exit.

Sipping the hot coffee, Commander Boland said, "You asked for it, so here's the poop on your ghost. You can take it for what it's worth, but I guess I know as much about Henderson as any living person. As gunnery officer, I was his department head. He was chief torpedoman and a plank owner on the *Field*. A typical thirty-year man, he'd started out in 1917 on four pipers. He was on the old

Fanning when she sank *U-58* and he let everybody know it. Unfortunately, he was also the *Field's* chief master-at-arms, and he worked at that job with a vengeance."

Boland leaned back in his chair. "When we weren't at G.Q. you'd find him strutting all over the ship writing up white hats for the most minor infractions. He even went after petty officers and other C.P.O.'s. Of course, our ships' company was almost ninety percent reserve, and I guess old Henderson just couldn't adjust to all those civilians coming aboard a 'can' that he helped put into commission."

The *Wayne's* C.O. poured extra milk into the coffee as he spoke. "Henderson kept piling on the report chits," Boland continued. "There were so many captain masts scheduled each day, our C.O. could have spent all his time just holding court. Finally, the old man blew his top. He reminded Henderson in rather colorful language that they were out in the Pacific to fight Japs, not the crew, and with the ship dead center in a shooting war, there was much more important things to worry about than a sailor wearing a frayed hat, or leaving a magazine on his sack after reveille. Chewing out Henderson didn't do much to improve the situation. In fact he got worse, so the captain finally relieved him of the job and gave it to our chief metalsmith. To add insult to injury, the metalsmith was a reserve."

"That must have gone over big," Royal smiled.

"It certainly didn't improve Henderson's disposition. From that day on until our little run-in with the Kamikaze, he spent all his time hating everybody on the *Field*, reserves and regulars alike."

"But how did the Kamikaze change the *Field's* luck?" Royal was puzzled more than ever.

"We were in the picket screen off Okinawa when it happened. As I remember we had just secured from G.Q. when our surface search radar picked up this bogey heading straight in towards our stern. He was winging along just over the water and at first, until they clocked his speed, C.I.C. thought a Jap P.T. or one of those suicide boats was making a run at us. Anyway, the old man started zigzagging all over the place," Boland gestured with his hands to show the *Field's* evasive maneuver. "Our lookouts finally identified the plane as a 'Claude.' Just about then, Henderson jumped down from his G.Q. station in the torpedo director and ran aft to the fantail. He must have remembered that the safety's for the stern depth charges had been left off. Well, just as Henderson was turning the lock on the last 'ash can,' Captain Gillig threw the helm hard starboard. The turn was just in time. That 'Claude' passed right over the fantail, sheared its fixed landing gear off on our number "5" gun and hit the water just a few feet off the port side of the fantail. The plane pancaked on the surface of the water, then ricocheted two hundred yards smack into the *Collsgrove* which had just started an emergency turn to avoid colliding with us. That 'Claude' must have had a bomb attached to its belly because the *Collsgrove* disintegrated and went down with almost all hands. I figure that the Jap must have hit one of her ammo lockers. My brother was ashore with the Sixth Marine Division. He told me he could hear the explosion over all the noise that was going on around him on the beach."

Boland stopped to smear some strawberry jam on his cornbread. "Getting back to Henderson," he paused, biting into the bread, "I'm not sure if it was our abrupt turn or the shower of water that knocked him over the side, but when the smoke and spray cleared, Henderson was gone. We didn't even find that crumpled-up chief's cap he always wore that looked like it'd been run over by a tank."

"Nobody saw him go overboard?" Royal quizzed.

"No, not even the crew on the stern 20-millimeters, and they were only a few feet away from him. With a ton of water cascading down on the fantail, I guess they were too busy trying to keep from getting washed over the side themselves."

"I still don't see why the crew came up with this ghost story," Royal shrugged.

"Well, Henderson had the dubious distinction of being the *Field's* only fatality in the entire war, and from that day on the ship continually broke down. Our steering casualties began to occur almost on a weekly basis. Instead of being known as the luckiest, everyone starting calling the *Field* the most fouled-up 'can' in the Fifth Fleet. Nobody on the ship could figure out why her luck had suddenly changed. Finally, the crew decided it had to be Henderson's doings. They reasoned that he was so damn mean when he was alive, it must have really fried his ass to have to 'buy the farm' for a crew he hated so much."

Boland poured Royal a second cup of coffee. "The fact that nobody actually saw him go over the side added to the mystery, and pretty soon a fair portion of the crew really started to believe that Henderson was causing all our trouble. They were sure that the old torpedoman was doing his damndest to deep-six the *Field* and everyone aboard her. Fortunately, he didn't have much time left to do it. The war ended and the *Field* became one of the very first ships to go into 'mothballs'."

"Too bad when she was re-commissioned, she didn't leave her ghost back in Charleston," Royal said in a brooding tone. "I expect I'll have enough to worry about with obsolete equipment and a new and inexperienced crew, not to mention the North Koreans and the Chinese. I don't think I'll have any time left over for ghosts." Royal hesitated for a moment, then said, "My big worry's not Henderson, its that 'Claude'."

"What do you mean? The damage the plane did to the *Field* was only minor."

"I've always been a firm believer in the law of averages," Royal explained in a soft tone. "You mentioned that the *Field* came through a lot of major engagements without getting a scratch. The way I see it, she used up the last of her nine lives that day off Okinawa. I'd say that Kamikaze had the name *Charles P. Field* inscribed across its nose but the postman fouled up and delivered it to the *Collsgrove*. I just hope there isn't another postman waiting for us somewhere around Wonsan with orders to rectify his mistake."

●   ●   ●

Candace regretted that she had gone drinking with Garrett after the play the night before. It was close to 1:30 by the time she finally got to bed. She thought she'd felt Garrett slip out sometime during what might have been the middle of the night. One thing was certain, she'd never understand how he could function with only two or three hours sleep; she chalked it up to his navy training.

At least Garrett would be away for the next two weeks, maybe she'd manage to get some sleep, she thought, squinting into a small hand mirror. Candace felt a little guilty about being glad she wouldn't see him for awhile. This unexpected reprieve should give her the necessary time to get up enough strength to tell him what she would have told him the morning he met her at the airport. This duty he was being sent to perform at Eniwetok, she wondered if it would be dangerous. She'd never heard of an island with that name but after seeing "*South Pacific*" the night before, she almost envied him. Candace wondered if it would be anything like "Bali Hai". With the war over, she imagined that navy duty in those islands must be pretty easy to take. Afterall, he was fortunate that they weren't sending him off to Korea. One thing was certain, she'd have to tell him before he left on May 26th.

She shuffled through some papers on her desk. This was going to be one of *those* days, she told herself. Dammit! She'd even slept through the alarm she'd set for 7:30. Good thing the office was so close to her apartment. She knew she couldn't crack down on her staff's tardiness if she began coming in late herself. From what she'd observed of their performance so far, it probably wouldn't make much difference whether they showed up late or not, she decided.

Candace looked into the large mirror mounted on the wall of her private lavatory, her status symbol as chief honcho of B.B.Y. and S.'s West Coast enterprises. And as if to reinforce her omnipotence, the board of directors had appointed her account management director as well as president. She didn't feel too omnipotent on this particular morning as she stood before the mirror rubbing her finger under her left eye which she was certain looked bloodshot.

Walking back to her desk, she slinked down in the enormous fan-shaped chair which still held a strong odor of cigars, a lasting memorial of her predecessor who had recently been forced into retirement. After a week of careful observation, Candace was convinced that the action by the B.B.Y. and S. board was more than justified. She'd never seen such a slipshod operation. Her new staff wouldn't last a day back on Madison Avenue, she told herself as she picked up a hefty folder of account profiles, accounts that had been targeted but not ensnared. The way things looked to her, they'd be lucky to hold on to the few decent accounts they already had. She knew she had quite a challenge facing her and for the first time she wasn't fully convinced that she would come out on top. She put the folder down and reached for the intercom. "Tracy," she called, "please ask Greg and Conrad to come into my office."

"Yes, right away," her secretary answered. Starting to summon the director of marketing services and his counterpart in management/finance, she hesitated, then buzzed Candace back. "I'm sorry I forgot to tell you earlier, the receptionist gave me a message for you yesterday afternoon shortly after you left the office. She said a gentleman came by to see you."

"Did he leave his name?"

"No, but he said he was an old friend of yours from New York."

"What did he look like?"

"I really don't know, I never saw him. The receptionist seemed quite impressed though."

"Alright, thank you. I imagine if it was important he'll be back," Candace said flipping down the intercom switch. She was really curious now, an old friend from New York? She found this little mystery quite perplexing. If it was anyone from the home office, she was certain that she'd have been told in advance. Well, she couldn't sit there thinking about it all morning. There were several high salaried executives, which, to borrow a phrase from Garrett's branch of service, would have to be told to either shape up or ship out!

Candace took most of the day to work her way through a series of conferences with B.B.Y. and S.'s key staff. A little after three, she gave audience to Troy Foster, the director of creative services, and Ronald Paradise, the agency's copy chief.

Foster, handsome and fortyish, was first into the room. "Candace, I'd like to take this opportunity to tell you that you really add a welcome touch of charm to this office," Foster's smile seemed more like a leer.

"Thanks, Troy, you're very gracious. However, I didn't travel three thousand miles just to charm the staff." She shot an annoyed look at Troy. "I'm much more interested in getting this agency back on track."

Ronald paradise quietly slipped into his seat, primly crossing his legs. He sat there simmering like water in a kettle as his new boss lady set about the task of systematically shredding to bits the entire promotional campaign for Cherokee motorcycles which he and Foster had spent six weeks formulating.

Troy, who had quite a reputation around the office as a lady killer, continued to fondle Candace with his eyes, seemingly oblivious to her scathing evaluation of his department's performance. Paradise continued to pout, evoking little sympathy from Candace.

Finally coming to the defense of his proposal for Cherokee, Foster proclaimed, "I have it on highly reliable authority that Columbia Studios is planning to film a Brando flick about motorcycle gangs right here in California. Brando's the number one box office attraction these days and our campaign will be timed to come out just before release of the picture."

"That would be great if we were out to promote black leather jackets," Candace retorted in an apathetic voice. "You know, somebody out there must buy motorcycles besides the Hell's Angels."

"I suppose you'd like us to feature some old lady riding one of those noisy things in a Mother Hubbard and a bibsy hat," Paradise sneered, raising his eyebrows.

"Well, Ronald, I'm not too sure what a bibsy hat is, but maybe that might be an idea worth consideration. Troy, I'd like you to pick up the ball and run with that one. It has possibilities."

"Alright, Candace, I'll get my people moving on it right away. Is there anything else?" Foster asked, suddenly conscious of the sweat that had formed on his forehead.

"Yes there is," Candace answered coolly. "That art department of yours is pathetic. I've known eight-year-olds who could do a more professional job in their drawing class. The story boards they've prepared for the Layton Tea commercials don't even relate to the copy. Do they even bother to read the copy before they go ahead with the art work?"

"Of course they do," Troy stuttered nervously as he reached for the huge story board Candace was handing him.

Looking much like a tigress preparing to swallow the great white hunter, she said, "This copy describes two teenagers sitting by the lake sipping tea from a Thermos bottle while the story board shows them in a canoe drinking out of glasses. Doesn't the left hand of your department know what the right hand is doing?"

"Yes, eh, I see what you mean," he mumbled in an almost inaudible voice. Pale and confused, Troy Foster had the sick look of someone who had just come out of an anesthetic. "Is that all?" he asked feebly.

"Not quite," Candace said as she took back the story board. "I think that footage your team took up at Ford Ord last week put too much emphasis on the tank and not enough on the sports car. Remember, the tank was just a gimmick to highlight the ruggedness of the auto. If the Detroit Tank Arsenal gets around to assigning us their account, your photographers might be able to justify shooting a tank from forty different angles. Do you realize that the car doesn't even show up in half of the footage?"

"No, Candace. I haven't had a chance to review the film with my art director yet," Foster answered in a near whisper.

"What's the name of that Colonel at Ford Ord...the one you said was so cooperative?"

"La Roche."

"Well, call him right away. Tell him we'd like to send the photographers back up to Monterey. Get them moving as soon as he gives you the okay...and this time, Troy, make sure they know what product they're selling!"

Kevin Logan wondered if the large watercolor on the wall behind the receptionist's desk had been mistakenly hung upside down. He'd never been able to understand modern art even after taking that elective art course during his junior year. That was understandable since he had no interest in the subject and only signed up for the course because he'd been told the instructor used nude female models. He leaned back in his seat and studied the painting again. The splatter of yellow cubes and orange triangles made no sense whatsoever. He wondered if the shapes were intended to convey something Freudian.

He glanced at his watch once more, it read 4:37. Too bad the cute receptionist from the day before wasn't still holding down the fort, Logan thought. In her place sat a thin young woman with rather nondescript features and the slight trace of a mustache. It wasn't important, after all, she'd treated him coolly when he asked about seeing Miss Moffet. He decided he'd wait a few more minutes before approaching her again. Tired of trying to figure out the meaning of the painting, he started wondering what kind of legs the receptionist had. Her desk completely obscured his view. Sometimes these plain Janes turned out to be over-sexed, regular little firecrackers in bed, he told himself. His thoughts were broken by the sharp metallic crack of a door closing down the hall on his right.

He looked up just in time to see the creative services director scurry by with the copy chief close at his heels. As they passed, Kevin heard Paradise demand, "Well, what do you think of Miss Bitch from New York City, now? Are you still determined to get into her pants, if she wears any?"

Kevin wished he could have heard the reply but the two disappeared down another hallway at the far side of the receptionist area. The door to his right opened and closed again with the same piercing crack. Logan sprung to his feet, immediately recognizing the tall blonde who approached the reception area.

"Candy bar, you're as fetching as ever," he said eagerly, causing the recep-tionist to lower her copy of *Colliers*.

"What are you doing here?" Candace gasped. Breathing rapidly, she tried to maintain her composure, conscious that the receptionist was taking everything in.

"Well, I just..."

"I don't want to discuss it out here!" she snapped. "Come into my office," she said in a slightly less frantic tone, grabbing at the sleeve of Kevin's brown sports jacket.

The receptionist leaned out as far as she could but the door of Candace's office slammed shut before she could see what was happening.

"You know, you ought to do something about that door," Kevin said smiling. "It really makes a hell of a noise when you're sitting out there in the reception area."

"I'd much rather do something about you! Now what are you doing here?" she demanded, retreating behind her massive desk.

"I don't know if I should bother to tell you after that greeting you just gave me. I bet Harry Truman would be nicer to Stalin."

"I told you to stay out of my life two years ago!" shouted Candace in an exas-perated tone. "Didn't I make it clear to you that day in New York?"

"Yeah, you made it clear alright, especially after you stole the second biggest account in the agency from me. You're the reason I had to leave B.B.Y. and S."

"I had nothing to do with your leaving," she said almost sympathetically. "They weren't going to assign it to you, anyway."

"How are you so sure? Did old man Barlow tell you that while he was bang-ing you?"

"You're the same crude bastard, Kevin, you haven't changed a bit."

"That's funny, I remember when you thought I was the greatest thing since bubble gum."

"That was back in college. I've changed quite a bit since then, or haven't you noticed? And speaking of college, don't you ever call me 'candy bar' again. You know how much I hate it!"

Kevin laughed to himself, remembering how she had picked up the nickname. It was the year she'd been chosen "Home Coming Queen." Soon after, the word got around campus that the football team had given her that appellation because half the squad had managed to take a bite. With that in mind, Kevin always thought it fortunate that Candy hadn't been named "Queen of the R.O.T.C."

"Okay, Kevin, I'm sorry I popped off like that out in the hall. It wasn't very professional of me, but you really caught me off guard," Candace said softening her tone. "Look, let's get something straight once and for all. I had absolutely nothing to do with your leaving the agency. Besides, I was told that you resigned of your own accord to go work on the United Cyclotron account at Brice and Gwin."

"I didn't have much choice; I was too embarrassed to stay at B.B.Y . and S. After you grabbed that Cola account right out from under me, your buddy, big daddy Barlow kicked my ass over to the General Standard and Sanitary account where another one of your cronies, Madeline Clausen, put me to work writing promotional brochures."

Candace was well aware of what happened. As Kevin spoke, she made a vain attempt to hold back the broad smile that was forming around her gorgeous mouth.

"And I guess you're going to tell me that you knew nothing about the first assignment that bitch girl friend of yours gave me to do?" Logan bantered.

"No, I never asked Maddy anything about you. As far as I was concerned, you and I were ancient history. I hope you understand that I still feel the same way."

"Don't flatter yourself," he shot back angrily. "Anyway, you asked me why I left the agency so at least let me tell you, not that I think for one moment that your deft hand wasn't behind the whole thing."

"I told you, I knew nothing about it." Her expression belied her protestation.

"It was the first assignment that did it," Kevin continued. "Clausen told me to prepare a sixteen page brochure on bidets!" his eyes flashed with rage. "Can you imagine some flat-chested bleached blonde like Madeline Clausen telling me, Kevin Logan, to go write about bidets? I didn't even know what a bidet was! I thought it was a fancy name for a bathroom cabinet or one of those little trays that hold soap. How do you think I felt when my little snot-nosed secretary started giggling all over the office just because I asked her what a bidet was? You know, I'm still sure you put Clausen up to giving me that assignment. She had two women working on that plumbing account besides me. She could have at least given me something masculine sounding to write about like urinals!"

By now Candace was laughing almost uncontrollably. "I'm sorry, Kevin, I really don't mean to laugh, I can appreciate how you must have felt, especially you," she replied, wiping huge tears of laughter from her blue eyes.

"Within a month, every guy in the place was making wise cracks. I heard they were even referring to me as the bidet king. Even the fairies, who probably envied the assignment, were making remarks," he snarled. "That's when I knew I had to switch agencies. I hope you're aware that I took a big drop in pay when I went over to B. and G."

"That still doesn't tell me what you're doing here in my office. I happen to know that Brice and Gwin doesn't have a West Coast operation, and if they were planning to start one, they wouldn't be sending out copywriters to lay the ground work."

Sadly Kevin realized that Candace had just torpedoed the snow job he was about to lay on her. He knew he'd have to think of something fast. The truth was out of the question. How could he tell her he was a swabby again? Maybe he'd say that he had accepted a navy commission, no that might get too hairy. Suppose she suggested they go to the officers club...besides, there was a persistent rumor floating around Madison Avenue that she had quietly married some army brass during a trip to Europe. Dammit, he'd have to come up with something in the next few seconds.

"Have you read the "*Caine Mutiny*" yet?" he asked, playing for time.

"No, but I'm planning to. Everyone's been telling me how good it is. In fact, I saw something in the paper the other day about Columbia purchasing the movie rights."

"Exactly!" Kevin's face brightened. "That's why I'm out here." Good old Candy, he thought, she sinks me one minute, then throws me a life raft the next. "I'm going to work on the script," he said confidently. "Remember when we were dating back in college, I always told you my main ambition was to be a screen writer, especially on movies where I could utilize my experiences from the war."

"No, I only remember you talking all the time about how you were going to write the great American novel."

"Well, yeah, that too, but this is sort of a short cut until I really get my book underway."

"Okay, so that's why you're in California, but how did you know where to find me? I've only been out here a little over a week."

"Oh, that was easy. You got a ten-line blurb in last week's *Advertising Age.* It mentioned your promotion, and that you'd be wearing two hats directing the B.B.Y. and S. operation out here. Don't tell me you didn't see it."

"No, I saw it. I just forgot all about it, that's all."

"I'm glad to see that success hasn't gone to your head. What does your husband think about your coming out here to play queen of the hill?" Logan asked with a smirk, deciding to broach the subject he had sidestepped for so long back in New York.

"That's nobody's business but mine!" she snapped back viciously.

"Calm down, Candy. I'm not getting nosy. You don't have to tell me anything you don't want to. Did you forget that you and I go back a long way together? Once I even wanted to pop the big question, remember?"

"Well, you said you wanted to marry me, but I was never really certain you meant it. Anyway, we were dumb college kids then, at least I was. You'd been through a war and everything," she hesitated, "that seemed to make you older. Besides, it was a safe proposal on your part. You knew damn well that my parents would have gone through the roof if their little wasp princess came home and announced that she wanted to marry an Irish Catholic, one with a brother a priest no less," she grinned.

"Don't feel bad, my family wouldn't have been jumping for joy about the idea either. I could just see Aunt Maureen pulling out her beads for my lost soul. It is a shame though," he shrugged.

Candace discreetly let the remark pass unacknowledged even though she knew he was right. Nobody before or after Kevin had been able to turn her on the way he could. When they were making love, every inch of her body became erogenous. Religion was only an excuse...an easy out...far easier than admitting, even to herself, that the guy she was so physically attracted to was probably the world's biggest heel. Even back in college, she knew that in Kevin's eyes, women only had one function, and it certainly wasn't to eat. Not that she was any saint herself, afterall, hadn't she cheerfully given it away to a delivery boy behind her uncle's barn when she was only fifteen.

Dammit, she thought, here she is making small talk with this bastard, listening to his phony line, knowing that he's here for one reason only, to get her in bed. Worse yet, after a token display of resistance, she knew she'd probably let him.

Hell, what a screwed up world, she thought. Garrett was the only really decent man she'd ever met, the only one who hadn't been out just to make her. He was everything Kevin would never be, yet, she couldn't bring herself to love him no matter how hard she tried. She even welcomed his long tours of duty overseas. They made the situation much easier for her. She dreaded the possibility that someday Garrett would resign his commission. Fortunately, for both their sakes, she would tell him very soon. All she needed was the courage to do it. Kevin's unexpected appearance wasn't helping things, she thought. But Kevin or no Kevin, she knew she could blame no one but herself for marrying Garrett.

She often wondered why she had gone through with it. She never really loved him, even in the beginning. She had broken up with Kevin for the third time, then Garrett walked through that French perfume shop just in time to catch her on the rebound. Garrett was the white knight she had dreamed about when she was a little girl, and the way he looked that day in his dress white uniform did nothing to dispel the illusion. Those two weeks that followed were possibly the most pleasant of her life. Garrett was such fun to be with, yet even then, she didn't love him. Candace suddenly realized that Kevin was asking her something.

"Hey, are you alright? You look like you're off in the clouds somewhere," Logan said angrily.

"No, I'm sorry, I've had a pretty rough day, that's all, now what were you asking me?"

"I asked why you've always been so secretive about that husband of yours. What's the matter, does he have two heads or something?"

"You should look half as good," her eyes flashed defensively.

"The way I heard it, he's a high ranking army officer, someone you met in the south of France when you were handling that perfume account."

"Yes, that's right. What else do you know?" her eyelids fluttered nervously.

"Not very much. In fact, I don't even know your married name."

"No, and you're not going to know it either," she shot back.

"Why not? Think I might embarrass you?"

"Exactly."

"You're not very secure in your marriage," Kevin taunted.

"Of course, I am!"

"Okay then, what's your name and where's your husband?"

"La Roche! He's a colonel and he's stationed up in Monterey at Ford Ord. Anything else?"

"No, Mrs. La Roche," he laughed. "By the way are you seeing him tonight?"

"I won't be seeing him for two weeks. He's going off on maneuvers." She said the words, fully conscious of the consequences.

It was a little past eight when they arrived at Terryhill Drive and entered Candy's apartment. Kevin was impressed with the airy floor to ceiling windows and especially the stained walnut walls that formed an ideal backdrop for the brightly colored furniture. Candy excused herself to go to the bathroom, instead she hurried into the bedroom where she quietly locked the door of the closet that contained Garrett's clothes, including two blue uniforms. She returned to the living room just as Kevin finished mixing her an extra potent version of what he remembered was her favorite drink. Handing her a Brandy Sling, he reached for the half-empty fifth of Canadian Club in the well stocked liquor cabinet and poured himself a generous shot.

They settled down on the sofa ostensibly to watch television though their thoughts were far removed from whatever program they might have tuned in on. Kevin met little resistance as he kissed her, eased her down across the massive red cushions, and pulled her skirt and slip back above her waist. She made a feeble attempt to push his hand away as he deftly slid it up her leg. As he tugged at the elastic top of her silken underpants, he suddenly recalled the caustic remark made by the swishy ad exec earlier that day. Too bad he couldn't gift-wrap them and send them to the little weasel, he laughed to himself as he slipped the panties down along her thighs. She kicked out one leg, catapulting her shoe out into the middle of the floor. Kevin reached down, removed the other shoe, and gently dropped it next to the sofa.

Candy's hair, piled high and carefully coiffured in beehive fashion came unfastened, hanging down across her face in long golden strands to give her a helpless, almost ravaged look. Kevin could feel the warmth of her thighs pressed hard now against his. He unzipped the back of her dress and pulled it down off her shoulders. He had trouble unsnapping the hook of her bra, finally she reached around and unfastened it for him. Just like old times, Kevin thought, his fingers gently racing across her bare breasts. She moaned loudly and Logan knew that he had found a new home away from home for the next two weeks.

It was almost six the following morning when Logan departed for Point Loma. Just before leaving the apartment he quietly walked back into the bedroom and looked down at Candy. He kissed her gently on the cheek and she rolled over with half-closed eyes. "Will I see you tonight?" She asked through a sleepy mist.

"You bet you will, Candy bar," he winked, gently squeezing her hand.

Logan was quite pleased with himself as he waited a few blocks from Candy's apartment for the bus that would take him back to the Point Loma Sonar School. He thought of the next two weeks, and hoped his system would stand up under such steady wear and tear. He certainly wasn't going to pass up the opportunity to find out. He spotted a coin booth at the Esso station across the street. Obtaining the number from information, he passed it on to the long distance operator, then deposited a hefty pile of coins.

"Orderly room, Fort Ord, Corporal Rice speaking, can I help you, Sir?" the voice boomed over the wires from Monterey.

"Yes, this is Major Barrington down in San Diego," Logan spoke up. "We have some training materials we'd like to return to one of your colonels but we don't have his full name. We'd also like to verify that he's still at Fort Ord before we send it up. His last name's La Roche."

"Yes, Sir. I'll check the roster, please hold on, Sir...yes, Major, we do have a La Roche, but he's a Lieutenant Colonel. His full name is Arthur M. Do you want me to find out if he's presently on post, Sir?"

"No, Corporal. You've been very helpful," Kevin said, placing the receiver back on the hook.

So "Candy bar" really was telling the truth about her hubby, Kevin grinned. All the years he'd known her, even back in college, she'd thrown the truth around the way other people tossed volley balls. He hated to admit it but even he had never been able to snow people with such skill and aplomb. He just hoped she wouldn't decide to call Columbia and check on that screenwriter's line he had dropped on her. He stepped into the bus and headed back to Point Loma.

The next two weeks went much as Logan had anticipated, and it was easy to come up with a plausible excuse to explain his appearance at her office each afternoon. Aware that Candy would never believe he was commuting daily between L.A. and La Jolla, Logan told her that the studio had appointed him as its liaison with the 11th Naval District. His assignment, he said, was to scout out suitable locales at the San Diego Destroyer Base that might lend themselves to the film. Logan hoped Candy wouldn't ask him anything about the story line. Between his attendance at school each day, and his attendance in Candy's bed each night, he hadn't even found time to hunt up a copy of "*The Caine Mutiny*," much less read any of it.

On Candy's part, even the mere mention of the word destroyer made her nervous. Suppose, she thought, that by some damnable coincidence, Garrett's destroyer should be chosen to serve as the *Caine*. From the description Garrett had given her, his ship, the *Field*, was pretty much of a sea-going antique...probably the very thing that Columbia was looking for...and the kind of ship that the Navy wouldn't even miss. If that happened, Kevin and Garrett were bound to meet. No! She couldn't let that happen. She wanted a divorce, but she didn't want it that way, Candy reflected worriedly.

On the final night before DesDiv 291's scheduled return to San Diego, Candy and Logan drove north to Carlsbad for a candlelight dinner overlooking the rolling Pacific. Half-way through the *scampi* and *fettuccine verde*, Candace solemnly announced her intent to terminate their current liaison, especially since her husband was returning from his "army" maneuvers the following day. She and Logan were cutting things rather close as it was, she suggested coyly.

Much to her surprise as well as her disappointment, Logan accepted her pronouncement without any show of emotion. Such nonchalance was a stunning blow to her ego, especially since she had anticipated a long drawn-out argument. Candy had no way of knowing Kevin's brief "season in the sun" was slated to end the next day anyway when he would have to report back to Dry Dock Number 5 to help prepare the *Field* for sea.

In Kevin's eyes, things had worked out far better than he had expected. Certainly the timing was perfect with hubby off playing soldier the same two weeks that he had been assigned shoreside duty at Point Loma. Besides, after thirteen nights of bedding the beautiful Candace, Logan mused, his libido was in dire need of respite.

Driving back along S21, which runs along the California shore line, Candy said icily, "I don't think Garrett would appreciate your staying over tonight. Besides," she sulked, "you've gotten more than enough of the only thing you ever wanted from me." Dammit! Candy cursed under her breath as Garrett's name slipped out. She hoped that Kevin hadn't caught it.

"I don't remember twisting your arm to get you into your bedroom," Logan shot back. "By the way, who's Garrett? Isn't your husband's name Arthur?"

"Yes, but he doesn't like it. He prefers his middle name!"

"Strange middle name for someone who uses M for a middle initial."

"How do you know his middle initial, and his first name for that matter? I never mentioned anything but his last name. Have you been checking up on me, you bastard?"

"You really are a magnificent beast when you get fired up," Kevin smiled.

"Just answer my question!" Candy demanded, her eyes flashing.

"You mentioned it when you told me he was a colonel at Ford Ord. You mean you don't remember?"

"No, I don't remember! You obviously telephoned Ford Ord to see if there was really a Colonel La Roche up there, didn't you?"

Kevin immediately pleaded the Fifth Amendment with a broad grin that immediately confirmed her accusation.

"Well, when I said middle name I meant to say it's his confirmation name," she snapped back.

"Confirmation name? Don't tell me you actually went ahead and married a papist. Your old man must have had a stroke." Kevin couldn't hold back his laughter which infuriated Candace all the more.

"No, I didn't marry a papist as you put it! Garrett happens to be an Episcopalian!" she angrily retorted, her face flushed even through her deep tan.

Pretty fast on her feet, Kevin thought, convinced more than ever that Candy wasn't married to a light colonel named La Roche. However, the name Garrett did have a nice "waspie" ring to it, he acknowledged, but the army was a hell of a big outfit. Without the last name to tag onto Garrett, Logan knew he didn't have the chance of a snowball in hell of ever coming across the guy, not that that was really high on his list of priorities. It was strictly a matter of curiosity. Besides, ever since "Candy bar" dumped on their engagement, Logan had gotten an almost sadistic delight out of bugging her at any opportunity.

Back at the apartment, Candy was still miffed at Logan for making the phone call to Monterey. On the other hand, she thought, the call actually may have worked to her advantage since it did confirm the existence of the fictitious husband, and she was certain that Kevin had swallowed that bit about the Confirmation name. Even so, there was really no reason why he shouldn't have trusted her, she told herself with total conviction.

For the rest of the evening, Logan employed every subtle device he could muster to overcome her hostility. Aware that this might possibly be his last chance to bed her, at least for the foreseeable future, he had no intention of dropping the ball while only inches from the goal line. The fact that she let him into the apartment when they returned from Carlsbad told him that Candy wanted it as badly as he did. A firm believer in a popular quip of the day that advised "candy is dandy but liquor is quicker," Kevin lost no time in mixing the drinks. As usual with Candy, the Brandy Slings acted as an aphrodisiac, and soon any enmity for Kevin was forgotten. Logan left the apartment the following morning, happy but thoroughly spent. He hoped he would gain his strength back in time to take on the North Koreans.

Logan thought he detected a few drops of rain in the air as he approached Dry Dock Number 5. The abundance of staging and other work platforms rigged around the *Field's* wheelhouse gave her normally austere bridge structure the topsy-turvy, pagoda-like appearance of a Jap battleship, he decided, as he passed over the gangplank that stretched from the side of the dry dock to the destroyer's quarterdeck. On the floor of the huge concrete basin, yard workers were busily applying the final coat of dark red paint to the now barnacle-free underhull.

He wondered if they'd manage to complete their work before the approaching rain clouds unloaded.

After checking in with Ensign Daly at the quarterdeck, Logan proceeded to the combat-information-center where he joined Howie Murray and the four third-class, already hard at work checking out the various pieces of electronic equipment crammed within the very limited space that served as the *Field's* brain.

•   •   •

By mid-afternoon, *Halsey Wayne, Abner Ward* and *John Morgan* were securely nestled once again along the side of the long quay at the destroyer base. Aboard *Halsey Wayne*, Owen Garrett Royal bid adieu to Sandy Boland, his friend and host for the past fourteen days. As he left the *Wayne*, Commander Boland called after him, "Be sure to give my best regards to Chief Henderson."

Within a short time, Royal was back aboard the *Charles P. Field* listening to a lengthy recital of problems and discrepancies related to the ship's overhaul. Work had been sped up considerably, Cobb informed him, since the dry dock was urgently needed to accommodate another destroyer currently enroute to San Diego. The new tenant was literally limping home after colliding with a North Korean mine. The ship had received temporary repairs at Yokosuka and Pearl Harbor, Cobb reported.

Now the yard will really cut corners, Royal grimaced, and the *Field's* limited refit will be limited still further, he told himself, finally convinced that his ship had a definate propensity for "Murphy's Law." Even so, he was still not ready to give any credence to *DD-505's* phantom chief torpedoman. Realizing there was nothing he could do about the reduction in the ship's refit time, he carried out a brief inspection of her spaces, then headed off to see his wife.

Candace went through all the motions of a loving, dutiful spouse and gave Royal no hint that she was looking for an opportunity to terminate their union. At one point, while they were touring the Palomar Observatory, she decided to tell him then and there but was unable to phrase the words. Ashamed of herself for coming so close and then chickening out, she knew she couldn't avoid telling him much longer.

As they drove back to La Jolla, Candace lowered the volume of the radio so she could listen to Garrett describe some of his recent experiences aboard the *Halsey Wayne*. When she turned the sound back up, Guy Mitchell was half-way through a song about a golden-haired angel and "*A Pawnshop 'Round the Corner in Pittsburgh, Pennsylvania.*"

Chapter IV - "On Target!"

The yard period continued without incident, and at the end of the third full week, each member of the ships' company had reported back from his assigned school, or from temporary duty with the local Armed Forces Police contingent. By this time most of the *Field's* equipment and machinery had been activated, serviced and tested. The final two days were set aside for "field day" routine, a grossly misnamed term used by the navy to designate the day or time period during which a ship is thoroughly cleaned from truck to keel and bow to stern. As the crew "turned to," each man knew that within a matter of hours, the dry dock's door-like caisson would be moved aside and the blue water of San Diego Harbor would rush in to lift the destroyer from the docking blocks.

The day for *DD-505* to get underway came sooner than anyone expected. Commander Royal and the dock master examined the tide charts for that day and soon agreed on the most opportune time to flood the dock. A good half hour before special-sea-detail was called away, the *Field's* sailors were at their assigned stations at the ship's outboard valves to ensure that not a drop of water would penetrate the interior of the hull. At the same time, bluejackets from the yard were positioned at the various wale shores and hauling lines to prevent damage to ship or dock should there be a sudden shifting of weights or an unexpected alteration in wind or tide.

At 11:15, the dock master allowed the water to slowly enter the graving dock, and, when the water integrity of the destroyer's sea-valves was confirmed, a heavier volume was admitted. Within a short time the water level inside the dock had risen to the height of that outside; the caisson was floated and removed, and a gray tugboat with an unpronounceable Indian name towed the destroyer out into open stream. As soon as the *Field* was free of the dry dock, the tug cast off her lines and quickly scurried out of the way. The starboard screws began to kick and the destroyer lazily turned toward the channel, her slow movement affording the *Field's* sailors a panoramic view of the San Diego Naval Base and the surrounding shore area.

On her return passage down the channel, Commander Royal decided to test the capabilities of his C.I.C. team by requiring that they assist the bridge with course and speed recommendations during the *Field's* transit to YE-953, an ammunition lighter standing by in San Diego's outer bay. Thanks to Logan's skill at the maneuvering board which impressed the captain almost as much as it mystified Coates and Murray, the destroyer soon reached her allotted mooring place beside the ugly black-hulled barge waiting with her lethal cargo.

As soon as the ammo barge had been made fast along the *Field's* starboard side, the two tugs used to propel YE-953 loosed their hawsers and headed off in the direction of North Island. The barge, a long rectangular hulk, was topped by a house-like structure which sheltered a vast quantity and variety of ammunition. At each end of the structure, a red swallow-tailed "Baker" flag cautioned anyone within visual range that ammunition was being handled. A third Baker flag flapped from *Field's* yard, looking like one more smear of blood on the cloudless blue sky.

Because the *Field* still carried only a fifth of her allotted wartime complement and since the next two weeks called largely for simulated gunnery practice, only a limited amount of 5-inch and 40- and 20-millimeter ammunition was taken on board; the loading of torpedoes and depth charges deferred for a later date. By late afternoon, the destroyer had freed herself of the barge, refueled from a small yard tanker, and provisioned from a refrigerated stores lighter. These laborious but indispensable tasks completed, *DD-505* slipped past the outermost channel marker, receiving an indignant yawp from the shaggy pelican that made its home atop the tall buoy.

By 18:00, the knife-like edge of the destroyer's bow was slicing through the shallow swells beyond the harbor entrance, tracing a greenish-white wake on the ruffled velvet of the Pacific. Point Loma's familiar outline quickly faded astern as word to secure the special-sea-detail was passed over the general address system. Those not assigned to the first underway watch section staggered down to the mess deck for a bowl of *chili con carne,* Turk's "specialty" and a common item on the *Field's* bill of fare.

The chart house, which doubled as the torpedo tracking room, was sandwiched between the pilot house and commanding officer's sea cabin. As Royal and his executive officer entered, Ensign Warden was hard at work checking the several course changes the ship would be required to make between their present position and their destination, the Hunters Point Naval Shipyard at San Francisco. Cobb tried to hold down a queasy feeling as the *Field* heeled slightly to starboard. Hunched over the large hydrographic office chart, Royal took careful note of the various depths and currents they would encounter in the California coastal area.

"What time will we initiate the speed run, Captain?" Cobb asked as he checked Warden's dead reckoning.

"When we steady up off Point Conception," Royal said glancing up from the chart. "We'll be pretty far out so we shouldn't have to worry about tangling our screws in any stray fishing nets. What do you think?" he asked.

"Course looks good to me," Cobb said. "It's the speed run I'm nervous about. I just hope her sides don't break off when we take her up to thirty knots."

"Thirty-three," Royal smiled confidently, remembering the encouraging words from Sandy Boland about the *Field's* reputation as a greyhound. He glanced down at the chart, his eyes tracing the thin penciled line that indicated the ship's intended route. The line ran parallel to the mainland, windward of Catalina Island, then on to the lee of tiny Santa Barbara where it slanted seaward avoiding the larger islands of Santa Rosa and Santa Cruz with their heavy concentration of fishing boats. At a point sixty miles off Point Conception, the course once again roughly paralleled the curvature of the mainland but at an angle calculated to progressively lessen their distance from the coastline by the time they reached San Francisco.

The captain's night intentions called for maintaining a 15-knot cruising speed followed by a three-hour high-speed run during which all her boilers would be "lit off" and maximum steam pressure applied. At the time of the *Field's* first commissioning she had been able to exceed her designed speed of 35 knots. This fact had also been confirmed by Commander Boland. However, this was before the wear and tear of extensive wartime service when C.O.'s were constantly demanding "flank speed" from their "black gangs." Royal also knew that her engines had sat idle for five years in a state of dehumidification, and he found scant encouragement in her engineering logs which showed that during the last nine months she had seldom exceeded 20 knots. Royal's concern was well warranted, since he knew that the *Field* would soon be screening the fast carriers, the big sledge hammers of the Seventh Fleet.

The *Field's* combat-information-center, like that of most naval vessels in 1952, was cramped beyond comprehension and submerged in darkness, the latter to eliminate distracting reflections from the glossy surface of the radar scopes. The one small light, its goose-neck extension arched over the plotting table, did little to relieve the somber atmosphere created by the flat black wash of the bulkheads.

Murray, Bacelli and Paulsen, a radar striker, shared the first underway watch, rotating each hour between the "Sugar George" surface search radar, the maneuvering board and the dead reckoning tracer. Not officially on watch, Logan was utilizing the little light available to leaf through a well worn copy of "*From Here to Eternity*" which Nugent had deposited on the plotting board when he secured from special-sea-detail. As Logan expected, the steamier passages had been underlined. Unfortunately, Nugent had used a grease pencil from the plotting table and had inadvertently obscured most of the lines he had intended to highlight.

It was a quiet watch and the only contact on the radar scope had long passed her CPA, or "closest-point-of-approach." The contact, which C.I.C. had designated "Skunk Easy," had indicated a steadily opening range and therefore had been officially "scrubbed" by the officer-of-the-deck.

"So what do you think I should name my new son?" Murray asked Logan, nervously scraping the pointed tips of his steel dividers through the thin paper which covered the plate glass surface of the plotting table. "When we named Deirdre for Mary Alice's mother and then Jenny after my mom, I promised Mary Alice that we'd name the next one after her father, but tell me, Kev, can you imagine the poor kid going through life with a handle like Willis?"

"Why don't you name him after your father?" Bacelli cut in.

"Finbar?"

"Sorry I asked," Bacelli grunted, pointing his face back down at the radar scope.

"Cheer up," Kevin laughed, still scanning the best selling novel. "It will probably turn out to be another girl and your problem will be solved."

"Oh, no, this one's going to be a boy. I can feel it," the first-class radarman replied eagerly. "Willis though, I wouldn't even wish that on MacKinlay or the exec."

"Speak of the devil," Murray muttered half under his breath, then swinging around on the stool and stretching toward the funnel-shaped opening, he acknowledged, "Combat, aye!"

"Combat, we've been trying to get you on the phones for the past five minutes! Haven't you got them manned?" MacKinlay's voice was clearly discernable.

"Yes, sir, it must be the jack-box," Murray replied. "I'll check the plug, it must be loose."

"Very well, Combat, be more careful in the future," MacKinlay warned sternly.

Murray reached for one of the sound-powered telephones coiled and hung on the bulkhead rack. "MacKinlay's breaking balls again," he snapped. "The old man or the exec must be up on the bridge. He's trying to show them he's on the ball by giving us a blast. We've got a voice tube, squawk-box and handset. He knows we never man these damn head phones until we pick up a contact. He must think we're going to be torpedoed by the Catilina yacht club or something," Murray mumbled, slipping the uncomfortable metal band with the two earpieces over his head. "I'd like to shake that bastard up by reporting a new skunk closing on a collision course. Bet he'd turn three shades of green with the old man up there watching him."

"Don't you think you'd better tape another piece of paper over the plotting table just in case you really do pick up a new skunk?" Logan suggested.

Murray nodded in agreement as he glanced down at the large area of glass visible where his divider had scraped through the tissue. "Say, I noticed before that you're pretty sharp at maneuvering board problems," he said as he extracted a long role of white plotting paper from the draw under the DRT. "I never had much experience plotting," Murray shrugged. "We had so many radarmen in our C.I.C.'s aboard the *Enterprise* and *Franklin* that most of us became specialists at a particular station. I spent most of my time on the air-search radars, so I'd like you to handle the maneuvering board during special-sea-detail and general quarters. Mr. Coates says we won't be getting any additional pip-jockeys when the draft reports aboard up at Frisco, and he wants me to submit a finalized watch, quarter-and-station bill before we tie up at Hunters Point. I don't want you to think I'm trying to dump my job on you. It's just that C.I.C. will run a lot smoother with you working out the maneuvering board solutions, especially during G.Q. All of this polar coordination crap confuses the hell out of me, and when it comes to anything besides dames, Bacelli here and his buddies Nugent, Holiday and Gardiner are completely useless."

"Hey, I'm pretty good with the maneuvering board," Bacelli said in a hurt tone which was completely ignored by Logan and Murray.

"What about Ensign Coates?" Logan asked.

"He doesn't know his ass from an ice cream cone," Bacelli interjected sourly.

"That's probably why they made him C.I.C. officer," Murray laughed as he smoothed out the ruffles and taped the edges of the fresh tissue to the redwood border of the plotting table.

"Combat, bridge!" MacKinlay's voice interrupted again. "We'll be coming left to three-two-five in six minutes so keep a sharp watch ahead. You should be picking up several fishing trawlers on our new course!"

Murray looked up at the rectangular gray box mounted near the overhead. The button-sized light on the box flashed red as the words blared out from the speaker. "Combat, aye," Murray answered dully, then turning toward Logan, growled, "That damn MacKinlay chews us out for not manning the phones, then as soon as we do, he starts sending his messages down to us over the bitch-box." Then turning to Bacelli, he cautioned, "Keep your eyes glued to that scope! I don't want that ex-gyrene up there finding any more excuses to ream us out!"

"The OOD's prediction was incorrect and the next hour passed quietly without a single contact.

"This last hour's really dragging. Dammit, I'll be glad to hit the sack," Murray said, watching the bulkhead clock. "You were on a 'can' during the war, weren't you, Kev?" Murray asked, trying to keep awake as the luminous clock hands moved closer to 23:45, the time the mid-watch section would relieve them.

"I was on the *Laffey*," Logan half mumbled.

"Was she a *Fletcher* like this tub?"

"No, a class later, same hull but a different superstructure."

"Did you ever operate with the Charlie P.?" Murray quizzed.

"Probably, for that matter, she must have screened you more than once when you were on those two flattops."

"I don't know about the *Field*," Murray frowned, "but there's one *Fletcher* class destroyer I'll never forget...old 673, the *Hickox*," Murray said the words slowly and with obvious reverence.

"I thought you only liked 'bird farms'?" Bacelli piped up. "What's so special about the *Hickox*?"

"What's so special? She only saved my life, that's all."

"How'd that happen?" Logan asked, knowing that Murray would tell them anyway.

"It was March of '45. I was on the *Franklin* then. We were operating with Task Force 58 only fifty miles off the coast of Japan. We were getting ready to launch an early morning strike against some Nip battleships holed up in Kobe Harbor. I'm not superstitious or anything, but 'Big Ben's' number was thirteen. Unlucky thirteen," he groaned. "She'd already suffered over a hundred casualties from a kamikaze hit she took the previous October. I wasn't on her then. I transferred over to her from the *Enterprise* just about the time she completed her repairs at Puget Sound."

"Come on, Murray," Bacelli balked. "Get back to how the *Hickox* saved your ass. You're keeping us in suspense."

"Well, like I said, we were loading our planes up with bombs, and things were going along without any hitches. The Japs had made a few scattered attacks earlier but they didn't bother us much. We couldn't work up much of a sweat over a few screwball Nips anxious to get their suicide vows over with. As I remember it, the 'airedales' were getting the lead plane in position on the flightdeck when it happened. We weren't even at G.Q. If we had been, I wouldn't be here talking about it because everybody in C.I.C. was wiped out to a man."

"Didn't anybody pick the Jap up on radar?" Logan asked.

"No, the bastard dropped out of a cloud then sped in fast and low. He wasn't a suicider. He just dropped his two eggs and then flew off. I'm not even sure our fighters ever splashed him. The story is one of our Hellcats chased after the guy for almost an hour before he finally shot him down. I've always suspected that the bastard got away. He's probably back in Japan right now, hustling up geishas for G.I.'s."

"You're a full-fledged cynic," Logan shook his head.

"So where's the *Hickox* come in?" Bacelli implored impatiently.

"Hold your water, I'm getting to that," Murray snapped back. "Like I said, one of the bombs killed everybody in C.I.C. Luckily, I had just come off a watch in C.I.C. and didn't feel like any breakfast that morning, so instead of going down to the messhall, I decided to stroll back to the fantail to get some air and watch the carriers astern of us launch their planes. I was standing back there when the two bombs hit. The second one dropped right through the elevator and exploded on the hangar deck right in the middle of some TBM's that were being fueled and armed. The explosion wiped out the messhall which was also being used as an auxiliary magazine for bombs and rockets 'cause it was so close to the hangar deck. Just like with C.I.C., everybody down there got killed. Within a couple of minutes, the whole ship was turned into a giant blast furnace. I guess there were about forty of us trapped back there on the fantail. A cruiser, the *Santa Fe*, came alongside but there was no way we could get back through that blazing hangar deck with its exploding bombs and fuel lines. If we tried to jump off the fantail into the water astern, we'd have been sucked down into the screws and ground up like chopped meat. I told myself that there was no way I was going to get out of this one. I just started to pull out my rosary when I see this destroyer, the

Hickox, come tearing around into our wake. Her old man aimed her bow right at our stern and comes steaming up until she's practically touching us. Both ships are whipping along at a pretty fast clip and 'Big Ben's' popping off like Vesuvious on the Fourth of July. But that didn't bother the skipper of the *Hickox*. He nuzzled her nose right up between our two stern sponsors and holds it there until every one of us trapped back there could jump down to her foc'sle. They even rigged up a line from her forward gun mount so the stretcher cases could be transferred over. I never saw such a great piece of shiphandling. I tell you, when I hit that foc'sle, I knew God had reached down with his hand and plucked me right out of hell."

"You're confusing God with the *Hickox*," Logan snickered.

"No, I'm not," Murray said shaking his head. "We had almost eight hundred killed on 'Big Ben' that day. That was seven years ago; I've had a lot of time to think about things."

"That sounds very profound," Logan grinned. "Come to any conclusions?"

"Yes, I decided that it's the little things in life that make all the difference," Murray said, his tone grim. "The kid who relieved me on the air search radar that morning told me the messhall was serving 'shit on a shingle' for breakfast. I hate 'S.O.S.', especially first thing in the morning. That's why I decided to skip chow and go aft for some fresh air. Do you realize that my daughters Deirdre and Jenny would never have been born if I had liked 'shit on a shingle'?"

"Are you saying that God put 'S.O.S.' on the menu that morning?" Kevin taunted, deciding to play devil's advocate.

"Well, maybe he did, who knows?" Murray grunted, just as Nugent and Holiday came bounding through the hatchway to relieve the watch.

"What's the gloomy expression for, Murray?" Nugent laughed. "You look like you just found out that the world's gonna' end tomorrow or something."

"Do I have to be thinking about the end of the world just because I don't go around with a silly shit eatin' grin on my face all the time like you do!" Murray snapped angrily.

"Hey, don't bother him," Bacelli said plaintively. "Murray's been philosophizing. He's been telling us that it's the little things in life that really count."

"I'll buy that," Holiday chirped up.

"Yeah, the only little thing Holiday's interested in is right between his girlfriend's legs. Right, Holly?" Nugent asked with a smirk.

"How about cutting the bullshit and relieving the watch," Murray retorted. "I don't know about your buddy Bacelli over there, but I want to get some sleep. We're on course three-two-five, fifteen knots. Bridge says we should be running into a bunch of fishing boats but we haven't had a contact for well over an hour. That was 'Skunk Easy' so your next contact should be designated 'Skunk Fox'."

"Who's got the conn?" Nugent asked.

"MacKinlay," Bacelli sneered, handing over his set of sound-powered phones. "You better wear these while he's up there. He should be getting relieved any minute now, so you should have an easy watch. I imagine the all-American boy, Lieutenant Stockwell, will be taking over the conn for the next four hours."

Logan had the four-to-eight watch, which meant he'd have to relieve Nugent and Holiday at 03:45. This gave him a chance for three hours sleep if he hit the sack right away. However, he didn't feel much like sleeping. He'd been reading about the army captain's wife who was having an affair with a sergeant in the novel noted earlier. The girl in the book, Karen Holmes, had been treated really badly by her husband. Logan wondered how "Candy Bar" and her army husband were getting along. If one of them was getting pissed on, he'd bet a year's pay it wasn't Candy. He looked at his watch and figured that she was probably making it with somebody right at that moment back in La Jolla...back in the same bed he'd gotten so use to over the past two weeks. With all her faults, he had to admit she was fantastic to look at and by far the best lay he'd ever had.

Candy certainly knew how to utilize those looks, he mused, remembering the night back at B.B.Y. and S. after the Christmas party when he and a receptionist, looking for much-needed privacy, wandered into old man Barlow's office and found the ad agency head plowing Candy right on that big pink couch...the one so many of the agency's top clients sank their fannies into during business hours.

And Barlow, with a daughter two years older than Candy, Logan reflected as he peered out from the open signal bridge at a sea washed silver by a full moon.

Sunrise found the *Field* running parallel to a trio of sperm whales prompting the OOD to have the announcement of reveille accompanied by a hearty "Thar she blows!" A few of the early risers took a moment to inspect their three uninvited consorts before hurrying on to the morning shower line. In a short time a sizable chow line began to form along the starboard side of the main weather deck, this, in spite of the nauseous smell of incinerated bacon sifting up through the galley vents where it blended in with the equally unappetizing smell of stack gas.

At 09:30, the *Field* commenced her speed run. Royal, leaning over the bridge-wing bulwark watched the water fall away in long white ribbons. He could feel the violent vibrations, the whining of the turbines straining at their casings as the speed increased. He gripped the steel shielding that girded the bridge wing; even the plating beneath his feet seemed to rattle in protestation as the destroyer moved faster and faster over the calm blue water.

"We're making thirty-three knots, Captain," Lieutenant Stockwell shouted through the open door of the wheelhouse.

"Very well," Royal replied, turning towards his conning officer. "Maintain our present speed until 11:30, then take her up to thirty-five."

"Thirty-five, Captain?" the executive officer, standing nearby, questioned nervously. "The way she's vibrating now, I don't see how we'll even be able to hold our present speed."

"You don't have much confidence in the Charlie P., Aub," Royal said good-naturedly.

"It's not that; I just think we should quit while we're ahead."

With a little coaxing, the *Field* was soon bounding across the water at speeds she hadn't known since the days before the Japanese surrender. By 12:30, her trial successfully completed, the destroyer settled back down to a leisurely 15 knots, and course was resumed for San Francisco.

"Told you the old girl's still got a lot of kick left in her," Royal said with a broad smile as he handed a copy of the engineering officer's report to Aubrey Cobb. The paper showed that the ship had held a steady 37.1-knot speed for over eighteen minutes. For the first time since taking command, Owen Royal felt completely at ease. Tension and anxiety were gone as he reviewed the details of the morning's speed run. He was reassured, not only about the *Field*, but even more importantly, about himself.

During the afternoon, the *Field* carried out a series of general drills including simulated firing exercises during which the long gray barrels of her main battery were swung about and elevated at every conceivable angle. Commander Royal was reasonably satisfied by the prompt response of the gun crews and the manner in which the damage control parties were executing their various drill assignments. And while the ship was now proceeding at a moderate speed, to Royal, she seemed to be flying over the water like some majestic sea bird.

Because of the *Field's* unexpected performance, Cobb's ETA was inaccurate by almost two hours, and the *Field* slipped past the little mission church at Point Lobos just as the chimes of the evening Angelus drifted across South Bay. It was still quite light, the sky astern not yet taking on its evening glow although the beacons at the harbor entrance were already blinking.

The ship slowed her engines to rendezvous with the approaching pilot launch, and soon the destroyer was steaming under the Golden Gate, her puny mast pointing audaciously at the colossal crimson span. Entering the harbor, *DD-505* rounded North Point and slid by Blossom Rock and the tall beige smoke stacks rising up from Alcatraz Island. Ahead lay the Oakland Bay Bridge, and a little beyond, the unmistakable outline of an *Essex* class carrier. Anchored in the bay, the lights from her hangar deck were clearly visible through the gap-like openings in her side where huge steel doors had been slid back to expedite unloading operations. Royal observed the four barges nestled along her waterline waiting to receive the thousands of tons of munitions which had to be removed before the flattop could enter the huge graving dock at Hunters Point. As the *Field* drew closer, the white number on the carrier's stack took the shape of a "31" identifying her as the *Bon Homme Richard*. Royal wondered if the "Bonnie Dick," only recently back from Korea, would complete her stateside rest period in time to return and operate with the *Field*.

Minutes later, the *Field's* signal bridge received a blinker message from the closest of the three DesDiv 291 destroyers which had left San Diego two days earlier than the *Field*. Moored down the channel, the trio was barely visible through the gray curtain that was starting to mask most of the harbor. Royal could see that the flashing light was coming from the bridge of *DD-503*, the *Halsey Wayne*.

"WELCOME TO SAN FRANCISCO—WE HAVE BEEN KEEPING A RED LIGHT OVER THE DOOR FOR YOU."

The captain read and deciphered the message even before the signalman standing nearby had handed him the clipboard with the message pad, "Send this back to Commander Boland," Royal grinned as he hastily scribbled a reply.

"I AM CERTAIN THAT THE CREW OF THE FIELD WILL DO THEIR UTMOST TO KEEP THAT RED LIGHT BURNING."

Corny but appropriate, Royal thought, as his signalman rattled out the message on the shuttered searchlight nearby.

By 19:30, the top loops of the *Field's* six starboard hawsers were firmly secured around the big black mooring dolphins which stood quiet sentinel along the pier's edge. A sullen mood of disappointment was evident throughout the entire crew as the executive officer announced that no liberty would be granted until each man in the new draft was fully billeted and assigned to his respective division and duty station. With almost two hundred and fifty men reporting aboard, ship's company was uncomfortably aware that this could be a time consuming operation. The first of Cobb's directives called for evacuation of the Operation Department's after berthing space to make room for a now greatly expanded Deck and Gunnery Department. Murray, Logan and the rest of the Ops department's enlisted personnel were assigned quarters in a smaller berthing area directly under the ammunition-handling room for the number "3" gun, three spaces forward of their previous residence.

At 21:30 (9:30p.m.), a convoy of seven gray buses from U.S. Naval Receiving Station, Treasure Island, pulled through the main gate at the Hunters Point Naval Shipyard, proceeded on past the ghostly silhouettes of "mothballed" cruisers and auxiliary vessels in the reserve ship basin, and stopped abruptly, squeaking almost in unison, at the foot of the pier. Several of the Charlie P.'s now "old timers" leaned over the life lines, some curious, some resentful, as they eyed the new arrivals filing from the buses and unloading their sea bags from a large truck that had suddenly appeared on the scene. Within a few minutes, the chiefs and leading petty officers accompanying the draft formed the men into three sections and marched them to the destroyer's midship's gangway; seven feet of blue-gray planking by which the novice entered a unique adventure he would always remember, and the veteran returned to that unique hell he could never forget.

The attachment for the plan-of-the-day, Tuesday, April 29, listed billet and station assignments for each of the 243 "white hats" who had reported aboard the previous evening. Included was a modified division roster with the names of the four lieutenants and one lieutenant (jg.) now added to the destroyer's complement.

Department	Department Officer	Assistant
Deck & Gunnery	Lt. (jg.) Alan MacKinlay, USN	Ens. George Ritter, USNR
Operations	Lt. Donald Stockwell, USNR	Ens. Donald Coates, USNR
Engineering	Lt. Oscar Kimmick, USNR	Lt (jg) Andrew Phelan, USNR
Damage Control	Lt. Rolf Sternhagen, USNR	Ens. Micheal Daly, USNR
Navigation	Lt. Philip Oetjens, USNR	Ens. Richard Warden, USNR
Supply	Lt. Jesse Fickett, USNR	CWO Joseph Canavan, USNR

A brief note at the bottom of the P.O.D. listed the *Field's* shore patrol contribution for that evening in San Francisco and nearby Oakland. Among the petty officers assigned was Kevin Logan.

It was almost nine by the time Logan and Sammartino, a metalsmith 3rd, were dropped off at the amusement park just behind Harding Boulevard and the Pacific Ocean. Included in their patrol area was a 200-yard stretch of shooting galleries, hot dog stands, a Ferris Wheel and other mechanical contraptions and fun houses usually associated with an amusement park. A roller skating rink bordered one end of their route. The other end was terminated by an ornate and squeaky carousel.

"Hell of a lot of jail bait," Sammartino scowled as two teenage girls gave them the eye. "Can't make out around this place, that's for sure. My cousin Tony shacked up with a broad he picked up in Coney Island. Built like Marilyn Monroe, told him she was twenty-two, and she looked every bit of it. Then just when she and Tony started rollin' around in the sheets, her old man shows up with the cops. Turned out she was only fifteen. Most expensive piece Tony ever had, cost him two years in Dannemora..."

The metalsmith rambled on but Logan paid little attention, contributing no more to the conversation than a casual nod. The hours dragged and the patrol passed uneventfully. The most serious breech of military discipline encountered came in the form of the occasional sailor who had to be told to "square" his hat or a marine with an open collar button.

This was not the first time Kevin had visited this particular section of San Francisco. For him, it had been the scene of many a happy liberty. As the two petty officers walked toward the carousel, details of past visits began to return. Logan remembered a pair of windmills, gaunt and deserted in a field further down the road. He could still recall the loose shingles, the paintless hide, warped and bleached by years of sun and salt air. He vaguely remembered someone telling him that they had been built for the Golden Gate Exposition, and he wondered if they were still there, futilely waving their tattered arms at the sea. But even in the moonlight, it was impossible to observe their spectral outline from Logan's prescribed route.

As the patrol continued, Kevin became increasingly aware of his surroundings, particularly the forgotten melodies that seeped from the carousel and the numerous speakers positioned throughout the park. It was an old music roll, and Logan would have been happier had it been sealed away with other forgotten things like ration books, swing shifts and little flags with gold stars. The carousel continued to grind out the same seven songs:

"Let's Remember Pearl Harbor"
"No Love, No Nothing"
"Coming in on a Wing and a Prayer"
"Don't sit Under the Apple Tree"
"You'll Never Know Just How Much I Miss You"
"You'd be so Nice to Come Home to"
"Praise the Lord and Pass the Ammunition"

How many times had this contraption spun round and round since he'd been here in 1944, Logan wondered, honking out its songs from another war...from another time. Logan found himself wondering if even the two windmills really existed. Maybe they were from some vague dream. He wasn't certain, and the feeling made him uneasy.

"Ever read Quixote?" Logan suddenly asked his fellow shore patrolman.

"Who's he? I'm strictly a Mickey Spillane man," Sammartino snapped indignantly.

"Nobody important, just a guy who went around chasing windmills a very long time ago."

• • •

Owen Garrett Royal met his executive officer in the lobby of the Mark Hopkins and proceeded up to the roof.

"Haven't been to the Top-of-the-Mark since the war," Royal smiled raising a scotch and soda to his lips. "Tell me Aub, and don't hold back, how do you think our new two stripers stack up?"

"Well, they're reserves, and from what I can tell from reading over their service records, only one of them has had combat experience."

"Oetjens?"

"Yes, as ensign he was exec of an LSM during the D-Day landings."

"Sounds like a good man to have on board. At least, he shouldn't be a stranger to shore batteries after Normandy," Royal paused then said, "I noticed you place a special emphasis on the word reserve."

"No, not really, Captain. As you know, I was originally USNR myself."

"Yes, but you've chosen the navy as your profession. Been on active duty since '49, haven't you?"

"Yes, Sir, but I think you probably also know that I was in my final year at Kings Point when the war ended. I never did reach the forward area until well after the Japs surrendered, and that was on a merchant ship. I've always deeply regretted missing the war."

"I don't know why you regret that," the captain smiled good naturedly. "I never cherished my tours in the Pacific, especially those in the Solomons. The mosquitoes out there were really rugged, far bigger nuisance than the Japs."

"I think you misunderstand me, Sir," Cobb answered, not certain if Royal was toying with him. "My only interest is in the navy. I just think I'd be a better officer with some combat experience under my belt."

"Combat isn't always the best teacher, Aub. Unfortunately, sometimes it kills off the student before he has a chance to graduate. Anyway, from what I've observed so far, I think you're doing a pretty good job of getting the crew shaped up for Korea, especially since we're not officially allowed to tell them," he laughed.

"Thank you, Sir, but to be completely honest, I am concerned about the large percentage of reserves we've been assigned. I'm sure they're all well motivated, but I'd feel much better if we had a few more professionals aboard."

"I understand how you feel, I had the same qualms myself on my first wartime patrol on the *Honolulu*. If you think we've got a lot of reserves, you should have been along on that little joyride. Next to Okinawa, I guess it was the roughest tour I ever had. Jap dive bombers all day and the Tokyo Express all night. Yet in spite of our heavy complement of reservists, I'm still alive to joke about it. You'd be surprised, Aub, those civilians make damn fair sailors in a scrap in spite of their amateur standing. Besides, I'm willing to bet that most of the reserve P.O.'s that reported aboard yesterday have had more than their fair share of combat in the last war."

"What do you really think our chances are of getting clobbered over there?" Cobb asked pensively.

"I don't think we'll ever get that close to their guns to worry about that. They'll probably use us only for screening the carriers. I've heard that every once in a while they lob some shells out at the flattops but they never hit anything at that range."

"What about mines? A friend of mine on the *Antietam* wrote me that the Reds have strewn them all over the place. He mentioned several close calls the *Antietam* and the other carriers have had with floating mines. The *Field's* had a lot of wear and tear. Do you think she could stay afloat if she hit one of those big influence mines?"

"Certainly, Aub," Royal countered with exaggerated reassurance. "As I said yesterday before the speed run, you should have more confidence in the old girl. I've got a special feeling about her. She's a good ship, she's not going to let us down. I have to admit I was a little disappointed that first day I went out to look her over. That was about a week before I relieved Commander Carver."

"I didn't know you'd been aboard before the change of command," Cobb answered with obvious surprise in his voice.

Choosing not to embarrass his executive officer, Royal decided not to describe the laxity he encountered during his initial visit. Changing the subject, he said, "You're married aren't you, Aub?"

"Yes, my wife's back east."

"Wouldn't it be more convenient to bring her out here?"

"Not really. Renee's doing quite well back in Roslyn. She's an assistant principal in a high school. She wouldn't want to give that up. Besides, we can use the extra income. If all goes well after this tour, I'm hoping to draw a billet with the Atlantic Fleet again. Before I got shanghaied to the *Field*, I was exec of another reserve 'can' out of Whitestone, New York. You know, the *Field* was originally slated to work out of New York with reservists. That's what I was told when we reactivated her at Charleston. The navy really fouled me up when they sent her to San Diego instead."

"Maybe it will be a shorter tour than we expect. The war might end before we even get there. Don't worry, we've got to stop off at Hawaii for a least three weeks of O.R.I. I doubt if we'll even get to Korea before August. I read in the papers this morning that the armistice talks at Panmunjom had started up again," Royal advised.

"Yes, but you know how often those truce talks have been on and off. I'm really afraid that we're in for a long haul."

"Well, if you're right, Aub, I'm certain the *Field* will come through for us. Now tell me, what looks good on the menu?"

After dinner, Lt. Commander Cobb placed a long distance call to his wife. Then the two officers caught the Humphrey Bogart film playing on Market Street. Set in the period of the 1914-18 War, the movie climaxed with a battle between a broken-down river steamer called the *African Queen* and a large and formidable German gunboat. Royal was keenly interested in this remote phase of the "war to end all wars," and he soon found himself closely associating the puny little underdog with the *Charles P. Field*.

By 09:00 the following morning, the *Field*, with her three sisters, was swinging out of the inner bay, her bow pointed on a westerly course toward deep water. From the bridge her bare jackstaff looked like a gun sight aimed at the vast blue expanse of Pacific visible ahead through the rapidly widening gap between Points Lobos to port and Bonita to starboard.

By early afternoon, the four ships were knifing through a sun glazed sea in a standard column formation with a 100-yard interval between each destroyer. Because Commander Royal was senior in time of rank to the commanding officers of the other three ships in DesDiv 291, the *Field* was accorded the honor of steaming in the number "2" position directly behind division flagship *Abner Ward*. The commodore's vessel, being the foremost unit in the column, served as guide ship for the formation. Astern, the *John Morgan*, and further back, the *Halsey Wayne*, obediently followed in the creamy wake churned up by the two lead destroyers.

The drill scheduled for that day was a surface firing exercise devised to test the accuracy of each vessel's main battery. A small raft with a square red canvas screen placed in the water by *Halsey Wayne* would serve as target. The operational plan called for each ship to fire five rounds from each of her largest weapons, which in the case of a *Fletcher* class destroyer, were the five-inch dual-purpose guns. Because modernization of the *Field's* three consorts entailed the removal of their midship's mount to compensate for the added weight of a new and heavier anti-aircraft battery, tripod mast, and more sophisticated electronics system, each of these ships was scheduled to fire only twenty rounds to the *Field's* twenty-five.

At 14:00, after the radars had scanned the area and reported no contacts within fifty miles, the baker flag was two-blocked on each destroyer. Seconds later, yellow-brown blotches could be seen flashing out from the *Abner Ward's* starboard side as her main battery opened fire. Rather than hit and destroy the costly float, the intention of the exercise was to place the fall of shot within a pre-scribed area relative to the target's location. To Royal and the others observing the ship ahead, the marksmen riding Commodore Price's mount seemed to be achieving their goal quite expertly.

The *Field's* C.O. made careful note as each snowy plume danced high in the designated target area a hundred yards short of the float.

"Right on," Aubrey Cobb announced, focusing his binoculars.

"*Ward's* dropping them through the hoop, alright," Royal said, turning toward Cobb and the gunnery officer, Lieutenant MacKinlay. "Gil Hedling must have a pretty sharp gun club on the *Ward*. Hope we can put in a respectable per-formance," he continued in a noticeably worried tone as he thought about his untried crew and a main gun battery that had not been fired since the bombard-ment of the Kamaishi Iron Works in July of '45. As he steadied his binoculars on the small red rectangle some four miles distant, the warning buzzer informed him that his own guns were now swinging around into position, their slender gray bar-rels leaning out over the sea.

"Where the hell did it go to now?" Holiday cried in an annoyed voice as the thin sweeping-line on the radar scope passed full circle without disclosing the green smudge that would indicate the position of the target.

"We'll be firing any second now," Mister Coates shouted angrily as he turned from the plotting table. "You'd better find it pretty damn quick."

"Radar won't pick it up, Sir. Must be too low in the water. Got a hell of a lot of sea-return showing up all over the scope."

"Sea's calm as glass. I don't know why you'd have any sea-return," the ensign barked back.

Murray went over to the Sugar George. Glancing over Holiday's shoulder, he studied the sweep for a few seconds, then turning to the young officer confirmed the operator's appraisal.

Over the TBS, the short-wave radio speaker located in both the bridge and C.I.C., came the voice of Commander Price.

"SHIFTLESS, SHIFTLESS, THIS IS BIRDBATH. YOU MAY COM-MENCE FIRING, OVER."

"BIRDBATH, THIS IS SHIFTLESS, ROGER, OUT," Royal quickly acknowledged.

There were a few seconds of silence, then…"Combat, Bridge, have you deter-mined the range and bearing of the target yet?" Royal questioned impatiently over the squawk-box.

"Negative, Captain," Ensign Coates answered with a quiver. "The target seems to be lost in the sea-return, Sir."

"What sea-return? The ocean's smooth, not a whitecap in sight!"

"Well, Sir, the Sugar George must have crapped out…eh, I mean defected, eh, become defective, Sir. Can't the Mark 37 get on target without an assist from us, Captain?"

"Unfortunately, the fire-control radar in the director has, as you put it, Mister Coates, crapped out also. We've got the E.T.'s up there working on it now."

In the wheelhouse all eyes focused on the captain.

"Shouldn't we request a delay until we repair our radar casualties?" Cobb asked.

"No, we'll fire using visual ranges and bearings," Royal answered calmly.

"Visual bearings, Captain?" MacKinlay asked with a shocked expression.

"Didn't the Academy teach you that naval gunnery existed long before radar came along, Lieutenant?" The captain then turned to the young apprentice sea-man standing nearby. "Tell Mister Ritter in the director to get on target immedi-ately with his optics. He's to open fire the instant he feels he's computed a cor-rect target solution."

"Aye, aye, Sir," the bridge-talker replied, then slowly delivered the message over the phones, syllable by syllable.

Thirty seconds later, the sharp slam of the most forward mount jolted the entire ship. The concussion of the ear-splitting bang kicked at the stomach of each man on the open bridge. Inside the wheelhouse, the thin bulkhead plating seemed to expand and contract with each loud report, and a piercing smell of cordite filled the nostrils of everyone in the forward part of the ship.

Owen Royal, bracing himself against the metal shielding that served as a wind guard, pointed his binoculars to starboard and waited eagerly for the mush-room-shaped towers of water that would mark the placement of number "1" gun's lethal cargo within the prescribed target area. The seconds ticked by but no splash appeared within his field of vision. He lowered his glasses just as the splash-es erupted…not short of the target as Royal had expected but three hundred yards beyond and two hundred yards to the left.

"What does the crew on number one gun think they are shooting at?…Korea?" the captain growled, his face almost as red as the baker flag flying over his head.

"Sorry, Captain," MacKinlay replied meekly. "They're mostly all new men on that mount."

"Well, what about Ensign Ritter?" Royal countered. "He's supposed to be putting them on target."

"Yes, Sir, I'll have him recheck his solution. I'm sure the number two mount will put in a better showing. It's being manned by our original ship's company."

"I certainly hope so. I expect Commodore Price has duly noted our initial performance. Tell Mister Ritter to take his time on this one and make it look good."

A moment later the long rifle projecting from the face of number "2" gunhouse elevated slightly, swung right almost 90 degrees, and coughed out a loud angry puff of brown smoke speckled with orange and yellow. An instant later, another sharp bang announced that a second round was off and on its way. Then, before this second projectile had completed half its journey, the target, float and all, ascended high in the air, shattering into a thousand tiny fragments that floated back down to rest upon a wide area of water.

"Cease firing!" Royal shouted.

"Sir, I don't know what could have happened," MacKinlay volunteered, stepping aside as the captain rushed passed him into the wheelhouse to answer a frenzied call on the TBS.

"SHIFTLESS, SHIFTLESS, THIS IS BIRDBATH," Commodore Price's voice thundered. "IT WAS OUR INTENTION TO FIRE ONE HUNDRED YARDS SHORT OF THE TARGET, NOT BLOW IT TO KINGDOM COME, OUT!"

Price's message terminated without the customary "OVER" which would have permitted Royal to reply. A few seconds later a second message came from the commodore.

"CAPRICORN, CAPRICORN, THIS IS BIRDBATH. MESSAGE TO FOLLOW, EXECUTE TO FOLLOW — ABLE-CHARLIE FOUR, I REPEAT, ABLE-CHARLIE FOUR. OVER."

"CAPRICORN" was a collective call name for all four destroyers in the division, and Royal didn't have to consult the general signal book to learn that translated, ABLE-CHARLIE 4 meant, "break off present exercise and prepare to return to base."

"BIRDBATH, THIS IS SHIFTLESS, ROGER, OUT," Royal answered.

"BIRDBATH, THIS IS TENNIS-COURT, ROGER, OUT," came the message from the *Morgan*.

"BIRDBATH, THIS IS SMUDGE, ROGER, OUT," said the OOD of the *Wayne*.

Down in the *Field's* combat-information-center, all was quiet as Ensign Coates and his "radar gang" listened to the verbal exchange between the flagship and the other destroyers.

"Old man's gonna get his ass chewed, that's for sure," Gardiner prophesized, his voice descending to a whisper.

"He can't blame us," Holiday flared. "It sure wasn't our fault that the radar conked out."

"Nobody's blaming you, Holiday," Coates counseled as he nervously watched the hatchway, anticipating an angry visit from his commanding officer.

At the plotting table Logan busied himself laying out a navigation chart of the San Francisco bay area in preparation for their return, while Murray fired up the dead-reckoning-tracer. The four third-class were still at their various G.Q. stations, while the quartet of young radar strikers quietly observed what was happening while doing their utmost not to become directly involved. The novice radarmen were in their teens; Belton, Farber and Paulsen were "Johnny Rebs." Patterson was from Trenton, New Jersey.

"How do you think the skipper will make out tonight, Sir?" Murray asked.

"Well, I'm willing to bet the *Field* gets a message from the commodore that he wants to see the old man as soon as we get back to port."

"I wouldn't take that bet, Murray, I'm sure you're right," Coates replied. "It's a funny thing though, I'm reading a novel right now about the captain of a destroyer-minesweeper who gets in trouble for the same reason, well, almost the same reason. His ship doesn't blow the target up like we did, instead, she ran right over the towing cable and cut the target loose."

"What book is that?" Logan spoke up.

"*The Caine Mutiny.* Have you heard of it?"

Before Logan could answer, the C.I.C. officer went on to explain most of the general plot. Kevin listened closely, smiling to himself as he remembered how completely he had "snowed" Candy.

"Well, I think I'll pass that one up," Howie Murray grunted. "It sounds too navy for me," he added as he coiled the seemingly endless extension cord on his sound-powered telephone.

The conversation was abruptly interrupted.

"CAPRICORN, CAPRICORN THIS IS BIRDBATH, ABLE-CHARLIE 4...I REPEAT ABLE-CHARLIE 4, STAND BY TO EXECUTE...EXECUTE! OUT!"

Seconds later, with their baker pennants hauled down and tucked neatly away in their flag bags, the four destroyers reversed their course, secured from general quarters, and proceeded at 12 knots toward San Francisco Bay and their respective mooring buoys off Alameda. Logan, assigned to the first watch section, relieved Holiday at the SG radar still strangely clouded with sea-return. As was his habit when relieving a man on the scope, Logan twisted the small black dial marked focus control and the sweep-line immediately sharpened. Then he reached for the gain-control knob, turning it slightly to the right. Suddenly, the sea-return vanished, the presentation on the scope brightened and the *Field's* three sister destroyers clearly appeared in their relative positions. Now Kevin knew why Holiday hadn't been able to pick up the raft; why the captain had to rely on inaccurate optical ranges and bearings from a not-too efficient gunnery officer. And Murray, with all his experience, hadn't even bothered to check the two knobs, a basic procedure taught to radarmen the first time they sit at a scope.

Korea could be quite hairy if this was a sample performance of *DD-505*'s Ops and Gunnery departments in action, Logan thought, his face suddenly flushed.

The *Field*'s radio room with its adjoining space called radio-central, occupied almost all of the deck in the bridge structure directly under the wheelhouse.

"Turn that damn music down a second, we got ourselves a message from the flagship!" 'Little Gilly,' the *Field*'s senior radioman, and no relation to 'Big Gilly,' a pipe fitter in the engineering department, shouted to his fellow watch stander. Buckley, a tousled haired radioman-third, frowned over the top edge of the comic book he was reading but reluctantly complied with the instruction. 'Little Gilly' frantically typed the incoming jumble of letters and numbers, keeping pace with the dots and dashes as they flashed from his headset. Then carefully retyping the message, he folded it neatly in an oversized envelope marked "Confidential" and handed it to one of his strikers who would hand carry it the short distance to the captain's cabin. As soon as the messenger departed Buckley turned the volume back up on the long range receiver. Picking up the comic book, he resumed reading even though it had become annoyingly obvious that Clark Kent was never going to make it into Lois Lane's pants. He flipped through the pages, lazily humming along with the music from Station KECA, Los Angeles. The song, a rouser from a new Broadway musical, emphatically told all within hearing that "*They Call the Wind Ma-ri-a.*"

30 April, 1952

REQUEST YOUR PRESENCE ABOARD ABNER WARD

AS SOON AS CONVENIENT FOLLOWING MOORING.

W.A. PRICE, CAPT. USN

To Owen Royal the message bore little surprise. He read it quickly, refolding it, then sent for his steward, Chief DelRosario. Like most of the young stewards aboard the *Field*, the chief was from the Philippines. Highly respected among his peers, Del Rosario was particularly proud of his service with Motor Torpedo Boat Squadron 3, the "Expendables" immortalized in the book by William L. White and on screen by MGM. The little Filipino, his sleeves covered with gold "hash marks," removed the newest of his commanding officer's three blue uniforms and carried it below for pressing.

By sunset, the *Field*'s heavy mooring chain had been "unbent" from the starboard anchor, passed through the bull nose, and shackled securely to the steel ring on buoy "21". Fifteen minutes later, Commander Royal alighted from the *Field*'s motor whaleboat and climbed the short accommodation ladder to the flagship's main deck.

"Good evening, Commander," the natty young ensign assigned to *Abner Ward*'s quarterdeck greeted, his gray gloved hand fanning the air in a snappy salute. "The commodore is expecting you, Sir. The messenger will show you to his cabin." Royal knew the route quite well by now but in keeping with naval protocol, he permitted the young seaman to lead the way.

Within a few minutes, Owen was sitting across from his division commander who was slowly leafing through an Office of Naval Intelligence manual entitled, "Destroyer Types — U.S. Navy." Price closed the long rectangular publication and looked up smiling. "Owen, eh," he fumbled momentarily for the right words. "I guess you think I called you over here to put you on the carpet for what happened at the shoot today." His tone was disarmingly friendly.

"Well, yes, Sir, since you asked, I did expect that..."

"Forget it, Owen," Price interrupted good naturedly. "I understand about what happened today...new crew, untried equipment, and I'm fully aware that the other three ships have gotten well over a month's jump on your people as far as training is concerned. But getting back to the purpose of this meeting," he paused, then said, "Owen, I've always believed in talking things over with my officers. I prefer to ask their opinion before I make decisions concerning their command."

"Decisions, Commodore?"

"Well, I guess that's the wrong choice of words. Actually, what I'm going to ask concerns a change in our current steaming disposition. As senior of my four C.O.'s, I realize your ship rates the number two spot, astern the flagship."

Since Price brought up the subject, Royal wondered if he should mention that it was customary for a commodore to fly his flag from the ship with the most senior commanding officer. Since Royal's date of rank preceded Gil Hedling's by a full year, the choice of *Abner Ward* as flagship over the *Field* was already an obvious slap in the face. Royal decided not to mention it however, knowing that the commodore would cite the importance of having access to more sophisticated communications equipment. Of course, that still wouldn't answer the big question in Royal's mind...why of the four C.O.'s was he the one chosen to command a ship that seemed long overdue for the boneyard.

Commodore Price hesitated, then picked up the O.N.I. manual once more. Swallowing hard, he looked straight at the commander. "Owen, I'd like the *Field* to steam in the number four slot. Do you have any objections?"

"No, Sir," Owen answered in an even tone, trying to mask his disappointment. "May I ask your reason, Sir?"

"Certainly, Owen, and I know you think it's related to what happened today, but I assure you there's absolutely no connection. Since the *Field* is the only five-gun *Fletcher* in the division, I'd like to keep her in the rear. In case we should draw a fire mission over there, I want to be certain that the last ship in the line has enough fire power disposed aft to cover the division's withdrawal. That number three gun the *Field* is still carrying could prove quite useful. I've been told that those Commie battery commanders, especially around Wonsan and Hungnam, have a cute trick of rolling their big guns out of their caves as our ships were withdrawing. Quite a few of our ships have been hit that way. Then there's another sound reason for putting the *Field* in the rear of the column. At first you might regard this as unimportant but after I explain my reasoning, I'm certain you'll agree with me."

"Yes, Sir," Royal answered with discernible feeling.

"I'd like to show you exactly what I mean," Price said in slightly rising inflection as he turned the oblong pages of the O.N.I. manual. He smiled as he reached the page with the heading "*Fletcher Class DD's*." "Here's the unmodified *Fletcher* like your *Field*, tall pole mast, high round bridge, two banks of torpedo tubes, five gun houses...now look at this rebuilt *Fletcher*," he instructed forcefully, pointing to the photograph on the opposite page. "I know I don't have to tell you how different the silhouette is. Now, considering this strictly from the standpoint of smart naval appearance I'm sure you'll agree that with the *Field* steaming in the second slot, the military bearing of the division is completely lost. Since the *Ward*, *Morgan* and *Wayne* have identical profiles, I've decided to position them in that order. I just want to be certain that you don't misconstrue my motive...that you fully understand there's nothing personal about it."

"Why would I think there was something personal about it?" Royal asked, scrutinizing Price's face for a reaction.

Price glanced down at his hands. They clamped tightly, then opened again. "Of course there's no reason to think that," he smiled. "Well, how about some fresh coffee before you take that ride back to the *Field*."

The two men sipped coffee and passed the next twenty minutes discussing the week's schedule of exercises. At 20:30 (8:30p.m.), the neatly uniformed coxswain of the *Field's* motor whaleboat clanged the brass bell mounted near the tiller, the boat's engineer spurred the snarling motor, and soon Owen Royal was being sped through the blackness of the harbor. As the twenty-six footer approached the gray blur mooring beyond buoy "21", the commander carefully reviewed the audience he had just had aboard the flagship. His conclusion was simple though discouraging. Price, while tactful and polite, had clearly made his point and Royal knew he had just been put on the carpet as surely as if he had received an official reprimand.

During the next three days the *Charles P. Field*, steaming astern of her three sisters, carried out all scheduled exercises without further incident but also without particular distinction. By Friday evening, the division's overall score for the week was tabulated aboard the flagship and dispatched to each destroyer where it was prominently posted on all bulletin boards except that of *DD-505*.

Results of Surface Firing Exercises 30 April - 2 May 1952

U.S.S.	5" Expended	Hits Recorded
Abner Ward	100	54

Charles P. Field	108	24
Halsey Wayne	100	41
John Morgan	96	43

Monday morning, 5 May, had a gray beginning but by 13:15 (1:15p.m.), when the quartet of warships neared the firing zone, the mist evaporated making way for a fine clear day. Soon the *Field* was cutting through the choppy blue water. Her bow dipped deep into the milky wakes of the ships ahead, then jumped to bite the air like a kitten leaping after a dangling string.

C.I.C. was hot; the large blower mounted over the Sugar George radar scope did little to lower the temperature in the dark over-crowded compartment. There was still almost twenty minutes left before the division would rendezvous with the tow-plane from Alameda; twenty minutes before the *Field* would have a chance to show how well she could repel enemy air attacks; and twenty minutes to make up her poor showing during the previous week's surface shoot.

Ensign Coates informed the bridge that the "combat-information-center was manned and ready," then glanced around nervously, hoping his report had not been premature. Murray and Logan beside him at the air-search radar, Bacelli and Gardiner at the vertical air plot, and the four strikers manning the various status boards and sound-powered telephone positions...everyone was there. The young officer could stop worrying for now anyway, he thought, wiping beads of sweat from his forehead.

"Nugent!" he called out. "Any sign of the plane on the SC yet? You should be picking him up any time now."

"No, Sir," Nugent responded as he studied the moving sweep line on the Sugar-Charlie air-search radar.

"Well, keep your eyes peeled! Just for once let's see if we can beat the other ships to the initial contact report," Coates implored.

..."BIRDBATH, BIRDBATH, THIS IS SMUDGE...I HAVE A BOGEY AT TWO-TWO-ZERO, SIXTY-EIGHT MILES, CLOSING, OVER..."

"SMUDGE, THIS IS BIRDBATH. DESIGNATE YOUR BOGEY, RAID ONE...TRACK AND REPORT, OUT..."

"That's the target plane," Ensign Coates cried out. "Nugent how come that pip jockey on the *Wayne* managed to pick it up before you?"

"It was just showing in my scope, Sir. I was just about to call it out to you when that feather merchant on the *Wayne* sounded off. Another second and I would have been able to give you the range and bearing, too, but I wanted to make sure I had an accurate fix before I said anything."

"Yeah, I'll bet you did. Cut the gab and start singing out his position."

"Yes, Sir, he's showing up real sharp now."

"Then start giving me a range and bearing every thirty seconds," Bacelli yelled over from the air plotting board.

"Start singing those ranges and bearings out, Nugent!" Coates ordered. "Maybe we'll be able to work out his course and speed for the bridge before the *Wayne* can send it over the..."

"BIRDBATH, BIRDBATH, THIS IS SMUDGE, RAID ONE SQUAWK-ING FRIENDLY AT TWO-THREE-EIGHT, THIRTY-ONE MILES...COURSE ZERO-EIGHT-FIVE...SPEED TWO-FIVE-FIVE, OVER."

"SMUDGE, THIS IS BIRDBATH, FRIENDLY AT TWO-THREE-EIGHT, THIRTY-ONE MILES IS TOPMAN NINER. CEASE REPORTING BUT CONTINUE TO TRACK, OUT."

Dammit, Coates thought, realizing that the *Wayne's* radar gang had beaten them again.

Murray looked at the list of names scribbled with yellow grease pencil on the Plexiglas surface of the air-status board. "Topman 9" was the call name for one of the two tow-planes slated for the day's exercise.

"Looks like we'll get a chance to see if we can screw up an air shoot as well as we screwed up the surface shoot," Gardiner observed. "Think our 40's and 20's can shoot any better than our five-inch?"

"The five-inch guns will be firing in this exercise, too, Gardiner," Coates said as Murray slipped a set of sound-powered phones over his head, connecting him with the "JA", or captain's command circuit. At the same time Kevin Logan, standing nearby, plugged his headset into the jackbox marked "JC" which put him in communication with main-battery control and Ensign Ritter.

Up on the bridge-wing, Owen Royal anxiously watched the small black dot grow larger in the sky off the starboard bow. Ahead, a bright new string of flags had been broken out on *Abner Ward*. It was quickly followed by a similar display of color aboard the *Wayne and Morgan*. Behind him came the scraping noise of brass snap hooks as his own signal flags flew skyward, the sharp squeak of running halyards announcing that the commanding officer of the *Field* had understood the flagship's message and was standing by to execute the afternoon's scheduled gunnery exercise.

The dot in the sky was closer now and within seconds took the shape of a single engined monoplane. Owen recognized at once the fat round fuselage and long tapered wings of a Grumman Avenger. He had seen thousands of this type of aircraft during the Pacific War. It seemed only yesterday that they had black-ened the sky above the carrier task groups as they formed up for a strike against the Emperor's proudest warships. It was sad, Royal mused, that the victor over the mighty *Yamato* and *Musashi* was now relegated to the inglorious task of tow-ing targets, and he thought it not too unlike harnessing a former Derby winner to a junk cart. As the aircraft drew closer a second speck appeared in the same area of sky. This the captain knew would be "Topman 6."

While the four destroyers held their position in column, the first Grumman TBM circled overhead waiting for his partner to catch up. Both of the TBMs were painted a bright yellow; the nylon target sleeve that trailed over 6,000 yards behind each plane was an equally brilliant orange although it looked more like a drab hyphen to the gunners on the destroyers below.

Each ship had been assigned a specific area of fire as prescribed by the "*Target Procedure Manual*" for destroyers steaming in column. Designated safety arcs covering relative bearings on both port and starboard beam were intended to safeguard each vessel from a stray burst or an unexploded round that might fall back to sea. For purposes of identification, each destroyer in the division would fire nonfragmenting projectiles with a distinctive color burst: *Ward* - green, *Morgan* - red, *Wayne* - orange, and *Field* - blue.

Commodore Price, in direct control of the exercise, had radio contact with the pilot of each plane. Because each aircraft carried only two target sleeves, the initial hour's firing would call for placing 5-inch shell bursts 200 yards astern but at the same altitude as and directly in line with the target.

Suddenly, a new set of signal pennants whipped the breeze from the flagship's halyard. The message was quickly relayed down the line by *Morgan* and *Wayne*. Then to give the flagship's signalman additional practice, the *Ward's* two all-directional blinkers, high atop her foremast, began to flash.

"The *Ward* says the first run will be an 'Uncle-run', Sir, down the starboard side, 'round astern, then up the port side. All ships will fire," continued Anderson, the *Field's* chief signalman in a pitch not too unlike that of a foghorn. "That was from her blinker, Cap'n, flag hoist reads…normal firing interval between all units." As he spoke, the pot bellied C.P.O. felt around the edge of his pants to make sure his shirt tail was still tucked in.

Captain Royal instructed the OOD to adhere to the commodore's instructions. Lieutenant Oetjens, who had the conn, immediately gave the lee-helmsman an order for the engine-telegraph, decreasing the number of shaft revolutions and widening the gap between the *Field's* foretip and the stern of the *Halsey Wayne* directly ahead.

A helmeted Cobb and MacKinlay joined Royal on the open bridge just as *Ward's* Baker flag raced to the yardarm.

"We're off to the races," Royal said glancing up to see his own red pennant flutter free of the wire rigging. As the officers watched, the first TBM, "Topman Niner," skimmed in low over the water flying parallel to the line of destroyers. *Abner Ward's* 5-inch battery, already pointing to starboard opened fire immediately. An instant later, green spots began to puff astern of the swiftly moving target.

"*Ward's* bursts look far off the mark," MacKinlay snickered, fixing his glasses on the sky behind the sleeve.

"Yes," Royal smiled. "Gil Hedling's boys don't seem quite as sharp on aerial targets as they were on surface sleds."

As the captain aimed his binoculars at the swiftly moving target, the *Morgan* and *Wayne* commenced firing almost simultaneously. To the observers on the *Field*, both ships appeared to be placing the majority of their shots near the prescribed distance astern of the sleeve, although one exceptionally large burst tore a hole in the sky almost a mile off the mark. The blood-red smoke clearly indicated that the misplaced round had come from the *Morgan.*

Then the *Field's* five-inch sounded off in rapid tempo. In the seconds it took for the narrow length of orange nylon to pass across the *Field's* allotted firing zone, her gunners quite handily managed to get away four rounds from each of her five main mounts.

"Eighteen…nineteen…twenty…" Commander Royal countered in a tone mixed with as much surprise as pleasure, as each blue orchid blossomed precisely 200 yards astern of and directly in line with the sleeve. "I had them work overtime to make up for the last shooting, Captain," MacKinlay piped up in relieved bewilderment.

"I don't believe it!" Cobb shouted aloud, losing momentary control. "A couple of days ago they couldn't handle a stationary target float, now twenty perfect placements? That can't be our gun gang, can it?"

Bet Billy Price swallowed his uppers on that one, Royal muttered to himself, wishing he could be aboard *Abner Ward* at that instant to see the commodore's reaction. "That was really fine shooting, Mister MacKinlay," he congratulated the gunboss. "I don't think they could have done any better if they had an actual kamikaze coming at them. Let's hope they can keep it up for the rest of today's exercises."

Five minutes later, the second Gumman TBM, "Topman 6," commenced it's Uncle-run. This counter-clockwise approach down the port side and up the starboard, passed much closer to the four destroyers, and was intended only for the ship's secondary or anti-aircraft batteries. Again, to the complete amazement of all hands in DesDiv 291, the *Field* put in the outstanding performance of the quartet, even though handicapped by an armament of obsolete 40- and 20-millimeter guns while her three sisters carried the new rapid-fire 3-inch/50's.

At 15:30 (3:30p.m.), Commodore Price signaled for a Zulu-run which called for both aircraft to pass directly over the column. The *Ward* and *Morgan* were assigned Topman-9's target, while the *Wayne* and *Field* would fire at the sleeve that dragged behind Topman-6. A second message from the flagship instructed that this drill as well as all the day's subsequent exercises would call for direst fire at the sleeve itself. At 15:33, a sharp snarl of motor announced that the two TBM's were passing overhead. Then as the sleeves flew on, both *Ward* and *Wayne* sorted out her respective target; green and orange poker dots decorated the sky around the swiftly moving sleeves but neither target received a hit.

The two Grummans banked sharply and approached from the opposite direction. Now the *Field's* big box-like director atop the bridge revolved around until its telescopic sights and radar-scan pointed directly at the oncoming sleeve. All five gun barrels moved in perfect sync with each minute variation in the director's train. At the same time, the 40-millimeters, controlled and aimed by small local directors, elevated their distinctive steel-coiled barrels and waited for the approaching target.

The next instant both planes were overhead, their long wire cables tracing a thin penciled line across the sky. As Royal turned his head to watch the bright gun flashes from the *Wayne* ahead, his own batteries suddenly opened fire.

Bang - Bang - Bang...the sharp slam of the five-inch jolted the entire ship, partially muffling the more rapid **Bam - Bam - Bam** of the *Field's* numerous 40-millimeter guns. Then, as *Wayne's* target escaped unscathed, a five-inch burst from the *Field* sent Topman -6's nylon cone plummeting to the sea like a lifeless gull.

Royal found this sudden renaissance on the part of his gunnery department almost incredible. Five minutes later, the *Field's* sharpshooters put in a repeat performance, this time splitting the orange sleeve dead center. At the same time, *Halsey Wayne* managed to bring down Topman-9's sleeve with a near-miss that parted the tow cable. Topman-6, now having expanded both it's targets, requested permission to return to Alameda. Permission was immediately granted by the commodore, and the aircraft quickly disappeared over the horizon.

As the aircraft departed, Topman-9 opened her torpedo bay and trailed out her second sleeve for a final Uncle-run down the starboard side of the column during which the entire division was scheduled to fire. With a few minutes respite before this last shoot, the *Field's* gunners, smoke and cordite fumes eddying around them, opened the small slit-like hatch covers in the face of each five-inch gun house. Anticipating the usual post exercise clean-up, some of the seamen were already stacking the brass cartridge cases that had rattled to the deck each time a crimson nosed practice round had departed the muzzle.

"Captain," the bridge-talker cried out, tugging at the long extension cord on his headphones, "number three-mount reports an unexpended round. They request permission to empty their bore before the next firing."

"Very well," Royal answered, glancing aft in the direction of number "3" gun which was located on the center line about 20 feet aft of the second stack. "Instruct them to fire on a safe line of bearing."

The talker repeated the message slowly into the mouthpiece, his small young face peering out from beneath the oversized helmet, especially enlarged to allow for the extra space taken up by the headset.

An instant later, a thunderous blast told all aboard *DD-505* that number "3" mount had emptied its bore.

Royal and his officers on the bridge watched the ocean to starboard waiting for the tall white geyser to appear.

"Those damn fools!" Cobb exclaimed.

Owen Royal looked up to see the gray-blue burst scar the sky just feet below the Grumman which had been in a tight orbit off the *Field's* starboard quarter.

Royal closed his eyes, opening them seconds later, expecting to see the flaming carcass of the TBM spiraling downward, but the chubby ex-bomber was still airborne, although beating a hasty retreat from the area of the flak burst which looked like blue pepper as it began to dissolve and float lazily aft.

"BIRDBATH, THIS IS TOPMAN-NINER, I AM RETURNING TO ALAMEDA TO ASCERTAIN EXTENT OF DAMAGE TO AIRCRAFT, OUT!" The radio message from the pilot of the tow plane to Commodore Price was short but not sweet, its torrid tone heard on all four destroyers. The pilot's words were followed immediately by a flag hoist from the *Abner Ward* which instructed that "the day's exercises be terminated and the division prepare to return to San Francisco."

"I wonder who our new skipper will be," Holiday announced with a smirk as word was passed down to C.I.C. to secure from general quarters.

"I feel sorry for the old man," Murray cut in. "From what I've seen of him in the short time he's been aboard, I have to admit he's really my idea of what a naval officer should be."

"Well, that may be," Holiday answered, "but you know what they say about nice guys finishing last."

"I'm with Holly," Nugent chimed in. "The commodore will throw his ass to ComDesPac, you watch."

"Unless ComAirPac claims it first," Logan joined in. "I don't suppose they're too happy about having one of their tow planes clobbered."

"It certainly wasn't the captain's fault," Ensign Coates said, deciding afterall to throw his two cents in.

"Yes, Sir," Murray agreed. "How's he supposed to be up on the bridge and back there supervising those clowns on number-three-gun at the same time?"

"A commanding officer's responsible for anything that happens aboard his ship. You know that, Murray," Coates said dogmatically.

"Well, maybe it's my civilian outlook, Mister Coates, but I still don't think it's fair."

"Okay, Murray," Holiday exclaimed, "we all bleed for the old man but right now I'm more interested in securing from G.Q. and getting down to the shower line. I want to be waiting at the quarterdeck the second the OD sounds liberty call."

• • •

Within seconds of the time Topman-9 departed the firing area, air control personnel at the Alameda Naval Air Station received a wordy dispatch from Commodore Price informing them of the returning craft's dubious condition. A half hour later, after an uneventful landing, the portly old torpedo plane was thoroughly examined and found to have suffered no more damage than a few scorch marks on its belly and lower tail section. Damaged far greater was the pilots feelings, for as he strolled toward the hangar he was heard to mumble several unflattering comments about certain of his fellows in the black shoe navy.

At 17:00 (5:00p.m.), with an hour's steaming time remaining before the division would slip back through the gaping entrance to San Francisco Bay, a report was neatly typed aboard *DD-505* for immediate dispatch to the flagship upon the evening's mooring.

To: Captain William A. Price, U.S.N. ComDesDiv 291

Subject: Accidental Firing by U.S.S. Charles P. Field, DD-505, at
           Towing aircraft. Lat. 38 N., Long. 130 W., 5 May 1952

1.) While clearing bore, subject ship fired single round of 5"/38 D.P. (non-frag. practice A.A.) which burst in proximity of tow plane.
2.) Investigation shows the cause to be a faulty stroke cylinder which jammed hydraulic rotation system, resulting in a sudden jolt while gun was in process of being trained to a safe bearing. Gun was in local control and abrupt jolt caused pointer to accidentally depress foot-treadle firing mechanism, resulting in premature discharge.
3.) This particular mount has been activated only three weeks and because of abbreviated shake-down period allotted this command, proper detection of all deficiencies in hydraulic equipment has been difficult. However, efforts will be redoubled to avoid such an accident reoccurring.

Owen Garrett Royal, Commander, U.S.N.

That evening, Commodore Price read Royal's report and decided the captain's explanation sufficient to warrant no further action on his part, especially since he had just been informed by ComAirPac that no damage had been incurred by plane or pilot. Also, with the division leaving for Korea in exactly three weeks, he decided that calling the incident to the attention of ComCruDesPac would not be advantageous to the command or his own career.

Within a few days the matter was forgotten by all except a few of the more imaginative members of the *Field's* ship's company who insisted that the near catastrophe must certainly have been the work of *DD-505's* vindictive phantom. And while none of her crew had served aboard the destroyer prior to her recommissioning, and despite the fact that Chief Henderson had been a torpedoman, not a gunner's mate, several had it "on good authority" that the number "3" mount had been the old C.P.O.'s battle station until that fatal day when he went aft to adjust the depth charges.

For the remainder of the week DesDiv 291 was busily engaged in similar antiaircraft exercises, although radio-controlled target drones were employed in lieu of towed sleeve targets. While no officer aboard the *Field* would admit openly, it was accepted generally throughout the wardroom that the use of pilotless drones was prompted by consideration on the part of ComAirPac for the unpredictable nature of the Charlie P.'s gun club. One anonymous member of the ship's company went so far as to paint a small white silhouette of a Grumman TBM on the port side of number "3" gun house where during the Pacific War proud marksman had painted small Japanese flags to signify enemy aircraft destroyed. Strangely enough, the *Field* managed to outshoot her three competitors by a wide margin during each of the week's subsequent air defense exercises, but the following week, when called on to fire at slow moving surface sleds, ordinarily the easiest to hit of any naval target, *DD-505* chalked up what stands to this day as the poorest gunnery score ever tabulated for an American destroyer.

On this sour note, the *Field*, trailing far behind her three sisters, showed her fantail to the city of the Golden Gate for one last time. As each destroyer picked her way through the sluggish harbor traffic, frantic quartermasters tried not to trip over nervous JOD's as they sought to determine their ship's position by taking geographic fixes from various high points and elevated structures discernible around the harbor. One such reference point was "Land's End," a 450-foot cliff overlooking the Golden Gate. There, mounted within a shrapnel-scarred bridge bulwark was a compass that had once functioned in the wheelhouse of heavy cruiser *San Francisco*. Its needle now soldered, pointed forever in the direction of Guadalcanal where nine years before, the cruiser had limped home in gory triumph from one of history's most savage sea battles. To a frustrated passerby who had mistaken the mounted compass for a drinking fount, the four little warships looked pathetically insignificant as they slid passed a big white Matson liner inbound from Hawaii.

As the *Field* rounded Point Lobos, her sailors could discern the same chimes that had greeted them only two weeks before. Somehow, the peel of the evening Angelus seemed more somber and so much further away.

Chapter V - Anchors Aweigh

"Reveille!...Reveille!...All Hands
Heave out and thrice up! The smoking
lamp is lighted in all berthing
compartments!"

As suddenly as the words blared out from the *Field's* speaker system, the lights flashed on throughout the ship, and faint signs of life began to stir in the various compartments. The groans heard by Pheifer, the chief-master-at-arms, as he made his unwelcome rounds through the berthing spaces were much louder on this particular Friday morning since reveille was an hour earlier than usual.

"Turn to! Scrub down all weather decks!
Sweep down compartments! Empty all trash cans!"

Dawn found the four destroyers moored in a compact nest, beam to beam, with *Abner Ward* inboard next to the quay. A wooden "camel" and several large cane fenders kept the flagship's thin gray side from scraping against the high concrete wall at the San Diego destroyer basin. The *Field* was outboard ship in the group. As her yawning sailors stumbled and stretched on their way to their pre-breakfast cleaning stations, the ship's position in the nest afforded them an unobstructed view of the channel via which, in three short weeks they would leave to join the Seventh Fleet.

The *Field's* 5 a.m. reveille was more than compensated for by the announcement in the plan-of-the-day which happily proclaimed that weekend liberty would commence that noon and expire on board at midnight, Sunday. This was unexpected but highly welcome, especially since the tars on the *Field* knew that liberty call would not be piped aboard the other destroyers until four that afternoon. Captain Royal, fully aware that his crew's departure would attract unfavorable attention from Commodore Price, nevertheless decided that granting his men the longest possible time ashore during these last stateside weekends far outweighed any risk of personal embarrassment.

In keeping with Commodore Price's directive, prominently tacked to each destroyer's bulletin board that morning was a special informational sheet which detailed climatic conditions prevalent around Eniwetok Atoll. In a vain attempt to further the deception, small film badges used to detect radiation were distributed to all hands.

Commodore Price was completely unaware that at that precise moment some 6,400 miles away in the port city of Yokosuka, Japanese tailors sedulously labored to finish a batch of silk club jackets of a type highly favored by souvenir conscious G.I.'s and sailors. Artistically embroidered across the backs of each jacket, along with a multi-colored outline of Korea and a Task Force 77 emblem, were the names *Abner Ward, John Morgan, Halsey Wayne,* and *Charles P. Field.*

It was a quiet weekend for *DD-505* with only two officers and fourteen enlisted remaining aboard; an on-board strength far below that prescribed by ComCruDesPac for a *Fletcher* class destroyer in a U.S. port. As always, Owen Royal was quite anxious to see his lovely wife. Unfortunately, a mountain of paperwork requiring his personal scrutiny delayed his arrival until after eight that evening. Again, Candace had made up her mind that she would definitely ask him for a divorce before the weekend passed.

On Sunday evening they went to see "*With a Song in My Heart.*" Loosely based on events in the life of singer Jane Froman, the Susan Hayward film dealt with the singer's frustration over her marriage to a man she did not love but was afraid to hurt. At the end of the film, the husband, aware of his wife's feelings, gracefully bowed out without Miss Froman having to say a word. Why couldn't life be as simple as it is in the movies, Candace thought, as the two walked from the theatre lobby. Now quite depressed, she knew she would have to put off telling him once more. Noticing his wife's pensiveness, Owen attributed it to her disappointment over their impending separation. It was a nice feeling to be loved so much, he smiled, as they drove back in silence to La Jolla and the apartment.

Kevin Logan's weekend would never go into the log books as one of his all-time best. After telephoning Candy's apartment three times he concluded that she was probably off somewhere with the mysterious colonel. By noon he began to detect an uncomfortable tickle in his throat. By mid-afternoon he was clawing furiously at his chest and back through his most expensive custom-made shirt. Purchase of a Chinese back-scratcher did little to alleviate his sudden affliction. If he hadn't just showered and changed at the locker club, he would have been certain that one of his more envious shipmates had decided to sabotage his weekend by slipping itching powder into his clothing. By 4p.m., the irritation had progressed to the point that professional help became mandatory.

Sharing Balboa Park with the San Diego Zoo and the sprawling Municipal Golf Course, the U.S. Naval Hospital at San Diego is surrounded by a lush green forest that persuades patient and visitor alike to forget that they are just a short walk away from one of the most bustling areas of downtown San Diego. In spite of its beautiful setting, however, the hospital had no place in Logan's game plan. Robust and healthy, he viewed such institutions only as places for picking up attractive nurses.

After a lengthy wait in the incoming patient's reception area followed by a very brief examination by the admittance physician, Logan was given the word, or more precisely, the words..."chicken pox."

•   •   •

To Logan, each day in the hospital's quarantine ward seemed like a week, and he found it hard to believe that only three days had passed since he'd checked in Saturday afternoon. In spite of an assortment of greasy pastes and liquids applied liberally to his chest and back three times a day by the pharmacist mates, the itch showed little sign of lessening.

The principal aggravation for Logan, besides the itch, was the cleaning detail he'd been assigned by Lt. (jg.) Cynthia Osbourne, the nurse in charge of the ward. As a second-class petty officer and hot-shot Madison Avenue ad man, swabbing down the entire floor of the ward twice a day was definitely degrading, he sulked.

He'd let Miss Osbourne know it pretty damn soon, too, Logan decided. A real martinet, next thing she'll be assigning him to the bed pan detail if he's not careful, he shook his head in disgust. Hell, she couldn't be more than twenty-two or three and here she was pushing her rank all over the place. Probably what she really needed was a good bounce in the hay, Logan smiled at the thought. Too bad she was a little flat chested. She did have a hell of a pretty face behind those glasses, pert little nose, big green eyes, perfect skin, a well-scrubbed all-American girl look. And he had always been hot for brunettes...hell if he wasn't careful he'd start falling for her, he mused softly.

Dressed only in pajama bottoms, Logan slid his feet into the paper throwaway slippers and wandered over to the window to peer in the direction of the zoo. He shook his head, his blue eyes brooding and distant. Chicken pox, he grimaced, a kid's disease at twenty-nine. How the hell could he have caught it, he wondered. He hadn't been around any kids in years...then it hit him; that damn shore patrol he'd had up in Frisco. Sure, that had to be it. There were hundreds of kids running around that amusement park.

He wondered how hard the navy would try to get him back to the *Field*. She'd be weighing anchor for Korea in just a little over two weeks. One of the pharmacist mates had told him that it would be close to three weeks before the hospital would turn him loose. He knew they couldn't take the chance of letting him go back too early; suppose he did and infected the entire ship? Hell, being a Typhoid Mary might prove a blessing in disguise, he smiled, aware that if he played his cards right, the good old Charlie P. would be long gone by the time he left the hospital. Poor Murray, Logan laughed, he'll split a gut when he finds out that he won't have anyone to work the plotting board for him. One thing's for sure, he'd have no guilty conscience about missing Korea. He'd more than paid his dues in the last one, he told himself, aware that there were a hell of a lot of guys his age who hadn't. Some of them were back at B. and G. right now, he thought, fat and happy, sniffing after his job like sharks after a bleeding porpoise. Then, he heard the sound of steps coming up behind him, the distinct tap of a female's shoes on the well waxed floor.

"Logan, get away from that window," Miss Osbourne said in a feminine but authoritative voice. "You know you shouldn't be standing there without your pajama top. You've given us enough trouble with your chicken pox. Do you want to get pneumonia on top of it?"

"I just wanted to get some air, Lieutenant, that's all."

"Well, come back over here and sit on the bed. I've got to rub this on your back," she said holding out the small bottle.

"What happened to the hospital corpsman? He's been doing it since I checked into this hotel," Logan snickered.

"Sturgis went on early leave. If you'd prefer that one of the corpsmen do it, I can send in Pelcher," she said with a coy smile.

"No, Lieutenant, you go right ahead. I was just worried that you might catch the chicken pox if you got too close," he smiled as he felt her soft young hands rub the salve across his shoulder blades.

"You don't have to worry about that; I had it when I was eight. Besides, I've been inoculated against anything you could give me," she answered in a stinging tone. "Here, you're a big boy, Logan, you can do your chest yourself," she said, thrusting the bottle into his hand before turning away.

Her back was to him now as she bent to adjust the bed next to his. He studied her closely, she was fairly tall, about five-eight, he judged comparing her to the perfect Candy who he always used as a yardstick. Like Candy, she had excellent legs and a small waist. He watched her walk over to the bed across the aisle where she took the temperature of a sad-faced motor mack. Maybe it was those white stockings, he mused. Hell, whatever it was, he knew he'd have to figure out a way to get into her pants before he left the hospital.

Finishing her rounds, the young nurse walked over to the window and adjusted the blinds. Logan noticed a trace of lace just below the hem of her white uniform. "Your slip is showing, Lieutenant," he grinned, waiting for a reaction. Miss Osbourne didn't grin back, but she didn't look offended either. As she walked away, she glanced around at the bare chested radarman, her gaze as appraising as his own. "Thanks," she smiled.

• • •

Owen Garrett Royal lost no time departing the *Field*. Unfortunately, the day's maneuvers had stretched out an hour-and-a-half longer than anyone had anticipated. If he was lucky, he thought, there wouldn't be any traffic jams between the destroyer base and La Jolla. He was especially leery of that intersection at Mission and Turquoise. He'd been tied up there a couple of times before. Even if traffic wasn't bogged down, he knew he'd still be cutting it close. In spite of the cool breeze, he could feel himself perspiring on this, his last night with Candace for nine, possibly ten, months. He refused to think the "unthinkable."

It was also the first opportunity he'd had to show off the Charlie P. to Candace. In the past she'd always managed to come up with an excuse to side step his invitations. Although she knew it bothered him, and he gave it much thought, he was never able to ascertain the reason for her reluctance. Now that she'd finally consented, he hoped she'd be impressed. Freshly painted from bow to stern, his old war horse didn't look half bad, he smiled confidently as he saluted the watch at the quarterdeck and headed for his car.

Royal hoped Candace would be ready to leave as soon as he reached the apartment. He appreciated Chief DelRosario's staying on board to oversee preparation of the special dinner in honor of Candace's visit. Valencia too, the wardroom's leading steward; it was damn good of him, Owen mused, to give up his last Stateside liberty to help with the big event.

Candace pursed her lips as she applied the final touch of lipstick. Picking up the largest of two blue combs, she ran it slowly through her hair now tumbling loosely around her bare shoulders. She brushed it for a few minutes until she was satisfied that the wealth of long golden strands hung straight without curls or kinks. Candace was quite pleased with the blonde rinse she'd tried for the first time that morning, and wondered which competitive ad agency was handling the account. Maybe they were vulnerable; she'd have to look into it, she decided as she finished brushing.

"Dammit!" she muttered aloud, glancing at the small clock on the corner table. Here she was, still running around in nothing but bra and panties with Garrett due to show up any minute. She scrambled for her garter belt and stockings. She was in no mood to put temptation in his path...not tonight, she decided, fully determined that she would ask him for a divorce before the evening was over. Candace wondered how he would react. Anyway, he'd have a lot of time to adjust to the idea while he was out there sailing around those South Sea Islands. It wasn't as if he was going off to war or something really dangerous, she rationalized. Garrett was still a terribly handsome man, and there were probably a lot of pretty nurses on those islands. Maybe he'd meet somebody like Ensign Nellie Forbush in "*South Pacific,*" she smiled, a little uneasily.

Candace pulled the second stocking on, making certain it was taut over calf and thigh. As she fastened it to the garter stay, she unexpectedly found herself thinking about Kevin Logan. She hadn't heard from him in over five weeks, not even a phone call. That was typical of that heel, she thought. He appears out of nowhere after almost three years, makes out with her like a Burgundian bandit every night for two weeks, then disappears without even a goodbye. He's probably back in L.A. screwing some eighteen-year-old starlet with king size tits, she frowned. At least that would keep him away from the destroyer base, she thought hopefully.

She'd been giving Garrett flimsy excuses for a month now about why she couldn't go see his ship. Kevin certainly should be through scouting out "*Caine Mutiny*" film sites by now...what if he wasn't! She didn't even want to think of that possibility. Suppose she and Garrett should bump into him tonight at the naval base. She had no idea how she would handle such an eventuality. She slipped the moss green dress over her head just as she heard Garrett's key jiggling in the door lock.

"Garrett!" she cried. "You've arrived just in time to help a lady in distress. Come here and help me with this damn zipper. I must have put a pound or two on since I left New York." She kissed him quite tenderly. "You know it's your fault that I'm having trouble fitting into my clothes. You've been wining and dining me every night in the most elegant restaurants in Southern California."

"And you deserve it, too," he smiled giving her a loving pat on the derriere.

"You've turned into quite a flatterer lately. If you were Irish, I'd tell you to cut the blarney," she retorted. "You know you look pretty damn good yourself. I really like that brown sharkskin you're wearing. I think it's my favorite of all your suits."

"I know, that's why I wore it," he said, adjusting the points of the white handkerchief in his breast pocket.

"I like your tie, too," she smiled.

"You should, you bought it for me for Christmas last year, don't you remember?"

"Of course I do. I bought it at B. Altman's. I was just testing you. Say, with all the expensive clothes you've been wearing around here lately, aren't you afraid that somebody might accuse you of selling secrets to the Russians?" she quipped.

"No chance of that. I don't think the Russians would be interested in any of the gear we're carrying aboard the *Field*. We supplied them with later equipment during World War Two," he said, handing Candace her purse from the table.

She snapped off the lights and they left the apartment.

"Well, tonight's the night that I'm going to meet my competition," Candace smiled.

Owen didn't notice that her mood had changed until they were well along Mission Boulevard. "Why so serious, sweetheart? Is it my leaving tomorrow?"

"Of course, I'm always sad when you leave on one of your overseas tours." Why did I say that, she thought, aware that this was not the night to feed Garrett a line, not when she had spent most of the day priming herself to tell him that she wanted a divorce...that she wanted to leave him for good.

"You've gone through this before," he said calmly, touched by her sadness. "I'd think you'd be accustomed to it by now."

"Well, it's not just your leaving. I had a really rough day at the agency."

With all the trials and tribulations Owen was experiencing each day aboard the *Field*, this was the first time that he gave any thought to the fact that Candace was probably encountering more than her share of problems at B.B.Y. and S.

"Why don't you tell me about your day at the office," he said. "I hear problems get a lot smaller when you share them with someone who loves you very much," he added, as they drove past Pacific Beach and the big Crystal Fishing Pier.

"Oh, there's this devious little worm in my office named Ronald Paradise. I caught him in another lie today."

"That doesn't seem serious."

"It is when it comes from Ronald. He's our senior copy chief. Every time I ask him why a particular ad or promotional brochure is late, he looks me straight in the eye and without hesitation, tells me something like he's just finishing talking to the printer and we can expect delivery this afternoon or tomorrow morning at the latest. Then I find out that he hasn't spoken to the printer in over two weeks, and that we won't even see the proofs for five more days much less the finished piece. I'm afraid he's just a pathological liar. If you were to show him a piece of green paper and then ask him what color it was, he'd instinctively say red."

"Maybe he's color blind," Royal laughed.

"He's not color blind. He's just got a mental block when it comes to telling the truth. How am I going to deal with our clients if I can't depend on the information I receive from my key staff? Hay," she smiled, "I thought you were going to sympathize."

"I am sympathetic...really, see, you're smiling about it now yourself. Say, if this little weasel is such a problem, why don't you fire him?"

"I'm certain it's going to come to that soon," Candace said. "Right now he's too deeply involved with the planning stages of two campaigns we're preparing for a couple of our most important clients. It wouldn't help our cause if word leaked out right now that we were getting ready to dump our senior copy writer. Once the campaigns are approved, Ronald Paradise will be just an unpleasant memory. Anyway, now that you've got me smiling about my problems, how are you doing with that destroyer of yours? I'll bet your crew's excited about calling at those islands with all those hula girls in grass skirts."

"That's something I've been wanting to talk to you about, but I couldn't before tonight."

"You wanted to talk to me about hula girls in grass skirts?" she stared at him, obviously intrigued.

"No," he laughed good naturedly. "I'm afraid there aren't going to be any hula girls in grass skirts, except maybe while we're in Hawaii. Where we're going, the female uniform of the day's more likely to be kimonos or whatever it is they wear in Korea."

"Korea?" Her face turned ashen white.

"Yes, I've known about it almost since the day I took command of the *Field*. The commodore clamped a heavy blanket of secrecy over our deployment. We were ordered to tell everyone that we were going to Eniwetok."

"Even me?" she asked with hurt in her tone.

"Yes, sweetheart, everyone. Even our crew and most of our officers aren't supposed to know until after we clear Pearl Harbor. Of course, I'm certain that everyone in the division right down to the lowest seaman deuce has known that we're joining up with Task Force Seventy-Seven since day one. In fact, most of the crew's been to school studying procedures that are only being employed in Korea. Our good commodore's a bit naive thinking that he could keep the word from leaking out."

"This commodore of yours doesn't sound very bright. Will we meet him on your ship tonight?" she asked, trying to get her thoughts together after Owen's unexpected disclosure. She knew now that she couldn't tell him she wanted a divorce...not the night before he'd be sailing off to war. Suppose he should get killed with that thought on his mind, she mused, how would she ever live with herself.

"To answer your first question," Royal said, slowing down for a red light. "I'm not really certain about the commodore. At times I'm convinced that he's not playing with a full deck. For example, just this morning he summoned all the C.O.'s in the division to a meeting aboard the flagship. Naturally, we were all expecting to hear important news about our upcoming deployment. Instead, he wasted over an hour showing us the various entries from a contest he's been running for a division shoulder patch design. The winning patch wasn't very imaginative, maybe that's why it appealed to Commodore Price."

"What was the winning design?"

"A silver sea horse superimposed over a red two-nine-one. The commodore couldn't have made a bigger fuss over it if it had been the Mona Lisa. That meeting was the main reason I was so late picking you up tonight. It caused us to reach the operating area more than an hour late. The C.O. of the sub we were supposed to play war games with assumed that the exercise had been called off, so he started to head back to the barn. Luckily we got there before he'd left the operating area, but it threw everything off schedule."

"Did someone on your ship win the contest?"

"No, it was a sailor from the *John Morgan*. That's part of the problem," Owen frowned.

"What do you mean?"

"Well, there were at least fifteen or twenty entries from each of the other three destroyers. Unfortunately, my crew's not artistically inclined. There were only four designs submitted from the *Field* and two of them came from Don Stockwell, my Ops officer. After the meeting, Commodore Price took me aside to tell me he was highly disappointed in both my officers and enlisted because of their apparent lack of interest in his contest. He implied that I had let both him and the division down by not impressing my crew with the contest's importance. He also let me know that our lack of participation shows how little esprit de corps we have aboard the *Field*.

"Can he cause you any trouble, you know, like with your future promotions?"

"Yes, unfortunately, but that's enough doom and gloom for the evening. I don't want to bother you with any more of my problems, not after just hitting you with the news about Korea. Besides, we'll be at the base in just a few more minutes."

Hardly had he gotten the words out when he saw the bright white and yellow lights that illuminated the main gate. He glanced over at his wife, the green skirt was almost up to her hips. Eyeing her smooth thighs, he stroked them gently, then running his fingers playfully along the garter strap, tugged the hem of her skirt down closer to her knees. "You wouldn't want to give those poor marines at the gate the wrong idea, now would you?"

Candace smiled that mischievous smile of hers, the one he always found irresistible.

The marines quickly passed them through the gate and in a few minutes they were at the pier.

A squadron of *Sumner* class destroyers had left for the Far East earlier in the week so there was ample room to berth the four *Fletchers* bow to stern along the quay rather than in the customary nest. This afforded each of 291's bluejackets convenient and direct access to the quay.

Before boarding *DD-505*, Owen took Candace for a stroll along the quay, pointing out the salient features of the ship's superstructure and external equipment. Even though the sun had long retreated, the destroyer was amply illuminated, both by her own lights and also by a generous string of floodlights rigged at twenty-foot intervals along the ship's entire 377-foot length and a bit beyond illuminating the name CHARLES P. FIELD emblazoned in black steel letters across the stern.

"Didn't you tell me in Nice that all navy ships have the letters U.S.S. in front of their name?" she quizzed.

"They do. At least American warships do," he quickly amended.

"Okay, then why doesn't your ship have a U.S.S. up there with it's name?" she asked with child-like inquisitiveness. "What happened? Did the navy run out of letters?" she teased.

"No, it's sort of a tradition...that is, not putting U.S.S. on the stern." Royal was deeply embarrassed not knowing the answer, and he hoped Candace had not picked up on his bluff.

Candace asked about the "funny looking gray barrels" perched in steel "cages" on the fantail just above the lettering.

"Those are depth-charge racks," he smiled, "the barrels are the depth-charges, we use them to destroy submarines. In fact," he snickered, "those depth-charges and that rack are almost identical to the equipment the navy mounted on its old 'four pipers' back in 1918 during the First World War."

"Oh, come on, Garrett, the navy wouldn't send your ship over to Korea with World War One weapons, would they?" she asked wide-eyed.

"It's not as bad as it sounds. Except for those stern racks, most of our equipment goes back to about 1942."

"That's ten whole years. Didn't the navy give you anything new for the ship?"

"Yes, the crew," he frowned. "Most of them reported aboard just three weeks ago when we went up to San Francisco."

"How are you going to fight the Koreans with old equipment and a new crew?" She asked in a genuinely worried voice.

"Oh, I don't expect that we're going to do much fighting. I'm pretty certain that they'll keep us out with the carriers beyond the range of their shore batteries."

"What about those things that float in the water and blow up ships when they bump into them?"

"You mean mines," he smiled. "Well, I have to be honest with you. They are all over the place, even in the area where the carriers operate. Unfortunately, not even our very latest ships are immune to being sunk by mines. At least the *Field's* age won't be a special handicap as far as they're concerned."

Candace shifted her attention back to the depth-charge racks, and Royal recountered the essential details of the Chief Henderson legend.

Quickly concluding that her husband was pulling her leg, Candace suggested that he should put the story on paper and submit it to one of the weekly magazines. "You know *Colliers* or the *Saturday Evening Post* would probably pay a heap for a weird tale like that one," his wife advised, trying unsuccessfully to keep a straight face.

Ensign Coates was assigned to the quarterdeck along with Bites. Both saluted smartly as their commanding officer and his wife alighted from the gangway. Commander Royal introduced Candace to the young OOD who nervously welcomed the charming visitor. Though sensitive to the pungent smell of the freshly painted quarter-deck, Candace returned the greeting and extended her hand to the *Field's* C.I.C. officer. Uncertain if he should shake it or kiss it, he hesitantly opted for the former. A few feet away, Bites stared at and mentally undressed the fabulously beautiful Candace. The young bo'sun continued staring as Royal and Candace departed for the wardroom where candlelight and braised duck awaited them. Because U.S. Navy regulations prohibited any type of alcoholic beverage aboard ship, Chief DelRosario prudently substituted a decanter of California grape juice.

"Wow-eeee, Mister Coates," the petty-officer-of-the-watch cried out, "Ah never seen anythin' like her 'cept maybe in the movies or up on one o' them billboards holdin' up a bottle o' Pepsi Coley. Ah tell you, ah'd eat live bees fer somethin' like her."

"Calm down, Bites, you're talking about the captain's wife, you know," the OOD cautioned sternly.

"Yes, suh, but did you ever see anythin' as pretty as that little ole' gal? If ah had a wife that looked like that, you'd never find me goin' off a year at a time and leavin' her untended."

McAlleney, the messenger for the evening watch, had been below in the electricians' shop finding out what the night's movie would be so word could be passed over the speaker system. When he returned to the quarterdeck, Bites gave him an anatomical description of the golden haired visitor replete with details that would make a second-year medical student blush.

"Think the cap'n will be takin' her fer a tour o' the bridge?" McAlleney asked.

"Ah 'magin' so, why?" Bites answered with a puzzled look.

"Well, if'n she's half the looker you say, Ah might just accidentally find myself at the bottom o' one o' those straight ladders she's gonna have to climb up," the messenger replied with a sly smile.

"Now stow that kind of talk, McAlleney or I swear I'll put you on report!" Ensign Coates snapped. "Better yet, I'll refer the matter to your department head, Mister MacKinlay! Do you read me?"

"Yes suh, loud and clear. Ah was only funnin'. Ah just wanted to get a rile out o' ole' Bites here."

"Okay. Just keep your mind on your watch," Coates said in a calmer tone. And while the OOD decided to ignore any further remarks made by his two watch standers, the young officer soon found himself fantasizing about how she would look climbing those outside bridge ladders in that clinging knit dress. Of course, there was no chance of that ever happening, he sadly concluded, certain that the captain would take her no higher than the wheelhouse, and she could use the stairway inside the bridge structure to get up there. One thing was indisputable, he knew she was the most fantastic looking female he'd ever seen in all his twenty-two years.

Coates wondered what it would be like to go to bed with someone so incredibly beautiful. He hoped he'd find out for himself in the not too distant future. Hell, the way he was picking hair out of his comb lately, he'd better find the right girl pretty damn quick. He wondered if he'd be completely bald by the time the *Field* returned from Eniwetok.

After dinner as expected, Owen Royal took his lovely wife for a comprehensive tour of the bridge. Candace showed a keen interest in the wheelhouse, especially the glistening gold binnacle that housed the gyro-compass. Royal enjoyed describing the functions of the various navigational aids. He explained how the magnetic compass differed from the gyro-compass, and how the radar repeater was like a remote television screen, duplicating the exact picture being seen on the radar scopes below in the combat-information-center. Amazed at how fast she digested each new piece of information, Owen decided she had more questions than a nine-year-old.

"The *Field* seems terribly small after the *Coral Sea*," Candace said as the two stepped out on to the open bridge. Her blonde hair gleamed magnificently in the moonlight.

"Well, comparing the Charlie P. to my old flattop is like comparing Kent Falls to New York City. Do you still remember that night in Nice?"

"How could I ever forget it. You know you really swept me off my feet. I had never met anyone quite like you. You'll always be very special in my life."

To Owen, Candace's words seemed strangely foreboding, like something someone might say if they were saying goodbye.

Candace detected his sudden uneasiness. She hadn't intended to hurt him, not now...not before he sailed off to Korea. She raised her face, eyes closed, and kissed him deeply.

"You know, I'll never be able to stand out here without remembering this evening," Owen said. "Every place on this ship where you've been will always have a special significance." They kissed again and she found herself wondering if she really did want him to leave...if she really did want a divorce. Maybe she'd give it a little more time. Her indecision was abruptly interrupted by a blast of static from the horn-shaped speaker mounted atop the wheelhouse a few feet above her head. The static quickly subsided...

"Now hear this! The movie on the fantail tonight will be 'A Yank in the R.A.F.' starring Tyrone Power, Betty Grable and John Sutton. The movie will begin in approximately ten minutes!"

"Isn't that an old movie?" Candace asked.

"I imagine so. The commodore seems to get all the new ones over on the *Abner Ward*. They're supposed to be rotated among the four ships in the division but somehow none of the newer films ever get to us before they have to be returned to the facility ashore that issues them. Say, to change the subject for a moment...have you ever had chicken pox?"

"Chicken pox?" Candace was completely bewildered. "Yes, I'm pretty sure I did. I had the measles, too. But why would you ask me that now?"

"One of my radarmen came down with the chicken pox a few weeks ago. We had to keep him over in the quarantine ward at the hospital. In fact, we'll be sailing tomorrow without him. I was planning to take you down to our C.I.C. That's the brains of this ship, especially when we go into combat. I'm pretty sure you'll find it quite interesting, and as long as you've already had chicken pox, it should be safe enough for you to go down there. Besides, we've had medical teams swarming all over the ship since the radarman reported into the hospital. Nobody in the crew has shown any symptoms so I've stopped worrying about an epidemic breaking out."

"Tell me one thing, Garrett, just how young are you taking people into the navy these days?"

"Oh, you mean the fellow with the chicken pox," Owen laughed. "He's certainly not a kid. I'd say he's just about your age. Come to think of it, I believe he's also from that nutmeg state of yours."

"Well, I'm glad to see that my homestate is represented by at least one member of your crew," she smiled.

"Oh, I think if I looked around, I could come up with at least two or three more. I'm really sorry about losing this man though. From what I've observed, he was by far the sharpest radarman in our C.I.C. team. I tried my damndest to get the hospital to release him so he could leave with us tomorrow morning but they wouldn't budge. I think the hospital's just being over cautious. From what I know about chicken pox, he should be well recovered after three weeks. I even asked the commodore if he could pull some strings. He didn't seem very concerned...suggested that I could get a perfectly good replacement from the personnel pool at Pearl. The last thing I want now is a new radarman. Those fellows train as a team and my radar gang's been training together since early March."

On the way to the Combat-Information-Center, Owen showed Candace his stateroom.

"I certainly won't have to worry about you getting some sexy geisha in here," she joked, "you wouldn't have enough room."

"You don't have to worry about that. The only woman I'm interested in is the one in that picture over there," he said pointing to a large framed photograph of Candace, the one she had sent him when he was serving aboard the *Buffalo*.

She straightened his necktie. "Who'll do this for you when you're over there?" she smiled.

"I don't expect to be wearing a tie in Korea."

"Oh, I wasn't really thinking of Korea," she laughed. "I've been reading a lot about those R and R's the G.I.'s have been having in Japan. That stands for rest and recreation, right?"

"Yes, you're well informed."

"Well, I don't mind the rest part, just make sure you don't get too much recreation."

"I could always stay aboard if you prefer, but then how could I buy you all those silk dresses, you know, the oriental kind with the sexy slits up the side."

Candace put her hands on his shoulder and he thumbed her chin playfully. They kissed. It was a long kiss, one Owen knew would have to last him a very long time.

Below in the combat-information-center, Howie Murray scribbled out the final lines of a rambling, repetitiously affectionate epistle to Mary Alice. Just an hour before, he had told her exactly the same things over the phone at the petty officers' club. He drummed on the plotting table with his fingers, thinking of the numerous times Bacelli, Gardiner, Holiday and Nugent had tried their damndest to get him to stray. And while he had no definite proof, Murray suspected that the four third-class had a bet going as to which one of them could get him to go over on the beach and cheat on his wife. He guessed they'd been working hard at it since he'd reported aboard back in January. Well, they could try all they wanted, he smiled, confident that his love for Mary Alice and the girls would continue to withstand any test in Hawaii, Japan, Korea, or any other place the navy might decide to send the Charlie P.

In the coffee locker, a closet size space adjoining the C.I.C., Gardiner thumbed through the now well-worn paperback edition of "*From Here to Eternity*." Sulking because he'd been stuck with the duty during his last night in

San Diego, he seemed determined to constantly interrupt Murray's letter writing with question after question.

"Say, Murray," he shouted, "you must have spent a lot of time in Hawaii during the war, did you ever hear anything about throwing one of those flower things you put around your neck into the water? You know, when you're sailing out of the harbor at Honolulu?"

"I don't know what you're talking about," the *Field's* senior radarman murmured, as he licked the sealer on the envelope.

"It's right here in the book, right at the end of the chapter. It's just after the Japs creamed Pearl Harbor. This broad, her name's Carol Holmes, is sailing back to the States' in case the Japs come back. She's on this big passenger liner loaded with dependents and she throws this lei over the side of the ship. There's supposed to be some old Hawaiian legend that says if you throw a lei overboard as you pass Diamond Head, it will tell you if you're ever coming back to Hawaii."

"I still don't know what you're talking about. Anyway, I don't believe in legends."

"Well, it says if the lei floats in towards the shore, then you'll return to Hawaii some day, but if the lei floats out to sea, then you're never gonna come back to the islands again."

"That's a lot of bunk. I don't believe in that stuff. I'm not superstitious. Didn't I survive the *Franklin*, and her with the number thirteen?" Murray snapped. "Besides, we'll all be back in Hawaii next spring on our way home. Coates told me we're good for about a four-day stop-over."

"Attention on deck!" Gardiner gasped aloud, his usual blank expression changing to one of utter astonishment.

The first-class turned his head just in time to see his commanding officer step through the door.

Murray and Gardiner instantly jumped to their feet and stood rigidly at attention.

"Carry on," Royal said in a warm friendly tone. "Just continue with what you were doing. I'm going to show Mrs. Royal what our C.I.C. looks like," he smiled.

"Yes sir, good evening Mrs. Royal," Murray replied nervously. "I was just leaving, Sir. I have to go over to the base post office. There's a mailbox out front. I want to make sure this letter to my wife and daughters gets off before we sail tomorrow morning. Gardiner here has the duty. He's monitoring the harbor and C.I.C. nets," the *Field's* senior radarman explained, wanting to be certain that the captain didn't think he was leaving the ship while on watch.

Owen went about the enjoyable task of showing Candace the specific function of each G.Q. station in C.I.C., explaining its contribution to the overall information gathering process so vital to a modern warship's performance.

Candace shook her head in amazement. "This is fascinating," she said, her blue eyes glowing with excitement. " I think you must be a genius to be able to run a ship like this and know so much about each piece of equipment."

Royal was embarrassed at the praise, unaware that Gardiner was paying little attention to what was being said. Like everyone else who crossed Candace's path aboard *DD-505* that evening, the third-class was completely overwhelmed. Nobody could look that good, he told himself as the two visitors took their leave. Too bad that smart ass Logan couldn't be around to get a look at her, he thought, convinced that the captain's wife had to be even more beautiful than any of those New York models Logan was always shooting his yap off about.

Lieutenant Commander Aubrey Cobb spent a turbulent Saturday afternoon trying to break 80 at the Coronado Country Club. At six o'clock that evening, he placed a long distance call to his wife Renee in Roslyn, but got no answer. Maybe she'd gone off to Boston for that teachers' conference she'd written about, he thought. No matter, he didn't have time to waste in a telephone booth anyway, he mumbled angrily as he hurried off to Chula Vista for a pressing appointment with a chilled Dubonnet and a warm platinum blonde named Carol Ritter.

It was almost 3a.m. Cobb plucked his watch from the dresser drawer and quickly slipped the expanding metal band over his wrist; then tightened the knot in his black tie until it pinched his collar. He could hear Carol's heavy snoring. That always happened when she slept on her back with her mouth open. She looked so silly and adolescent in those peppermint striped pajamas, he decided, glancing back at the bed. It almost made him feel a little guilty when she looked that way. He rubbed his face, felt the beard stubble and wondered if he should have taken the extra time to shave. Quarters wouldn't go until 7:30, he remembered. There would be ample time to take care of that minor detail aboard ship, he reassured himself. Slipping into his jacket, Cobb quietly snapped out the small table lamp and tip-toed to the door. He wondered if Carol would miss him when she awoke. Probably not, he concluded indifferently, aware that the pretty young wife of the *Field*'s assistant-gunnery officer had a well-deserved reputation for quickly making male friends.

Outside the young woman's apartment, the *Field*'s executive officer hailed a passing cab. When he reached the foot of the quay where the division was berthed, he handed the driver a five-dollar bill. "Keep the change, fella," he instructed good-naturedly. "I'm leaving for Korea in about six hours so I won't have any place to spend it."

The cabbie's face twitched in annoyance. The meter read $4.85.

As Cobb gripped the cold chain railing of the gangway that linked the pier with the *Field*'s quarterdeck, he suddenly wondered if Renee had gone to Boston for anything besides business.

•   •   •

Munching on a leathery piece of smoked beef, Major Mychenko was fully convinced that Maksan had to be the worst hell-hole on the face of the earth. He opened his traplike mouth to spit a huge chunk of the unpalatable meat into a metal bucket he specifically kept next to the table for that purpose. Looking up at the roof of the small hut, he hoped that the repairs he'd made earlier that morning would keep out the rain which he knew would come before nightfall.

Mychenko pondered which of his comrade colonels had been responsible for his being packed off to this miserable place. Probably that Siberian pig, Nikilayev, he quickly concluded. After all, how could you expect any consideration from anyone who came from Strelka.

It had been weeks now since he'd dispatched his recommendations to General Svobni back in Pyongyang. He wondered when the comrade general would get off his fat ass and send him the equipment he needed. Maybe then, he could get the work completed and be able to say *proshchuy* to this misbegotten little harbor with its rat-infested village and its ugly toothless women.

Chapter VI - "Far Away Places"

Monday, May 26th came faster than anyone in DesDiv 291 could ever have imagined. To commanding officer and seaman "deuce" alike, the two months of intensive training seemed far more like two weeks. And, as if to announce the opening of this special day, dawn burst forth with a crazy quilt of crimson and rose, causing more than one sailor aboard the *Field* to recite aloud the time-worn rhyme of the seafarer that cautioned:

> *"Red sky at night, sailor's delight,*
> *Red sky in the morning, sailor take warning."*

Personnel on each of the four destroyers were lined up by departments well before the call to quarters which wasn't piped away until 07:30. Erected at pierside was a flag-draped speakers' platform, and atop the tall poles that lined the concrete basin, loud-speakers were strategically rigged so that all hands might hear the Commandant of the Eleventh Naval District wish them the traditional "smooth sailing and good hunting." Listening to the admiral's parting words, Ensign Coates wondered just what they could possibly be called upon to "hunt" at Eniwetok Atoll.

Assigned quarters for *DD-505's* Operations Department was on the port side of the bridge-wing. Since the *Field* was berthed with her starboard side to the quay, this location was as remote from the festivities as was possible. Nugent and Holiday made no secret of their annoyance at being denied a view of the baton-twirling, short-skirted drum majorettes from the local high school who were patriotically demonstrating their God-given talents in front of the speakers' stand.

The navy band rambled its way through a short medley of Sousa marches followed by a lively selection of sea chanties. At precisely 09:00, the band shook the air with a lilting rendition of *"The Girl I Left Behind Me."* Then, as the bandmaster signaled for a second playing of the old Irish air that had sent so many a lad off to battle from Waterloo to the Little Big Horn, a screech of whistle announced special-sea-detail. Bluejackets on all four destroyers scampered to their assigned stations, and the serious business of getting underway commenced.

Seconds later, Owen Royal, taking his cue from the ship ahead, gave the order to "cast off all lines," and soon the *Field* was sliding out from the quay stern first. Standing out several hundred yards, *DD-505* slowed her engines as each of her sisters maneuvered away from the quay. As she waited to take her position in the number four slot astern of the other three *Fletchers*, all hands topside, even McAlleney, put extra starch into their stance as the militant strains of "*Anchors Aweigh*" drifted out from the shore. And, Turk, who had been slouching near the open bread locker, set aside his tray of freshly baked biscuits and unconsciously straightened his posture until the final notes had faded away amid the harbor noise.

By four that afternoon, the division was far at sea racing into a cool west wind that whipped the waves and capped them with milky white spray. An ideal day to be at sea, thought Royal as he climbed the ladder to the wheelhouse. He wondered what Candace was doing about now. The feeling of her was all over the bridge. He missed her already, and he wondered how well they'd both be able to adjust to this fifth separation since their marriage.

The four destroyers were running in line-of-bearing formation which placed the ships beam to beam as if they were racing. Rather than attempting to surge ahead, however, the OOD on each of the four ships was striving to keep his vessel perfectly parallel to the vessel abeam. Before entering the wheelhouse, Royal paused to watch the *Field*'s consorts. All three were to starboard. *Halsey Wayne*, closest of the trio, obscured a clear view of *John Morgan* and *Abner Ward*. Now and then the *Wayne* would rise on a wave and dip her stern deep into the sea, sloshing green water over her depth-charge racks. Then her bow would plunge steeply, affording Royal a few seconds glimpse of the two more distant *Fletchers*. Lieutenant Sternhagen, the ship's damage-control officer, was standing the 16:00 to 18:00 (4 to 6 p.m.) steaming watch. Assisting him as JOD was Ensign Daly. After briefly observing the wheelhouse activity, the captain moved on into the adjoining chartroom to study Commodore Price's schedule of drills for that evening and to write up his own "night intentions."

Night steaming would be a new experience for many of the *Field*'s younger tars. To them, it would seem quite strange at this time of the day not to be dusting off their dress blues and hurrying on to ship's office to pick up their liberty cards for the evening's adventure along San Diego's Broadway or Market Street. It seemed stranger yet when twilight dissolved into a vast black void without revealing the reassuring contours of Point Loma and the California shoreline.

After dinner the officers sat in the wardroom discussing the *Field*'s impending operations with Task Force 77. It was general opinion that *DD-505* would never fire a shot in anger, and all were agreed that Korea was a land war and the navy was only being called upon to support the army and marines. After dinner Lieutenant Stockwell retired to his room to write a long letter to Cassy Jean, his college sweetheart and, he hoped, future bride. Cassy Jean was flying out to

Hawaii with her mother to see him. Stockwell had heard all about how beautiful the captain's wife was. Well, just wait till his fellow officers on the *Field* got a look at Cassy Jean, he told himself. After all, hadn't she just been named "Miss Talladega County," he smiled confidently.

By nine the conversation in the wardroom had finally persuaded Ensign Coates that the Charlie P. wasn't really bound for the Marshall Islands. Promptly burying himself in a corner of the wardroom with "*Awards and Decorations — U.S.N. and U.S.M.C.*," he wondered how many ribbons he would earn while helping to liberate the South Koreans from their communist aggressors. Peering over the black leather cover of the NavPers manual, he asked, "Do you think we'll rate the 'China Service Medal' if we pull any patrols in the Formosa Strait?" His companions were unable to answer his question with any certainty, though all agreed that the young ensign was the only man aboard the *Field* who could be wounded in the head and not rate the "Purple Heart."

• • •

While Mr. Coates was contemplating future glory, Cynthia Osbourne was affectionately taking Logan's arm as he escorted her from the dance floor to their table in a secluded corner of the Del Coronado. Lieutenant (jg.) Osbourne, the iron-fisted disciplinarian of Ward 8 had succumbed to Logan's charms in just half the time the radarman had anticipated. What he had viewed as a possible challenge had turned out to be a total rout.

Hailing from a small town on the fringe of Lake Erie, the young nurse had never encountered anyone as fascinating or as worldly as Kevin, she thought. Not that she was a naive little virgin; at twenty-three she'd had more than her share of doctors tripping over their stethoscopes trying to get her bedded. Even as a candy striper back at Cleveland General, she'd become well accustomed to the passionate ramblings of most of the hospital's interns. Several of the officers that hung out at the hospital O-club had also made a try for her, usually without much success. Kevin though, he was completely different. She'd sensed that the first time she stopped to talk to him. He was so interesting. She could listen to those amusing stories about Madison Avenue all day, especially how he helped develop those big ad campaigns like the one for Coca Cola, and the one to introduce General Motors' lineup for 1952. The world of advertising had captivated her ever since she'd read "*The Hucksters.*" She never thought she'd ever get a chance to meet somebody as high up in the agency business as Kevin.

Her roommate Betsy Chadwick had warned her about dating a sailor. Betsy had even quoted verbatim the navy dictum that said, "Thou shalt not fraternize with enlisted men." Well, she actually didn't think of Kevin as being in the navy. Afterall, he is a reserve, and that's practically a civilian, she reasoned. Besides, he does have a college degree, and he could be an officer if he wanted to spend that extra time in the navy. She certainly could understand his being anxious to get back to Madison Avenue and that penthouse apartment with the maid and valet he had told her about.

It didn't hurt that Kevin was so good looking either, she thought, hating to admit, even to herself, that she'd been physically attracted to him since the first morning he'd smiled at her from his hospital bed. She'd never fallen for anyone like this before. She wanted him so badly, so sexually, she told herself, but Kevin was such a gentleman, she doubted that he'd try to take advantage of her even if she did invite him back to her apartment. The thought of enticing Kevin to her place suddenly excited her. She knew Betsy had the duty in the emergency ward from midnight until eight.

She wondered what it would be like being married to a leading ad executive like Kevin. Living in New York City would be great fun, but then maybe he'd want to get rid of the penthouse and buy a big house in Westchester. She'd read that that was where most of the important advertising people lived.

The lieutenant sipped her Singapore Sling through a glass straw while Kevin savored his Prior's dark. What a lucky break, Logan thought, coming down with chicken pox just before the *Field* hauled out for Korea. He wondered how far at sea the destroyer was by now. They should be hitting Hawaii in four or five days, he thought, providing the commodore didn't come up with a lot of underway drills. Anyway, the *Field* was past history, a small but definitely closed chapter of his life. He'd wish them all luck but that was as far as he'd go, Logan decided.

Watching the reddish liquor slowly inch its way up the straw to Cindy's pretty mouth, Logan was convinced that his biggest problem now was just remembering not to call her Candy. He'd almost slipped twice already. Too bad their names were so damn close. He knew that with or without an assist from the Singapore Sling, he'd have to be more careful if he was going to make it into her skivies. One thing was certain, she was exceptionally attractive when she wasn't wearing her glasses. Logan found her eyes particularly bewitching. They seemed to change from green to hazel then back to green again depending on the light. The idea of making it with a nurse particularly appealed to him. It was like having an insurance policy that would protect him from getting a dose, he reassured himself.

The eyes he was admiring so much studied his face in objective silence. "You know, I could really get hung if anyone saw me sitting here with you, and recognized that you're a white hat," she said.

"That's unlikely since neither of us is in uniform. Besides, there's nobody around here to recognize me. They're all way out there on the deep blue sea," Kevin smiled, glancing toward one of the picture windows that faced the Pacific.

"Aren't you a little sorry that you're not going with them?"

"Not inthe least. They really don't need me. Anyway, the navy got more than it's money's worth out of me in the big war. The Japs and the krauts both got to use me for target practice, and if Italy hadn't gone belly up half way through the war, Il Duce probably would have gotten a crack at me too. Besides, if I was way out there with them, I couldn't be sitting here with someone as special as you," he added never being one to miss an opportunity.

She tried to keep from blushing but was unsuccessful. "You don't know that I'm going to Japan in August, do you?"

"No, how would I know that?" Logan winced, caught completely off guard by the unexpected announcement.

"Oh, I just thought some of the enlisted personnel at the hospital might have told you. I know they don't like me very much. I've heard them refer to me as Lieutenant Bligh behind my back more than once. I'm certain that they'll throw a big party the day after I leave."

"Don't be so hard on yourself. From what I've observed, I'd say you're doing a damn good job of running that ward."

"Thanks, I like to think I am. I guess I'm a little strict. You know, I'm the oldest of five kids. My father died when I was eleven so I had to help my mother bring up my four younger brothers. Running the ward with a bunch of groaning sailors and marines is a picnic after that," she laughed.

"How come you're going to Japan?"

"Oh, it's only a one-year tour. Actually, I requested duty in Korea but they gave me the naval hospital at Yokosuka. A lot of the Korean wounded get sent there before they're flown back to the States."

"I'm a little ashamed now, after what I said a few minutes ago," Logan said, trying his utmost to fake a contrite expression.

"There's nothing for you to feel ashamed about. I'm sure you did more than your share in World War Two. Incidentally, did you know that your commanding officer really holds you in high esteem?"

"What do you mean?" Logan looked completely puzzled.

"He must have called the hospital six or seven times in the last two weeks trying to find out if he could get you back before your ship deployed. That's the first time I can recall a C.O. ever personally going to the trouble of trying to get an enlisted man back. That sort of thing is always handled by the ship's exec or the sailor's department head. You must be quite a hot shot radarman," she smiled affectionately.

"The old man really tried hard, heh?"

"Yes. He even dropped by to see you one evening but we couldn't let him in the quarantine ward. Didn't the corpsman on duty that night mention it to you?"

"No, this is the first I've heard about it." Logan started to sweat as he realized how close he must have come to being sent back to the ship. "Tell me, Cindy. How come Doctor Geiger allowed me to leave the hospital tonight but wouldn't let me rejoin the ship before she sailed this morning?"

"Oh, you're completely cured of the chicken pox. You don't have to worry about that. It's just that the doctor didn't think you're quite ready to go back to a ship, especially a little ship like a destroyer where you're in such close proximity to everyone. In such confined spaces, he's afraid that if you're still even slightly contagious, you might infect the entire crew. He just wants to keep you ashore for one more week to ensure that there's no chance of you causing an entire destroyer to be pulled out of service. If that ever happened, that would be the end of Geiger's naval career and he's really got his mind set on making admiral someday."

"How about you?"

"What do you mean?"

"Do you have your mind set on making admiral someday?"

"No, of course not," she laughed. "In fact, when my tour in Japan ends next year, I think I'm going to get out of the navy. I'd like to work in New York. That's always been a big ambition of mine. I think New York must be the most exciting place in the world. You're really lucky, working there. Maybe I'll get to visit your office on Madison Avenue someday. You can show me how you make all those great television commercials."

"Sure, I'd be happy to. Even if you don't leave the navy, you could always put in for duty at the naval hospital at St. Albans. That's only a subway ride away from Madison Avenue, you know."

"Do I," she smiled, "I've requested duty at St. Albans three times. Everyone wants to get up to New York. There's a waiting list five miles long."

"I'm sure you'll find Japan exciting."

"Yes, I've been looking forward to it. You know, it's too bad in a way that you're not going to Korea on the *Field*. I understand that almost all of the navy ships over there come into Yokosuka for their R and R's as well as to get their battle damage repaired. See, if you were on the *Field*, you and I could go explore Tokyo together. Oh, but that wouldn't work, would it? You're not allowed to have civilian clothes aboard ship, are you?"

"Oh, I had that problem licked. My C.I.C. officer," he laughed, "I mean my ex-C.I.C. officer, Ensign Coates, is just out of college and he's really hot to trot. He's been pestering me to set him up with a model when the ship gets back and he goes up to New York on leave. I once showed him some head sheets I had with pictures of the models at Powers and some of the other agencies. He really flipped over one of the girls. I didn't tell him that the particular young lady he fell madly in love with would be much more interested in meeting you than in meeting him," Logan grinned, aware that she perceived his inference. "Anyway, I made a deal with Coates. I promised to introduce him to his dream girl and he agreed to stash one suit and some shirts and ties for me in his stateroom. He also agreed to smuggle the clothes ashore for me any time I asked." Logan tipped his glass as he emptied the bottle of beer.

"You really know how to play all the angles, don't you, Kevin?"

"Do I detect a criticism?"

"No, not at all. I admire somebody who knows how to take command of a difficult situation."

"Don't give me too much credit. If I really knew how to play the angles, I wouldn't be running around San Diego these days in a blue monkey suit. If I'd been smart, I wouldn't have stayed in the reserve once I graduated from college and didn't need the drill pay anymore."

"Why did you stay in the reserve?"

"I enjoyed getting away each year on those two-week training cruises. We usually went to places like Bermuda or Nassau or Montego Bay. Besides, going to sea on a destroyer escort or a sub chaser for two weeks was fantastic therapy. It gave me a chance to get out from under the pressures of the agency. I always had enough money to go first class once I got ashore, so I considered those cruises little vacations paid for by Uncle Sam. It was such a different world from the office, and as I said, it allowed me to unwind. Of course, by the time the two weeks were up, I'd have had the navy right up to my eyeballs and I'd be quite happy to leave the discomforts of shipboard life behind me for another year. Say, how about another Singapore Sling?"

"No thanks, one's my limit. I wouldn't want you to have to carry me home, especially since you don't know where I live."

"I don't see how one more drink would possibly hurt you. What's the matter, don't you trust me?"

"Of course I trust you, Kevin. Believe me, I'm not being a prude. It's something in my metabolism. If I'm not really careful about how much I drink, I pass out cold, and I mean cold," she giggled as she emphasized the word. "Now, you wouldn't want that to happen, would you?"

"Oh, I don't know, it might be fun," he winked, giving the nurse a sly smile.

"Honestly, Kevin, I'm not exaggerating. The night I graduated from student nursing, I konked out on just a couple of beers. And when I pass out, it's impossible to bring me around. I just have to sleep it off. I'm told that at my graduation party, half the interns at Cleveland General took turns examining me, ostensibly to find out if I was still alive, of course," she quickly added with a noticeable blush.

"Who finally undressed you?"

"I'm not really certain. I heard it was a collective effort," the nurse grinned.

"Yeah, but you were a few years younger then. I'm sure your system's adjusted by now."

"Don't believe it. Just last month my roommate Betsy had to put me to bed, and that was after a little wine and cheese party. You probably think I'm kidding but I even have to watch myself when I'm eating rum-raisin ice cream," she laughed. Then, sucking on the orange slice from her Singapore Sling, Cynthia asked, "When we discharge you from the hospital Thursday, do you have any idea what kind of duty you'll get?"

"Your guess is as good as mine."

"Do you have any preference?"

"Well, after being with you this evening, I think I'd like to get something that would keep me around San Diego for awhile, at least until August. When I was taking the course at Point Loma last month I heard that the school had a critical need for radarmen with instructor's experience. I've been an instructor in the reserve program for almost seven years. I even graduated from the navy's instructor's training school, so I think I should have a pretty good crack at it."

"That would be very nice. Maybe sometime we could go out for dinner again. You know, Kevin, a girl shouldn't be so candid on a first date, but I really enjoy your company very much."

"Thank you, Cindy, but I'm the one who should be telling you that. You know, I think you're a very special person. Besides being very gracious, you're one of the prettiest young ladies I've ever seen, and that includes those models on the head sheets I showed old Coatsie."

"I think I'm going to be sorry about leaving for Japan," she frowned.

"We've still got two months to see each other, that is if you'd really like to."

"Of course, I would," she blurted out. "I think you know that, don't you? Did you really mean it when you said I was as pretty as all those models?" the lieutenant asked shyly.

"Yes, I wouldn't have said it if I didn't mean it."

This is like shooting fish in a barrel, Logan told himself, realizing that the young nurse was beginning to act like a moon-struck teenager. The symptoms were not unfamiliar. The next two months should be fantastic, he thought. Maybe if he planned his operations carefully, he'd be able to alternate between Candy and Cindy, providing he had the stamina, he snickered to himself. Cindy and Candy...Candy and Cindy...the names danced through his brain. Maybe life in the Korean War navy wouldn't be too hard a pill to swallow after all, he smiled triumphantly.

Tastefully furnished, the small apartment that Cynthia Osborne shared with Ensign Betsy Chadwick was conveniently located within one mile of the hospital.

Logan stood there in the bedroom, his eyes fixed on the young lieutenant as she unfastened each button of her blouse. He kissed her gently on the forehead, his lips sensing the satin softness of the chestnut-brown hair that so attractively framed her face. He reached around and unhooked her brassiere. It fluttered to the floor. Neither made an effort to retrieve it. They kissed for several minutes until she pulled back from him and walked over to the small table by the window. She snapped out the light.

Cynthia wiggled out of her skirt, the slip quickly followed. She slipped off her panties, and Logan continued to stand there watching her in silence as she sat down at the dressing table and slowly peeled off each stocking. She was aware that she possessed exceptionally well shaped legs and it was her intention that Kevin Logan should also be made fully cognizant of that fact. The nurse walked back to him, her naked body awash in a silvery glow from the friendly moon. He could see the traces of her ribs, her small but well turned breasts. She was very slim but also very enticing. Logan quickly slipped out of his trousers.

· · ·

Monday, May 26th, had been a day of confusion and deep depression for Candace. She couldn't believe that she had acted like a lovesick schoolgirl the night before...that she had allowed Garrett to sail away thinking that all was well with their marriage. She paced the floor in her office. Now that Garrett was gone she realized that she really didn't miss him, yet, she was genuinely worried that something might happen to him. Why couldn't he really have been going to those tropical islands, she thought. It would have been so much easier all around.

She fidgeted uncomfortably, then stiffened. She hated to admit, even to herself, that it was that damnable, philandering son-of-a-bitch Logan whom she really wanted. She'd thought she'd finally gotten him out of her system. She had too, she mused...then he had to pop into her office that day with that Charlie Charm act of his that even a retard could see through. Not that she was a poor little innocent, she'd used sex and her looks to get ahead many times, but at least there was some logic to that, she reassured herself. But Logan, there was nothing he could do to help her career. If anything, he could only screw it up. Afterall, wasn't that the reason she'd worked on Ham Barlow to cut Kevin out of the Cola account.

"Oh, hell," she muttered aloud, then looked at her watch. It read 9:38. She sat down and reached for the intercom. Tracy, please tell Troy that I'd like to see him as soon as possible."

The secretary acknowledged and within three minutes Troy Foster was seated opposite her. "Tracy said you wanted to see me right away, anything wrong?" he asked with bemused puzzlement.

"I hope not," Candace frowned. "I'd just like you to clear something up for me."

"Certainly, I'd be happy to."

"I'd like you to tell me who this Bailey Hubbard is?"

"Bailey Hubbard, oh, he's an advertising consultant. He's a friend of Ronald Paradise. At least I think he is. Ronald introduced him to us last year."

"Did Ronald also fix it up for this Hubbard character to collect a hefty payment from this agency every month?" Candace asked staring straight into Troy's face.

"Well, I think there were competitive bids. Ronald showed me a list of about ten other consultants he said he interviewed."

"You mean you took his word that he interviewed these other people? You didn't check, or at least have the final bids published?"

"No, I trusted Ronald. I guess it didn't occur to me at the time."

"Your trust in your subordinates is quite admirable. However, I'd like you to tell me why this agency, one of the biggest in the world, had to hire an outside advertising consultant in the first place?"

"That's a good question," Foster's voice fell to a strangled whisper. "Ronald came up with the idea. He gave me a big sales talk about how this Hubbard had lots of good ideas. More important, he said Hubbard had some really good business contacts and he'd be able to swing a couple of major accounts for us. I spoke to Hubbard myself. He spouted off a list of companies and contacts a mile long."

"How long has Hubbard been on our payroll?"

"I guess about a year, or maybe a little more."

"How many accounts has he brought to us so far?"

"None, as far as I know," Foster's voice was almost inaudible.

"I've been asking around the office about the relationship between Paradise and this Hubbard. Everyone I spoke to told me that this guy had a habit of hanging around Ronald's office three or four times a week for at least a year before Paradise put out any bids for an ad consultant."

"I guess that's possible. Come to think of it, I did see him with Ronald quite a bit. I really never gave it much thought. I certainly wasn't going to tell my copy chief who he could have in his office," Troy said defensively. "You don't think Paradise had an arrangement with Hubbard, do you?"

"An arrangement?" Candace asked with faked innocence. "I certainly hope not. Anyway, as of today, any arrangement this agency had with Mr. Hubbard is terminated!"

"What about the terms of his contract?"

"I think you can explain things to him. Just tell him that if he doesn't agree to the termination, we'll take steps to learn just how competitive his competitive bid really was. Oh, and be sure to pass that on to Paradise. In fact, I think it might be a good idea if you told him to personally inform his buddy that his services are no longer required...at least by B.B.Y. and S."

"Is there anything else?" Foster sighed heavily.

"No Troy, I think that's enough for now. Don't you?"

•   •   •

During the night, the division shifted into a column disposition with the lead ship *Abner Ward* acting as guide. When daylight broke over the formation, the OODs on each of the four destroyers discovered that the large pip they had been watching for hours on their radar repeaters and had plotted as being on the same course and speed as DesDiv 291, was now visible to the naked eye. The contact was still miles ahead but had apparently slowed her speed, for the division was now slowly overtaking her. In a few minutes the lookouts and bridge watch on each of the destroyers were able to identify the stranger as an escort carrier. Soon they were able to make out a tall white 86 on the jeep carrier's small box-like island. The number identified her as the *Sitko Bay*. By 08:00, the division was steaming close abeam of the squat little flattop affording several of the newer men their first glimpse of a carrier at sea. In coming months they would have countless such opportunities.

The *Sitko Bay* was much smaller than the *Essex* class carriers the division would be escorting off Korea. Like the Charlie P., she was a retread from the Pacific War recently activated from the mothball fleet for the Korean emergency. Too slow for fast carrier operations with Task Force 77, she was presently employed as a ferry carrier shuttling small single-engine aircraft that lacked the necessary range to fly the Pacific. As each destroyer passed alongside, the customary salutes were exchanged for men-of-war meeting at sea. As the *Field*, bringing up the rear of the column, pulled abreast of the carrier, her crewmen curiously eyed the P-51 Mustangs that crowded her flight deck. These propeller-driven fighters, their wings detached to permit a maximum number of aircraft to be accommodated, were en route to the fledgling Republic of Korea Air Force. They looked like huge blobs of chocolate in their brown plastic coating which had been sprayed on to protect them from salt corrosion during their long ocean transit.

After the noon meal, all hands aboard *DD-505* somewhat reluctantly lined up to receive the countless injections necessary to safeguard their health during an extended tour in the Far East. Tetanus, typhoid, diphtheria, yellow fever, small pox...the *Field's* sickbay even managed to come up with a vaccine for something called Chinese Coolie Fever.

As with most destroyers and other small naval vessels, there was no doctor aboard the *Charles P. Field*; her entire medical department consisted of a chief pharmacist mate named Claccum, and two third-class, Fiske and Parish. The latter, with three years of pre-med at N.Y.U., had refused a college deferment his senior year so that he could request active duty, specifically in the Korean war zone. While his action was prompted partially by patriotism, it was initiated even more by the conviction that duty on the battlefields of Korea would afford him far better opportunities to advance his medical knowledge than he could ever experience dissecting frogs in a bio lab. Anticipating assignment to a marine unit ashore, Parish was bitterly disappointed at being sent to the "non-combatant" *Field*, and he planned to negotiate a duty swap with the first marine-attached navy corpsman encountered upon the ship's arrival at a Korean port.

Towards dusk, the Pacific winds, as unpredictable as ever, grew warmer but steadily more intense, and by 20:00 (8 p.m.), were kicking up a moderately choppy sea which kept the fantail awash. This necessitated that the evening's movie be transferred from the Spartan area under the stars to the shelter of the crew's messhall. Cramped and humid below decks, few of *DD-505's* white hats waited for the final reel of another vintage movie, "*The Lady Eve*," with Henry Fonda and Barbara Stanwick. During the night the sea worsened and several of the *Field's* complement became seasick, including Aubrey Cobb.

When morning finally came, the winds had settled to little more than a zephyr, and the ocean was glassy calm. The wake from *Halsey Wayne* just ahead, was snaky and ragged. Owen Royal observed the other destroyer from the starboard bridge-wing, a slight smile forming on his face as he watched *Wayne's* stern pitch out of line, first to the right, then to the left.

"Commander Boland must be breaking in a new helmsman," the captain said to Lieutenant Stockwell, the Ops department head, who was OOD for the morning watch.

"Yes, Sir," agreed the two-striper. "*Wayne's* been zig-zagging like that since I came on watch. I've dropped a knot off our speed to compensate," then turning to the bridge talker, he shouted, "range to the ship ahead!"

The sailor quickly relayed the request over his sound-powered-phone to the radarmen below. "Combat reports range to the *Wayne* is five-nine-ooh, Sir," he answered after a short silence.

Stockwell, embarrassed at being 90 yards behind station, nervously snapped instructions to the man at the engine-order-telegraph, increasing the *Field's* rpm's to a sufficient number that would bring her bow up to the prescribed steaming interval 500 yards astern of *Halsey Wayne*. The latter now appeared to have recovered from her steering difficulties.

"I see that the other ships are flying the 'stars and bars' from their port yards again, Captain," Stockwell commented, his binoculars dangling loosely around his neck as he stepped back out to the sunlit bridge-wing.

"Yes, Commanders Boland, Fenchurch and Hedling are all true blue, eh, guess I should say true gray, sons of the South. They've been trying to convert me to the ways of the Confederacy since I joined the division," Royal laughed, "but I'm afraid their campaign hasn't met with much success. Last week a messenger from the *Morgan* brought over one of those rebel flags for the *Field*, courtesy of Commander Fenchurch. In retaliation, I dug up a phonograph record of 'Marching Through Georgia,' and sent it over to Archie, gift wrapped for his wardroom. I don't imagine it will get worn out from too many playings," Owen said, still smiling.

"Well, Sir, being a Johnny Reb myself, I'm kind of disappointed that you didn't accept Commander Fenchurch's gracious gift," Stockwell replied with a good-natured grin. "From what you've said, Captain, may I assume you hail from Yankee country?" the OOD asked.

"That's a fair assumption, Mr. Stockwell. I've lived in Idaho most of my life but I was born in Portland, Maine. My father's company transferred him to Boise when I was eight, so I guess you could say I'm a dyed in the wool Yankee. Even my wife was born and raised in New England."

"Guess I can understand why they haven't been able to convert you, Captain."

"Yes, but I expect they'll keep right on trying. They seem determined to make this the first division of *Fletcher* class destroyers in the Confederate Navy."

"Is Commodore Price from the South?" the lieutenant asked.

"No, he's from Omaha. I suspect he's just a victim of circumstances. If Mr. Cobb comes up to the wheelhouse, please tell him I'd like to discuss our ETA for Oahu. I'll be in the chartroom," the captain said, departing the wing.

Ten minutes later he was joined by a pale and watery-eyed executive officer who appeared not completely recovered from the rough seas of the night before. The two men, along with the navigator, Lieutenant Oetjens, discussed the feasibility of the commodore's estimated time of arrival. Eight-thirty Saturday morning seemed cautiously realistic to all three. Then the captain and Cobb set about making preparations for the C.I.C. and communications drills Price had scheduled for later in the day.

"Aub," the captain said casually, "I imagine you noticed back in San Diego that each of our three running mates had campaign ribbons tacked up to her bridge."

"Yes, Sir. Most of the ships in the fleet seem to be doing it these days."

"Well, last evening I started reading the BuShips history of this division and the wartime records of those three souped-up yachts we have to play tail-end Charlie for. It only took a few minutes to discover that the three of them together couldn't match the combat record this old girl chalked up with Arleigh Burke's 'Little Beavers' in the Solomons, to say nothing of her performance off Okinawa. Before we reach Hawaii, I want you to have the metalsmith get up a set of ribbons for the port and starboard wings. You have a complete list of all the decorations she's earned, haven't you?"

"Yes, Gordon has one somewhere in the ship's office," Cobb answered dully, clutching the canvas coated railing as the two men descended the ladder to the lower bridge level.

"Make certain he follows the proper order of precedence," Royal instructed. "We'll really give Price and the rest of the division something to look at when we tie up next to them at Pearl. She rates six ribbons," he continued, "that will mean two rows of three with the Presidential Unit Citation she won at Empress Augusta Bay leading off. Tell the metalsmith to use the brightest paint we've got onboard. I believe each ribbon should be about a foot-and-a-half long and five inches high."

"Yes, Sir, I think the latest issue of *All Hands* has something about the prescribed dimensions. I'll turn it over to Chief Monaghan, along with the list of citations. Monaghan's the best metalsmith we've got."

"Good. Our little black sheep may not be the prettiest 'can' in the division, but she sure as hell is the fightin'est," Royal declared proudly as the two officers entered the wardroom for a quick cup of freshly brewed coffee.

The remaining days at sea passed uneventfully. Few ships, naval or merchant, were encountered and activity was confined to the daily slate of C.I.C. drills mandated by the commodore. These drills required that each destroyer's C.I.C. team demonstrate its proficiency at solving a wide variety of maneuvering board problems. However, before they could begin each problem, they had to speedily decipher the coded radio-telephone messages that originated in rapid succession from flagship *Abner Ward*. This required expert knowledge of the General Signal Book, which, to Murray and the rest of the radar gang aboard *DD-505* might just as well have been printed in Bantu. With Logan now detached, the book suddenly became little more than an incomprehensible collection of numbers and phonetic word combinations. By trial and error, mostly the latter, Coates and Murray were usually able to translate the messages. Unfortunately by the time each was fully deciphered, the radar teams on the other three destroyers were already hard at work on the next exercise in the series. It was only during general quarters drills when Lieutenant Stockwell was manning his battle station as the C.I.C. evaluator that the *Field's* 'pip jockeys' were able to put in an acceptable performance.

On Friday afternoon, traffic began to pick up and several freighters were sighted, a certain sign that a landfall was not far away. That evening the majority of the crew bedded topside taking advantage of the warm trade winds that greeted the destroyer as she drew closer to her destination.

Nugent, Holiday and Belton were holding down the mid-watch. Shortly after 1 a.m., they were joined by Howie Murray, who, too restless to sleep, had decided to ready the navigation charts for the *Field's* entry into harbor later in the morning.

"See the movie, Murray?" Nugent asked, glancing at the unexpected visitor.

"No, I decided to turn in early but it didn't do much good, I still couldn't get to sleep," the first-class answered in a quiet voice, rising from the pub locker with several rolled charts under his arm. "It must be the tropics. They always affected me that way."

"Spend much time at Pearl during the war?" inquired Nugent.

"A little when I was on the *Enterprise*."

"Think it's changed much?" Holiday piped up, looking over at Belton to make sure the young striker wasn't dosing at the surface scope.

"I imagine it's pretty much the same except for the hotels. I guess the navy's given them back to the tourists by now." Murray's tone was casual as he unrolled the largest of the charts, the one marked Oahu and Related Sea Approaches.

"I see you're in the first liberty section. Are you going ashore tomorrow?" Holiday asked.

"Yes, I think I'll go over to the petty officers' club for a beer. As I remember, there was a pretty nice club on Ford Island. What I really want to do though is find out how much it will cost to call home," Murray said, fitting the chart over the plotting table.

"You know, Murray," Nugent frowned, "I'll bet you could spend a night with the best looking hooker in Honolulu for what one long distance call to Ohio's gonna' cost you."

"I told you guys a hundred times, I'm not interested in fooling around! I've got too much respect for Mary Alice and my girls to do something like that, so lay off before I really get pissed!"

"Okay, but it just don't seem normal," Nugent replied in a half-whisper. "Don't you ever get the urge to go over on the beach and get some nookie?"

"Of course I do! I'm not queer, you know. It's just that I take my wedding vows and my religion seriously. Besides, I've got no intention of going over on the beach and getting all clapped up. When I get out of this damn outfit and go home for good, at least I won't have to worry about giving Mary Alice a dose. Now, how about handing me that roll of tape hanging over there on the jack-box so I can get this chart squared-away."

The scent of hibiscus grew stronger during the night and the wakes of the four little ships took on a fluorescent glow which turned silver-white in the moonlight.

Back in San Diego, Kevin Logan had been discharged from the hospital and was temporarily assigned to shore patrol duty while the navy decided what it would do with him for the remainder of his active duty tour. Chances are good, he decided, that he'd get that instructor's billet at Point Loma. He'd contacted the training officer at the school who remembered the high marks he'd racked up there in April. The officer had assured him that he'd do his best to get his request approved. Unfortunately, the instructor Logan would be replacing wasn't slated to ship out for another six weeks. All he had to do now, he told himself, was to coast along with this damn shore patrol assignment. If he could get through the next month-and-a-half without some drunken swabby or jarhead breaking a beer bottle over his head, he should really have it "made in the shade." So what if he went back to Madison Avenue next year without ever having been near Korea, Hell, the only action he wanted these days he knew he could get under the sheets with Lieutenant Osbourne.

And Cindy, what an unexpected but highly rewarding diversion she turned out to be, Logan grinned, savoring the realization that he'd been getting vengeful pleasure out of literally screwing a member of the navy's officer elite. She could be a problem, though, he mused, aware that the nurse was obviously in love with him. He knew all the signs. She'd started buying him little presents like after shave-lotion and a "Box Brownie" camera, and calling him "sweetheart" and "darling." Damn it, why couldn't she be more like Candy, just interested in good honest sex without messy complications, he shook his head in annoyed puzzlement. Well, it can't last much longer, he reassured himself. Cindy would be shipped off to Japan soon. Till then, commissioned officer or not, Miss Osbourne, the terror of Ward 8, was a guaranteed lay whenever he wanted her. Hell's bells, what's so bad about that, he asked himself, as he headed off for his evening's assignation with the amorous Jaygee.

Later that night, lying in bed next to Cynthia, Kevin Logan was finding sleep an elusive quarry, and the situation wasn't being helped by his pretty bedmate who appeared to be in an exceptionally talkative mood. Indeed, it was Logan's latest theory that the more sex Cindy experienced, the more loquacious she became, and thus he was now reconciled to the prospect of a long and sleepless night. Initiated on the living room floor, their evening's love-making had gradually worked its way through the foyer, kitchen and finally on into Cindy's bedroom. He could hear Betsy now, moving around in the adjoining room. He wondered what her reaction had been when she came across his pants and shirt, and various items of Cindy's underwear strewn around the floor. He remembered tossing Cindy's panties up on to the coffee table. That must have gone over big with Betsy, he grinned broadly. If it embarrassed her, too bad, he thought. After all, who asked her to stick her key in the door an hour early.

"Just think, Kevin," Cynthia said in a sweet whisper. "Maybe someday you and I will be doing this in your apartment in New York."

"You might not like New York. You know winters back there are far different than here in California."

"Oh, cold weather doesn't bother me. Did you forget I grew up on Lake Erie. I remember plenty of winters when the snow was so high we had to enter and leave our house by a second floor window. I learned to walk in snow shoes almost as soon as I learned to walk in regular shoes. Bet you never had winters like that in Manhattan, did you?" she teased, cuddling up closer to him.

"No, New York never gets that bad. I still don't think it's as great as you seem to think."

"No matter what you say you can't discourage me one bit. I think being with you in New York will be fantastic," she giggled like a little girl as she ran her fingers under his T-shirt and stroked his chest. "Do you love me, Kevin?" she asked suddenly, her fingers now entangled in the chain that held his dog tags.

"Now that's a damn silly thing to ask. You know I wouldn't be here in bed with you if I didn't think you were really special."

"I don't want to be special. I just want a direct answer. DO you love me, yes or no?" Her tone was impatient as she drew her hand back.

"Hey! Watch it! That hurt!" he cried, rubbing his neck where the chain had chafed. "What brought this on all of a sudden?"

"It's not all of a sudden. You've made love to me six times now, counting tonight. Even Betsy thinks you're just using me."

"Well, what do ensigns know anyway?" he smiled as he moved his hand down between her legs. "Of course I love you, you should know that," he winced as he said the words, hoping that she wouldn't see his expression in the darkened room.

"You really love me?"

"Yes, really, now get some sleep."

"Wouldn't you rather make love some more?" she asked coyly.

"Cindy, babe, we've been making love for the past two hours. I'm worn out," he said, withdrawing his hand from her crotch. "Don't you want me to be at my best when we go to Tijuana on Sunday?"

"I guess so," she said with marked disappointment in her tone.

"Well then, try to get some sleep. You know you won't be able to crack the whip at the hospital tomorrow if you're bleary-eyed. And besides, I've got eight hours of shore patrol coming up that I'm not exactly looking forward to."

"I guess you're right, darling," she said drowsily. Stretching her long legs under the sheets, she sighed and rolled over until she lay almost on top of him. In a few minutes, he noticed her body slacken. Her soft breathing tickled his neck, but Logan was afraid to move and waken her. He lay very still, trying not to get aroused as he felt her nakedness through the very abbreviated night dress she was almost wearing.

He couldn't hear Ensign Chadwick moving around her room anymore. He guessed she'd finally gone to bed. He'd never met Betsy and he wondered if she was as fetching as her roommate. He also wondered if she was as easy a lay. Maybe if he played his cards right, he'd find out in August when Cindy flew off to Yokosuka to play Florence Nightingale.

All was quiet now except for the rhythmic purr of Cindy's breathing. He started to feel horny again as he sensed the weight and feel of her bare thigh pressed against his own. She mumbled something in her sleep but Logan couldn't make it out. One thing he did know...he'd better try to get some sleep. Otherwise, he'd find himself climbing back in the saddle, and at this point, he wasn't at all certain that his system could stand an encore performance.

Logan's mind focused on the Charlie P. He wondered if the old bucket could make it all the way to Pearl without springing a fatal leak. Poor Murray and that equally inept bunch of clowns he called his C.I.C. team...the blind leading the blind, he grinned, wondering if any one of them had yet learned to properly set up the DRT. Anyway, it was probably a good thing that the *Field* would be trailing along behind the rest of the division. At least that way they'd have less chance of getting lost, he concluded.

Cindy made a slight grunting sound. He wondered what she was dreaming about. After another hour, he finally dozed off.

Under a canvas tent at Panmunjon, U.S. and communist truce representatives remained deadlocked over the sticky problem of prisoner exchange. Observers reported that there was little hope for an early peace.

Chapter VII - "Name, Rate and Horsepower!"

Throughout recorded history, warriors have journeyed to the land of the ginger lei; Cook and his "hearts of oak;" the Tahitians in their giant *pahi*; and Nagumo and his carrier pilots; some to remain, some to linger briefly before passing on to join the distant thunder. To this roster on a bright Saturday morning in the spring of '52, add the names of the men of DesDiv 291, or as they had come to call themselves after being exposed to the *Field's* indiscriminate gunnery — "Price's Expendables."

By 08:00, with engines slowed to less than two knots, the four destroyers stood by off Diamond Head, their crews impatient to "get the show on the road." As the mahogany-cabined pilot-launch nudged up to the port accommodation ladder of the flagship, "Quarters for entering port," boomed over the *Field's* speaker system, and all hands not assigned to a special-sea-detail scurried off to their stations along the ship's rail. Aboard each of the four *Fletchers*, bridge personnel watched the small red and white pilot's flag climb to the two-block position at *Abner Ward's* starboard yard. Moments later, *John Morgan, Halsey Wayne,* and *Charles P. Field* fell in line as the flagship began to make headway, her twin screws churning the emerald water which rippled out from San Souci and Kapiolani Park in clearly defined and progressively lighter shades of green.

"All engines ahead one-third," Royal ordered. "Make turns for six knots."

The division picked up speed and Diamond Head slowly slid astern, forming a majestic backdrop for the luxurious pink and white hotels that fenced the surf along crescent shaped Waikiki. During the Pacific War, these structures had been requisitioned by the navy for use as convalescent quarters and to give combat weary sailors, especially submariners, a much needed morale boost after extended combat patrols. Several of the division's reservists had enjoyed such a stay at Waikiki; few ever expected to return some day aboard another man-of-war.

Trailing her sisters, *DD-505* steamed by Sand Island, Keehi Lagoon, and on around Fort Kamehameha, finally entering the narrow channel that led to Pearl Harbor. Slipping to the right of Waipio Peninsula, the column of destroyers snaked its way passed Hospital Point with its clustered jacaranda, then cut to the right of Ford Island. Outboard of the island and clearly visible were ten concrete blocks which, until transformed into tombstones by the Japanese, had served as mooring quays for "battleship row." On the bridge wing, Ensign Warden, the JOD, zealously called out each new bearing, pointing his pelorus first toward the training tower at the submarine base, then left to the Koolau peaks, then further left to an abrupt break in the mountain ridge through which Kakuichi Takahashi had led his "Vals" on history's fateful "Day of Infamy."

"Sound attention to port, Mister MacKinlay." The captain instructed the OOD in a somber tone.

"Sound attention to port!" barked Lieutenant MacKinlay to the bo'sun-of-the-watch, standing just inside the wheelhouse.

An instant later, the shrill notes of the bo'sun's pipe escaped from the various speakers located throughout the *Field*, instantly bringing each man topside to the position of attention. A second signal, calling for a hand salute, followed an instant later. Object of this courtesy was battleship *Arizona* which, with her silent complement of bluejackets and marines, lay entombed off Ford Island in 70 feet of blue water. Still carried on the navy's register of active warships, the murdered old dreadnaught rated the same honors due any other naval vessel, and Owen Royal, never one to neglect military protocol, was especially conscientious when it concerned the ship on which he had spent his fledgling days as an ensign. Protruding slightly above the surface and barely visible to Royal and the others aboard the *Field* was the outline of a black and rusted control tower. The flag atop its mast seemed to beat the tropic sky with greater ferocity than any of the many other flags in view around the harbor.

As Commander Royal glanced aft down the starboard side, he chuckled to himself at the sight of one of the ship's motor whaleboats, fully secured with heavy hurricane lashings. Shortly after midnight of the previous day, Ensign Coates, coming off his stint as JOD, had had occasion to pass the radio shack and overhear "Little Gillie" discussing a hot flash from an associate at Radio Station N.O.B., Oahu. The message reputedly told of a tempest storm that was expected to reach Honolulu by noontime. Without questioning the *Field's* leading radioman or awaiting further clarification of the message, Coates excitedly informed Lieutenant Oetjens and Ensign Daly who had just assumed watch that a typhoon was bearing down on the islands.

Within seconds, all deck and gunnery department personnel were hustled out of their bunks, as were Commander Royal, Aubrey Cobb and almost everyone else not already on watch. By 01:11, life rafts, depth charges and all non-structural fittings and equipment had been securely lashed down, and Condition "Able," which called for maximum watertight integrity, was put into effect throughout the destroyer. Royal, concerned that the other ships in the division might not be aware of the potential danger, made a hasty trip to the radio shack where he found Little Gillie, Turk the cook, and two other radiomen casually engaged in a game of blackjack. Speedy interrogation disclosed that the tempest storm about to hit Honolulu was in reality Miss Tempest Storm, a personality of no small renown among burlesque enthusiasts. In the opinion of a very tired and equally sullen deck force, it was indeed a pity that Ensign Coates' proclivity for television did not extend to other and more artistic facets of the entertainment industry.

In a little while, the *Field* and her sisters had nosed their way into East Lock, nesting beam to beam midway between Ford Island and McGrew Point.

"Ever hear of an old Hawaiian yarn about throwing flowers in the water Mister Stockwell?" Gardiner asked phlegmatically as the radar gang sat around C.I.C. waiting for the word to secure from special-sea-detail.

"Funny you should ask that, Gardiner," the operations officer replied. "Just last night at dinner Mister Kimmick was talking about the same thing. According to legend, you're supposed to throw a lei over the side as your ship leaves Oahu. If it floats in toward the shore, it means you'll come back to Hawaii some day."

"Don't believe it, Mister Stockwell," Murray grunted discontentedly. "I never tossed as much as a banana peel over the side when I came through here in forty-five, but here I am, back again! How do you explain that?"

The Ops officer was spared that hopeless task as word to secure from special-sea-detail finally blared over the ship's address system. Liberty call quickly followed and all hands not assigned to the duty section made flank speed for the beach which in this instance meant Honolulu or its plush neighbor, Waikiki.

DesDiv 291's first evening in Hawaii was not without incident. Shortly after nine o'clock, Lieutenant (jg.) Phelan, OOD for the 8 to 12, was hurriedly summoned from the wardroom by a very flustered petty-officer-of-the-watch.

"It's the army, Mister Phelan," Puchalski, a machinist mate second, shouted, half out of breath. "Some captain, he said he was in security or intelligence or some jazz like that. He wants to speak to Captain Royal." The motor-mack's voice lowered to a whisper as Phelan picked up the quarterdeck phone.

"Lieutenant Phelan speaking, Sir, can I help you?"

"I'm Captain Himmel, G-two, Fort Shafter. I'd like to speak to your commanding officer, Lieutenant."

"I'm sorry, Captain, but the skipper's over on the beach. He and our executive officer left word they could be reached anytime up to eleven at the Royal Hawaiian. Can I be of any help, Sir?"

"No, thank you. I'd prefer to deal directly with your C.O. I'll ring him up at the Hawaiian. Good evening, Lieutenant, thanks again for your assistance."

"Wonder what that's all about?" Phelan muttered, scratching his neck as he hurried back to the wardroom before Ensign Coates could completely rearrange the figures on the chessboard."

Owen Royal's table at the Royal Hawaiian's glass enclosed dining room was in direct line with Diamond Head which jutted seaward. As Royal and his executive officer savored their *mahi mahi*, the captain watched the winking lights and torches from the nearby Surfrider and Moana Hotels.

"Seems to be a big blow-out behind the Moana tonight, Aub."

"Yes, I guess they're holding a luau," answered Cobb, his glance temporarily falling away from the towering redhead struggling to teach her much shorter partner how to execute a Hawaiian version of the mambo.

At the far corner of the dance area on the beachside oval, a mixed assortment of newly weds and nearly deads lounged in beach chairs, casually sipping rum and pineapple juice concoctions from bulging coconut shells. A soft concerto of ukuleles and hissing surf completed the illusion of a Paramount set for a 30's Crosby flick.

Royal was relating a humorous incident involving a WAC lieutenant that took place eight years earlier on that same terrace, when he noticed a Hawaiian page approaching their table. The boy seemed hesitant as he appraised the rank on the black shoulder boards of Royal and Cobb who were dressed in their whites. Before speaking, the messenger's eyes searched the area one last time to be certain that there were no other commanders present among the five or six naval officers seated within the room.

"Excuse me, Sir," the bushy-haired lad interrupted. "Are you Commander Owen Royal?"

"Yes, that's right."

"You are wanted on the telephone, Commander."

"Thank you," said Royal, taking a final sip from his drink as he rose from the chair. "Coates has probably gotten word of another typhoon," he smiled. "Be back in a few minutes."

As the bellhop led the commander to the lobby, Cobb settled back to enjoy the slow shuffling hula now being performed on the terrace. Before the first dance had been completed, Owen Royal, noticeably worried, returned to the table.

"I'll have to run over to Fort Shafter, Aub. Seems the army picked up a couple of our boys on a security charge."

"Security charge?"

"Yes, I couldn't get any more than that out of them over the phone. You stay here and finish your dinner. There's no sense in both of us missing out on this good chow."

"That's alright, Captain. I'm beginning to bulge anyway, and you know the army, you certainly wouldn't want to go over there outnumbered" the *Field's* exec laughed.

"Okay, Aub, if you really don't mind, I think it might be a good idea to have you along."

Royal easily won the brief argument for the check, and within minutes they were in a cab speeding along Kalakaua Avenue. At Fort Shafter, a corporal of military police politely ushered the two naval officers down a dimly lit second floor corridor to the office of Major Sanford Eberle, USA.

After an exchange of cordialities, the major, a slightly built bald-headed gentleman with a thin mustache, said, "Commander, I hope you realize we're not trying to embarrass either the navy or your command by bringing in these two men, eh, this Orville McAlleney and Ashton Bites."

"Yes, Major, I'm certain that's not your purpose. Are Bites and McAlleney being detained in this building?"

"Yes, Sir," Eberle answered, handing Royal a mimeographed sheet of charges. "We're holding both men in a room down the hall. We'll be happy to turn them over to you for disciplinary action anytime you want."

As the major spoke, the *Field's* C.O. read the lengthy list of security violations. "How did you happen to pick my men up, Major?" he asked, noticeably annoyed.

"Two of my people were disguised as merchant seamen. They were in the Golden Hula. That's a bar on Hotel Street in downtown Honolulu. We do this sort of thing quite regularly. Can't be too careful after what happened December seventh, you know."

"Oh, yes, you mean 1941?" Cobb snickered.

"The major smiled meekly, pretending not to have noticed his visitor's sarcasm. "My two men engaged Bites and McAlleney in casual conversation," Eberle continued. "After a little while, they asked them several rather sensitive questions about your ship. Those are the questions," the major said, pointing to the paper Royal was scanning. Owen didn't answer.

"Both men were very talkative," the army officer went on, "told my people anything they wanted to know about the ordinance aboard your ship."

"So I see."

"Needless to say, my men were forced to place them under military arrest."

"Were Bites or McAlleney drunk or causing any kind of disturbance?" Cobb cut in with exaggerated concern.

"No, according to the report, they'd only had a beer or two."

"Well, Major, your men certainly didn't waste any time. We only arrived in the islands this morning," said Royal, handing the list of violations back to his host. "I must congratulate your people on the thoroughness of their report. The only thing I don't understand is why my men were brought in for answering questions about unclassified information."

"Unclassified information?"

"Yes, there's not one question on this list that couldn't be answered by a visit to a library. The question about our main battery consisting of five five-inch dual-purpose guns, for instance, a copy of *Jane's Fighting Ships* will give you that information and quite a bit more. Major, except for her paint, my ship hasn't received anything new since 1943. Anybody sitting in a fishing dinghy when we entered the harbor this morning could have seen that for themselves. During the war, we loaned the Russian Navy the cruiser *Milwaukee* as well as a countless number of frigates and smaller combat vessels. I doubt there's a single piece of gear aboard the *Field* from her guns to her radars that we didn't at one time or another furnish the Russians."

"That may be, Commander, but it's the principle."

"What principle? These particular men don't work in sensitive areas. They have no access to classified information. If they did, I'm certain they would be much more careful about discussing their shipboard duties. Now, if you'll turn them over to me, I'll see that the matter is taken care of to everyone's satisfaction."

"Very well, Commander. If you'd like, I'll have your men driven back to your ship immediately."

Their business with the army finished, the two officers waited at the Notley Street Gate for the staff car assigned to transport them back to the Royal Hawaiian.

"The commodore will really blow his tubes when he learns about this little episode," Royal commented sourly. "He's extremely touchy when it comes to anything that might embarrass the division. Besides, I don't think I have to remind you about his devotion to matters of security."

"Yes, but I really don't think you have anything to worry about. There's no way he can learn anything about what happened tonight. That smug little major looked quite willing to forget the whole matter when you informed him that his men had arrested Bites and McAlleney for disclosing unclassified information."

"Yes, but as much as I hate to admit it, Major Eberle was right. It was only a matter of luck that those two didn't blab out something important. Suppose the army had picked up a couple of our radarmen. That really could have been embarrassing if they started talking about radar frequencies or IFF codes. Before you release the next plan-of-the-day, you'd better make sure it carries a strong reminder about not discussing anything concerning the ship or our itinerary when they go ashore. Remind them of that old World War Two slogan that says loose lips sink ships. And while I'm on the subject of directives, here's one for you. The name's Owen. You don't have to keep addressing me as captain or sir when we're off the ship."

"Fine," Cobb smiled. "It will make conversation a lot easier. Say, I just thought of something. Eberle mentioned he was sending our boys back to the ship in an M.P. car. What about Price?"

"We're in luck for once. The commodore left word that he'd be spending the weekend with friends. The address was way out on Kalanianole Drive beyond Koko Head so I don't think we'll have to worry about any untimely observations. And most of the officers are ashore, so Bites and McAlleney should have an uneventful homecoming."

"What are you going to do about punishment for those two idiots?" Cobb asked heatedly.

"Oh, they're just a couple of kids bragging about their ship, Aub. I'm certain they didn't mean any harm," Royal said, as a khaki Dodge sedan pulled up to the curb. "I'll give them a lecture about the importance of security and toss in a couple of hours extra duty. Try to schedule the mast for sometime this week before we get underway for our O.R.I."

135

"Anyone ever tell you you're a soft touch?" Cobb asked good-naturedly as the two climbed into the back seat.

Sunday, 1 June, was Commander Royal's thirty-seventh birthday. It was uncomfortably humid for Oahu, and most of the *Field's* company headed for any of the various beaches in the area. Though only casually acquainted, Aubrey Cobb managed to persuade Lieutenant-Commander "Skate" Robbins, Commodore Price's staff assistant, that the afternoon was ideal for a round of golf. Soon, both men were matching their skill on the luxurious green at Walalae. The game, an easy victory for Cobb, was followed by dinner with the loser picking up the tab at the swank Coral Strand. After an ample helping of roast pig and salted butterfish wrapped together in taro leaves, both officers returned to their respective ships. By ten that evening, Commodore Price was fully cognizant of all the details relating to Owen Royal's recent encounter with army intelligence.

The division passed its first working days at Pearl Harbor taking on heavy ordinance, primarily torpedoes, depth charges, and hedgehog rockets. The rest of the week was spent preparing for the exercises slated to commence the following Monday.

No doubt the most noteworthy event to take place during the *Field's* second weekend at Pearl Harbor was the visit to the ship by Lieutenant Stockwell's fiancee, Cassy Jean Cooper. As promised in so many of her letters, "Miss Talladega County" arrived via Pan Am clipper to spend two glorious weeks in Honolulu. On Sunday the *Field's* operations officer proudly escorted Cassy Jean aboard the destroyer for an above deck inspection followed by a luncheon in the wardroom with the captain and several of his fellow officers. Everyone seemed duly impressed with her physical attributes, if not her intellect. Tall and curvaceous, the young Alabamian could modestly be called a show-stopper, with strawberry-blond hair that framed a delicately sculpted face, and skin as smooth and wholesome as freshly whipped cream.

Later that afternoon, after a thorough inspection of the foc'sle machinery, the young couple took their leave of *DD-505*. As Cassy Jean gingerly stepped upon the tarry plank leading to the *Halsey Wayne*, she attracted more than a few appreciative glances from the crewmen aboard the two destroyers. Most ardent of her admirers that afternoon was Turk, who, taking a breather from his hot chores in the galley, was unexpectedly confronted by the tantalizing spectacle of the flustered young lady's crinolines in violent conflict with a sudden but persistent rush of wind. To the complete delight of the on-lookers and the total embarrassment of the *Field's* Ops officer, the gust of wind seemed to be winning out.

• • •

Operational Readiness Inspection, more commonly referred to as O.R.I. by the abbreviation-prone American bluejacket, is that period during which a warship and her personnel are put through the most stringent exercises devised to test their capabilities and their fitness to engage in actual combat. During this trying period, specialists in particular areas of shipboard operations, are assigned to each unit as observers. At termination of the three-week long exercises, evaluatory reports are submitted to pertinent authority indicating whether or not the performance of the warship observed was efficient enough to get her through a shooting war. Theoretically, any vessel deficient in a major category such as gunnery or engineering would be detached from fleet operations and hurriedly sent home for further training. However, not a man in the division could name a vessel ever to warrant such punishment, though several of the *Field's* white hats were convinced that the Charlie P. was about to set a precedent.

Each day the *Field* and her sisters would weigh anchor long before the first rays of sun had climbed the Pali, and the ships would not return to port until the hills beyond Pearl City were splattered with the red and yellow patches of early evening. Each night their sailors would swarm into Honolulu to restlessly stroll River and Hotel Streets in quest of diversion from the day's pressures and those they knew would come on the morrow. A few of the thriftier and perhaps wiser men would pass their leisure time at the Navy "Y" with its modest swimming pool, phonograph record library and ancient but free motion pictures. Others would journey out to Waikiki, some to sit near the beach behind the Moana and watch the moon hover over Diamond Head. And perhaps in some far-off time, a farmer plowing grain in Indiana or a mailman making his rounds on a dusty Appalachian road, might take time from his chores to tell pumpkin-faced youngsters about an incredible voyage to the magic islands where people talked to flowers and waterfalls fell upside down.

The first week of O.R.I. consisted primarily of multi-air and surface gunnery runs. Consistent with her performance off California, *DD-505* set the pace in the former, but as usual scored far below her sisters in the much easier surface shoot. When the week's totals were tabulated, including a night firing session during which her gun club seemed utterly confounded, the *Field*, to everyone's surprise, managed to eke out a qualifying score.

The following week passed lazily. After a day of surfing, Don Stockwell and Cassy Jean Cooper waited on a lengthy line at Waikiki Cinema to see another Cooper, no relation, keep a deadly appointment in Hadleyville at "*High Noon.*" The same evening just a few blocks away, Owen Royal watched Jimmy Cagney and Dan Dailey battle the Hun in the latest remake of "*What Price Glory?*" In months to come, the *Field's* C.O. would have numerous opportunities to recall Cagney's haunting words..."It's a lousy war but it's the only one we've got!"

Monday morning began with a series of anti-submarine exercises that stretched through most of the week. The *Field's* sonar, though archaic, "pinged" beyond anyone's expectations, and this, combined with Royal's prowess as a ship handler, enabled the Charlie P. to lead the division at week's end with two undersea kills and three confirmed assists. Torpedo drills were the order of the day for Friday. In this competition the *Field* racked up a qualifying but not impressive score.

During the next weekend, the division managed to acquire a berth in Quarry Lock near the submarine base, thus eliminating the long and tiresome wait for the liberty launch. Even so, the weekend passed much too quickly. Lieutenant Stockwell and Cassy Jean shared an emotional farewell at the Honolulu airport; Cobb broke his usual eighty-five at Waialae; Ensign Coates finally discovered what Hawaiian girls wear under those wavy grass skirts; and Howie Murray came dangerously close to "bankruptcy" thanks to three more lengthy calls to Mary Alice.

The division's final week of O.R.I. called for high speed maneuvering and screening drills. Each morning the four destroyers sped through Kaiwi Channel which separated the large islands of Oahu and Molokai. At a point due north of Makanalua Peninsula, they would rendezvous with heavy fleet units and other destroyer divisions engaged in large scale task force operations similar to those they would encounter off Korea. The first two days saw the *Field* and her sisters puff their way from station to station, executing the many and varied screening formations dictated by SOPA who flew his flag from light carrier *Crown Point*. Sharp right angle turns and sudden bursts of speed became the order of the day aboard each destroyer as she raced at a moment's notice from the carrier's flank to a post far in the van, only to be ordered at top speed to a new position astern.

Those sailors expecting Friday afternoon to bring some respite from the week's turbulence were sadly disappointed. In the *Field's* combat-information-center, Coates and Murray busily worked out one change-of-station solution after another, vainly trying to keep pace with each urgent request from the bridge; while above in the wheelhouse, a perplexed Lieutenant Sternhagen ordered without question each new course and speed recommendation his bridge-talker passed on from C.I.C.

By 14:00, the formation had settled down to a circular screen with each destroyer, in turn, being ordered to come alongside the carrier to simulate an underway refueling operation. It was almost five when the signalman aboard the *Crown Point* gave the *Field* her cue, and Mr. Cobb, feeling surprisingly chipper in spite of the fast running sea volunteered to take the conn for the approach which would put the *Field* in position parallel to and between 60 and 100 feet from the carrier's starboard side.

Because of the *Field's* present screening station far ahead of the carrier's port bow, the maneuvering required a 360-degree turn to starboard which would permit the destroyer to slip around astern of the relatively fast moving flattop, then execute a standard approach by overtaking the larger ship. Owen Royal, never given to back-seat driving when one of his officers had the conn, leaned back in his bridge-chair trying to appear completely detached from the wheelhouse activities. Sternhagen, quite happy to be relieved of the tricky task of drawing alongside the carrier, stood stiffly at the exec's side, striving his utmost to look actively involved in the execution of the complex maneuver.

The helmsman responded to Cobb's order and the *Field* abandoned her forward station in the screen, swinging sharply from formation course. To the men on the bridge, it seemed that the other warships had all suddenly changed direction to zigzag recklessly about *DD-505*, which, as long as they didn't look aft toward her curving wake, appeared still to be galloping over the water on a fixed course. As the *Field* swung around further and further to the right, ships that had been cruising comfortably distant off her port quarter an instant before, unexpectedly appeared dead ahead or close to her starboard bow. This phenomenon was not uncommon to men engaged in high speed encounters with the principles of relative motion, and even to seasoned mariners like Owen Royal, such maneuvers always proved a bewildering experience when transformed from the polar-coordinate plotting table to the boundless expanse of the Pacific Ocean.

"All engines ahead full, right standard rudder, come to two-four-zero," commanded Cobb hoarsely.

As he spoke, the *Crown Point* disappeared from the conning officer's line of vision to emerge seconds later off the starboard beam as the *Field's* stern pivoted around in a sudden jerking motion which slapped the waves and washed the side of her aftermost gun-house with green water. For a few moments the two ships were roughly parallel though traveling in opposite directions.

"Right full rudder!" shouted Cobb.

"Right full rudder," repeated the helmsman.

Turning to the bridge-talker, Cobb said, "Ask Combat for the course and speed of the carrier."

"Combat reports the *Crown Point* is on course zero-five-zero, speed eighteen knots. Combat recommends steadying up on course zero-five-zero, and reducing speed to twenty-two knots for the approach, Sir."

"Negat!" snapped Cobb curtly. "Inform combat we are coming right to zero-five-zero, twenty-six knots!"

Moments later the *Field* completed her wide circular turn, pitching heavily as she finally steadied in the carrier's tossing wake; her bare jackstaff pointing directly ahead at the square box stern of the flattop.

Royal said nothing even though he knew that the recommended procedure was to advance parallel to the wake of the vessel being overtaken. His exec still had time to shear out to starboard, the captain reassured himself, certain that Cobb would give that order to the helmsman any second now.

"Combat reports that our present course and speed are collision, Sir!" the bridge-talker shouted nervously.

Cobb's face reddened. "Of course it's collision! We're in her wake, aren't we?" he glared at the young sailor. "Inform combat that since we're making eight more knots than the carrier, any fool would know that we're on a collision course! I'm conning this ship, not combat," he muttered half under his breath. Then turning to the captain, he softened his tone and said, "That's the trouble with those damn pip-jockeys, they all think they're indispensable."

"Sir," the talker broke in with noticeable hesitation, "Combat requests permission to call your attention to the fact that if we don't come right immediately and reduce our present speed, we will run right up the carrier's stern."

"That's ridiculous! I know when to change course!" Cobb said, turning to the captain for some sign of agreement.

"Range to the carrier," Royal suddenly asked the talker.

"Four-hundred-and-fifty-yards, Sir," came the quick reply.

"You'd better come starboard, Aub," Royal advised.

The exec gave no indication that he had heard the C.O.'s recommendation.

"Mr. Cobb, combat says we can expect a collision in the area of frames one through twelve in approximately three minutes," the talker's voice squeaked fearfully, yet with a taunting air that said I told you so.

"I have the conn!" the captain spoke up suddenly. "Left full rudder!" Royal shouted to the helmsman. "Port engine stop!" he ordered turning to the man on the engine telegraph. Aware that *Independence* class CVL's such as the *Crown Point* have four trunked stacks projecting far out on the starboard side, Royal knew that in this close he had no chance of clearing the carrier if he came right as had been the prescribed plan. He was also cognizant of the strong wind now blowing from the starboard quarter which could set the *Field* hard against the carrier, slamming her midships or after section into the larger ship's side.

Still bearing down on the ship ahead, Royal could see white dots moving swiftly near the carrier's fantail. In a few seconds the dots took the form of sailors scrambling out of the flattop's stern gun sponsons.

Years of shiphandling had taught the captain how to make the wind work for him. Now coming left, he would use it to accelerate his turn; to carry the *Field* on to a safe, though unscheduled appearance along the carrier's port flank.

The *Field* continued to close the carrier.

"Get those two men off the foc'sle!" Royal's voice thundered at Sternhagen, as the captain noticed two seamen emerging from the hatch that led to the bo'sun's locker.

The destroyer's stern tilted upward free of the sea, her screws bit the air and an instantaneous vibration shook the entire ship. Then her stern plunged back into the water and the *Field* heeled sharply to port.

"She's turning," cried Sternhagen as he felt the reassuring motion of the destroyer pivoting beneath his feet, her stern swinging around like the spoke of a wheel. Then to the helmsman and the man at the engine-telegraph, Royal commanded, "Starboard engine stop! Shift your rudder! All engines back two-thirds! Rudder amidships!"

The *Field* steadied, then with a sudden burst of forward thrust, bolted out on a tangent that brought the tip of her starboard yard within an uncomfortable ten feet of the port edge of the *Crown Point's* overhanging flightdeck.

Royal's eyes focused on the small blue flag with the two white stars flapping from *Crown Point's* halyard. He sighed bleakly, painfully aware that SOPA was riding aboard the carrier.

On the CVL's hangar deck, crewmen assigned to the starboard fueling rig waited at their station in open-mouthed bewilderment for a destroyer that did not appear. They could recall many an occasion when the conning officer of an approaching vessel had misjudged his distance and paralleled their flattop by too wide or too close a margin; this, however, was the first time a maneuvering ship had completely missed the prescribed beam. To the tars on the *Crown Point*, the old quip about "missing the broad side of a barn" seemed particularly appropriate.

High above the hangar deck, a paunchy little man with satanic eyebrows and a fluorescent nose angrily paced the carrier's narrow flying-bridge. Unfortunately for Owen Royal, the satanic eyebrows and fluorescent nose were the property of Rear Admiral "Tailspin Tommy" Tebbens, Training-Coordinator for ComAirPac.

"What's the name of that 'can'?" the admiral bellowed at his flag-lieutenant.

The young officer hurriedly stuck his head through an open hatchway and repeated the question to his people in flag-plot.

A sailor in undress whites rushed to the huge surface-status board, studied the numerous names and numbers scribbled in yellow grease pencil, then shouted "Five-0-five's the *Charles P. Field*, Lieutenant Gilhooley!"

"*Charles P. Field*, Sir," said the lieutenant.

The admiral stopped pacing, put his fingers to his lips, paused, then scowled, "Who's her commanding officer?"

Lieutenant Gilhooley nervously thumbed through the Ops plan he'd picked up in the flag-plot. "Royal, Sir," he answered, "Commander Owen G."

"Reserve?"

"No, Sir...U.S.N."

"Incredible!"

The *Field* was now approximately a hundred yards broad on the carrier's port beam. "Tailspin" examined her closely with his binoculars, then charged into flag-plot. There was a momentary burst of static as the admiral turned up the volume tuner on the radio-telephone. "What's her call name?" he asked impatiently, clutching the phone with a motion one might use to strangle a chicken.

"Shiftless," came the synchronized reply from flag-plot's six occupants.

Back in the *Field's* wheelhouse, the same loud burst of static warned Royal that he could standby for a blast from the carrier's skipper, or at least from Commodore Price whom he was certain had observed the entire fiasco.

Cobb, his face flushed with rage, had already excused himself from the bridge and had started down the ladder when the red button beneath the speaker began to flicker... "SHIFTLESS, SHIFTLESS, THIS IS DOWAGER. YOUR SHIPHANDLING WELL BEFITS YOUR CALL NAME. OVER."

Commander Royal pressed the small button on his mouthpiece. "THIS IS SHIFTLESS, REQUEST PERMISSION TO TRY AGAIN. OVER."

The admiral hesitated, studied his surface plot, then, in an exasperated tone, answered, "PERMISSION GRANTED, BUT EXPEDITE! I HAVE TWO MORE SMALL BOYS STANDING BY TO DRINK."

"THIS IS SHIFTLESS, ROGER, OUT." Royal acknowledged, then checking the call name "Dowager," swallowed hard as he read the words — Rear Admiral Thomas J. Tebbens, U.S.N. on the day's Ops sheet.

Lieutenant Sternhagen and the JOD, Ensign Ritter, prudently positioned themselves as far out of the way as possible as the captain retained the conn for the second approach which was executed flawlessly.

Below in his cabin, Aubrey Cobb lay in his bunk staring up at the pale green overhead. Never known for any propitiousness towards the radar gang, they, and especially Ensign Coates, now held undisputed first place on his "enemies list" with Owen Royal moving up fast. Achieving such status was no minor accomplishment since Cobb's list encompassed almost everyone aboard the *Field*, the one possible exception being the ship's gun boss, Alan MacKinlay. Giving new credence to the "birds of a feather" maxim, this concession was prompted purely out of a perceived need for a henchman. Even so, MacKinlay's privileged status was on shaky ground since the executive officer had long harbored a burning envy of all Naval Academy graduates.

As Cobb listened to the erratic purr of the engines, the afternoon's events flashed through his brain. Where the hell did Royal come off embarrassing him like that in front of Sternhagen and those other idiots up there, he fumed. There was no need for Royal to have taken the conn, he told himself over and over again, firmly convinced that if left alone, he would have had more than enough time to come right of the carrier and properly complete the maneuver. Hadn't he carried out that approach hundreds of times, hell, he'd never had any problem in riding up a wake before!

It was quite obvious to Cobb now as he lay there that the captain had pulled his rank just to show off in front of that misfit crew. Well, he wouldn't let it bother him. He knew he was superior to the whole lot of them. At least he had one consolation, Royal's ass is really in the grinder now, he smiled, convinced that Price would never let the captain get away with embarrassing the division in front of Admiral Tebbens and a fair portion of the Pacific Fleet. One more nail in Royal's coffin...Cobb took great relish in the thought.

By 17:30, the last two destroyers had completed their fueling exercises and the various divisions were detached one by one to steam back independently to Pearl Harbor. A few minutes before the blunt smudge of Barber's Point took shape on the *Field's* surface-search radar, a tersely worded message was received from *Abner Ward*.

· · ·

The white hands on the flagship's quarterdeck clock indicated five after nine as Commander Royal made his way to the commodore's cabin.

"Sit down, Owen," Price said in a peeved tone. "Here, take a look at this, it's from Admiral Tebbens."

Royal read the short message which ended with, *after thorough consideration it is my conclusion that shiphandling in your division leaves much to be desired.*

"I imagine you know what prompted this," Price said with a frown.

"Yes, Sir," Royal answered softly, his fingers moving nervously over the raised gold leaves on his cap visor.

"Any explanation?"

"No, Sir, I had the conn at the time. I'm fully responsible."

"With all your experience, I find it hard to understand how you could have run up her wake like that. You had plenty of room when you steadied around to the carrier's course."

"Yes, Sir."

"Is that all you have to say?"

"I'm afraid I have no excuse, Commodore."

"Well, if you insist on taking the blame, so be it. I just want you to remember that today's little happening will receive due consideration when it comes time to make out your fitness report."

Royal said nothing as he leaned forward to place Admiral Tebbens' message on the commodore's desk.

"Do you realize that today's incident, combined with the division's mediocre gunnery performance, could strike us out as far as this O.R.I. is concerned?" Price scowled, glancing red-eyed at the sheet of paper.

"Yes, Sir, I suppose it could," Royal answered in a penitent voice.

"I won't know where we stand until sometime tomorrow, but it won't surprise me if the entire division is sent packing for a refresher thanks to this afternoon's screw-up, and one-fouled-up crew that thinks it's open season on target planes and aircraft carriers." Price squashed out his cigar in the brass tray, then pointing his finger at Royal, said, "Look, Owen, I tried to give you a hint right after your boys clobbered that target float. Apparently, I wasn't forceful enough. Well, this time I want you to know I'm not kidding around. If you can't get that pig-iron aviary squared-away, I'll see to it that she gets a C.O. who can! Now I want to be fair about this thing," Price continued after a short pause. "If you have anything to say in your defense, say it, but please don't bring up that tired bit about mothballs and a limited refit. I let you squirm off the hook on that one after your gun gang tried to splash Topmannine." Then before Royal could answer, Price flailed out again. "In all my years in the navy, I've never seen a ship with such incredibly poor surface gunnery. The very fact that your gun club can tag a fast moving sleeve, to say nothing about it's tow-plane, and yet can't handle a slow moving surface target only serves to underscore their ineptness."

"I'll see that the crew shapes up, Commodore," Royal said after a long silence, but as he spoke, he wondered if the *Field* and the odd collection of eccentrics she'd been given for a ship's company really could shape up. Maybe there was something to this Henderson foolishness after all, he mused.

"While you're here, there's one more thing," said Price with a slight shudder. "It's come to my attention that two limped-brain members of your crew managed to get themselves arrested by army intelligence the very first night we arrived here. Now, anyone who knows me can testify to the fact that I would be the last one to interfere in a matter between one of my captains and his ship's company. However, in a case where the security of the division is threatened, I mistakenly assumed that the commanding officer of the men involved would have notified me immediately. In case you've lost track of time, Owen, that little incident took place almost a month ago."

"I'm sorry, Commodore. The matter was minor and I didn't think it warranted disturbing your weekend."

"Nothing that concerns security is ever minor," Price said glumly, then stood up abruptly, a signal to Royal that the meeting was over.

As Owen Royal rose from his chair, he wondered why Major Eberle had gone to so much trouble to hunt down and inform the commodore of a matter already settled to everyone's satisfaction.

Price held the door for his visitor. "Oh, and Owen," the commodore smiled, "next time you try to chew up the ass end of a carrier, make certain there isn't a two-star on board."

The commodore's final words, an attempt to soften the severe reprimand he had just delivered, did little to alter the commander's expression, that of a whipped cocker spaniel. Royal returned to the *Field* still wondering what Eberle had hoped to gain by reporting the incident to Price. He had no way of knowing that neither the major nor anyone else in Army Intelligence was responsible.

A short time after the captain returned to the shadowy comfort of his cabin, he heard the metallic sound of a signet ring tapping on his door.

"Come in," Royal said, his back to the door as he placed his tan uniform blouse on a coat hanger.

"Captain, could I talk to you about today?" his exec's voice sounded a little stronger than a whisper.

"The less I hear about today, the better, Aub. I just finished a command performance for the commodore, so I'd appreciate it if we could make this as short as possible." Royal loosened his black tie. "I'm going to hit the sack in a few minutes and try hard to pretend that I'm still on the *Buffalo* and the most pressing decision I have to make is whether I should go view the ruins at Pompeii or take the bus up to Rome." He smiled wearily as he sat on his undersized bunk.

"Yes, I imagine Commodore Price made things pretty nasty for you." Cobb sat down opposite his C.O. "There was no excuse for what I did today, Sir, I'm only sorry that you had to suffer any embarrassment over what happened. I've been sitting in my cabin for the last three hours cursing my own bullheadedness up there this afternoon." Shaking his head in disgust, he said, "If it's alright with you, I'd like to request permission to go over to the *Ward* tomorrow and explain how I messed up the refueling drill."

There was a long silence. The expression of humble contrition on Cobb's face suddenly changed to fright as he waited for Royal's answer. Had he mis-judged the C.O.? Maybe Royal wasn't the soft touch he appeared to be when dealing with the white hats. Cobb wondered and worried.

Finally the captain broke the silence. "Aub, the navy means a lot to you, doesn't it?"

"Yes, I plan to stay in for at least twenty, maybe more." Cobb chose his words carefully.

"Well, I don't see any need for you to talk to the commodore. I'm sure he's already forgotten the incident."

Cobb breathed much easier.

"There's one thing, though," the captain said. "I'd like you to go a little eas-ier on Coates and his radarmen. You know as well as I do that they're only doing their job when they send up course and speed recommendations. You've done enough time in C.I.C. yourself to know that."

"I know you're right. All I can say is that today was just one of those unex-plainable days. I promise you, I'll be much more careful in the future."

"I'm sure you will, Aub."

As they spoke, Cobb's eyes focused on the large picture of Candace on the captain's desk.

"Your wife is very beautiful." The words burst forth almost as a reflex action.

"Thank you," Royal smiled. "I'm sorry you weren't aboard that last night in San Diego. I would have asked you to join us for dinner."

"Coates told just about everyone in the wardroom that she was fantastically attractive but after seeing this photo, all I can say is that he didn't exaggerate one bit." Cobb continued staring at the framed picture. "Well, Captain, I know you want to get some sleep, so I won't take up any more of your time."

"You'd better get some sleep yourself. We should be finding out how we scored on our O.R.I. tomorrow."

"I'm certain we'll get a passing grade," Cobb said as he departed the cabin. Then walking aft to supervise the post-movie clean-up, he congratulated himself on how thoroughly he had "snowed" the captain. He was fully aware however, that he had experienced one hairy moment when it appeared his bluff might backfire. But in keeping with the philosophy of the *Field's* gunnery department, Aubrey Cobb that evening believed that a miss was every bit as good as a mile.

Before turning out his light above the bed, Owen Royal decided to scan a few back issues of *Life* which he had borrowed from the wardroom. As he thumbed through the May 12th edition of the weekly magazine, one article attracted more than his casual attention. The headline read "*Wasp Splits Hobson — 176 Men Lost in Oil-Soaked Sea.*" Above the headline, a two-page illustration depicted a huge aircraft carrier knifing through the mid-section of a destroyer-minesweeper. The captain noted that the smaller ship was not unlike the *Field* in general appearance.

Saturday morning came and the *Field's* number "2" mount received a fresh coat of haze gray; sections one and three were granted weekend liberty; and Howie Murray scraped up enough money to put in another call to Mary Alice. At two minutes before noon, word was received from the flagship that all four destroyers had passed O.R.I. and the division would weigh anchor in nine days for Yokosuka, Japan.

The extra week in Hawaii was necessitated by an unexpected modification to each destroyer's radar, making it compatible to the up-dated I.F.F. system going into effect in Korean waters as of July 1st. The modification called for replacement of the responder and interrogator units used to challenge and identify aircraft as friend or enemy. The work in the yard would be followed by a day at sea during which the new system would be tested against naval aircraft flying out of Ford Island.

• • •

"They can't do this to me!" Logan cried out as he read the orders handed to him by the marine sergeant at the shore patrol headquarters where he had reported for what he expected would be a routine patrol. Three hours later, the radarman was in a telephone booth at North Island frantically placing a phone call to the San Diego Naval Hospital.

"Cindy, baby," he announced sadly, "I don't think we'll be able to go to that play you wanted to see tonight. I just got orders to report back to the *Field*."

There was dead silence from the other end of the line.

"Cindy, are you there?"

"Yes," she said feebly. "I don't understand. I thought you were all set for that instructor's billet at Point Loma?"

"I thought so too," he answered through lips tight with anger.

"Where is the *Field* now...Korea?"

No, Pearl Harbor. I'm at the North Island Naval Air Station. My plane leaves in a few minutes."

"Damn," the nurse cried aloud. "When did you find out?"

"A couple hours ago. I had to scramble to get my gear packed back at the base."

"Couldn't you have stopped at the hospital to see me on your way to North Island?"

"Hell, I barely had time to stop at the locker club so I could pick up a set of civies. I made arrangements with the manager to have the rest of my clothes sent back to New York."

"What about us?"

"What do you mean?"

"Kevin, you must know by now that I'm in love with you. You do, don't you?"

Logan was embarrassed, and for the first time in his life he wasn't certain how he should respond.

"You love me, too, don't you?" Cindy waited nervously for the answer.

"Well, yes, of course I do, but now that I'm going to be so far away, I don't want you to think you have to...you know, keep yourself for me. It's not like we're engaged or anything, you know," he said almost cheerfully. "Anyway, I've got to run, they're calling away the draft for my plane."

"Don't forget, I'll be flying to Japan in August. We can still see each other."

"Yes, that's right," he answered dully.

"Please take care of yourself, darling. I love you."

"Okay, Cindy, I've got to go now. Goodbye," he clicked the phone, hoping he'd still have time to telephone Candy.

Convinced that it was a good idea to touch base with her once more, he decided to tell her that Columbia was sending him to Pearl Harbor and Japan with his *Caine Mutiny* assignment. He was certain she'd swallow it. Hell, he'd even drop her some postcards. That would convince her, he smiled. Then when he showed up again in eight or nine months, maybe she wouldn't be too pissed. After all, "Candy bar" was still the best damn lay he'd ever had, he reflected, as he dialed the La Jolla number.

"Baker, Barlow, Yeager and Sigsbee," came the prompt reply.

Logan wondered which receptionist was answering, the cute one, or the nasty little bitch with the mustache.

"Miss Moffet, please," he asked politely.

"I'm sorry. Miss Moffett is in New York on business."

"Shit," Logan snarled.

"Excuse me?" came the indignant response.

"Never mind, that's alright, sorry, I've got to go!" he slammed the phone back in its cradle.

Twenty minutes later, Logan was staring up at the gleaming silver fuselage of the R4D Skymaster that would carry him to Hawaii. A chief petty officer stood at the base of the four-engine transport's mobile staircase. Smiling, he glanced down at the list of passengers on his clipboard, then back up at Logan. "Okay, sailor," he said, grinning like the proverbial Cheshire cat..."Name, rate and horsepower?"

Chapter VIII - "Aloha Oe"

It had been a red-letter day for Hampton Barlow. Candace Moffet had arrived from California. He'd cleared the decks for her, had even put off an appointment with the sales V.P. of a major razor blade manufacturer, an account B.B.Y. and S. had been courting for more than a year. It was also a big day for Candace who spent most of it in Barlow's office bringing him up to date on her plans for the coming year. She was certain that Cherokee would renew the account. The campaign for their new line of motorcycles had them ecstatic, she happily reported. She also felt that the agency had an excellent shot at a new California fast-food chain which was planning to go nation-wide by late '53.

That evening Candace and Barlow met "under the clock" at the Biltmore. After cocktails at the hotel's Palm Terrace, they caught a cab to the Three Crowns where they dined on a sumptuous smorgasbord, serving themselves from the restaurant's huge revolving table. Next on the evening's agenda was the Midston House on Madison Avenue, home of Candy's favorite watering hole, the Whaler Bar.

Rigged out to resemble a Yankee whaling bark, the ingeniously designed cocktail lounge featured a sound effects system that reproduced the hissing drone of the ocean while portholes with moving seascapes convinced customers, especially after a few drinks, that their "ship" was actually rolling. To complete the illusion the Whaler's serving staff were decked out in Jack Tar jumpers and bell-bottoms that would have made Lord Nelson proud.

"Damn but it's great being here with you again, Candy. This evening's been wonderful," the gray-haired executive said, raising his gin-and-tonic in a gesture of a toast.

"Thanks, Ham. I always enjoy your company, and it's nice being back in New York even if it is only for a few days. You know you really look terrific. With all those two martini lunches, how do you manage to keep that lean and hungry look?"

"A few of our competitors have described it as lean and mean," Barlow smiled, obviously flattered. "Actually, I try to work out at least two evenings a week at the New York A-C. I'm afraid at my age, the ivy league look doesn't come without a little effort. Now, if you'll permit me to change the subject to something more important," Barlow said nervously, "I hope you've given some serious thought to what I asked you the last evening we were here." His lips drew into a small, crooked smile. "You know, all you have to say is yes, and you'll make me the happiest guy on Madison Avenue."

"What about Bettina?"

"You know as well as I do that there's nothing between me and her. There hasn't been for fifteen years," he added in a plaintive tone. "She'd have no qualms about giving me a divorce just as long as I agree to a big enough settlement. All she really cares about these days is cruising off to Europe on the *Liberte* or one of the *Queens*. Right now she's on an around-the-world cruise aboard the *Coronia*. Last card I got was post-marked Port Said. I think she's got more time at sea than that husband of yours."

"What about your children? How do you think they would feel?"

"Children? Josh and Miranda are both older than you are." Gently squeezing her hand, he said, "For the last three years you've been the only woman in my thoughts...in my life for that matter."

"Are you completely discounting Garrett?"

"You've repeatedly told me that you don't love him...that you never did," Barlow countered ruefully. "That wasn't a lie, was it?"

"No," she answered softly, tracing her finger back and forth over the rough gray surface of the driftwood table top.

"I don't know why you're so concerned about your husband. He obviously doesn't give a damn about you. If he did, do you think he'd be gallivanting all over the globe with the navy every chance he gets. You know, I'm damn sorry I sent you to France on the *J'Attendrai* account," he said angrily. "If you hadn't gone over there, you never would have met him."

"I don't think Garrett has very much to say about how much time he spends overseas. You should know that. You were in the service, weren't you, Ham?"

"No," the ad executive smiled. "I was born at a very fortunate time. I was too young for the First World War and to old for the Second. I did my bit though," he added quickly. "You probably aren't aware of it but during World War Two B.B.Y. and S. turned out more public service messages for the armed forces than any other agency on Madison Avenue. In fact, it was our agency that made America air minded with the slogan 'keep 'em flying.' I don't think I'm taking any undeserved bows when I say that we probably helped recruit half the flyers in the army and navy with that little gem." Then beaming, he added, " Hitler may have had his Goebels but luckily F.D.R. had his Barlow." Gripping her hand once more, he asked, "Speaking of the armed forces, did you know your old friend Kevin Logan has gone back into the navy?"

"Oh, no," she laughed loudly, "He's not in the navy. He's just working on the script for a navy movie...*The Caine Mutiny*. I saw him a couple of times recently. He was in San Diego gathering material for the screenplay."

"That's funny," Barlow said with a puzzled grin. "I could have sworn Tommy Ives told me Logan had rejoined the service. I had to admit it didn't make any sense. I couldn't imagine anyone giving up a good job in advertising to go back into the navy. I understand he was doing quite well at G. and B. Oh, well," Barlow shrugged, "I guess he must have found Hollywood a little more lucrative." The ad exec signaled the waiter for a fresh round of drinks, then turning back towards Candace, he said, " You know, that smug son-of-a-bitch was the only one I ever really worried about."

"Logan? Why would you worry about him? You helped me fix things so he had to leave B.B.Y. and S."

"Don't try to kid a kidder, Candy. I always felt that you and Logan had something going even after he left the agency. I understand you were engaged to him once."

"Twice, if you want to count college," she answered wearily.

"How come you saw him in California? I thought you told me he was definitely out of your life?"

"He was, I mean he is," she quickly corrected herself. "He was just in the area one day so he dropped in for a chat, that's all. I supposed he wanted to rub it in about how good he was doing in Hollywood. He knew that when I entered that Miss Connecticut contest I had great ambitions to be the next Lana Turner or Rita Hayworth. From what I've been reading in the papers these days, it looks like Marilyn Monroe has beaten me to it," she quipped.

"I hope you're telling me the truth, Candace. I don't know why he'd just come traipsing into your office unless he was after something."

"Oh, come on, Ham, you're too suspicious," Candy laughed. "Kevin knows there's nothing left to salvage of our relationship."

"Did you tell him that?" he asked anxiously.

"I didn't have to," Candy smiled. "There was no reason for the subject to come up. He was only in my office ten minutes or so."

"I thought you said you saw him a couple of times," Barlow grumbled, his face solemn.

"Oh, the second time was in a restaurant. He had somebody with him. We just waved. He didn't even come over to my table, honestly," she said, squeezing his hand affectionately.

Apparently satisfied with her explanation, Barlow quickly shifted the subject back to Candy's appraisal of the agency's West Coast prospects. When it came time to escort her back to her hotel room, Candace observed that with a busy day looming ahead, it made little sense for him to take the midnight train all the way up to Darien. As a practical alternative, she suggested that he share her digs at the Biltmore. The charitable offer was immediately accepted.

•   •   •

When a warship is at sea her combat-information-center is a dark and mysterious place glowing with greens and yellows and pervading the aura of an alien space ship. In port, with the lights on, C.I.C., much like Cinderella's carriage, suddenly turns back into a pumpkin...or more specifically, a windowless, metal box crammed with electronic gadgetry, steel tables, soiled charts, and dirty coffee cups. Thus, back into this "pumpkin" on a sunny June morning unhappily stepped Kevin Francis Logan, his expression matching that of the death-row inmate just denied his final reprieve. Lowering his sea bag and a small leather satchel to the deck, he looked around at the drab gray compartment. "This must be a bad dream," he said gloomily, his eyes homing in on its four occupants.

"Lover boy Logan's back, lock up your wives and daughters," Holiday yelled from the adjacent coffee mess to Gardiner and Bacelli who were on their knees clumsily fitting fresh strips of black rubber matting around the base of the Sugar-George.

"Fucked again by the fickle finger of faith, heh, Logan?" Gardiner asked with great glee.

"I think the word is fate, but the substance of your observation is essentially correct," Kevin said dryly.

"What happened?" Bacelli joined in. "We thought you'd be back on Madison Avenue knocking out Kotex ads by now."

"So did I," shrugged the second class. "I guess I'm being punished for an ill-spent youth."

"We really bleed for you, Logan," Gardiner sneered, "having to come back here and associate with us peons again. What'd you do, screw up on the beach?"

"No, apparently the old man just decided that I was indispensable to the proficient operation of the Charlie P. Can't say I blame him now that I look around at you brainless wonders."

"Hey, Kev, welcome back! Coates said you'd be reporting aboard sometime today," Murray beamed as he vaulted through the open doorway. "You're looking great. Guess you got plenty of rest, heh," the first-class asked, slapping an arm over Logan's shoulder. "It'll be great being a team again. We can really use you."

"Speak for yourself," Gardiner muttered half under his breath.

"How come this bucket's still in Hawaii? I thought you'd be well on your way to the big-K by now," Kevin quipped, smiling for the first time since he'd left San Diego.

"We would have pulled out this morning except for some new I.F.F. gear they'll be installing this week. Then, of course, we wasted a week sitting around Pearl Harbor before we even began our O.R.I."

"How'd you do?"

"Oh, okay, I guess. At least we passed."

"What Murray means is that we squeaked through by the skin of our teeth." Bacelli piped up.

"That's about it," Murray agreed in a somber tone. "To make matters worse, we really pissed off the exec. He's been gunning for us for almost a week now.

Seems we embarrassed him in front of the old man during our refueling drill. Cobb had the conn at the time."

"What'd you do? Send up the wrong course and speed recommendations?"

"No, just the opposite. We tried to keep him from running us right smack into the ass-end of a carrier. As it was the skipper had to take the conn away from him right in front of everybody on the bridge. Otherwise, there would have been one hell of a collision. We were in so close, I still don't know how the old man was able to pull us out of it. He must be one hell of a shiphandler," Murray smiled vaguely. "And Coates, I take back anything negative I ever said about him."

"Yeah, he's really got balls for an ensign," Nugent cut in. "I wish I could have been up in the wheelhouse and seen Cobb's expression when old Coatsie had the word passed up to standby for a collision between frames one and twelve."

"Coates is okay for my money," said Holiday. "That proves what I always said. There's two kinds of officers...good guys like Coatsie and turds like Cobb."

"The only thing in common between those two is that they're both losing their hair," Bacelli said, lighting up a cigarette for his buddy Holiday.

"I'll bet Cobb's bald spot got a little bigger when the captain grabbed the conn," Kevin laughed.

"Unfortunately, poor old Coates is paying the penalty," Murray said grimly. "Cobb never liked him before but he's really on his back now. Every chance he gets he chews his ass out, and he made sure that Coates got stuck with the quarterdeck watch all last weekend."

"Why's the old man letting him get away with it?" Kevin asked.

"Who knows? Guess the captain's so busy getting ready for Korea, he hasn't noticed what's going on. Maybe he doesn't care," Murray shrugged, hooking his thumbs into the waist of his dungarees.

"Coates isn't the only one on the exec's shit list," Nugent joined in. "Last Friday night just before liberty call, Cobb made a surprise visit to our compartment and all of a sudden he decided he needs a complete paint job from deck to overhead."

"That's crazy! The whole compartment was just painted last month!"

"Try telling that to Cobb," Murray said. "Belton, Paulsen and Farber are back there painting right now. You better leave your gear here in C.I.C. We'll be sleeping on cots topside. It's a good thing the weather's nice and warm here this time of year."

"Yeah, I guess things could be a lot worse," Bacelli smiled. "Suppose this happened next December when we're up off the top of North Korea somewhere. I hear those Siberian winters run as low as 50 degrees below zero."

"Shut up, Bacelli!" Gardiner barked. "That bastard Cobb might have this place bugged and I don't want you giving him any ideas."

"Wouldn't surprise me if that prick really did have us bugged," Nugent snapped. "You know I don't think he has one friend on this whole ship, 'cept maybe MacKinlay," the third-class snickered, wiping a wet rag over the residue of yellow wax left on the vertical plot by countless grease pencils. "Cobb thinks he's some kind of fuckin' big shot 'cause he's number-two honcho on this bucket. Can you imagine how he'd act if he got to be C.O.?"

"Well, I don't know what Cobb has to feel so superior about," Murray grumbled. "It certainly can't be his looks. Ever notice the way he looks at you with that dumb vacant stare, and with his mouth hanging half open?"

"You're right, Howie," Nugent struck in. "I can't figure out who in the navy ever made him a lieutenant-commander, much less put him in the number-two-slot around here. All I can figure is he must have connections somewhere," pondered the third-class aloud.

"Personally, I think Cobb and the navy deserve each other," Murray growled. "By the way, when I was hunting up a name for my kid, I happened to come across Aubrey. Know what it means?"

"No, tell us, Howie. You will anyway," Holiday muttered.

"Elf ruler!"

"Elf ruler?" Nugent boomed indignantly.

"What's a fuckin' elf?" Gardiner asked, pressing down a strip of matting.

"Boy, you're stupid," Bacelli cut in. "Weren't you ever a kid? Everyone knows an elf is like one of those little midgets with the pointed ears in the *"Wizard of Oz"*. Right Logan?"

"Guess so," Kevin answered, his face flushed with laughter.

"Well, if Cobb's the ruler of the elves, what's that make us...a bunch a fuckin' pixies?" fumed Nugent.

"Now don't take it personally, fellas," Logan said, vainly trying to control his laughter. "See what you started," he chuckled, turning towards Murray who was also laughing almost as much as Logan. "Well, maybe we'll all luck out and somebody will send Cobb on an all-expense paid cruise aboard a torpedo," Kevin said, hiking himself up on a stool next to the D.R.T. "I see that you got a new clock," he yawned, his eyes re-examining the surroundings he'd thought he'd left forever behind. "By the way, Howie, you didn't mention Patterson before. I'm surprised you don't have him down in the compartment slopping paint around with the other strikers."

"He's not down there because I've got him mess cooking," Murray answered smugly. "I assigned it to him a week ago."

"How come? Didn't he spend just about all of May down in the mess decks?"

"Well, he's not much good for anything else," the first-class frowned.

"From what I remember, he was every bit as sharp on the scopes as Belton, Farber or Paulsen. And he didn't have the advantage of a nine-month class-A radar school like they did. You're being a little tough on the kid, aren't you?"

"I don't think so. Besides, he's a real jerk. He likes the navy too damn much as far as I'm concerned."

"Come on, Howie, that's a hell of a reason for sticking him down in that lousy scullery every chance you get. You know navy regs say you can't assign a non-rated man to mess duty for more than ninety days during any one year."

"Well, I'm going to make sure he puts in his full ninety days!"

"You're a bit out of character, aren't you, Howie? What happened to that mister nice guy image?"

"Patterson's not getting anything he doesn't deserve. Besides, he's not even officially assigned to the Ops department. Technically, he's assigned to deck under MacKinlay. We only got him because we were short one radar striker."

"Yeah, and because he's got a high I.Q. and a G.C.T. higher than any of the other deck apes that decided they wanted to be radarmen! You know, the kid hero-worships you. Why do you think he's always asking you about the *Franklin* and *Enterprise?*"

"I don't know anything about that! All I know is that he annoys the hell out of me."

"What's the matter, Howie? Does he remind you a little of yourself when you were seventeen and starting off on the greatest adventure of your life? Come on, admit it. You were just as gung-ho back then as he is today. I know I was."

"I told you, Kev. He's down there because I think he should be and as long as I'm wearing this first-class crow, I'm the one who decides who mess cooks and who doesn't!"

"Okay, you're calling the shots. It's just that it's refreshing to see that my brother Brian's not always right. I told him there was no such thing as a Twentieth Century saint."

"What's that mean?" Murray quizzed, gnawing at his lower lip.

"Don't worry about it, Howie. Now what was it you wanted to change the subject to?"

"Oh, yeah, I wanted to ask if you'd like to chip in a few bucks towards some phonograph records. We picked up that forty-five player at the exchange last week," he said pointing towards the small table in the coffee mess. "Me and the other guys here agreed that we can't take much more of the 'shit kickin' music' the radio shack keeps piping all over the ship."

"In polite circles, it's referred to as country and western," Logan announced with a fake solemnity.

"We're not in polite circles, we're in the navy! Milk is 'cow,' coffee's 'Joe,' ketchup's 'blood' and chocolate milk, not that we ever get any, is 'panther piss,' but most of all...country and western's 'shit kickin' music'!" Murray scowled. "Anyway, every time I go down to the mess hall, I have to eat chow to the accompanyment of *'Your Cheatin' Heart'* or *'I'm a Long Gone Daddy'.* Turk's cooking is bad enough by itself. If I have to listen to *'Detour, There's a Muddy Road Ahead'* just one more time, I swear I'll toss my whole damn tray at the first 'oakie' I see!"

"You sound like you want to start the Civil War again," Logan laughed.

"I don't think it ever ended, at least not around here. I'll bet that close to two-thirds of the ship's company hail from south of the Mason-Dixon Line."

"I'd say it's probably more like three-fourths," Kevin half-whispered. "What about your three pet strikers? They're rebels aren't they?"

"They're out voted!" Murray made the pronouncement with all the finality of a chief justice rendering a Supreme Court decision.

"Okay, Howie, I'll be glad to help the cause. When I go over to Waikiki tonight, I'll buy an album of "*South Pacific.*"

"Hey, that'll be great. I knew we could count on you. Now, let's get this C.I.C. squared away before the E.T.'s arrive with the new electronic gear," exclaimed Murray, snatching a coffee-stained chart from atop the plotting table.

•   •   •

It was Thursday before the modifications of the I.F.F. systems on all four destroyers were fully completed. By that time, Kevin had reacquainted himself with Oahu, his last visit having been back in May of '45 while nursing a wounded and bleeding *Laffey* home to a Seattle repair yard. Except for a much smaller military presence, Honolulu and Waikiki appeared much the same as they had seven years earlier.

He mailed Candy a post card showing a Moanalua sunset. Wondering what she had been doing in New York besides putting out for Ham Barlow, Logan dispassionately deposited the card into the Surfrider's lobby mail slot, then cut a course for the plush hotel's Captain Cook Bar and what he hoped would be another memorable evening.

Friday morning, *DD-505*, with her three sisters, sailed forth to an area in Kauai Channel miles northward of Kaena Point. There they would test their new electronic identification equipment in consort with a Douglas JD-1 flying out of Kaneohe.

The radar shack seemed much hotter than Logan remembered it. Always the realist, he had already reconciled himself to the next thirteen months...to the discouraging but unalterable fact that he was stuck with the *Field* and the *Field* was stuck with him.

Leaning over Paulsen's shoulder, Logan peered intently at the scope of the Sugar-Charlie air-search radar. "There it is," Kevin smiled, pointing to a distinct pattern of minuscule yellow bars now discernable just below the target blip. "Mode-one's showing up strong and clear on the scope, Sir," Logan reported to Ensign Coates as Murray joined him at the radar console.

"Very well," the young officer replied casually. "Let's hope the other three modes come in just as clear. Get ready to interrogate using mode-two."

"Yes, Sir, we're doing that right now," Murray said as a smaller, less complex pattern of bars appeared on the scope in response to the *Field's* challenging signal. The cycle was repeated numerous times during the course of the afternoon - the electronic challenge, then the identification reply, and finally the recognition - as the ex-bomber carried out a wide variety of approaches from various bearings and assorted altitudes.

Concentration was on the "Mayday" or emergency I.F.F. mode when Owen Royal entered the darkened radar shack.

"Carry on," the captain said in a friendly tone. "Just continue as if I wasn't here, Mr. Coates."

"Yes, Sir," the C.I.C. officer replied, glancing sideways at Farber and Belton who had already slouched back down to a sitting position on the rubber deck-matting, their backs propped against the base of the plotting table. Then perceiving a message in the ensign's eyes, both strikers shot back to their feet with all the thrust of a missile launch.

The exercise continued for another hour allowing each radarman a turn at the new identification gear. Challenging signals originating in the interrogator unit aboard each destroyer continued to trigger the identification component in the aircraft until 15:30 at which time the twin-engined Douglas was detached and sent home with a hearty "well done" from Commodore Price. Moments later, the regular underway steaming watch was resumed and the *Field* and her sisters set a leisurely course home to Pearl.

"Logan," said the captain jauntily, "this is the first chance I've had to welcome you back to the *Field*. How was your trip out?"

"Fine, Sir, it was a very smooth flight," Logan said, glancing for an instant at the bulkhead clock

"You know," Owen continued, "it took more than a little pressure but I was finally able to persuade the commodore that it didn't make much sense to have to break in a new radarman when a trained member of our C.I.C. team was still unassigned and within flying range."

"Yes, Sir, I see what you mean," Logan said plaintively.

"I understand your wartime service was on destroyers. Is that right?"

"I served on one 'can,' Sir, the *Laffey*."

"The *Laffey*?" Royal's eyes brightened. "Do you know that we'll be relieving the *Laffey* in Korea? She's one of the ships in the division we've been ordered to replace."

"I'll be damned," Logan wrinkled his nose. "I didn't even know the *Laffey* was still around. When I left her at the Todd Yard in Seattle, I assumed the navy was planning to scrap her. She looked more like a floating junk-heap than a destroyer," Kevin shrugged. "I sure as hell never thought they'd bother to repair her, especially with the war winding down and all."

"As I recall didn't she take a terrible beating off Okinawa? What was it, five kamikazes?"

"I don't think anyone knows for sure, Sir," Logan frowned, scratching the nape of his neck. "Those suicide planes came in so fast and from so many directions, it was impossible to tell. One official report I read said we were hit by six kamikazes, another said only five crashed into us. I know we spent five days just picking apart pieces of Jap planes and pilots. It looked to me like they hit us with everything they had...'Judys,' 'Jills,' 'Zekes,' 'Oscars'...hell, I think the whole Nip air force crashed us. Then to add insult to injury, they also clobbered us with four or five bombs. Frankly, Captain, I was so damned scared that morning I never bothered to count."

"That's understandable. I was serving aboard the *O'Bannon* at Okinawa. I guess we were one of the few destroyers lucky enough not to take a hit off that bloody island." Owen Royal looked a little embarrassed and Logan wondered if his commanding officer could actually be apologizing for escaping the terrible wrath of the *kikusui*.

After a short silence the captain said, "It seems a shame that you won't get a chance to see your old ship. Her division detaches on the twenty-second. We won't reach Japan by then. I also understand that her division will be returning to the East Coast rather than to California. Unfortunately, there's no chance that we'll even pass them in transit since they're going home via the Suez Canal and Mediterranean."

"That's okay, Sir. I'd just as soon not see her," Logan said with a heavy sigh. It's funny, though, during the last seven years I don't think I ever shaved once without looking at the razor blade and wondering if it was made from the old girl's hull. By the way, Sir, how'd she do in Korea?"

"Quite well," Royal nodded. "I spent a good part of last night going over her division's battle records. In addition to screening the carriers with Task Force 77, they were also quite active with Task Force 95. That's the bombardment group," Royal added. "I remember one report credited the *Laffey* with knocking out several shore batteries at Wonsan Harbor. Well, I'll leave you men alone so you can get on with your watch," Owen announced with a flourish as he took leave of his C.I.C. team. A moment later Ensign Coates departed for his JOD stint in the wheelhouse.

Pouring himself a cup of coffee from the Silex, Gardiner looked at Logan and said, "Now if you really want to see what a beautiful broad looks like, you ought to get a load of the skipper's old lady. She'd make those Madison Avenue models you're always bragging about look like a troop of Brownies."

How do you know what the old man's wife looks like?" asked Logan, a little sullenly.

"He had her aboard the night before we left San Diego. She was some piece, right, Murray?"

"Well, she certainly was attractive."

"Attractive! Hell, next to her, Marilyn Monroe looks like a Ubangi!" snapped Gardiner just as Bites, attracted by the smell of coffee, entered the radar shack.

"Ah never knew you damn Yankees could grow 'em that purty," Bites smiled, moistening his lips with his tongue. "Lookin' like that, she's gotta have some country blood in her. Ah know one thing, if she was my ole' lady, ah'd be all over her like flies on cow-flop."

"Anyone ever tell you you've got a way with words?" Logan asked curtly.

"Not that ah know of."

"Well, don't worry, they won't."

"I've got to admit, Kev," Murray joined in, "she looked good enough to be a movie actress. She had some body," he took a deep breath as he stretched. "And she was tall and blonde and I don't think I've ever seen anyone with so perfect a face, not even Mary Alice," the first-class conceded in a rasping whisper as if he was afraid his wife was within hearing.

"Speaking of movies," Bacelli prodded. "Did you hear about what Hephaistos brought back when he went over to the base yesterday for the movies?...a personal hygiene film for female military personnel," he continued before anyone could answer.

"How'd he get a hold of that?" Gardiner's eyes squinted. "It's not even listed in the training film catalog!"

"Yeah," Nugent interjected. "I heard they always keep that one locked up in a safe."

"Hephaistos spotted it laying on the shelf right next to the stack of films marked for the *Field*. Some Wave or Bam was probably supposed to pick it up. Anyway, the guy who signed out the movies turned around to answer the phone so 'Greek' slipped it into the sack with the other films he was bringing back."

"Hell, they'll trace it right back to him," Nugent sneered. "Hephaistos will really find his ass in a sling."

"Nah, he's not sweatin' that," Bacelli smiled. "He said there were at least five or six other guys coming in and out for films while he was there. Greek says there's no way anyone can trace it back to the *Field*. All we have to do is keep the officers from finding out so watch what you say when Coates or Stockwell are around."

"Where's the film now?" Logan asked.

"In the I.C. shack. Greek and the other electricians are going to keep it stashed away until we get to Korea," Bacelli explained. "Then they're gonna' have private showings at a buck a head."

"Hell, that I.C. shack can't hold more than eight or nine people at any one time," Nugent scowled.

"So what," countered Bacelli. "The damn thing only runs twenty minutes. They can fit in five or six showings a night. By the time we get back to 'Dago' next year, those electricians will be able to split a bundle."

"You guys are really sick!" Murray thundered. "Why don't you try to get your minds up out of the gutter! This isn't a floating porno house, you know!"

"Nobody's twisting your arm, Howie. You don't have to watch it," Bacelli said brusquely.

"Don't worry, I don't intend to!"

"You know, a dollar is a lot of dough to pay just to watch some Wac or Wave soapin' up her privates," Holiday shrugged. "A first-run movie over on the beach doesn't cost any more than that."

"Well, I don't know about you guys," Gardiner grinned, "but after thirty or forty days of steaming with the task force, I'd be happy to pay a buck just to watch a chicken piss."

"Combat, bridge!" the words suddenly blared over the 'squawk-box.' "We'll be coming around to course one-one-five in three minutes. Keep a sharp eye for any surface contacts." Lieutenant (Jg.) Phelan's voice was clearly discernable. "We should be encountering a lot of small craft and sailboats off Kepuhi Point," the OOD cautioned. "There's a yacht club in that area."

"Combat, aye," Logan answered as the *Field* fell in line, her bow knifing its way through the milky wake left by the three ships ahead.

•   •   •

The division's final weekend in Hawaii passed without incident. Sunday evening was warm and quiet and there were so many last details to take care of, Owen Royal was afraid he'd never get finished in time to go ashore and put a call through to Candace. Luckily California was in an earlier time zone. He'd still be able to talk to her before she went to bed.

To Owen, it seemed that the operator was taking forever. He had telephoned his wife several times since the *Field* had arrived in the islands. The connection had never taken more than thirty seconds before, he reflected, nervously rubbing the back of his hand across his brow. Suppose there was a foul up and he was unable to get through, he thought. He doubted that he'd be able to make any long distance calls from Japan. Then he heard the buzzing sound of the phone ringing, a voice followed...it was Candace.

"That's alright, operator, that's my wife," he quickly cut in as the operator sought to verify the number.

Candace's voice sounded clear and strong. She said she'd been waiting by the phone for his call. She missed him terribly. Yes, she was glad to be back from New York. No, she didn't miss Madison Avenue at all. It had been a hectic trip, she said. She'd worked around-the-clock the few days she was there. No, her busy schedule hadn't allowed her time to catch a Broadway show or even enjoy a decent meal. She reminded him not to do anything dangerous while he was sailing near Korea. He assured her that he wouldn't and reaffirmed the fact that there was little if any chance the *Field* would encounter hostile action.

Rain suddenly began to splatter against the glass of the telephone booth. The shower was short and intense and typical of a June evening in Hawaii. With the rain thumping heavily against the roof and sides of the booth, Owen found it difficult to hear Candace's words. He managed to tell her how much he loved her and strained to hear her reply, but between the rain and the operator interrupting to tell him his time was up, Owen wasn't certain what she had said. Hardly had he placed the phone back in its cradle when the rain stopped with all the abruptness of a faucet being turned off.

The wet pavement glistened in the moonlight as he walked back to the *Field*.

A few minutes after Owen Royal returned to his stateroom, Howie Murray crossed the shaky gangplank and saluted the officer-of-the-deck. "What do you have in the bag?" Ensign Daly asked. "I hope that's not a bottle of booze."

"No, Sir," grumbled Murray squeezing the brown paper bag to show it didn't contain a bottle or anything solid. The bag made a soft rustling sound.

"What ya' got, Howie, a hula skirt for Mary Alice?" Van Ginderen, the petty-officer-of-the-watch stammered.

"Yeah, that's right," Murray nodded dolefully as he stalked off towards the hatch that led to the Ops berthing compartment.

. . .

Monday morning blossomed with a blaze of sky that splashed zig-zag patterns of color on the water off Ewa. At 06:30, special-sea-detail was fully secured and the destroyers steadied up on a westerly course for Japan. Far astern, a huge orange ball hung low over Diamond Head as Murray made his way aft along the main deck to the starboard depth-charge rack. He looked around cautiously, then waiting until he was certain no one was paying him particular attention, the radar-man carefully reached into the crumpled bag he had hidden beneath his jumper and quickly tossed its contents over the stern.

An uncomfortable shiver twitched his entire body as he watched the pale-white ginger lei bob up in the *Field's* churning wake and float out towards the open sea.

Chapter IX - "Lotus Land"

These days at sea were bright and warm. Between working hours, a shirtless sailor would sprawl on scorched deck-plating or lie in the concave of the torpedo tubes, his head pillowed deep in the lazy comfort of a kapok life jacket. Except for sporadic drills this "calm before the storm" was a quiet time aboard the *Field*. Many passed it sun-bathing and thinking of home. Others contemplated shore leave with a seductive geisha. The more practical just slept. A few like Howie Murray watched the sea and remembered red fireballs on the horizon...and cotton candy clouds pocked with a million black sores.

Don Stockwell spent much of his day wondering if Cassy Jean had received that hula outfit he had sent special delivery from Honolulu. Even on his watch he would find himself thinking of her body, the grass skirt clinging snugly along her well-rounded hips and long tanned legs. He wondered if it itched, then embarrassed turned to the helmsman and instructed the sailor to check his course. In the evening after dinner, the young lieutenant would rush to the cloister of the cryptoshack and write Cassy Jean about the elaborate plans he had for their future. By the time the *Field* would reach Japan, the Ops officer would have ten more amorous but rather repetitious letters to entrust to the tender care of the Fleet Post Office, Yokosuka.

On Tuesday morning the destroyers steamed within the sight of Polynesian fishermen tending their nets off Gardner Island. Later in the day the ships were reviewed by a solitary beachcomber on Layson. By sundown Wednesday, the division had cleared the last island outpost of the Hawaiian chain and entered the shadowy waters north of Midway where they unknowingly passed over carrier *Yorktown* and a family of giant sea squid completing a tenth year of residence in her gutted carcass.

By the fifth day of their journey they had encountered but two other travelers, a tired old coaster off Ocean Island and a Dutch cargo-split puffing her way from Nagoya to San Pedro with a belly full of china. With no contacts to plot and scant likelihood of finding any until they neared Japan, each watch in C.I.C. seemed to the *Field's* radarmen longer and more wearisome then the one it succeeded.

Indeed, there was little the men would remember about the 4,000 miles of ocean that lay between Hawaii and Japan. Narcotic temperatures prevailed and even the North Pacific, strangely placid and unreal, seemed reluctant to disturb the malaise of shipboard routine. Each day the deck-log opened and closed with the same entry, *steaming as before*; and each night an identical wind strummed identical notes on the *Field's* salt-parched halyards.

But other more pleasing notes were also being strummed aboard the destroyer, mostly by a boiler tender named Culpepper who each evening, guitar in hand, positioned himself in a secluded spot near the base of the bridge. His favorite song these nights seemed to be a traditional cowboy ballad called *"The Trail to Mexico."* No one who had heard the song knew its name, nevertheless, since the May morning the *Field* had departed San Diego, the old ballad had mysteriously climbed to first place on *DD-505's* hit parade, even beating out Hank Williams' *"Jambalaya."* And while nobody could accurately pin a name on the song, a few who heard it, such as Owen Royal, recognized the haunting melody as that which served as background music for the John Ford classic *"Stagecoach"* and numerous other westerns.

Softly fingering the strings of his "gee-tar," the Texan drawled on through the song's many verses. Standing two decks above the signal bridge, the captain listened, trying hard to catch the words:

> *"It was in the merry month of May,*
> *When I started for Texas far away,*
> *As I left my darling girl behind,*
> *She said her heart was always mine.*
>
> *When I embraced her in my arms,*
> *I thought she had ten thousand charms,*
> *Her caress was soft, her kisses sweet,*
> *Sayin' we'll be married next time we meet."*

...and the *Field* slid silently through the night.

The following morning, the division's lookouts spotted another traveler, the first they'd seen in almost a week. The ship, a two-stack trooper out of Yokohama wore the blue and yellow funnel bands of the Military Sea Transport Service. As the big *General*-class hurried by, the bronze tips of her enormous screws were barely visible above the whipped cream they churned, and her speed seemed to highlight a haughty impatience with anything that might slow her ETA for San Francisco. On her decks combat-proven veterans of the 24th and 25th Infantry Divisions waved and hooted at the small gray warships and speculated as to their type and destination.

Later that day the destroyers passed far north of Okinawa Gunto and the geographic point where seven years earlier the *Collsgrove* had been ripped asunder by the fortunes of war and a misplaced kamikaze intended for the *Field*.

•　　•　　•

Dawn of July 2nd broke with all the grandeur of a DeMille production. Ahead lay Fujiyama, a purple giant astride a pillowed throne of moss.

By 07:00, a spirited breeze was fanning the *Field's* starboard flank, cooling the sailors as they waited in line for morning chow. As the men queued up, they watched a cluster of miniature islands take form amid the pink-gray haze...hump-back little islands that more closely resembled stepping stones in a pond. Then the ships heeled to starboard. It was a wide lazy turn, and to the pilot of a Mariner flying boat passing overhead, their curving wakes seemed little more impressive than the rippled inscriptions left by water bugs.

The maneuver completed, the ships steadied off Izu Peninsula on a course parallel to the Honshu coast. All about them were fishing craft; junks and sampans of infinite variety and improbable description. One, a black-hulled monstrosity with tattered red sails and huge painted eyes which seemed to accent her determination to weave between the column, narrowly missed colliding with *Halsey Wayne*; the latter equally resolute in maintaining speed and station.

The destroyers were closer to land now, yet the orange pagodas nestled along the hillside and on many of the off-shore islands, still seemed as artificial as ceramic miniatures in a goldfish bowl.

The ships moved over the flat water at a leisurely ten knots and crossed the broad entrance to Sagami Bay following a course that ran through the smaller opening at Tokyo-Wan, then left to the naval shipyard at Yokosuka.

Aboard each of the four *Fletchers*, the officers and men were at quarters-for-entering-port a good half hour before word was formerly passed over the speakers. On the *Field's* bridge, Royal, Navigator Oetjens, OOD MacKinlay and JOD Warden, watched anxiously as each new signal pennant flew to flagship *Ward's* yard. Sagami-Wan was to their left now; a wide patch of murky gray water which the Japanese often referred to as a sea. For Owen Royal, nearly seven years had passed since that Monday morning in late August when he rode *O'Bannon* as she escorted battleship *Missouri* to Latitude 35 degrees, 21 minutes, 17 seconds - Longitude 139 degrees, 45 minutes, 36 seconds...the most memorable anchorage of World War II.

•　　•　　•

Shortly passed noon the sky above Yokosuka shaded to deep gray heralding a heavy rain which within seconds had saturated the entire shipyard. The destroyers were moored along the dock in pairs, *Wayne* and *Field* forward, *Ward* and *Morgan* aft.

The *Field's* plan-of-the-day announced that liberty would commence promptly at four and be granted in three sections. Those men in section 1, the last to have the duty in Hawaii, would draw overnight liberty expiring on board at 07:45. The remaining sections would rotate the duty during the division's three-day-stopover. The POD also carried a wordy message from the commodore warning all hands that "because of Japan's proximity to the fighting in Korea, each man **will** be especially alert and security-conscious." Noticeably absent was any reference to Eniwetok or nuclear energy experiments.

The rain had lessened to a fine mist by the time the last hawser from the *Wayne* had been made fast around the *Field's* port bitts. Moments later, special-sea-detail was secured and word to set the in-port watch was passed over all circuits. Moored to Berth 7 in the yard's Truman Bay area, the destroyers were a short distance from and directly opposite Piedmont Pier, a long hilly finger of rock jutting out into the bay with accommodations for the largest and most powerful warships in the Seventh Fleet.

After much coaxing, Logan finally managed to persuade Murray to set his unfinished letter to Mary Alice aside long enough to accompany him topside for a quick inspection of their new surroundings. From the *Field's* open wing, looking acrossed the roof of *Halsey Wayne's* number "2" five-inch gun-mount, the radarmen enjoyed a clear view of carrier *Boxer* newly arrived from Korea and occupying almost the entire length of Piedmont's Berth 12. At the dock's edge, two mammoth cranes, black and ominous in appearance, towered high above the flattop's island. The larger and most prodigious of the pair displayed a weather-beaten sign with the greeting, WELCOME TO JAPAN in faded blue letters.

"There were a few days back in forty-five that I'd have laughed in the face of anyone who ever told me that I'd ever be reading a sign like that, especially here," Murray shrugged.

"That crane to the left might even be bigger than Brooklyn's hammer-head," said Logan, wondering as he spoke just how many of the emperor's "elite" warships once rested alongside that same pier to be serviced by these same two giants that now tended their new masters with all the impartiality of Aladdin's genie.

They watched the larger machine swing its long steel arm out over *Boxer's* flightdeck to lift a damaged Corsair and gently lower the dark blue fighter plane to a barge moored outboard of the carrier.

"With a little imagination, Kev, you can almost see a bloody Zero dangling from that hook," Murray sneered, wiping the rain from his eyes with his sleeve. "Wonder how many of the pips I tracked on Big Ben's air-search-radar once dangled from that hook, maybe even the plane that clobbered us off Kyushu."

"Hope you're not going to get philosophical again," Logan laughed as the two crossed the bridge to the inboard wing to observe the activity on the pier below where a detail of seamen in dungarees hurriedly unloaded canvas mail sacks from a gray Ford pick-up. Crowded around the *Field's* quarterdeck, noisy gobs, many from *Halsey Wayne*, eagerly counted each bag as it was passed aboard, at the same time arguing whether its contents were letters or packages. A loud groan of disappointment was heard whenever a sack of official correspondence, marked guard mail, crossed the gangway.

"I'd better get below for mail call," Murray beamed. "I'll bet there's a pile of letters from Mary Alice. Aren't you expecting any mail?"

"Yeah, I imagine there's a letter or two from my folks," Logan answered casually. "I'll be down in a little while. If I get anything, just toss it on my rack."

By the time Murray departed, the rain had stopped except for an occasional pellet that clinged loudly against the thin metal of the wheelhouse. The wind that blew in from sea was crisp and fresh and for the first time in many months, Logan felt strangely at ease which caused him to wonder if he was actually looking forward to this new and unexpected adventure.

He watched the main road which intersected the foot of the pier and his glance fell upon a jeep cruising the area on security patrol. From their sodden appearance, it was evident that its two marine occupants had been caught without rain gear. Kevin's eyes followed the jeep in its rounds until it was no more than silver tracks on wet pavement. His attention shifted next to the group of gulls screaming wildly overhead as they glided and swooped at the destroyers. One bird, displaying particular audacity, claimed squatters' rights on the muzzle of the *Field's* number "2" gun. Another perched briefly atop the gun-director, then flew off as if dissatisfied with the limited accommodations the Charlie P. had to offer.

"Going ashore, Logan?" inquired a friendly voice from behind.

Kevin turned to face the captain. "Yes, Sir, providing the weather clears."

"I'm certain it will. There's a strong wind blowing. It should move the clouds out to sea."

"Excuse me, Captain," DelRosario half whispered as he strode up to Royal. "I have your mail, Sir," the chief steward advised, saluting as he handed a letter to the *Field's* C.O.

Logan caught a whiff of perfume from the scented blue envelope.

Glancing at the letter, obviously embarrassed by the pronounced aroma of lilies," Royal said with a good-natured grin, "My wife's stationary must really perk them up at the LaJolla post office."

"Yes, Sir," Logan smiled back, suddenly reminded of the fabulous Miss Moffet and the two weeks they'd spent in the sack together back on Terryhill Drive. It'd be quite a coincidence if Candy and the captain's old lady turned out to be neighbors, he mused. But then, LaJolla's not exactly Manhattan, he laughed to himself.

"Well, enjoy your liberty, Logan," Royal said, anxious to get below so he could read Candace's letter.

"Thank you, Sir," Logan saluted, then watched the captain disappear through the wheelhouse doorway.

•   •   •

On Sherman Avenue near the foot of Pier 7, a noisey swarm of bluejackets from the four destroyers waited impatiently for the base bus; this, combined with an aching restlessness induced by twelve days at sea prompted Logan and Murray to undertake the twenty-minute walk to Carney Gate. Their route down Forrestal Street took them close by Berths 8 and 9 and *Sitko Bay*, the carrier the destroyers had courted briefly off San Diego the second morning of their odyssey. Moored along the finger pier just forward of heavy cruiser *Bremerton*, the stubby little flattop presented an innocuous appearance in contrast to the lethal look of her fellow lodger.

Sailors from the two vessels trickled down the pier to join the ever-growing procession to the main gate. From a short distance away, their round white hats glistened like so many sugar bowls as the afternoon sun pushed away the last gray smudge of sky.

"Looks like every road on this base is named for some navy or marine brass," Murray observed as he and Logan continued along Howard Street passing gaunt black buildings once used for servicing the machinery and ordinance of the *Rengo Kantai*. "I wonder if Sherman Avenue back there is named for Ted Sherman or Forrest Sherman?" Murray puzzled aloud.

"What's the difference, an admiral's an admiral," Logan laughed.

"I guess so, it's just that I served under old Ted for awhile in forty-three when he was flying his flag on the *Enterprise*. I reported aboard at Espiritu Santo just before he took our task force out on the Solomons sweep. We lost the cruiser *Chicago* on that one," he said pointing to one of the battle stars on his Pacific Campaign ribbon.

Quickening their pace they took only hasty notice of the many relics left along their way as rusty reminders of Yokosuka's former masters. Mounted on lawns or propped up alongside entrances of various buildings were midget submarines, suicide torpedoes, 18-inch projectiles, and even a small tank or two.

"Hey, did you see that old hulk back near the *Bremerton*? She looked like something left over from the Spanish American War," Murray said, instinctively squaring his hat with both hands as a sudden gust of wind brushed his face.

"That's the battleship *Mikasa*. She was Togo's flagship when the Japs beat the Russians back in 1905. They've kept her here as a memorial."

"How do you know so much about old Jap battleships?" asked the first-class, his tone one part awe, two parts dubiety.

"You'd know them too if you bothered to read the hand-out sheet ship's office sent around this morning. There was also a note on today's plan-of-the-day outlining Yokosuka's tourist attractions," Logan smiled indulgently.

"I don't have time to read all that junk. I had nine letters from Mary Alice to read and they're a hell of a lot more important than old Jap battleships."

"How is Mary Alice coming along?"

"Great, she wrote that the doctor told her everything should be right on schedule."

"Speaking of everything, have you decided on a name yet?"

"Yeah, I have. That's what I'd like to speak to you about."

"Me?"

"Well, I've already written to Mary Alice and gotten her okay, but she says I ought to talk it over with you first. You don't have any objection about our naming him Kevin, do you?" the first-class asked shyly. "You know, it goes kind of nice with Murray, and you're just about the only guy on the *Field* I can really talk to anymore. The rest of the reserves are starting to act as gung-ho as the regulars. And another thing," he hesitated for a few seconds, then said, "Guess I shouldn't admit this but you're a lot sharper in C.I.C. than I am."

"That's a lot of crap."

"The hell it is. You should be wearing this first-class crow, not me. I'm sure they only gave it to me as a reward for surviving the *Franklin*. Besides, you know how easy they handed out rates during the war. I didn't even have to pass a written exam. Anyway, what I'm trying to say is that I really appreciate your taking over so much of the work I should be doing. Anyone else would be bitchin' all over the place. You know, when it comes to plotting anything more complicated than course and speed or maybe a simple change-of-station problem, I'm up shit's creek without a paddle," Murray said shakily. "I'd sure hate to screw up and lose the little bit of dough the navy's paying me, especially with the baby coming and all."

"Don't worry about it, Howie. I enjoy working the plotting table. Besides, I'd be a little rusty too if I hadn't stayed in an active reserve unit for the last seven years. Actually, under the circumstances, I'd say you're doing a damn good job of running things, especially with that quartet of meatballs the navy decided to stick you with."

"Yeah, I guess our third-class will never win any medals for efficiency," Murray shrugged, "But getting back to our naming the baby Kevin, you really don't mind?"

"Mind? Hell, I'd be honored."

"Too bad we won't be back in time for the christening. If we were, I'd ask you to be the godfather."

"Well, I'm not too sure about that. You know the church expects the godfather to set a good Christian example. I'm sure you wouldn't want your kid to model his life after me," chided Logan.

"Have you ever considered changing your life a little, Kev? You know, there's a lot more to life than just trying to make it into the pants of every broad you see."

"Oh, I don't do that. I only try to make it into the pants of the good looking ones," Logan smiled.

"Come on, Kev, be serious. You can't laugh everything off with a wise-ass remark. You're going to have to make an accounting with God one of these days. You know that as well as I do. Sometimes it's hard to believe you could have a priest for a brother."

167

"Well, I do and you're starting to sound just like him."

"You still consider yourself a Catholic, I hope."

"Sure, of course I do," Logan nodded.

"Then why don't you start living up to what's expected of you as a Catholic? You know, this time next week, you're gonna' be ass-hole deep in another war."

"Oh, come on, Howie. The *Field's* not going to see any action."

"I hope you're right, but from what the skipper was saying in C.I.C. that day about your old ship and the other destroyers we're relieving, it sounded to me like they were doing a lot more than just screening carriers."

"Well, that may be but I'd appreciate it if you'd stop trying to save my immortal soul. You know the navy decided a long time ago that destroyers are too small to carry chaplins. Now do me a favor and change the subject."

Few words were exchanged as the two radarmen continued on past the fleet gym and the newly completed C.P.O. club. A final turn and a brisk walk down King Street brought them to Carney Gate named in honor of the American rear admiral who, in August '45, had accepted the surrender of the massive naval base from Japan's Vice Admiral Totsuka.

Exiting the yard, the two petty officers immediately found themselves on Honcho-dori, Yokosuka's principle thoroughfare and one of the city's few paved roadways. Just as Yokosuka had been bastardized to "Yo-kuss-ka," Honcho-dori's pronunciation also had fallen victim to "G.I.-ese," quickly becoming "Hunky-dory Street."

"Never thought I'd ever be taking an afternoon stroll around here," Murray snickered. "I still remember the fly-boys on 'Big Ben' saying how they couldn't wait to get a crack at this place. They called it the Jap's Norfolk."

"They must have really hated the Japs," Logan quipped, "comparing it to Norfolk."

"What have you got against Norfolk?" Murray asked, with an expression of complete puzzlement.

"I was there last year for reserve training. On the lawn in front of one of their buildings was a real cute sign. It read 'dogs and sailors keep off the grass.' I assume it was there with the blessings of the town fathers."

"Talk about biting the hand that feeds you!" Murray blurted out angrily. "I bet three-fourths of Norfolk's population owes all if not part of its income to the navy being there. I'd sure like to get my hands on that sign," the first-class scowled.

"Don't sweat it, Howie. It's not there anymore. One of the New York newspapers got wind of it and sent a photographer down. The paper plastered the picture all over its front page...really caused quite an uproar. The American Legion and the V.F.W. got into the act and that sign came down faster than a hooker's drawers. I'm surprised you didn't hear about it back in Ohio," Logan grinned as the two crossed to the far side of Honcho-dori.

"This place sure stinks," grumbled Murray hoarsely.

"Must be the sewers," Logan answered, calling his companion's attention to the shallow gutters covered partially by stone slabs.

They continued on past countless shops and grinning gold-toothed tradesmen who hawked everything from pearls and silk kimonos to bathtub models of the battleship *Missouri*. Most of the shops were small and flimsy, reminding the radarmen of stalls found along a carnival midway. In spite of the cramped quarters however, each establishment had ample space for a prehistoric gramophone machine which appeared capable of playing but one selection...the hauntingly beautiful "*China Night.*" By this troubled summer of '52, every United Nations ground unit and ship's company engaged in the Far Eastern conflict had fashioned its own lyrics to this old Japanese tune which reportedly had even been adopted by the Chinese and North Korean enemy. "Shi-a-na-na yuro," usually sung "she ain't got no yo-yo," by the more creative G.I., was destined to become the "*Lily Marlene*" of the Korean War.

"How do you like this military script?" Murray asked, extracting a few of the small pink and purple bills from his pocket for the purchase of two small geisha dolls for his daughters.

"It reminds me of monopoly money."

"I don't care what it looks like. It's just that we lose a hell of a lot of time exchanging it for greenbacks aboard ship. Coates said it's a court martial offense to get caught ashore with even a single American bill. I guess they're really afraid of the black market getting hold of any U.S. currency. Hey! Look at that!" Murray said excitedly, pointing to a row of gaudy club jackets with the name *Charles P. Field* handsomely embroidered above a not too unfamiliar silhouette of a *Fletcher* class destroyer and the word KOREA. Similar jackets honored each of the other three members of DesDiv 291, though in the case of *Halsey Wayne* an obvious breakdown in intelligence occurred since the jackets were produced with the name "Harry Wayne."

"I'd like to send one of those jackets to Commodore Price," Murray laughed. "I wonder if he really thought he was snowing anybody with that stuff on the plan-of-the-day about atom bombs and Eniwetok."

Many of the shops displayed photographs of naval vessels engaged in the Korean fighting. One record store proudly exhibited large photos of the *Antietam*, *Leyte*, *Wisconsin* and *Worchester* surrounding a water color of Douglas MacArthur. To the Japanese, the Americans were an adopted navy, the ships that replaced *Kaga, Akagi, Haruna* and *Suzuya*, pictures of which at one time had hung just as proudly on this same wall.

Hunky-dory's curb was lined with bicycle-rickshaws, their grim-faced owners lustily cursing the rains for stopping and depriving them of so many potential customers. Occasionally a rickshaw boy would shout at the radarmen, "Hey, Joe! You go station, one hundred yen only, yes, very cheap!" The overtures were in vain as Logan and Murray continued on to the enlisted men's club and it's navy operated gift shop, camera exchange, liquor store and beer hall. During World War II, the building had served another navy as was evidenced by the large bronze chrysanthemum still hanging majestically in the club's theater. This aesthetic symbol of Imperial power was similar to the figureheads once prominently displayed on the bows of all Japanese warships.

Their inspection of the E.M. club completed, Logan and Murray turned down Shioiri Street, unknowingly entering one of Yokosuka's more active red light districts.

"Hey, guy...you like nice clean girl me think, maybe, heh? I take you to mamma-san. She fix, ichiban number one girl, very clean, short time plenty cheap...long time, little yen more, yes?" The proposition was repeated over and over again as the two trudged on.

Murray was reminded of a hobo village he had seen by a railroad siding near Akron. There seemed little dissimilarly between the yellow mud streets and the paper-mache huts leaning loosely together like a toppled stack of egg boxes. At the foot of Shioiri, two Japanese girls in tight western style dresses waited to greet them. The girls appeared to be in their late teens but were closer to their mid-twenties. A natural look of youthful innocence was something Yokosuka belles capitalized on.

"What you know, Joe...you from big Mo?" inquired the more buxom of the two. The second girl just smiled and tried to look seductive.

To Logan's astonishment, Murray gave the talkative one a playful slap on her girdleless buttocks. The girl giggled almost shyly and asked, You 'rike, heh, sailor boy?"

"Yeah, but Mary Alice wouldn't!"

Logan and Murray walked on and in a few minutes were back at Hunky-dory.

"You kinda' surprised me back there, Howie," Logan laughed good-naturedly.

"Oh, you mean patting Tokyo Rose on the rump," he smiled. "Hell, there's no harm in that. Actually I probably boosted her morale a little. How come you didn't decide to hop into the saddle?"

"I've never had to pay a broad for her wares, I certainly don't plan to start doing it now. There's one possible exception though," Logan's face relaxed and his eyes lit up, "I've always been real hot to make it with a geisha, not just any geisha but one with a lot of class, you know the kind that only cater to captains of industry or old Jap generals."

"You must have read 'Terry and the Pirates' too much when you were a kid," Murray said briskly.

"If you mean 'Dragon Lady' she was Chinese and not a geisha, but you've got the general idea."

"Yeah, but I thought geisha's weren't hookers."

"They're not, but I understand if you've got the right connections, special arrangements can be made."

"What special connections do you have over here?" Murray looked at Logan quizzically.

"Last year my boss roped me into taking a couple of big-shot Japanese businessmen around New York. I wined and dined them and took them to El Morocco and a couple of Broadway shows, all on B and G, of course. I even shot a whole afternoon taking them for a ride on the Staten Island ferry. By the way, during that ferry ride, we passed pretty close to your *Franklin* and *Enterprise*. Do you know they're mothballed right next to each other at the Bayonne Naval Base?"

"Yeah, I saw them two years ago when I took Mary Alice to New York to celebrate our wedding anniversary. It was really depressing."

"Your wedding anniversary?" Logan feigned innocence.

"No, of course not! I mean the ships. It was depressing to see what miserable condition they were in. They looked like two gray ghosts sitting there with a bunch of sea gulls nesting on their flightdecks, and their paint all faded and peeling off."

"*Sic transit gloria mundi*...it happens to the best of us sooner or later, Howie," muttered Logan as the two re-entered the naval base.

The petty officers club was drab and gray but within an easy walk of Carney Gate. Fortunately for its bluejacket clientele, what it lacked in ambiance and decor it made up for in the excellence of its table. The *piece de resistance* that evening was pan-fried rainbow trout squired by giant frogs legs of a quality and meatiness rarely encountered outside Japan. Logan and Murray were debating whether they should split a second helping when they were interrupted by a familiar voice.

"Great chow, heh," yelled Bacelli anxiously as he and Gardiner plopped down at the table.

"How come you two are still haunting the base?" Logan asked in a vexed tone. "I figured you'd be well-established with one of the local mamma-sans by now."

"Can't work on an empty stomach, you know," Gardiner smirked.

"Yeah, we just finished eatin', except for dessert," Bacelli added. "We're on our way back to Hunky-dory now. We found a fantastic place about three blocks from the base. Loaded with broads...and hey, I thought the Jap babes were supposed to be flat-chested. You should see the knockers on this bunch!" Bacelli held out his hands to emphasize his point.

"Well, don't let us keep you," Murray said.

The two third-class ignored the barb.

"What'd you try, the trout?" Bacelli asked, staring queerly at the eyes in the fish heads left on the two plates.

"That's right," Murray said in a guarded tone calculated not to prolong the conversation.

"How was it?" Bacelli persisted.

"A lot better than your buddy Turk dishes out," Kevin shrugged.

"Hell, the chow we get ain't so bad," Gardiner cut in. "You should have been around before Royal came aboard."

"I hate to have to agree with him, but he's right," Murray said swiveling around in his chair. "I've fed my dog better chow than the swill we got while Carver was C.O."

"Yeah, it was so bad we couldn't even attract any sharks when we dumped the left-overs off the fantail," said Bacelli.

"That's funny," Logan said lighting up a cigarette. "The reserve DE's I've cruised on always served passable chow. It wouldn't win any awards from Duncan Hines but at least it was eatable."

"Well, your DEs probably didn't have a prick like Cobb for exec," Gardiner snapped. "We'd still be eating moldy bread and rubber frankfurters if it wasn't for Royal."

"Yeah, those hot dogs were green inside," Bacelli cried out. "One thing though, you've got to give Cobb credit for being shrewd. He knows he doesn't have the free hand he had when Carver was skipper. He's playing it close to the vest these days but that doesn't mean he won't slip it to the old man first chance he gets."

"Hell, he already has," Gardiner said with a low, rumbling laugh. "The story's all over the ship how the captain took the rap for that near collision with the *Crown Point* while old Cobb came out of the whole thing smellin' as rosey as a French whorehouse."

"They're not exaggerating about the chow," Murray frowned. "The *Field* was probably the only ship in the whole damn navy that served powered milk and powdered eggs while we were in port. And even worse than that," continued Murray, "we never had half enough silverware. If you weren't in the first part of the chow line, you'd have to stand around waiting until somebody finished eating. Then if someone else didn't beat you to it, you might be able to grab his knife and fork. It was bad enough when we only had ships' company aboard. You can imagine how it got when we were carrying our full quota of reserves."

"What about the supply officer?" Kevin asked. "Didn't you have one when Carver was C.O.?"

"Yeah, that was Lieutenant Maye, but he was only aboard a few months when he got transferred to 'Gitmo.' I always figured the exec had something to do with getting Maye shit-canned. I heard them talking a few times. From what they said, I'm sure they must have sailed with each other in the merchants before they joined the navy. Anyway, I could tell they knew each other real well."

"Think Cobb was pocketing part of the ship's commissary allotment?" Logan probed.

"I've got no way of knowing that," Bacelli replied in a half-whisper. "One thing I do know, he sure wasn't spending the money on our chow."

"How'd he ever keep the reserves from complaining?" Kevin asked. "I can see how he could make it tough on ships' company but what could he do to reserves? He only had them under this thumb for two weeks. And I know from the cruises I took, the navy always had us fill out a form on the last morning of the cruise just before we were released from active duty. The form was a regular critique. It gave us a chance to complain about the food, the quality of the training, the berthing arrangements...hell, just about everything. Then the form got forwarded to the local naval district and the reserve training command. How could he get around that?"

"Oh, that was no problem for Cobb," Gardiner said. "Instead of giving the form to the reserves that last Saturday morning, he'd have it distributed on Wednesday. Then he'd personally examine each critique and if he found a complaint, he'd pressure the reserve to change it."

"How could he do that?" Kevin asked.

"He'd call the reserve into his cabin and question him about any negative comments. If the reserve wouldn't fill out a new critique, he'd threaten to write the guy up for everything from wearing non-regulation dungarees to allowing himself to get sunburned while on watch. Most of the reserves were non-rated men with no active time in the navy. It was a breeze for Cobb to buffalo them. He found it tougher with petty officers. He'd usually ask one of the reserve officers taking the cruise to advise the guy to tone down his complaints. If the reserve still wouldn't change what he wrote, Cobb had almost four days to build up a case against the guy. You know how easy that is to do if you're really looking to hang something on somebody," Gardiner smiled. "And the exec could always give the guy an 'unsat' on his performance while on the cruise. That would fuck him up for taking any future tests for promotions. If the guy bitched when he got back to his training center, Cobb would say he was just a trouble-maker trying to get even for being put on report. And he had another cute trick...his ace in the hole. You know when a reserve goes on training duty, he's legally drawing pay for two full weeks."

"Yeah, so what?"

"It's usual policy throughout the navy to let the reserves off on Saturday morning as soon as the ship gets back from the cruise."

"That's right," Logan nodded.

"Well, whenever Cobb came up against a tough cookie who wouldn't change his critique, the exec would threaten to keep the guy working aboard the ship until one minute before midnight. No matter how pissed-off the reserve was, he'd be so damn glad to get off the *Field* that a little thing like changing a few remarks on a piece of paper wouldn't seem like such a big deal. The guy would just chalk the two weeks up to experience and remember not to ever sign up for another reserve cruise aboard the Charlie P. Occasionally, a reserve would gripe when he got back to his reserve center, but from what Gordy says, his training officer, not wanting to rock the boat, would just stash the complaint away in the old circular file."

"Even the reserve officers got a lousy deal when they came aboard for their two weeks active duty," Murray explained. "I guess it didn't pay for them to bitch though. They had that old fitness report to consider and Carver and Cobb were the boys who made it out. Like the white hats, I imagine they just figured the two weeks were past history and not worth involving themselves in navy red tape and a possible court of inquiry. You know, one foul ball like Cobb could screw up the navy's entire reserve training program," Murray shrugged. "I guess the *Field's* being sent to Korea is the luckiest break the reserves could have gotten."

"Carver's foul-up in Catalina was a real bad break for Cobb," Bacelli laughed. "I don't think he'll ever adjust to not being kingfish on the *Field* anymore. I've noticed he's been twice as obnoxious since we left Pearl. Either that or he's starting to go 'ape shit.' He jumped all over Ensign Daly Monday because he asked the *Ward* for a repeat on the TBS message, and yesterday he gave Ritter a royal blast for a little thing like the gun-director being secured a degree or two off the ship's centerline."

"I heard he chewed out Kimmick and Phelan during special-sea-detail this morning," said Gardiner eagerly. "Sammartino says he called them a couple of lint-brained reserves in front of half the 'snipes' in E division. Hey, there's Parish," Gardiner said, motioning to the pharmacist mate.

"Sit down and pull up a frog's leg," Bacelli greeted the newcomer.

"No, thanks, I've eaten. I just stopped in for a beer."

"Where you been all day...out trying to learn if there's any scientific validity to that old quip about Chinese girls?" Logan laughed.

"No, I've been at the base hospital," Parish answered, not entirely certain which quip the radarman had referenced to, especially since they were in Japan, not China. "Things look pretty good," the young sailor continued excitedly. "I met a corpsman at the hospital who's got a buddy with the First Marine Division. He thinks he can arrange a swap within a month or so. His friend's a third-class, same as me, so there shouldn't be any complications. We'll just have to get an okay from his C.O. and Commander Royal."

"Now why do you want to go over there with the mud-marines and get your tail shot off?" Gardiner grinned. "Stick with us. The navy'd never dare let the Charlie P. get in range of any real shooting."

"I didn't leave college to go sightseeing," Parish declared sternly. "Korea's the only place I can really learn something about being a doctor. And at the same time, I'll feel I'm paying my own way."

"Soon as you get a bullet bouncing inside your tin bonnet," Bacelli laughed, "you'll wish you were back on the *Field* with us free-loading tourists."

"I'm not worried. Anyway, you guys don't need me. Chief Claccum and a couple of shots of penicillin will take care of the worst thing the *Field's* ever going to encounter."

"When the 'gooks' start chopping you up for chow mein, just remember we warned you. Brrr," quivered Gardiner. "I don't like the idea of getting stuck with a bayonet. Otherwise I might have joined the jarheads and become a 'grunt' myself. I always liked that dress uniform the marines have. You've got to admit it's a hell-of-a-lot sharper looking than this monkey suit."

"Yeah, that may be if you don't mind looking like a sea-going bellhop," Murray shot back, his face suddenly flushed. "What makes you think the navy's such a soft racket? Ever have to ride out a full-fledged typhoon like the kind we had in the Pacific in '44 and '45? Why don't you ask Kevin here about the pleasure cruise he took to the picket line at Okinawa aboard the *Laffey?* Do you guys have any idea what it's like when a ship gets turned into a giant blast furnace in a matter of seconds, or how it feels to float in water ass-hole deep in sharks, with maybe a half gallon of fuel oil in your lungs? When it comes to fighting...and dying too, the navy doesn't have to take a back seat to the gyrenes, the army, the Toonerville irregulars or anybody else!"

"Bravo, Howie," Logan laughed loudly. "You really put your heart into that one. I don't think a spokesman for the Navy League could have phrased it more eloquently. But aren't you the guy who hates the navy so much?"

"You're damned right I am, and I still do! I just wanted to set these morons straight, that's all."

"Okay, okay," Bacelli agreed with a sheepish grin. "You're talking about the big war. We were still in grade school for that one. You know as well as I do, that the Charlie P. will never get anywhere near any North Koreans. Now, before Gardiner and I take off for Hunky-dory, let's see what's for dessert."

•　　•　　•

Thursday, July 3rd was an easy day for Destroyer Division 291. Since the men would not be in port to celebrate the upcoming holiday, maximum liberty was authorized on all four ships. Among the events scheduled for enlisted personnel was a Fourth of July Eve dance, replete with attractive young hostesses, mostly Japanese girls employed in clerical positions by the base administration or as members of the sales staff at the navy exchange.

Due to the division's imminent departure for Korean waters, only commissioned officers were afforded the privilege of traveling beyond Yokosuka's immediate boundaries. With only one day at their disposal, Commanders Royal and Boland opted to forgo the slightly longer trip to Tokyo or Yokohama in favor of a visit to Kamakura, a quiet little town overlooking Sagami Bay and famed for its great Buddha, or *Daibutsu*. After climbing inside the 42-foot-high bronze figure, the two officers went on to the nearby Hase Kannon temple and then to view the Hachimangu shrine, one of the oldest in Japan.

It was late afternoon when Royal and Boland made their way back through the grove of cherry trees that served as a delicate setting for the shrine.

"How's my old buddy Henderson doing?" Sandy Boland asked with a chuckle.

"Frankly, I hope he's not doing well at all," Owen retorted with the faint hint of a smile. "Maybe he'll lay off us for awhile. After all, he got his licks in pretty good that day we almost totaled the *Crown Point*."

"That's my boy," said Boland breezily. "Speaking of boys, what'd you think of Price's little pep talk this morning?"

"Well, I can't say it did anything to brighten my day, especially that bit about the shore batteries increasing in number and accuracy during the past six months. It's almost like the Reds knew we were coming."

"Cheer up," Boland laughed, "maybe we'll earn that forty-five dollars a month combat pay after all. Hell, according to the rules the navy's set up for us, all we have to do is take a direct hit from the enemy or else be bracketed by enemy shell fire six days a month. Sounds easy, doesn't it?"

"Yes, and Price emphasized that when the navy says bracketed, the navy means bracketed. The shell splashes have to fall on both sides of us. Now what imbecile back in the Pentagon do you suppose came up with that little gem?"

"I don't know, but I'd like to hang the son-of-a-bitch out on the edge of my bridge-wing with a ruler in his hand and let him measure each splash so he can tell whether or not the shell fell close enough for us to qualify," said Boland angrily. "Do you realize the way those rules are set up, we could come under direct fire fifty times a day for five days and not rate combat pay?"

"That's right, and apparently mines don't count at all...that is, unless we actually run into one."

"A lot of our ships seem to be doing that lately," Sandy Boland grinned wryly.

"Well, at least our men might have a chance to pick up a little extra cash, even if it is only forty-five bucks a month," Owen said.

"Personally, I hope they keep us out with the carriers and we don't qualify at all," Sandy laughed. "I had enough people shooting at me in the last one to do me for my lifetime. I'll be perfectly content just screening the airedale navy. They can keep their lousy forty-five dollars."

"You know, except for pilots, the carrier crews aren't drawing a penny of combat pay even though they're attacking up and down the coast in easy range of Red aircraft," Royal observed as he and his companion approached the small touring bus which would take them to a local hotel for dinner.

"From what I've been reading in those ComNavFe dispatches," said Boland, "the flattops are taking more casualties from flightdeck accidents than the 'cans' and 'sweeps' are taking from shore fire."

"I guess that's understandable when you consider the conditions the carriers are operating under. I imagine on an average, each one must be launching well over a hundred sorties a day in every type of weather. And of course what goes up must come down. Can you imagine how hairy it must be bringing in a shot-up jet with live ordinance under its wing?"

"And they've been doing that in pitch blackness with snow and ice on their flight decks," Boland shrugged. "How long do you think this damn war's going to drag on anyway? Think anything will come of those talks in Panmunjom?"

"Nothing has so far," Owen answered almost gruffly. "It seems to me the Reds are just using the truce talks as a sounding board for their propaganda."

"I really feel sorry for those poor guys over on the beach," Boland said. "From the pictures I've seen, Korea's just one rocky hill after another. It sure must be rough, fighting in terrain like that. We've got it soft compared to what those 'dog faces' must be going through over there. My brother was almost caught by the Chinese up near the Chosin Reservoir. He was lucky to make it out via Hungnam.

Unfortunately, he lost all the fingers on his right hand...frostbite. They discharged him from the marines last month. My sister-in-law wrote and told me he's taking it quite badly. Tom was really gung-ho about the Corps. He'd made all the nasty ones from Guadalcanal right on through Okinawa without getting a scratch. He had a good shot at making flag-rank, too, if it hadn't been for this dirty little war that nobody back home even cares about. I'm sure, thirty years from now nobody in the States will even remember that there ever was a Korean War."

"I'm not certain they're aware of it now. The newspapers certainly have put it on the back burner. Marilyn Monroe gets more publicity these days than 'Punchbowl' and the 'Iron Triangle' combined. For that matter, I suppose we shouldn't even be referring to it as a war," said Owen bitterly. "After all, our commander-in-chief, Harry Truman, insists on calling it a police action."

"Well, then as one cop to another, how good do you think those Red shore batteries really are? From that intelligence report Price passed around this morning, I got the impression that most of their costal guns lack radar."

"They don't need it. They've seeded range buoys all across the harbors and along the coast to mark our position. Besides that, they've started using VT-fuzed ammo so any shells passing overhead will burst like flak showering the whole ship with shrapnel. With that stuff, they won't have to score a direct hit to hurt us," Royal said gravely.

"How effective do you think our five-inch will be as far as counter-battery fire's concerned?"

"Not very. I doubt if anything less than a cruiser's eight-inch will do any real damage. If I read that report correctly, most of their guns are mounted on railroad tracks and hidden deep in caves dug in the face of cliffs. The openings are small, just large enough to give the gun a wide arc of fire. With the entrance covered by camouflage netting and drop cloths, there's no way we're going to spot them till their muzzles are pointing down our throats."

"Looks like this could turn out to be a real fun cruise," Boland sighed.

"Cheer up, Sandy. With all those mine fields we're going to run into over there, we won't have time to worry about little things like shore batteries. And besides, aren't you jumping the gun?"

"If that's a pun, Owen, it's in damn poor taste."

"As far as I know, nobody's assigned us to the blockade force. The only orders I've seen say we'll be operating with Task Force 77, not Task Force 95."

"Hell, most of the 'cans' with 77 rotate over to 95 sooner or later," Boland grunted.

"Well, if we do, it'll break the monotony of screening the carriers forty or fifty days at a clip."

"Good old Owen...always the optimist."

The two officers boarded the bus for the short ride to the hotel.

● ● ●

Hardly had the men of DesDiv 291 turned out of their bunks when word blared over the speakers on all four destroyers announcing that special-sea-detail would be set at 06:00, a full hour earlier than the time listed on the plan-of-the-day for 4 July.

"What a kick in the ass," Bacelli barked loudly as he bounced into the combat-information-center.

"Hook into that JA circuit and make sure Farber's manning his talker-station up in the bridge," Murray instructed, tossing a set of sound-powered phones in Bacelli's general direction. "Anybody see Mister Coates?" the first-class asked, slipping a set of phones over his crew cut.

"Who knows?" Holiday growled back. "He's probably in the wardroom enjoying a leisurely breakfast with the rest of the officers while we're down here breaking our hump an hour earlier than we were supposed to!"

"Yeah, Murray, how come special-sea-detail went so damn early?" Gardiner snarled from his perch near the DRT. "When the hell are we gonna' get some breakfast?"

"Don't sweat it. From the looks of that pot-belly you're starting to develop, I don't think waiting an extra hour or so is going to kill you," Murray retorted, prompting an exuberant "amen" from Logan.

"Hey! Turn those lights down a little," Nugent yelled from the inner sanctum of the Sugar-George surface radar. "How do you guys expect me to focus this scope if you're gonna' keep all the lights on out there?"

"Hold your water," Logan shot back. "I'm still looking for the chart of the inner harbor!"

"I wonder if those Jap broads got off okay," Holiday pondered aloud as he squeezed behind the vertical status board.

"What Jap broads?" boomed the question in perfect sync from Murray, Logan, Nugent, Gardiner, Bacelli and Belton.

"The two that Hauser and Goff snuck aboard last night. They picked them up at the dance over at the base."

"How do you know?" Nugent asked indignantly.

"Goff told me. I got up to take a leak about four o'clock, and when I got down to the head, Goff and Hauser wouldn't let me in."

"What do you mean they wouldn't let you in?" asked Murray.

"Well, the showers were running. They said they had made it with these two Jap girls in the gun shack and the girls were taking a shower before they left the ship."

"That's rich, shackin' up in the gun shack," Gardiner laughed.

"Shut up, Gardiner!" Nugent cut in, "Let him finish! Did you see the girls?" he asked eagerly.

"Well, kinda'," Holiday answered through the Plexiglas of the vertical plot, "at least I saw one leg. It was stickin' out of the shower when she reached for a towel. Personally, I was wishing those two bastards would get caught with the broads. Can you imagine, when I told them I had to piss real bad, Goff told me to go find a Dixie cup!"

"How'd they get them aboard?" Logan asked.

"They did it after ten when there was no officer on the quarterdeck. Their buddy, Van Ginderen, had the watch. Since we're the inboard ship for a change, they didn't have to sweat taking them across the *Wayne*. They told me they were gonna get them off the ship before reveille. Since there wouldn't be an officer at the quarterdeck until time for colors, they figured they had it made in the shade."

"Well, did they get them off okay?" Bacelli asked.

"Guess so, I don't know. I went aft and pissed off the fantail. When I went back to the head to wash up, they were gone. Next thing I know, the *Field's* sounding early reveille and the lights are poppin' on all over the ship."

"Goff and Hauser can't be playing with a full deck, pulling a crazy stunt like that," Murray shrugged. "I always thought those damn fire-controlmen were a little ape shit. Must come from being up so high in the gun director."

"Hey, watch it, Howie," Logan laughed. "I spent the best part of World War II inside a Mark 37."

Hitting the steel bulkhead with a loud snapping sound, the door to the radar shack suddenly flew open.

"All manned and ready in here?" Ensign Coates asked, heading directly for the plotting table.

Three decks above the radar shack on the open bridge, Owen Royal leaned far out over the wind guard, his eyes taking a quick accounting of the sailors on the foc'sle and the other line handlers stationed strategically along the inboard side of the main weather deck.

"Single up all lines!" the captain ordered, pointing the bullhorn at the seamen below. Glancing to the outboard side, he watched *Halsey Wayne* slip neatly away. Within minutes, Sandy Boland's destroyer was well out in mid-channel, pivoting slowly, bright pennants fluttering from her taut halyards.

"Cast off the stern lines!" Royal bellowed. Then in rapid succession, he gave orders to the line handlers on the pier who instantly complied by loosing the five remaining hawsers. An hour later all four *Fletchers* were steaming in the familiar column formation, the *Field* as usual, bringing up the rear.

The black smokestacks of a sooty Yokosuka were fading in the morning haze as Royal joined Cobb in the wardroom for coffee and a discussion of their upcoming meeting with the fast carriers. The two officers were studying a chart of the Sea of Japan showing the North Korean coastal area near Yang Do just below the 41st parallel, their point of rendezvous with Task Force 77. It was just past ten when Ensign Ritter entered the wardroom, his face pasty white, his expression that of someone about to light a very short fuse.

"What's up, George?" Royal laughed amiably. "You look like you just had an encounter with our resident phantom, Chief Henderson."

"Sir, I wish that was all I had to report," the young officer stammered nervously. "Mister MacKinlay sent me to tell you that we've got two unauthorized civilians on board."

"We've got what on board?" Cobb asked incredulously before Royal could respond.

"We've got two foreign nationals on board, Sir." The words came out slowly as if he was forcing them through a strainer. "I think they're Japanese."

"What do you mean you think they're Japanese?" the captain exclaimed. "don't you know?"

"Eh, yes, Sir, they're definitely Japanese."

"Well, Mister, are you going to tell me what this is all about or do I have to pull it out of you word by word?"

"No, Captain. They're Japanese females. They work at the navy exchange in Yokosuka. They were hostesses at the dance on the base last night, and two of our men, Goff and Hauser, brought them back to the ship. I imagine they thought they could sneak them off before we went to special-sea-detail but leaving an hour early must have screwed up their plans a little."

"Should we ask if anything else got screwed in the course of their overnight stay, Mister?" the exec cut in.

"I don't know about that. Goff and Hauser didn't say. I kinda' suspect they were fooling around, though. The four of them spent the night in the gun shack."

"Where are the two young ladies now? I assume they are young," Royal said, trying to retain his composure.

"Yes, Sir, I'd say they're about twenty."

"I guess we can be thankful they're not underage," Royal sighed.

"Yes, Sir. They're down in the messhall. Mr. MacKinlay and Chief Pheifer are questioning them now. Goff and Hauser are down there, too, Sir. Pheifer's instructed his master-at-arms force to keep everyone out of the messhall."

"Did you get the names of these girls?" Owen asked.

"Yes, Sir, I have them here on this paper. One's named Keiko Hayama. The other's Ayako Ishihara," the ensign said, glancing at the small pad he was carrying.

"Who had the quarterdeck when they came aboard?" Cobb demanded.

"Goff and Hauser were deliberately vague about that, Sir."

"Oh, they were, were they! Well, it had to be sometime after Daly secured so we shouldn't have any trouble finding out who the watch P.O. was," the exec grinned smugly.

"Mister MacKinlay said to ask if you want Chief Pheifer to bring the four of them up here?" Ritter asked, looking at the *Field's* C.O.

"No! If I get within ten feet of those two cretins, I'm liable to boot both of them overboard! Too bad this ship doesn't have a brig. If it did, I'd lock them in it and toss the key off the fantail. Have the stewards feed our two visitors and try to make them comfortable till we decide what we're going to do," said Royal with a worried look. "Right now, my biggest concern is how to spring this piece of news on the commodore. We obviously can't take two young women into a combat zone."

"Yes, Sir," Ritter agreed meekly, then departed.

"Maybe we can detour over to Pusan long enough to drop them off. I'm sure arrangements can be made to have them flown back to Japan," Cobb suggested trying hard to conceal the delight he was taking in his C.O.'s predicament.

"No, that's not practical," Royal frowned. "Pusan's two day's steaming time from here. That means we'd have to arrange overnight berthing for our two Madam Butterflies. Besides, Pusan's a good ten or twelve hours off our base course."

"Yes, I didn't think of that," Cobb said, wondering if Royal would be able to weather this latest ill fortune.

"Well, no point in postponing the inevitable," Royal forced a smile. "I'm going to call Price and ask permission to return to Yokosuka so we can say *sayonara* to our uninvited passengers. Hopefully, we'll be able to catch up to the division before Wednesday morning when they hitch up with Seventy-seven."

·   ·   ·

It was sunset when *Charles P. Field* slinked back into Yokosuka and hastily discharged her two unwelcome guests. The warships moored all around them in the bay and those on berth at the base were taking down their holiday bunting as *DD-505* once again knifed her way back down the channel towards Sagami Wan and the open sea beyond.

Sometimes radarman, presently mess cook Patterson, taking a moment's breather from his chores below in the scullery was saddened to see the flamboyant little pennants come flapping down all around the harbor. Few sights in life he would argue were as breathtaking as that of a fleet at full dress, and he felt the same discomforting twinge of melancholy he always experienced as a child whenever it came time for his parents to discard the Christmas tree.

The wind was dead astern, humid and dense, as the young sailor secured a line to one of the dirty swabs he was carrying. He gingerly lowered it over the fantail into the destroyer's cleansing wake, then watched the mop smack up and down as it skimmed along the surface of the water. His line of sight followed the *Field's* white track back towards Yokosuka and suddenly he was aware that he was leaving the security of the stockade...that at last he was heading for "Indian Country."

Chapter X - Indian Country

Murray flattened his back against the steel bulkhead at the base of the bridge trying unsuccessfully to avoid the spray that swirled up over the foc'sle in thick green sheets. He could see *Halsey Wayne* up ahead, heeling from side to side, as were *Morgan* and *Ward* further up the column. His eyes still smarted from the salt as he entered the radar shack.

"Hey, Howie," bellowed Bacelli from the plotting table, "what's with this speed run? I thought we were gonna' slow down once we caught up with the division?"

"That's what I thought," Murray frowned. "I guess the commodore wants to make sure we reach the task force on time tomorrow. What's our position now?"

"We're forty miles due east of Kosong...that's Kosong...like in Kosong, North Korea," Bacelli announced solemnly, glancing down at the penciled track line on the chart.

"Anything on the scopes?" the first-class asked.

"No, and that's okay by me," Holiday quickly added from his seat at the Sugar-Charlie air search. "I'd hate to get caught up here by a bunch of Migs, especially since nobody's bothered to give us any air cover."

"There's nothing to worry about," Murray retorted dryly. "This war's been on two years now and you can count the number of air attacks against our ships on the fingers of one hand. When I was on the 'Big E,' we'd fight off more than that in a single hour."

"Yeah, but you old salts didn't have jets to sweat back in the stone age," Bacelli quipped. "The pop guns the Charlie P.'s toting around are completely obsolete against the kind of planes they're flying today."

"Speaking of obsolete," yelled Gardiner from the adjacent coffee mess, "I know a couple of fire-controlmen and a pipe fitter-second who are gonna' be obsolete pretty damn soon."

"Where'd you hear that?" Bacelli asked.

"From Gordon. He told me all three of them are getting a summary court martial."

"Van Ginderen, too?"

"Damn right. Gordon says the old man's even more pissed off at him than he is at Goff and Hauser."

"What about Mister Daly? He was OD for that watch," Holiday asked, glancing up from the SC-radar.

"Gordon says Cobb wants to ream his ass, too."

"What's new about that?" Bacelli snickered. "Cobb wants to ream everybody's ass. He gets his jollies out of shafting people."

"Gordon overheard Cobb and the captain discussing Daly this morning," Gardiner said, placing an Eddie Fisher record on the small 45-player. "You know, with that open vent they got up there, Gordon can sit in the personnel records office and hear every word that's being said next door in the ship's office."

"Yeah, I know, get on with it! What'd he hear?" Holiday demanded irritably.

"He heard Royal tell the exec that it's been accepted procedure aboard the *Field* for the officer-of-the-deck to shift his watch to the wardroom after ten at night, providing the ship's at a safe berth at a US base and as long as he checks the quarterdeck watch at least two or three times each hour. The captain said he was satisfied that Daly followed those guidelines."

"Did Cobb buy that?" Murray asked.

"Hell no! Cobb said he still thinks Daly should be charged with dereliction of duty as an example for the other reserve officers who he said are always slackin' off."

"The exec sure hates reserves," Bacelli grinned.

"Except for the captain and that prick MacKinlay, every officer on board is a reserve," Holiday interjected.

"Well, what'd the old man finally decide?" Murray grumbled impatiently.

"Royal said he wasn't gonna' punish Daly for what's been standard procedure up till now, but in the future he wants an officer at the quarterdeck right around the clock no matter where the ship is berthed."

"Did Gordon tell you who's going to be the summary court officer?" inquired Murray.

"No, that's still up in the air. He did say that old Cobb didn't lose any time volunteering for the job."

"Too bad he wasn't around during the Spanish Inquisition," Murray smiled. "He would have had a field day."

"Gordon said Cobb tried his damndest to talk the old man into putting the three of them up for a general court martial instead of only a summary so the navy could really throw the book at them. Cobb suggested that the charge should specify that through their willful actions, the ship was almost late in meeting her combat assignment."

"Wow," Murray exclaimed. "He's really out for blood, and I mean that literally. A charge like that could bring the death penalty."

"You're kidding, aren't you?" Bacelli asked hesitantly.

"The hell I am! Just take a look at the UCMJ manual. Your buddy Gordon's got a copy in ship's office."

"Well, at least they won't have to sweat that," Gardiner grinned wryly. "Gordon said the old man flatly refused to give them a general. He told Cobb that a general court martial would mean that Goff, Hauser and Van Ginderen would have to be transferred ashore, and with trained fire-controlmen at a premium these days, to say nothing of pipe fitters, he didn't want to take the chance of permanently losing them and maybe not getting equivalent replacements. Gordon doesn't really think that's his reason, though," Gardiner added, slowly sipping black coffee from a colorful mug the size of a small bucket.

"What do you mean?" asked Murray.

"Gordon thinks that the captain's really afraid that a general court martial would screw them up for the rest of their lives. The least punishment they could expect would be a couple of years on the rock pile at Portsmouth, followed by a dishonorable discharge. The captain told Cobb that he considers that a hell of a price to pay for a quick roll in the hay."

"It hurts me to admit this, especially about anyone in the regular navy, but the skipper's my idea of what's meant by the expression an officer and a gentleman," said Murray. "One thing's certain, he cares a lot about the welfare of the crew. It's a shame they can't reciprocate a little. You know, since Royal's been on board, this bucket's become a floating example of Murphy's Law...if anything can go wrong, it will. The sad thing is that none of what's happened has been the old man's fault. Of course, the navy won't look at it that way. They'll see it as an indication of piss-poor leadership. Hell, if Bull Halsey was our skipper, I don't think he'd even be able to avoid the screw-ups we've had in the last few months." Then, in a choked tone, Murray added, "I really felt sorry for Royal the other day...the way the commodore chewed him out over the radio telephone. Can you imagine how embarrassing it must have been."

"Yeah," Gardiner laughed. "I bet the whole Seventh Fleet heard it."

"That's not likely since the transmitting range is only line-of-sight, but it's a safe bet anyone anywhere near the receiver on the other three 'cans' heard it," the first-class snapped.

"I thought officers weren't supposed to chew out other officers, especially ship's captains in front of white hats," Holiday interrupted eagerly. "When Price started screaming and ranting all over the circuit, I was sure he was havin' some kind of fit. Personally, I don't know what all the fuss is about. I bet we're not the first ship that ever started out for war with a couple of broads," the third-class said in a vain attempt at humor.

"If you think Price sounded mad over the TBS," Gardiner cut in, "can you imagine what it must have been like in the *Ward's* wheelhouse. Can't you just see him jumpin' up and down like a virgin makin' the most of her first goose."

From behind them in the coffee mess came the voice of Eddie Fisher telling the radar gang that "they're not making the skies as blue this year."

• • •

"Tracy...I need something quick and light, just enough to hold me until I get to L.A.," Candace told her secretary, a fortyish woman with ruddy cheeks. "What do you recommend?"

"How about shrimp and avocado with Norwegian flat-bread? That's today's special at Leonard's."

"Alright, and some coffee, black as usual. I'm going up to Ronald Paradise's office. I should be back before it arrives."

"Oh, they've also got a special on passion fruit cheesecake. It's really great. Want them to put in a slice?"

"I'd better pass on that. I may need my bathing suit this weekend. I want to be able to fit into it," she said exiting.

Dressed perpetually in a dark suit and vest, Ronald Paradise was on the phone, his back to Candace as she entered his doorless office. Reconciled to the unpleasant reality of Candace's reign, Paradise had quickly made the conversion from sulking antagonist to fawning sycophant, a shift in attitude that gained him no favor with the perceptive Miss Moffet.

As Candace settled her well-rounded bottom in a leather studio chair, Ronald swiveled around. "Good morning, Candace," he beamed, replacing the receiver. "How do you always manage to look like you just materialized from the cover of *Vogue?*"

"I take a special pill," she said unsmiling. "Now that the bullshit's out of the way, what time this afternoon can I expect to have the final proposals for the Cherokee contest? You know, I'm booked on a six-fifteen flight to Los Angeles, and Bill Lydecker expects me to have the complete format on his desk at nine tomorrow morning."

"Tomorrow? I thought we had at least another week? I'm sorry," Paradise swallowed hard.

"Another week! You've had three weeks already!"

"Well yes, but a contest as big as this one needs a lot of thought. We can't just ask the public to come up with a slogan for a motorcycle, you know."

"Why can't we?"

"Let me see how Beerey's doing," Ronald said after a long pause.

"Beerey? What's Beerey got to do with the Cherokee contest? I thought he was all tied up with Dandy Andy frankfurters? We've promised Dandy Andy triple spotting on "*Beat the Clock*" for August, and we'd better deliver or a half-million dollar account goes down the tubes. J. Walter and B.B.D. and O. are both breathing down our necks on this one."

"Oh, you don't have to worry about Dandy Andy," Paradise bluffed, feeling the blood pumping in his head. "Beerey's got the entire promotion well in hand."

"Have you seen the copy?"

"Yes, I certainly have. In fact, I just finished checking it over. It plays like Beethoven. I'm sure it's exactly what they're looking for."

"Can I read it?"

"I don't have it here."

"Well, when can you get it? Beerey does still work for us, doesn't he?" she asked sternly, her blue eyes afire.

"Yes, of course he does. Only right now I think he's working on the Valtex copy."

"Valtex? Didn't you tell me last week that you were personally preparing all the copy for that account?"

"Yes, but I've been up to my neck with Baker's Dozen. I had to reluctantly pass Valtex on to him."

"From what I remember, the Baker's Dozen material was pretty straight-for-ward. They didn't even ask us for a jingle this time. I assume you have the copy finished," she smiled, then said softly, "Mike Bannon said he gave you the video over a month ago. He'd like to know when he can go ahead with the dubbing? Well, answer me!" she snapped. "Is it ready?"

"Yes, I was just going to ask Marianne to bring it down."

"You can give it to me. I'm going down there now. I'll give it to him."

"On second thought, I'd better proof it one more time before I let Bannon's crew get their hands on it. I wouldn't want any foul-ups," said Paradise, his voice quavering noticeably.

"I'm beginning to think the only foul-up around here is you!"

"Now, I don't think that's completely fair, Candace. I believe I've done a pretty good job of coping with an exceptionally heavy workload."

"From what I've observed so far, your idea of coping is to pass all your work off to your subordinates! In two hours, I expect to see the complete Cherokee for-mat, sample questions and all, on my desk. Do you read me loud and clear?"

"Yes," Ronald frowned.

As Candace took her leave, Paradise made a solemn vow to fix his boss lady's wagon, for good!"

• • •

"Skunk Jig...2-9-1...22,000 yards, Skunk King...2-8-5...21,300 yards, Hold it! I've got another one," Nugent exclaimed from his perch at the surface search. "New skunk bearing 2-9-7...range 44,000 yards. New skunk's a cluster...two or three pips. Yes, I make the new skunk out to be three large!"

"Bridge, combat! We hold a new contact which appears to be three large ships at 3-9-7...44,000 yards!" Ensign Coates shouted into the open mouth of the voice tube.

"Bridge, aye," came the acknowledgement in blase tone from the executive officer three decks above in the wheelhouse. "Designate your new contacts Skunks Love, Mike and Nan...track and report!"

"We've sure got ourselves a lot of company all of a sudden," Coates said, turning to Logan who was hunched busily over the plotting table. "That's the task force, all right. Give me a relative bearing to the closest contacts," the young officer yelled back at Nugent.

"They're all ahead...relative bearings anywhere from 3-4-5 to 0-1-5," the third-class replied in a begrudging manner.

"CAPRICORN...THIS IS HARLOT...WE HOLD VISUAL CONTACT WITH MANY SKUNKS...3-5-5 RELATIVE...LONE SKUNK AT 0-0-5 RELATIVE. OUT."

The message from *Abner Ward* was addressed to CAPRICORN, joint call-name for all four destroyers in DesDiv 291.

"Bridge, combat...*Ward's* lookouts hold visual contact with skunks at 3-5-5 and 0-0-5 relative," Coates eagerly relayed the information into the voice tube.

"Bridge, aye. We heard *Ward's* message," Cobb replied tartly. "Skunks have been identified as Task Force 77. You may cease reporting but continue to track until we are on station."

"Combat, aye," Coates answered, then turning to Logan. "Mr. Sternhagen's supposed to have the conn this watch but the exec seems to have taken things over up there so we'd better be on our toes. I imagine the task force commander will be assigning the division's screening stations any minute now. Think you can handle it, Logan?" the ensign questioned nervously. "You know, our station should..."

"CAPRICORN...THIS IS JEHOVAH. STAND-BY TO EXECUTE...ITEM-ABLE FIVE."

As the words flashed from the speaker, Murray fumbled through the *General Signal Book* to "Item-Able 5." There he found a reference to a page in the *Maneuvering Board Manual* and a particular anti-aircraft screening formation.

"HARLOT—ZEBRA SEVEN." the message continued. "SHIFTLESS—ZEBRA NINER...TENNIS COURT—ZEBRA ELEVEN...SMUDGE—ZEBRA THIRTEEN... REFERENCE GRID ABLE JIG...OVER!"

"JEHOVAH, THIS IS SHIFTLESS...ROGER, OUT," answered Sternhagen over the *Field's* wheelhouse TBS.

"JEHOVAH, THIS IS SMUDGE...ROGER, OUT," squeaked *Halsey Wayne* amid a jumble of static.

It took Murray several excruciating seconds to decode the message from "Jehovah," voice-call for the admiral in tactical command of Task Force 77 and a name the Charlie P.'s radar gang would soon come to know as well as their own. The *Field* had been assigned "Zebra niner," or station-9 in the circle of destroyers which formed a protective screen around the larger ships, especially the navy's sacrosanct carriers. On the day's grid-chart, the phonetic "Able-Jig" translated to the numerals two-zero, indicating twenty minutes, the division's prescribed time to get on station.

Logan studied the relative positions of each of the numerous contacts plotted on the maneuvering board. Inscribed upon this translucent table-top was a polar-coordinate chart, basically a large circle with lines of bearing spaced 10 degrees apart and radiating out from the center of the circumference. Inside the circumference, concentric circles spaced at equal intervals served as range markers for plotting the relative position and distance of contacts from the circle's center point which represented the position of the plotter's own ship, in this case the *Field*.

"CAPRICORN...THIS IS JEHOVAH. EXECUTE ITEM-ABLE FIVE...OUT!"

"Recommend coming left to one-three-one," Logan announced, sliding his parallel rulers across the surface of the maneuvering-board. This was only an initial course recommendation intended to start the *Field* turning in the general direction of her assigned slot in the task force screen. It took Logan 30 seconds more to skillfully execute the geometric and arithmetic calculations involving time and relative motion which would determine the course and speed *DD-505* should utilize to reach station-9 within the prescribed twenty minutes maneuvering time.

"Recommend steadying up on one-four-five, twenty-six knots to get on station," advised Kevin Logan. Coates, without checking the solution, speedily passed it on up to the bridge. Cobb acknowledged, and an instant later, readings from the gyro-repeater and pitometer in C.I.C. confirmed that the executive officer intended to follow his radar team's council.

"Old man must be up in the bridge," Murray said.

Coates shrugged.

"Only reason Cobb would ever take our recommendation," grunted Murray. "Guess he's afraid to foul-up again like that day he did with the *Crown*..."

"They're all over the place!" Paulsen interrupted excitedly from the open hatchway leading into C.I.C.

"Yeah, flattops, battleships, cruisers, 'cans'...hell, they're all over, any direction you look!" Farber agreed as he and Paulsen entered from the sun-drenched passageway. "Must be the whole fuckin' navy out there. Ah, never seen such a mess of ships. Not even when we were takin' our ORI off Hawaii!"

"Ha," Murray frowned. "There's no more than thirty, maybe thirty-five ships out there. That's kid stuff. You should have seen Task Force 58 back when I was on 'Big Ben'. We never had less than a couple of hundred ships with us at a time. Hell, just one of our task groups was over twice the size of this outfit. I remember when we'd pull into Ulithi Lagoon to rearm before a strike. We'd anchor off Mog Mog in a line...ten...fifteen carriers deep. The navy P.R. people came out and photographed us...called us 'Murderer's Row'. Now that was a fleet. Thirty-five ships. hell...you could lose that just in one corner of Task Force 58 and never even know it was missing. Ain't that right, Kev?"

"I'd say that was a pretty fair description," Logan nodded with a mirthless smile, marking in the position of the latest contact.

Above on the open bridge, quartermasters and signalmen hurried frantically from blinker to flag-bags and back to blinker again as a flurry of signals appeared from every point on the compass. The *Field* was close to the tail-end of the screen now and *Ward*. *Morgan* and *Wayne* were already sheering off to starboard.

Dick Warden, JOD for the morning watch, trained his binoculars on the carriers, the rationale for the task force's existence. "*Philippine Sea, Bon Homme Richard, Princeton,*" the young ensign loudly proclaimed as his glasses swept the island structures of each flattop, focusing for an instant on her I.D. number. At the far side of the formation and slightly astern of *Princeton* steamed a haze gray mountain of steel called battleship *Iowa*; her multi-platformed control tower dominating a cluster of cruisers just beyond. Still further off behind the most leeward destroyer in the outer screen, a hint of green rode the horizon.

Songjin, Ensign Warden reckoned, recalling the radar fix he and Sternhagen had entered on the wheelhouse chart a few minutes earlier. Songjin...the word seemed suddenly as familiar as the name of the town in Indiana where he had spent all his twenty-two years. Yet it was only a matter of hours since he had come across the funny sounding name in a fleet intelligence memorandum. Not as infamous as Wonsan or Hungnam, he thought, nevertheless its shore batteries had gained a lethal reputation after battering numerous U.N. warships.

Aiming his binoculars at the hilly ribbon of coastline that divided sea from sky, Warden gazed hard and long, searching for the tell-tale flashes that would allow him to savor this special moment to the fullest. But there was nothing...no lightening...no thunder...no Wagnerian chorus to tell him that he was now a participant in a shooting war. The Charlie P. might just as well be back steaming off Santa Catalina, thought Warden, only half believing that he was looking at land occupied by a hostile enemy.

He found it equally hard to believe he was now standing on the open wing of a twenty-one hundred-ton destroyer skimming breezily across the Sea of Japan. A little over a year ago his most pressing problem was a hundred and twenty-pound blonde named Wendy Torgersen, and whether or not she'd let him take her to the senior prom. Now Wendy Torgersen was on the other side of the world, undoubtedly giving it away to Billy Begley in that damn Nash of his with the fold-down front seats, he mused.

"What's all the fuss about, Mister Warden?" grunted McAlleney, the messenger-of-the-watch, who was standing nearby. "The way ah look at it, joinin' up with an outfit like this is only gonna' mean a lot o' extra work 'n a bunch of admirals breathin' down our necks."

The junior-officer-of-the-deck was too busy contemplating the erotic image of Wendy Torgersen fornicating in a Nash "Statesman" to reply.

McAlleney turned towards Ashton Bites, "What's that big 'un out there?" the seaman-apprentice said, pointing to the battleship which was galloping by en route to her new station astern of the three carriers. "She sure is a mean lookin' ole gal, heh, Bitesie," he drawled, "mean as spurs in a henhouse."

Before the boatswain could answer, the roar of jet engines flashed overhead. Grumman Panthers, Commander Royal observed as he twisted around on his stool to watch the four fighters in the combat-air patrol circle over the task force on the prowl for any venturesome Migs. The planes were sleeker and a lot faster,

Owen decided, but he doubted that they could ever surpass the portly old Hellcats for reliability. Beyond the outer rim of the screen almost diagonally opposite the *Field's* quickly changing position, an early-warning patrol plane moved slowly in a wide orbit counter to that of the Panthers. Royal could make out the modified Skyraider's pregnant under-belly, the awkward almost immodest bulge that housed the single-engined aircraft's mammoth radar.

"Two hundred yards to station, Captain," Sternhagen advised stepping part way out of the wheelhouse.

"Very well, inform the flag as soon as we're on station," Owen answered.

"*Ward* and *Morgan* are already on station, Sir," the OOD said worriedly.

"Yes, well they didn't have quite as far to go, now did they, Mister Sternhagen?" the captain smiled.

"Just about on station, Mister Sternhagen," a quartermaster interrupted and the lieutenant bolted back inside.

"JEHOVAH, THIS IS SHIFTLESS...ZEBRA STATION...OUT!" he bellowed into the radio-telephone only seconds before *Halsey Wayne's* OOD sent a similar announcement that his ship was also on station.

Cobb's overseeing in the wheelhouse finished, the executive officer joined the captain on the open wing. "Seems we've picked up a few hitch-hikers," he grinned.

"Our old girl's back in the big leagues, alright," Owen answered, swiveling his stool around towards the open wheelhouse door. "Mister Sternhagen," he shouted, "you can secure all hands from general-quarters but standby for a fueling assignment from Jehovah and set a mine watch on the foc'sle."

"Yes, Sir," the *Field's* damage-control officer obeyed with all the ardor of a dragoon about to lead his brigade to immortality, but before he could have the captain's orders passed over the intercom an air-contact report was flashed to all ships from the *Iowa*.

Below in C.I.C., after lengthy coaxing, Holiday was finally able to locate "many bogeys" closing swiftly from the northwest. Before he could determine their precise range and bearing, the intruders were challenged by the air-defense ship in the outer screen and were found to be "squawking friendly."

"For a few seconds I thought the Reds were sending their chamber-of-commerce out to greet us," said the exec aiming his binoculars in the anticipated direction of the approaching aircraft.

"The Commies are much too smart to try a silly stunt like that now that they know the Charlie P.'s joined up," Royal chuckled. "It's only one of our own strikes coming home to roost. Don't you remember mention of a morning launch on today's op-plan?"

"Yes, you're right...a flak suppression raid around Kilchu as I recall," said Cobb, screwing the prisms into focus. "I hold them now," he said, "about one-eight-zero relative ...seems to be three groups, fifteen or twenty to a group. Can't make out their type yet but they're moving in fast. Must be jets."

"We can forget about refueling for awhile, Mister Sternhagen," the captain advised and swung his legs to the deck. "I expect Jehovah will be sending out a course change for the formation any second now. What direction do we hold the wind?"

"Wind's blowing from two-two-five true, Captain," the OOD reported after checking the aerovane indicator in the wheelhouse.

"Very well, Mister Sternhagen. Then that's the direction we'll be turning."

"Yes, Sir," the lieutenant replied in a questioning tone as if unaware that fundamental maneuvering doctrine always required carriers to speed directly into the wind during landing operations to set up a natural barrier to safely slow the speed of the descending aircraft.

"First group's jets, second and third look like ADs and Corsairs," Cobb corrected his earlier observation as the planes maneuvered into a tight circle to await the landing signal from the force commander.

"SPECTACLE, SPECTACLE...THIS IS JEHOVAH...EXECUTE TO FOLLOW ...CORPEN CHARLIE-NAN-OBOE, SPEED XRAY-DOG. I SAY AGAIN...CORPEN CHARLIE-NAN-OBOE, SPEED XRAY-DOG, OUT!"

"OTC to all ships, standby to execute...come right to course two-two-five, speed thirty, Captain," the lieutenant hurriedly translated from the day's grid-chart.

"SPECTACLE, SPECTACLE, THIS IS JEHOVAH...STANDBY TO EXECUTE CORPEN CHARLIE-NAN-OBOE, SPEED XRAY-DOG...EXECUTE!...EXECUTE!... OUT!"

"Come right to two-two-five...make turns for thirty knots!" Sternhagen instructed his bridge watch, and the *Field* leaned sharply as each ship in the task force pivoted about with "Rockette-like" unison. The destroyer's bow reared high in the air as she straightened on her new base course broadside to the waves. Now, racing into the wind, her keel squashed each oncoming crest with a flat uncomfortable thud.

"Twenty-four knots, Sir," Sternhagen called out as the *Field* worked up speed. "Twenty-eight knots," he amended moments later, the *Field's* deck plates now quivering as if the old ship had suddenly been taken with palsy.

"Making turns for thirty knots, Sir," the man at the engine-telegraph reported, and the OOD immediately passed the news on to Commander Royal.

"I imagine they'll bring the jets in first, Aub," the captain said. "They burn fuel up so fast, they're probably flying on vapors right now," he smiled, remembering his days aboard *Coral Sea* in the Mediterranean.

The course change now placed formation-center, with its triangle of carriers, broad on the *Field's* starboard beam. The planes were already setting down on "Phil Sea" when Howie Murray pushed his head through the starboard hatchway at the base of the bridge. He watched the display of color, yellows, whites and reds flying up *Princeton's* halyards announcing that she too had a "ready-deck" and would commence receiving aircraft.

As Royal predicted, the jets, always high on fuel consumption, were the first to enter the landing pattern. The F9F's were followed closely but at carefully synchronized intervals by the prop jobs; the cumbersome Douglas Skyraiders, the navy's answer to many a foxhole prayer.

Finally, the Corsairs filed out of their swarm, each lowering its flaps and gear to touch down to a jerky stop near the rear of *Princeton's* flightdeck. Murray vividly remembered these last from his final days on *Franklin*. Retreads like himself, he thought, watching the three big *Essex* class carriers charge the wind. And, for one long moment he was seven years younger and leaping wildly for the haven of *Hickox's* oil-splattered foc'sle.

"Close that fuckin' hatch! You're screwin' up my pop-overs!" came an impassioned growl from Turk in the galley-way, and Murray's ghosts departed as suddenly as they appeared, leaving him once again on *DD-505* with a definite mission to perform.

"Belly-robber!" he snarled back at the cook, then reached into his hip pocket for the folded sheet of paper. Glancing back down the ladder to the combat-information-center and satisfied that no one had followed, he quickly made his way through the passageway that led to "officer's country." With everyone either on watch or topside taking in the big show, the area was deserted just as he expected. A few more steps and he was at the curtained entrance to the executive officer's stateroom. He scanned the passageway a final time, then entered.

A popular calendar of the day depicting a nude Marilyn Monroe adorned the bulkhead next to Cobb's bunk. An ideal place to leave his calling card, Howie thought, grinning as he pressed the tack into the most provocative portion of the illustration. His mission completed, he moved out with prudent speed.

A clean getaway, the first-class decided, ducking back into the radar shack. Every bit as clean as the night he had painted the silhouette of the target-towing TBM on the side of the Number-"3" mount, Howie concluded happily.

An hour later, Ensigns Coates and Ritter passing near the executive officer's stateroom narrowly missed a possibly fatal collision with the *Field's* number-two honcho.

"Some smart son-of-a-bitch just stuck his ass in the chopper! Hear me loud and clear about that!" Cobb thundered, still mumbling threatening oaths as he disappeared down the passageway.

"What's biting him?" Coates frowned bewilderedly as his companion bent to pick up the ball of paper the exec had thrown at their feet. Flattening out the creases on the wardroom table, the young officers were able to make out the neatly typed stanzas of a poem addressed to "Mr. Cobb-alias Captain Queeg."

The poem, an old chestnut popular among carrier pilots and other flattop personnel during the Pacific War read:

> *You can take away my ribbon,*
> *And eliminate my star,*
> *But protect me from the villain*
> *Who would drop that precious "R".*

Foul up my pay account
Refuse me at the bar,
Send me off to Mandalay,
But save that lovely "R".

Deny me ration books and stamps,
And tires for my car,
Take my blessings one by one,
But leave me with my "R".

Do what you will, please, Captain,
But this symbol, Sir, preserve,
That warm and tender "Roger"
Which indicates "Reserve".

The paper was signed: The lint-brained reserves of *DD-505*.

By sunset, *Charles P. Field* and her sisters had "Topped-off" from the larger units assigned; *Bon Homme Richard* had recovered all but one AD from the mid-afternoon launch against the marshalling yards at Kowon, and cruiser *Juneau*, with destroyer *Orleck*, had been detached to investigate a suspected barge build-up near Tanchon.

Now the *Field* was running with the pack...running north to bring the carriers within easy striking range of the seemingly endless truck convoys that nightly snaked their way down from Manchuria.

And half a globe away in Ebbets Field, Americans munched popcorn and watched a pitcher's duel between Joe Black and Sal Maglie as the Brooklyn Dodgers and the New York Giants battled it out for top slot in the national league.

Chapter XI - Task Force

Candace had never imagined that anything this luxurious could float. Lying in bed next to Bill Lydecker, she found it hard to believe that they were actually somewhere off the California coast. Except for the huge brass portholes and the purring of the yacht's twin diesels, she could be waking up in the master bedroom of a Park Avenue townhouse, she thought blissfully.

"Are you awake, Darling?" Lydecker asked, moving his body tenderly against her. For a man in his mid-forties, the heir to the Lydecker Industry fortune and president of Cherokee Motors, Inc., was in peak condition as Candace had just learned first hand during an evening of prolonged love making.

Brushing a golden thread from her eyes, she focused her gaze on the mahogany cherubs perched atop each of the tall bedposts.

"No, not now...not in front of the angels," she said playfully, gently moving his hand from between her legs.

"What's the matter, don't you believe in sex before breakfast? Besides, the angels didn't seem to bother you last night," he said smugly, his fingers gliding back up her inner thigh.

"In the dark I thought they were devils," Candace teased, disentangling herself and rolling away. "I think it's raining. Make it stop," she pleaded with the little girl giggle she'd managed to perfect so well over the years.

"That's not rain, it's just sea-spray. I've instructed the captain to increase speed a few knots. I want to be sure we reach San Francisco by sunset. You haven't lived until you've sailed under the Golden Gate just as the sun's going down," he said eagerly.

Candace did not reply, and although her gaze was now trained away, Lydecker could detect a sudden coolness.

"Why the doldrums? Do you have something against sailing into San Francisco?"

"No, no, of course not. It's just that someone else I know recently described how beautiful San Francisco's harbor is at night. I was just reminded of it, that's all."

"Sounds like I might have a little competition. Who is he, a fellow yachts-man or one of those dashing buccaneer-types adolescent girls hope will snatch them away to Pago Pago," he smiled cavalierly.

"Now you're being silly," she bubbled happily, "and what do you mean... competition? I thought you agreed last night that we'd keep this relationship purely business?"

"I did?"

"Yes, and then you went right ahead and seduced me," she said with a ravishing smile.

"Hmmm, I could have sworn it was you who did most of the seducing," he grinned back.

"Now that's not a very gallant statement."

"Oh, I've been accused of a lot of things. Being gallant has never been one of them. Just ask any of my ex-wives about that," said Lydecker with a measured touch of arrogance.

"Paula, Caroline or Denise?"

"You haven't done your homework very well. You forgot Francine."

"Francine?"

"Yes, she was number three. Tremendous personality. Good mind for business, too. She knew what she wanted and she went right out and got it."

"And what was that?"

"Oh, about half a million dollars in alimony," he laughed. "Well, one thing's certain. It's true what they say about you advertising people."

"Now just what do they say about us advertising people?" Candace mischievously retorted.

"That you cleverly maneuver a conversation around to any topic you want," he beamed. "Here I was, asking you about this mysterious friend of yours with a penchant for my favorite harbor and the next thing I know you've got me talking about my ex-wives."

"Well, if it will make you feel any better, the mysterious stranger you're so concerned about is just a casual friend. He's in the navy. In fact, he's over in Korea right now."

"That's good. I wouldn't want him bumping into us in San Francisco. I'd like to keep you all to myself for the next few days."

"That sounds quite inviting but I've got to be back in the office on Tuesday. You know, I've got to look after a few other accounts besides Cherokee Motors."

"May I ask you one very important question?"

"Of course, go ahead."

"What's your biggest account?"

"Cherokee Motors. You know that," she answered carefully.

"Well then I don't think it would be out of line if the owner and senior executive of your biggest account asked you to spend a few extra days with him. You know, there's several points in your program that I'm not entirely clear about."

"Oh, really. I got the impression yesterday morning that you thought our proposals were the greatest thing since mother's milk," she smiled coyly.

"Yes, overall they're fine. It's just that I think you might be able to help me raise my level of enthusiasm still further. Now I don't think that's too much to ask, do you?"

"Well, since you put it that way, I suppose I could call Tracy and tell her to keep my other appointments on hold for a couple of days."

"Now, that's the kind of progressive thinking I admire in the people I do business with."

"Business?" she said curtly.

"Sorry, that was a poor choice of words. How about associate with?" Lydecker replied flashing a broad smile.

"Yes, I think associate with would be far more preferable."

"Okay, now that we've agreed on that, let's see if I can change your mind about sex before breakfast," he said, lying back on the bed and tugging her gently towards him.

It was well past noon before the corporate head got around to taking the exquisite Miss Moffet on a close inspection of his 920-ton *Cherokee Maiden*, pride of the Lydecker fleet which included two cabin cruisers, a speed boat, a 60-foot sailing yacht and a moderately-sized catamaran. First stop was *Cherokee Maiden's* bridge. Rich in burnished oak and gleaming brass, it was the exact antithesis of the drab off-white that Candace remembered adorned the interior of the wheelhouse aboard her husband's destroyer.

"That's a radar scope. I know how that works!" she exclaimed excitedly as she spied the dark gray machine that looked decidedly out of place amid this delicate marriage of wood and metal. "And that gold stand over there," she said pointing, "that's a binnacle. It holds the compass. Isn't that right?" Her eyes lit up like those of an excited child.

"Yes, but how do you know so much about ships?" Lydecker snorted quizzically.

"Oh, in my business you have to know a little about everything. After all, you never can tell when someone might walk into your office and ask you to advertise a new line of yachts," she laughed softly.

"Are you putting me on?"

"No, of course not. I wouldn't do that to the most important client we've got," she grinned, causing Lydecker to wonder what sardonic double-entendre was masked behind the word client.

Damn but she's fantastic looking, he thought as he mentally undressed the superb body he had known intimately less than an hour before.

Also eyeing the young woman now hunched over the compass stand were the yacht's master, a gravel-faced veteran mariner, and the mate, a thin lantern jawed type. And while both strained to appear totally unconcerned, each found it impossible not to risk an occasional furtive glance at the superbly curved calves, the trim yet pronounced buttocks and the patrician features of a face they could only dream about. Both would agree later that their present passenger far surpassed any of the numerous models, starlets and chorus girls their fickle employer had paraded before them over the past four years.

"I hope you realize that you've managed to do it again," Lydecker said, assisting his guest down the well varnished wooden steps that led to the boat deck.

"What did I do again?" asked Candace solemnly.

"You've managed quite adroitly to avoid answering my question. I asked you how you know so much about things like radar scopes and binnacles and you come up with what can best be called an evasive answer."

"I wasn't trying to be evasive. I just didn't think it was that important, but if you're really interested, that fellow I know in the navy happens to be captain of a destroyer, and one night when his ship was in San Diego, he invited me aboard for dinner, that's all."

"And you picked up that much nautical lingo on a single visit?"

"Of course. Why not? I'm a fast learner. You have to be if you intend to be president of the country's second most important ad agency." Then pointing aft, she said, "That area back there near the stern is called the fantail. The equivalent area up near the bow, we can't see it from here because the bridge is in the way, is called the foc'sle. That's where all the chains and machinery for hoisting and lowering the anchors are kept, right?" she smiled smugly.

"Right," he laughed. "The way you were able to rattle all that off, maybe you will be president of the country's number two agency someday."

"Oh, there's no maybe about it. Only when I become president, I'll see to it that B.B.Y. and S. is number one. Second place to me has always been synonymous with also ran."

"Then I guess you don't agree with all those people who say it's a man's world," chided Lydecker.

"No, and I never will," she shot back sternly. Not certain how her candor was being interpreted, she gave her host the sweetest smile she could muster. Taking his hand she led him back to a small open area on the boat deck abaft *Cherokee Maiden's* tall primrose stack.

They kissed for several moments.

"Think your destroyer captain would approve of this?" Lydecker teased.

"I don't think he'd care one way or the other. I told you he and I are just good friends. Actually, he's very happily married. I happen to know his wife quite well."

"Hmmm, this sounds more and more interesting. Does she know her husband had you on his ship for dinner?"

"Yes, of course. Actually she and I are very close," Candace said, enjoying her little joke.

"Speaking of wives, how come a woman as beautiful and desirable as you isn't married? It certainly can't be because you're afraid of sex."

"That was a bit crude, don't you think?"

"Possibly, but we've already agreed that I'm not gallant, so why don't you answer my question?"

"How do you know I'm not married?"

"Well, isn't it customary to wear a ring?"

"I wouldn't know, I've seldom done what's customary. If I had, I'd still be a junior copy writer back on Madison Avenue. But, if you really want to know, yes, I am married."

"The navy guy in Korea?"

"Yes," Candace answered, her sudden frankness prompted by realization that Lydecker's money and governmental connections could get him a detailed dossier on her entire life in just a matter of hours if he so desired.

"Then adultery doesn't bother you?"

"No, does it bother you?" she snapped back.

"Of course, can't you tell," he chuckled softly. Then looking at one of the two canvas covered lifeboats, he asked, "How about doing it in one of the boats?"

"What?" she smiled quizzically.

"In the boat, under the canvas, like a couple of stowaways. It's great...adds a touch of adventure to the sex. Sorry it's not raining. That's when it's really fun!"

"I'll take your word for it. Why don't we wait until sometime when it is raining," she said skittishly, wondering if her host had lost all his marbles.

Before Lydecker could press the issue further they were interrupted by a white-jacketed steward.

"Lunch is ready, Sir," the little black man announced cautiously, deducing from his employer's sullen expression that his arrival on the boat deck may not have been too timely.

"That's terrific," Candace beamed. "I can't remember when I've been this hungry," she said, taking Bill Lydecker's arm.

With her Krupp diesels humming contently, *Cherokee Maiden* kicked up a frothy wake and continued on towards San Francisco Bay.

• •· •

In the make-up of Task Force 77, the attack carrier reigned supreme and duty aboard these big *Essexes* was fast and frantic. All-weather round-the-clock launches and recoveries of jet aircraft still in the teething stage; flak-torn Corsairs chewing up a hundred yards of deck timber in early morning blackness; a Banshee fighter jumping the barriers at ninety miles an hour to hurdle headlong into rows of aircraft parked forward; the sudden jerking stop of a big AD caught in the wires, a "Hunger" slithering out from beneath its wing to bounce end-over-end across the flight deck as sweating sailors matched speed and skill against nose fuse and detonator; a wounded pilot to be pulled from his flaming bird; that one spark that must not reach the fuel and ammo stores — this was life on a Ko-war flattop, the daily operational fatalities that never won a Purple Heart...the routine that never quite became routine.

For the men of DesDiv 291 however, screening duty with Task Force 77 was an endless lethargy broken only by spasmodic drills, fitful course-changes and the momentary anticipation of battle evoked by the returning "friendly" with an inoperative IFF. To "Price's Expendables," Korea by mid-August had become as intangible as Oz. By day it was a peak-studded smudge punctuated at irregular intervals by spiraling stalks of oily brown smoke. By night it was the direction of the orange flashes and the rumbling thunder.

And while the crews of *Ward*, *Wayne*, *Morgan* and *Field* seemed fated to suffer the unrelenting monotony of squiring carriers in a war completely void of major enemy air or submarine attack, they watched and waited as each day sister units detached to test their metal against the crack North Korean naval batteries at Hodo Pando...to intercept a puffing locomotive at the Pukchong junction...to sauté a column of T-34 tanks caught in the open Chocho plain. As the long August days marched on, they would read the daily reports that told how other destroyers from the screen were rendering vital support to beleaguered army positions below Kosong, or supplying harassing fire for the marine advance along the Imjin Estuary. One report would detail the exploits of the destroyers "riding shotgun" for the feisty little minesweepers that worked inside the dragon's throat. Still another would tell of destroyers navigating obscure inlets to land recon parties far behind enemy lines, or of darting between giant shell splashes to pluck a single downed pilot from the angry waters of Wonsan Harbor.

The more they read the reports, the more the men of DesDiv 291 complained about "having to wetnurse the birdfarms," unaware that in doing so, they were being spared many tribulations then plaguing their counterparts in the bombardment force. Not having experienced a turn with Task Force 95, they could not know the discomfort of nearly baking alive inside a destroyer, DE, or cruiser tightly "buttoned up" during lengthy periods at general quarters.

Air-conditioning aboard most naval vessels this blistering summer of 1952 was still viewed as something out of *Buck Rogers*, thus sleep was often impossible with temperatures in the ships often well over a hundred degrees. To compound the problem, it was not uncommon for the bombarding ship's own gunfire to jar loose the glass wool insulation in the overhead, causing it to rain down on bunks and fill the closed compartments with millions of splinter-like fibers.

By late-August, no such annoyances had yet befallen Price's division, and as long as the *Field's* main deck hatch was kept open, Murray, Logan and the others in the Ops department were usually able to maintain a modest but steady stream of fresh air flowing through their berthing space. Such a stream was cooling the compartment as Vinny Bacelli entered with the bulging sack of mail he had just picked up in the *Field's* small post office, a deck above. Transferred earlier that day from a navy supply ship, the letters and packages were distributed in record time to the several Ops department sailors who had eagerly assembled for mail-call.

"Hey, Logan, you really got a bundle this time," Bacelli cried out, tossing half a dozen identical envelopes on Kevin's bunk.

"Must be one of lover boy's famous models," snickered Gardiner, eyeing the pink envelopes.

"Nah," Bacelli grinned, twisting one side of his mouth. "Logan's got himself a Wave officer, a lieutenant Jg. no less," he quipped, eyeing the neatly printed return address on the nearest letter.

"Like me to read them to you?" Logan snapped angrily, snatching up all six letters.

"Hey, knock it off, fellas," Murray called out. "I'm trying to read this letter from Mary Alice!"

"How's she doing?" Logan asked, still glaring at Bacelli.

"Oh fine. The doctor says everything's coming along right on schedule. Say, I don't want to be nosey but who's the Wave officer Bacelli's talking about? You never told me you were dating a Wave lieutenant. When did that happen?"

"Back in San Diego after you guys took off for Hawaii, and she's a nurse, not a Wave. I met her when I was in the hospital. By the way, she's from your home state of Ohio," Kevin smiled, opening the fattest of the envelopes. "Here's a picture of her," he said, extracting a small colored snapshot from the envelope.

"Very nice," Murray said, shaking his head in approval. "Where was this taken?"

"Tijuana. We spent the weekend down there."

"Hard to believe that's commissioned pussy," Gardiner announced, peering over Murray's shoulder. "She's some piece, and look at those legs," the third-class said, eyeing the photo.

"She sure likes her shorts nice and short, doesn't she?" Bacelli leered. "How good a lay is she?"

"Yeah, do you have to salute her before or after you screw her?" Gardiner snickered.

"Blow it out your ear!" Logan barked, snatching back the photo.

"What's biting him?" Bacelli shrugged as Kevin departed the compartment.

"Most likely your big mouth!" Murray scowled tucking the letter from Mary Alice in his shirt pocket as he followed his friend Logan up the ladder.

Logan was above decks sitting near the practice loading machine for the 5-inch gun as Murray approached.

"Hey, Kev, why'd you blow your tubes down there? You've never let those two retards get to you before."

"I really don't know," Logan laughed. "I even surprised myself."

"Maybe it's the nurse. You kinda' like her, heh?"

"Come on, Howie, you've got to be kidding."

"Why would I be kidding? From that picture, I'd say she's an extremely pretty girl even if she happens to be a navy officer."

"Oh, there's nothing wrong with her looks. In fact, she'd give some of the models I've dated back in New York a good run for their money, but I've certainly got no serious interest in her. For one thing, she's immature."

"Immature?"

"Yes, totally."

"Then why'd you go out with her, or should I ask that question?" Murray half whispered.

"Believe me, I'm sorry I ever did! It's just that she looked so unattainable prancing around the hospital ward bossing us all around like a little tin general. And, I have to admit, she looked kind of sexy bending over the beds in those white stockings. Frankly, I really didn't think I could score but I was fascinated by the challenge. It was kind of a game to me, so I pulled out all the stops. Unfortunately, I guess, I overdid it. Next thing I knew she'd completely flipped. By our third date she was talking about marriage and our living in New York. Hell, whenever I'd kiss her, I could feel her going limp all over. I have to admit I was pretty flattered by it all, and you know, there did seem to be something a little special about her."

"What do you mean, special?"

"Well, she had such great skin and she always smelled so feminine, you know like baby powder."

"Sounds like you're the one who's flipped," said Murray, greatly amused by his shipmate's situation.

"You're off your rocker! I've never flipped over any broad in my life and I'm not going to start doing it over some silly little nurse who's read too many dumb novels about Madison Avenue. Far as I'm concerned, there's still a lot to be said for that old battle cry of the four-Fs…you know, find 'em, feel 'em, fuck 'em, and forget 'em."

"You seem to be having a lot of trouble forgetting this one," Murray grinned.

"Yeah, well she seems determined to try to keep me from doing just that. Do you see the post mark on this letter?" Logan said, handing Murray the envelope.

"Yokosuka?"

"That's right. According to this letter she arrived last week."

"Well, that doesn't mean you have to see her, does it?"

"How am I going to avoid it? If I know Cindy, she's already got a pipeline to base operations. I bet she finds out what time we're scheduled to tie up in Yokosuka next week before the old man does," said Logan with marked frustration. "Hell, every time we pull in for R and R, she'll be down at the pier waiting for me. I might just as well be married!"

"Are you sure this steady steaming isn't getting to you, Kev?"

Logan raised his eyebrows. "Why would you ask that?"

"Cause I can't imagine you getting upset just because a good looking girl wants to spend a little time with you."

"A little time? She's not interested in a little time! She's only interested in till death do us part!"

"Well, I still don't see what you're so shook up about. Ten to one she'll be so busy taking care of wounded from Korea that she won't have any time to go gallivanting around Japan with you. Besides, she's an officer and you're just a peon. She can't be seen with you."

"That didn't stop her back in San Diego," Logan said grimly.

"Yeah, but you had civilian clothes in San Diego, and there was nobody around to recognize you after the *Field* hauled ass for Pearl."

"I've still got one set of civies, only I can't get my hands on them. They're in Coates' stateroom," said Logan plaintively.

"I thought you had a deal with him?"

"I did, but he chickened out. He says our agreement was only for Stateside and Hawaii. He's afraid of what might happen if he got caught taking the clothes ashore for me in a foreign country. I guess he doesn't want to give Cobb an excuse to nail his hide to the mast."

"You can't blame him for that," Murray shrugged.

"Maybe not, but after this, the only model I'm going to introduce him to will be the kind that poses for kitty litter!"

"Well, if you're serious about not wanting to meet your little J-G, then it looks like Coatsie's actually done you a favor."

"A favor?"

"Yes, don't you see, he's solved your problem for you?" Murray said, leaning back against the dummy loader. "All you have to do is write and tell her one of her fellow officers reneged on the agreement he made with you. There's even a little irony in it," he grinned.

"That won't work," Logan shook his head negatively. "Cindy will just suggest that we travel up to Tokyo or Yokohama separately. Nobody will recognize us up there, and since she can wear civies, the military police won't bother us. They'll think she works for one of the American companies that have offices over here. There is one way I can get rid of her, though," Logan said with a devilish smile. "Only thing, it's a bit drastic. Do you remember I mentioned to you once that I had a buddy on a carrier...the *Oriskany*?" Logan asked.

"Yeah, so what?"

"Well, he and I were both radar instructors in the same reserve unit. When we were activated, he went to 'shit city' for duty on the 'Big O', while I wound up in 'Dago' aboard this gray vale of tears. This friend of mine really hates carriers. He wrote that with air ops, they keep him on watch practically all the time. Besides, he's always been hot to serve on a 'can'. I'm sure he'd jump at the chance to swap with me if I asked him. We're both second-class so all we'd have to do is get Royal and his C.O. to okay it."

"Where's the *Oriskany* now?" asked Murray in a noticeably disturbed tone.

"They should just about be leaving North Island to come over here. In his letter he said they sailed around Cape Horn from Norfolk because the ship was too wide for the Panama Canal. He said the waves were so big below the Horn they wrecked her bow guns and buckled the forward part of the flight deck...cost them close to three weeks in 'Frisco' getting repaired. That's probably why the *Bon Homme Richard* cut short her Stateside stay and rushed back over here. Anyway, figuring on a few weeks of O.R.I. off Hawaii and her transit time, she should be joining the task force by late September."

"Well, I don't see how jumping over to a carrier is going to help you. The *Oriskany* will be pulling into Yokosuka for R and R too, you know," Murray grumbled.

"Sure, but Cindy's got no way of knowing that I'd be on her. Besides, the *Oriskany* carries three thousand men. I could get lost in the crowd."

"I thought you and I were buddies?"

"We are. You know that."

"Then why are you so hot to transfer to some damn carrier?"

"I thought you liked carriers?" Logan laughed.

"I do. It's just that friends don't run out on friends. You know you're the only one on this damn ship I can even have an intelligent conversation with. I'm even going to name my kid Kevin."

"Well, don't worry about it, Howie. It was just an idea. Looking at it realistically, I doubt the old man would approve the swap so I guess I'm back to square-one," Logan frowned as the two radarmen headed for the base of the bridge and the ladder leading down to C.I.C.

The days dragged on and except for the daily dawn and dusk alerts, the men of DesDiv 291 felt they might just as well be on the other side of the world operating with the big showboats of the Sixth Fleet. At least in the Med, as Nugent caustically put it, they could help the navy's three newest and largest carriers, the *Midway*, *Roosevelt* and *Coral sea*, shore up the morale and economic well-being of America's allies in Southern Europe.

The most anxious moments for Owen Royal and the C.O.'s of the other ships in the screen came each evening shortly past eight, the time Jehovah consistently chose to radio his night intentions and operational orders for the following day. Information included in this cryptogram ranged from target selection to steaming formations and combat-air-patrol assignments. Transmitted also were the many and varied "special jobs" for the escorting battleship, cruisers and destroyers.

After almost six weeks of continuous steaming with the task force, Commodore Price and the rest of DesDiv 291 had given up all expectation of ever tangling with anything more provocative than a delinquent shoal of porpoise. Then on 19 August, two days before the division was scheduled to depart for Japan for a brief rest and overhaul, *Abner Ward* , with heavy cruiser *Bremerton* and another destroyer, the *Hollister*, was ordered to Hangwon for a pre-dawn bombardment of a freshly rebuilt railroad trestle destroyed by air attack only two days earlier. *Ward* and *Hollister* were to supply illumination fire for *Bremerton's* big rifles but halfway to the target city, Price's destroyer was abruptly and much to his displeasure detached from the mission to hunt for a B-29 believed down in the area. The search was fruitless and *Ward* rejoined the task force the following noon. Operationally the division flagship had accomplished nothing. She had been denied her shot at Hangwon and had failed to find even the slightest trace of the luckless bomber or its crew; yet to all hands, her mission had been a thunderous success for at last "291" had won Jehovah's recognition.

• • •

"I told you the caves have to be much deeper and wider at the base," bellowed Major Mychenko at the North Korean lieutenant who was his interpreter and liaison with the small army of laborers assigned to the work at Maksan. The lieutenant bowed, seemingly courteously, but with a hint of insolence in his bearing.

Damn this glut of imbeciles, Mychenko thought as the lieutenant relayed his criticism to the comrade foreman. "Tell him each cave must be deep enough for its own generator. And I want those tracks firmly imbedded!"

Again the Korean officer passed on the message and again his Russian overseer hoped nothing had been lost in the translation.

Walking back to his hut, Mychenko wondered how his request for duty in Hungary was progressing. If he could get it passed Colonel Nikolayev, there was every chance that he would see Budapest by late spring, he told himself, smiling as he recalled several of the plump Hungarian women he had gotten to know so well during his stint as artillery instructor at Jeszbereny. Here in Maksan, his only pleasure was an American-made phonograph "requisitioned" from a mission-school at nearby Chuuronjang. Tonight, it would be Tchaikovsky even if he was decadent and Czarist, the major decided.

Later that evening, Mychenko listened to a badly scratched recording of *"Dance of the Mirlitons,"* totally unaware that four American destroyers were passing less than thirty miles away. As the last of the warships slid by, her radar watch paid little heed to the glowing green sweep on the Sugar-George, their attention focused on the voice of Jo Stafford and her latest hit *"You Belong to Me."*

Chapter XII - "Small Boys"

Sitting in the main waiting area at Tokyo's Shimbashi Station, Cynthia Osbourne looked even more attractive than Logan remembered. Her chestnut brown hair seemed a bit shorter than it had been in California, he thought, but she still maintained that clean-cut all-American girl look that he always found so alluring. Her legs were crossed with one foot swinging, and the short wine colored skirt had fallen open along the slit, attracting several admiring glances from passing G.I.s.

She was not wearing her glasses and a slightly worried look was etched on her face as she wondered if Kevin would really keep his promise and meet her. "Kevin, darling!" she cried out excitedly, jumping from the wooden bench and rushing into his arms.

"Hi, angel face," Logan said softly, then sensing the presence of two M.P.s a couple of aisles away, he abruptly broke off the kiss. "We'd better wait until we have a little privacy. We don't want the army checking our I.D.s and discovering you're an officer," he cautioned, picking up her small suitcase along with his own.

The taxi driver who "piloted" them to the Ambassador Hotel stuck to the standard line prevalent among Tokyo cabbies of post war Japan; that being that he was an ex-Kamikaze pilot. Taking his hands off the wheel several times in the course of his pronouncement, he related how the war had ended just one day before he would have taken off on his first and final mission. After ten minutes of dodging in, out, between, around and seemingly "over" Tokyo's bustling traffic at break-neck speeds, Cindy and Kevin quickly concluded that they at least had come upon the real thing.

Recommended to Cynthia by a friend at the hospital, the Ambassador Hotel was an attractive Western style structure with most of the creature comforts Americans had come to expect. It was also just far enough off the beaten path so that there was little chance of any embarrassing encounters as most of the naval officers from Yokosuka took their lodging at a local B.O.Q. or at a highly prestigious hotel like the Imperial or the Hotel Tokyo.

Having secured separate but connecting rooms, Lieutenant Jg. Osbourne and Radarman second-class Logan lost little time in amalgamating their respective quarters.

The bed had no headboard but was a third again larger than what would be found in an American hotel room of comparable size.

Cynthia fluffed the small round pillow and turned to Kevin laying half-naked next to her. "I never thought I could love someone as much as I love you," she said, refluffing the pillow before lying back again. "Making love with you is so special," she smiled tenderly.

"Shh...not so loud. The walls in these Jap buildings are only paper, you know."

"You're not mad are you?"

"Of course I'm not mad," he smiled and patted her bare bottom as she rolled over against him.

"Well, you sounded mad," she started to giggle a little nervously.

"Now why would I be mad? Here I am in bed with the most beautiful nurse in the navy...in the army and air force too for that matter," he smiled.

"Is it special when you make love to me?"

"Super special," he said in an amused tone.

"Can I ask you something personal?"

"Why not? I'd say we've had a very personal relationship so far. Wouldn't you?"

"Have you made love to any other girls since you met me?" she asked forcefully.

"No, how could I? I've been at sea."

"Well, you were in Hawaii, and you told me you were in Japan for a few days before you went to Korea."

"Sure, but believe me, I haven't made love to anyone else since that night back in San Diego when you let me take you home to your apartment."

"Really," her face lit up with bright affection. "You're not just saying that? You know, Kevin, I love you so much I could never think of going to bed with anyone but you ever again."

"Ever again? You sound like a woman of great experience, and here I thought I was the one who deflowered you," he laughed good naturedly, pulling her firmly against him.

"Well, you practically were. Promise you won't laugh if I tell you something?" she asked shyly.

"I won't laugh...honest."

"I'm afraid I'm not very experienced at all. Before I met you I only had sex three times...well, actually only two. One of the times was when I was practically passed out, so that really doesn't count. Besides, all that happened mostly when I was a student nurse. I've done a lot of growing up since then. I know now that sex can only be special if it's shared between two people who are deeply and completely in love with each other."

Another recruit for Howie and Father Brian, Logan laughed to himself, gently massaging the nurse's smooth abdomen.

"You've been so quiet, Kevin. Was Korea terrible?" Cindy asked wide-eyed. "If you don't want to talk about it, I'll understand," she said, pressing her naked body close against his skin.

"Heck no," he smiled. "To quote a line I remember from an old World War Two movie, I've seen more action on the Albany night boat. As far as Korea's concerned, we didn't get to see very much of it except as a hilly patch of land far off on the horizon."

"I don't understand. You were operating as part of Task Force 77, weren't you? They fly in navy wounded from Task Force 77 two or three times a week. Most of them are really in a bad way. They're usually terribly burned or missing an arm or leg... sometimes both. I'm a nervous wreck every time the list of names comes in. I think I'd fall dead right there on the spot if I ever saw your name on that list," she said, tears suddenly clouding her expressive green eyes.

"You don't have to worry about me, Cindy. All the action with 77 is on the carriers. That's where those casualties are coming from. They rack up flight deck accidents every day. I watched a Panther come barreling into the *Boxer* the morning we detached. That jet went jumping over about ten wires right smack into the plane that had landed just before it. There was a fireball on the *Boxer's* deck about the size of a small atomic blast."

"Can't they do anything to stop that sort of thing?"

"I don't know. I just read an article in *All Hands* about putting angled decks on carriers so that when a plane misses the arresting cables it can just take off again without crashing into any of the other aircraft parked forward. It's a British idea. The *Antietam's* supposed to be on her way to the Philadelphia Navy Yard to get fitted with an experimental deck of that type. It may help them out in some future war, but unfortunately, I don't see it coming on line in time to help us out with this one," Logan said, staring up at the ceiling. "By late November or December when those Siberian winters start hitting those flight decks, I'm afraid you're going to get a lot more casualties from the carriers than you're getting now."

She listened to each word in total awe of Kevin's vast knowledge about the navy, feeling a bit like an Annapolis plebe in the presence of a Nimitz or a Halsey. "What about destroyers like your ship, the *Field*?" she asked in a deeply concerned tone. "From what I've been reading in *The Navy Times*, they've been going right inside the Communist harbors to duel with shore guns. They do, don't they?"

"Sure, the 'cans' assigned to Task Force 95 see combat almost every day, and just about every night since that's when the bulk of the Red troops and supplies are moved down from Manchuria. But that doesn't mean the navy will ever let the bucket I'm on see any action. The screen commander will make sure the Charlie P. does nothing but escort duty and maybe go searching for a downed pilot or two once in awhile. So far though, he hasn't even let us do that."

"Isn't escorting aircraft carriers dangerous?"

"Not unless the Commies start sending out Migs or those W-class subs we've been hearing about lately. I really don't think there's much chance of that," Logan said. "Actually our biggest danger is probably from our own conning officers. Ours aren't the most proficient. I just hope one of them doesn't order the helmsman to turn to port some night when the other thirty ships in the task force are turning to starboard. If that ever happened, there's a good chance we'd wake up to find a flattop right in the middle of our messhall," he said in a rather callous tone.

"Something like that happened earlier this year, didn't it?" asked Lieutenant Osbourne with marked concern.

"Yes, last April when the *Wasp* sliced right through the *Hobson*, and they were operating in the Atlantic off the Azores where they could keep their mast-head and running lights on. Off Korea, every ship in our task force is completely blacked out. We're not even allowed to light a cigarette above decks after dark," he explained. "What really makes it scary is we have to follow a zig-zag plan each night that calls for a complete change of course at least eight or nine times between sundown and dawn."

"Why do you keep changing course?"

"That's standard operating procedure in a war zone. We did it in the Pacific too when I was on the *Laffey*. Say, didn't you get any of this stuff in your naval orientation course when they made you an officer and a lady?" he laughed.

"No, they were too busy teaching us about naval traditions and customs and saluting and things like that. After all, it's not like a nurse is ever going to command a battleship, silly," she smiled coyly, running her index finger across his bare chest. "Now tell me why you have to change course so much each night."

"The navy figures if there are any subs in our area trying to draw a bead on us, a sudden unexpected turn will screw up their torpedo solution. Of course, zig-zagging occasionally backfires and causes a ship to get sunk," said Logan with the faint trace of cynicism.

Cynthia looked at him quizzically.

"That's how the Jap navy lost the world's largest aircraft carrier, the *Shinano*," Kevin grinned. "The *Archerfish*, that's the sub that got her, had been chasing after the Nip flattop for almost six hours but the range kept opening. The C.O. of the *Archerfish* finally realized he couldn't catch up and was just about to break off the chase when the Jap skipper decided to zig-zag. The sudden turn by the *Shinano* brought her within easy torpedo range and *Archerfish* put six 'fish' in her belly."

"I think there's got to be a moral in that story but I'm not certain I can find it," Cindy frowned.

"Oh, there's a moral alright," Logan laughed. "The flattop was okay as long as she just kept running down the Honshu coast fat, dumb and happy. As soon as the Jap captain started worrying about subs and decided to follow the proper procedure, wham-o, he gets an express ticket to Davy Jone's locker."

"For someone from Madison Avenue, that sounds a bit anti-establishment. Aren't you in favor of rules and regulations?"

"When they work, I am," he said smugly. "Unfortunately, it's luck more than rules that determine how well things are going to turn out for you in life. Too bad one of my shipmates isn't around. I'd let him tell you his famous story about how not eating creamed beef on toast once saved his life. Getting a little closer to home, I doubt that I'd be lying here in bed with you right now if my G.Q. station had been twenty feet further forward on the *Laffey*. For that matter, if the ship had been going half a knot faster, two of those kamikazes that crashed us would have landed right in my lap. Since I had no say whatsoever in how fast we were moving that morning, wouldn't you agree that luck was much more important than whether or not I was wearing a regulation set of dungarees?"

"I only had one semester of philosophy. I wouldn't even try to answer a stickler like that one. All I care about is that I'm lying here in your arms right now," Cindy smiled lovingly. "I wish we would just be together like this forever. Are you certain the navy won't send your ship into combat?"

Kevin's expression changed for the slightest instant. "Yes, I'm pretty certain," he answered slowly.

"Why? Is the *Field* too old for anything but escort duty?"

"No, there are plenty of *Fletcher* class destroyers operating with us in the screen that take their turn with Task Force 95. It's just that we seem to have picked up a reputation for being unreliable."

"Unreliable?"

"Actually, that's an understatement. Dangerous would probably be more accurate," he chuckled. "The Charlie P.'s been doing a lot of little things that seem to annoy the navy...like shooting at target planes instead of their targets, and almost ramming aircraft carriers with two-star admirals on board. To top it off, we came pretty close to missing our rendezvous with Task Force 77. I'm not sure the navy's found out about that, though," Logan snickered.

"What do you mean came close to missing your rendezvous with your task force? That couldn't happen, could it? You're kidding, aren't you?" asked Cindy, her eyes fired up with curiosity.

"No, I'm not kidding, really," Logan said, grinning broadly at his bedmate's incredulity. "A couple of idiots on our ship decided to sneak two Japanese girls aboard the night before we left for Korea. We pulled out earlier than scheduled and they didn't turn the girls in until we were out about six hours. Naturally, we had to go back to Yokosuka to dump the girls off, then go racing after the other three ships which by then had a twelve hour jump on us. For awhile, I really thought they might join the task force without us. You should have seen our 'snipes' push those old engines. Luckily, we caught up to the division a day before the rendezvous. If we'd missed it, or even showed up late, the navy would have made the old man walk the plank. That's for sure."

"Do you still have the same C.O. you had back in San Diego...the one I met when he came to see you in the hospital?"

"Yes, I forgot. You did meet him, didn't you? What'd you think of him?"

"He was very nice, even when I refused to let him see you after he'd taken the time to come all the way over to the hospital. You know, it's not very often a J-G can get away with telling a three-striper, and the C.O. of a ship at that, what he can or can not do. He was very polite. He told me he understood about the quarantine and fully appreciated the situation. He even thanked me for my help, and frankly Kevin, I wasn't very helpful to him at all. Say, if I wasn't so madly in love with you, I think I could get interested in someone like him. Is he single?" she asked in a teasing tone.

"No, I'm afraid you're out of luck there, I understand he's married to a fantastically beautiful woman. He had her on board the *Field* for a visit when I was in the hospital being subjected to your tender mercies," he laughed. "Everyone who saw her that night still talks about her. To hear some of their descriptions, you'd think Helen of Troy had paid a call on the Charlie P."

"Really?" There was a hint of peeve in her tone.

"Yes, even Coatsie, my C.I.C. officer flipped over her. One thing's certain, she sure made a lasting impression on everyone who met her. Anyway, I don't think anybody could be as good looking as they say she is. I heard the old man's got a photo of her on his desk in his stateroom. I'll have to figure out a way to get in there and see it one of these days."

"You sound like you're really sorry you didn't get to meet her. If she's as beautiful as you say, maybe you could have spent that time in San Diego with her instead of with me," the young lieutenant said with a sudden pout.

"I suppose that was a possibility. Hey, what's the matter? Those aren't tears I see streaming out of those big beautiful eyes, are they?" Logan laughed, hugging the former terror of Ward 8 who was now sobbing uncontrollably.

"Come on, Cindy, stop crying. You know I was only kidding."

"No, you weren't," she said, pushing away from him and rolling over on her stomach. Burying her face deep in a pillow, Miss Osbourne continued to cry.

Logan gently patted her small but well shaped derriere.

"Stop that!" she snapped, as she reached back to remove his hand from her buttocks.

"Damn it, Cindy! Stop acting like a baby! You're twenty-three years old and you're an officer in the United States Navy. Now stop acting like some spoiled little brat!"

"I want to go back to Yokosuka. I don't want to see you anymore," she grumbled, her words slightly muffled by the pillow.

"Now come on, stop being silly. We've got two whole days to see Tokyo and have fun. Now stop crying. I was only teasing you. I've got no interest in my C.O.'s wife. I was just curious about what she looked like. That's all."

"You aren't really interested in meeting her?" Cynthia's voice squeaked plaintively as she tried to stop crying. Struggling for breath, the J-G pushed herself up from the pillow. Then, resting on her elbows, she turned towards Logan. "I love you so much, Kevin. You must know that by now. I just wish you could love me the same way. If you did, you wouldn't be teasing me about other women. I see you looking them over whenever we go anywhere. I tried not to let it bother me back in San Diego, but it really hurts me very much."

"Come on, sweetheart. You're imagining things. Besides, aren't you the one I'm spending my few days in Japan with?"

"Yes," she answered with a feeble smile.

Logan watched her as she dried her eyes with a tissue from the box next to the bed. She was not as incredibly beautiful as Candace, nobody could be, Logan thought, but this girl who now shared his bed exuded femininity like no other woman he had ever known. In spite of all the sex they shared, to Logan, Cynthia retained an innocence that both captivated and disturbed him.

"There, that's better," he said, dabbing at her wet cheeks with a tissue.

"You know, Kevin, sometimes you can be very sweet and considerate, but other times, I think Betsy is right about you when she says that you're just using me for sex."

"Ah, come on. I've never even met Betsy. I don't know why she keeps butting in between you and me, even over here."

"Betsy's very protective of my feelings."

"Hell, Betsy's only a dumb ensign. Besides, she's two years younger than you are."

"That's alright, she knows I'm very sensitive. Anyway, she still thinks I'm making a big mistake. I got a letter from her yesterday. I had written and told her I'd be seeing you this weekend."

"Well, I don't know why she seems to dislike me so much. I only spoke to her on the phone a couple of times when I was calling you, and she happened to answer. I certainly was polite. I don't think it could have been anything I said," Logan shrugged.

"Oh, it wasn't what you said. I think she's mostly upset about my panties." Cindy tried unsuccessfully to stifle a giggle.

"Your panties?"

"Yes, she didn't appreciate finding them on top of her toaster that night when she came home. She's convinced that you threw them up there to show that, as she put it, you'd made it all the way to home plate. Betsy feels that you're the kind of a fellow who doesn't want a permanent relationship. She says your throwing my underpants up on the toaster was the equivalent of a Sioux Indian hanging a scalp on the top of his wigwam."

"Well, if you'll excuse me for saying so, your former roommate doesn't know anything about me or my intentions. In fact, you can tell Ensign Chadwick for me that she can...well, just do me a favor and make up your own mind about seeing me. If you decide you don't want to continue our relationship, I'll fully understand."

"I didn't say I didn't want to see you anymore. You know I do. I don't have to tell you that," the nurse said meekly.

"Yeah, I know," Logan answered in a soft voice. "If I do seem inconsiderate, I want you to know it's not intentional and I'm sorry. Now that you've stopped trying to compete with Niagara Falls," he said, giving her cheek a final pat with the tissue, "how would you like to spend the rest of the day? It's only two-fifteen so we've still got a good part of the afternoon left to see Tokyo."

"Oh, there's a whole slew of places I think we'd both enjoy. They gave me this list back at the hospital." She reached for her purse and hauled out what was evidently an encyclopedia of notes. "Now we definitely have to see the Imperial Palace. That's an absolute must," Cynthia announced excitedly.

"The palace isn't open to visitors," replied Logan blandly.

"Oh, I know that, but we can go right up to the edge of the moat. It's supposed to be like something out of the middle ages. I hear there's a big stone wall with castles and pagodas and things like that. And the Palace Gardens are really worth seeing...and we have to go shopping on the Ginza. They say you can buy almost anything there. Then, after that we can go visit the Zojo-ji Temple in Shiba Park. That's world famous, you know. Of course, we should try to see the Diet Building, and the building where MacArthur had his headquarters."

"Cindy, honey, don't get carried away. We've got all day tomorrow to fit in the places we don't get to today."

"Oh, no, we really don't," she frowned. "We'll need tomorrow for visiting the National Museum in Ueno Park, and the Zoological Gardens, the Tokyo Art Gallery and Hibiya Park and the Imperial Library, and..."

"Take it easy, Lieutenant, slow down," Kevin laughed. "We've got to catch a seven o'clock train tomorrow evening. We'd need at least a week to get to half the places you'd like to see. Let's just play it by ear this afternoon. I'm more concerned about this evening. Do you have any ideas how we can spend it?"

"Of course I do, silly," she grinned mischievously.

"I mean before we do that. Where would you like to have dinner? That could be a real problem with me wearing a white hat's uniform. For instance, I hear the dining room in the Imperial Hotel is out of bounds for enlisted personnel."

"Oh, I wouldn't feel comfortable there, anyway. Actually, I've got a real crazy idea for this evening if it's okay with you."

"You know, Cindy, I'm certain I shouldn't ask but just what is this crazy idea of yours?"

"Why don't you take me to the Rocker-Four Club?"

"The Rocker-Four Club? That's a club for non-coms. It's run by the army. I can't take you there. You're a commissioned officer."

"Of course you can. You're a petty officer. That's the navy equivalent of a non-commissioned officer so you're eligible to go in. Since I'll be wearing civilian clothes and going as your guest, there's no reason for them to ask me anything about rank. Come on, Kev. It'll be fun. I've never been in an E.M. club," she smiled wickedly.

By nine that evening, Cindy and Kevin had decimated a mountain-size serving of Rocker-Four cheeseburgers and fries and were now gently swaying to the foxtrot beat of the small Japanese orchestra that entertained the club's G.I. clientele and their guests each Saturday night. Cynthia felt secure in Kevin's arms as he guided her into a dark corner of the crowded floor. Their bodies pressed tightly together, he could feel the top edge of her girdle pushing against him and he wondered why a girl as trim as Cindy bothered to wear one. Probably to hold up her stockings he concluded as he kissed her gently on the ear.

"Are you enjoying yourself?" Logan asked.

"Yes, I want to thank you for taking me here, and for all the other places we went to today," she answered just as the orchestra stopped for a momentary breather before undertaking the next Glenn Miller medley.

"I should be thanking you. I have to admit I really had a great time today. Besides, you've got the best pair of legs I've ever seen on a tour guide," Kevin grinned.

"Thank you, kind sir. As the old expression goes, flattery will get you anywhere," Cynthia beamed. "You know, Kevin, this is the first time I've ever seen you wear your ribbons. You've got so many. Which one is for Korea?"

"None of them are. The navy won't give us the Korean Campaign Medal until we've put ninety days in Korean waters. So far, we've only had about forty-five with the task force. We'll get it on our next tour, not that I really care one way or another. I got enough ribbons on the *Laffey* to last me for a lifetime. Some of the younger guys on the ship are hot to get some 'fruit salad' on their chest though," he laughed. "Do you see that blue and white ribbon on that Wac sergeant over there? That's the Korean Campaign Ribbon."

"How come she's got one?"

"The army gives the Korean medal to its personnel stationed in Japan. They don't have to get anywhere near Korea. They get it for what the army calls direct support," Kevin smiled.

"Well, I'm glad the army's so liberal. With all the Korean wounded we've been taking care of, I don't see the navy giving us any medals," Cynthia frowned. "Anyway, I don't care about getting a medal. I'm just thankful I'm able to help those poor guys a little. I just wish I could do more for them."

The lights darkened and spotlights from the balcony played over the dancers as the music resumed. The beat picked up with a bouncy "*Moonlight Cocktail*" and "*Chattanooga Choo Choo*," then settled back down with a wistful "*At Last*" and "*Moonlight Serenade*."

This was what real love was all about, Cindy was certain as she let Kevin pull her in close.

Logan could feel the brush of her hair against his cheek, the softness of her body now almost limp as she swayed against him. She smelled real nice, he thought soapy clean, yet quite seductive. Her perfume seemed familiar. "Is that *J'Attendrai* you're wearing?" he asked.

"Yes, it is," she answered with a surprised expression. "You really are a ladies man, aren't you, Kevin? You're even able to identify perfume."

"Now, don't go writing anything into that. I was working at B.B.Y. and S. when they introduced *J'Attendrai* to the American market. For months, every female in our office smelled like she'd just taken a bath in it," Kevin explained, all the while thinking about the fabulous Candace and wondering what she was presently up to.

They danced silently.

"Glenn Miller's music really takes me back to the war years," Kevin said after a few moments.

Cynthia didn't answer.

•   •   •

Once the exclusive stomping ground of the Emperor's top brass, the single-storied Taishokaku squatted somewhat awkwardly along five choice acres of Lake Kawaguchi shoreline. Regarded by insiders as the finest of the many Japanese resort establishments catering to Americans on R and R, the hotel, with its misty ponds and hanging gardens, radiated a story-book image at least a planet removed from recollections of Korea's battle-scorched countryside.

From its sprawling dining room, the Taishokaku's patrons enjoyed a peerless view of legendary Fujiyama. Among the many guests enjoying the sacred mountain's grandeur that Saturday evening were Commander Owen Royal and Captain Tim Barrett, the latter just topping off his dinner with a third bottle of *Asahi* beer. "I've never associated beer with Japan, but this isn't half bad," the four-striper commented. "Sure I can't pour you one, Owen?"

"No, thanks," the commander declined good-naturedly. "You know I've never been much of a beer drinker, especially after a meal as big as the one we just put away. So then, Tim, you were talking about Korea. When do you think you'll have to head back out to the 'Land of the Morning Calm'?"

"The yard-boss at Yokosuka figures the repairs to our boiler could take up to another week. The evaporators are my biggest worry," Barrett frowned. "Seems we no sooner get them working when they crap out again. Having to take salt water showers in hot weather is bad enough, I can't expect my crew to start drinking salt water too. If worse comes to worse, I'll have to figure out a way to store extra water on board. I know we can't sit on our duffs back in Yokosuka while the task force is screaming for fuel oil," Barrett scowled.

"I guess I should consider myself lucky. So far, the Charlie P.'s evaporators have been performing right on the mark. Of course, like every other ship out there, we've had to observe rigid water hours."

"Glad to hear your 'vaps' are working so well," Barrett smiled slyly. "When you bring that kitty car of yours alongside to drink, maybe we can strike up a deal...our fuel oil for your water."

"Okay, that is providing we ever get to refuel from that floating gas station you insist on calling a ship. Three times this month we were slated to fuel from the *Chickamauga* and each time we were diverted to another oiler...twice to the *Aucilla* and the other time to the *Cimarron*."

"That's only because the replenishment force commander likes to save his real pros for the carriers and 'wagons.' Any rinky-dink oiler with a complement of piss-eyed green reserves can top off you 'small boys.' It takes experience and skill to service the first team," Barrett loudly laughed. "Tell me, Owen," the captain's tone suddenly took on a serious note, "now that you're part of the big show again, have you been able to shake off those ghosts you told me about that night in Coronado?"

"I guess so," Owen smiled a little uneasily. "Truth is this so-called police action has kept us so busy with drills, especially gunnery exercises, I haven't had any time left over to reminisce. You know, Tim, I'm certain the *Field's* expended more rounds at radio-controlled drones during the past six weeks than the total amount of shells all four of my ships fired at the Japs in the Pacific. And don't forget...two of those ships were cruisers."

"I can believe that. They've been keeping my gun crews hopping too and we stay well below the thirty-eighth parallel. The sad thing is there's not a ship over here that could stop a Mig if the Reds ever do decide to mount a major air campaign against the task force. For some damnable reason, the navy seems determined to keep all our newest and most efficient ships in the Mediterranean."

"Are you referring to my old ship, the *Coral Sea?*" Royal grinned.

"Yes, and she's not very old, nor are her two sisters, but I'm not only talking about carriers. We've got the three newest, most powerful cruisers in the world sunning themselves in the 'Med' when they should be pounding the hell out of Wonsan with those new rapid-fire eight-inch guns the navy's so proud of."

"I have to admit, I've been wondering why the *Newport News, Salem* and *Des Moines* haven't pulled at least one Korean tour."

"While you're at it, you can wonder about the *Roanoke, Fargo, Huntington, Albany, Oregon City* and a few more post war commissionings I could name that should be over here," Barrett interjected, almost angrily. "You know, Owen, being regular navy all my life, I'd like to assume that the C.N.O. and the rest of the brass back in Washington know what they're doing. Maybe they don't really want to win this one," the four-stripper said with a frown.

"Of course they do. Actually, if you think about it, they're being surprisingly logical. They're sending forgotten ships to fight a forgotten war. Except for a few of the carriers, and a couple of cruisers, just about every ship over here is a World War Two retread...either a refugee from the mothball fleet or just one jump ahead of a ship-breaker's torch."

"From what you've told me about the *Field*, she seems to qualify on both of those counts."

"Oh, she's not a bad ship. I just wish the screen commander would release us for duty with Task Force 95 so I could prove it."

"You're starting to sound a bit bloodthirsty in your old age," Barrett laughed.

"Come on, Tim, you know me better than that. I'd just like to see the Charlie P. get her licks in before this thing ends. Afterall, we did come a hell of a long way to fight a war. That should rate us something more than just wet nursing the carriers. Besides, there's the question of morale. My crew's mostly disgruntled reserves who still haven't figured out why they were suddenly uprooted from their jobs and families and sent over here. I'm certain their attitude would be a little different if they were fighting some tangible enemy like a lot of them were doing in the last war," Owen shrugged.

"Well, you've still got at least six months left on your tour. The *Field* should be seeing more than her share of action in that time. Have any of the other 'cans' in your divisions pulled duty with the bombardment force?"

"Yes and no. Just before we left the task force, our flagship, the *Abner Ward*, was ordered to bombard a railroad trestle near Hangwon but her mission was aborted."

"Aborted? Hah! That must have boiled old Billy Price's beans." Barrett's face grew bright red as he chuckled.

"Do you know the commodore?"

"Of course, I do. That supercilious jackass! Did you forget, he and I were in the same class at the academy?"

"That's a long time ago, Tim. Somehow I thought you were a class ahead of his."

"Hell, no. I even remember how pissed he was at you over some girl you took away from him. It really punctured his pride, losing her to a plebe."

"I really didn't take her away from him. It was just one army-navy game. In fact, he eventually married her. I think he told me they've got twin sons prepping for the academy."

"Twins? I certainly hope they don't take after their father. Can you imagine two more Billy Price's in this man's navy?"

"You do have a point. Say, speaking of sons, how's your boy doing at Pensacola?"

"Great. Lee's almost through basic. He's already fully qualified in SNJ's...starts his jet training in two weeks. From his letters, he's really gung-ho on aviation. I just hope this thing is over before he gets assigned to an air group."

"I don't think you have to worry about that. The navy wouldn't send him to a WestPac carrier straight out of Pensacola. If he does go to sea, I'm certain it will be aboard one of the Mediterranean 'showboats' you were blasting just a minute ago."

"I sure hope so," Barrett said worriedly. After a brief silence, he looked up and asked, "How's that beautiful wife of yours adjusting to California?"

"Fine. I doubt she misses Madison Avenue at all. In her last letter, she mentioned that she had just gotten her agency's biggest client to extend their contract for another two years."

"See, I told you back in Coronado that you were worrying for nothing. You know, Owen, I'm really happy that things are finally working out for you. You really deserve the best," Barrett smiled warmly, pouring himself another tall glass of *Asahi*.

.   .   .

An astute G.I. once philosophized that R and R, like youth, be a fleeting thing. Indeed, it would have been hard to convince anyone aboard the *Charles P. Field* that they had just experienced five full days of R and R, or that a little more than two weeks had passed since they had detached from the task force to seek the transitory pleasures of post-war Japan. Now back on their familiar slot in the screen four-thousand yards out in front of the carriers and the larger gun-ships, the men of the Charlie P. were painfully aware that they had little to look forward to except another 45 days of gray seas, incessant drills and interminable watches.

It was during one of these watches that Bacelli, sitting at the Sugar-George, announced gleefully, "I finally got a look at Cobb today. I had to deliver a message to the old man and I passed Cobb on his way to the head. Boy, what a shiner. No wonder the son-of-a-bitch has been hiding in his cabin since we left Yokosuka."

"If you think he looks bad now, you should have seen him when he came back to the ship that night," Nugent piped up from the Sugar-Charlie. "He told Phelan at the quarterdeck that he'd been mugged by a gang of ex-Jap navy guys. That's not what I heard the next day when I pulled shore patrol."

"What was that?" asked Patterson, who had finally completed his stint in the mess hall.

"One of the gyrene M.P.s told me that Cobb spent the weekend in a cathouse, then refused to pay the mamma-san the full amount they'd agreed to, so her goon-squad waylaid him on his way back to the base."

"Well, it couldn't have happened to a nicer guy," Murray cut in just as the *Field* took a heavy roll, causing a stack of black loose-leaf books to come crashing down from the overhead pub-cabinet.

"Get those damn pubs off the deck, Patterson!" Murray enjoined, grabbing the steel-rimmed edge of the plotting table to keep from tumbling off his stool.

"I sure wish we'd slow up a little," implored Bacelli. "Those damn carriers can go plowing along through this rough a sea at twenty-eight knots just as if they were cruising on Prospect Park Lake, but it sure knocks the hell out of the destroyers. Doesn't Jehovah know that?"

As if in answer to his question, the large gray speaker mounted above the D.R.T. began to cough and cackle. A few more seconds of static were followed by the words...

"BIRTHRATE...THIS IS JEHOVAH. HOW ARE YOUR 'SMALL BOYS' RIDING? DO YOU SUGGEST WE REDUCE PRESENT SPEED? OVER."

"JEHOVAH...THIS IS BIRTHRATE." boomed the reply from the screen commander. "MY SMALL BOYS ARE TAKING A BEATING AT OUR PRESENT SPEED. IF CONDUCIVE TO OUR MISSION, I STRONGLY RECOMMEND WE REDUCE SPEED. OVER."

"BIRTHRATE...THIS IS JEHOVAH. I CONCUR. PREPARE TO REDUCE SPEED TO XRAY-PETER KNOTS. OUT."

"What's xray-peter on today's grid?" Murray asked Patterson who was standing near the status-board.

"Twenty-five knots," the young radar-striker quickly replied.

"Big deal," Nugent sneered as *DD-505* slammed headlong into another oncoming wave. "Three lousy knots, hell, Jehovah should cut our speed down to no more than fifteen knots in this kind of a sea. What's he care, anyway? Hell, he's sitting high and dry in a comfortable cabin on the *Iowa*."

"Knock it off, Nugent," shot back Murray. "I'm sure we wouldn't be steaming up north this fast if the carriers weren't really after an important target. Who knows, maybe the Commies are moving down another fresh regiment of troops like that time last month. If our planes can catch them on the roads again before they reach our front lines, some of those dogfaces in the foxholes might live to get home and see their folks this Christmas." Then turning towards the metal squawk-box, Murray shouted, "Bridge...Combat. Jehovah has informed the screen commander that we will be reducing our speed to twenty-five knots."

"Bridge, aye," Ensign Daly replied blankly.

"SPECTACLE...THIS IS JEHOVAH. SPEED XRAY-PETER. I SAY AGAIN, SPEED XRAY-PETER. STANDBY TO EXECUTE!...EXECUTE!"

"Bridge, Combat...Jehovah to all ships...reduce speed to twenty-five knots," reported Murray instantly.

"Bridge, aye," again came the response from the JOD, and within minutes, the dial on the speed-indicator was steadying on the numeral 25.

"Dammit, tonight's watch is really dragging," Nugent sulked as he looked up at the bulkhead clock to discover that it was not yet seven o'clock.

"What's the difference? You've got nowhere to go," Murray grunted.

"Hell, he hasn't," Bacelli said, bracing himself as the *Field* took another heavy roll. "Nugent's hot to get back to the electrician's shack. He's trying to set the all-time record for seeing that Wave hygiene flick. He's seen it fourteen times already."

"Fifteen!" Nugent angrily corrected. "Besides, you should be the last one to talk. You've seen it at least twelve times, yourself."

"Yeah, but I'm just about sick of watching it. Hell, you can't even see their faces."

"Since when did you start looking at faces?" Nugent countered.

"Far as I'm concerned, you're both a couple of sex perverts," Murray shook his head in disgust. "Why don't you two start thinking about something constructive like maybe going to college next year when your enlistments are up. At least I've got a job waiting for me. What are you two going to do, qualify as experts on female anatomy?"

"I don't know about Nugent over there, but I'm going into business introducing those neat little bite-size Chinese egg rolls...the kind they had back at 'Don the Beachcomber's Dagger Bar' in Waikiki. Boy, they were great. They're gonna really love them back in the States," Bacelli smiled smugly.

"What's a guinea like you know about chink food anyway?" Nugent snapped indignantly.

"A hell of a lot more than you micks do! Did you forget, I grew up in Brooklyn in a neighborhood that was about eighty percent Jewish? Nobody gobbles up as much Chinese food as the Jews. We had at least one Chinese restaurant on every block along Flatbush Avenue. Just wait until they get a taste of those little egg rolls. I'll make a fortune."

"Don't you think you ought to let 'Don the Beachcomber's' in on your grandiose plans?" Murray interjected.

"Sure, that's the first thing I'm going to do when we stop off at Pearl on our way home. I'll make a deal with them to act as their Stateside rep. You just watch, Howie. Three years from now when you take your wife and kids to a baseball game, those little egg rolls will be out-selling the hot dogs. You can tell your family that you knew the guy who started it all."

"Speaking of baseball games," Nugent called out from the air-search radar, "I'm really getting sick of this damn screening duty. All the other destroyer divisions have had their crack at the Reds. When the hell are we going to get our turn at bat?"

The inning came sooner than anyone aboard DD-505 had expected. That evening, only minutes after Nugent and Bacelli had each paid a dollar fee that would gain them entrance to the electrician's shack, the Ward, Wayne, Morgan and Field received the long awaited word. The four destroyers would detach at ten the following morning; their course 320 true to a point just north of Songjin; their target, a newly located ammunition bunker and the carefully camouflaged spur track used to feed it.

Chapter XIII - Fire Mission

Daylight emerged with a warm westerly wind that spindled whitecaps on the tossing gray sea and swept the sky blue but for one ball of fluff that seemed painted to the horizon.

At precisely 10:00, the message, "CAPRICORN...THIS IS BIRTHRATE... XRAY-LOVE-FOUR," poured out of the tin-faced speakers on board *Ward, Morgan, Wayne* and *Field*. Within minutes, all four destroyers had vacated their slots in the screen to slip neatly astern of the task force which, with eerie dispatch, had faded completely from view in a wall of haze that formed suddenly to the north. In a short time, even the radar scopes would surrender any trace they had held of the armada, the presence of which had become as accepted a fact of life to the men of DesDiv 291 as the daily rising and setting of the sun.

Steaming in a loose column with a thousand yard interval between each ship, the gray quartet soon steadied up on course 320 true; flagship *Ward* in the lead, the Charlie P. bringing up the rear.

Aboard the *Field*, helmets and kapok life jackets flew haphazardly through the air as ship's company, in their inimitable Keystone Cop fashion, scrambled to "clear the decks for action." Far below the bridge in the radar shack, Howie Murray's attention focused on one of the hurtling gray helmets. He watched it fall from Gardiner's hands to bounce clumsily across the black rubber deck matting until it finally collided with the leg of a chair. What was he doing in this dark little room amid all this insanity when he should be home reading the comics to Deirdre and little Jenny? What unspeakable sin could he have committed to cause God to punish him this way, Murray asked himself as he adjusted the khaki cloth liner in the helmet he was holding. All this was supposed to have ended for him back in forty-five. That final morning on Big Ben had to make up for anything he might experience in a thousand purgatories, the first-class mused as he wiped the sweat from the back of his neck.

He looked across the plotting table at Logan who was entering a status report in the C.I.C. log. Cool as the proverbial cucumber, Murray thought, amazed at his shipmate's casualness. Around him, the other eight enlisted members of the

Field's radar gang were putting on a great show of excitement. This was understandable, Murray reasoned. After all, these imbeciles had never seen a ship torn inside out. They'd never smelled burning hair and flesh, nor heard the whine of dying men trapped in a flaming compartment. But Logan, he'd lived through this obscenity. Granted, his friend had little sense of genuine values. Even so, it wasn't natural for anyone to appear this unconcerned about sailing into a gun fight on an obsolete "honey barge" like the *Field*. Just what was on Logan's mind, Murray wondered, convinced that the only thing that would shake Kevin up would be the realization that if he "bought the farm," there'd be two or three hundred females back on Madison Avenue he'd never get a chance to screw.

Murray remembered the lei, and how it had floated out to sea that morning off Oahu. Hell, that was only superstition, he told himself. How could he, a practicing Catholic, put any stock in something like that? Besides being totally illogical, it was probably just something the natives made up to get the tourists to buy their damn flowers...still, wouldn't it be a bitch if he was to get snuffed out in this dirty little war after making it all the way through the Pacific.

"How's things coming along in here, Murray?" shouted Ensign Coates, sticking his head through the small doorway.

"We're just about squared away now, Sir. Do you know what time the captain's planning to officially call away G.Q.?" Murray asked, again feeling a pang of nausea.

"No idea. Guess you'll just have to play it by ear. I've got the afternoon bridge watch. If anything develops, I'll send word right down to you," Coates said jubilantly, then quickly disappeared from the doorway.

That damn fool's actually enjoying all this, Murray shook his head in total despair.

By mid-afternoon the four destroyers were galloping across the water at a brisk twenty-six knots. Up on the starboard bridge-wing, Commander Royal peered aft over the flag-bags to watch the midship and two stern mounts swivel noisily back and forth between port and starboard, their long gun-barrels ceaselessly elevating and depressing as the *Field's* gunners flexed their muscles.

Ahead, *Abner Ward's* signalmen were breaking out pennant after pennant; a pale spiral of smoke danced atop *John Morgan's* after stack, and from *Halsey Wayne's* outermost halyard, a Confederate flag whipped the Korean sky with unremitting ferocity.

"So this is the land of the morning calm," exclaimed the *Field's* executive officer, loosening the chin buckle on his helmet strap. He leaned forward and gripped the metal splinter screen that girded the bridge-wing. "I don't think I've ever seen an uglier stretch of coastline anywhere," Cobb scowled.

"I've a strong hunch it'll get even uglier around seventeen-hundred," Royal answered grimly, then turning abruptly towards the wheelhouse door, he asked, "Are all stations manned and ready, Mister Kimmick?"

"Yes, Sir," the OD reported from his conning station. "Radio-central was the last and they checked in a few minutes ago. Condition-one has been set throughout the ship," the lieutenant continued with a broad smile, "and I'm happy to add, Sir, that all hands are eagerly waiting at the post."

"For the sake of all those eager hands, we'd better be certain we make the winner's circle," the captain replied as the navigator, Lieutenant Philip Oetjens, joined the small huddle of officers on the open bridge.

Oetjens quickly slipped into one of the bulky kapok life-jackets that had been splotched with bright "red-lead" for easier spotting in the water. The other officers, including the captain, were wearing the inflatable and more comfortable "Mae West" which Oetjens considered far less reliable.

"Look anything like Normandy, Phil?" Royal queried the new arrival.

"To be honest, Sir, I was so busy ducking, I never really did get a good look. As I remember, though, the land seemed much flatter with sheer cliffs that dropped down to the beach. Now that over there," he said pointing, "reminds me of broken glass on a backyard fence."

"Don't look so grim, Phil," Owen Royal counseled in a tone of calculated reassurance. "I don't expect we'll be running into anything comparable to what the Germans threw at you."

"No, I guess not, but when I was at Normandy, I went in with a crowd...at least four thousand other targets. I figured the Krauts wouldn't waste too many shells on my innocuous little LSM with that many tempting targets to shoot at," he frowned, tugging at the dangling straps of his life jacket. "Somehow, the odds aren't too comforting today."

A loud grinding noise announced that the *Field's* two forward gun houses had also come to life.

"The old girl sounds pretty pugnacious," Royal laughed as he watched the guns swing back to center-line, stop with a loud squeak, elevate, then train once more to starboard.

Ahead, the five-inch rifles on *DD-505's* three consorts spun and stretched in similar fashion, then as Royal and his officers watched, *Morgan* and *Ward* joined *Wayne* in hoisting the "Stars and Bars."

"Okay, Anderson, you can run it up now!" shouted Owen Royal to his chief signalman, and to the squeal of well-worn halyards, a gold-bordered blue flag with the national eagle in its center flew quickly to the *Field's* starboard yardarm.

"What the hell's that?" exclaimed Cobb, wrinkling the inch of red forehead that showed below his helmet and contrasted so markedly with the purplish-blue skin around his still-swollen right eye.

"It's a Union cavalry flag," Royal smiled proudly. "I got it from a mail-order house at Gettysburg that specializes in that sort of thing."

A flashing light suddenly appeared on *Halsey Wayne's* signal bridge. Anderson snatched the clipboard from Bodine, a signalman-third who was standing nearby. Scribbling down the message, the chief looked up and said, "*Wayne's* confused as hell, Sir. They just sent us an interog on our last signal."

"We didn't send a signal."

"No, Sir. I think it's that flag we just two-blocked. Do you want me to answer with the blinker?"

"No, Chief, the commodore might see it and get confused. I'm certain Captain Boland on the *Wayne* has caught on by now. Afterall, we didn't send out an interog when those three canoes hauled up their 'Johnny Reb' flags."

"Aye, aye, Sir," the chief shrugged.

"Captain," petitioned Coates from the wheelhouse doorway. "All hands are already at battle stations except for the bridge watch. When should I have the bo'sun sound general-quarters, Sir, you know, just in case some straggler below decks hasn't gotten the word?"

Royal tried to suppress a grin. "Why don't you call G.Q. away yourself, Mr. Coates," the captain suggested, adding "and use that bugle recording, the one we keep in the charthouse. I suppose we might just as well do this in the regulation manner."

"Yes, Sir. Thank you, Sir," the young officer beamed happily.

"What's gotten into him?" Oetjens puzzled.

"Nothing, Phil," said Royal. "It's his first police action and I imagine he just wants to make the most of it."

Seconds later, the blast of bugle and clang of bells escaped from every speaker above and below decks. "Now hear this!...Now hear this! General-quarters!...general-quarters!...all hands man your battle stations!"

"Well, he certainly did it in the regulation manner," Owen chuckled.

"He couldn't have been any more regulation if John Ford had been directing the scene," Cobb added dryly.

Surrendering his watch on the bridge to Andy Phelan, Coates flew down the ladder, eager to take over his station as C.I.C. officer alongside Lieutenant Stockwell and the radar gang. At the same time Oetjens relieved Kimmick as OD, the latter scampering off to the main engine room.

"Mister Phelan...range to the beach!" Owen Royal shouted to the wheelhouse as Cobb departed for his G.Q. station in after-steering.

"Twenty-two thousand, five hundred yards, Captain. That's to the nearest point of land, Point Ko-cho, bearing 328 to 331 true, Sir," the JOD replied, reading the range and bearing directly from the radar repeater.

"Almost eleven miles, Captain," Lieutenant Oetjens said staring in the direction of Phelan's bearing. "I understand long range batteries clobbered one of our 'cans' at almost this range near Hungnam last week."

"Yes, from here on in our men should start earning their free mail privileges."

The *Field's* bow dipped and a veil of spray saturated the face of the wheelhouse.

"You lookouts on the foc'sle!" the captain suddenly barked, aiming a weatherbeaten megaphone at two seamen squatting on the taut black links of the anchor cable. "Keep a sharp eye for mines, especially in the wakes of the ships ahead!" He placed the megaphone down heavily on the lid of the bulkhead telephone box and turned to the navigator.

"Some of those Red influence mines won't activate until a specific number of ships have passed within range...then wham!" the captain gestured with his fist. "It could be the third or fourth ship in column that triggers the damn thing. That way they get a crack at a cruiser or wagon being led in by a line of cans. If they're lucky...Mister Oetjens," the captain's voice suddenly took on a tone of anger. "That foc'sle lookout pointing his binoculars back at number-two mount...what's his name?"

"He's one of Mister MacKinlay's boys...I think his name's McAlleney."

McAlleney, one of the two men who caused all the fuss with army intelligence, Royal remembered. "You! McAlleney!" he shouted hoarsely and without the megaphone. "That's not Moonlight Bay out there! Stop the skylarking and keep your eyes glued on that water or else you might find yourself swimming in it!...and us right alongside you," he uttered half under his breath.

"Shucks," McAlleney drawled, sucking in his mouth as if he was chewing on a lemon. "What's the ole man getting up such a head a steam about, anyway?" he asked Sweetpea Hopkins, the other lookout.

McAlleney reluctantly raised his binoculars pointing them at the pitching stern of *Halsey Wayne*. He studied the black lettering along the stern and watched the sun expose the skeleton beneath the destroyer's paper-thin hide. Bored with his assignment, he began to drawl his favorite song, one alerting all in the foc'sle area that shrimp boats were a'-comin'.

From the bridge the land seemed less gray than muddy now.

"When do you think they'll open up?" asked Oetjens. "That beach is starting to look awfully close, Captain."

"Intelligence says most the radar around here is restricted to their anti-aircraft batteries. I imagine they won't disclose their positions until we've closed within easy range," Royal answered coolly. "Besides, Phil," he smiled, "there's nothing to worry about, don't you read the papers? This is a non-naval war, remember?...Range to the nearest point of land, Mister Phelan!" he snapped suddenly.

"Point Ko-cho...eighteen-thousand yards, bearing 329," came an instant response.

"Nine miles to touch-down," the captain exclaimed, darting to the port wing. "They're almost in range of our fives now but our orders say we don't fire unless they do," he muttered aloud.

"Signal from the flagship, Captain," shouted Anderson from the flagbags. "Increase speed to twenty-eight knots!"

"That's it, Phil. We'd better button-up," Royal said with a sudden tone of urgency. "You lookouts on the foc'sle...get to cover!" the captain directed with the megaphone, dispatching McAlleney and Sweetpea down the starboard side to their G.Q. stations on the Bofors twin-40 millimeter mounted abreast the second stack.

"We're making turns for twenty-eight knots, Sir," JOD Phelan announced as Royal and Oetjens entered the wheelhouse.

"Very well, watch your range to *Halsey Wayne*. Make sure we're not tailgating just in case Captain Boland should have to slow up for any reason," the captain warned.

Towering high above the wheelhouse, the Mark-37 main battery director spun noisily around to starboard until it reached a bearing facing Point Ko-cho. The five 5-inch rifles; two forward; one midship; two aft; immediately trained around to an identical bearing. The smaller Mark-51 directors followed suit and within seconds, the twin-forties, starboard and aft, were showing their muzzles to the rocky finger of land, the name of which to McAlleney, sounded more like a sneeze than a geographic location.

Suffering the confines of the wheelhouse and the limited field of vision that it afforded, Owen Royal was soon back out on the open bridge, his binoculars sweeping the enemy shore and the ships ahead.

Ensign Ritter poked his head through the hatch atop the big box-shaped Mark-37, spotted his commanding officer prancing the wing below, and retracted back into his gray shell with turtle-like animation.

"Mister Ritter!" shouted the captain, and the closely-shaven head of the *Field's* assistant-gunnery officer popped once more into view.

"How are your communications with Mister MacKinlay in gun-plot and Mister Stockwell in C.I.C.?" Royal inquired loudly.

"Excellent, Sir. We just tested all circuits a minute ago."

"Good. Remember, we'll be constantly selecting new targets so keep your guns loose. There should be plenty to go around for each mount. And get a helmet on! And that means now, Mister!"

The ensign whined an acknowledgement, and submerged once more among the jumble of computers and cables that were the heart and arteries of the *Field's* main-battery director.

"There's a flashing light three points off the starboard bow, Captain!" a lookout positioned atop the wheelhouse excitedly announced.

"Yes, I see it," acknowledged Royal, lowering his binoculars, then turning towards Oetjens who once again had ventured out on to the open bridge, the captain said, "That light seems to be blinking at irregular intervals. Inform gun-plot and tell Mister MacKinlay to mark its position on his grid."

"Yes, Sir. It's probably a fire-control station of some kind," Oetjens suggested nervously. "Some Red battery commander's telling his boys that they can expect company for dinner."

"I think they're a lot sharper than that, Phil. More likely, it's some coolie perched in a tree with a lantern so he can draw our fire while they zero in on us. It's the places where we don't see any activity that we'll have to sweat." Royal looked back towards the signal bridge. "Make any sense out of that flashing light, Anderson?"

"No, Captain," the old chief shrugged. "It's not Morse...more like chow-mein!"

"Mr. Phelan," the captain cried out as he stepped into the wheelhouse. You can secure the port hatch but keep this one on one dog. I'll be constantly shifting between here and the wing."

The *Field's* C.O. took a stance in the center of the wheelhouse between the helmsman and his mate on the engine-order-telegraph.

"Combat, Bridge," he shouted into the long brass-necked funnel that arched python-like from the overhead.

"Combat aye," came a nervous giggle from Ensign Coates.

"Watch those hills at zero-two-five for low flying aircraft. Be certain whoever you've got on the air-search radar knows how to get the most out of that gain-control knob," Royal cautioned.

"Yes, Sir," replied the C.I.C. officer almost before the captain had finished the order.

"We're getting excellent resolution on the A-scope, Captain," Lieutenant Stockwell's voice cut in over the squawk-box from C.I.C. "We should be able to pick out any air contact from the land mass without too much trouble."

Coates wiped the sweat from his receding hairline as he turned toward the third-class on the Sugar-Charlie. "Holiday, you heard Captain Royal! Are you sure you know how to work that gain-control?"

"Yes, Mister Coates," the radarman sighed with discernible exasperation, then drooped back over his scope.

"Don't know why Stockwell told the old man that," Holiday scowled to Nugent on the nearby surface radar. "There's more grass on this damn scope than Carter's got little liver pills!"

"I'll be needing steady ranges and bearings, Nugent," Coates grunted angrily, "so stop bull-shitting with Holiday and get ready to read them off! Where do you hold Point Ko-cho, now?"

Nugent sullenly cranked the radar dial on the Sugar-George, then adjusted his bearing cursor until it had dissected the image on the scope. "Point Ko-cho...three-three-eight, sixteen thousand yards," the sailor announced with little emotion.

"Give me a reading on that piece of land just north of Ko-cho!" Lieutenant Stockwell shouted, standing beside Coates and Logan at the D.R.T. "There's a hill near the water. The strip of land behind it has a pretty low elevation according to this chart so the hill will probably show up on your scope looking like an island."

"Yes, Sir, I've got what looks like an island at three-four-five...sixteen thousand, eight hundred yards," Nugent informed the *Field's* Ops officer, who, during general quarters, functioned as C.I.C. evaluator and as liaison with MacKinlay and his people in gun-plot. The gunnery officer, in turn, had direct link-up with the Mark-37 as well as all other fire-control stations throughout the ship.

"Any luck finding that hill, Nugent?" Stockwell called out impatiently. "That's where the spur track starts," the lieutenant explained, indicating the location on the chart with the points of his dividers. "The ammo bunker is further north...here behind this hilly area," he drawled, penciling in an X and measuring its distance from a dead-reckoning fix on lead-ship *Abner Ward*.

"With us being low-man on the totem," Murray questioned, "do you think they'll be anything left worth shooting at after *Ward, Morgan* and *Wayne* get in their licks?"

"We aren't going after the bunker," said Stockwell, surprised that Coates hadn't familiarized his C.I.C. team with the details of the operation. "That job belongs to *Ward* and *Morgan*. We're along strictly for counter-battery fire. Our assignment is to knock out the guns and director system on Point Ko-cho. The *Wayne's* tackling the Mop-cho batteries opposite."

"Might have known we wouldn't be carrying the ball," Bacelli scowled from the vertical plot. "We just pull the messy job of running interference."

"That's enough griping!" Coates warned. Then glancing towards Murray, the ensign instructed, "You'd better check Nugent and Holiday. See that they've got those scopes in focus."

"Range to Point Ko-cho!" Logan requested loudly from his station at the dead-reckoning tracer.

"Range to *Halsey Wayne!*" demanded Coates.

"Let me have a quick range and bearing to Mop-cho Peninsula!" ordered Stockwell.

"Range to the nearest point of land!" came an urgent summons from the bridge via the squawk-box.

"Check that range you gave me to Mop-cho! It can't be right!" Stockwell snarled.

"Range to *Abner Ward!*" the captain's voice boomed from the spout of the speaker-tube.

"Give me a new range to Ko-cho!" Logan yelled.

"What happened to that range to Mop-cho? Did you check it out yet?" Stockwell implored.

And Nugent swallowed hard as he cranked the dials positioning the cursor, and twisted the countless knobs and buttons on the Sugar George.

They were moving in fast and on the open bridge, Royal aimed his glasses at the halyards of the ships ahead, awaiting the commodore's signal for independent action.

"Be ready for some split-second maneuvering, Mister Oetjens," Royal cautioned the officer-of-the-deck. "Remember, if the Reds don't disclose their gun layout, we'll hold fire until we've closed to eight thousand yards. We'll open up with number one and two guns, then swing forty-five degrees to port and give them the full treatment broadside from all five mounts. We'll follow that with another turn to port, this time ninety degrees. This will allow us to steer an evasive course seaward with one-eight-five as our base course. On the way out, our stern mounts should get their licks in at Mop-cho. If all goes according to schedule and we don't get hit, the entire maneuver should take approximately twenty minutes. Second time around, we'll reverse the circle trading places with *Halsey Wayne*. We'll be making starboard turns with Mop-cho first on the agenda while the *Wayne* tackles Ko-cho. Halfway through the second run, we should be in position to cover *Ward* and *Morgan* during their withdrawal from the inner harbor. You'd better inform Combat to make certain our DRT plot is right on the mark. Tell them to let us know if our turning diameter closes within a thousand yards of *Halsey Wayne* any time during the maneuver."

"Sir," Lieutenant Phelan petitioned from the wheelhouse doorway, "Radio-telephone message to all ships from *Abner Ward*...They hold an air contact at zero-five-five true, twenty miles...no IFF!"

"Twenty miles," Royal flushed angrily. "Ask Combat if they hold anything at that range and bearing!"

"I've got them," Oetjens announced, his binoculars squeezed tightly to his eyes. "There's three of them...prop jobs...they look like Mustangs."

Phelan rejoined Royal and Oetjens on the bridge-wing. "Mister Coates reports his air-search radar is useless for low-flying contacts within twenty miles. He says it's because of the hills."

"I think Coates and that radar gang of his are useless within twenty miles," Oetjens muttered half under his breath.

"I was afraid those hills might give us trouble, although they don't seem to have bothered the C.I.C. team on the *Ward*," Royal frowned. "Mister Phelan...you're the resident airplane buff, take a look...would you say they're Mustangs?"

"No, Sir, they're definitely not P-51s," the JOD answered worriedly as he focused his glasses on the three specks. "I think they're Yaks, Sir,...Yak-9s!" Phelan suddenly sang out.

Oetjens ran into the wheelhouse and returned seconds later with an O.N.I. identification manual. "Yak-9P, Russian-built...fighter bomber," the OD said, scanning the oblong-shaped book. "Maximum speed 414 miles per hour, armament one engine-mounted 20-milimeter cannon and two 12.7-milimeter machine guns. This type of aircraft is capable of carrying light bombs or rockets for ground attack," he read slowly.

"Very well, pass the word to MacKinlay to get his guns locked on. They look like they're getting set to make a strafing run. As I recall, it was Yaks that bombed the *Rochester* and the British *Jamaica* at Inchon," Royal advised.

"Think those planes will really make a pass?" Oetjens asked, his glasses still fixed on the distant intruders.

"They don't seem to be closing. I imagine they're trying to determine if we've got a combat-air-patrol in the vicinity."

"We do...don't we, Sir?" Oetjens asked hopefully.

"The air force was supposed to keep a standby cap within calling just in case we ran into anything like those three up there. Unfortunately, the carriers have all gone north. They went after a string of bridges at some place called 'Carlson's Canyon.' Anyway, I'm certain the commodore's put out a call for air cover by now."

Royal's assumption was confirmed a moment later when Little Gilly puffed his way up to the bridge to deliver a freshly decoded cryptogram from the commodore to the Fifth Air Force area commander.

"That's a relief," sighed the OD, wiping the wrinkle of neck between the bottom of his helmet and the top of his life jacket.

"Our hosts must be monitoring our frequency," Royal observed. "Even if they can't decode Price's message, they must have figured out that he'd called for air cover. They seem to be calling the hounds off." The captain paused and watched the three black specks quickly disappear beyond the northern-most fringe of mountains. The respite was short-lived.

"Captain! Many bogies closing at two-nine-five, seventy miles!" shouted Phelan from the wheelhouse doorway.

"Is that from our radars?"

"No, Sir, *Halsey Wayne's.*"

"We hold them now, Captain!" the JOD amended seconds later. "Combat reports bogies at two-nine-five, sixty miles...course one-one-five, speed five hundred...no I.F.F.!"

"Very well. Get MacKinlay and Ritter on them right away!" Royal turned to Oetjens. "Those first three could have been decoys sent up there to distract us. This could be the first string...probably Mig 15's. One-one-five will put them right overhead in a matter of minutes. Looks like we're in for a little skeet shooting."

The directors and guns on all four destroyers swung in unison to bearing 295 and a new string of flags flapped and fluttered their way up *Ward's* halyards.

"Here's where we cash in on all that practice with the drones," Royal smiled.

"I hope so, Captain," Oetjens shrugged. "The only thing though, those drones couldn't shoot back."

Commander Royal aimed his glasses at the anticipated bearing. "I'm sure the commodore would never admit it, but I bet right now he's damn glad our gun gang's along to keep his roof swept clean," he said with a faint smile.

"Gun-plot reports all guns locked on, Sir," the bridge-talker announced with an adolescent squeal.

"Signal from the flagship, Captain!" cried Phelan. "Execute to follow, reduce speed to eighteen knots."

Royal acknowledged, then turned towards Oetjens. "I assume the commodore doesn't want us bottled up inside the harbor if we have to maneuver to avoid those planes."

"That makes two of us."

"Mister Phelan!" shouted the captain. "Be prepared for a hundred and eighty degree turn. I expect the commodore will signal formation X-ray, so work out a solution that will put us in station-four with as little maneuvering as possible. Get Mister Coates and his radar gang hot on it, too. The turn will probably be to starboard so..."

"CAPRICORN, THIS IS BIRDBATH. NEGAT MY ITEM-ZEBRA-SPEED LOVE. BOGIES AT TWO-NINER-FIVE, FORTY-EIGHT...SQUAWKING

FRIENDLY...OUT," rang loudly from the wheelhouse speaker.

Royal understood the meaning even before Phelan and Coates and his radar gang had translated the phonetic word combinations from the general-signal book. The message from Price to all ships in the division cancelled the standing order for a speed reduction. More important, it informed all concerned that the flagship's radar had picked up the proper electronic recognition signal from the approaching aircraft.

"Guess you'll have to wait a little longer for the answer, Phil."

"What answer is that, Captain?"

"Whether or not our gang will be as good against live game as they were against drones."

"Frankly, Sir, I'm in no great hurry to find out. I'm perfectly happy to leave that one up to conjecture," Oetjens laughed.

"I think I see the planes now," Royal said, adjusting the focus on his binoculars. "They're just in that open area between the two highest peaks."

"Yes, Sir, I see them. They sure are moving in fast. I can't make out their type though. Do we have any fighters with twin jet engines?"

"Mister Phelan!" Royal called. "Come out here! We need your expertise again. The Reds may be trying to give us a fast shuffle. What do you make them out to be?"

Phelan raised his glasses and with a broad smile, he announced, "Meteors, Captain...it's okay, they're Gloster Meteors...British, but most of the Commonwealth Air Forces use them too."

"Captain." interrupted the young bridge-talker, "Combat reports the approaching aircraft are now squawking friendly. The *Abner Ward* has contacted them on the fighter-director net and they're Australian. Their call name is Titan-one, Sir."

"Very well. Ask Combat for a range and bearing to Point Ko-cho."

"Point Ko-cho now bears three-four-five, range twelve-thousand, three hundred yards, Sir," came the almost instant reply.

"About six miles," Royal muttered. "Have Combat pass up a range and bearing every thirty seconds."

"Combat reports that the range to *Halsey Wayne* is three-hundred yards, and Point Ko-cho now bears three-five-one, eleven thousand, two-hundred yards, and *Abner Ward* has requested Titan-one to orbit overhead, Sir," the young sailor proclaimed in a single breath, trying not to confuse the details.

"Very well. Has Titan-one acknowledged the flagship's request?"

"I don't know, Sir. Combat didn't say," the bridge-talker answered nervously.

Royal re-entered the wheelhouse, heading directly to the squawk-box. "Combat, bridge, this is the captain. What's the story on Titan-one? Are they going to cover us, and if so, at what altitude? I don't want our gunners scratching any of the few allies we've got over here."

"Yes, Sir," Stockwell answered. "Titan-one informed the flagship that they only have enough fuel to stay on station for thirty minutes. Their flight leader said that they would orbit overhead with two sections, one at angels-one-eight, and one at angels-one-five,"

"Have you passed that on to MacKinlay and Ritter?"

"Yes, Sir. Just a second before you called."

"Very well, keep me informed of all transmissions to and from the flagship."

"Yes, Sir," Stockwell sheepishly acknowledged, not certain if he had just been put on the carpet for not getting the word to his commanding officer.

Royal returned to the wing in time to see the first four jets roar over "Price's Expendables." With an ear-shattering blast, the planes made a second pass at the destroyers. Skimming over the water at masthead level, the Meteors banked sharply, then climbed to their assigned patrol altitude of 15,000 feet. The four Meteors that made up the two sections of the second division repeated the maneuver, almost decapitating the *Field's* bedspring antenna in the process. The planes then raised their noses just short of the Ko-cho peaks, and rocketed skyward to orbit the area at 18,000 feet.

Royal and Oetjens trained their glasses on the black rock; the muddy uneven splashes of grays, greens and browns that cloaked Ko-cho Peninsula. They watched and waited for the anticipated flashes which would disclose their opponent's anti-aircraft batteries and hopefully some of his other defensive positions. To their total surprise, the Australians soared unopposed.

"Looks like Uncle Joe is saving all his apples for us," said Oetjens.

"Point Ko-cho now bears three-five-eight...ten thousand, one-hundred yards, Captain," the talker announced on his thirty-second schedule.

Ashore, the solitary blinker remained the only sign of human habitation.

Ahead, *Wayne, Morgan* and *Ward* suddenly began to slip to the right of the *Field's* jackstaff.

"Mister Phelan!" shouted Royal, "Did we receive a turn execution from the flagship?"

"No, Sir," came a bewildered reply. "Formation course is still three-two-zero, twenty-eight knots."

"Well, something's fouled up! Either the column's moving off to starboard or we're falling out of formation! Helmsman!" the captain bellowed, brushing past Oetjens and Phelan as he charged the wheelhouse. "What course are you steering?"

"Three-two-zero, Sir," Goodfellow, the boatswain at the helm answered with a bewildered expression.

"We're at least five degrees off course! Come right to three-two-five on the double!"

"Coming right to three-two-five," the helmsman repeated as he turned the rubber rimmed wheel. "Steady on three-two-five, Sir," he added seconds later.

"Very well...Mister Phelan, you'd better get someone on the gyro right away. We seem to be carrying a five degree deviation. Have combat..."

"Ship's not answering the helm, Captain!" Goodfellow interrupted loudly. "I've lost all rudder control! We're passing three-three-zero and we're still swinging fast!"

Royal lunged at the squawk-box panel. "After-steering, bridge! You have control! Steady up on three-two-five!"

"After-steering, aye. Steady up on three-two-five," came the executive officer's instant acknowledgement.

Bridge-talker! Inform all stations that we've switched control from the bridge to after-steering...Helmsmen! Keep singing out those bearings. Let me know the second after-steering steadies up on..."

"SHIFTLESS, THIS IS BIRDBATH. INTERROGATIVE YOUR PRESENT COURSE AND SPEED...OVER," came Price's voice via the TBS in a tone more astonished than annoyed.

Royal thumbed through the section in the general-signal book dealing with breakdowns. Opposite steering casualty was the code George-Item-love-4.

"BIRDBATH...THIS IS SHIFTLESS. GEORGE-ITEM-LOVE-FOUR...MY SPEED SHACKLE MIKE-ABLE KNOTS. WILL FURTHER ADVISE IN SHADOW... OUT," he replied without rendering the customary "over".

"Bridge, after-steering! We've lost all control down here, too, Captain!" Cobb's voice came over the bridge-speaker in a frantic pitch. "Rudder appears to be jammed over. Sternhagen and his people are checking it now."

After what seemed an eternity, the red button on the squawk-box flashed once more and Sternhagen reported, "Oil line to the starboard ram is ruptured, Captain. It's gushing like 'Old Faithful' down here. Request permission to cross connect gear to the port ram."

"Permission granted, Rolf, but do it fast! We're moving in a pretty wide circle and I don't feature piling up on Point Ko-cho. I'm cutting speed to fifteen knots while you make repairs...Lee-Helmsman! Make turns for fifteen knots!"

"Mister Phelan!" instructed Royal. "Get radio-central to send the following to the flagship in crypto. We have a ruptured oil line on the steering engine and we're reducing speed to fifteen knots. We expect repairs to be completed momentarily. Estimated time to rejoin the column at flank speed is twelve minutes."

"Engine-room reports we are making turns for fifteen knots, Sir," the lee-helmsman loudly announced.

Commander Royal eyed the formation through the open wheelhouse doorway. *Wayne*, *Morgan* and *Ward* were far off the port bow.

"Combat, bridge," the C.O. beckoned through the voice-tube. "If we continue around at our present angle of turn, how close will we come to Point Ko-cho? Also, how close will we come to Area-Dog on your chart? It's suspected of containing a mine field."

Anticipating the captain's questions, Logan had already worked out both problems on the maneuvering board and had passed the answers on to Stockwell and Coates.

"We'll clear Point Ko-cho by three thousand yards, Sir...the extreme outer fringe of Area-Dog by less than one-hundred yards," reported a noticeably worried Stockwell.

"Bridge, after-steering!" Sternhagen's voice rang out. "Captain, we're in big trouble down here! We can't cross connect to the port ram. The valve was frozen so we tried to turn it with a pipe wrench. The valve stem split and the handle flew off!"

"And just how soon do you think you can make it fly back on?" Royal's tone was now void of all patience.

"Don't know, Captain. Valve stem's shot. Only thing I can suggest is to have a patch welded on to the starboard fuel-line, but that will take close to an hour."

"An hour!" the captain yelled into the squawk-box. "What the hell do you think this is...a naval reserve training cruise? I'm sure the North Koreans already have us zeroed in, and if we keep going around in this circle we'll wind up right in their laps!" Royal slammed the speaker switch to the off-position.

"Sir," Oetjens spoke up, "what if we cut our engines completely?"

"If we were further out that might work. In this close it would be suicide. Anyway, you'd better call radio-central and kill that crypto to the commodore."

"It's too late, Captain. The radio shack just reported that they transmitted the message."

"Dammit!" Royal fumed. "Any other time they'd take a week just to encode it! Now all of a sudden they have to get efficient!" Royal paused, then said, "Send another message canceling the first. Tell the flagship we've had a total breakdown in the feeding system for the steering engine. Inform Commodore Price that I am requesting permission to complete the circle at our best possible speed taking the Ko-cho batteries under fire for as much of the turn as possible. Tell him that I also request permission to continue around for as many full circles as it takes to deliver effective counter-battery fire."

Down in after-steering, which doubled as the *Field's* secondary-conn, Aubrey Cobb turned milk-white when advised of his C.O.'s decision. "Bridge, after-steering," he called, experiencing a sudden trembling in his arms and body. Hoping Sternhagen and his damage-control team had not perceived his near state of panic, Cobb took a deep breath and exhaled slowly. "Captain," he said, "why not stop here, back down, and steer our way out with our engines?"

"I've already considered that," Royal answered in a calmer voice. "Coming to a full stop in this close would make us a sitting duck. In the time it would take for us to push our stern around with our engines, the Reds would have us skinned, quartered and hanging on a hook to dry. Our only chance is to keep moving as fast as we can, at the same time putting out as heavy a volume of fire as possible. Besides, a steering casualty doesn't relieve us of our primary mission...counter-battery support for the force"..."Mister Phelan!" Royal turned to the JOD. "Get as many men back to after-steering as you can. Anyone who's not manning an essential battle station. See if they can move that rudder manually to hard starboard. The way we're heading now could bring us right into that mine field!"

"SHIFTLESS — THIS IS BIRDBATH," came Price's voice amid a flutter of squeals and static. "AFFIRM YOUR SHADOW ALL BEFORE WORD

ZEBRA...BREAK... NEGATIVE ALL AFTER WORD ZEBRA...BAKER-XRAY-
FIVE. I REPEAT, BAKER-XRAY-FIVE. OVER!"

"BIRDBATH — THIS IS SHIFTLESS...ROGER, OUT," Commander Royal
acknowledged.

"The commodore has given us an okay to complete the first circle as a firing
run, Captain, but he's refused our request to repeat the maneuver," Oetjens
called out, his eyes still fixed on the General Signal Book. "Baker-xray-five means
withdraw from present exercise as expediently as possible and await further tactical instructions."

"As expediently as possible?" Royal grimaced, then leaned towards the speaker. "All stations, Bridge...this is a firing run...God be with all of us," he added in a
half-whisper, releasing the central-communications switch.

Then pressing the lever marked main-battery control, Royal instructed,
"Mister Ritter...be ready to let fly with everything you've got. When this turn is
completed I don't expect to see anything left of Point Ko-cho but a cloud of red
dust!" Depressing the next lever, he instructed, "Combat, this is the captain. Be
certain you pass each contact on to main-battery control the second you have it
on your scope. Remember the Ko-cho directors and guns are your priority targets,
and you're only getting one crack at them! There's always the chance we might
encounter torpedo boats so keep an eye peeled for small craft."

"CAPRICORN...THIS IS BIRDBATH. ITEM-JIG-CHARLIE!...OVER."

"THIS IS SHIFTLESS...ROGER, OUT," answered Royal.

"THIS IS TENNIS-COURT...ROGER, OUT," acknowledged Commander
Fenchurch on *John Morgan*.

"THIS IS SMUDGE...ROGER, OUT," came the familiar baritone of *Halsey
Wayne's* skipper, Sandy Boland.

"THIS IS HARLOT...ROGER, OUT," Gil Hedling shouted into the TBS
speaker aboard *Abner Ward* even though the commodore ("Birdbath") was standing but a few feet away in the flagship's wheelhouse.

"Commence firing, Mister Ritter," Royal ordered calmly, and the *Field's* two
forward 5-inch rifles snarled and flashed at the enemy shore. The midships and
after mounts added their sharp **Bang-Bang-Bang** to the din, not quite muffling
the more rapid **Bam-Bam-Bam** of the 40 millimeters, and soon even the smaller
twenties were clawing out angrily at the Ko-cho coastline.

Oetjens swallowed hard as round after round flew off towards the rocky
shore. He flinched noticeably with each concussion that shook the stomach
he had cushioned so well beneath his kapok and an ample roll of premature
middle-age fat. Cordite fumes pinched his nostrils and vivid recollections of
the Normandy Beachhead rushed his brain, while all around him, hellish
thunderclaps announced to anyone who cared, that the Charlie P. had gone
to war.

"Flank speed!" ordered Royal, and the *Field's* snipes pushed the old destroyer faster and faster along her circular course.

234

Far off to port, a forest of shell splashes blossomed around *Halsey Wayne*, obscuring Sandy Boland's ship for what had to be the longest thirty seconds Royal could remember since his days off Okinawa. Beyond his friend's destroyer, Mop-cho sparkled with countless orange blotches as battery upon battery shifted its attention to the *Ward* and *Morgan*, both of which were displaying a remarkable proclivity for broken-field running as they raced towards their targets in the inner harbor. So far, only *Charles P. Field* ventured unopposed.

The range to Ko-cho was less than 4,000 yards now, Owen Royal conclud-ed, as his 40-mm gunners arched their tracers into the beach with the lazy, weav-ing motion a gardener might use to hose down a hedge row.

4,000...3,900...3,800 yards...still the *Field* closed the enemy shore, and still the Point Ko-cho batteries remained silent.

What are they waiting for? Murray wondered as he handed a fresh grease pencil to Gardiner who was marking in the latest positions of the orbiting Aussie Meteors on the vertical air plot.

"Dammit, but we're getting close," Nugent muttered as he cranked the range dial on the Sugar-George.

"We get any closer, Turk will be handing out chopsticks for use with our evening chow," Bacelli replied from the status board.

"Great! While he's at it, maybe he can rustle up some of those midget egg rolls that are gonna' make you a millionaire," Nugent shot back with a snicker.

"Knock it off, you two!" yelled Coates. "Now if you can get back to the busi-ness at hand, Nugent, what's our present range to Area-Dog?"

"Range to Area-Dog is 400 yards, Sir," replied the third-class placing sarcas-tic emphasis on the word sir.

"Bridge, combat," Stockwell called into the squawk-box. "Range to Area-Dog is 400 yards, Sir."

"Very well. Let's hope our intelligence boys were wrong about those mines," Royal advised as the *Field* charged on; her engines thumping, deck-plates rattling and guns lashing out at a thus far silent enemy.

"I think I've got a small target dead ahead!" Nugent warned, genuinely star-tled by its sudden appearance.

"What do you mean a small target?" quizzed Coates. "Is it moving?"

"I don't know. I don't think so. Every time I try to range in, our guns toss out another salvo and the vibration distorts the hell out of the picture on this scope."

"What do you expect with the prehistoric gear we've got on this tub," scowled Holiday.

"Well, you'd better check that target out," Stockwell cut in coldly. "If it turns out to be a PT-boat, we could be in bad trouble!"

"Bridge, combat," Coates called through the intercom. "We hold a small tar-get dead ahead. It doesn't seem to be moving."

"Bridge, aye," Royal replied. "We hold it visually. It's a sandbar. At our present rate of turn we'll clear it by fifty yards. The chart indicates an abrupt drop in depth to twenty fathoms just seaward of the bar so we should be alright."

"Sir, our chart indicates another set of reefs close by the land," Coates shouted, hoping to be heard over the unremitting **Bang, Bang, Bang** and **Bam, Bam, Bam** of the guns. "If we pass any closer to Ko-cho, we'll run aground," the ensign said hesitantly.

"If we pass any closer to Ko-cho, Mister Coates, we'll all qualify for the Combat Infantryman's Badge," Owen grimaced, turning his head just in time to see a blinding flash off in the direction of the inner harbor. A second later, came a cracking sound like the world had just split open.

Now back on the open bridge, Royal watched as oily black smoke, mixed with flame, billowed skyward. He knew it could mean only one of three things: the *Abner Ward*, the *John Morgan*, or the ammunition dump. He felt immense relief an instant later when he heard over the TBS that it was the ammunition dump.

Royal clutched at the rim of the splinter screen, painfully aware that his destroyer was swiftly completing the curve which would bring her closest to Ko-cho and this strangely silent enemy. The *Field's* shot continued to fall in flaming clusters of red and orange but still aroused no response from an apparently indifferent foe.

Royal was well aware that his ship's reception was far different than that being afforded *Halsey Wayne* off Mop-cho. In less than four minutes of battle, Sandy Boland's destroyer had already taken two major caliber hits and several smaller ones. In the inner harbor, flagship *Ward* and *John Morgan* were undergoing similar attention from the carefully concealed guns that poked their muzzles from every cave and crevice, coughed their brief lethal message, then retracted back to obscurity. Miraculously, neither ship had so far taken a major hit. High overhead, the Australians twisted and swerved and chalked white vapor trails across the blue summer sky.

"There's somebody on that damn sandbar, Sir," a bridge lookout shouted excitedly over the roar of a five-inch barrage.

An artillery spotter with a walkie-talkie, Royal concluded as the *Field* bore down on the hapless Red non-com. The next instant, spotter and walkie-talkie were dancing high in the air, courtesy of a well placed round from number-"2" gun. A small cloud of sand and powder, all that remained of the offshore shoal, floated lazily down the destroyer's port side.

The faces in C.I.C. were much brighter now as Nugent read off successively opening ranges to Point Ko-cho. Then, amid audible expressions of relief, Logan, working the D.R.T., coolly announced that the ship was passing well clear of Area-Dog. Even so, the sound of the two after mounts pounding away at the receding coastline reminded the radarmen that the fire mission was not yet over. In actuality, this last hurrah by the *Field's* gun gang was comparable to a small boy trying to chip marble with a toothpick.

By 18:00 (6p.m.), after a series of time-consuming half-circles during which the destroyer would stop; back down on one engine; go forward on the other; move her stern around a few precious degrees, then thrust ahead until the entire cycle had to be repeated again, Lieutenant Phelan was finally able to report to Commander Royal that the after-steering engine was again "back on line."

It was about this time that *DD-505* was joined by a battered and smoking *Halsey Wayne*, and a somewhat less bruised *Morgan* and *Ward*. Commander Royal's destroyer slipped in column astern, and the ships moved out into the Sea of Japan heading for a point off Iwon and their scheduled rendezvous with Task Force 77.

The following afternoon while cruising once more in their screening stations, a detailed dispatch based on South Korean intelligence was forwarded from Jehovah, now aboard carrier *Princeton*, to Commodore Price for further dissemination throughout the latter's command. It answered the question of why the *Field* had encountered no opposition, noting that two days prior to the operation, the unpredictable enemy had decided after a prolonged bombardment by cruiser *Toledo*, to move all guns and equipment from untenerable Ko-cho to far more formidable Mop-cho. This also accounted for the existence of two gun-laden barges and their tow which *Abner Ward* had reported blasting from her path during her charge to the inner harbor.

With the dispatch was a breakdown of the results obtained. Commodore Price augmented the report with information supplied by the four C.O.s, and ordered that "for purpose of morale," the following be posted prominently aboard each destroyer:

To: All Officers and Enlisted Pers. DesDiv 291
From: Capt. W.A. Price, U.S.N. ComDesDiv 291

All hands are to be heartily congratulated on their splendid show of valor and determination, which is in keeping with the finest traditions of the Naval Service during this Division's operation of 12 September 1952. The following are the results of the operation as reported by reliable informants and units participating:

Unit	Major Caliber Rounds Expended	Results Obtained	Casualties Suffered
U.S.S. Abner Ward DD-506	149-5"	Assist on Ammo dump, 2 Barges plus tow, 2-7.7" naval rifles confirmed 2-7.7" naval rifles probable	4 wounded
U.S.S. John Morgan DD-504	162-5"	Assist on Ammo dump, 1-R.R. spur track	2 wounded

237

		1-boxcar	
		1-3" battery-director	
U.S.S. Halsey Wayne DD-503	159-5"	Total destruction of 4-directors for main battery. (Mop-cho) 1-7.7" naval rifle 1-122 mm. howitzer 1 barge	9 wounded
U.S.S. Charles P. Field DD-505	249-5"	1 sandbar and occupant Possible damage to undeter- mined shore installations.	none

Prior to posting the commodore's message aboard the *Field*, Owen Royal made one slight alteration — the word "sandbar" was deleted and replaced with the words "forward-observation post."

That same evening *Halsey Wayne*, her wounded personnel already transferred to *Princeton* and *Bon Homme Richard*, was detached and sent to the harbor of Sasebo in western Kyushu. Damage to *Ward* and *Morgan* was not extensive enough to warrant a yard period, thus both destroyers remained with the task force.

It was raining heavily as Murray, Bacelli and Belton, relieved Logan, Nugent and Patterson for the mid-watch, and the squall area on the long range scale of the Sugar-Charlie indicated to Murray and his watch-mates that they could expect the rain and fog to last the duration of their four-hour tour.

In the wardroom, Lieutenant Stockwell set about recreating his first naval action in his daily letter to Cassy Jean, while his commanding officer, three decks above in his sea-cabin, labored over a detailed report of the recent and untimely breakdown to the steering machinery on his destroyer; a report which would be dispatched in triplicate to Commander DesDiv 291, Commander Task Force 77, Commander Task Force 95 (Bombardment Group), Commander 7th Fleet, and Commander-Cruisers-Destroyers-Pacific.

Hundreds of miles away in Tokyo, American naval personnel at ComNavFe carefully monitored the day's broadcast from Radio Peiping. It began:

"Yesterday, near the peaceful village of Songjin, units of the North Korean People's Militia and volunteers from the People's Republic of China banded together to repulse a massive amphibious assault by barbarian elements of the American Navy. During the course of this action, the People's forces destroyed the infamous American warship known as Missouri, three vessels of the heavy cruiser type as well as innumerable escort vessels and troop carriers. Proof that the Wall Street mercenaries lack all stomach for a fight was amply displayed by the cowardly conduct of one American cruiser which bore the number 505. Even before the People's forces began their devastating fire in defense of their threatened home land, this vessel broke formation and attempted to

flee, deserting the rest of the gangster clique it was assigned to protect. While racing wildly from the scene of battle, this treacherous vessel and its crew were blown from the water by the deadly accurate fire of the People's Artillery. In this action which lasted but ten minutes, total casualties inflicted on the People's forces were three soldiers killed and one wounded. In addition, fourteen children and their teacher were murdered when the reactionary sadists destroyed a clearly marked schoolhouse during their frantic withdrawal from the scene of their overwhelming defeat."

The winds increased and a stale black rain lashed the *Field* and the other ships of the task force as they journeyed through the night.

Chapter XIV - A Fish Story

A cloudless sky and fast running sea greeted Owen Royal as he mounted the sunlit bridge-wing. To starboard and slightly forward, he could see a thoroughly mended *Ward* and *Morgan* as they charged the wind at a pounding thirty knots, hurdling each crest like practiced jumpers in the *Grand National*, as was his own ship and the dozen additional small boys that formed the bent-line screen out in the van of the task force.

The three carriers far astern were riding hard, gluttonously spooning up white mountains of water and sloshing it down their bulbous gray snouts. *Essex*, closest of the big flattops, was in the midst of a maximum-effort launch. Royal and the others on the open wing watched each blue speck catapult from her deck, climb high above the task force, circle, group, then fade from view in the direction of Wonsan. *Boxer* and *Princeton* in the more distant corners of the triangle formed by the three carriers completed their respective contributions to the mid-morning strike, then, in unison with *Essex*, pivoted abruptly from the direction of the wind. On cue, the fifteen small boys raced to new stations in a maneuver designed to keep them at all times in front of the carriers and the other heavies in their charge. The maneuver, called screen re-orientation, was executed whenever the larger ships came about to a new course. Requiring the utmost skill on the part of each destroyer's bridge watch and C.I.C. team, this reshuffling of escorts usually resulted in numerous near-collisions as the little ships crisscrossed each other's wakes scurrying to their new slots in the screen. And although Owen Royal had carried out the maneuver a thousand times during his naval career, it never failed to remind him of so many gray mice dashing frantically about a barnyard floor to escape the thwack of a farmer's broom.

Royal looked down at the foc'sle. He watched the two mine lookouts carefully sweeping the water ahead with their binoculars. This was one morning when he was certain he would not have to remind them of their responsibilities even though the task force was operating many miles out from the coast. The night before while cruising these same waters ninety miles east of Wonsan, the *Barton*, only a short distance away in the screen, had a 40-foot long hole ripped in her hull by a floating mine. Suffering five dead and seven wounded and with her forward engine room flooded and completely gutted, the ship had detached to limp low in the water back to a friendly haven. The explosion had been clearly heard aboard the *Field*, even down in the crowded messhall where most of the crew were deeply engrossed in watching a thunderous charge by Cheyenne and Sioux during the climatic finale of "*They Died with Their Boots On.*"

Three days had passed now since the *Field's* inauspicious combat debut against the North Koreans, and in spite of the *Barton's* lethal encounter of the night before, an obvious aura of lethargy seemed to have settled once more over Owen Royal's radar team. Like Bacelli, most of the Charlie P.'s complement were happily convinced that even if Jehovah was unaware of the "Henderson Jinx," he certainly must realize that the *Field* was no longer capable of close combat with the enemy. Indeed, their biggest worry now, besides floating mines, was the thought that the jury-rigged steering-engine might let go any time and send them off in another wild circle, one culminating in a disastrous collision with some other unlucky unit in the task force.

Manning the Sugar-George on this particular morning was Holiday, who in the midst of a yawn, asked, "Did you hear that Goff, Hauser and Van Ginderen got off with only a reduction in rate?"

"Yeah," Gardiner answered from the D.R.T. "They really made out dropping just one grade. They were damn lucky getting a soft touch like Mister Kimmick as the summary court officer."

"That wasn't luck," grunted Murray. "I'd bet a month's pay the old man assigned the job to Kimmick knowing he wouldn't rack them up too much."

"How come you're always sticking up for the old man?" Gardiner asked sourly. "You always say you hate the navy. Don't you know Royal's part of the navy?...regular navy, that is."

"Well, that may be, but Royal's different. You can trust him."

"Don't you trust anyone else?" Holiday asked in a deliberate attempt to badger the *Field's* senior radarman.

"Not in the navy I don't! I learned that a long time ago."

"Hell, Murray, you're just a cynic," shot back Gardiner, pouring more coal on the fire.

"It's got nothing to do with being cynical."

"Come on, Howie, admit it. You're just bitter 'cause the navy yanked you back and stuck you over here," Holiday snickered.

"You're right about that. I'm damn bitter! Tricking me into signing those reserve papers was one thing, but I've learned that you can't even trust the navy when it comes to little things."

"Little things?" Belton asked from his seat at the Sugar-Charlie.

"Yeah, little things...steak and eggs, for instance."

"Steak and eggs?" the entire radar watch asked incredulously.

"That's what I said, steak and eggs. I can't count the number of mornings back on the *Enterprise* and *Franklin* that some hair-brained master-at-arms would come bouncing through my compartment at reveille, snapping on the lights, banging on my bunk with his flashlight, and yelling 'steak and eggs for breakfast.' You know, I'm still waiting for those steak and eggs."

"Well, you'll wait forever on this bucket. Best Turk can rustle up is powdered eggs and a tired slice of Spam," Holiday frowned and shook his head in apparent sympathy.

"Combat, bridge!" came a sudden blast from the squawk-box. Lieutenant MacKinlay's voice was clearly discernible.

"Combat, aye," Murray acknowledged.

"The carriers will be turning back into the wind in approximately one hour. I expect Jehovah will call for formation Coke again. This time when we shift stations, I want to hear that course and speed recommendation before Jehovah gives the execute... not ten seconds after the maneuver's underway! Do you know what the word before means?" MacKinlay snapped in his usual belligerent fashion.

"Yes, Sir, we know."

"Well, just make sure that you do!" the OD said, releasing the lever. The *Field's* gun-boss glanced out the open wheelhouse door just in time to see one of the strikers from radio-central hand his commanding officer a sheet of paper. From its size and color, MacKinlay was certain that it was an operational dispatch. With only a make-shift repair to the steering-engine, he doubted that the ship would be off on any more fire missions for awhile. Maybe Jehovah was detaching them a little early so they could get patched up properly in Sasebo, or maybe alongside one of the tenders in Pusan or Inchon.

"From Jehovah, Sir?" the executive officer asked, joining Royal on the starboard wing.

"No, it's from the screen commander," the C.O. said with a puzzled expression, handing the paper to Cobb.

"Prepare to detach from task force at 10:35 and proceed independently to latitude 40 East, longitude 129 North. Additional instructions to follow..." Cobb read in a jittery tone. "Where the hell are they sending us now? Don't they know we've got a touchy steering-engine?" asked the exec hesitantly.

"The engine will hold," Royal smiled. "What ever they've got planned for us, at least this shows the screen commander considers the *Field* an effective member of the team. If he wasn't confident that we can do the job, he'd have given it to the *Ward* or *Morgan* over there," he smiled, glancing in the direction of the two destroyers. Turning to Ensign Warden, JOD for the morning watch, Royal said, "Let me know where latitude 40 East, longitude 129 North is please."

"Yes, Sir," the junior-officer-of-the-deck replied, departing for the chart on the table in the wheelhouse.

"Captain, if we're going in on another fire mission, the timing couldn't be any worse," Cobb cut in. "The morale on this ship is just about non-existent after what happened the other day off Mop-cho. That's what I came up here to talk to you about."

"Come on, Aub. Aren't you exaggerating a little?"

"No, Sir, there's a distinct undertone throughout the ship. I'm pretty sure it's this Henderson stuff again."

"That doesn't make any sense. We were the only ship in the division that didn't take any casualties."

"Yes, Sir, but I'm afraid a lot of these meatheads don't see it that way. The story that's floating around is that old Henderson jammed our rudder and tried to run us aground right in the middle of the whole Chinese army."

"Well, at least it shows that the crew has a little imagination," laughed Royal, his eyes suddenly focused on the approaching radio-striker, the same young man who had delivered the message earlier.

Royal returned the sailor's salute and took the dispatch, his smile quickly changing to a frown as his mind reluctantly grasped its contents.

Cobb's eyes focused unsteadily first on the sheet of paper, then on the captain's expression. With a nervous grin, he asked, "What are we going after? Shore batteries again?"

"No, our job's bigger than that," Royal smiled in a vain attempt to mask his disappointment. "In contrast to Mop-cho, we should have more targets than we can handle this time. I'd say a million might not be too far off the mark," he answered, handing the paper to the exec.

"Pollack!" exclaimed Cobb seconds later, his eyes almost popping from their sockets.

"Not just pollack, Aub...Alaska bluefin pollack." Then walking to the wheelhouse door, Royal asked, "Do you have that fix yet, Mister Warden?"

"Yes, Sir. It puts us 32 miles off Songdo Gap. That's just off area 'Engine-Block,' Captain."

"Very well," turning to MacKinlay, Royal asked, "Are your depth charges in order, Alan?"

"Yes, Sir. I have my people always check them first thing after muster each morning. Are we going after a possible sub contract, Sir?" the *Field's* gun-boss quizzed with obvious surprise in his tone. "I just checked with the sonar shack. As of three minutes ago, they weren't pinging in on any contacts."

"No, unfortunately we're not hunting anything as glamorous as *untersee-booten* this time, Mister MacKinlay. Read this and have your ordinance people stand by."

Warden peered over the OD's shoulder as the latter digested the meat of the dispatch from Birthrate. The amplifying message succinctly related that a South Korean gunboat had encountered a massive shoal of Alaska bluefish pollack moving slowly down the coast near "area Windshield," heading southwest towards "area Engine-Block." Royal's instructions were simply stated — he would destroy or disperse said fish by any means he deemed appropriate. Allowing for its rate of speed, direction, and the prevailing currents, Birthrate estimated that the shoal of pollack should reach latitude 40 East, longitude 129 North at approximately 15:00 (3p.m.).

The dispatch went on to stress the urgency of the operation, outlining the basic rationale for its undertaking:

1/ Fishing restrictions have been a prime concern of the United Nations naval blockading force since September, 1950.

2/ Fish is the main staple of the Korean diet; annual pre-war consumption exceeded 300,000 tons.

3/ The Red Chinese and North Korean armies rely heavily on an unrestricted supply of fish for food. Elimination or drastic reduction of said supply will greatly complicate the enemy's logistics problem, forcing him to import additional food from Manchuria and the U.S.S.R., thereby utilizing truck and rail transport otherwise allocated to the movement of troops and munitions.

MacKinlay reflected on the nine months of instruction he'd received in some of the navy's most advanced gunnery schools. He remembered the many tests, the long hours of study, all so he could be sent to the other side of the world to kill some fish. Handing the paper back to the captain without comment, he mopped his brow and wondered if maybe he had made a mistake not choosing to accept his commission in the Marine Corps when he had the opportunity back at the academy.

The next quarter-hour passed swiftly and at precisely 10:35, *Charles P. Field* kicked her stern around neatly to move away from the task force on a north-westerly heading.

A course and speed recommendation was promptly worked out by Logan and sent up to the bridge where Navigator Oetjens concurred, noting that it coincided exactly with his own course and speed solution.

Gardiner looked at Logan curiously. "You really know that shit don't you," he said, shaking his head in dismay as Logan produced the course and speed in a little under twenty seconds.

"Hey, Logan," Holiday cut in. "What do you really think of the old man?"

"He seems okay," answered Kevin in an even tone. "What brought on that question all of a sudden?"

"Oh, we were having a discussion about Royal just before you guys popped in," Holiday glanced at Bacelli and Nugent who had squatted on a pile of kapok life jackets. Then turning to Kevin again, the third class said, "Howie thinks the old man's the greatest thing since bubble gum."

"I didn't say that!" Murray exclaimed heatedly. "I just think he cares a little about the crew, that's all."

"Do you think he knows what the hell he's doing?" Bacelli jumped into the conversation.

"Of course I do," Logan shot back. "I've watched him on the bridge. He's real sharp."

"How come he almost piled us up on that Commie beach last week if he's so sharp?"

"He had nothing to do with that," Murray snapped. "It was a screwed up steering-engine that almost piled us up on the beach."

"You're both wrong," Nugent frowned. "That was old Henderson's work, sure as hell."

"Come on, Nugey," Holiday laughed. "You don't really buy that ghost crap do you?"

"Hey, don't be so sure Henderson's not haunting this bucket," Gardiner chimed in. "With the whole Sea of Japan, to say nothing of the Pacific Ocean, it seems awfully strange to me that our steering-engine waits until we're right smack in the middle of an enemy harbor to crap out. Besides, Bites and Chapman both think they saw him that afternoon."

"Saw him?" Logan snorted.

"Yeah, and they weren't the only ones who said they saw some weird looking chief prancing around the passageway below the torpedo shack right after the ship went to G.Q."

"Come on, Gardiner," Murray smiled. "There's twenty-two CPOs on this tub. Do you know each one?"

"Maybe not by name, but I'd certainly recognize all of them."

"That lower deck passageway's not well lighted even under ordinary conditions. During general quarters, it's practically blacked out. They probably spotted one of those three new chiefs...you know the ones that reported aboard just before we left Pearl. Now, I couldn't tell you what any of those three looked like if my life depended on it," Murray explained determinedly. "Besides, there's a lot of weird looking chiefs prancing around this ship. Did you ever take a really close look at old Anderson, the terror of the flag-bags?" Murray grinned, "Or Chief Becker, the Charlie P.'s very own porn king? I'd hate to bump into him in a dark alley."

"Becker may be a weirdo," Bacelli scowled, "but by the time he gets off this bucket, he'll be a mighty rich weirdo thanks to that Wave V.D. flick."

"That might be but getting back to the old man," Murray snapped, "you guys are mighty quick to blame him for anything that goes wrong, but you've got a convenient lapse of memory when he does something like saving you all from an assend collision with the *Crown Point!*"

"Yeah, Murray's right," Nugent piped up. "Royal's a pretty good skipper. You should have had that character I had on my first ship, the *Pelican Bay.*"

"Your first ship?" Bacelli questioned indignantly. "What are you trying to do, sound like an old salt? Next you'll be givin' out with that tired line that you've rinsed more salt water out of your socks then we've ever sailed on."

"Well, maybe I have. At least I put in a year-and-a-half on that seaplane tender before I got transferred to this tub. With the exception of Murray and Logan here, the Charlie P.'s the only ship you dumb asses know. Hell, you came aboard right out of radar school or boot camp!"

"Calm down, Nugent, and tell us about the character you had on the *Pelican Bay*," Logan laughed.

"Character is putting it mildly. He'd make that guy Queeg in 'The Caine Mutiny' look like Captain January from the Good Ship Lollipop." Nugent paused, then asked, "Any of you guys ever been to Gitmo?"

"Of course, hasn't everybody?" Logan chuckled.

"Then you probably remember that Cuban beer with the label that had a picture of the Indian with the patch over his eye?"

"Sure, you mean *Hatuey Beer*," replied Logan. "Anybody who's ever sailed into Guantanamo Bay knows that."

"Well, that was our name for the old man on the *Pelican Bay*...Ha-tuey," Nugent pronounced the name slowly. "You see, he had this one bad eye. I don't know if it was glass or what, but it use to stare at you like it knew you were trying to get away with somethin'. All the while his good eye'd be rollin' around in another direction like it was lookin' for somebody to come sneakin' up on him like when he was a fighter pilot in the war."

"How come the navy let a guy without sight in one eye skipper a ship? You know how strict BuPers is about having twenty-twenty eyesight," Bacelli asked, taking an extra long drag on his cigarette.

"Ha-tuey was a war hero...shot down a bushel of Japs. They say that's how his eye got messed up...he crashed a shot-up Hellcat into the island of his carrier. Anyway, he had a hell of a good war record so the navy gave him a medical waiver on the eye. Besides, he was a four-striper when he took command of the *Pelican Bay*, and I think he was close to being retired."

"Why do you say he out-Queeged Queeg?" Murray asked impatiently.

"Well, what would you call a C.O. who'd pop into the wheelhouse unexpected, then put everybody on report including the OD and JOD just because he found a couple of pencils in the chart table drawer without points on them? Twice the exec was up there when Ha-tuey decided he didn't like something like some sailor's shoes needing a shine, so he goes right ahead and puts the exec 'in hack' too, and the exec was a three-striper." Nugent waved away the smoke that had drifted over from Bacelli's cigarette, then said, "I remember one time Ha-tuey came bustin' into C.I.C. and spots one of our strikers sitting over in the corner reading a comic book. The guy wasn't even on watch but the old man was so pissed-off, he wrote up everybody in the radar shack, even the two guys sitting at the scopes. Then Ha-tuey orders the next watch-section to immediately relieve everyone in C.I.C. Now don't tell me that isn't wackier than Queeg counting strawberries," said Nugent in a perky, challenging voice. "I tell you, Ha-tuey was living proof that truth really is stranger than fiction," the third-class sighed.

"Got to admit, you present a strong case," Logan said reflectively.

"Hell, you guys haven't heard anything yet," Nugent boomed. "Once when we were up in Halifax, Ha-tuey came back to the ship about three in the morning with half-a bag on. He orders the OD to call away G.Q. Then, while we're all runnin' half-ass naked to our battle stations, and thinkin' the Russians have just launched World War Three, we see Ha-tuey standing down there on the pier, cursing a bloody blue streak and throwing empty beer cans at the side of the ship."

"Damn," Holiday muttered, "if you put that in a book, nobody'd ever believe it."

"Like I just said, truth is a lot stranger than fiction."

"Speakin' of truth, Logan," Gardiner said glibly, "when are you gonna' fill us in on all the gory details of that Tokyo weekend you spent with that leggy lieutenant?"

"Yeah...did you get to do something kinky like humping her on the palace grounds?" asked Nugent, positioning one of the kapoks as a backrest.

Kevin looked at him coldly, then went back to updating the C.I.C. log.

"Don't look so pissed, Logan," Nugent continued. "Actually, I think it would have been kinda' fitting...you know, making up in a small way for the fact that old Bull Halsey never got to ride the emperor's horse like he wanted to do."

"Yeah, Logan, what the hell are you so secretive about?" Holiday joined in. "You don't see Vinnie here refusing to tell us about his latest love."

"She's not my latest love," Bacelli cut in, then closing his eyes said, "Ediko is my only love...my final love...*mio amore eterno*," he sighed.

"Bullshit!" snapped Gardiner. "I don't know what that guinea lingo means but you say that about every broad you make it with. I remember you used to describe that hash slinger up in Frisco...what was her name?"

"Marlene, but she was no hash slinger! She was a waitress in a real high-class joint. She made more in tips in one night than you make in a whole month," Bacelli bristled.

"Sure, and we all know what she did to get those tips," Gardiner said smirking. "As I remember, you had another everlasting love not too long ago...that broad you picked up in the bowling alley in Chula Vista...the midget with the big tits and the Adolph Menjou mustache."

"You mean Angela...she was no midget, and she didn't have a mustache! The skin above her lip was just a little dark, that's all. Anyway, look at Holiday here. He's always shooting off his mouth about how he's going to marry into Philadelphia society next summer. That doesn't stop him from trying to screw every female that will let him get in range!"

"Hey, you leave Toby out of this conversation!" Holiday snarled. "She's not a cheap whore like you guys are use to. Just keep it up and none of you will get invited to my wedding!"

"Ah, we've ruffled poor Holiday's feelings," Nugent grinned mischievously. "Remember fellas, no wise cracks about Toby. She goes to one of those exclusive girl's colleges back east... Right?"

"Right!"

"What's it called again?" quizzed Nugent.

"Chestnut Hill, but I don't expect you low-lifes would know anything about a school like that."

"Hey, Holly, tell us again about Toby's daddy," Gardiner snickered. "Didn't you say he was going to make you a vice president of his bank some day?"

"You got that right!" Holiday struck back angrily. "When you and Nugent are still sweating it out on this rust bucket, and Bacelli over there is trying to persuade his little Jap cookie to help him peddle his greasy egg rolls, I'll be dining at *The Fish House* with Philadelphia's elite."

"Combat, bridge!" interrupted Ensign Warden's voice via the speaker-box.

"Combat, aye," answered Murray.

"Keep alert for small craft. There's a fair chance we'll be encountering some of the North Korean fishing fleet. And make sure whoever you've got on the Sugar-Charlie keeps his eyes peeled for low flying aircraft. We'll be operating approximately thirty miles from land," the JOD cautioned.

"Combat, aye," Murray again responded.

"Hey, I don't like moving in that close," Holiday called out from the air-search radar.

"What are you sweating?" Logan shot back. "That's still well beyond the range of their guns."

"You never heard of mines?" Holiday carped. "What about the *Barton?* We were ninety miles out when that mine got her," the third-class grunted.

"How come they're sending us to a point thirty miles from the coast?" asked Gardiner at the surface-search radar. "Our main battery can't reach a third that far."

"Who knows," Murray shrugged. "It's probably to take up life guard station in case any of our planes ditch near "Engine-Block." He glanced over at Bacelli and Nugent, still comfortably planted atop the pile of kapoks. "Who's turn is it in the coffee mess?"

"Vinnie's. I got stuck in there for most of yesterday," scowled Nugent.

"Okay, Bacelli, get your ass in gear and hustle us up some coffee," Murray bawled, "and make sure you don't forget to clean out the grounds this time!"

"While you're at it, stick a record on the player," Nugent interjected with an exaggerated tone of authority.

"Yeah, Vinnie," Gardiner cut in. "Play that Frankie Layne record of 'High Noon' that I like."

"Up yours!" replied Bacelli with an appropriate gesture.

Within a few minutes, the turn-table began to spin, and, in spite of a scratchy needle, all in C.I.C. could clearly hear Perry Como warn them not to let the stars get in their eyes.

A deep swell was running steadily off Songdo Gap and the *Field* rode the crest of each wave flopping bow first into each fresh trough. The cool breeze was a welcome stimulant to Aubrey Cobb as he climbed the outside ladder to the bridge-wing.

"Range to the nearest point of land?" Cobb heard the captain ask.

"Combat reports the range to Songdo Gap is sixty-four thousand, three-hundred yards, Sir," the bridge-talker replied just as the exec stepped on to the wing.

"Hello, Aub," Royal greeted in a friendly voice.

"Afternoon, Sir," Cobb flipped a casual salute. "Will we be staying at condition-two for this operation?"

"I had hoped we could. Unfortunately, I don't see any pollack out there, do you?"

"No, it looks like Birthrate figured wrong this time."

"Well, I doubt we've missed them by much. We are exactly thirty-two miles off Songdo Gap. I've requested an aerial reconnaissance of the immediate area. In fact, the plane should have been here by now," Royal frowned. "Anyway, if we do move in any closer to the beach, we'll have to shift to condition-one. I know how hot it is below decks and in the gun-houses, so I don't want to call away G.Q. and button up the ship unless it's absolutely necessary."

"Captain," the bridge-talker spoke up excitedly. "Combat reports an air contact squawking friendly at one-two-eight, fifty miles...contact is closing fast," the red-headed seaman quickly added.

"That should be Gold Digger-Five, our spotter plane," Royal said to Cobb, aiming his binoculars along the reported line of bearing.

Minutes passed before the dot appeared midway between the horizon and a low hanging cloudbank. In another minute, this seeming imperfection in God's sky took on the unmistakable outline of a Neptune patrol bomber. Engines droning, the P2V-3 moved in from seaward, then banked sharply, trapping a spark of sun on its glossy blue hide as it passed less than a mile ahead of the *Field's* jackstaff.

Royal heard the loud hum ooze from the wheelhouse speaker, the annoying but familiar preamble to each transmission received via the destroyer's radio-tele-phone.

"Shiftless...this is Gold Digger-Five," came a distinct southern voice. "Get out your nets, ah see your fish...approximately eight miles due east of your present position. Over."

"Gold Digger-Five...this is Shiftless," Royal replied, Cobb and MacKinlay standing inches away, "can you estimate size of school? Over."

"Shiftless...ah sho' hope you 'black shoes' like fish. There's enough down there to feed every parish in New Orleans, and maybe Baton Rouge thrown in for good measure. That school's got to be almost a half mile wide."

"Gold Digger-Five...thanks again for your help. We've got the ball...out," Royal acknowledged. "Now let's see how well we can run with it," he muttered, turning towards the exec and OD. "Mister MacKinlay, I relieve you of the conn. Bo'sun, sound G.Q. Helmsman, come left to two-six-five. Make turns for twenty-eight knots."

"Now hear this! Now hear this! General quarters! General quarters! All hands man your battle stations. Set condition-one throughout the ship!" The words bellowed from every corner of the destroyer, from bull-nose to stern-post, from truck to engine room.

..."Clang! Clang! Clang! Clang! Clang!" followed in fierce staccato as sailors scrambled to their posts.

Anticipating their C.O.'s next command, the signal gang had already two-blocked *DD-505's* unofficial battle-flag...a replica of the "blue belly" banner that fanned the air above Buford's Brigade at Brandy Station, and flew to glory, or some might say perdition, with Phil Sheridan on his mad gallop through the Shenandoah. With the *Field's* complement predominantly southern, this Billy Yank relic was to many aboard the destroyer just one more irony in a war already steeped in irony.

"Mind if I stay up on the wing for this one, Captain? Sternhagen and Chief Whittington are both in secondary conn," Cobb added. "I'm sure they can handle things without me. Afterall, it's only fish we're after," the exec said shakily.

"Sure, if you'd like," Royal smiled. "You'd better hang on to that tin hat though," the captain cautioned glancing at the gray helmet dangling from Cobb's right hand. "I intend to get in fairly close to the beach."

"You do?"

"Yes, but there's still time to get back to secondary conn if you've changed your mind," Owen said, not certain if he'd detected a trace of alarm in Cobb's voice.

"No, no, of course not," answered the exec aggressively. "Actually, I'd really welcome a chance to get a good look at North Korea."

"Well, then you've picked the right time to do it. I intend to slip in between the school and the shore. That should put us just about four miles off the beach."

"Why can't we just cut right through the middle of the school and blast it with our 'ash cans'?"

"I don't want to kill or even stun the fish. That would make it too easy for the Koreans to send out their sampans to scoop the fish off the surface the minute we haul out. And, from a purely practical standpoint, if we blast the school itself, we'll most likely end up knee-deep in pollack. So, I intend to move in between the fish and Songdo Gap, lay a full pattern of depth charges then get the hell out of there before the Commies can figure out what we're up to."

"Yes, but I don't understand why we're dropping our depth charges where there aren't any fish?" puzzled Cobb.

"What's the matter, Aub? When you were a kid, didn't you ever go to those Saturday afternoon westerns where the cowboys were always able to turn away a herd of charging cattle by shooting their pistols in the air? Basically, we'll be doing the same thing, only on a much larger scale. The concussions and underwater turbulence created by all that T.N.T. popping off should send those fish racing for Japan faster than if they had rockets attached to their tails."

As Royal spoke, he could feel the growing vibration in the steel beneath his feet. Even the chest-high splinter screen that fenced in the bridge-wing seemed to quiver with each additional knot of speed. The *Field* came alive when she was flying over the water. Royal sensed it during that first speed run off Point Conception. Now he was certain of it.

"What about shore bombardment, Sir?" The words intruded upon his thoughts.

"I'm sorry, Phil. What did you say?"

"I asked about shore bombardment, Captain," repeated Oetjens who had just relieved MacKinlay so the latter could man his G.Q. station in gun-plot.

"This one's not a fire mission, Phil. This time discretion really is the better part of valor. Besides, there's a new directive out from ComSeventhFleet forbidding surface ships from seeking out shore batteries just for the sake of having gun duels. The navy figures it doesn't make much sense, tactically or economically, to have a destroyer or cruiser knocked out of action or possibly sunk just for the chance of destroying a few relatively inexpensive artillery pieces. A ship in Japan having battle damage repaired can't do much to stop a red supply convoy from moving down the coast. If we're engaged, we will, of course, follow standard counter-battery procedure. Songdo Gap and the adjacent coastal area supposedly have seven-point-seven-inch guns. That's the same caliber as the main battery on those new *Sverdlov* class cruisers the Russians are so proud of. That type of gun tagged one of our 'cans' almost eight miles out last week. That's just about the range we're at right now..."

Royal saw the fish the precise instant he heard the lookout atop the wheelhouse call out the sighting report.

"Sweet shit!" cried Cobb, almost dropping his helmet as all eyes focused on the gleaming silver blanket that suddenly seemed to cover the entire surface ahead, twinkling and reflecting the rays of the sun like some mammoth sheet of aluminum foil.

"Just our luck," Royal laughed, "all this fish and it isn't even Friday."

"Dammit. I've never seen anything like this before," said Cobb blankly as the animated patch reached out on both sides of the *Field* like the grasping tentacles of a colossal sea monster.

"I hope there isn't a couple of floating mines in the midst of that school," Oetjens exclaimed as the *Field* knifed through the thrashing silver specks that fragmented against her smooth gray hull leaving transient splotches of blood.

"We're killing a hell of a lot of fish," Oetjens shook his head.

"Don't worry, Phil, they're Ruskie fish," Royal grinned. "they follow the cold currents down through the Liman Straight between Sakalin Island and Siberia, though I don't think the schools usually run quite as big as this one."

It was several minutes before the destroyer passed into clear blue water. A tight turn to starboard brought the *Field* around to a course parallel to the widest axis of the school which was now seaward of the ship and almost a half mile distant. Following their cue from the Mark-37 director, all five gun-houses now faced Songdo Gap. Royal, with Cobb and Oetjens close at his heels, quickly shifted to the port wing.

"In spite of that directive I'm tempted to lob a few rounds into that jetty," Royal announced, sweeping the hostile shoreline with his glasses. He noticed a steam-powered fishing trawler large enough for minelaying lazily swinging at anchor just inside the tip of the breakwater. He wondered how such a plum of a target had managed to survive this late into the war, especially with all the air strikes that had been launched against this portion of North Korea. He focused his binoculars carefully on the hills and cliffs behind and to the right and left of the jetty. Not a gun muzzle anywhere, he thought, trying to make out the lines of what appeared to be a small tanker truck nonchalantly bouncing along a dusty road, apparently heading for the jetty.

Walking briskly to the signal-bridge, Royal leaned over the flag-bags. He could see the sailors in a tight huddle near the two stern racks, each of which housed eight 720-pound depth-charges. Although he had the option of releasing the lethal gray barrels by remote control from the bridge, he decided to let the men on the fantail have that honor.

Turning to the bridge-talker, the captain ordered, "Stand by to fire a shallow pattern, six charges from each rack, five-second intervals, set depth at thirty feet."

The bridge-talker relayed each word, syllable by syllable, to the chief in charge of the fantail detail. A similar message was promptly passed over the sound-powered phones to the gunner's mate overseeing the three mortar-like K-guns mounted along the starboard edge of the main deck. The command to fire came an instant later, and every five seconds, a big Mark-7 started rolling down the rack to plop with a sizeable splash dead center in the *Field's* milky wake. Simultaneously, a trio of the smaller teardrop-shaped Mark-9s, soared skyward, then after following a high looping arch, plummeted end-over-end into the sea in the general direction of the pollack.

Though muffled by the water, each blast managed to send a clearly dis-cernible shudder through the thin-hulled *Field*. One charge, a Mark-9, fell closer than intended, jostling the ship a few degrees off course and up-ending more than one hapless sailor caught in the open with nothing to grab on to.

Owen Royal's attention once again shifted to the jetty and the fat trawler bobbing peacefully nearby. Taking targets of opportunity under fire certainly could not be construed as violating the recent directive forbidding deliberate encounters with shore batteries, he reasoned. Hell, such tactics were the very bedrock of the naval service...the stuff of Barry and John Paul Jones, he quickly decided.

Scanning the hills and rocks once more from the port wing, Royal was still unable to pick out anything that even slightly resembled a gun emplacement. He focused his glasses on a small hut at the ridge of the highest hill, a disguised fire-control station? he wondered. And the guns, those big seven-point-sevens...could they be tucked away in caves behind camouflaged drop cloths, the kind he'd been briefed about?

Slipping into the wheelhouse, he reached for the squawk-box lever that linked the bridge to gun-plot. "Mister MacKinlay!" he called loudly. "Can you and your gang toast that trawler on a single pass. I have no information on the minefields around here so I don't want to push our luck by going in any closer."

"Yes, Sir, I'm sure we can hit the trawler," the gun-boss answered without hesitation.

"Good, I'm going to come around a full hundred and eighty degrees, so you'll be firing to starboard. You should be able to get off several broadsides. Make sure you and Mister Ritter keep C.I.C. informed as to..."

Royal saw the yellow-red flashes an instant before he heard the sharp, thunderous crack, before he saw the three tall pillars of water leap high above the *Field's* bedspring antenna. The flashes seemed to be coming right out of the side of the cliffs, the same cliffs he'd so carefully scrutinized just moments before. A second and third enemy salvo fell, like the first, two-hundred yards short on the port side.

The Commies had sucked him in beautifully, he painfully conceded to himself. "Mister Ritter!" Royal yelled into the speaker. "I'm coming hard right in ten seconds! Get your stern mounts on those guns! Pronto!"

"What about the trawler, Sir?"

"Forget the trawler! The enemy batteries are your only target! I repeat! Get those bloody guns!" Turning to Ensign Warden, Royal ordered, "Make smoke, Mister! I want a screen so big the Reds will think they're looking at the Chicago fire! Helmsman, hard right rudder! Steady up on zero-eight-five!"

"Coming hard right to zero-eight-five, Sir!" the helmsman called out, swinging the rubber-rimmed wheel with a vigor seldom observed aboard the Charlie P.

Now the hills beyond the jetty literally blossomed with brilliant bursts of color. At least twenty guns were lashing out at the twisting, turning destroyer, Royal was certain.

Zig-zagging from port to starboard, the *Field* was giving as good as she got, pouring out a remarkably steady return fire from her two after five-inch, with an occasional assist from midships whenever a sharp change in course unmasked number-"3" gun.

Tall stalks of white water were erupting ahead, astern, and on both sides of the *Field*. Miraculously, none had yet come closer than a hundred yards. Wondering how much longer her luck could hold, Royal commenced another series of left and right turns, hoping the enemy gunners would not be able to calculate his new base course. The steering engine was now of paramount concern, for Royal was keenly aware that so many rapid course changes, especially at flank speed, could knock out even the best machinery.

It was then he saw the fish. For some reason completely unfathomable to him, the school had suddenly reversed course; instead of making for open sea, it was now swimming back in towards Songdo Gap. Once again the *Field's* bow began to force a path through the suicidal pollack, pushing aside the thick layers of fish that caked the water's surface like some living ice floe.

The *Field* swung jerkily from left to right, then back again in still another series of short evasive turns, zigzagging furiously through cascading sheets of water that showered her decks with shell fragments and bloody, grotesque chunks of fish.

Oily black smoke poured from her two funnels, mixing with the white smoke now streaming out of the smoke generator mounted on the fantail. Within moments, the massive man-made cloud forming astern had completely obscured any visual contact with the Korean coastline.

Again Royal vacated the confinement of the wheelhouse for the "wide open spaces" and flexibility of the port bridge-wing. Accompanied by a helmeted Oetjens and an eager young bridge-talker, the C.O. gripped the canvas-covered rim of the flag-bags as he peered aft at the thickening gray curtain.

"Maybe we'll get out of this, afterall," Oetjens beamed, obviously reassured at seeing the wall of smoke. "One thing's for sure, if we can't see them, they can't see us," the navigator shouted over the continuous bark of the *Field's* after battery.

"Providing they don't have radar," said Royal dubiously even though the enemy fire was now falling completely off the mark. He stared up at the gun-director which was almost facing dead aft. Ritter's gang's doing okay up there, he thought, before glancing aft again to observe mounts - "4" and - "5" firing blind-ly into the gray infinity formed by the smoke screen.

Eyeing his wrist watch, Royal darted back to the wheelhouse door. "Rudder amidships! Steady up on zero-seven-zero!" he yelled to the helmsman, hoping the Red battery commander would be expecting him to make another radical zigzag to starboard.

Cobb, ambivalent about joining the others on the open wing, finally decided that it was the most prudent action to take. "We seem to be out of the worst of it," he said, holding his helmet in one hand while clumsily bracing himself against the pelorus stand with the other.

Royal said nothing, still not convinced the North Korean gunners had lost the scent.

"Don't you think you ought to put your helmet on, Sir?" suggested Oetjens in a friendly voice.

"I hate these damn things! They always make my head itch," the exec protested, unwilling to admit that his main concern was a worry that wearing the helmet would accelerate the size of his already ample bald spot.

Hardly had Cobb finished his explanation when three black specks came burrowing through the blanket of smoke, heading straight for the retreating destroyer.

Royal and the others on the wing watched the first projectile snip the outer-most halyard on the port yard before continuing on to chip an ugly black hole in the sea directly ahead of the *Field*. The second passed well above its intended vic-tim and burst against the surface of the water far off the port bow just as the third looped in to explode less than twenty yards to starboard.

Aubrey Cobb, almost to the wheelhouse door when the third shell detonated, fell to one knee dropping his helmet as a fragment struck him hard across the back of the neck. It was cold and sticky. He pulled his hand away, looked at his wet palm and saw it covered with blood. "I'm hit! I've been hit!" the exec cried out as Ensign Warden and Doneggan, a quartermaster-second, pulled him up under the arms and helped him reach the psychological security of the wheelhouse.

"Helmsman! Come right to zero-eight-five!" shouted the captain scrambling over a thousand thrashing pollack that had come raining down amid the great gouts of water thrown up by the last shell. Two more seven-point-sevens came spinning in to crash to the port side, dumping tons of water and even more fish upon the retreating destroyer.

Owen fought to keep his balance, the deck now completely covered with dancing, squirming pollack. He felt something tug hard at his ankle and he went tripping down among the fish, his left foot painfully entangled in the bridge-talker's long extension cord. Oetjens slipped and stumbled as he went to the captain's aid. Another shell landed close-by and another thousand pollack came cascading down.

The shells were sailing through the smoke in two's and three's as Royal, Oetjens and the bridge-talker struggled over the small hill of fish that now claimed squatters' rights to most of the open wing. They had almost reached the wheelhouse door when a pair of seven-point-sevens arched over the full length of the ship barely clearing the air-search antenna before spiraling down to meet in one tremendous eruption just yards ahead of the destroyer's bow. Too close to turn, the *Field* ducked under and through the geyser as tons of water crashed down heavily to the foc'sle and mounts-"one" and -"two", before splashing up over the wheelhouse and gun-director, and washing many of the fish down the open ladder-ways into the port and starboard motor-whaleboats hanging in their davits on the deck below.

For the next few minutes Royal skillfully parried each lethal thrust of the enemy battery commander. Ordering another change in course, he looked over at Cobb. "How do you feel, Aub?" he inquired as Parish, the pharmacist mate-third, busily applied a compress to the back of the exec's neck.

"I'm still a bit foggy. I didn't think it was serious until I reached back and saw all that blood on my hand. That piece of shrapnel must have torn a vain in my neck."

"You weren't hit by shrapnel, Sir," Parish cut in. "You must have been hit by a piece of fish. There's no skin broken."

"What about the blood?" snapped Cobb indignantly.

"That was from the pollack, Commander. All you've got is a slight swelling. It should be down in a day or two."

"You imbecile! Don't you think I know human blood from fish blood? Get down below and send up Chief Claccum. Maybe at least he'll know what he's doing!"

"Calm down, Aub," the captain interjected. "You've had a nasty crack on the neck, that's all. I'm certain Parish here is doing a competent job," said Royal, glancing at the now sullen pharmacist mate. Then quickly turning to the helms-man, he ordered, "Come left to zero-nine-five!"

Once again he had outguessed the North Koreans as a string of shell splash-es rose up far off the starboard beam.

"Their aim's falling off," Oetjens exclaimed cheerily.

"Ask combat what the range to the nearest land is," Royal instructed the dripping-wet bridge-talker.

"Combat holds Songdo Gap at two-seven-two...twelve thousand, five-hun-dred yards, Sir," came an almost instant reply.

Royal depressed the lever on the squawk-box which opened the circuit to gun-plot. "Mister MacKinlay. You may cease fire but keep all stations manned and ready. We're not out of this yet."

"Confirming the captain's appraisal, a shell flew out of the smoke to explode close off the port beam. One large chunk of Russian steel bounced off the base of the Mark-37, clanked noisily across the deck above the wheelhouse, then fell back into the sea.

For another five minutes, great plumes of white boiled up on both sides of the *Field*. Then, as if to punctuate the engagement, a final enemy round whistled into the sea astern, skipped twice along the length of the wake and sank without exploding only yards from the destroyer's churning screws.

"Mister Warden!" the C.O. called out. "Pass the word to all stations to report any casualties and battle damage."

When the *Field* reached a point forty-miles from land, she turned north toward her scheduled rendezvous with the task force off Chuuronjang.

"Now to deal with the pollack," Royal grunted bewilderedly, stepping back out on the bridge-wing.

"Excuse me, Cap'n, but they are not pollack," Gadberry, the chief quarter-master piped up dogmatically. "They are mackerel, sure as shooting."

"Mackerel?"

"Yes, Sir, Pacific mackerel."

"Are you absolutely certain?"

"Cap'n, I am a Gloucester man. I was weaned on cod and mackerel. These are a bit larger than the mackerel we use to take off Georges bank, but they are mackerel. No doubt about that."

"Looks like we chased after the wrong school, Captain," Oetjens volun-teered.

"If we did, we're not going back to rectify our error," Royal answered sourly as he held up a large specimen by its tail before hurling it back into the sea.

While the captain and his party were busily surveying the situation on the bridge-wing, equally perplexed crewmen were emerging from deck hatches throughout the ship to discover a scene of indescribable carnage. Battered demol-ished mackerel hung limply from every rail and platform, drooped over splinter shields and radar screens, dangled from the roofs of gun-houses and gun-directors, their giant eyes bulging nightmarishly as if in haunting protestation for the slaughter of the non-belligerent. All weather decks and gun tubs were covered at least five-deep, and Lieutenant Phelan, many decks below in the forward boiler-room, reported that numerous mackerel had fallen through the clinker screens atop the *Field's* two funnels. Here and there the moribund thrash of a tail could still be seen among the mounds of shiny fish as all hands, from seamen-deuce to petty-officers first-class, turned-to.

Those unlucky enough to be assigned the bridge clean-up did so under the close supervision of Chief Gadberry who, inspired by the events of the day, felt compelled to continuously serenade his workers with song. Unfortunately, only one song, an old sea chantey, was in his repertoire.

"Gloucester girls they have no combs,
Heave away, heave away,
They comb their hair with codfish bones,
We are bound for South Australia."

Fire hoses, brooms, swabs, buckets and waste-paper baskets were put to maximum employment. Even so, countless mackerel still adorned the antennas, stack tops and more remote extremities of the upper superstructure the following afternoon when the *Charles P. Field* rejoined the task force. Fortunately, the executive officer aboard the *Princeton* was an old chum and classmate at Annapolis. After a good-natured exchange of academy reminiscences via the TBS, Royal managed to recruit the services of the carrier's mammoth flightdeck hoses for washing-down the *Field's* inaccessible upperworks while she refueled alongside.

Aubrey Cobb, *DD-505's* only "casualty" of the Songdo Gap operation, opted to pass up the evening's movie and retire early to nurse his wound.

The flick being viewed in the wardroom was the venerable "A Yank in the R.A.F." Owen remembered it had been playing on the fantail that very special evening Candace had come aboard for dinner. This recollection gave the classic war film new significance, and hours after its conclusion, Royal found himself unconsciously humming its background theme, *"These Foolish Things Remind Me of You."*

•   •   •

Candace Moffet Royal was also contending with fish that night only it was broiled Rocky Mountain trout stuffed and wrapped with mint, and it was not aboard a destroyer off North Korea but in the elegant Crown Room of the Hotel del Coronado.

"It looks fabulous, Ham, but you don't really expect me to eat all this now do you?" Candace smiled. "How am I going to lose those extra three pounds I've targeted if you insist on wining and dining me every night?"

"Personally, Candace, I don't know why you'd want to lose any weight. You're perfect exactly the way you are."

"Thank you kind, sir. You're always gallant."

"It's easy to be when I'm with you. Tell me, Candace, did you know that the Prince of Wales met Wallis Simpson for the first time right here in this very room?"

"No, I didn't."

"And did you know that arched ceiling up there," he pointed, "is made of natural sugarpine, fitted together entirely by wood pegs? In fact, this room is said to be the largest pillarless room in the United States?"

"For a New Yorker, you seem to know an awful lot about this place. How come?"

"Oh, back before the war Bettina and I use to vacation here quite often. Tell me, have you eaten here before?"

"Yes, several times with Garrett. This seemed to be a favorite place of his and I don't think he even knew about the Duke and Duchess of Windsor."

"How's he coming along? From what I hear the navy isn't doing very much over there. At least you won't have to worry about getting one of those telegrams from the Defense Department, though it would solve things rather neatly," he muttered half under his breath.

"I hope you really didn't mean that," Candace snapped.

"Don't get sore. You know I was only kidding. Hell, I hope you don't think I'd really wish something like that on him, now do you?"

"Well, that's not something I'd even like to joke about."

"Of course not. Have you heard from him lately?"

"Yes, I get a stack of letters every two weeks. He writes almost every day, but I guess the navy waits until they can consolidate all the mail."

"Hell, if he's able to write every day, he must have it pretty soft. I don't think you have to worry about anything happening to him. I'm probably in more danger every time I cross Madison Avenue," Barlow laughed.

"I'm not so sure. He never writes anything about the war but I know that's only because he doesn't want me to worry."

"Nor do I," said Ham, tapping out his cigarette. "Remember, worrying makes wrinkles and I'd hate to see any imperfections in that beautiful face of yours," Barlow teased.

"Why? Would you lose interest in me? You know nobody keeps their looks forever. Is that why you've fallen out of love with your wife?"

"Don't be silly. I've told you hundreds of times I never really loved Bettina, not even at the beginning. Ours was the classic marriage of convenience. Bettina woke up one morning in her father's twenty-room townhouse and decided she wanted to get married. I just happened to be nearby and convenient. She might just as well have decided that day that she was going to buy a new hat in Lord and Taylor's."

"Were you that easy a conquest?"

"Well, let's say that I was just a junior account exec and the fact that her father was chairman of the board for our biggest account didn't exactly stifle my interest. Besides, in her younger days she was sensational in bed."

"You're certainly very candid."

"Why not? You know how I feel about you. I imagine you've always known, probably since your first morning at B.B.Y. and S. when you stopped me in the elevator and asked me what a 'brainstorm session' was. Most of the agency staff would piss in their pants if I as much as looked in their general direction. You know, I've always suspected that you knew more about 'brainstorm sessions' that morning than I did. Am I right?"

"Now, Ham. You wouldn't want me to tell you and ruin all the mystery, now would you?" asked Candace with a saucy smile.

"No, not really," he grinned, lighting up a fresh Camel. Taking a drag on the cigarette, he asked, "Speaking of mysteries, have you seen your friend Kevin Logan lately?"

"No, I guess that movie script's keeping him busy," she answered, deciding not to mention the postcards she'd received from Japan and Hawaii. "Why do you consider Kevin a mystery?"

"Well, I had occasion to handle some publicity for Columbia Studios recently and when I mentioned Logan's name, nobody had ever heard of him. They said the screen play for the '*Caine Mutiny*' was well underway but it was being written by a guy named Stanley Roberts."

"Maybe he's assisting this Roberts fellow," she answered with a puzzled expression.

"I asked about that. The fellow who's working on the dialog is named Blankfort. I even asked if they had a technical advisor named Logan and they said no."

Candace turned milk-white.

"What's the matter, did I upset you by bringing up Logan?"

"No...no, of course not," she said, forcing a smile.

"You really scared me. For a second you looked like you were going to faint. Are you sure you're not still carrying a torch for that heel?"

"Don't be silly, Ham. I never carried a torch for Kevin. I was the one who broke our engagement...twice in fact," she laughed. "What you said just surprised me, that's all. I can't imagine why he'd go to the trouble of making up such a story. It just doesn't make sense."

"You don't think he really joined the navy like I heard back in New York, do you?"

"No, of course not. Would you give up a top-paying job in an agency to go into the service. Especially if, like Kevin used to say, he'd already paid his dues in the last war?"

"No, it doesn't seem very logical," Barlow shook his head.

"I wasn't going to mention this but I recently got a card from him...from Japan," she added sheepishly.

"Japan. What would he be doing over there, unless maybe he's hired himself out to stud in a geisha house," Barlow quipped.

"Very humorous," said Candace sardonically.

"Hey, cheer up. I thought this was going to be a fun night. I'd hate to think Logan could throw a damper on our evening even when he's six thousand miles away."

"I'm sorry, Ham. It's got nothing to do with Kevin. I've been having some personnel problems at the office and they're really starting to get to me."

"Personnel problems? Hell, you ran your accounts and supervised your people back in New York better than anyone else at the agency. That's one of the reason's you're here now. From what I've seen so far, you've done one hell of a job. You've not only saved the accounts we'd already written off but you've managed to lasso two we've been chasing after for five years. As far as I'm concerned, you've got a free hand. If anyone's not pulling his weight or giving you a tough time, just get rid of him. You won't have to answer to anyone back in New York. Don't worry, I'll see to that!"

"Thanks, Ham. I know I've got your support. It's just that I hate to fire somebody who has been working at the agency as long as Paradise has.

"Paradise! Is that weasel giving you a tough time? I never did like the guy but I've never known him to be insolent. Actually, he's probably the biggest ass-kisser in the agency. That's why your predecessor kept him on. He was good for his ego. What's Paradise been doing to get you this upset?"

"Probably his biggest problem is he never tells the truth. He can stare you straight in the eye and look completely sincere, and yet you know he's lying through his teeth."

"What about his work? Is it up to snuff?"

"He doesn't do much work. He prefers to push everything off on his subordinates."

"Well, Candace, I don't see that you have any choice. I say go ahead and can him. Give him two weeks salary and show him the door. A con artist I can take. Hell, that goes with the territory. One thing I won't tolerate is a con artist who doesn't produce! Now let's forget about Paradise and the agency and just spend the rest of the evening enjoying each other's company."

Since Barlow was well known at the del Coronado, Candace could understand his reluctance in taking her up to his room. Therefore, it was mutually agreed that her apartment on Terryhill Drive would be a prudent substitute.

•   •   •

It took two full days to remove the mackerel from every crevice, crack and void. Even so, most of the *Field's* crew insisted that their ship smelled less appetizing than a Campeche shrimper. The ill aroma did little to discourage Culpepper who still took relish in strumming his guitar and wobbling his favorite ballad, "*The Trail to Mexico.*"

"Well it was early in the year,
When I started out to drive those steers,
Through sleet and snow was lonesome goin',
As the herd rolled on to Mexico.

Well when I got to Mexico,
Wished to see my gal but could not go,
I wrote a letter to my dear,
But not a word for years did I hear."

The task force steamed on, moving south over a calm level surface that gleamed like brass in the evening sun.

Chapter XV - "Pigboat"

By mid-October, the presidential campaigns of Eisenhower and Stevenson had swung into their final and most critical phases. In Korea, the war had settled down to a continuous series of fierce small-scale battles fought along what had come to be known as the MLR or "Main Line of Resistance." Stretching 155 miles across the Korean peninsula from the Yellow Sea to the Sea of Japan, the MLR, which roughly ran along the 38th parallel, was in many ways reminiscent of the terrible trench warfare of World War I. Here, dogface and gyrene, ROK and highlander, engaged in massive artillery duels, and in infantry contests where bayonet or trench knife became the ultimate weapon. They launched patrols into no-man's land and slugged it out on rocky, oddly shaped crags of land to which they gave names like "T-Bone," "White Horse Hill," "the Hook," "Bloody Ridge," "Big Nori," "Old Baldy," "Jane Russell Hill," and the especially appropriate — "Heartbreak Ridge."

On the day that 7th Division infantry was probing Red outposts near Kumwha, and the marines on "Bunker Hill" were hearing the bugles and whistles that heralded a Chinese charge, the *Field* was far away, steaming 60 miles out in front of the task force in the "Tomcat" slot; her assignment twofold, to provide early warning radar coverage and to act as reference point for aircraft returning to their carriers.

Almost a month had passed since Songdo Gap. During that time the *Field* had resumed her role as screening ship for the task force except for three days when she accompanied cruiser *Toledo* on a series of hit and run strikes along the bombline from Yang do to Chuuronjang. Again, superb shiphandling on the part of Commander Royal saved the destroyer from sustaining any damage more serious than the loss of one RCM antenna, and a large but patchable hole in the side of the port motor-whaleboat.

Abner Ward and *John Morgan* were also seeing their share of action this October of 1952. Both ships had again detached from the task force...this time to provide much needed artillery support for embattled army units holding the right anchor of the MLR. They'd been gone eight days now, and scuttlebutt had it that both destroyers were taking heavy and accurate return fire. One story circulating around the ship was that the *Morgan's* profile had been drastically altered by a passing 3-inch shell that had removed nine feet of her after stack leaving only a twisted stump. Casualties, including two fatalities, were rumored but not confirmed.

There was a strong bite of salt in the air as Commander Royal worked his way up the foc's'le. Standing by the jackstaff, he peered ahead at a dark gray sea and an equally somber sky. Out here all alone on "Tomcat," the ship would be a sitting duck should the Reds decide to send out attacking aircraft. Luckily, this wasn't Okinawa and such an eventuality was unlikely, he smiled, fully aware that aerial strikes against UN surface units had thus far been limited. Even so, he could not discount the possibility, and he hoped Coates and his people in C.I.C. were keeping wide awake.

In spite of the dreary atmosphere of their solitary assignment, Owen was feeling quite chipper. In his pocket were two letters from Candace he'd received the evening before while the *Field* was refueling alongside *Kearsarge*. As an added bonus, he'd finally learned the results of his ship's unscheduled encounter at Songdo Gap. The information was contained in a dispatch from Jehovah routed via the screen commander. The commodore had also been copied, Royal noticed, but with *Abner Ward* frantically dodging Chinese metal off Chumunjin, Owen doubted that Price would have much time to read it.

The score confirmed by South Korean and U.S. intelligence sources listed the complete destruction of a three-hundred-foot-long jetty, two prime-movers, a gasoline tanker truck, a lighthouse, a mine- and net-control station and most important, a large trawler which had been last seen in a highly restricted area at Vladivostok. However, conspicuously absent was any mention of damage to the enemy's gun emplacements or fire-control system, and Royal was well aware that the shore batteries, not the jetty and trawler, had been the *Field's* actual targets. In this regard he lost no time in scheduling a thorough critique of the operation for the specific benefit of Messrs. Ritter and MacKinlay.

The watch in the combat-information-center was passing uneventfully. The only aircraft detected on the *Field's* Sugar-Charlie was a flight of Air Force Sabres out of Kimpo, heading north for the Yalu River and "Mig Alley."

"Think those F-86s will bag any Migs up there today, Mister Stockwell?" Gardiner asked from his seat at the air-search radar.

"They usually do. I don't know why today should be any different," the Ops officer remarked as he inspected the latest entries in the C.I.C. log.

"Hey, Howie," Bacelli called from the surface-search. "How come you're so quiet today? I haven't heard a squeak out of you in the last hour."

"I didn't know I was being timed," snarled the first-class.

"Sorry I asked," Bacelli muttered sullenly. Then turning to his mate at the SC, said, "How come Murray's got the rag on today? I just asked him a perfectly harmless question and he practically bites my head off."

"Who knows?" Gardiner sighed. "He chewed my ass out ten minutes ago, and all I did was step away from the radar for two seconds to get some sugar for my coffee."

"Do you still hold those Sabres?" Lieutenant Stockwell asked in a quiet tone as he leaned over Gardiner's shoulder to squint at the greenish scope. "I seem to have lost them on the repeater."

"Yes, Sir. Right up here at three-four-eight…sixty miles," the third-class said cranking the range dial.

"Murray," Stockwell called out. "You'd better call an ET and have that radar repeater checked out. While he's at it, have him take a look at the whole radar console," the lieutenant instructed, emerging from the blackness of the alcove that housed the two search radars.

Kevin Logan arrived just as Farnsworth, an electronics tech-second, began checking the thousands of tiny wires and connections that formed the guts of the main radar console.

"What's with the repeater, Howie?" he asked, hiking himself up on the stool near the plotting table.

"Mister Stockwell says it's not working right. Hell, I'm not surprised. All this gear dates back to World War Two. Of course, when you go over to the *Oriskany*, you'll have a chance to see what new radar equipment looks like."

"*Oriskany?* Who said I was going to the *Oriskany?*"

"You did. You said you were going to work out a swap with that buddy of yours," Murray grunted. "Mister Coates told me the 'Big O' will be joining the task force on the thirty-first. Her call name's 'Childplay' in case you want to give them a buzz on the TBS," he added sarcastically.

"No, after I gave that idea a little thought, I realized that Cindy would be able to track me down just as easily when the *Oriskany* pulled into Yokosuka for R and R. Besides, now that I've ridden out a few fire missions on this pig-iron honey barge, I suddenly find that I've developed a warm spot in my heart for the old girl."

"Then you're not putting in for a transfer?" Murray's face suddenly brightened.

"Of course not. How could I ever leave my old friend, Chief Henderson?" Kevin laughed.

"Logan. Did I hear you mention you've got a girl in Yokosuka named Cindy?" Stockwell glanced at the radarman curiously. "Isn't that an unusual name for a Japanese girl?"

"Oh, she's not Japanese. She's a wave."

"A wave? That's strange. I was told that there aren't any waves stationed in Japan at this time except medical personnel."

"Did I say wave? I meant to say wac. I'm always lumping those female outfits under one acronym," he replied quickly, hoping that no one in the radar shack would disclose his blatant breach of navy regs for Lieutenant Osbourne's sake as well as his own.

"Mister Stockwell. Can you come back in here for a minute," Bacelli called out with a tone of urgency. "Sir, I think I've got a contact out at three-five-three, twenty-five thousand yards," he explained as the Ops officer stooped over the scope. "It only shows up every third or fourth sweep...See! There! It just came in again on that last sweep!" Bacelli's voice bounced with excitement.

Stockwell studied the Sugar-George for a long minute, then looked up at the adjacent A-scope. "There's something out there, alright," he muttered before dashing back out to the plotting table. "Bridge, combat...this is Lieutenant Stockwell," he yelled into the squawk-box. "Is the captain on the bridge?"

"No, Sir. He's on the foc'sle. If it's important, I'll send the messenger down to get him," Phelan, OD for the afternoon watch, offered.

"Yeah, Andy, I think that might be a good idea. It looks like we've picked up a contact twelve-and-a-half miles dead ahead. It's probably just a couple of 'gooks' in a junk, but it could be a sub with only its periscope and snorkel showing."

"You know, we're blind up here with our radar repeater down," Phelan complained. "Do you have any idea when the main console will be back on line?"

Stockwell glanced down at the ET who was crouched under the console stand, probing a jungle of tubes and wires.

"At least another hour, Sir," Farnsworth volunteered.

"Another hour, Andy," the Ops officer called into the speaker.

Hardly had Stockwell finished the sentence when the captain entered the radar shack.

"The messenger said something about a sub on the radar?" quizzed Royal, walking straight to the Sugar-George.

"Well, I'm not sure it is a sub, Sir," Stockwell replied in a shaky voice. "It's probably just a small fishing boat. The way it's not showing up every sweep, maybe it's a floating mine."

"At what range do you hold it?"

"Twenty-five thousand, two hundred yards, Sir," Bacelli spoke up.

"You'd never pick up a mine at that distance with this old gear," Royal said to Stockwell.

"There it is again, Captain," Bacelli cried out.

"Yes, I see it. You'd better start plotting it's course and speed," Royal instructed, turning to Murray and Logan at the plotting table. "Mister Stockwell, I think we've just picked up out first pigboat," the captain said in a calm voice. Seconds later, he was reaching for the "to-speak" lever on the squawk-box. "Mister Phelan," he called. "This is the captain. We may have a submarine out there. Please call away general quarters." Then turning to Stockwell, he said, "Don, I suggest you get your RCM gear fired up. If that skunk out there is a sub, he's undoubtedly tracking us with his radar. Let's see if we can pick up his signal."

"Yes, Sir." Looking at Murray, Stockwell ordered, "Get somebody on that SPR-2. If that skunk is echoing in on us, I want to know his frequency pulse width and wave band, pronto!"

Royal departed for the bridge to the nerve-bending blast of general quarters, barely avoiding what might have been a catastrophic collision with Ensign Coates, the latter barreling into C.I.C. in a manner worthy of the "Red Ball Express."

"Damn!" exclaimed Coates, catching his breath. "Was that the old man I almost ran into?"

"That's affirmative, Mister Coates," Holiday said with a smirk as he and Nugent, followed closely by the radar strikers, joined their comrades for G.Q.

"Well, what's taking you so long to man the SPR-2?" Stockwell demanded, looking first at Murray, then at Logan.

"There's nobody here who knows how to work that damn thing, Sir," Murray said, wiping his brow.

"Is that right, Mister Coates?"

The ensign shrugged. "I guess so, if Murray says so."

"How the hell did you people pass O.R.I. off Hawaii?"

"Beats the hell out of me, Sir," Nugent grinned.

Murray scratched the back of his neck. "The RCM exercise they had us slated for sort of got lost in the shuffle," explained the first-class. "Actually, it was cancelled so we could get extra practice coming alongside large ships. Remember, Sir, that was the afternoon we almost kamikazed the *Crown Point?*"

"How could I forget," Stockwell mumbled, looking around at his now fully present but obviously incompetent C.I.C. team. "Can you at least get that thing working?" he said, turning towards Farnsworth.

"Yes, Sir. That's no problem. Only once I get it turned on, I'm not really sure what to do with it," the electronics technician explained with a blank expression.

While Farnsworth went about firing up the SPR-2, Stockwell, Murray and Coates started flipping through the Procedures Manual, hoping to learn the secrets of this strange, alien-looking apparatus.

Wading through voluminous sections on "harmonic responses," "super-heterodyne receivers," "panoramic adaptors," and "oscillator image recognition," Stockwell, always the realist, shook his head in utter frustration, realizing that there was no way he or his radar gang would be able to produce the information the captain expected within the next few moments.

While contemplating how best to apprise the bridge of this unfortunate circumstance, he heard Bacelli shout, "That skunk's completely faded from the scope. I've lost it on both the PPI and A-scope!"

"Saved by the bell," Stockwell sighed aloud, wiping the perspiration from his face with one of the monogrammed handkerchiefs he had just received as a birthday gift from Cassy Jean. "Bridge, combat," he called cheerfully, "that skunk at three-five-three has faded."

"Bridge, aye," acknowledged Royal. "It must have been a sub after all. She's obviously picked us up on her radar and decided to dive. Get your sonar people pinging right away!"

"Combat, aye," Stockwell said, then flipped a different lever. "Sonar, combat," he called.

"Sonar, aye," came the prompt reply from Liebing, *DD-505's* leading "ping-jockey."

"Sonar...we've just lost a possible submarine contact bearing three-five-three, twenty-seven thousand yards. Do you have an echo?"

"Affirmative, combat. It's just coming in now," Liebing sang out with unabashed satisfaction. "We hold a strong echo at three-five-eight, twenty-six thousand yards. Contact appears to be crossing from left to right."

Liebing's words were also heard in the wheelhouse since ASW operations aboard *DD-505* were handled by a triumvirate made up of the bridge, C.I.C. and sonar-control, the latter also functioning as underwater-battery-plot, which for reasons unfathomable to Owen Royal, had never been incorporated into his ship's design.

Hunched over the chart table, Royal listened to sonar's report as he flipped the pages of the O.N.I. manual entitled "*Russian Submarines and Their Equipment.*" A recently inserted addendum noted that Chinese Communist Naval Forces had taken delivery of a small number of Russian submarines. Naval intelligence believed the recent transfer included "S"-, "MV"-, "Shchuka"-, and "M2"- class submarines.

It wasn't very likely the Chinese would be operating any of these basically obsolete types in the Sea of Japan, especially this far north, Royal quickly concluded, certain that the Chinese would prefer to keep their fledgling undersea force closer to home in the Yellow Sea. In view of his contact's relative nearness to Vladivostok, Royal decided she was most likely a Russian snooper out to spot the Sabres so she could alert the Mig bases around Antung. He wondered if the sub was one of the new "W"s he'd been hearing so much about. If so, there was a good chance the *Field* might soon become the quarry instead of the hunter. His thoughts were suddenly distracted by the pencils rattling loudly against the inside of the coffee mug that served as their holder. Royal could hear the racing propellers, the creaks and squeaks of a much used wheelhouse straining under the vibrations of a 30-knot charge.

"Radio-central, bridge!" Royal called impatiently into the bridge-speaker. "Has Jehovah replied to my message yet?"

"No, Sir," Little Gillie answered, recognizing his commanding officer's frustration.

"Get it to me the second it comes in!" Turning to Oetjens and Phelan, Royal said, "When we get within four thousand yards of the target, we'll reduce speed to fifteen knots for the attack. I plan to fire both hedgehogs, a full twenty-four projectiles from each. We'll use a standard pattern, 160-feet long by 195-feet across."

"If we miss with the hedgehogs," Oetjens asked, "will we follow up with both the K-guns and stern racks, Captain?"

"Yes, but I pray to God we don't miss on our first run. If that target does turn out to be one of the new "W"-class our cloak and dagger boys are so worried about, we could be buying ourselves a batch of trouble. Supposedly, this type incorporates all the latest advances the Germans were able to come up with by the end of the war, plus a few the Russians tossed in for good measure." Royal checked the latest contact fix on the maneuvering board as he spoke. "You know, Phil, I wasn't overjoyed last March during our refit when we swapped the two twin-forties at the base of the bridge for that pair of hedgehogs. Maybe it wasn't such a bad deal after all," he smiled, his eyes still following the contact's estimated track line as he listened to each new range and bearing blare out from the special ASW-command speaker mounted in the wheelhouse. Decks below, the same information was being plotted on the D.R.T. by Kevin Logan.

"Those hedgehogs might get into the history books someday," Oetjens said hoarsely.

"What do you mean?" asked Phelan, standing just behind the helmsman.

"Well, if we do sink that baby out there, those hedgehogs could very well have the distinction of having fired the first shots of World War Three."

"There's not much chance of that," Royal answered curtly. "The Russians know that their subs are fair game any time they send them into the war zone."

"Yes, Sir, I understand that," Oetjens said in a troubled tone, "but with a volatile old cutthroat like Stalin running the Kremlin, who knows what might happen?"

"I'm afraid that's for the politicians to work out," Royal replied. "Our job's clear-cut, we find a bug in our rose garden, we stomp on it." The captain reached for the speaker button. "Sonar, bridge. Do you have a course and speed on that contact yet?"

"Sonar, aye. Contact is heading zero-two-eight, twenty-two knots, Sir."

"You'd better check that speed, sonar," Royal answered sourly. "even those new "W"s can't move that fast submerged!" The captain pushed the lever for C.I.C. "Combat, Bridge! Have you worked out a course and speed on the D.R.T.?"

"Combat, aye," Stockwell acknowledged. "We concur with sonar on a course of zero-two-eight, but we show her making fifteen knots."

"Very well," Royal said. "Mister Phelan, I have the conn. I'll take her in for this one..." "Talker. Pass the word to all A-S-W stations to stand by to fire on command."

"Yes, Sir," the young sailor replied, immediately relaying the captain's instructions via the sound-powered phone circuit.

Like an old hound chasing after a fox, the *Field* leaped along towards the point of interception. Maintaining a base course of zero-four-zero, Royal weaved to right and left at irregular intervals, each change in heading short and abrupt. It was a safe assumption that his adversary had a sting in her tail, and Royal was determined not to give the Russian an easy shot.

Narrowing the range to the contact, he was aware that they were far enough out from shore for the Russian to pull the plug and dive deep. Closer to land in shoal waters, the sub's skipper would not enjoy such freedom of maneuver.

Royal knew that choosing the proper setting for the depth charges could be a tricky proposition, especially considering the limitations of the *Field's* antiquated sonar and the "W"-class boats' reputed capability of reaching depths of 500 feet or more. At least with the hedgehogs he knew he wouldn't have to worry about selecting the wrong setting. Thrown 280 yards out in front of the ship in a wide fan-like pattern, these 7.2-inch projectiles were strictly contact weapons, exploding only when they collided with the solid mass of the submarine. On the debit side, Royal had had no actual combat experience with this type of weapon even during his two years aboard *Remey* and *O'Bannon* since hedgehogs had not been fitted to most *Fletcher* class destroyers until well after the conclusion of the Pacific war.

They were almost four-thousand yards from the target now, and the *Field* had slowed her engines to the prescribed attack speed of 15 knots. Even at this moderate speed the ship quivered and thumped as if she was getting ready to come apart at the proverbial hinges. Royal interpreted this as an impatience for the kill.

"Bridge, sonar-control."

"Bridge, go ahead sonar," Royal replied.

"Target is altering course to port, Sir...target is fading. Captain," Liebing's voice rose sharply. "Sir, there's no echoes! We've lost contact!"

"Hard right rudder!" Royal instantly commanded. "Increase speed to twenty-five knots!"

The *Field* responded quickly, swinging around to point her bow at the sub's last known position. It was Royal's intention to give the Russian as small a target as possible, but where was the bastard, Owen asked himself. Was the Red skipper getting ready to serve up a spread of high-speed torpedoes at that very instant? Had he turned the *Field* in the wrong direction, Royal wondered. Was he showing a broad beam to the sub's commander instead of a slim bow?

Below in C.I.C., Stockwell was passing on to sonar-control an estimated search arc which Logan had worked out by drawing a circle about the point that represented the last known position of the submarine. The radius of this circle was equal to the fastest possible speed the contact was likely to make. In the wheelhouse, Navigator Oetjens had prepared a similar search arc for the captain's perusal.

Royal swung the destroyer hard around in a tight 180-degree turn, making certain the *Field* did not cross her own wake and thereby cause a baffle that would interfere with the sonar operator's ability to ping back on to the target. Skillfully, the captain coaxed the ship around in a semi-circle, continuously using just enough rudder to avoid leaving a strong knuckle in the water...a knuckle that could create a false target for his sonarmen and their highly temperamental equipment.

The *Field's* affinity for "Murphy's Law" sprung to mind as Royal hoped this last turn had not put the Russian dead astern in the blind spot caused by the ship's twin screws. If the sub was tagging along back there, the captain knew there was no way his sound gear could ping through that churning uproar.

"Bridge...sonar!" came Liebing's voice from the speaker.

"Sonar, bridge, what is it?" Royal asked, masking his anxiety from Oetjens and the others in the wheelhouse.

"We've regained contact, Sir! Submarine now bears zero-zero-nine, twenty-six thousand yards! Contact is definitely opening, Captain!"

"Very well. Give me a course and speed on the contact as soon as possible," Royal ordered smiling, relieved that he hadn't set the ship up for a torpedo, and knowing they were back in the ball game once again. He wondered why Jehovah was taking so long to acknowledge his report that he was preparing to attack a possible Russian submarine, as well as his request for air assistance from the task force.

The captain glanced over at Oetjens. The navigator had just marked a fresh X on the large white sheet that covered most of the chart table, and was waiting impatiently for the next range and bearing so he could D.R. a new track line.

Turning to the helmsman, Commander Royal ordered another 180-degree turn, this one geared to allow the *Field* to literally run right up the pigboat's stern, an ideal approach when attacking with hedgehogs. Hardly had he uttered the order when Little Gillie burst through the doorway connecting the wheelhouse with the inside stairway.

"Sir! This just came in from Jehovah! I decided I'd better run it right up from the crypto-shack myself," the radioman announced, still gasping for breath.

"*Action: Shiftless — Originator: Jehovah — Info: Birthrate — Message follows: Break — Do not initiate hostile action against reported contact — I say again" Do not initiate hostile action against reported contact. If you are attacked you may take any means necessary to safeguard your command. Under no circumstance is this last to be interpreted as authorization to provoke offensive action on part of contact — Break — Air assistance is not authorized at this time. — Break: Over.*"

"Damnation!" exclaimed Royal. "Helmsman! Belay that last order. Come left standard rudder! Steady up on course one-seven-five!"

"One-seven-five, aye!" repeated the helmsman, yanking hard at the wheel to counter the turn already initiated.

"One-seven-five will open the course to the sub, Captain," murmured a perplexed Oetjens.

The *Field* rolled hard and with a terrible rumpling sound as if all her machinery was rearing up in sudden protest.

Royal ignored Oetjens' confusion for the moment as he turned to Little Gillie, the latter waiting with pad and pen poised in anticipation of his C.O.'s acknowledgement to the Task Force 77 commander.

"Send this to Jehovah with info to Birthrate...Your message received and understood. Over and out...Get that coded and off right away!"

"Aye, aye, Sir," said the radioman rendering an unusually snappy salute before diving for the stairway.

"Sir, I take it that action report says we should hold off our attack until the A-S-W planes arrive?" Oetjens asked in a respectful but still puzzled tone.

"Not exactly, Phil. Here, read it," Royal frowned, resisting the temptation to crumple the paper up into a small yellow ball and toss it over the side.

"Did I say action report? Inaction report would be more appropriate! Why do you think they've pulled us off? That sub is well within the area the U.N.'s declared out of bounds to non-belligerents, not that those damn Ruskies could be considered non-belligerents. They're involved in this thing right up to their armpits!" Oetjens shook his head wearily.

"You won't get an argument from me on that score. However, with a lame duck sitting in the White House, and the election just three weeks away, I'm not surprised Jehovah isn't predisposed to letting us create an international incident."

"Do you think the order Jehovah sent came all the way from ComSeventhFleet?"

"No," Royal said amicably. "I think it came all the way from U.N. Command headquarters in Tokyo. That's probably why Jehovah took so long to reply."

"Hell's bells!" exclaimed the navigator eagerly. "The Charlie P.'s made the big times. Maybe this will get into the papers back home. You know, I'll bet they're even keeping Harry Truman informed of what we're up to right this very minute."

"I'm afraid what we're up to right this very minute is withdrawing from the scene of a possible confrontation. If the *Field's* going to make the papers, let's hope it's for something a bit more commendable," said an annoyed Royal as he leafed through the O.N.I. manual to the section on the capabilities of Russian torpedoes.

"Sonar, bridge," he called into the special ASW speaker.

"Sonar, aye," Liebing's voice flew back.

"What's our present range and bearing to the contact?"

"Zero-one-three, twenty-six thousand yards, Sir."

"Very well. Inform me if the range closes by as much as two hundred yards. Also, be especially alert to any major course changes the contact might make. We've got no guarantee that she won't reverse course and head down south again."

"Yes, Sir. We've been getting a strong echo. We should be able to keep an accurate track."

Turning to Phelan, the captain said, "You can secure the ship from general quarters and reset condition-two. That pigboat's almost thirteen miles away. Russian torpedoes are effective up to ten miles according to this manual. Even so, I intend to maintain our present distance. That should be more than enough of a safety margin just in case O.N.I. has underestimated the range of those Red fish."

"How could they do that?" Phelan quizzed.

"Quite easily. I remember during the war our intelligence manuals listed the displacement of the Jap super-battleship *Yamato* at forty-six thousand tons. We learned recently that she actually weighed in at close to seventy-two thousand.

And if you think they were off on that one," Owen smiled at Oetjens and Phelan, "just ask some fighter jock who flew in the Pacific how many Joe's, Adam's, Steve's, Omar's and Ione's he shot down. Each of these code names and at least a few more were assigned to what the intelligence boys thought were new hot planes rolling off the Jap assembly lines when in actuality the planes never existed. Those manuals carried detailed drawings and silhouettes of what the aircraft supposedly looked like. O.N.I. even went so far as to issue recognition models of some of these fictitious planes to hang from the overheads in carrier ready-rooms and lookout training spaces. Soon our pilots started reporting that they were encountering some of these types, and you know, they really believed that they were," Royal smiled. "Occasionally, a pilot would even report shooting down a nonexistent Ben when he was actually splashing the usual Zeke or Oscar he'd been flying against for months. In the heat of a fast-moving dogfight, it's understandable that a pilot might make an occasional misidentification, especially if he's anxious to be the first flyboy to come up against a new type. Of course, such false sightings just gave more credence to those Jap phantoms."

"I'm amazed you were able to fight a war with that kind of intelligence, Captain," Phelan said in a sympathetic tone.

"On the contrary, Andy. Our intelligence gang in the Pacific were top notch, the best in the entire war as far as I'm concerned. What they could do with seemingly insignificant scraps of information was close to miraculous. For example, if they hadn't cracked the Nip code just before Midway, we might still be out here fighting the Japanese instead of the Koreans."

The remainder of the day passed without incident. By 18:00, the contact was well north of the 49th parallel, and what might have been the spark to light World War III had now become nothing more than cold ashes. In another few hours, the *Field* was back in the screen, zigzagging through the night's black void with the thirty other gray entities that collectively comprised Task Force 77.

•　　•　　•

The order came suddenly and without a hint or warning. It came before Owen Royal could wipe the sleep from his eyes or write a short pre-breakfast letter to his wife in La Jolla. A stoop-shouldered radio-striker had handed it to him with a nervous gesture that suggested that the messenger was aware of its content.

"Has Mister Cobb seen this?" the captain asked, tightening the silk cord on his robe.

"Yes, Sir, both he and Mister Stockwell were in radio-central when the message was broken-down," said the sailor a bit uneasily.

Royal dismissed the young man, then reread the dispatch. This was one morning he'd have to skip his shower, breakfast too, he decided, quickly slipping into the light tan pants and shirt that served as underway uniform for American naval officers and CPOs.

The executive officer was already in the chart house, thumbing through a hefty ATP-manual, the one entitled *"Amphibious Operations — Tactics and Equipment."*

"Guess this is it," he said solemnly as Owen entered.

Royal had hoped Cobb wouldn't utter that damnably mawkish cliche. When he did, the captain found it impossible to suppress a broad grin, which in turn, confounded the exec who stared blankly at Royal, wondering what the C.O. could possibly find humorous about orders to participate in an all-out amphibious assault against some of the most heavily fortified real estate in North Korea.

"They've certainly sprung this one on us out of nowhere," moaned Cobb. "How can they expect us to pull off something as complex as an amphib landing without at least a half-dozen practice runs?"

"I guess they're counting on the element of surprise."

"They're the ones who'll be surprised if this turns out to be another Gallipoli. You know, I suspected something big was brewing the other day when Admiral Radford joined Jocko Clark on the *Iowa*. That's probably the only time this task force ever had both a 'four-star' and a 'three-star' riding herd on it at the same time."

"Yes, poor Jehovah must have felt like a seaman-deuce in that kind of company," Royal laughed good naturedly. "I took a look at *Iowa* from the bridge a few minutes ago. She's only flying Clark's ComSeventhFleet flag so Radford's obviously moved on. As commander of the Pacific Fleet, I imagine he's either over in the Yellow Sea inspecting Task Force 90 or ashore in South Korea giving the look-see to one of our shore bases. My main gripe with this message," Royal frowned, "is that it doesn't tell us anything about our specific role in the operation. Right now, I don't even know if they want us to be part of the bombardment force or the escort group for the transports." Royal examined the message again, hoping to pick up a clue he might have missed during the earlier readings. Dated 13 October, the message from Birthrate to Shiftless instructed:

> *"You will detach from Task Force 77 at 09:30 this date and proceed to latitude 39 East - Longitude 129 North where you will rendezvous with Joint Amphibious Task Force Seven. This force, supported by coordinated joint action, will seize by amphibious assault, occupy and defend a beachhead in the Kojo area with the Eighth Cavalry Regimental Combat Team in order to:*
>
> *a. Create an enemy psychological reaction favorable to the United Nations.*
>
> *b. Draw enemy reinforcements to the defense of objective area.*
>
> *c. Fully exploit the enemy's physical and psychological reaction.*
>
> *For purpose of this operation and until directed otherwise, you will be under the direct command of Commander Joint Amphibious Task Force Seven.*

"Well, one thing's certain. This invasion's not going to be anything on the scale of the Inchon landing," Royal observed in an edgy voice.

"Why do you say that?"

"According to these orders, they've only assigned a regimental combat team to the operation. At Inchon, they put two reinforced divisions and most of an army corps ashore. Kojo's defenses and its strategic position in relation to the MLR certainly warrant more than a token landing force," Royal shrugged. "Somehow, I can't help feeling that there's something a bit odd about this one."

A bit odd or not, the *Field* was eleven miles off Kojo at the appointed time, wallowing clumsily under heavy gray clouds and an overcast that made Royal strain his eyes to see the bombardment force which was busily engaged just a little over a mile away. A misty rain was fanning the open wing as he aimed his binoculars at the closest cruiser. He could sense the jolt of her guns each time they spewed out a new salvo, and he wondered if she was the *Toledo*, the ship the *Field* had recently squired during a three-day stint along the bombline. Focusing his glasses on her bow, the big white "135" told him instantly that she was not the *Toledo* but her identical sister, the *Los Angeles*. Beyond the cruisers, he discerned the unmistakable outline of Jocko Clark's *Iowa*, her nine 16-inch rifles unleashing broadside after broadside at the enemy's coastline.

Royal was aware that the 7th Fleet flagship, along with a bevy of cruisers and destroyers, had spent the previous twenty-four hours laying down a pre-invasion barrage. He wondered if the battlewagon or any of the other ships in the bombardment group had taken any hits. Earlier, he had read an action-dispatch that reported heavy casualties aboard the *Perkins*, one of the destroyers assigned to cover the minesweepers. Two near misses had sprayed the unlucky tin can with shrapnel, killing one crewman and wounding 17 others. The battle update also noted that minesweeper *Osprey* had been damaged by Communist gunfire.

"Right standard rudder!" a helmeted Royal called out from the port wing, sending the *Field* off on her fourth circle around the transport group. "Mister Phelan. Please inform combat once again that I don't want to pass closer than half-a-mile to any of those transports. They'll have a tough enough time putting their landing craft over the side in this kind of sea. I don't want our wake adding to their miseries."

Now Royal turned his glasses on the big troop carriers. The bow numbers on the three closest APAs identified them as the *Bayfield*, *Mountrail* and *Okanogan*. He was focusing in on the latter vessel, a navy-modified Victory Ship, when the bridge-talker announced almost casually, that C.I.C. had detected another bogey...this one at two-eight-one, twenty-two miles.

"Tell combat to keep a close watch on the new bogey and inform me if it points its nose in our direction," Royal answered, still studying the activity taking place aboard the *Okanogan* in preparation for the ship-to-shore maneuver which was still scheduled for 11:00.

Normally the report of an unidentified air contact, especially one that placed the aircraft within minutes flying time, would have caused all hell to break loose aboard the Charlie P. However, this latest bogey was the ninth to intrude upon the destroyer's radar screen in the seven hours since the *Field's* sailors had scampered to their battle stations. Like its predecessors, the plane briefly appeared over Kojo before fading beyond the spired crest of the Taebaek Mountains, adroitly avoiding the combat air patrol from *Bon Homme Richard* that droned reassuringly overhead.

The boatswain-of-the-watch struck two bells and Royal glanced instinctively at his watch to make certain it read exactly 10:00.

"Coffee, Captain?" Oetjens asked, approaching with two white mugs, each giving off more smoke than a smoldering volcano.

"Yes, thank you. The transports look like they're just about ready to put their boats in the water. Too bad we won't be leading them in," Owen said, sipping the coffee.

"Why didn't we get the nod?" grumbled the navigator, glancing at a destroyer bobbing like a plastic toy off the port quarter. "What's that *Sumner* class over there got that we don't?"

"Four five-inch guns forward of the bridge," Royal snickered. "She can throw out twice the volume of fire that we can going in. I imagine that's mighty comforting if you're a G.I. trailing behind in one of those little assault boats. Besides, somebody's got to stay out here and protect the transports, especially with all those bogeys that have been popping up on the radars all morning."

"Sir," interrupted Phelan from the wheelhouse door. "We just received a message from the force commander. H-hour has been postponed until fourteen-hundred."

"Very well," the captain said, his acknowledgement half muted by the cacophony of jet and piston as Corsairs, Skyraiders and Panthers broke through the overcast, disappearing seconds later in the gray midst that blotted out any suggestion of Kojo or its adjacent shoreline.

By noon the sea had stopped heaving and spears of bright sunlight began to stab through the low cloud cover. The *Field* had just moved abeam of the *Bayfield* when the speakers throughout the transport group boomed out the traditional battle cry of the "gator navy," the order to "Land the landing force."

"There they go over the side. Sick 'em army!" Oetjens cried out, a sudden glare of excitement lighting his eyes as he and Royal watched the first boats, those that had been rail-loaded, descend to the murky gray water. Within minutes, the LCVPs and two LCPRs were untethered from the transports to gather in clusters 500 yards astern of the larger vessels.

"That's strange," Royal shook his head. "They're sure not playing this one by the book."

"What do you mean, Captain?" quizzed the navigator.

"The way those loaded boats are all ganging up in little groups behind each transport. They should be moving off to one general assembly area so they can form into assault waves. Isn't that the way you did it at Normandy?"

"Yes, I think so. Of course, being on an LSM, I didn't get directly involved with any of the boats from the transports. We hauled out of Weymouth with ten other LSMs and sixteen LCTs, and crossed the English Channel in our own convoy. We didn't shift into assault waves until we were ten miles off Ravenoville. That's where we picked up the four PCs that were assigned to ride shotgun for us."

"Which beach did you land on, Omaha or Utah?"

"Utah, thank God. As bad as that was, at least we didn't run into anywhere near as many underwater obstacles or mines as the boats that hit Omaha. I guess you're aware, Sir, that the entire attack force at Utah landed on the wrong beach. The reference points we were using were pretty ambiguous. Then to top it off, we encountered a southerly tidal set that put us ashore almost a mile south of our assigned area. Actually, what should have been a disastrous screw-up turned out to be a blessing in disguise," he laughed. "We learned later that the beaches we'd been assigned to hit were as heavily fortified and mined as Omaha. The area where we went in turned out to be the weak link in Hitler's Atlantic Wall. By the way, I remember the *Bayfield* over there from Utah," Oetjens said, pointing at the pudgy C-3. "She was flagship for the transport force commander, Admiral Moon. I think the army's Lawton Collins was riding her too."

"Well, that's one nice thing about Korea. You certainly get to meet a lot of old friends," said Royal with an arid smile.

The *Field* had almost completed her ninth loop of the transports, and was now passing closest to the *Mountrail*. Royal took a compass bearing on the troop carrier, another navy-rigged Victory Ship, just as the last of her landing craft hit the water. Launched with only their navy crews, these LCMs and LCVPs were moving away, one-by-one, to take their place in the queue before coming back alongside to pick up their allotment of G.I.s. As each of the boxy landing craft cuddled up to her mother ship, Eighth Cavalry shock troops began scrambling down the cargo nets which had been spread against the ships' sides like huge black spider webs.

To Orville McAlleney, watching from his midship G.Q. station without benefit of binoculars, the Khaki swarm reminded him of moonshine boiling over the rim and down the sides of a huge gray still.

By 13:00 (1 p.m.), the final LCVP had taken on her 36 G.I.s, and with a sooty blast of diesel smoke from her stern exhaust, had roared off to join the other boats astern of the transports.

Royal glanced aft at the *Field's* ensign which, when the ship was underway, always flew from the gaff attached to the second stack. Drooping limply only moments before, the five-by-eight-foot flag was now standing out freely, its stars and stripes clearly discernible. "Those people in the landing craft better get their show on the road pretty soon. I think that water's going to start kicking up again," the captain said in an anxious voice.

"Kelty!" Oetjens called to the wiry quartermaster-third hunched over the chart table in the wheelhouse. "What's the wind doing?"

"Eight knots, Sir," the third-class reported as he read the anemometer.

"I can't figure out what they're waiting for," Royal said, raising his binoculars once more.

Hardly had he gotten the words out when the landing craft began returning to the APAs. To the complete bewilderment of all watching, the boats immediately commenced transferring their assault force back to the transports.

"Mister Phelan!" Royal beckoned to the OOD. "Has anything come over the T-B-S or via radio-central about canceling this operation?"

"No, Sir. Not a word." The young officer stared vacantly passed his commanding officer at the transports and at the soldiers in full combat gear climbing back up the assault nets.

"Are they really doing what it looks like they're doing?" exclaimed Phil Oetjens. "What the hell's going on here anyway?"

"I'm reserving my opinion until I see whether or not they start hauling those boats back on board," said Royal with a crafty grin.

"Why wouldn't they haul the boats in? What good are landing craft when they don't have anybody in them to land?" the navigator asked, seeking some logic in the clearly illogical.

Like a dutiful policeman patrolling the beat, *DD-505* continued around past the ungainly-looking transports while off to port, *Iowa* and her entourage had stepped up the bombardment, their thunder rumbling across the water to tell all within hearing that the operation was still very much underway. Overhead, additional strike waves of ADs and Corsairs reaffirmed that the landing was imminent.

In a little while the boats from all the transports had assembled in the rendezvous area, their navy crewmen seemingly oblivious to the absence of their army passengers. Forming a series of assault waves, ten boats to a wave, the landing craft proceeded to the geographic reference point designated to be the "line of departure." Royal and the others on the *Field's* bridge watched as each new wave moved up in a wedge formation, the boats quickly shifting into line abreast as they approached the LOD (Line of Departure) where the *Sumner* class and an APD waited to lead them in. The latter vessel, a destroyer-escort converted to the high-speed transport role with special navigation and communications equipment, would serve as primary control ship for the landing operation.

"Gentlemen, I think we've been had," Royal said with an easy smile. "It appears we've been participating in what the navy likes to call a demonstration."

"A demonstration?" puzzled Ensign Phelan.

"Yes, in boxing, I guess you'd call it a feint."

"What do you suppose the objective is?" Oetjens wondered aloud.

"Most likely the brass hopes to draw out the Chinese and North Korean reserves so our planes and the air force can clobber them on the roads while they're rushing to reinforce Kojo. Up till now, the Reds have been careful not to expose their reserve divisions. That's why they've been moving their troops only at night."

"Why couldn't they tell us, Sir?" OD Phelan asked in a slightly annoyed tone.

"I guess it was a matter of security. This way they don't have to worry about any leaks. Besides, the operation is much more convincing if everyone participating thinks it's the real thing."

"Why do you think they made those soldiers scramble up and down those nets like that?" asked Oetjens.

"Practice, I imagine. Anyway, don't feel too sorry for those G.I.s. They're safe and sound back on their transports. I doubt any of them are bitching about the change of plans. If you want to feel sorry for anyone, I think it should be for those swabbies who have to take the empty boats back in..." Royal paused to look at his watch..."in just about six minutes."

"Do you really think they're still going to make a run at the beach?" Oetjens quizzed, aiming his binoculars at the assault wave closest to the APD.

"They'll have to. That's the only way they can make this thing look convincing. Besides, there's no way the Reds can see over those boat ramps to tell if the boats are empty or not," Royal focused his glasses on the APD, then beyond to the destroyer which had just two-blocked a colorful new array of signal flags.

At precisely 14:00, the charge for the beach commenced...the destroyer...the APD ...then wave after wave of landing craft...all heading in towards Kojo at fifty-yard intervals.

In the 45 minutes it took the assault group to reach the turn away line 5,000 yards from shore, the velocity of the wind had accelerated to 40 knots. Now the danger from the sea far outweighed the danger from the enemy guns which fortunately and to everyone's surprise had been firing ineffectively. By the time the boats got back to their respective transports, the wind was whipping in at a full gale force of 55 knots. Recovering the landing craft in the tossing sea proved a perilous undertaking, a fact brought home to Royal and the others on the open wing as they witnessed four boats smashed and totally destroyed against the steel side of the *Okanogan*.

After much speculation aboard the *Field* that their destroyer would now get the word to join the *Iowa* group and get her licks in at the beach, a message was received from the force commander ordering the ship to accompany the transport group to Pohang-dong where the Eighth Cavalry Regimental Combat Team was slated to disembark. At 16:00, *DD-505*, sharing the escort assignment with the APD, departed the Kojo area without having gotten off a single round. As the vessels trudged seaward, the crashing sound of *Iowa's* 16-inch salvoes was still audible even to Oscar Kimmick and his snipes in the seclusion of the forward engine room.

• • •

The small wooden stool came flying out of Mychenko's hut. The Korean woman who had come to clean stood outside, afraid to approach any closer as she wondered what this bear of a foreigner was raging about in such a manner. Indeed, nothing seemed to please him in the months since he'd first come to poke and pry around the caves that overlooked the water. Her husband had cautioned her to put up with the Russian and his temper outbursts. After all, his presence did mean work for all the people of the village... work that might compensate a little for the recent loss of Maksan's small fishing industry.

A fresh string of Caspian curses flew from the major's mouth as he damned the American navy, his North Korean allies, and most of all, Comrade Colonel Nikolayev and those nits on his staff in Pyongyang. He had warned them that it would be a mistake to try to move the range-finding radars and the technicians who would install them all the way from Vladivostok by trawler. He'd told those imbeciles that the safest route would be by truck. It was little consolation to learn that the trawler had made it all the way to Songdo Gap, less that thirty miles away. He wondered how the Americans were able to time their attack so accurately...how that Yankee destroyer was able to sail right into Songdo Gap and blow the trawler out of the water moments before the range-finders were to be off-loaded. Obviously, the American intelligence system was far more capable than he's been led to believe, Mychenko concluded as he tried to accept the gloomy prospect of spending an additional month or two in this damnable exile.

Chapter XVI - Flower Covered Hills

Owen didn't know why he felt so uneasy or why this mood of depression had plagued him since late afternoon and all through dinner. It seemed to be getting worse as the evening progressed, and to add to his general discomfort, he could now detect the start of a headache. Maybe he'd have to break down and see a doctor about getting reading glasses, he told himself, frowning as he entered his stateroom. Taking off the tan shirt, he tossed it over the chair, then walked to the well-polished metal sink which he half filled with water. Within seconds, he was scooping soapy water up to his face. As refreshing as it felt, it did nothing to lighten his mood.

The captain had little liking for his present task, escorting a gaggle of slow-moving transports south through waters he considered about as perilous as Central Park Lake. Certain that the APD could easily handle the job alone, he wondered why the *Field* hadn't been ordered to augment *Iowa's* bombardment group, or at least been sent back to help screen the fast carriers. He'd been in the navy long enough to know that a record of second-string assignments like his present one, no matter how capably preformed, was bound to have a damning effect when the next selection board measured him for that fourth stripe.

Still wearing his trousers and T-shirt as he settled back in his bunk, he wondered if the evening movie might be the medicine he needed. He reached over to the desk for the Plan of the Day which informed him that the movie to be shown in the wardroom at eight was "*Northwest Mounted Police.*" He'd seen the old DeMille film three times in almost that many months. Entertaining as it was, he decided to forego a fourth viewing. The movie scheduled for the crew's mess was a John Payne-June Haver flick called "*Wake Up and Dream.*" Certain he had never seen it, he nevertheless opted to pass, knowing how uncomfortable the men would feel with the C.O. sitting in their midst.

He tossed the sheet of paper back on the desk top, and his gaze beamed briefly at the framed photograph. Even Candace's smile did little to shake off his melancholy.

A loud and rapid knock suddenly told Royal that he had an impatient visitor. "Yes?" he called out, sitting up in his bunk and slipping back into his shoes.

"It's Aub Cobb, Captain. Can I talk to you for a moment?"

"Sure, come on in."

The exec closed the door behind him. "Sorry to disturb your rest, Sir, but something's been bothering me..."

"I know the feeling, Aub," Royal cut in, almost smiling. "Sorry, I didn't mean to interrupt. Go ahead. You were saying that something's bothering you."

"Yes, I was just up in ship's-office," he said in a low, urgent tone. "I asked Gordon if he'd gotten any word yet on my Purple Heart. He said he didn't know anything about it."

"What Purple Heart?"

"The one I asked you about the day after Songdo Gap."

Owen looked up, his expression an equal mix of astonishment and amusement. "You weren't really serious about that, were you?"

"Of course, I was!" Cobb replied, unable to mask his anger. "Captain, I'm up for commander next year. You know as well as I do that a Purple Heart might make all the difference. Besides, it's not like I'm asking for something I didn't rate. That fish really knocked me for a loop. The back of my neck was covered with blood. You saw that yourself."

"That was fish blood. I watched Parish wipe it off your neck. He mentioned at the time that there was no skin broken. No, Aub, I'm sorry, I'd like to help you out, but there's no way in good conscience I could put you in for a Purple Heart."

"But you told me that morning you'd do it. You promised, Captain," Cobb's eyes glared as he spoke.

"I was being facetious. I thought you were putting me on, so I decided to go along with the joke. If I misled you in any way, I'm really sorry."

"Captain. I've already written to my wife, Renee, that I'd been recommended for a Purple Heart. By now, it will be all over Long Island. Knowing Renee, she's probably phoned it into all the local papers, to say nothing of the alumni news at Kings Point. Everyone I know will be laughing at me!"

"I can't help that, Aub. You never should have told anyone. Even if I had recommended you for the medal, it would still have to be approved by the Bureau of Personnel."

"I'm sure they'd approve it, Sir. I've a friend who works in the Medals and Awards section. He told me they're asshole deep in Purple Hearts. He said towards the end of World War Two, BuPers had several thousand Purple Hearts made up in anticipation of heavy navy and marine casualties during the invasion of Japan. Of course, when they A-bombed Hiroshima and Nagasaki, the invasion plans were cancelled. My friend says there's a couple of warehouses filled with Purple Hearts they don't know what to do with."

"You make it sound like it's my patriotic duty to recommend you for the medal so they can free up those warehouses," Royal said with a smile.

"I don't think this is funny, Sir."

"No, it's not," Royal said haltingly. "I guess I was being a little facetious again. That's a bad habit of mine. I'll have to try and break it."

"Then you will send the recommendation in?" Cobb prompted.

"No, Aub! I'm sorry about your embarrassment, and your school paper and all that, but there's no chance I'm going to change my mind. For one thing, half the men above deck that afternoon got clobbered with those fish. If I put you in, every one of them would be pounding on the door of the ship's office looking for their medal."

"Well...do you have any objection to my writing a letter to the bureau? I'd like them to decide if I have a valid claim or not," asked Cobb, raising his voice.

"No, of course not. Go right ahead if you think it will make you feel better. Only I doubt it will do any good without my endorsement." Royal felt a sudden surge of annoyance at Cobb's unbridled obstinacy.

"That's all I came to talk to you about, Captain," Cobb exhaled heavily. "If you'll excuse me, I'll be leaving. I have to check the charts for Pohang."

"Aub, before you go, there's something I've been wanting to talk to you about, and this seems to be as good a time as any."

"Yes?" the exec asked, his tone still testy.

"It's about your GQ station."

"Is there something wrong with it?" Cobb grinned nervously.

"Yes, decidedly so. I don't know what my predecessor had in mind when he allowed such a screwed-up organization for this ship. It's a miracle nothing was said about it during our O-R-I off Hawaii."

"I still don't understand what's wrong, Captain?"

"You don't? Then just answer one question. If the wheelhouse was ever knocked out, how could you conn this ship from way down in after-steering? To conn a ship you have to be able to see where you're going."

"Yes, naturally. That's why I'm connected via the sound powered phones to Ensign Daly up in the auxiliary secondary-conn."

"The auxiliary secondary-conn?"

"Yes, the platform on the second stack."

"Dammit, Aub! Are you trying to play games with me? That platform is secondary-conn! There's nothing auxiliary about it! You know that as well as I do," Royal lowered his voice trying to contain his anger. "Now, I don't know how to put this delicately, but I've been hearing wise cracks around the ship about you burying yourself down in after-steering whenever we get anywhere near the Red guns. I'm sorry I had to mention it. Naturally, I know there's absolutely no truth to any of those remarks. We both know how white hats thrive on shooting off their mouths about officers. I hate to think what they must say about me when I'm not around to hear them. However, I've come to the conclusion there's only one way to squelch that kind of talk, and that's to shift your GQ station. As of tomorrow, I'd like you to takeover the evaluator slot in C.I.C. Stockwell can move to secondary-conn and Ensign Daly can takeover your old post in after-steering. I'm sure you know that the recommended ship's organization from DesPac prescribes that the executive officer be in charge of C.I.C. during GQ."

"Yes, Sir. Whatever you think best." Cobb could feel the numbness creeping up through his cheeks as he tried to force a smile.

A moment later the discussion was terminated on a seemingly friendly note, and the executive officer departed for the chart room. And while the *Field's* number-two honcho was conjuring up a hefty new list of obscenities to prefix to the name Owen Garrett Royal, he was also breathing a lot easier, relieved that his new GQ station was not to be up on the exposed platform that served as secondary-conn.

The sea was calm but for a single swell when the *Field* reached Pohang-dong late the following morning. Freeing herself from the transports, the destroyer refueled and took on fresh water while captain and crew awaited word of their next assignment. The word came precisely at four; the *Field* would proceed 70 miles south to the port of Pusan where the crew would be given four days R and R. To sailors eagerly anticipating respite in Japan, the news came as a bitter disappointment.

•   •   •

The war by late October had moved far north of Pusan and the many vessels swinging peacefully at their moorings in the harbor. Sprinkled among the prim gray men-of-war were a score of merchant ships, their white upperworks and orange booms incongruous as bowling shirts at a formal wedding.

Near the north channel outboard the tender *Piedmont*, the *Field* was sandwiched in between two destroyer escorts and a South Korean PC. The repair crew from the mother ship had finally completed their work on her steering engine, and liberty launches were swarming around *Piedmont's* gangway to ferry restless sailors to whatever adventures awaited them on the nearby shore.

To the bluejacket stepping foot on the fleet landing for the first time, there was little to distinguish Pusan Hang except its smell, which Murray insisted was even fouler than that they'd encountered in Yokosuka.

"Too bad we can't bottle this air and use it against the North Koreans," quipped the first-class as he and Logan trudged along the dirt road that led into town and the non-commissioned officers club. "Hey! Look at all those tanks!" Murray suddenly exclaimed, sighting what appeared to be a vast staging area.

Many of the tanks were newly arrived from the States, their virgin shells spotless and glistening in the noonday sun. Others, their treads and hulls heavily crusted with the red mud of Chorwon or the "Punchbowl," were waiting to be shipped home for reconditioning or more likely the scrap heap.

"Let's go take a look. It will only take a few minutes," coaxed Murray. "They'll still be plenty of cold beer left when we get to the club."

"Okay, but what's this sudden interest in tanks?" Logan puzzled, shaking his head in the patronizing way one might address an impulsive child.

"Oh, it's not sudden. I've been fascinated with tanks since I was a kid. Back in Warren before the war, I used to spend just about every Sunday afternoon watching the local guard unit put their M-2s through their paces."

Murray's few minutes stretched closer to an hour-and-a-half, especially after the radarmen discovered several vehicles of Russian manufacture that were slated for evaluation testing at the army's Aberdeen Proving Grounds.

"When we get back to the States, I'll have to introduce you to my brother, Neal," Logan said as the two resumed their trek into town. "He drove a Sherman across North Africa and half of Italy during the war."

"That would be great. Incidentally, those last two rows back there are all Shermans," Murray said pointing. "They're a later version than what your brother had in Italy, though."

"How can you tell?"

"Easy. These have a much larger turret to accommodate the long barrel seventy-six. They didn't come into service until around the Battle of the Bulge. Your brother's Sherman would have been the earlier version with the short barrel seventy-five millimeter gun."

"I guess you really do know your tanks," Logan smiled. "To me they all look like big olive-drab blobs."

"If you ever get a chance to come visit my neck of the woods, and I certainly hope you will, I'll show you the exact type of Sherman your brother fought his war in. There's one in Warren sitting on the lawn in front of the National Guard armory." Murray hesitated, then in a somber tone, said, "You know, I had a couple of close buddies on the *Franklin*. When we were discharged, we all agreed to get together at least once a year. Needless to say, we never did. In fact, after a couple of years of exchanging Christmas cards, we lost all contact. The last card I sent came back with a note saying the addressee had moved without leaving a forwarding address. I hope that doesn't happen with you. I'd really like to keep in touch after we get out of this thing. It would be great if you could meet Mary Alice and the girls, and young Kevin, of course."

"Speaking of young Kevin," Logan laughed, "you and Mary Alice must be getting down to the wire about now."

"Yeah, according to the doctor, it should be about three more weeks."

"Are you going to put in for emergency leave?"

"No, if we were in the States I would, but not while we're over here. Now that we're in a shooting war, I don't want anybody saying I used the baby as an excuse to save my ass. By the way, when we get to the club, make sure I don't drink more than a couple of beers. After dinner, I'd like to find a church and light a candle, you know, for Mary Alice and the baby."

The two radarmen soon reached downtown Pusan which, except for the picturesque Yongdusan shrine, held little to attract the sightseer. By five, Logan and

Murray were enjoying the luxury of real eggs and fresh milk.

It was about this time that the *Field's* whaleboat slid neatly alongside the big fleet oiler, depositing Commander Royal on the small wooden platform at the bottom of *Chickamauga's* gangway.

Tim Barrett's stateroom was as plush as a carrier skipper's, and more spacious than the *Field's* entire wardroom, Royal observed as he compared it to his own cramped quarters.

"Looks like you've really struck oil on the *Chickamauga*, Tim, excuse the pun," Royal smiled, stepping aside as his host's steward flapped open the table linen and juggled the silver to carefully assigned stations on the snowy white spread.

"Ha, you'd be bored within a week, shuttling back and forth between here and the replenishment area every four days. If it could be arranged, I'd swap duty with you in a minute. From what I've been reading in the combat reports, the *Field's* been seeing more than her share of action, just like I told you she would."

"We still haven't qualified for combat pay," Owen answered with a sardonic grin.

"How come?"

"We don't have six days under direct fire. Counting the three days we were with the *Toledo*, and a little slug fest we had at Songdo Gap, we only racked up four days for October. According to the rules, that leaves us two short. Of course, we did lose an R-C-M antenna, and the Reds shot away one of our halyards, but the navy says neither case qualifies as taking a direct hit. I certainly don't give a damn about the forty-five dollars, but I'd like to see my crew collect. I'm sure some of them could really use it."

"Well, funds are a little tight these days, especially now that the navy's embarked on its nuclear program."

"You mean the *Nautilus?*"

"Sure do," Barrett's face brightened. "They've already started work on her. When she puts to sea in about two more years, the navy as you and I know it will be a thing of the past. Your destroyer will become as obsolete as 'Old Ironsides,' and there won't be much need for oilers like this one," the four striper said leaning back in his chair. "A nuclear-powered task force will be able to stay at sea indefinitely. Ships won't be dependent on underway fueling like they are now."

"You really think nuclear propulsion will work?...even in subs?"

"I've no doubt about it. Take my advice, Owen. The next time you get a chance to attend a course ashore, put in for anything you can get on nuclear theory and practice. Believe me, that's where the future lies. But enough about the future, I'd like to hear a little about the recent past. How about filling me in on that little donnybrook you got yourself into at Songdo Gap. The way I heard it, you practically pulled a Teddy Roosevelt and tried to go charging up San Juan Hill with that tin can of yours," Barrett chuckled loudly.

"Guess you mean Point Ko-cho," smiled Royal. It's easy to laugh about it now, but at the time it didn't seem very funny. Take it from me, Tim, if you ever have a steering-engine conk out on you, make sure it doesn't happen dead center in a Commie harbor."

"You must have pulled off a damn nice piece of ship handling to get out of a situation like that."

"Frankly, what really saved us was that oversized rudder they fitted the ship with when she went into dry dock last spring. The *Field's* original rudder, like that of every other wartime *Fletcher*, had an atrocious turning radius. I can testify to that from my *Remey* and *O'Bannon* days. I know damn well that without that new rudder, our turn would have been so wide, we'd have cut right through the mine field. If the mines didn't get us, we'd sure as hell have piled up on the rocks at Point Ko-cho."

"And I remember when you were complaining about only getting a limited refit," Owen's host laughed.

"Well, they really didn't do very much to update our equipment. Outside of the rudder, the only other new gear we received were a couple of hedgehogs, but we had to swap our forward forties to get them...not that they'll ever do us much good. The only sub contacts around here are Russian, and it's not likely that Jehovah's going to let us attack one of them. We recently learned that firsthand."

"Ha, so it was you," Captain Barrett said agog. "I read that report last week about one of our cans coming close to clobbering a Red pigboat up near Chongjin but I never stopped to think that it might have been your ship," he shook his head in an approving manner. "You're really having quite a time for yourself," Barrett said midst a robust laugh. "Hell, in the couple of months you've been over here, you've taken a couple of Jap nationals, female no less, on an unauthorized cruise, you've almost run your ship aground behind enemy lines, and now I learn that you were the joker that almost rang the gong on World War Three. Tell me, Owen, what new little adventure do you have cooked up for us? You know, you're really starting to put a little life back into this humdrum war."

"I don't think there's much chance of that," Royal frowned. "It took Jehovah two months to let us take a crack at the coast. Even then he used us begrudgingly. Every other can in the screen, including the *Ward* and *Morgan*, have been pulling fire mission after fire mission. For some cockamamie reason, Jehovah and the screen commander have decided the *Field's* strictly second string. Just this past week during the Kojo operation, Jehovah made sure we stayed well out of harm's way. Then, instead of calling us in to help the bombardment force, he detached us and sent us south with the transports."

"Do you think your problem might be Billy Price?"

"No, except for one operation, we've had hardly any contact with the commodore or the rest of the division for that matter. The destroyers have been operating independently, taking assignments directly from the screen commander. *Halsey Wayne*, of course, hasn't been taking assignments from anybody. She's been back in Yokosuka getting repaired. She took quite a pasting during our first fire mission. No, I'm more inclined to think it's the *Field* herself. The brass takes one look at her and they see that pole mast and that high silhouette with the two banks of torpedo tubes, and they think they're looking at something from the stone age."

"Well, if you want to get that fourth stripe next year, you've got to do something special...something that will make you stand out from all the other tin can jockeys over here." Barrett paused for a few seconds, then exclaimed, "I know! You've got to get yourself a train!"

"A train?"

"Yes, trains are priority targets these days. The bombardment force has even formed what they call the Trainbusters Club. You mean you haven't heard of it?"

"I do seem to recall some mention of it one night at the O-club in Yokosuka, but I didn't take it very seriously."

"Well, I advise you to start taking it seriously. For one thing, that club's the brain child of Harry Baker, Task Force 95's operations honcho. For another, it's received full endorsement from Jocko Clark." Barrett's jaw stiffened. "Why, it's even attracted the attention of the army. Just last week I read in the '*Navy Times*' that Van Fleet took the time to congratulate the skipper of the *Orleck* for knocking out two ammo trains north of Tanchon."

"The *Orleck?*" Royal's eyes brightened. "We were in the screening slot next to her when we first joined up with Seventy-Seven. Ed Yates is her CO."

"Well, you can bet your brass binnacle it will be Captain Ed Yates when the next board sits, and if you want to get that fourth stripe, I strongly recommend you follow his example," said Barrett, a trace of imperiousness in his tone.

"Your recommendation is duly noted and appreciated," Royal said with a look of bemused patience. Then, hoping to change the subject, the captain said, "If your chef ever feels inclined towards destroyer duty, tell him he can always find a billet on the Charlie P. This *vichyssoise* tops any I ever had on the Riviera."

"Not on your life, Owen. Friendship goes just so far," laughed Barrett. "I had one hell of a time getting him transferred with me from my last command. The captain who relieved me sampled his talents and tried every trick in the book to keep him on board. Luckily, I had a friend at BuPers who owed me a favor. Hell, my biggest worry now is that some admiral will find out about him and snatch him away," Barrett said settling back in his chair. "Now, getting back to the *Field*...any chance that bum steering engine will send her back to the States?"

"No, certainly not," Royal answered indignantly. "The repair boss on the *Piedmont* assured me this morning that the steering engine is as good as new."

"Now don't get your dander up, Owen. I was just thinking that maybe they'd retire the old girl and give you a nice new *Gearing*."

"I don't want a nice new *Gearing*. I'm perfectly satisfied with the *Field*. You know, Tim, when I'm standing out there on the open bridge, she's more than just so many tons of pig iron. Skimming over the water, she's a living thing. I almost feel like talking to her."

"Well, if you do, make sure nobody sees you," chuckled Barrett loudly. "With half the country reading about that Queeg character, it's going to be hard enough convincing the general public that navy skippers aren't all wacko."

"Hell, there's nothing wacko about my having a special feeling for the *Field*. You know, the yard where she was built is only twenty miles from where I was born. Granted, we've had our share of mechanical failures," Owen continued, "but that's understandable considering her limited overhaul after being laid up in 'mothballs' for six years. The important thing is she's always pulled us through when the chips were down."

"Sounds like a real love match, but didn't you offer to trade her for the *Chicamauga* just a minute ago?"

"Oh, it wasn't the *Chicamauga*," Royal beamed. "It was the *vichyssoise*."

As if on cue, a steward carried in the entree, a *bouillabaisse* Owen Royal was certain had never evolved from the unpretentious recipes of "*The Navy Cook Book.*"

After dinner, Captain Barrett escorted his guest topside for an inspection of the tanker's massive wheelhouse.

"How's the family, Tim?"

"Fine. Carolyn always asks about you in her letters. I wrote her that you were over here. She probably thinks you and I get together for a poker game every other night. Joanne's gotten engaged and unengaged, and Lee's got his wings. He's at Oceana waiting to get assigned to a squadron. Naturally, he's put in for fighters. I sure hope you were right, you know, what you said back in Japan about the navy not sending him over here. The way these truce talks are going, this thing could drag on for a long time."

"If it's any consolation, I'll make sure the Charlie P. does her utmost to shorten it."

The evening's movie aboard the tanker was the recently released "*One Minute to Zero.*" Royal and Barrett watched with great amusement as Robert Mitchum sang "*China Night*" in Japanese to Ann Blyth.

"Sure you don't want to stay over for the night. You're welcome to use my exec's cabin. He's over on the beach, got himself a nifty little air force nurse at K-9," Barrett smiled as the two officers made their way along the rain-soaked catwalk.

"Thanks, it sounds tempting but I'd better start back. I left my engineering officer knee-deep in *Piedmont* paperwork. I'd better help him wrap it up. Can't tell when we might want to use *Piedmont's* repair gang again. Besides, I expect we'll be getting orders to rejoin the task force tomorrow. Now that our steering engine's on line, there's no reason for Jehovah to let us sit out the war in Pusan."

"Well, if you're determined to go back to that cramped little tin can of yours, I'd better not hold you up. The last weather report said this rain's going to get a lot worse before it gets any better," Barrett groaned as the two reached the gangway. "I'll be looking for your pocket-battleship at the next replenishment. Maybe you'll get lucky and top-off from this baby. Then you'll really see what state-of-the-art refueling's all about. Anyway, like they say in the flicks, get out there and give 'em hell."

The two COs clasped hands warmly and Tim Barrett watched his friend's launch quickly disappear in the fog and rain that hung drearily over Pubong-Mal.

By eleven, the downpour was tapping a hollow crescendo upon the corrugated tin roof of the roadside shelter where Logan and Murray awaited the shuttle bus to the fleet landing. Behind them, a young Korean girl stood in the shadows clutching at a huge bundle of rags and humming the same morose chant the two radarmen had heard several times since they'd come ashore. As their eyes focused in a darkness reddened by a nearby road flare, they became aware that the monotonous melody seeped not from the lips of the young girl but from the bundle of rags on the floor, which on closer examination, they discovered to be an indescribably round old woman squatting in the classic pose of a Buddha.

"Good evening, Mamma-san," Murray greeted, as he fumbled through his Korean Language Guide for an appropriate phrase. "There's not enough light; I can't read this damn thing," he grunted, holding the thin blue covered paperback up to the glow from the flare.

"Do you speak English, young lady?" Logan asked, and the girl, in her late teens, stepped forward from the shadows.

"Ah, yes, very much English I speak. I work at K-9 air force base with many G.I.," she volunteered with an eager smile that etched its way across her wide flat features.

"Mamma-san, there," Murray asked with obvious concern in his voice, "she doesn't live in here all the time, does she?"

"Ah, no. She is my harmony...eh, I think you say grandmother," she pronounced the English translation slowly and with obvious difficulty. "We live on Nokchong Street. Not far. We wait for the rain to stop. We wait now."

"Tell me. That song your grandmother is singing. We've been hearing it all day. Is it your national anthem?" Murray quizzed.

"National anthem?" the girl puzzled.

"Yes, eh, your number one patriotic song."

The girl's eyes glazed and she seemed deeply embarrassed at not understanding the question.

"Eh, is it the chief song of your country?" Kevin interjected with equal difficulty.

"Song is *Arirang*."

"Onigong?"

"No," she giggled, "song is *A-ri-rang. Arirang* is big hill. Song is very old. For many hundred years is favorite of my people."

"Does the song have a meaning?" A long pause followed Murray's question.

"Oh, yes," her black eyes sparkled. "There is many stories told by this song. Story I like most is of young girl who loves sodja. Is very long time ago, maybe thousand years. Sodja likes to march away and fight enemy. This makes girl much sad. Song tell how she pray her tears for his going will wet all the flowers on the *Arirang* hill. Then each time her sodja climb hill on way to war, his feet will slip

on flowers made wet by her tears and he will roll back down to where she is waiting. *Arirang* is very happy hill with many beautiful flowers. *Arirang* keeps sodja
always home with girl that loves him. No let him go to war and be taken from her."

"Have you ever been to this *A-ri-rang* hill?" Howie asked.

"No, *Arirang* very far from here, but someday maybe I see."

A loud rumble from down the road announced the approach of the deuce-
and-a-half that would carry the two petty officers to the fleet landing.

Bidding *adieu* to the Koreans, the radarmen mounted the huge vehicle which
smelled like it had been used to transport four-legged passengers in the not too
distant past.

"Goo-da-by," the girl shouted until her words were swallowed up in the dis-
cordant roar of a faulty ignition.

"I'm learning quite a bit about you today," Logan quipped. "First I find out
you're a tank buff, and now I learn you're a music lover."

"I'm not a music lover," Murray said, frowning. "I just figured it might be a
smart idea to learn a little about the local history. Suppose little Kevin or the
girls ask me someday about my time in Korea. What am I going to tell them,
that every time their old man got close enough to make out what the shoreline
looked like, somebody tried to blow his head off? How's that going to sound to
my kids?"

"More realistic than flower-covered hills," Logan shrugged, and the truck
bounced on through the rain.

• • •

Benny Margolis was a fat and sweaty little man, hardly the image Ronald Paradise
had held of the typical private eye.

"You're sure this broad's not your wife?" Margolis asked, a mug of tomato
juice clutched in his hand.

"Don't be absurd! I told you, she's the manager where I work…I mean where
I did work. The bitch fired me yesterday!"

"I've been in this business over twenty years," Margolis shook his head, "this
is the first time anyone ever asked me to do this kind of job on his boss."

"Well, there's a first time for everything, now isn't there," Paradise's mouth
tightened. "Look, I didn't come all the way from La Jolla just to watch you drink
tomato juice out of a dirty coffee cup. I was told you specialize in this sort of thing.
If you don't want to handle it, I'm certain I can find somebody else who will."

"I didn't say I didn't want to handle it. Just as long as you know this kind of
work doesn't come cheap."

"I'm well aware of that. Now specifically, this is what I want you to do…"

• • •

Commander Royal leaned over the splinter screen and studied the fast black current. The bells of the wheelhouse telegraph jingled and the *Field's* screws kicked up huge bubbles of water as they pulled her free of the *Piedmont*. She backed out slowly until her bow was parallel to the stern of the tender. The bells rang again...the throbbing stopped...another clang of bells...her decks shuddered as the engines changed direction and pushed her forward toward the opening in the breakwater off Choryong Island.

The rising sun speared the mountain ridges beyond Pusan City as Owen Royal's destroyer glided through the outer harbor to enter the tiderips off Oryuk-To. An R.A.F. Sunderland flying boat circled low off the port quarter as the *Field* came about to a northerly heading.

There was the faint hint of snow in the air.

Chapter XVII - Many Bogies Closing

It was the 18th day of a very gray November. The morning sea was flat calm as the *Field* steamed independently toward her lifeguard station off Najin — her assignment, to cruise in a specified pattern ready to fish up any hapless airmen forced to ditch on the way home to his carrier. Twenty miles away, cruiser *Helena* was performing similar search and rescue duty, while up and down the coast, destroyers scurried to picket stations as Task Force 77 launched a maximum effort air strike against industrial targets in the far northern cities of Chongjin, Kilchu and Hoeryong. This was the furthest north the *Field* had yet ventured, and her mission would place her well above the 42nd parallel within an uncomfortable 50 miles of Vladivostok.

The Gods of War were indeed fickle, thought Owen Royal, reflecting upon his ship's performance of the past two weeks, contrasting it with the relative inaction of the preceding months. Making his way up the ladder to the open bridge, he smiled assuredly as he recalled Tim Barrett's parting words at the *Chicamauga's* quarterdeck. Well, the Charlie P. may not have gotten a train but she's sure given them hell and then some, he chuckled under his breath wondering if his friend had been keeping abreast of the *Field's* recent activities via the daily battle reports circulating among the Seventh Fleet C.O.'s.

If so, Tim would be aware that within three days after leaving Pusan, the ship had been dispatched to "Engine Block" to join destroyer *Walker* in bombarding coastal roads, rail lines and trestles in the Sinpo area. On the 1st of the month, the same day the world's first hydrogen device was being exploded at Eniwetok, the *Field* was creating pyrotechnics of her own with three direct hits on a major ammo dump north of Hungnam. On the following day, the ship blasted a radar station and transformer on the island of Mayang-do, then paired up with H.M.S. *Charity* to pound Chinese infantry crossing the Hamhung Plain. Impartial, the two destroyers passed the remainder of the day harassing a North Korean signals unit bivouacked a few miles away.

Eisenhower's election to the Presidency on the 4th was celebrated by interdicting a small truck convoy, then after replenishing and four more days of carrier screening, the *Field* made a return engagement off Mayang-do, this time to scatter a newly discovered sampan anchorage. The following afternoon her 5-inch guns were again in action providing covering fire for minesweepers working the pestilent waters off Hongwan. In the course of two weeks, she'd also managed to rescue the pilot and radar operator of an AD-4N that had overshot the *Essex's* flight deck. The *Field* had dodged everything the Reds had thrown at her, too, thought Royal staring at the white wake spreading out behind his racing destroyer. Most important though, not a man had been lost or even wounded. Old Henderson must have effected a transfer to some other ship, the captain smiled as the *Field* galloped on.

Below in C.I.C. Ensign Coates gripped the edge of the plotting table and studied the fathom markings off Najin on the chart spread out before him. "How far do you hold the nearest land?" he shouted across the darkened compartment.

"An even twenty-two miles at two-eight-one!"

"You've been in the navy long enough to know how to report a radar range, Nugent!" the C.I.C. officer grumbled. "Didn't Mister Cobb chew you out yesterday for not following proper procedure?"

"Yes, Sir," replied Nugent in a tone just shy of insubordinate. "Nearest land bears two-eight-one, forty-four thousand yards, Sir."

"Very well," answered the ensign glancing again at the chart.

"Mister Coates," Patterson exclaimed, the metal braces of his sound-powered phone creasing his reddish-blonde crew cut, "bridge wants to know how long it will take to reach our assigned station if we maintain our present course and speed?"

"You want to take care of that, Logan," the officer instructed in a quiet voice.

"Forty-four minutes to station," Logan answered without looking up from the maneuvering board. "That will put us off Najin at thirteen-fifteen," Kevin looked at the bulkhead clock as he spoke.

"Hey, Logan," Bacelli called out from his seat at the air-search radar. "How much homework did you have when you went to college?"

"Too much."

"Come on Logan, be serious. I'd really like to know."

"What's this sudden interest in higher education, Bacelli?" Coates asked, eyeing the third-class curiously.

"Bacelli's decided he wants to go to college," Nugent interjected with a smirk.

"That right, Bacelli?"

"Yes, Sir, providing Congress passes a Korean G-I bill," Bacelli replied hesitantly.

"What about those midget egg rolls you were so hot for?" Kevin laughed.

"Oh, I'm still going to handle them. In fact, I might take up marketing. That way I'll be able to run the whole sales operation after I make my deal with Don the Beachcomber's."

"Did I hear you say you're going to college when you get out?" asked Murray entering the combat-information-center.

"Yeah, I already spoke to Mister Daly about it. He's going to give me a list of colleges that I can write to."

"Now that's the first smart idea I've heard around here," Murray looked at Gardiner and Nugent contemptuously. "It wouldn't hurt you two any if you followed Bacelli's example." Then turning to Bacelli, Murray said proudly, "I'm glad you paid a little attention to what I've been saying about getting a decent education and improving yourself when you get out."

"Don't go taking any bows, Murray," Gardiner scowled. "You didn't have anything to do with Vinny's wanting to go back to college, did he Vinny?"

"Well, yeah, kinda' in a way maybe," Bacelli replied sheepishly.

"Bullshit!" Gardiner shot back. "Why don't you tell them the real reason you're so hot to get to college."

"Yeah, Bacelli," Nugent joined in. "Cut the crap and tell them what you told us at chow this morning. You know, about wanting to major in panty raids."

"Panty raids!" exclaimed Murray as Logan and Coates literally doubled over laughing.

"Show them the article you cut out of that newspaper you got back in Pusan," Gardiner yelled aloud. "The one you got tucked in your shirt pocket."

"I don't know what you guys are talking about," Bacelli frowned.

"Boy, what a liar this guy is," Gardiner shrugged. "Just before we came on watch, Bacelli here was going into great detail about how he's going to introduce a whole new element into those panty raids."

"Yeah," Nugent joined in. "Vinny says when he gets back, instead of standing under some dormitory window waiting for some college broad to toss out her skivies, he's gonna' lead the charge upstairs and take them off her himself."

"I never said anything like that!" Bacelli replied angrily.

"The hell you didn't!" Gardiner barked back.

"Okay, you two, knock it off and get your minds back on your work," Ensign Coates instructed coldly. "I expect that we'll be going to G-Q any minute now and I don't want you people fooling around like this in front of the exec."

"We weren't fooling, Mister Coates," Gardiner protested. "Everything we said about those panty raids was gospel...honest."

"Okay, okay, just knock it off and keep an eye on those scopes. You know we're way out on a limb by ourselves up here if the Reds decide to send out any Migs or PT-boats!"

"How's everything coming along in here?" asked Don Stockwell stepping through the doorway.

"No problem, providing a couple of our watch standers pay attention to what they're supposed to be doing," answered Ensign Coates with a touch of frustration.

"Say, Mister Stockwell," Nugent called out in a shaky voice, "do you mind if I ask you a question?"

"I don't if it's related to your work here in C.I.C."

"Oh, it's related. That's for sure."

"Then ask away."

"How come Mister Cobb's been made the C.I.C. evaluator during G-Q?" Nugent asked with a conspiratorial wink at Gardiner.

"The captain's just following recommended procedure," Stockwell said. "The organizational chart for Pacific Fleet destroyers calls for the executive officer to be in here during general quarters."

"Yeah, but since you're the Ops department head, shouldn't you be in here too?" Gardiner interjected in his best "sea-lawyer" tone.

"I would be if we were carrying our full complement of officers. A *Fletcher* class DD rates twenty. We've only got thirteen."

"How come we're short so many officers, Sir?" Patterson asked after a pause.

"Oh, we're not the only can out here operating with a reduced complement of officers, especially ensigns and J-Gs. A large percentage of the officers in the reserve had been in the Second World War. Even if they came out as junior officers in forty-five, by the time they were called up for Korea, most of them were at least two-and-a-half-stripers."

"How did you get your commission, Sir?" asked Paterson, feeling a bit awkward with the headset pressed tightly against his ears.

"N-R-O-T-C."

"Did you get your commission through the N-R-O-T-C too, Mister Coates?" Bacelli asked.

"No...O-C-S."

"Do you think I can get into O-C-S and get a commission too?" Bacelli's question had a tone of flippancy.

"You haven't been accepted to a college yet. You'd better start worrying about that before you start worrying about getting into O-C-S," the ensign answered coldly. "You know, even if Congress does go ahead and pass a G-I bill for Korea, from what I've been reading, it's going to be watered down quite a bit from the World War Two version. For one thing, there's no provision for a living allowance. You'd better plan on getting yourself a part-time job, one that will pay for your food and board while you're in school."

"Hell," Gardiner laughed loudly, "Vinny doesn't have to sweat getting food...not with all those egg rolls."

"Egg rolls my ass," Nugent broke in. "Now that this old bucket's really in the war, Vinny will be able to live off all that combat pay he's gonna' earn over here. Isn't that right, Mister Stockwell?"

"I don't think forty-five dollars a month will keep you in filet mignon," the Ops officer answered blandly. "Besides, we haven't qualified for combat pay yet, at least according to the rules the navy's set up."

"Haven't qualified?" Gardiner piped up. "We've been blasting the gooks since we left Pusan! Just what the hell does the navy call combat?" the third-class asked sullenly.

"I don't understand either, Sir," Murray joined in. "That day off Sinpo, we were dodging in and out between shell splashes for over two hours. Remember, that was the time I went sailing off the stool when the captain swung us hard around to avoid those seven-point-sevens. And the Reds bracketed us both times we hit Mayang-do."

"Yeah, and what about Hongwan?" Nugent cut in angrily. "The crew on mount-forty-one told me it looked like the Fourth of July up there with all those shells and tracers whizzing just over their heads. And don't forget the day we were operating with that limey can. A shell passed so close to the signal bridge, I hear Chief Anderson spit out his uppers."

"I'm not disagreeing with you about those five engagements," the lieutenant answered in an even tone. "Unfortunately, as far as combat pay's concerned, the navy says five days doesn't make it. The magic number is six. Don't worry though," he grinned. "There's still twelve days left in this month. That's plenty of time for the Reds to help you earn that extra cash."

"Twelve days?" Gardiner's voice was suddenly pensive. "Somehow that extra dough doesn't seem anywhere near as good as it did a minute ago." Then scratching the back of his head, he shrugged, "What really bugs me about this deal is the way the navy's so chintzy about handing out a lousy forty-five bucks. What do we have to do, get our asses shot off to collect? Back in Pusan, Holiday and I were talking to a couple of merchant seamen. Do you know they get double their base pay for just going to Pusan? And if their ship's carrying even a small amount of explosives, they get another fifteen percent on top of that!"

"Hell, this tub's crammed with ammo from stem to stern," Nugent sneered. "How come when we go south to Pusan, the navy calls it rest and recreation? Why is Pusan Las Vegas East for us and a bloody war zone for the merchant marine?"

"That's those fuckin' unions," Bacelli grunted. "If they weren't getting extra pay to deliver that ammo, you can bet your ass we'd be out here shooting paper clips."

"And another thing," Gardiner cut in. "How come the second we drop below the thirty-eighth parallel to rendezvous with the replenishment force, the word blasts over the P-A system that our free mail privileges are canceled till further notice?"

"Yeah, Mister Stockwell, isn't that a crock?" Nugent agreed. "When we're operating above the thirty-eighth, we're too damn busy going to G-Q all the time to write any letters. The second we slip below it to take on stores, the navy says we've got to pay for our stamps."

"What's the big deal about a couple of nickel stamps?" Bacelli shrugged. "Hell, we work harder loading all that food and ammo than we do when we're up north pounding the Reds. We don't have time to write any letters on the days we replenish, so what's the difference?"

"Yeah, well some of us who are literate can find the time," chided Nugent.

"Look, I'm not going to tell you two again. Now cut the skylarking and get your minds back on your jobs!" Coates burst out. "Next time I have to tell you, you're both going on report. And that's not a threat, it's a promise!"

"Yes, Sir," Bacelli frowned, turning his attention back to the air-search radar.

"Nugent made a vague acknowledgement, then continued wiping down the Plexiglas surface of the vertical plot.

By 13:00 the *Field* was nearing her assigned patrol area off Najin, billows of white smoke streaming back from both stacks. Logan had just finished taping a fresh plotting tissue to the DRT table when the overhead speaker began to cackle.

"Combat...bridge," the captain's voice rang out clearly.

"Combat, aye," Coates answered, looking up at the squawk-box.

"Are your people picking up any air contacts?" Royal's voice had a distinct tone of impatience.

"No, Sir," replied the young ensign, glancing nervously over his shoulder at Bacelli and the Sugar-Charlie.

"Well, they should be getting something!" barked the C.O. "We've received two radio messages from *Helena*. She's been tracking several high-speed bogies for the past ten minutes. She reports they're moving towards the task force."

"Yes, Sir," Coates replied, wiping the stream of sweat that was burning his eyes. "We've had no contact with the *Helena*, Captain. She's just beyond range of our C.I. net."

"Very well. I'll pass anything that we get from radio-central on down to you. I intend to have G-Q called away in exactly one minute," advised Royal. "Let me know the second you start getting anything on those scopes!"

"Aye, aye, Sir," Coates' voice trailed off as he slowly released the speaker-switch.

"Old man seems a bit pissed, Don," Stockwell grinned as he started for the doorway. "Hate to leave you in this zoo at such a critical moment but duty awaits. I've got less than forty seconds to get up to secondary-conn before G-Q sounds. Good luck!"

Murray joined Coates at the radar console as Stockwell disappeared in the passageway outside C.I.C. "Bacelli!" the first-class called out, peering at the repeater scope. "Check out zero-zero-eight about forty-four miles. There's something fading in and out...could be a bogey."

"Yeah, I see it," the air-search operator exclaimed, adjusting the focus and gain-control knobs. "It's faint but the way it's moving I think it is a bogey. Belay that! It's definitely a bogey! It's coming in stronger...it's more than one contact...it's several bogies...I estimate eight to ten. Sweet shit! I'm getting more! Hell, they're poppin' up all over the scope...everywhere from zero-zero-eight to zero-four-five! The scope's saturated with contacts, Mister Coates! It must be the whole fuckin' Red air force out there!"

"Okay, Bacelli, calm down," the ensign said. "Are any of those bogies squawking friendly?"

"No, Sir, there's no I-F-F."

"Okay, start calling out those ranges and bearings so we can determine their course and speed. Concentrate on bogies closing us or the task force. Designate the closest raid Raid-one"…"Bridge, combat!" the ensign shouted into the overhead speaker, his voice barely audible over the pandemonium that always accompanied the announcement of general-quarters. "Captain! We've got many bogies...could be up to fifty or sixty planes, Sir. They appear to be heading directly towards the task force."

"Where do you hold the task force now?"

"It's out of our radar range, but the last radio fix we had at twelve-fifteen placed it at latitude forty-one degrees, thirty-one minutes east, longitude one-thirty north," Coates read from the note Logan had hastily scribbled. "It should be approximately fifty miles southeast of us now, Sir, bearing one-one-five relative."

"How far is the task force from Vladivostok?"

Coates glanced at Logan who was penciling the answer on a sheet of maneuvering board paper. "Approximately ninety miles, Captain," the ensign quickly reported into the speaker.

"Very well," acknowledged Royal. "Jehovah's calling all his small boys home to roost. We've just been ordered to rejoin the task force. Work out a course at thirty-knots that will get us back to the screen, and let me know our E-T-A."

Coates acknowledged seconds before the executive officer came bounding into his new G-Q station, followed closely by Holiday, Paulsen, Garber and Belton. A moment later, the *Charles P. Field* heeled around a full 180 degrees to plunge ahead through steep gray waves and deep black furrows.

The *Field* was still thumping along at a brisk 30-knots when the messages from Jehovah and Birthrate started coming into the crypto-shack. Deciphered and relayed to the bridge, they soon dispatched any hope the captain had had that the Charlie P. would reach the screen in time to participate in history's first recorded jet attack against a carrier task force. Piecing each successive report together much in the matter one assembles a jigsaw puzzle, Royal and Lieutenant Oetjens were quickly able to gain a fairly accurate picture of what was going on 50 miles away.

Formed around fast carriers *Oriskany, Kearsarge* and *Essex*, Task Force 77 was waiting for its strike aircraft to return from their mischief up around Hoeryong when the *Oriskany's* combat-information-center detected various groups of bogies crossing from northwest to northeast at distances from 40 to 100 miles.

"It's obvious from this first message," Royal said, handing the yellow slip of paper to his navigator, "that Jehovah never received any of our contact reports. This credits the 'Big O' with making the initial radar contact. You did check with radio-central to make sure those bogey alerts went out, didn't you, Phil?"

"Yes, Sir, out initial contact report was sent at thirteen-oh-six. The two amplifying reports followed at thirteen-ten and thirteen-eighteen."

"No acknowledgement from Jehovah or Birthrate?"

"No, Sir," Oetjens grunted uneasily, recognizing the worried expression on his commanding officer's face.

"I'm certain someone's going to come down hard on us for this one," Owen said dejectedly. "If Jehovah doesn't give us a meaningful blast, we'll have to sweat ComSeventhFleet...at least, I will," Royal quickly corrected.

"Sir, I really can't see how they can stick it to us for those contact reports not getting through. We did transmit them."

"Forget about us, Phil. I'm the C.O. If there should be any flak over those messages, I'll see to it that nobody catches it but me."

"I really don't think they'll be a problem, Sir. It's pretty apparent that *Helena's* contact reports didn't get through to Jehovah, either, yet we received everything she sent out."

"*Helena* was only twenty-miles away from us and in a different direction. Besides, we've been receiving all of Jehovah's cryptograms without any trouble."

"Yes, but you know how unpredictable atmospheric conditions are, especially when it comes to fouling up radio transmissions."

"Let's hope the brass follows that line of thinking. Anyway, it looks like we're going to be sitting this one out," Royal frowned, glancing at a dispatch that had just been handed to him by the messenger from radio-central. "It appears the battle's been joined. Here, take a look."

The message Oetjens scanned reported that a group of 16 to 20 bogies designated Raid 20 had separated from the other unidentified air contacts, and had headed on a direct course towards Task Force 77. At a point 35 miles from the task force's formation center, Raid 20 had gone into orbit with eight aircraft breaking away to make a run on the ships. *Oriskany*, holding down the day's C.A.P. assignment, vectored four of her Panthers to intercept the oncoming jets. The Cap's flight leader identified the approaching bogies as Mig-15s. His tallyho was received at 13:50.

"Get this down to C.I.C. on the double," Royal instructed McGill, the messenger-of-the-watch, the instant Phil Oetjens had digested the contents of the dispatch. Walking to the wheelhouse squawk-box, he called his combat-information-center and recognized his executive officer's voice as it flew back out of the speaker in acknowledgement.

"Mig's have closed the task force, Aub," Royal advised. "First wave's been intercepted by an *Oriskany* Cap. Jehovah's latest update's on the way to you now."

"Right...McGill's just coming into C.I.C. We're still holding approximately fifty bogies on our screen. They're hanging up north in the vicinity of Vladivostok. My guess is they're Ruskies...probably flying barrier patrol for their naval base."

"I concur, but make sure your gang keep's on top of them just in case we're wrong and they turn out to be Chinese or North Koreans waiting their turn to hit the carriers. Right now, I'd like a good fix on that donnybrook up ahead. Got anything in the direction of the task force?"

"Negative," Cobb replied after a few seconds pause. "The dogfight must be northwest of the task force. Since we're forty-miles northeast of the ships, those Migs have to be well beyond the maximum range of our search gear."

"Very well. Anyway, I doubt they'll detour in our direction. If they're still flying after our Cap's gotten in its licks, they're much more likely to make a beeline north to whatever bases the Chinese have above the Yalu."

Owen Royal walked back out on to the open wing. Here, better than any other place, he could feel his ship's pulse, the throb and drum of her turbines. It was here he could listen to the grind and snarl of racing propellers pushing hard against sea and wind. Standing on the small walk-way directly in front of the wheelhouse, he watched the foc'sle drop, the bow slice deep into the water to hurl sheets of stinging green spray up and over the bridge. The captain braced his feet against the roll and pitch of the destroyer, and pointed his glasses dead ahead in the direction of the task force although he knew that the ships, and certainly the air battle, were many miles beyond the range of his binoculars.

"Captain!" Oetjens cried out from the open wheelhouse doorway. "Combat's reporting three bogies at zero-two-eight, thirty-six miles..."

Royal shot past the navigator and was clutching at the speaker switch on the 21MC before Oetjens could finish his sentence. "What do you have on those bogies, Aub?" he yelled into the squawk-box.

"I think it's that dogfight Jehovah reported, or at least part of it, Captain. It's coming our way," replied Cobb excitedly. "We had three distinct bogies just a few seconds ago. Now they've merged into a single pip...belay that, Captain. My air-search operator now says he's only got two."

"Two?" Royal fumed. "You better locate that third bogey damn quick! The bastard might be trying to slip in under the beam of our air-search. Have your man on the surface search scan the last bearing you had on that merged plot."

"Bridge, combat!" the exec called back after a seemingly interminable pause. "Captain, those two bogies we just reported aren't bogies. We're getting a definite I-F-F response...code three." The electric amplifier of the 21MC failed to mask Cobb's complete relief. "One of the planes seems to be in orbit just about where we had that merged plot. The other one's heading southeast in the direction of the task force...wait one, Captain, I'm getting another report from my air-search operator...now the plane that was in orbit is moving off too. It's following right after the other one. It's my guess they're going back to their carrier."

Again Royal was distracted by the messenger from radio-central. Saluting smartly, the helmeted sailor departed as his commanding officer perused the latest cryptogram.

Within minutes, DD-505 was pivoting around to a new heading worked out by Ensign Coates, one devised to expeditiously move the destroyer from point-Able, her present position, to point-Baker, the portion of water over which the "friendly" had so recently been orbiting. Steadying on the recommended bearing, the Field kicked up her heels as she worked herself up to flank speed.

Oetjens wondered why the captain was holding back the last message from Jehovah and why he had suddenly requested a course to some nondescript spot in the Sea of Japan. Was Royal being deliberately enigmatic or had the message been so startling it had shunted all other considerations from the C.O.'s mind.

"Captain, now that those two planes have turned out to be friendly and have headed back to their carrier, why are we pulling out all the stops to go racing off in the opposite direction from the task force?" asked the navigator haltingly.

"Sorry, Phil. I didn't mean to be mysterious. Jehovah thinks there's a Mig pilot floating around out there...bailed out of one of the bogies *Oriskany's* fighters shot down, probably the one that disappeared after that merged plot. That friendly was probably orbiting to show the task force where the Russian hit the water."

"Russian?"

"Yes, but the temperature of the water being what it is, I'm afraid he's already a very dead Russian. But dead or alive, we're the closest ship to where he went down, so when Jehovah says go fetch, we go fetch."

"How's Jehovah know he's Russian?"

"I assume the Mig pilots were talking in Russian during the dogfight."

"Sir, another message just arrived," the sailor from the radio shack breathlessly announced.

"Rest of the Migs must be closing the task force. This is an advisory from Birthrate. At least one of the ships in the screen has already commenced firing at unidentified air contacts."

Oetjens looked away, staring in awe at the way the destroyer seemed to be soaring over the water. The impact of what was taking place had not yet fully registered. Turning again to Royal, he asked, "Does this mean we're at war with the U-S-S-R?" The words came slowly, mixed with thoughts of his wife and five-year-old son back in Chevy Chase, and images of New York and San Francisco erupting in mushroom-shaped clouds.

"God only knows, Phil. There's a good chance this is an isolated attack, one without the Kremlin's blessing. Could be some hot headed Ruskie flyboys trying to get into the war. I think Jehovah's pegged it that way. If this was the opening curtain of World War Three, I don't think he'd be sending us off to find one frozen commie."

"Speaking of frozen commies, Captain," Oetjens scratched the fringe of hair showing below the back of his helmet, "if we do find him, what do we do with the body? Stash it in the reefers?"

"Can you think of a better place? It's not cool enough in the spud locker. Anyway, we'll get rid of it this evening as soon as we rendezvous with the carriers."

"Our food wouldn't win any prizes now, Sir. Putting a corpse in the reefer space is not going to make it any more appetizing. Couldn't we just tie a line around it and tow it astern?"

"I'm sure the sharks would love that suggestion," Royal smiled grimly. "One thing's certain, we've got to treat this bird like he's royalty. For two years now our people in the U.N. have been trying to prove to the world that the Russians are directly involved in this thing. If we can locate this Mig jockey or whatever's left of him, we'll have all the proof we need."

By 14:00 the *Field's* bow was knifing through the area prescribed by Ensign Coates' calculations. Carrying out a standard navy search pattern, Owen Royal's destroyer passed the next two hours criss-crossing a ten-mile square patch of gray water with nothing to show for their labors but an auxiliary fuel tank jettisoned almost a year before by an Air Force Thunderjet.

"I don't understand this, Phil," Royal said, lowering his binoculars. "Even taking the currents into account, there's no way we could have missed this joker."

"Do you suppose he could have sunk?"

"Not likely. I'm sure a Russian pilot wouldn't bail out over water without his Mae West anymore than one of our boys would. Besides, we certainly should have come across his chute by now." Turning towards the open wheelhouse door, Royal called, "Mister Phelan. How are things coming along in C.I.C.? Are they still tracking bogies north of us?"

"Affirmative, Sir. I just checked with Mister Cobb. They've got about forty to fifty bogies...none closer than fifty miles, but he says there are several other bogies within thirty-five miles of the task force."

"Very well. Let me know if there's the slightest change in the air picture."

"Aye, aye, Captain." Phelan then bawled an order to the helmsman to steady up on the next course in the search pattern.

The captain continued to pace the open wing as the *Field* swung around to her new heading. "Phil, go down to the crypto-shack and get an update off to Jehovah. Give him our exact position and that of the area we've been covering. Let him know that we've seen no sign of the pilot so far. With luck, maybe he'll call the search off and let us head back to the task force."

Royal was still scrutinizing the horizon when Oetjens came flying out onto the open bridge. "Whoa," laughed the *Field's* skipper, his navigator stopping abruptly. "I like to see my officers display eagerness, Phil, but aren't you overdoing it? You came through that doorway like you'd been shot from a catapult. What's up? Did the crypto-shack get that report off to Jehovah?"

"Eh, yes, Sir."

"Well?"

"They got it off alright, Captain. That's the problem."

"Problem?"

"Yes, Sir," the navigator answered, plainly flustered. "Jehovah says we've been searching the wrong area. Here, Sir," Oetjens said, grinning cautiously as he handed Royal the task force commander's reply.

"I don't understand this! Fifty miles? How the hell can we be off the mark by fifty miles?" yelled Royal, still reading the paper as he pushed past Oetjens to enter the wheelhouse.

"Combat, bridge!" he bellowed.

"Combat, aye," Cobb's voice came back through the 21MC.

"We just sent Jehovah a posit report. He responded by saying we're fifty miles away from where that Mig splashed. Can you give me an explanation?"

"Sounds like a screw-up on the maneuvering board. Mister Coates worked out the course solution," Cobb replied without hesitation. "I assumed he knew what he was doing."

"Well, put him on the squawk-box, pronto!"

"Captain, this is Ensign Coates."

"You'd better check that course you sent up," Royal tried to maintain his composure. "According to Jehovah, we're a good fifty miles off target."

"Yes, Sir," Coates stammered. "I'll check it right away."

"When you discover what went wrong, please see me on the bridge," Royal said calmly.

Several minutes passed. Then Coates, fidgeting nervously with the chin strap of his helmet, appeared on the starboard wing. Royal nodded at Phil Oetjens who discreetly retreated to the port side of the bridge, allowing the young ensign a modest degree of privacy for what was obviously going to be a few very embarrassing moments."

• • •

Murray glanced at his watch. The sun was up now and he knew the morning "heckler" strikes would soon be coming home to mamma, in this case *Oriskany*, *Kearsarge* or *Essex*. Standing on the fantail which was still wet and glistening from an early morning rain, Murray had skipped breakfast again, the third time in the five days the *Field* had been back with the task force. He'd keep skipping it too, the radarman vowed, just as long as that cretin Turk kept insisting on serving S.O.S.

However, the first-class had far more on his mind this third Sunday of November than creamed chipped beef. Mary Alice was almost four days overdue. Dammit, but he felt totally useless out here! What if something had gone wrong. Was that why he hadn't received any word? Hell, even the navy as devious as it was, wouldn't sink so low as to hold up a telegram so important, he reassured himself.

He could hear the hum of engines now. The planes were coming in from the west ...prop jobs, radar-equipped Corsairs and Skyraiders from the VC squadrons back from disrupting the milk run for the "Wonsan express." He watched them circling in the sky, queuing up to enter the landing pattern. Higher up, the four Banshees assigned to the day's Cap were doing their utmost to keep out of the way of the incoming aircraft. The Banshee's silhouette was distinctive, quite different than that of the stubbier and more familiar Grumman Panthers, decided Murray. The long nose of the McDonnell fighter made him think of Canadian honking geese, the kind he and Mary Alice watched each fall soaring southward over Lake Erie. He knew the Banshees belonged to the famed "Red Rippers," no extraordinary deduction since the *Kearsarge*-based VF-11 was the only squadron with the task force presently flying the twin-engine jet.

Lowering his glance, Murray peered to starboard across a gently heaving sea. *Halsey Wayne* was back, looking all prim and new after her two-month sojourn in the Japanese shipyard. There was something odd about her though, the radarman thought, quickly concluding it was her paint. It appeared several shades lighter than the standard haze gray of the other ships in the task force, and he wondered if the Jap yard had somehow screwed up. It gave the destroyer an ethereal look, and he knew it wouldn't take a soothsayer to predict that her crew would soon be laying claim to the much used title — "Galloping Ghost of the Korean Coast."

Most people squint when they pass from a darkened area to one of light. For an inexplicable reason, Howie Murray always squinted when he stepped from a lighted passageway into the blackness of the combat-information-center. So he did this morning as he entered the radar-shack and focused his eyes on its occupants.

Ensign Warden, C.I.C. watch officer for the 8 to 12, was seated at the plotting table reading the single mimeographed sheet that served as the ship's newspaper. A daily service of radio-central, it contained capsule reports of the day's news as selectively gleaned from the Armed Forces Radio Network.

Kevin Logan was taking what for him was a rare turn at the air-search radar while Belton sat nearby on the Sugar-George, studiously keeping tabs on each of the thirty-odd blips which that day composed Task Force 77. From the adjacent coffee-mess, tended this hour by Vinny Bacelli, flowed the plaintive lyrics of Sammy Kaye's "*Harbor Lights*."

Dick Warden happily observed that the ships were already heading into the wind when the returning planes began their approach. Greatly relieved, he knew he would not have to come up with a change of station solution since there was now no need for the carriers to alter course. In his anxiety, he'd completely forgotten that they were presently steaming in a circular rather than a bentline or horseshoe formation, thus reorientation of the screen would not have been necessary even if the carriers and other heavies had swung around to a new heading.

Ordinarily quite proficient at the maneuvering board, Dick Warden now approached each stint as C.I.C. watch officer with much trepidation, knowing that just a few days before, Don Coates had given immeasurable help to the enemy simply by drawing a five-inch-long pencil line in the wrong direction.

"You people all squared-away in here?" came the peculiarly whining voice of Cobb at the open doorway. An immediate chill flashed through C.I.C.

"Yes, Sir, the carriers are just roosting their birds," Warden answered, hurriedly slipping the news sheet he'd been reading under the green-covered C.I.C. watch log.

"What's that music?" Cobb asked, stepping up to the plotting table.

"Doris Day, Sir."

"I know it's Doris Day, dammit! I didn't ask you who it was. I asked what it was! Somehow I don't think it's conducive to a smooth running watch. Do you, Mister?"

"No, Sir,"..."Bacelli!" Warden called sharply. "Keep that door closed and turn down that phonograph so it can't be heard in here!"

Cobb spent the next five minutes prancing from station to station seemingly oblivious to the sullen glances he was receiving from the various enlisted members of the C.I.C. watch team.

"JEHOVAH...THIS IS TRUSTFUND," suddenly blared over the TBS. "XRAY-ABLE-FOUR. I SAY AGAIN...XRAY-ABLE-FOUR...OUT."

"*Kearsarge* says she's got a ready-deck, Sir," Gardiner reported, looking up from the radio-telephone.

"Very well," Warden replied, then reached for the squawk-box button. "Bridge, combat, *Kearsarge* just reported she has a ready deck."

"Bridge, aye," Stockwell's voice came back in an even tone.

"JEHOVAH...THIS IS CHILDPLAY. XRAY-ABLE-FOUR. I SAY AGAIN... XRAY-ABLE-FOUR...OUT."

"*Oriskany* to Jehovah, she's got a ready-deck now too, Sir," Gardiner reported.

"Very well"..."Bridge, combat!" Warden called again into the squawk-box.

"Bridge, aye."

"*Oriskany's* just reported a ready-deck."

"Very well," the officer-of-the-deck acknowledged once more.

"Mr. Warden," said Cobb, "are you aware that your man on the T-B-S just violated security regulations, to say nothing of standard C.I.C. procedure?"

Completely puzzled, the ensign looked at Gardiner wondering what the exec was talking about. Just as baffled, Gardiner merely shrugged.

"Eh, no, Sir," Warden groaned.

Cobb started to pace back and forth, seemingly disorientated. "Well, Mister, you'd better start boning up on proper procedure mucho quick or else you'll find yourself in hack right alongside your buddy, Ensign Coates!" The exec looked around the combat-information-center. "Is there anyone who knows what I'm talking about?"

Dead silence cloaked the C.I.C. except for the faint sound of Doris Day seeping out from under the coffee-mess door.

"Well, since it's obvious that nobody in here has the slightest idea of what's meant by proper radio-telephone procedure, I suppose I'll have to take the time to enlighten you," intoned Cobb with heavy sarcasm. "A few minutes ago, this man here," the exec pointed the pencil he was holding at Gardiner, "received two messages, one from Trustfund and one from Childplay. Both messages were the same."

"Yes, Sir, both carriers were reporting a ready-deck," Murray spoke up, still confounded by the lieutenant-commander's sudden outburst.

"A ready-deck...exactly my point! But how did he know that? I was watching him very closely when those messages came in. Even though he has a copy of

Janap-one-nineteen right in front of him, he never opened it to see which ships were using the call names Trustfund and Childplay! Nor did he check the surface status-board for the call names. Even worse, he never bothered to look up the meaning of the signal here in A-T-P-One," Cobb pointed to the general-signal-book on the table next to Gardiner.

"Sir, we receive the signal Xray-Able-four at least twenty times a day when we're out here with the carriers," Murray retorted. "Every time one of those flat-top's has a clear deck capable of landing planes, she transmits Xray-Able-four, just like if she's got a fouled deck, she sends out Tare-Oboe-three. I hear those messages so much I find myself repeating them in my sleep. As far as the call names are concerned, we hear them constantly all through our watch. It's ridiculous to waste time flipping through Janap or A-T-P-One when we already know exactly what the signal says and what ship is sending it."

"Are you challenging navy regs, Murray?" Cobb snapped angrily.

"I'm not challenging them, Sir, I just think it's stupid to have to look up something that you already know."

"I suppose you think I'm stupid too for insisting that this crew adhere to the rules the navy's laid down."

"As a white hat, it's not for me to say whether I think you're stupid or not," Murray found it impossible to suppress a grin.

"Okay, Mister Wise-Ass, let's see if you'll still have that smirk on your face when you go up before the captain. You're officially on report for gross insubordination. And you! What's your name?" the exec glared down at the third-class sitting at the TBS.

"Gardiner, Sir...Leroy H., Sir," the radarman said in a fumbling half-whisper.

"You're on report too!"

The remainder of the morning's watch passed without incident.

• • •

The *Field* remained with the screen for the rest of the week, taking on stores from the *Arequipa* on the 26th, a red-letter replenishment since the 27th was Thanksgiving Day. Two days each year the navy pulls out all the stops to make certain that its bluejackets enjoy a feast second to none. Thanksgiving was one of those two days and this being a war year, no efforts were spared to ensure that its personnel received a traditional turkey dinner with all the trimmings.

On the following morning after topping-off from *Essex*, Owen Royal's destroyer received two important messages — one from Jehovah dispatching the ship to a lifeguard station off Odaejin; the other, from the American Red Cross, informing Howard Murray that he had become the proud father of a seven-pound, eight-ounce baby girl. Both mother and daughter were doing fine.

• • •

"Really, Terry, I'd like to help you out but I'm not the least bit interested in dating any marine officers, or anybody else right now," Lieutenant Jg. Osbourne said in an apathetic tone, folding the white uniform blouse she'd just ironed.

"Come on, Cindy, you're a nurse not a nun. Give yourself a break," her roommate bristled. "It's not natural for someone with your looks to spend the little time off she gets hanging around some room here listening to Crosby records and mooning over some swab-jockey. Right now he's probably in a Pusan cathouse snuggled up to some little Korean cookie."

"You know, just because you were once a pharmacist's mate, you don't have to be so damn crude."

"I'm not being crude. I'm just facing life realistically. Hell, Cindy, you've been seeing enough of it slip away on operating tables these days. I don't see what you've got against having a little fun while you're still young enough to enjoy it," Terry said, vigorously toweling her bleached hair.

"Well, I'd appreciate it if you'd stop making snide remarks about Kevin. You're just as bad as Betsy back in San Diego. Besides, I've told you a hundred times to stop calling him a swab-jockey. He's a radarman, and anyway, he's getting out soon. He'll be going back to a top job at one of the most important advertising agencies on Madison Avenue. He even lives in a real neat penthouse."

"Yeah, along with a real neat wife, I'll bet," her roommate snickered as she left for the bathroom to get a dry towel.

Lieutenant Teresa Winfield was a big bosomed, rather hippy blonde with a passably pretty face that framed enormous blue eyes. Her looks were in stark contrast to the fragile wholesome beauty of the slender chestnut haired Miss Osbourne. In a few minutes, she emerged from the bathroom wearing a pink terry robe and with a towel now wrapped turban-style around her hair making Cynthia think of an old movie song about "*The Girlfriend of the Whirling Dervish.*"

"Look, Cindy, I really understand how you feel about your sailor boy, and I wouldn't ask you to go on a double date like this if the fellow I want to fix you up with wasn't really extra-special. Honest Injun," said the nurse, crossing her heart, "he's a real gentleman, and a fantastic looking guy. Tall, blonde, sort of a Sonny Tufts type."

"What's his rank?" Cindy asked casually.

"First-lieutenant. Does that mean you've changed your mind?" Terry's eye's brightened.

"No, it doesn't. I was just curious, that's all."

"Admit it, Cindy, you wouldn't be curious unless you were at least a little bit interested. Besides, you can always look at it as a patriotic gesture. After all, the poor guy just recovered from being shot. He's all healed now of course. It was a clean wound. The bullet passed right on through his arm without hitting anything vital. But instead of putting in a chit to go back to the States, he's requested reassignment to his regiment. They're in the thick of the fighting on Bunker Hill right now."

"That's very commendable, I'm sure, but if he's so terrific, how come you're not dating him?"

"Believe me, I would be if it wasn't for his buddy, Greg. Greg's the kind of guy I've been waiting for all my life."

"Is Greg in from Korea? How come this is the first I've heard about him?"

"Oh, we just met an hour ago over at the commissary...right between the Coke and the Campbell's beans. Why do you think I'm washing my hair again so soon?" the nurse's mouth fluttered upward in a half smile. "Greg's Bill's best friend. Bill's the guy I've been telling you about. Anyway, both of them are shipping back out to Korea next Tuesday and Greg kind of asked me if I could fix his buddy up with a real nice looking girl. Greg's got himself the loan of a car for a few days, and since I told him I didn't have duty this weekend and that my very attractive roommate was also free, well, you know," Terry said sheepishly, "one thing just sort of led to another. Actually, I told Greg that you'd be happy to meet his buddy Bill and go up to Kamakura with us for the weekend."

"You what?" Cindy's eyes flashed angrily.

"I told him you'd be happy to come along to Kamakura."

"I can't believe this. You know, you've really got a colossal nerve. Suppose Kevin's destroyer should come in this weekend?"

"You'd know by now if there was any chance of that happening. Hell, you bug base-operations just about every day. Larry Burke told me that you drive his guys crazy calling up so much to ask about the *Field*. He says he doesn't get half as many calls about the *Missouri* or even the carriers."

Cynthia wished the conversation would end. She folded the last of the three white shirts she had ironed, put it in the drawer and kicked off her shoes. "This morning was the roughest yet," she sighed. "If you don't mind, Terry, I'm awfully tired. I'd better get some sleep if I'm going to be of any use on the eight to twelve tonight."

Lieutenant Winfield smiled agreeably, "Well, before you drift off to never-never land, can I tell Greg you'll come with us on Saturday?"

"I don't know. You'll have to let me sleep on it."

Terry grinned contently as she closed the door and headed for the O-club.

•   •   •

The morning was clear with a high blue sky as the *Field* steamed independently to her lifeguard station off Odaejin.

"Where do you have the nearest land, Gardiner?" Ensign Daly asked from his perch at the plotting board.

"Nineteen-thousand, three-hundred yards at three-one-three, Sir."

The C.I.C. watch officer for the eight-to-noon mumbled a faint acknowledgement as he finished penciling in the *Field's* position on the chart spread out before him. He hoped Cobb wouldn't show up before G.Q. By then Don Coates would be there to relieve him. No sooner had he concluded that he would be blessed with a Cobb-free watch then the executive officer appeared in the passageway outside the combat-information-center.

"Your people all fully awake in here, Mister Daly?" Cobb asked from the doorway.

The ensign took a deep breath. "Yes, Sir," he replied, shifting nervously on the stool.

"I expect to hear G-Q called away any moment," Cobb grunted as he plodded up to the plotting table. "You'd better have your men switch into battle dress now so they won't waste time later. I'm not at all satisfied with the way this C.I.C. team's been operating lately. Everything they do, they do in second gear."

"Yes, Sir," Daly nodded, gripping the edge of the table. Then eyeing Murray, he said. "Make sure everyone has his collar turned up and his pants tucked under his socks."

Amid frowns and low-keyed moans, the radar team went about carrying out the navy's recommended procedure for protection against flash burns.

The *Field* moved four miles closer to her assigned station and at 11:25, general quarters was sounded throughout the ship.

"How long will we be off Odaejin, Sir?" Logan asked Daly from his position at the DRT.

"Why? Do you have a special appointment somewhere?" Cobb cut in with a snide grin. Logan didn't answer.

Excused from his punishment during periods of G.Q., Ensign Coates relieved Ensign Daly so the latter could scurry off to his battle station in after-steering, and by 11:27, phone-talker Patterson was able to inform the bridge that C.I.C. was "fully manned and ready."

The minutes passed with muffled voices, ship's sounds and the strong smell of coffee, the latter as much a part of the radar shack as the thousands of wires and cables that kept it functioning.

"Combat, bridge," Royal's voice suddenly blared out of the 21MC. "There's a minefield three miles off the tip of that hook jutting out from Odaejin. I assume you have it indicated on your chart?"

"Yes, Sir," Cobb answered into the squawk-box.

"We'll be maneuvering within two miles of it so keep an extra sharp eye on our track. I don't intend to close that unswept area by less than one mile. Comprende?"

"Aye, aye, Sir. We'll keep you advised. We've already marked it in on the D-R-T."

"As you know, the enemy has shore batteries in this area so there's every likelihood we'll be engaged," Royal cautioned.

"Yes, Captain," Cobb answered dryly, releasing the speaker-button and glancing around the C.I.C. to make certain that all stations pertinent to counter-battery routine were manned and ready.

"If those bastards shoot at us today we'll make the big six and qualify for that extra forty-five bucks!" Holiday beamed, evoking little enthusiasm from his fellow watch standers.

The *Field* steamed on and upon reaching her station off Odaejin, reduced speed to 10 knots to commence cruising in a series of figure-eights approximately a mile in length from loop to loop.

A minute past noon the distinct growl of aircraft engines became discernible over the rhythmic purring of the destroyer's geared turbines. To Royal, Oetjens and the others on the open bridge, the sixty dark specks in the northeastern sky looked far more like migratory birds than complex war machines on their way to obliterate the Funei power plant at Musan.

Hardly had the sound of the carrier planes died out when a radio-striker appeared on the bridge-wing. Taking a halting step towards his C.O., the sailor saluted. "Priority-one, action-immediate from Jehovah, Captain," the lanky teenager stammered slightly.

Royal's eyebrows rose a bit in surprise as he digested the content of the freshly decoded dispatch. His surprise quickly gave way to a broad smile. "Looks like we've drawn a real hairy one this time, Phil," the captain said, his words at odds with the obvious pleasure he was experiencing as he savored the prospects of his ship's next mission.

The navigator stood by, expressionless.

"Here's how this deal stacks up," Owen eagerly announced after a second reading. "Some air force bombers made a pass at a four-truck convoy on the coastal road just south of where we are now. The trucks ducked into a tunnel and the planes can't get a clear crack at them. The strike leader can keep them pinned down in there until thirteen-fifteen, but then he'll have to order his boys on to their primary targets at Kyongsong. Since we're the closest surface unit to the tunnel, Jehovah's given us the job. According to this dispatch, the main entrance to the tunnel is in a coastal ridge that juts out forming a small inlet. We should be able to slip into that inlet and lob a couple of five-inch directly into the mouth of the tunnel. Here's the position those fly boys reported," Royal said, handing the paper to his navigator. "Work out a course and speed that will get us there before thirteen-fifteen."

"Aye, aye, Sir," Phil Oetjens said, departing from the charthouse. In a few minutes he returned with a course recommendation which at 32 knots would put the *Field* abeam of the tunnel well before the time specified. "According to the position the air force gave, the tunnel is about eight miles north of a coastal village called Maksan."

"Maksan?"

"Yes...M-A-K-S-A-N," the navigator pronounced each letter slowly.

"I can't recall ever reading anything about a place with that name in any of the Op-reports," Royal frowned.

"There's not much reason why you would. It can't be much of a place. It wasn't even printed on the chart. Somebody had penciled it in, probably the South

Koreans. However, it is the closest town or village to the tunnel according to the fix the air force gave us."

"I wonder if those trucks were heading to this Maksan?" Royal puzzled aloud.

"I strongly doubt it. Hungnam's further south on the same route. I imagine that was their destination," suggested Oetjens.

Below in C.I.C., the tension grew as Donald Coates at the maneuvering board set about determining a course and speed to the inlet. With Cobb breathing down his neck, thereby eliminating any chance of help from Kevin Logan, the radar team watched and wondered if their C.I.C. officer's recommendation would duplicate that worked out on the bridge by Navigator Oetjens. Fortunately, their concern was unnecessary. Having just passed a week confined to his cabin with nothing for company but a two-pound packet of maneuvering-board-paper, parallel rulers and a new shiny set of dividers, the young ensign was now as adept at the plotting board as anyone aboard the destroyer, and his course and speed recommendation was right on the money.

The moments passed as the *Field* worked her way up to a rather shaky 32 knots. Farber behind the vertical plot and Belton, manning the surface-status board, could feel the Plexiglas quiver against the soft tips of their grease pencils as the ship's shafts spun round and round with accelerated frenzy.

"Bow-lookout's sighted a floating mine dead ahead!" shouted a wide-eyed Patterson.

Before Cobb or anyone else in C.I.C. could respond to the phone-talker, the *Field*, making a sound like scraping chains, lurched sharply to starboard. Books, charts, pencils and coffee cups sailed around the compartment as officers and enlisted instinctively grabbed at stanchions, grip-handles, or anything else that might prevent a bone-breaking encounter with the steel bulkhead or an intrusive angle iron. Then, as abruptly as the ship had rolled on her side, she snapped back up, green water pouring through her scuppers, to wobble briefly before steadying again on even keel.

"Anybody hurt in here?" Ensign Coates cried out, pulling himself up off the rubber deck matting.

"Negative, Sir," Murray groaned after a few seconds pause.

A white-faced Cobb, still clutching the stanchion that had saved him from colliding with Bacelli and the Sugar-George, looked around the radar space slowly surveying the damage which fortunately was minor. No sooner had the cursing, moaning members of the *Field's* brain trust uprighted their chairs and stools than Lieutenant Phelan's voice boomed out over the various speakers located throughout the destroyer.

"Standby for another sharp roll to starboard!" the OD warned via the ship's general address system.

"Lookout just reported two more mines a hundred yards off the port bow," Patterson excitedly announced, pushing the speaker piece of his headset down and away from his mouth.

Suddenly a deafening bang erupted from somewhere up forward, and although the occupants of the radar shack had heard the bark and crack of the *Field's* five-inch guns more times than any of them could count, this piercing explosion sounded entirely different...the way that running headlong into a floating mine might sound to someone anticipating such a catastrophic likelihood. Then came a second crashing blast, followed closely by two more, and as the destroyer leaned hard over to starboard, all in C.I.C. were relieved at the realization that the sound must be their own guns firing at the enemy mines.

Kevin Logan counted twelve distinct thunderclaps coming from the forward part of the ship before he heard the midships five-inch and port twin-forty join in. Like the two forward guns, they missed the bobbing blackball by a wide margin. Over the side went a smoke flare to mark the mine's general location. Even before it had hit the water, Logan had penciled in its reference point on the DRT overlay tissue.

Two earsplitting detonations rattled the combat-information-center informing all within its confines that the ship's gunners had been more successful in dispatching mines two and three.

Five decks above on the open bridge, a nervous Owen Royal searched aft in the direction of the first mine which by now was well out of sight. Even the smoke flare, floating on the surface of the water far off the port quarter, was barely a thin yellow wisp on his binocular lens. The captain knew he would have to make a choice...one that involved weighing the urgency of his present mission against the prospect of the first mine floating off to some lethal termination in the vastness of the open sea.

"How much time will we lose if we circle back and hunt for that damn mine?" Royal grumbled to his navigator.

"That's a pretty fast running sea, Captain. The mine's got to be back there at least a mile, maybe a mile and a half by now figuring on the wind and current," Oetjens frowned. "Even if we're really lucky and sight it right away, and our gunners can clobber it on the first pass, I'd say a half-an-hour would be the very best we could hope for...and that's not counting the time it will take to get us back to where we are now," he added with a shrug.

"Then we don't have much choice. If that floater drifts out any further, who knows what it might hit, maybe one of the flattops or an ammo ship." The captain took one last departing look at his ship's ragged white wake, then walked to the wheelhouse door where he ordered Phelan, the OD, to reverse course and head the destroyer to the mine's estimated position.

"Combat, bridge," Lieutenant Phelan's voice pierced the still ruffled radar shack. "We're going back after that mine we missed before. The turn will be to port. Have your phone-talker pass up a mark to the spot where we dropped the flare every thirty seconds!"

"Combat, aye," Ensign Coates acknowledged, looking past Cobb to Kevin Logan at the DRT.

"One-two-four...twenty-six hundred yards," Logan said, taking a bearing and range directly from the penciled fix with the drafting arm of the dead-reckoning-tracer. "One-one-eight...twenty-four hundred yards," he announced as Patterson relayed each new range and bearing to the bridge via his sound-powered phone.

"Recommend steadying up on course zero-nine-eight," Logan said.

"Are you certain?" Cobb questioned hesitantly, eyeing the track line the radarman had penciled in a wide circle on the plotting tissue.

"Yes, Sir, zero-nine-eight," Logan answered briskly.

"Bridge, combat," Cobb called, "we recommend steadying up on course zero-nine-eight."

"We concur, Combat, thank you," Phelan acknowledged and the destroyer came around in a wide circle reducing speed considerably as she turned.

"What speed are we making, Nugent?" asked Ensign Coates, the pitlog indicator on the bulkhead being obscured by Cobb's arm which seemed soldered to the stanchion next to the plotting table.

"Ten knots...guess the old man figures we should play it safe while performing our good deed for the day. It still wouldn't surprise me none if we ran smack into the fuckin'..."

"Let's eliminate all unnecessary chatter in here!" Cobb upbraided sharply.

"Aye, aye, Commander," Nugent responded coldly.

Logan continued to call out ranges to the spot where the flare was dropped as the *Field* followed the recommended course line.

"Starboard-lookout just reported that he can see the flare two points off the starboard bow...range about six-hundred yards. He said there's no sign of the mine," Patterson sang out loudly.

"Just watch, we'll get that damn mine right in the number-two frame...pow!" Nugent gestured.

"See anything that looks like a mine?" Cobb questioned worriedly, hunching over Bacelli's shoulder.

"No, Sir, I've switched to short-range search but it isn't doing any good." Bacelli peered at the scope. "Too damn much sea-return to pick up something that small, especially the way it's probably bobbing up and down...and I can't get a solid pip on the A-scope," he added, anticipating the exec's next question.

Coates and Murray moved aside as Cobb stooped over the Sugar-George for a closer inspection. "I don't know where all the sea return came from," the exec snorted angrily. "The sea's not that rough today. Are you sure you know what the hell you're doing? Have you checked your gain-control recently?"

"Yes, Sir," Bacelli answered sheepishly, hoping he wouldn't be joining Murray and Gardiner on the list of personnel awaiting Captain's Mast.

"Talker!" Cobb bellowed. "Ask the bridge what kind of sea we have running!"

"Bridge reports the sea state has increased to Beaufort-scale five," Patterson answered seconds later.

Cobb scowled and walked back to the plotting table. Turning to Coates, he said, "I understand one of our minesweepers detonated several brightly colored mines off ch'o-do a few weeks ago. One mine even had the bizarre eyes and features of some Chinese dragon painted on it...connected with some superstitious ritual I imagine. It turned out to be a lucky break for the sweeper though. Her lookouts were able to spot the mines at least a mile away."

"Hell, wouldn't you know with our luck we'd get the plain black unsuperstitious kind," Murray muttered in a low voice as he checked out the focus controls on the Sugar-George.

"Fantail lookout reports an object that looks like a mine floating in the water one point off the port quarter, about three hundred yards," Patterson said eagerly.

"The port quarter!" Cobb exclaimed querulously. "Are you sure that's what he said?"

"Combat, bridge...we've got sight of the mine. It's dead astern of us now, about four hundred yards," Phelan's voice came over the 21MC before Patterson could reply.

"Hell's bells, we must have almost passed right over it," Cobb mumbled, removing his glasses and patting the sweat from his brow.

An instant later, Commander Royal announced his intentions over the speaker, and the *Field* came around once again to her original course keeping a cautious distance from the mine as she swung about. On cue from Lieutenant MacKinlay, the 40-millimeter atop the after deckhouse and its sister mount abreast the second stack, discharged several noisy rounds that skipped off the water and exploded well beyond target. The captain, his patience exhausted, ordered the entire main battery into action. After the second broadside, the mine went off with a deafening bang and an eruption that shook the destroyer and jarred a mammoth length of firehose loose from its brackets, sending it crashing to the main deck near the base of the bridge.

Soon the destroyer was steady on her course again, heading for a dubious target in a nameless inlet.

"What's your range to the nearest land?" the executive officer called out from the plotting table.

"I'll have it in a second, Sir," Bacelli replied from the Sugar-George. "I'm switching back to long-range search now," the third-class announced, clicking the range selector knob.

"What do you mean your switching back to long-range search?" Cobb shrieked. "You should have done that ten minutes ago when we scratched that last mine!" The executive officer turned towards Ensign Coates. "You've got mucho work ahead of you, Mister! I want this C.I.C. team squared-away and on the ball by our next G-Q! Do you read me?"

"Yes, Sir," Coates answered in a guarded tone.

In the next few minutes, Cobb turned his wrath on the radar strikers, lashing out at Patterson for not relaying the phone messages in a louder voice, and at Belton for handing him a greaseless grease-pencil.

The *Field* rose and dipped steadily as she raced over the wind-stirred sea, and Cobb took a few moments leave to vomit into the metal bucket reserved for such emergencies.

At 13:58, the *Field* slipped cautiously within gun-range of the Kyongsong batteries, and galloped down the coast in search of the inlet and tunnel reported by the air force bombers.

"Captain," Phil Oetjens called, the wind whipping his face as he stepped out on the wing, "I think we've got a slight problem. The chart indicates a whole series of ridges jutting out for the next fifteen miles. Each one of them forms an inlet and unfortunately, there's more than one tunnel in this area. In fact, the chart indicates four large tunnels within two miles of the fix the air force gave."

"Why is it that nothing's ever simple over here," Royal muttered sourly as he followed his navigator to the small, closet-like chartroom sandwiched in between the wheelhouse and the captain's sea cabin.

"There's a highway tunnel here five miles below Kyongsong, two here at Chuuronjang and this one just above Maksan...you know, the place I mentioned to you earlier," Oetjens advised. "As you see, Sir, the trucks could be hiding in any one of them. Reminds me a little of that old story about the lady and the tiger."

"Yes, and I wonder what the consequences are if we don't pick the right tunnel," Royal mused aloud. "Every pound of supplies the Reds deliver along that road could very well mean another G.I.'s cross at Arlington. Guess we'll have to systematically tackle all four of the tunnels. I just hope the trucks are still in one of them. I assume the air force flew off on schedule." Royal had an uneasy expression as he studied the chart. "Let's hope those A-26s made a mess of the road near the tunnel. If the commies have to stop to fill in bomb craters, we've got a better than even chance of catching them. Anyway, we've got one good break. All those tunnels are within the same stretch of coastline. We should be able to make a clean sweep of all four while we've still got daylight," his face brightened slightly. "The closest to our present position is this one just below Kyongsong, so it's elected number one on our hit parade."

"Yes, Sir. Course two-nine-three at our present speed should place us in firing position in approximately fifteen minutes. According to this chart, the first inlet will be plenty deep enough, and we should have ample maneuvering area if we're taken under fire," the navigator advised.

"There's no indication of any gun emplacements along this patch of coastline, but we'll reserve the two after mounts for counter-battery fire just in case. The other three mounts should be able to work over the tunnels without any trouble. I'd like to move in as close as possible. That way our gun gang can fire straight into the face of each tunnel. I suspect our biggest worry is going to be mines and perhaps an uncharted reef or two."

The captain ordered the ship to course two-nine-three, and the destroyer wheeled around, a bit sluggishly thought Royal, as she pounded her way over white-capped water toward the notch in the enemy's shoreline. Topside, hatches slammed shut and gunlayers manipulated their complex sighting-gear as the destroyer neared the inlet and the first and largest of the four tunnels. Ten feet above the torpedo deck on the exposed platform that wrapped around the second funnel to serve as secondary-conn, a cold and windblown Lieutenant Stockwell reached inside his foul-weather jacket to take a clandestine peek at a much-worn snapshot of Cassy Jean. While the Ops officer shuddered in the dank November winds, down in the handling rooms sweating sailors stood by shell and powder hoists waiting to feed the hungry five-inch gun mounts just a deck above their heads.

"Captain!" Lieutenant Phelan called out from the wheelhouse doorway. "Radio-central's received an operational-immediate canceling our present mission."

"They've what?" Royal cried out as he bolted from the chartroom.

"Here's the crypto now, Sir," Phelan said as he spotted the messenger ascending the top step on the inside ladder.

Royal took the dispatch from the young radioman. "Task force radar has picked up several bogies to the north," the captain said, scanning the message. "Jehovah's calling in all his small boys including us. He obviously doesn't want to get caught with his screen down if there's a repeat performance of what happened on the eighteenth."

Royal walked over to the 21MC and pushed the lever marked radio-central. "Send this to Jehovah right away, use plain language," he instructed. "Request permission to carry out our present assignment. Estimate time to complete assignment...forty minutes," he added after a pause.

"Aye, aye, Captain."

Royal released the lever and pushed the one marked C.I.C. "Combat, bridge! What's the range to our first firing position?"

"Eight thousand yards, Sir," Cobb's voice came back. "Are we still going after the tunnel?"

"I hope so. I've requested...hold it, Aub, radio-central is flashing."

"Bridge, radio-central."

"Bridge, aye."

"Sir, Jehovah via screen-commander...your request is denied. Your present mission is cancelled at this time. You are to return to the task force immediately...assume screening-station-fourteen. Jehovah's repeated the ciphers for immediately, Sir."

"Did he conclude with an over or and out?" Royal asked.

"An out, Captain," Swarztrauber, the Field's chief radioman answered timidly. "Do you want me to send a copy up to you, Captain?"

"No, that won't be necessary, Chief. Thank you." Royal turned to Oetjens. "How long do you think it would take us if we just went after that first tunnel and skipped the other three?"

"About twenty minutes. But Captain, that would be direct disobedience of Jehovah's orders. If the word ever got back to the admiral, you could be brought up on charges."

"I understand that Phil and I appreciate your concern but I really wasn't planning to disobey any orders. Right now each of our five-inch guns has a shell sitting in it's breech. We can't go racing back to the task force like that. We'll have to empty our bores anyway in accordance with safety procedures. I think it would be much more practical to empty those shells in the direction of that first tunnel than just to make five big holes in the water. Hell, that would be a sinful waste of taxpayer's money, don't you think?" he said with an artful smile.

"Yes, Sir, but if we're going to line our guns up with that tunnel, we'll have to go right inside that inlet."

"Certainly, but there's no directive against our turning in a wide circle while we're reversing course. If that just happens to take us into the inlet, well, everyone knows that these *Fletcher* class are notorious for their wide turning radius," Royal snickered, conveniently dismissing the capabilities of his ship's new rudder. A loud flapping noise caught his attention and he instinctively glanced up at the dark blue banner of the Grand Army of the Republic streaming freely from the foremast. It contrasted starkly with the double pointed blood-red Baker pennant flying from the neighboring halyard. The captain watched the two flags for several seconds, then as the *Field's* bow approached the tiderips at the outermost reaches of the inlet, he stepped into the wheelhouse. "I have the conn, Mister Phelan," he informed the OD in a friendly tone. "All engines ahead one-third, left standard rudder," Royal ordered an instant later.

The *Field* steamed into the inlet past hills black as coal piles. At a point directly abeam the tunnel, Royal instructed Ensign Ritter up in the gun-director to "empty all bores." An instant later, each of the five-inch guns belched out a yellow flame and five 54-pound projectiles went spinning through the air to terminate in an enormous eruption of smoke, sand and flying rock.

Pleased with his gunners' accuracy, and satisfied that no living creature could have survived within or anywhere near the target, Royal was never-the-less certain now that the tunnel had housed nothing beyond some unfortunate hermit crabs and cave lizards. Certainly, there was no sign of a gasoline explosion or anything else to indicate the presence of even a single vehicle, he concluded despairingly as his destroyer followed around on her circular course which would soon take her back out into open sea.

The captain had almost finished scanning the receding shoreline with its iceladen cliffs when he saw the other tunnel. Almost a mile south of the one his gunners had just transformed into a rubble heap, this one appeared even larger, which made him wonder why his navigator hadn't mentioned it.

"Phil," he called out in a slightly agitated tone, "that tunnel over there..." he said pointing. "Why didn't you call it to my attention? We could have made our turn a little wider and clobbered it on our way out."

"I'm sorry, Sir, but there wasn't the slightest hint of anything on the chart to indicate a tunnel in that location," Oetjens protested, lowering his binoculars till they hung loosely against his chest. "As far as I could determine, the next closest should have been that pair just north of Chuuronjang, and that's at least seven miles down the coast from here. That's the trouble with these damn charts they've given us," he shrugged in utter frustration. "None of them are up to date. For example, the chart we're using for this area was issued in nineteen twenty-two."

"I know, Phil. I'm not blaming you. It's just that I've got a bad feeling about that tunnel...the way it popped up out of nowhere. I'd be willing to bet my next stripe that right this second, some Chinese or North Korean non-com is peering out at us, laughing about how well he was able to outwit the Yankee imperialist navy."

"I'm not so sure about that, Captain. The half hour we lost going after that mine gave those trucks plenty of time to hightail it. They're probably well on their way to Hungnam or Wonsan by now."

"Yes, you're probably right. Well, we'd better concentrate on getting back to the screen as quickly as possible. Let's see if we can make up that fifteen minutes we just lost reversing course and unloading our bores," Royal quipped, stepping quickly inside the wheelhouse.

· · ·

Because of the bomb craters and the generally poor condition of the road, the drive from the tunnel to the murky little fishing village took the four trucks several hours. During that time, a crisp orange dust had settled upon the snow already blanketing the hoods and canvas tops of the big ex-German Bussing-NAG and the three smaller Russian-built GAZ-51s that sputtered along at 100-foot intervals. To Senior Lieutenant Perekov in the lead vehicle, it looked as if some careless cook had sprinkled paprika on a delicate meringue.

It was impossible for the Russian or his North Korean drivers to keep speed on the continually twisting road made even narrower by steel spikes and the barbed wire that was strung at irregular intervals along its edge. To their left, the embankment dropped down almost 40 feet to a swirling black sea. And as the trucks climbed and coughed their way over the last but hilliest stretch of road, Perekov wondered what transgressions his Uncle Boris could have committed to have gotten himself assigned to such an abominable place.

Major Mychenko was waiting with the sergeant from the local militia and several civilian laborers as the four trucks bucked to a noisy stop in a designated area near the village.

"Strogi!" shouted the major eagerly.

"Uncle Boris!" the young officer responded just as excitedly as he leaped from the cab twirling about as he hit the soft snow, his arms flung wide in a dilettante's interpretation of the Cossack dance.

"How long has it been?...a thousand years?" the major exclaimed, hugging his visitor like an over animated bear.

"Actually, Uncle, it is no more than eight months, though from what I have seen so far of this sewer of a land, I can well understand your feelings. And to think I once thought that Vladivostok was the end of the earth," Perekov frowned as he led the major around to the truck's tailgate. "Come see the tid-bits I have brought you." Pulling back the flap he said, "Those crates contain the latest fire-control radars in the Soviet, fresh from the production lines at Tomsk. I've been told this system is far superior to the one that was originally sent to you. I understand it fell victim to an American warship."

"Yes, a destroyer sank the trawler that was transporting it."

"That is quite a coincidence," Perekov said pensively. "You know, Uncle, an American destroyer came uncomfortably close to destroying this shipment also."

"What?" Mychenko squinted, his face suddenly as red as a ripe apple. "What do you mean, an American destroyer?"

"Earlier today, a little below Kyongsong. We had been chased into a cave by six Yankee bombers. The planes finally flew off and I was just about to give the order to get back on the road when I heard the noise of guns. It was a ship firing at another cave less that two kilometers away. I was certain it was moving into position to take my cave under fire also when it suddenly showed its stern to us and disappeared over the horizon."

"You are very fortunate, Strogi," Mychenko said as the two walked on to inspect the cargo in the other three vehicles, component parts for five 152-millimeter rifles. Mychenko snapped instructions in acceptable Korean, and the laborers, joined by two additional squads from the village, set about the task of unloading the disassembled gun barrels and breechblocks.

"How long will you be here, Strogi?" the major asked as the two withdrew, leaving the role of overseer to the sergeant of militia.

"I leave tonight as soon as the guns are unloaded."

"Tonight?"

"Yes, I am due in a place called Hapsu this time tomorrow evening and my guide says it is almost seventy miles south of here. I am to turn the trucks over to a Chinese unit, then I must stay there for at least another day to offer my technical experience to our socialist cousins. It seems they are having trouble with the gun sights on a recent shipment of T-34s."

The Russians entered the major's hut.

"Uncle, I am astonished. Where are all those succulent geishas I have heard about?"

"Most likely with the capitalists in Japan," Mychenko shrugged, eyeing a half-empty bottle of *Stolichnaya*. "Yes, Strogi, believe me, this has been quite a tour. I wouldn't even wish it on Colonel Nikolayev. Well...yes, maybe in his case I would make an exception," the major grinned, pouring out two cups of vodka. "Women, pfff..." he said, holding the cup as if he was about to propose a toast. "You can tell your Aunt Tschanka she has nothing to worry about on that account. I might as well be a monk as long as I am in this place." He gulped the vodka. "When you see your aunt you can tell her to remind that straw-brained brother of hers, your Uncle Dmitri, to do something about my transfer."

"Come on, Uncle," the lieutenant laughed, "with your reputation for the women, a little rest will do you good. Actually, I feel sorry for the girls of Moscow. There must be broken hearts strewn everywhere."

"Enough talk about females, Strogi. It is not doing my constitution any good. You know, it is not very wise to leave Maksan before morning. These roads are bad enough in the daylight. At night they can be pure suicide."

"Yes, I have considered that. However, they told me back in Vladivostok that the Americans have made the roads almost impassable by day. After the close call I had this morning, I am inclined to believe our intelligence units for once." Perekov took another sip of his vodka. "Tell me, Uncle, how soon do you expect to get the guns and radars into place?"

"That's hard to determine now that the first snows have fallen. I'm certainly grateful that you were able to make this delivery before the blizzards moved down the coast from Siberia. They could come any day now. If I had to wait until after winter for this shipment, my schedule could be pushed back by four or five months. If that happened, I doubt the guns and radars would be ready for operation until mid-June the earliest. Even if we don't get a heavy snow in the next few weeks, it will take several days to haul the guns to a position from where they can be lowered into the caves. As far as the radar is concerned, I won't be able to do anything until the technicians arrive. They are due next week but if snow delays their arrival, I could be stuck in this stink-hole forever."

"Can you tell me why we are putting such sophisticated equipment into such a place? Coming down, my driver mentioned that Maksan is so insignificant it doesn't even appear on most maps of this area. He said that he was told that even the Fascist Rhee's gunboats give it no more attention than that required in their routine patrol."

"Ha, Maksan's insignificance is one of its major advantages. When the guns are in their reinforced caves, they will be able to fire point blank at any ship stupid enough to try to pass through the narrow opening at the entrance. The inlet itself is quite wide and deep. When these guns are strategically positioned, even the Yankee battleship *Missouri* will find it impossible to force a passage. Certainly, if a ship should be able to fight its way into the harbor, which I strongly doubt, it would be so badly mauled by our guns, it would have no chance of ever getting out."

"Yes, but why would anyone want to bring a ship in here? There is certainly nothing of strategic importance in a nondescript fishing village."

"There is nothing important here now, I agree. However, once the guns and radars are in place, Maksan will become the launching point for sea borne attacks against the Yankee aircraft carriers that have been crippling our supply lines. In a few months, four of our newest W-class submarines will be officially transferred to the North Koreans. Of course, the officers and crew of each will be Russian on, shall we say, voluntary leave from the Soviet to help our socialist allies. In the southernmost corner of the inlet, there is a natural overhang of cliff even thicker than the concrete used by the Germans to protect their U-boat pens. The cavern below the rock is over three-hundred feet wide. In such a base, our submarines would be completely immune from air strikes. The only way they could be attacked would be by surface ships. When the guns are installed, that possibility will also be eliminated."

"Why send the submarines down here? Wouldn't they be just as effective if they were operating out of Vladivostok?"

"Vladivostok is in the Soviet. I imagine Comrade Stalin does not want to show his hand quite so blatantly. As it is now, the Americans are reluctant to attack the Mig bases across the Yalu. Vladivostok might prove to be that famous last straw in the famous Yankee proverb."

"Well, Uncle, since you have no female diversion to offer me after a hard day's drive, I'd better be getting back to Elsa."

"Elsa?"

"Yes, the Bussing-Nag. I've named her Elsa. She's an ex-Nazi bitch the Germans left behind at Stalingrad. However, she's the only thing that's kept me warm since I left Vladivostok."

"Well, Nephew, before you leave, let me give you this very sound advice. No matter how boring some future assignment might be, and no matter how much time you might find you have on your hands, never...and I repeat, never under any circumstances volunteer to learn another language, especially Korean. That was what gave Colonel Nikolayev the excuse to ship me here."

"Ha, you need not worry about such foolishness on my part, Uncle." The lieutenant drained the last of the vodka, then raised his empty cup in a toast. "To those damn seventy miles between here and Hapsu!"

"And to those damn Yankee jets. May their cannons jam and their sights confound!"

"Better yet, Uncle. May their wheels stick to their flightdecks," the young officer laughed robustly.

The two Russians reached the clearing just as the last piece of ordinance, a hydraulic-recoil-brake for one of the 152-millimeter guns was being lowered by crane from the rearmost vehicle.

On the following morning, the *Field* and *John Morgan* slid through a heavy snowfront to a patrol sector near the Manchu-Siberian border where the two ships executed a repetitious series of early-warning search patterns. Still annoyed about being pulled off the tunnels for what proved to be a false alarm, Royal spent much of the day's tedious patrol wondering what valuable cargo the trucks must have been carrying to make their drivers risk a daylight passage.

Shortly before sundown, the ships were relieved on station by the *Rogers*, a specially equipped radar-picket, and the two destroyers rejoined the task force off Songjin with nothing to show for their day's effort but a 10-inch frosting of snow and ice. Shovels and axes were liberally distributed aboard both vessels and few crewmen below the rank of petty-officer first-class managed to escape the sub-zero sport of ice-chipping or the acquisition of a few blisters to remind them of their first encounter with a Siberian winter.

That evening as was customary, the box score of the day's carrier operations was circulated throughout the task force. One paragraph in the report held particular interest for Commander Royal. Upon reading it he immediately summoned Lieutenant Oetjens to his cabin.

"Take a gander at this, Phil," Royal said with a look of satisfaction as he handed the paper to his navigator. "Seems some of *Bon Homme Richard's* ADs caught a four-truck convoy on the coastal road just north of Hapsu."

"Yes, Sir," Oetjens replied, scanning the report. "It looks like a clean sweep. It says here they scratched all four...plastered the roof of the leader with napalm. What a bloody mess that must have been," the navigator said, still staring at the paper. "The report says the first truck was especially large. Do you think these were the ones we missed yesterday?"

"I'm certain of it. The important thing is they were heading south when the planes caught them. That means they were still in the process of delivering their cargo. If they'd unloaded it, they'd be heading back north to Manchuria. I must admit, those trucks have been on my mind since we pulled out of that inlet yesterday. I couldn't shake the thought that for a matter of another fifteen minutes we could have taken out that second tunnel, too. Well thanks to Bonnie Dick's ADs, I guess I can stop worrying about that truck convoy. Maybe I'll take in a movie," said Royal, forcing a smile. "What's on the marquee for tonight?"

Oetjens extracted a folded paper from his breast pocket. "Looks like another couple of clinkers," he frowned, eyeing the blurred typeface on the mimeographed plan-of-the-day. "The wardroom's showing 'The Crimson Key' starring Kent Taylor, Doris Dowling and Louise Currie. The crew's mess has something called 'Rendezvous Twenty-Four' with William Gargan and Marie Palmer."

"Sounds pretty much like a toss-up. Which is newer, Phil? Does it say?"

"Yes, Sir, the wardroom movie. It's a forty-seven release. The other picture was made in forty-six."

"Hmmm, at least that's a step in the right direction. Most of the movies we've been getting lately date back to the thirties," Owen grinned.

The two officers left the cabin and made their way to the wardroom. There, for an hour and fifteen minutes, they would escape the realities of a frustrating war as they tried to unravel the complex mystery of 'The Crimson Key.'

The snow had stopped hours before and the wind had lost the better part of its bite, even so, the captain knew it was much too cold to linger back there on the darkened fantail for more than a moment or two. The movie had been a welcome respite. Perhaps he was getting much easier to please in his old age, he chuckled, glancing up towards where the sky ought to have been. He looked for the stars. There were none to be seen, just a creamy blur he assumed must be the moon.

Bracing himself against the depth-charge rail, he let go quickly, its icy sting piercing his fur-lined gloves. He recalled the sun-drenched beaches around La

Jolla and the last time he'd gone swimming with Candace. Dammit, but he missed her! He could practically see her smiling as she modeled her bathing suit for him, the new red one she'd written about in her last letter. He wondered what she was doing at that precise moment. He had no way of knowing that she was in Acapulco with the advertising director of Gilray Pharmaceuticals, an account she'd soon be adding to the B.B.Y. and S. client roster.

Owen glanced at the black shapes around him on the fantail, not sure just what or who he was expecting to see. It certainly wouldn't be old Henderson, he told himself, paradoxically wondering exactly where the unfortunate CPO had been standing during those final seconds off Okinawa.

The *Field* shuddered and shook as she strained to maintain her precarious position in the "pouncer" slot midway between the screening ships ahead and the three racing carriers barely a mile astern.

Chapter XVIII - Season's Greetings

Another month had gone into the hopper, and again the crew of the *Field* had missed qualifying for combat pay by a single day. If it wasn't for that unhappy fact, November would have slipped away completely unnoticed amid the sleet and mist that swirled like a white gauze around the ships of the task force, soaking the sky of all color and leaving the sea as dreary and cheerless as the distant landscape.

But even this bleak November had had its brighter moments. Howie Murray and Lieutenant Sternhagen had both become proud fathers of bouncing baby girls — Mary Kathleen and Dorothy Veronica; and Navy's 7 to 0 upset win over Army was proving just the right tonic to lift Owen Royal's spirits, though not enough to offset the noisome task he must take care of this first day of December.

There was still a few hours left...enough time to head this stupid thing off, hoped Owen Royal, reaching for the phone in his stateroom.

"Wardroom, Beaumont speakin', Suh."

"This is the captain, Beaumont. Is Mister Cobb in the wardroom?"

"No, Suh, ah ain't seen him since breakfast, Cap'n," the steward's mate answered in a heavy Afro-American accent.

"Well, see if you can locate him for me. Tell him I'd like to see him here in my cabin. If you're not able to find Mister Cobb in the next ten minutes, tell the O-D that I'd like to have him paged over the address system."

Paging Aubrey Cobb was unnecessary. Within five minutes the exec was seated opposite the C.O.

"Aub, I hope you've given a little thought to what we discussed the other morning, you know, about going ahead with this thing this afternoon."

"Yes, Sir, I've given it quite a bit of thought and I'm more convinced than ever that I was completely justified in taking the action I did. As far as I'm concerned, those two are getting off damn light. Disobeying navy regs, especially when they pertain to classified signals, should really have gotten them a summary."

"In that case we'd have to court martial every signalman, radioman, radarman and any officer who has routine contact with the general signal book or T-

B-S. For that matter, I'm certain the Ops departments on every ship in the task force are just as guilty… and that goes for the Ops people on Jehovah's flattop and on Jocko Clark's *Missouri.*"

"Well, I don't know about the other ships, Captain. I'm not responsible for what their personnel do. However, as executive officer, I have been charged with maintaining order and discipline on this ship. That's all I'm attempting to do in this case."

"Of course, and naturally I appreciate the overall good job you're doing in that regard. However, as far as Murray and Gardiner are concerned, don't you think you're getting a little carried away?"

"No, it's not just a case of memorizing signals. One of them…the first-class, eh, Murray, he actually tried to defend their wholesale disregard of security regulations. Then, as if that wasn't enough, he had the gall to talk back to me. That's why he's also up for insubordination."

"Yes, but I don't see how you're going to make that one stick. I checked with Coates to see just what Murray said and…"

"You mean you don't take my word as your exec and as a naval officer?" Cobb burst out angrily.

"Of course I do, but don't forget, you were directly engaged in the …what should we call it," Royal paused, "confrontation? Anyway, Coates said you asked Murray if he thought you were stupid, and Murray declined to answer. The best you could charge him with is taking the Fifth."

"Well, it was the way he declined. You weren't there. You didn't see him smirk."

"Maybe it really wasn't a smirk, Aub. Maybe he only smiled a little and you misinterpreted it."

"Oh no! If there's one thing I know, it's a smirk, and that man smirked!…in a highly deliberate manner, I'd like to add."

"Okay, so he smirked. That's not the end of the world. You know, morale's pretty low on this ship right now. The fact that we've been dodging shore batteries and mines and still haven't qualified for a combat bonus hasn't helped to boost it, either," Royal frowned. "Most of this crew, like Murray, are reservists. Also like Murray, a lot of them have already had their war. Now they're pulled away from their families and stuck over here on what I'm sure they regard as a wet, smelly, uncomfortable little ship, fighting a war that hardly makes the newspapers anymore. Do you really expect me to keelhaul this man because you object to his facial expression?"

"Well, Gardiner's not a reserve."

"Great, we'll keelhaul Gardiner then."

Cobb continued to sulk.

"Look, Aub, just a few days ago, Murray was sitting right there on that same chair you're sitting on. You should have seen how happy he looked when I congratulated him about his new baby. Now you want me to rack his ass over the coals for some minor infraction of a rule nobody in the navy adheres to. You know, I was reviewing Murray's service jacket just before you came in," Royal said, glancing over at the reddish-brown folder on the desk. "By the time he was nineteen, he'd been in sixteen major engagements and earned a P-U-C and a Navy Unit Commendation."

"Captain, if you're bringing that up just to underscore the fact that I didn't get to see any combat during the war, I'd like to..."

"Dammit, Aub! Stop making this a personal issue! I don't give a rat's ass in hell whether or not you've ever gotten your tail shot at. What I do care about right now is the morale of this crew! As X-O, you can do a lot to see that it picks up."

"Ensign Daly is the morale officer, Sir," said Cobb blandly.

"A little over a year ago Daly had never seen a destroyer, except maybe in the movies. Anyway, it's quite apparent that he can use some expert help. Now with all the experience you've had in the merchants, plus your navy time, I'm certain you can do a lot to guide Mister Daly's efforts. Now, getting back to the mast that's scheduled for this afternoon. Have you reconsidered? I'm certain it would do a great deal to boost morale if you withdraw the charges against Murray and Gardiner."

"I'm sorry, Sir. I've got to be firm in this matter. If I were to back down now, discipline on this ship would become little more than a joke. The enlisted men would be tripping over each other trying to see who could get away with the most infractions."

"Alright, Aub, if you feel that strongly about it, I won't pressure you. I'll hold the first mast exactly as scheduled at fourteen-hundred."

"Thank you, Captain. If that's all you wanted to see me about, I'll be heading back to the ship's office."

Royal nodded, looking away vaguely as the exec took his leave.

Captain's mast commenced precisely at 14:00. Murray and Gardiner appeared separately. Both were instructed by the C.O. that in the future, they were to check the meaning of each radio-transmission before passing it on to the bridge or to their fellow watch-standers in C.I.C. A total of two hours extra duty to be spent updating the C.I.C. pubs was assigned as punishment. The captain also specified that no record of the mast was to be entered in either sailor's service jacket. In addition, neither radarman was to be denied the opportunity to take the next promotion exam providing he met all the other requirements for rate advancement.

Upon hearing of the exceptionally light punishment imposed on the two crewmen, Aubrey Cobb flew into a rage and disappeared into his cabin for the remainder of the day, not even surfacing for the evening's flick, a 1947 comedy called "Out of the Blue," with George Brent and Virginia Mayo.

The Second of December opened peacefully enough with a bright sun slanting across rolling blue waves. Now a "short timer" with only five months remaining on his enlistment, Howie Murray began the morning by eagerly X-ing out another day on the calendar taped to the inside of his locker door. Next to writing his daily epistle to Mary Alice and the girls, this ritual quickly became the highpoint of his day. Obliterating the calendar's symbolic representation of what he started calling his "hard time," Murray was totally unaware that this particular Tuesday would have special significance. Before its passing the *Charles P. Field* would suffer her first fatality since that day in April '45 when Wilbur Henderson came in second best to a hell-bent "Claude" off Okinawa. This time, however, the perpetrator was not to be a plane, nor a mine or shore battery.

"A Coke machine!" Commander Royal stared in disbelief at Lieutenant MacKinlay. "How the hell could anyone be killed by a Coke machine?" Half stumbling as he jumped up from his seat in ship's office, the captain plunged past the gunnery officer and headed towards the ladder that led to the crew's mess.

Grubbing coffee from the radar gang was by now standard operating procedure for Ashton Bites. Propped contently on the steel-legged stool near the door, the bo'sun had barely "cumshawed" his second refill when radar striker, currently mess cook Paulsen came tumbling into C.I.C.

"Hey! Watch it!" Bites snarled, splattering most of his coffee on the rubber matting as he tried to balance the teetering stool. "What's your problem, Boy? You look like you've been rode hard and put away wet!"

"Sweetpea Hopkins...he's dead," the young sailor shuddered noticeably.

"What are you talking about?" Nugent joined in. "I saw him this morning dishing out S-O-S on the chow line."

"Yeah, that's right," Bacelli agreed. "How could he be dead?"

"Two-hundred and twenty volts of electricity, that's how!" Paulsen shot back. "The captain and exec are on the mess deck right now. So's MacKinlay and Ritter and Chief Pheifer and his whole damn master-at-arms force," Paulsen gasped, still trying to catch his breath.

"Well, what happened to Sweetpea?" Murray asked sharply.

"It was on account of that damn Coke machine, you know how it usually gobbles up five or six nickels before you can get a drink out of the friggin' thing."

"Not if you time it right," Bacelli said smugly. "I've got that Coke machine down to a science. All you have to do is know exactly when to release the nickel." Bacelli looked around the radar space as if to check the attentiveness of his audience. "Like I was saying, all you have to do is judge the ship's roll, then release the nickel in the slot exactly three seconds before the ship gets on even keel. If you wait even a second too long and the ship continues her roll or slides back in the other direction, you can kiss that buffalo goodbye. It's all in the timing."

"Bullshit," Nugent laughed. "I watched you drop six coins in that nickel grabber just yesterday."

"The hell you did! I've never lost more than two nickels in all the time I've been on this bucket. Working that Coke machine's no different than playing pinball, and I was pinball champion for all of Flatbush."

"I repeat my last transmission — bullshit!" said Nugent, cupping his hands to his mouth as if he was talking through a megaphone.

"You think so, heh. Well, how about putting ten bucks where your mouth is. Next time we get up to Tokyo, we can use that pinball machine in the Rocker-Four Club and I'll top any score you can make!"

"You're on, only let's make it twenty bucks," Nugent retorted.

"I don't believe you two," Murray cut in angrily. "You meatheads get the word that one of your shipmates has just bought the farm and all you can do is argue about who's the better pinball player!"

"Well, it's not like we really knew the kid. He was only a seaman-deuce, and a two-year reserve at that," Bacelli replied a little sheepishly.

"Besides, Murray," Nugent glanced slyly at Bacelli and Bites. "Maybe it was the S-O-S that done him in."

"What the hell are you talking about?" Murray snarled, certain he was being put on.

"Yeah, Murray," Bacelli said, "you're always telling us about how you wouldn't be alive today if you'd gone down to the mess deck and eaten S-O-S that time the Jap bomber clobbered your flattop."

"Yeah, well I don't see what that's got to do with what happened to Hopkins."

"You don't?" Nugent exaggerated his surprise. "It seems to me that just about every time we've had S-O-S for breakfast, Sweetpea's been the guy behind the chow line dumping it on our trays," snickered the third-class.

"What happened with me on the *Franklin* had to do with fate, not superstition. There's a big difference you know. Hell, I've never been the least bit superstitious," Murray protested, hoping that nobody had seen him toss the lei from the fantail that last morning off Oahu.

"Well, all I know is whenever they're serving S-O-S, you won't step foot in the mess," Nugent teased.

"I know another place Murray won't set foot in...a cathouse, right, Howie?" Bacelli prodded.

"You're damn right. I never have and I never will!"

"Now, Murray, you shouldn't make an all-inclusive statement like that. You never know when you're gonna' really get that urge," Bacelli advised. "You know, it's still gonna' be a long time before you get back to Mary Alice and we're bound to hit Japan at least three more times before we haul ass for the States."

"I don't care how many times we go into Japan. I said I'd never step foot in a whorehouse and I never will. And if you guys think I'm just blowing off steam, I'm willing to bet each one of you a hundred bucks at ten to one odds."

"You mean if we lose, we each pay you ten bucks, but if you as much as set one foot inside the door of a cathouse, you'll give us each a C-note?"

"That's right!"

"Okay, it's a bet," Bacelli beamed as Nugent, Bites and even Paulsen joined in to accept the first-class's offer. Within the hour, Holiday and Gardiner made an unexpected appearance in C.I.C., quickly goading Murray into letting them join the wager.

Chief Timmermann was nervous. Even with eighteen years of sea duty under his belt, he got this way whenever he had to go see his commanding officer. Royal was easier than most he'd served under, he was certain of that, even so, talking to the skipper seemed something akin to appearing before the grand inquisitor. Standing out there on the sun splashed open bridge didn't make things easier either, he thought, blinking and fidgeting with his cap as he awaited the first question.

"Chief, I hate to put you on the spot like this, but you're the *Field's* senior electrician. Can you tell me exactly what happened to Hopkins? I want to be certain it doesn't happen to anyone else aboard this ship."

"Eh, yes, Sir," the CPO stared down at his feet. "I know exactly what happened, I'm certain of that," he said, talking quickly, as if anxious to get through. "That kid, eh, Hopkins I mean. He did a real dumb thing, real dumb."

"Yes, Chief, I'm sure he did. Can you be a little more specific?"

"Well, he had no business opening up that damn fuse box that supplied the power for the Coke machine. I imagine he was pissed, I mean annoyed about losing a nickel in the machine so he decided to try to get his money back. Guess he thought he was playing it safe by removing the fuse before he tried opening up the machine. Only thing is, he didn't use a fuse puller. He just stuck his claw into the box and grabbed at one of the fuses. You know, Sir, they're really cartridges, sort of like long cardboard tubes with brass at each end."

"Yes, Chief. I'm familiar with them. Go on."

"Well, I figure what happened is he touched one of those metal ends. His hands were probably still wet from mess cooking, too. Anyway, he must have taken the full shot, two-hundred and twenty volts. That's enough to kill a horse, you know, Sir."

"Yes, Chief. Thank you. That's really all I wanted to know. I'll see to it that it reads that way in the report I'll be making out shortly."

"Yes, Sir. Will that be all, Captain?"

"Yes, Chief. Thank you again."

A few minutes after the CPO left the bridge, Aubrey Cobb appeared. "We've got over two hours yet before sunset, Captain. That's more than enough time to hold burial services. I've told MacKinlay to have his division set things up on the fantail," the exec said loftily.

"The fantail? I didn't say anything about burial services. We'll keep Hopkins in the reefer until we get to Japan. That way, at least his parents will have the comfort of being able to visit his grave. God knows, that's little enough to give them back," said Royal reflectively.

"The reefer? How can we keep him in there? We're not scheduled for an R and R until Christmas. That's a good three-and-a-half weeks away."

"The length of time has nothing to do with it. It's the temperature that's important," Royal replied, a trace of sarcasm in his tone. "Unless I've been misinformed, our reefer is in perfect running order."

"Captain, I'd like to remind you that only yesterday you implied that I wasn't doing my job when it came to boosting the crew's morale. I certainly don't think we're going to improve morale by putting a corpse in with the crew's food."

"Hopkin's will be in a body-bag."

"Yes, but most of the smaller ships have been burying their dead at sea. Even the *Halsey Wayne* held an underway burial last week after she lost those three men at Tanchon."

"Forget it, Aub! I'm in no mood for a debate, and I'm not going to change my decision in this matter." Royal's voice rose sharply. "In an hour or so, I'll be writing a letter to Hopkin's parents. Right now they're probably wondering whether or not he'll like whatever it is they've sent him for Christmas. Now I've got to find a way around telling them that it doesn't make a difference anymore...that they've lost their son because of something as insignificant as a nickel soda. They won't even have the consolation of knowing he died in action against the enemy, and there'll be no Purple Heart to hang over his picture on the parlor table. I can't do anything about that. However, I'll be damned if I'm going to write them and tell them we just fed their seventeen-year-old son to the sharks! Now if you're a little squeamish about eating for the next few weeks, I suggest you consider going on a diet!"

"Will that be all, Captain?" the exec asked, his eyes glaring.

"Yes, that's all," Royal said, returning the salute in the same half-hearted manner it was given.

Three December found the ships of Task Force 77 on special alert. Combat air patrols in the area were doubled and the bulk of the carrier strikes scheduled for the day were abruptly canceled. It would be much later before Royal and the others would learn that on that day, President-elect Eisenhower, who had been in Korea on an almost clandestine inspection tour, had departed by air for Guam. There, he and Admiral Radford, along with future cabinet members, would board Cruiser *Helena* for passage to Pearl Harbor.

The remainder of the week passed uneventfully for *DD-505* until the morning of the sixth when she rescued the two-man crew of a Marine Corps OY-1 observation plane that splashed in the choppy waters off Wonsan. In the Honghung area that evening shortly past sunset, she provided illumination fire for battleship *Missouri* and in the process was credited with knocking out a mobile 3-inch gun and damaging a bunker. On the ninth, she saved another flyer, this time the pilot of a *Phil Sea* Panther that had lost power on take-off and had barely missed being plowed under by its' mammoth mother ship.

Earlier that same morning, a somewhat baffling piece of information gleaned from the Armed Forces Radio Network appeared as lead paragraph on *DD-505's* daily news sheet. The news brief related how "the officers and men of the *Ward*, *Wayne*, *Morgan* and *Field* had unanimously chosen a certain up-and-coming Hollywood starlet as the pinup queen of Destroyer Division 291 currently serving with Task Force 77 off Korea." The report was especially mystifying as no such poll had ever been taken aboard any of the four destroyers.

That evening while refueling alongside carrier *Oriskany*, the Charlie P. received five hefty bags of mail via high line. Included in the heftiest bag was a generous supply of glossy publicity photos showing the shapely young actress as she posed on an ice covered pond clad only in a one-piece bathing suit and a pair of ice skates. It took the slightest expenditure of thought, even on the part of Turk, to conclude that some studio press agent, along with a well intentioned Navy P.I.O. type, had hatched up the entire thing for the "morale of the folks back home." And while a few of the *Field's* crewmen, especially the Marilyn Monroe devotees, resented getting a "snow job" from their own newspaper, the majority of *DD-505's* bluejackets welcomed the pinup which within minutes adorned every bulletin board and numerous locker doors throughout the ship. A few cynics utilized one of the photos by tacking it to a dart board and awarding appropriate points for hitting appropriate areas of the young lady's anatomy.

•   •   •

Wearing only a pink slip, Cynthia Osbourne was sitting up in bed writing a letter on the hotel stationary when Terry Winfield stormed in.

"Cindy, would you please tell me what you think you're doing? Dammit, the guys think you're some kind of fruitcake or something, suddenly hopping up from the table and disappearing like that. What do you think we came here to Kamakura for? So you could write letters?"

"I'm sorry if I've upset your plans, but I made it quite clear when I agreed to come along that I had no intention of obliging you by going to bed with your friend's buddy. I certainly didn't think you were going to try to switch our room arrangements without even asking me."

"Come on, Cindy. Don't give me that little Miss Goody Two-Shoes routine. You knew damn well that when we registered, I'd be paired off with Greg and you'd be sharing the other room with Bill," said Lieutenant Winfield standing at the foot of the bed.

Cynthia looked up briefly, then resumed writing her letter without answering.

"Come on, get dressed. You can at least come back down to the lounge for a drink."

"You know I can't drink. I had my limit at dinner. I've certainly no intention of losing consciousness tonight, not with those two friends of yours," she pouted.

"Frankly, for all the fun and cheer you've added to the evening, you might just as well be unconscious."

"Good! I agree, so then why don't you go back down to the Marine Corps and let me finish this letter to Kevin. Then I intend to get some much needed sleep."

"I can't figure you out. You're totally moonstruck over that swab."

"That's my business, isn't it?"

"Okay, maybe it is but he's not here and Bill is, so why don't you come down and have a ginger ale or Coke. You know, you could at least be a little sociable. They've only got three more days left before they rejoin their outfit in Korea."

"Don't try to appeal to my patriotism. There's no way I'm going back down there. Why should I bother getting dressed just so your idea of Sonny Tufts can start undressing me again?"

"What are you talking about? Bill's been a perfect gentleman."

"Oh, really? Then why was his hand under my skirt all through dinner? Every time I raised my fork to eat, I had to put it down so I could stop him from unfastening my garters. Of course, I'm sure the garters were only his way of establishing a beachhead. It was when he decided to take the high ground that I jumped up from the table, just in case you're still wondering. You know, for someone who was recently shot in the arm, it sure hasn't slowed him up any," Cynthia added, unamused.

"Well, what about the sleeping arrangements?"

"What about them?"

"How are Greg and I going to...you know...if you don't let Bill spend the night in here with you?"

"I'm certain Bill would be content just watching you and Greg."

"Damn you, Cindy, you little bitch! Do you realize that if you don't help me out tonight, our friendship is a thing of the past?"

"If that's the way you want it, it's up to you. One thing's certain. Bill's not getting into this room tonight and he's not getting into me! Now please leave me alone so I can finish this letter!"

The paper thin walls of the Tomoduru Hotel quivered like an old saw blade as the door slammed shut behind a livid Terry Winfield.

•　　•　　•

The second week of December plowed ahead without major incident. The carriers launched and retrieved, and the *Field* shunted from screening station to screening station, her bridge watch pressing to keep their ship that one all-important jump ahead of the hard-charging flattops and cruisers.

Then on the 16th the men got their first hint that they were in for a change of scenery. The clue came at reveille, that most hated occurrence of shipboard routine. It came in the form of a Kay Kyser recording piped throughout the ship via the general address system. On it lead singer Harry Babbitt told all within hearing about the pleasures associated with a slow boat to China.

By the time the phonograph had spun its scratchy course, all aboard *DD-505* had correctly deducted that their destroyer would now take her turn as part of the Seventh Fleet's patrol force in the Formosa Strait. At ten past nine, the *Field*, *Ward*, *Wayne* and *Morgan* detached from the task force and headed south towards the Shimonseki Strait, gateway to the East China Sea.

Thousands of landing craft, composed largely of motorized junks, had been assembled at mainland coastal points opposite Taiwan, and all signs pointed towards an attempted invasion of the Nationalist stronghold as well as a grab at the Pescadores and Matsu. Air activity had greatly increased in the area recently and two U.S. Navy patrol planes had been attacked by Chinese Migs. With the helm of state conceived as possibly being a bit shaky under the hand of a lame duck president, it seemed a reasonable time for the Communists to make their move. So thought Owen Royal as he guided his pugnacious little man-of-war up and down the 100-mile wide strait tugging at the tail of the Maoist dragon. In contrast, his crew's main concern centered around their prospects of pulling an unscheduled liberty in exotic Hong Kong. If the scuttlebutt could be believed, a call at the British crown colony was imminent.

Within an hour of their arrival off Wuch'i, the destroyers topped-off from the *Cimmarron*, one of the navy tankers operating on a rotation basis between Korean waters and the Fomosa Strait. While refueling alongside the big oiler, Royal was disappointed to learn that he'd missed Tim Barrett's *Chicamauga* by only two days.

On the second morning of their patrol, the *Field's* bluejackets found themselves steaming directly under a wild dogfight between mainland Migs and a flight of Nationalist P-51s. The battle was inconclusive but the patchwork of vapor trails slowly dissolving against the winter sky reminded the onlookers that death was still well within reach.

It was precisely 14:00 when ship's company aboard the *Field* got the word. All speculation about sampling the forbidden pleasures of Hong Kong was quickly abandoned. Worse yet, the crew's Christmas R and R in Japan was also down the drain. Learning that the enemy was planning to take advantage of an anticipated U.N. slowdown on Christmas Eve to move massive reinforcements southward, Eighth Army headquarters had requested a maximum interdiction effort by the navy. As part of this effort, Commodore Price was ordered to immediately detach a unit of his force for duty with Task Force 95. To no one's surprise, the Charlie P. was chosen to make the speed-run to a point just north of the 41st parallel where, on the morning of the 24th, she arrived snorting and hissing like a hard-ridden horse.

Christmas Eve found carriers *Kearsarge, Oriskany* and *Essex* dispatching raid after raid against the enemy's troop convoys and rolling stock. At the same time, the lethal gun clubs of Task Force 95 were unleashing what history books would later record as the heaviest bombardment of the Korean War. Absent from the memorable assault was *DD-505*, which on special orders from the blockade force commander, was hurrying north to intercept a cluster of junks suspected of sewing mines in the coastal waters off Chuuronjang.

It was past ten when the *Field* reached the area where the junks had been spotted. A thorough search aided by an unusually bright moon revealed no hint of the enemy vessels, and Owen Royal was about to withdraw southward to a secondary assignment, a lifeguard station off Kilchu, when his combat-information-center reported a faint pip twelve miles ahead. The target detected on the Sugar-George was slightly seaward of the *Field* but moving in toward Chuuronjang at four to five knots speed. Additional turns were added to the propeller shafts and the *Field* lurched forward with a sudden shiver, her bow knifing through the black water towards the unidentified radar target which by now had been designated "Skunk-Able."

"Have the first-division prepare to lower the port motor whaleboat," ordered Royal, training his glasses at the darkness ahead.

"Combat reports range to Skunk-Able is now six thousand yards. Skunk-Able bears zero-one-five." The voice of the phone-talker pierced the darkness of the open bridge.

"All engines stop!" Royal called to the wheelhouse. "Mister Phelan, ask Lieutenant MacKinlay to step to the bridge."

A moment later, the *Field's* gunnery officer was shuffling over the soft snow that carpeted the open wing.

"All engines back full!" Royal ordered, slowing the destroyer's glide. "Skunk-Able's probably a large or medium-sized power-junk making for the beach," the captain advised, pointing as MacKinlay raised his binoculars. "The chart indicates a shallow bed to port so I can't risk taking the ship in any closer. Besides, there's every likelihood we're sitting in the middle of a minefield right now. Anyway, I'd like to catch this bird before he can get to shore. Maybe somebody on that junk can tell us where the rest of his buddies are hiding. Think Ritter can handle it?"

"Yes, Sir, he should be able to. I've a sharp enough gang in the Mark-thirty-seven. With some help from Commander Cobb and his people in C.I.C., they should be able to handle things up there without him," the *Field's* gun-boss replied, disappointing Owen who had hoped his ex-gyrene and fellow "trade school" alumnus would have better lived up to his gung-ho image by volunteering to take the whaleboat in himself.

In contrast, Ensign Ritter's eagerness to take on the assignment impressed the captain the second he began briefing the young officer.

"Alright, George, the show's all yours, but watch yourself, especially when you close to board. More than a few of these supposedly harmless fishing junks have turned up bristling with heavy machine guns and bazookas. According to a recent report, one of our ships intercepted a junk that was toting a twenty-millimeter gun and a recoilless rifle. Of course, there's an outside chance that Skunk-Able out there might really be just a fishing junk, so if possible, try and take her out without the six-shooters."

"Sir, does that mean we don't fire unless fired upon?"

"That's about it. Remember, your objective is to get us a prisoner, preferably a nice talkative one who can give us the scoop on the number and location of the mines in this area."

"Yes, Sir, I understand. If they do want to shoot it out, though, we'll be more than ready for them. I've been putting the landing force through its paces till I'm certain they can out marine the marines," Ritter said with an anxious grin.

"How many men will you need?"

"If I could, Sir, I'd like to take two gunners-mates, Wrigley and McNulty, and two seamen, Poole and Lockhart, plus the regular boat crew. That would be Bites as coxswain, Gist on the engine, Lucas as sternman, and McAlleney as bowhook. A B-A-R for Wrigley and carbines for the others should give us more than enough fire power."

Royal agreed, then ordered that a five-inch round be placed a hundred yards ahead of the target which now appeared to be increasing speed. Number-"2" gun complied with a thunderous blast and the motor-junk immediately hove to.

"I don't think you'll have to sweat any trouble from shore batteries, the *Rochester* and *Los Angeles* teamed up to give this area a terrific pasting just this morning. That's probably why the Reds are anxious to mine this stretch of coast. I imagine they're afraid the cruisers might come back for a repeat performance. The sea looks fairly calm right now but it could build up in a matter of minutes. If at any time you judge the whaleboat to be in danger, return to the ship immediately. Remember, George, that's an order not an option. The safety of you and your crew comes first. We'll keep as close as possible," the captain advised, escorting the assistant-gunnery officer back to the ladder that linked the signal bridge with the boat deck. "At least the snow's stopped and thanks to the moon you'll have good visibility," he added. "Just remember to stay out of the water. In this temperature, you'd be dead within minutes of immersion. I'm going to put the starboard whaleboat in the water as backup in case you get in trouble. If you need help let us know via your walkie talkie. If you really bite off more than you can chew, send up a couple of flares, pronto."

"Yes, Sir," said Ritter glancing at his watch. "In exactly thirteen minutes, it'll be Christmas."

"I'm afraid I'd forgotten. It doesn't look very much like the star of Bethlehem up there, does it?" Royal said as he studied the black clouds moving swiftly across the moonlight.

"No, Sir, I can't honestly say it does."

"Merry Christmas, anyway, George," Royal smiled as the ensign descended the ladder.

"Thank you, Captain. The same to you. I'll do my best to bring you back a prisoner to put under the tree in the wardroom."

"If you do, be certain he's an officer. Otherwise, we'll have to put him under the tree in the crew's mess," Royal laughed good naturedly. In a moment, the whaleboat with its nine occupants was free of its mother ship. A biting whiff of yellow smoke rose from her exhaust as the toy-like engine coughed and chugged pushing the 26-footer away from the destroyer. Royal watched the bobbing motion of the small white light as the launch heeled heavily from side to side in a rapidly rising sea.

The waves were much higher than Ensign Ritter had reckoned back on the open wing of the *Field* and their black crests, stirred by sudden winds, hovered menacingly on all sides obscuring horizon and quarry each time the whaleboat's stern slid back into a trough. To compound the problem, the wind and sea were forcing her head off to starboard.

"Left-half rudder, cox'sun!" Ritter shouted at Bites on the tiller. The boat rolled violently and a heavy vail of salt spray rattled off the helmets and pelted the faces of the crew and the armed sailors crouched well below the gunwales. Ritter sat aft, his fingers gripping the edge of the stern thwart, his feet braced hard against the deck as if to keep the little wooden craft on even keel.

"Reduce your speed, Bites!" Ritter's voice was barely audible against the roar of the sea, wind and engine, as the whaleboat scaled the next wave.

"Object…two points off the starboard bow!" Bites yelled anxiously.

"Left-full rudder!" Ritter ordered, and the boat swerved to port colliding with a wall of water that sloshed along the planked decking from gunwale to gunwale and from bow to stern thoroughly soaking all hands. Ritter checked the hooks of his kapok life jacket suddenly wondering if drawing this assignment had been such a break afterall. He thought of Carol. They'd been married less than two years. What if he didn't make it back to the *Field*?

The launch jumped atop another wave teetering for an instant like a child's seesaw before plunging bow first into the black trough that followed.

"Stop your engine!" Ritter screamed in total surprise. Directly ahead and dangerously close lay the junk. Its alien form bobbed defiantly in the moonlit swells, sending a sudden shiver up the ensign's spine. His fingers tightened around the metal hoisting shackle that protruded up from the stern thwart as he contemplated his chances of boarding this nautical abomination in such a tossing sea.

To McAlleney up in the bow, the junk's jagged black hide and jutting snout had the ominous profile of an "Okee" gator on the prowl.

Wrigley propped the heavy Browning automatic rifle near the bow, its muzzle ready to sweep clean the entire length of the junk's deck should the necessity arise. Poole, McNulty and Lockhart checked the safeties on their carbines.

The whaleboat wallowed throwing Ritter off balance as he rose to a standing position. He quickly righted himself and pointed the megaphone at the dark hump-like figures he thought he perceived hunched near the junk's stern.

"Kug-ee suk-guh-rah…nah-noon mee-gook sah-rahm-ee-yaw," Ritter shouted. It meant "Stop, I'm an American," and it seemed the most appropriate of the three Korean sentences he'd memorized since the *Field* had departed Pusan. The others concerned the ordering of food and drink and the whereabouts of the toilet.

"Ritter called out again. There was no answer. The two craft drifted closer.

"Get ready with that hook, McAlleney! Poole, when I give the order, you and I will go aboard. Once we're safe on deck, you two will follow," the officer commanded, glancing back at McNulty and Lockhart. "Wrigley, you stay here with the B-A-R. Keep us covered but don't fire unless…"

McAlleney and Gist were the only ones in the whaleboat to see the tubular object as it came somersaulting over from the general direction of the junk.

Visible for an instant as it caught the moon's glow, it looked to McAlleney like some kind of rolling pin.

"Watch out!" Gist shouted to Bites at the tiller. Before the warning could be heard, the object slammed with a muffled thud against the coxswain's kapok life jacket, bouncing back into the open boat where it disappeared somewhere in the inky wetness of the keelboards.

"Open fire!" Ritter shouted as he and Gist leaped for the "potato masher," but the order was lost in the thunderclap of Wrigley's Browning, already pumping a stream of red rivets into the shadowy forms frantically dashing to-and-fro along the junk's deck.

"Full astern!" the ensign ordered, praying that the elusive grenade would turn out to be a dud. It was Ritter's last command. Hardly had the words flew out of his mouth when a blinding silver flash ripped the bottom of the wooden whaleboat asunder.

The junk, a small fire now burning amidships, pulled away at flank speed only seconds before Ensign Warden and the starboard whaleboat appeared on the scene. The flames licking at her waist quickly vanished, but the embers glowing brightly in her bullet gutted stern persisted in betraying her position as she made for the safety of the Chuuronjang breakwater. The howl of the wind increased and the moon slid briefly behind a cloud. A flare tore a bright hole in the sky and yellow streamers cascaded down in all directions as Warden and his boat crew clutched for their shipmates in the freezing blackness. The frenzy of their search was such that they never heard the *Field's* first salvo whistle overhead. Five more projectiles flew from the destroyer's muzzles to hurdle down with damning fury on all sides of the zigzagging enemy. Warden watched the geysers dance along the water. They had a strange kind of beauty when set against the spectral light of the dying flare, he thought. Then, with terrible finality, the junk detonated in a starburst of exploding ammunition and gasoline spray. Sizzling streamers of teak and metal showered down around the whaleboat, and bodies, whole and in parts, dotted the surface of the water.

An hour later, after an intensive search, Warden rejoined the destroyer as anxious sailors crammed the deck-edge to count the whaleboat's occupants. Wrigley, Gist, Bites and Ensign Ritter were not among them.

Dick Warden rubbed his hair briskly, tossed the wet towel atop his bunk, and hurried to the captain's cabin where Royal and Cobb awaited his report.

"You say there was no trace of Ensign Ritter or the others?" questioned Cobb in a solemn tone.

"No, Sir, we searched the area thoroughly as soon as we picked up the five survivors. McAlleney said he saw the grenade go off right under Ensign Ritter," the young officer said pensively. "The others were blown right out of the boat. Poole tried to reach Wrigley but he went under too fast. I'm really sorry about what happened, Captain. I know it's partly my fault. If I'd caught up with Georgie's boat a couple of minutes earlier, I'm sure…"

"You had nothing to do with what happened," the captain cut in. "There are five sailors on this ship right now who wouldn't be alive if it wasn't for you and your crew. That was a fine bit of boat handling. It will be reflected in you next fitness report."

"Thank you, Sir," Warden acknowledged dolefully.

The captain's steward entered with a steaming pot of coffee, poured a round for the three officers, and departed.

"Now about the junk…you say it was transporting troops?" Royal said, holding the still wet cloth cap the ensign had salvaged from the water.

"Yes, Sir. We countered well over thirty bodies floating around our boat. Probably enough arms and legs and other pieces to make an additional ten or so."

"Were they all in uniform?" Cobb inquired.

"Yes, I think so. All except the women." Warden shrugged.

"Women?"

"Yes, there were two of them. I suppose they were camp followers."

"Possibly…more likely spies being ferried down coast to infiltrate our positions below Wonsan," Royal frowned, then picking up the khaki cap, he unfastened the metal insignia, a silver star centered on a gold circle. "This cap device indicates that the cap belonged to a North Korean officer so it's safe to assume that we intercepted KPA reinforcements, probably company strength. We're due to top off from the *Oriskany* tomorrow. I'll send the hat over to them. I'm certain the intelligence boys on Admiral Hickey's staff will find it of interest. At any rate, there's no sign of any additional junks in this area," said Royal reaching for his desk phone. He dialed the radio-shack and got Ensign Daly.

"Mike, I'd like you to get the following off in code to Jehovah via Birthrate…we have intercepted and destroyed one large motor-junk being used to ferry KPA troops and possibly infiltrators down coast. We have searched the area thoroughly and have not been able to locate any other junks reported in operational dispatch, this command, number one-eight-two-zero, Jehovah to Shiftless via Birthrate. We evaluate junks reported in subject dispatch to be engaged in troop transport rather than minelaying. We estimate their position to be somewhere in Area-Oboe…get that off right away!"

A few minutes later the messenger from the radio-shack entered with Jehovah's reply via the screen commander.

Royal read the message, then handed the paper to Cobb.

"Jehovah concurs. He's dispatching two small boys and some night fighters from one of the carriers to Area-Oboe for interception," the captain announced aloud for Ensign Warden's benefit. "We're to withdraw to a lifeguard station off Poha and remain there until oh-seven-hundred. We'll rejoin the task force a little south of there."

The two officers departed and Owen Royal returned to the bridge. It was snowing again as the destroyer wheeled around to point her nose towards Poha.

The captain reentered the wheelhouse. His watch read a quarter to four. Behind him, the bridge detail was just being relieved.

"Merry Christmas, Captain," Sternhagen, the on-coming OD offered.

"Merry Christmas, Rolf," answered Royal, his eyes peering through the port in search of some hint of sunrise though he knew it was well over an hour away. December had been a costly month for the Charlie P., he thought as he went below to check the condition of the men in sickbay. He tried not to think of the five letters he would now have to write.

Heavy swells rolled out to greet the *Field* off Poha. Pitching drunkenly, the destroyer commenced steaming in a standard box pattern calculated to keep her within her assigned patrol area until it was time to rejoin the carriers. Back on the bridge-wing, Royal was certain he could detect a weird creaking noise coming from the after portion of the ship, possibly the fantail.

The duty bo'sun, a lifeline hooked snugly to his waist, made his way gingerly over the rain-soaked deck to the stern racks. A brief but thorough investigation revealed nothing out of the ordinary, and after slipping twice, he returned to the after-deckhouse to phone in his report. Crewmen standing nearby were certain that they heard the bo'sun utter a short but colorful string of obscenities, all centered around a chief torpedoman's mate named Henderson. The creaking continued well on into Christmas day.

• • •

Christmas at the Plaza...California had nothing to match it. On that point Candace was unyielding, and her conviction was reinforced the instant she'd pushed aside the curtains to peer down at Central Park in all its winter finery. Sparkling like sugar crystals, the freshly fallen snow had transformed the park with its tree-fringed duck pond into a giant Christmas card, one created especially for her, she mused undisturbed by the dull buzz of Ham Barlow's electric razor.

It was hard to believe she'd slept till almost noon. She wished Ham would finish up in the bathroom. She was anxious to take a shower. Up in Kent, her parents and sister, Tammy, should just about be leaving services now, she thought, glancing at the clock near the bed. This was the first Christmas she hadn't spent with them. She'd let them think she was still in La Jolla rather than a relatively short distance away in Manhattan. Candace vowed to call them later, mentally noting not to make a slip about the time since there was a three-hour difference between Connecticut and out on the coast. "Out on the coast," she snickered at the phrase, telling herself that she was even beginning to talk like a Californian.

Her gaze shifted to the copy of the *Times* the bellhop had delivered a few minutes earlier. Without picking it up from the table, she began flipping the pages of the first section until her attention focused upon a small headline with the word "Korea" in it. The article went on to describe how, on Christmas morning, the army had been engaged in bloody hand-to-hand fighting near someplace with the astounding name of "Luke the Gook's Castle."

Suddenly she realized that Christmas had already come and gone in Korea. Over there it was now December 26th. Candace scanned the column to see if there was any mention of naval activity. There was none. Garrett had written that he expected to be in Japan for Christmas. At least he'd be safe there, she told herself, smiling, erasing any slight conscious qualms she might have felt about spending the holiday in bed with Ham Barlow.

Dinner at the Oak Room had been as deftly prepared and enjoyable as ever. She remembered the many evenings she had met Kevin Logan there for cocktails, and that he had slipped an engagement ring on her finger just two tables away from where they were now sitting. She wondered where Kevin was at this moment. There had been that card from Tokyo, then nothing.

"A penny," Ham muttered, eyeing Candace admiringly.

"What?"

"A penny for your thoughts. You were looking off into space. Aren't you enjoying the holiday?"

"Of course I am. It's been absolutely great. You know I always enjoy myself when I'm with you."

"Then why don't you say yes and make that a permanent condition? Now that Bettina's agreed to the divorce, there's absolutely no excuse for you to stay married to John Paul Jones."

"Don't be sarcastic, Ham. It's not becoming."

"I'll stop being sarcastic if you'll stop being so damn evasive. You know I'm only asking you to approach this thing sensibly. Take it from me, the kindest thing you could do for him right now would be to write him and tell him you want out. At least that way he'll have plenty of time to adjust to the idea. That would be a hell of a lot better than just springing it on him when he steps off that boat of his."

"Ship, Ham, a destroyer is a ship," said Candace with a teasing smile.

"There. That's exactly what I mean. You're being evasive again."

"No, I'm not. You've just got to give me a little more time. I've got to work this out for myself."

"You know, Candace, I don't really think your husband is the reason you've been putting me off."

"Why do you say that?" she asked hesitantly.

"I can't help thinking you've still got some strong feelings for Logan."

"Ham, I don't know what I can do to convince you that I haven't the slightest interest in Kevin Logan." Her tone was one of complete frustration. "Maybe you don't realize it but you manage to bring him up in every conversation we have lately. He's becoming an obsession with you and there's really no reason for it. I only saw him that one time in my office, and that's got to be at least nine months ago. I never would have mentioned it to you if I knew it was going to upset you so much."

"You're right. I'm sorry. I guess I have been getting a bit annoying. It's just that I know how close you two once were. I can't stand thinking that anyone, especially that skirt-chasing no-talent opportunist could have…"

"Known me in the biblical sense?" quipped Candace, suppressing a girlish giggle.

"If you don't mind, I think I'd like to change the subject," Ham replied dolefully as he experienced a sinking sensation in the pit of his stomach.

Nodding happily, Candace held out her cup which Barlow immediately refilled from the gleaming silver tea service. She gazed at her employer in that splendidly relaxed superior way she had, safe in the knowledge that she exercised complete control of the relationship.

•   •   •

The first thing Vincent Bacelli did upon learning they were going into Japan for a New Year's R and R was to toss a Frankie Laine recording on the phonograph.

Howie Murray's initial thoughts centered around the prospects of getting a telephone call through to Mary Alice and the girls. He'd tried the last time the ship was in Yokosuka, and then again in Pusan, but he'd gotten nowhere, being told that there was a waiting list a mile long for overseas calls. Blaming the navy's bureaucracy, and convinced that commissioned officers were being given preference, Murray vowed to pursue every angle he could think of this time even going to see the old man if need be. Right now, talking to Mary Alice and hearing her tell him about Mary Kathleen was the most important thought in his mind.

While working out a new E.T.A. to Tsugatu, the narrow band of water between Honshu and Hokkaido, Kevin Logan unexpectedly found himself thinking about Cynthia Osbourne's exquisite legs and how smooth they felt to his touch that last night they'd spent together in Tokyo. Judging by the content of her most recent letter, he felt safe in assuming that the comely Jaygee still had a first-class case of the hots for him. Hopefully, she'd be able to swing a couple of days off so they could steam up another one of those oversized beds at the Ambassador. While in Tokyo, he'd kill two birds with one stone and try contacting Okamura-san again. When he'd telephoned during the *Field's* first call in Japan, the Tozawa Heavy Industries bigwig had seemed agreeable to making the necessary arrangements. It was the least he could do, reflected Logan, remembering how lavishly he and his agency had wined and dined Okamura and his two flunkies back in New York. Always a realist, Logan knew his opportunity would soon be over and that he could only count on one or two more R and R's in Japan before the Charlie P. pointed her ugly gray nose stateside. He was determined now more than ever that he was going to make it into the pants of a four-star geisha, providing she actually wears any under all that exotic garb, he thought, smiling lustfully as he penciled in a light course line across the Sea of Japan.

Occupying the stool next to Logan was Dick Warden, C.I.C. watch officer for the noon-to-four. The afternoon was passing slowly, and with the *Field* steaming independently towards Japan the young officer anticipated a trouble-free watch. Better yet, with no drills scheduled, there was little likelihood that Cobb would be popping into the radar shack. He smiled contentedly as he decided it was safe to use some of the time to knock off a letter to Wendy Torgersen.

There was a rumor floating around the wardroom that the captain was putting him in for the Navy Commendation Medal with a combat-V. He also heard that Royal was recommending the Navy Life Saving Medal for each of the men that were with him in the boat the other night. Warden tried to imagine the look on Wendy's face when she finds out. Coming from a small town like Daleville, it was a certainty that the local newspaper would pick up the story. Hell, it might even make the bigger papers like those in Anderson and Muncie. After all, those cities weren't very far from Daleville, he reasoned.

Warden recalled the parade they'd had in forty-five for the men returning from World War II. He was only fourteen then but he still remembered the two tanks, and the army truck that was pulling the big field piece. Wendy would be all over him like a blanket, he grinned. Boy, would that draft-dodger Billy Begley burn. Coming home a hero would carry a lot more weight with Wendy then owning a Nash. Of that, he was certain, then he remembered Georgie Ritter who wouldn't be coming home at all, not even his body, and the feelings of guilt rushed back stronger than ever.

Dick Warden had never considered himself an insensitive person, yet here he was, only thinking about himself and some lousy medal. He wondered how Carol Ritter would react to the news. Just about every officer serving in the ship last year knew she was sleeping regularly with the C.O.; everyone that is except Georgie, Warden frowned, aware that his former roommate had never stopped to consider why he was always getting stuck with the in-port watch. Warden assumed Carol had quickly managed to find a replacement for Commander Carver when the navy relieved him of command and sent him off to the Great Lakes. It was a fair conclusion he told himself, vividly recalling the night she had come on to him in the parking lot behind the O-club. Always the personification of discretion, Carol had suggested they do it in the grass where there wasn't any light. He thought she was kidding at first. Now he was damn glad that he hadn't taken her up on her offer. Poor Georgie, Warden shrugged, then decided to postpone his letter writing until some time when he was in a better frame of mind.

"Say, Mister Warden," Gardiner called out from the status board which he was halfheartedly wiping down with water and detergent. "Is it true we're finally gonna' qualify for combat pay? You know, Sir, for losin' Mister Ritter and the men 'n all?" His tone was noticeably hesitant.

"I don't know, Gardiner. That's the least on my mind right now."

"Yes, Sir, I know how you feel. I don't give diddlely about the forty-five bucks, myself, I was just a little curious, that's all."

"Yeah, Mister Warden," Nugent piped up from the Sugar-George. "I don't give a damn about the dough either. I was just wondering if losing the whaleboat like that is considered the same as if the ship took a direct hit."

"Well, I really don't know. You'll just have to wait and see if the captain puts the ship in for it."

"If he doesn't, I doubt we'll ever get a bloody cent," Nugent said with an anguished look. "I'm positive those commie bastards are keeping close track of all the ships they shoot at."

"How can they do that?" blurted a puzzled Patterson.

"Simple. All they have to do is keep track of the bow numbers."

"Yeah, that's what I think, too," Bacelli cried out from the coffee mess, his voice having to compete with Frankie Laine. "The way I see it, the Reds record the bow numbers of each ship they take under fire. Then they pass the information up and down the coast to their various battery commanders. As soon as they figure out that a particular ship's been under fire for five days, the word goes out not to fire at her for the rest of the month. They do it just for spite so her crew can't collect the bonus."

"You've got to be kidding," snorted Patterson. "I've been reading the *Navy Times* and *All Hands* and they've been listing the different ships that have been coming under fire. Some of them have racked up over twenty days out of the month. Besides, how can they identify the bow numbers when they're firing at the ships at night."

"Don't try to confuse them with logic," Logan cut in, pouring himself a cup of coffee.

"Speaking of things that are logical, Mister Warden, what's your honest opinion about Henderson?" said Gardiner, smiling. "Do you really think he's haunting this bucket?"

"Yeah, what's the real scoop, Sir?" asked an eager Bacelli. "Do we have a ghost roaming around the Charlie P. or don't we?"

"Of course there's no ghost on the ship," the ensign shot back, certain that the radarmen were putting him on. "You two can't really be serious. You know damn well there's no such thing as ghosts."

"I wouldn't be too sure about that, Sir," Nugent joined in, his tone uncharacteristically humble. "I come from Canajoharie up in the Mohawk Valley. Hell, we've got ghosts up the ass up there. Redcoats, Colonials, Iroquois, Tories...you name 'em, Sir, we've got 'em. I know at least five people who'll swear that on almost any dark and rainy night, you've got a good chance of seeing old General Herkimer hopping along the Oneida trail looking for the leg he lost at Oriskany."

"Come on, Nugent, not you, too." A look of frustration crossed Warden's face. "Next you'll be telling me you believe in the headless horseman."

"I'm keeping an open mind on that one, Sir," the third-class shrugged indifferently.

In the coffee mess, the unattended phonograph played on and on as Frankie Laine intoned the many attributes of a "flower of Malaya" named Rose.

. . .

If it hadn't been for having to skirt around the fishing fleets, first South Korean, then Japanese, the *Field* might have reached Yokosuka in time for her crew to celebrate New Years' Eve ashore. Also contributing to her slow progress was a persistent beam sea that seemed to be doing its utmost to push the little ship back to the unfriendly waters she had so recently departed.

December 31st threatened to finish just as black and squally as it had begun. Kevin Logan was sure of that as he peered through the opening in the athwartships passageway, watching the gray waves climb high along the starboard side. He glanced at his watch. It was almost five after eight, the time Coates had said he'd like to see him. He wondered what the C.I.C. officer wanted, certain it couldn't be tutoring on the maneuvering board. That week in hack had made the ensign every bit as proficient a radar plotter as he was, Logan reflected as he entered the pale green domain of the *Field's* ruling class.

The area appeared deserted. The officers were either on watch or attending the evening movie, Logan reckoned. Then he noticed that the door to the captain's cabin was ajar. The room was pitch-black and obviously unoccupied. Royal was probably up in the wheelhouse making sure the ship didn't slice into a stray fishing junk, the radarman speculated, suddenly aware that this was the opportunity he'd been waiting for. It would take only a second or two to find the light switch and take a quick look, he told himself. After all, for months he'd had to listen to Gardiner and the others ramble on about what a piece the old man's wife was, and even Murray had recently commented about seeing her photograph on the captain's desk. Well, now he had a chance to find out for himself, he mumbled, reaching out to push back the door.

"Logan! Where the hell are you going? That's the captain's stateroom!" Logan turned to see Coates leaning half way out of his cabin at the far end of the passageway.

"Yes, Sir, I know that. I heard something falling to the deck when we took that last roll. I was going to snap the light on to see if there was any damage."

"Well, it was probably only a book. You'd better just let it lay. If the C.O. should walk in and find you in his cabin, he might get pissed."

"Yes, Sir, I'm sure you're right." Logan's voice trailed off as the ensign ushered him into his cabin. Pushing aside the dark green curtain that served as a door, Logan waited patiently, hat in hand, for the young officer to announce the purpose of the mysterious meeting.

"Look, Logan, I've got a favor to ask," Coates blurted out nervously.

"Yes, Sir, what can I do for you?"

"How good are you at poems?"

"Poems, Sir?"

"Yes, you know…like jingles. You must have written lots of them when you were at that advertising agency of yours."

"Well, yes, I did do some T.V. commercials, but most of my work was space ads."

"Space ads?"

"Yes, eh…written ads, you know, for magazines."

"Well, I'm sure you can handle this without any trouble. I didn't want to ask you to write this poem for me in front of Mister Warden or the other people in C.I.C. If I did, I know I'd never hear the end of it. Besides, as J-O-D on tonight's mid-watch, I'm the one who'll have to enter it in the steaming log…tonight being New Years' Eve and all."

"I'm sorry, Sir, I don't understand."

"Not being an officer or a quartermaster, I guess you wouldn't know about it," Coates said in a doleful tone. "The navy's got this old tradition that the deck log entry for the first day of a new year must be written in verse. I've got the mid-watch tonight with Mister Sternhagen, and whenever he's the O-D, he expects that his J-O-D make the log entry. Hell," he shrugged, "I never got past 'roses are red, violets are blue,' and I know the captain and the exec are both going to read the log first thing in the morning. After fouling up with that Ruskie pilot last month, I sure don't want to look like I can't even handle a little thing like a poem."

"I'll be happy to help you if I can, but doesn't the verse have to contain the same information you'd ordinarily be putting in the log…you know, like course and speed, the weather, sea state, what boilers are connected? Since you won't be going on watch for four more hours, how will I know what words you'll have to rhyme?" Logan looked doubtful.

"Well, can you write something with blanks that I can fill in? Once you get it started, I'm sure I'll be able to finish it."

"Okay, if you don't mind using something right off the top of my head," Logan reached for the small yellow pad he'd spotted on the ensign's bunk. "Let's try this on for size," he mumbled, hurriedly scribbling on the paper. "How's this sound?" He handed the paper to Coates who began to read aloud.

"Steaming along towards the coast of Japan, liberty is foremost in the mind of each man. On course blank-blank-blank and with a blank-blank knot speed, the Charlie P. strutted like a haughty gray steed. Numbers one and two boilers on line and the sea at scale four, our tin can rolls on towards Honshu's back door. Hey, that's terrific," Coates smiled happily. "Only one problem…what happens, if for instance, the sea disturbance isn't registering four. It's pretty rough out there. It's probably more like a six."

"Six? No sweat, just change the line to something like…we're R and R-bound after getting in our licks."

"You're really sharp. That ad agency of yours must hold you in high regard, being able to come up with stuff like that on a seconds notice."

"Mister Coates, if I ever came up with stuff like that back at the agency, I'd be out on my keyster on a seconds notice."

Departing officers country, Logan decided to take another try at the captain's cabin. The idea was abandoned the instant he noticed the blade of light seeping out from under the C.O.'s door.

.   .   .

It seemed as if the navy wanted to hide the *Field* away in the most remote corner of the sprawling shipyard complex. Assigned to Berth 3 way over in Yokosuka Cove, she had nothing for company but a motley collection of crewless *Tacoma* class frigates nested side-by-side out in the stream in long rusty rows. Loaned to the Soviet Navy in 1945 as part of the deal to secure Russian participation in the planned invasion of Japan, the blocky little one-stackers had been stagnating in the sooty harbor since 1949, the year they had been returned to the U.S. Navy in near derelict condition. By degrees, each of the escort vessels would be refurbished and, except for a few slated for South Korea, Thailand and Latin America, the bulk would form the nucleus of a reborn Imperial Navy now functioning under the less imposing name of Japanese Maritime Self-Defense Force.

Like *DD-505*, the *Oriskany* had had her Christmas R and R pushed back a week so she could keep a more pressing engagement with the North Koreans, but unlike Logan's destroyer, the Big-O had managed to reach Yokosuka in time to celebrate the New Year's holiday.

This was the first opportunity Logan had ever had to visit a carrier and view her combat-information-center. Having only destroyers and a few reserve DEs to use as a yardstick, his inspection of the ship's myriad of electronics and communications equipment proved a mind-boggling experience.

The train ride to Tokyo that evening seemed much longer than Kevin had remembered it being. Lieutenant Jg. Osbourne sat several seats away, and although she was not in uniform, both she and Logan were careful to avoid making eye-contact, or giving any other indication that they shared even the slightest acquaintance.

Such was not the case when the young nurse and the radarman finally reached the Ambassador Hotel and the room they had reserved for the next two days. Hardly had Cynthia removed her coat then she found herself sprawling with obscene abandon across the enormous bed, letting Kevin undress her in what she thought must be record time even for a sailor. She knew she'd made it easier for him this time, not wearing a girdle, but she wished he had allowed her just a few seconds more to slip out of her sweater as her hair and an earring snagged in the warm woolen jersey. Suddenly the sharp pain gave way to a feeling of complete excitement as every cell in her body became fired up. Then she stopped thinking about earrings, the Guinness Book of Records, or anything else except how much she loved Kevin.

"Beautiful, isn't it?" Cynthia asked, squeezing Kevin's hand as they made their way along the winding path in Tokyo's 300-year-old Shibarikyu Garden. "Did you ever see anything as intriguing as those pine trees? How do you suppose they manage to grow them in such odd shapes?" she asked, her face bright and happy.

"Beats the hell out of me," answered Logan dully, wishing that the afternoon would end so he could get her back to the Ambassador. Cynthia was really turning him on, he thought, sensing the dewy-eyed look of an innocent whenever she glanced in his direction. He wondered if it was that look that aroused him so much. Perhaps he was turning into a dirty old man at twenty-nine, he shrugged, then slipped his hand around her waist before moving it down to rest firmly upon her now girdleless bottom.

A mild breeze mixed with the wintery spice of chimney smoke greeted them as they left the park. Cynthia was suddenly very quiet and Kevin sensed that she wanted to say something. He hoped she wasn't going to bring up the subject of marriage or how much fun they were going to have together in New York. He was relieved when she started to ask him about Korea.

"I really worried quite a bit about you, you know," she said. "We heard at the hospital that your ship was in a lot of combat and had knocked out several enemy guns and other shore targets. Then last week, Commander Zandt from base operations was at our Christmas party. I told him that I knew someone serving aboard the *Field*. I guess he assumed it was an officer. Anyway, he mentioned that they'd just gotten word that the *Field* had taken several casualties on Christmas Eve. From what they told me at the hospital, I guess I must have taken the news rather badly, especially for a nurse who's supposed to be hardened and unaffected by death and things like that." She sighed and looked uncomfortable. "Anyway, by the time they'd gotten me calmed down, Commander Zandt had come back with a list of the men your ship had lost. He'd put a call through to Com-Nav-Fe in Tokyo. You can't imagine how relieved I felt when he showed me the list of names and yours wasn't among them. Were any of those men close friends?"

"No, not really," he answered in a flat tone, remembering his sharp dislike for Ashton Bites.

"Do you think you'll be seeing much action when your ship gets back to Korea?"

"It's hard to say. So far they've kept us away from the really hot spots like Wonsan and Hungnam." He pulled her in close to him. "Who knows," he said smiling, "maybe our luck will hold and we'll pull some more lifeguard assignments. They might even send us back to the Formosa Strait."

"Did you manage to get ashore at all in Korea?"

"Yes, we were in Pusan for a few days getting our steering engine repaired."

She smiled primly. "Did you get to meet any Korean girls?"

"No, I didn't find any that I considered interesting."

"What would you have done if you had? Would you have made love to them?"

"Probably."

Cynthia sensed he was teasing. "I know you're only trying to see if you can get me jealous. You can't. See," she said smiling. "You know, I went up to Kamakura one weekend with a marine lieutenant."

"That's nice. I hope you had a good time," he said calmly.

"You mean you approve?"

"It's not for me to approve or disapprove. I thought we agreed to that back in San Diego."

Cynthia glanced at him irritably. "Damn it, Kevin! Don't you care for me at all?" her voice flared angrily as she pushed his hand away from her buttocks.

"Of course I do. It's just that I don't have any ties on you. You're perfectly free to do anything you care to. It's not as if we were married."

"Well, for your information nothing happened with the marine!…nothing at all! Now Terry, my roommate, won't even speak to me. She hasn't for three weeks now. It's like sharing a room with a bloody zombie!"

"Your roommate won't speak to you because nothing happened between you and some gyrene lieutenant? Excuse me if I seem a bit confused…" Kevin couldn't contain his laughter which infuriated the nurse even more.

"I'm sorry I even brought it up," she said curtly. "Anyway, forget about it. It's too complicated to explain. Besides, I was only trying to make a point. Now if you don't mind, I'd like to change the subject."

"Okay," he said, a broad grin still etched on his face. "What would you like to do this evening?"

"I thought it might be nice if we could go to the Kabuki theater."

"Isn't that one of those deals where all the woman's roles are played by men?" Logan frowned noticeably.

"Yes, that's an important part of the Kabuki tradition. It's hundreds of years old."

"Frankly, I don't think I'd enjoy looking at a bunch of Japs in drag. Can't we go see something else? I understand there's a Japanese equivalent of the Rockettes. They're called the Takarazuka girls. Couldn't we try to get tickets to see them perform?"

"Perform? Don't you mean kick their legs up in the air?"

"Okay, we'll skip the Takarazuka girls."

"No, if that's really what you want to do, it's alright. That's where we'll go."

"You sure you don't mind?"

"No, I don't mind…really."

"Great. Let me call up the hotel and find out where they're playing. You're sure now?"

"Yes, I think it should be fun," she said with a forced smile, trying to conceal her disappointment.

Logan lost little time in finding a telephone.

•   •   •

Logan hooked the steel clip that served as a belt buckle, squared his cap, and officially relieved Puchalski as petty-officer-of-the-watch for the eight to noon. It was cold on the open quarterdeck and Coates, the OD, had wished he'd remembered to bring his gloves as he flipped open the deck log to review the morning orders and scheduled events. A few feet away, messenger-of-the-watch Dietz shivered and fidgeted with his flat hat, worrying that the gold U.S. NAVY emblazoned on the cap ribbon might be a little off center. A newly activated reservist, Dietz had been requisitioned from the personnel pool at Yokosuka as a replacement for the luckless Sweetpea Hopkins.

The reality that five days of R and R could have come and gone so quickly seemed incredible to Logan. His hands tucked well inside the slash pockets of his peajacket, he peered off in the direction of the hospital and wondered if Lieutenant Osbourne also had the morning watch. He envisioned her all prim and proper in a snug fitting uniform like the one she'd first turned him on with back in San Diego. She was probably wearing those glasses, too, thought Kevin, remembering how authoritive they looked perched on that small upturned nose. He assumed she was still playing the role of dedicated martinet, and he wondered if anyone else was aware of her true personality…her vulnerability. But what if she was playing games, he thought, considering for the first time that she might also be putting out for one of the doctors or some navy brass at the base. After due deliberation, Logan dismissed the notion with a snicker, smugly confident that Cindy would keep a tight lock on it until the next time he came sailing into Yokosuka for his R and R.

Ensign Coates finished a perfunctory review of the notations in the log book. Satisfied that none of them called for anything beyond his capabilities, he turned to Logan and said, "I haven't had a chance to thank you for your help the other night."

"That's okay, Sir. How'd you make out?"

"Great. I had no trouble at all with the poem. In fact, I was really surprised when the exec complemented me on what he called my literary bent."

Logan tried to keep from grinning, aware that the word bent could also be defined as meaning crooked. "I'm glad things worked out so well for you, Sir."

"Yes, I owe you one," Coates smiled, then asked, "what happened to Holiday? Did somebody hit him in the nose?"

"I don't know, Sir. I do know that he, Gardiner and Bacelli came barreling into the compartment about three this morning. They sounded like they had cornered the market on every bottle of sake in Japan. The lights were out so I didn't really see them. I told them to stop the racket they were making, then I rolled over and went back to sleep. I was pretty tired from my trip to Tokyo. I sure didn't get much sleep up there."

"Busy seeing the sights, heh?"

"Yes, I guess you could say that," answered Logan with a Leer.

"Well, the way Holiday was holding his hand over his nose and pounding on the door of sickbay a little while ago, something must have happened to him."

"Did you ask him?" queried the radarman.

"No, I didn't have the chance to. The second he saw me, he took off down the passageway. It was obvious that he wasn't in the mood for conversation," the ensign frowned. "Well, let's not worry about Holiday now. We've got a liberty party leaving in twenty minutes, and at ten, Commander Edwards from the base will be coming aboard to see McAlleney."

"McAlleney? McAlleney's only a seaman-deuce. Why would a three-striper be coming over so see him?" Logan puzzled aloud.

"Commander Edwards is a Protestant chaplain. I understand he's a Baptist like McAlleney."

"I still don't understand why he'd be seeing McAlleney. I'm sure we must have a lot of Baptists in the crew besides McAlleney, especially with all the Johnny Rebs on this bucket."

"Haven't you seen McAlleney the last couple of days?"

"No, Sir, remember...I've been up in Tokyo."

"Yes, well McAlleney's been walking around the ship in a virtual trance. He hasn't been able to do any work. He hardly eats, and Lieutenant MacKinlay told me he didn't even bother to pick up his liberty card."

"That sure doesn't sound like McAlleney," Logan shrugged. "I know that he and Bites were buddies, but I didn't think he had taken it that hard. It was only a day or so after we lost Bites that I heard him cracking a joke about what lengths Bites would go to to avoid paying up on a five-dollar bet."

"Oh, it's got nothing to do with Bites. It's because of Hank Williams," Coates replied matter-of-factly.

"Hank Williams?"

"Yes, didn't you hear about it? He died on New Year's Day. Half the ship's been in mourning. You'd think they'd lost their parents or wives. Even so, none of them have taken it anywhere near as badly as McAlleney. He's almost catatonic. It was the captain who arranged for Commander Edwards to come over. He thought it might save him from having to call the hospital for one of their psychologists."

By nine-fifteen, the last sailor in the liberty section had cleared the quarterdeck and headed for Carney Gate.

"I certainly hope we don't have the trouble Mister Kimmick had yesterday morning during his watch," Coates said grumpily.

"What was that, Sir?"

"Just about every man he cleared for liberty was sent back to the ship by the marines at the base gate. They said the men were improperly dressed. Most of them were wearing a pressed neckerchief, and the marines decided to enforce that old regulation that specifies that neckerchiefs have to be rolled."

"Nobody ever wears a rolled neckerchief anymore, except maybe during formal inspections," Logan replied angrily. "Those jarheads at the gate just wanted to show what ball-busters they could be."

"Exactly. When the captain heard about it he called marine headquarters over on the base and got a hold of the officer in charge of the guard detail. After giving him a royal blast, excuse the pun," Coates smiled, "he informed the marine captain that the ship had just returned from a combat assignment where she had taken casualties while intercepting North Korean ground reinforcements which could very well have been used against the First Marine Division. I understand that the marines that pulled that stunt yesterday morning are still standing guard duty as a reminder that they hadn't been posted there to play games."

"Mister Coates! Can I ask you a favor? It's an emergency," Holiday wailed breathlessly, suddenly appearing on the quarterdeck in dress blues.

"What are you all dressed up for? You're in today's duty section, and what are you holding your hand in front of your nose for? Is that supposed to be some new kind of a salute?" snapped a nettled Coates.

"It's my nose, Sir. Something happened to my nose last night and I have to go over to the base exchange and buy a few boxes of Band-Aids. I tried to get some from sickbay but it was secured, and all the corpsmen seem to be on the beach."

"That's no problem. If all you need is a couple of Band-Aides, I can let you have them as soon as I get off watch. I'm sure I have one or two in my desk drawer."

"Thank you, Sir, but with the ship heading back to Korea tomorrow morning, I don't think two Band-Aids will last me very long."

"Take your hand away from your nose and let me see the damage," the O.D. instructed briskly. "Even if the cut is deep, it will heal quickly if you wash it properly and use a strong disinfectant."

"It's not a cut, Sir…I wish it was…it's…it's a fly," the third-class answered in a half whisper as he moved his hand slowly away from his nose.

The statement did little to prepare Coates, Logan and Dietz for what they were about to see. Perched atop the fleshy tip of the radarman's nose was a full-scale replica of *Muscat domestica*, otherwise known as the common housefly.

Coates looked at him sharply. "What the hell did you do that for? Are you crazy…getting a fly tattooed on the end of your nose?"

"It really wasn't my fault. I was drinking and I guess I must have had a little too much saki. One thing I know, I'll never try mixing it with beer again," Holiday put his hand back over his nose.

"You mixed saki with beer?"

"Yes, Sir. I think they call it a kamikaze."

"I can understand why. Anyway, it doesn't take a genius to figure out what happened," the ensign said shaking his head in astonishment as Logan laughed robustly and Dietz stood by staring in total disbelief.

"I suppose Gardiner, Nugent and Bacelli talked you into this. What did they do, dare you, or did you lose a bet?" asked Coates who was about to dissolve in a helpless fit of mirth, himself.

"They dared me, Sir, only Nugent wasn't along. He had the duty. I'm pretty sure he was in on it, though," the sailor mumbled angrily.

"Alright, Holiday," Coates said smiling. "Get your peacoat. You can go over to the exchange and get your Band-Aids, but you'd better be back within half-an-hour. Remember, you've got to relieve Logan here in time for chow."

"Yes, Sir, thank you, Sir." Holiday moved his left hand up to his nose so he could salute with his right, then disappeared into the athwartships passageway.

The ensign glanced at his watch, Logan continued to laugh, and young Dietz began to wonder just what kind of floating madhouse the navy had banished him to.

• • •

Major Mychenko's ample hulk put the small wooden stool to the test. Each time he leaned forward to peer out the window at the falling snow, the stool squeaked like a small animal that was being stepped on.

Mychenko was content in spite of the snow. He knew that most of the work was ahead of schedule and that he would certainly be out of Maksan by early April when the guns and radars were all in operation. Happily, he wouldn't have to stay around while the submarine pens were being constructed. That was to be the responsibility of a senior naval engineer who would be arriving from Vladivostok in less than two weeks.

Mychenko resumed his favorite pastime of late, speculating about what his next assignment might be. Perhaps Bulgaria, he thought. He had never been there but he'd been told that Bulgarian women were relentless in bed. His chubby face twisted in lively anticipation.

Then again, why must his next assignment be restricted to a socialist country? Why couldn't he be sent to a capitalist country?…maybe even the United States, he reasoned, certain that he had all the qualifications to serve as military advisor on the embassy staff in Washington. After all, he spoke very acceptable English. He smiled as he remembered reading someplace that in Washington, women outnumbered men by at least three to one. American women, skinny as they were, should appreciate a vigorous man such as himself, he beamed as he lit a fat black cigar.

The major leaned back on the stool and listened to the dull hum of carrier planes passing high overhead. The Pukchong marshalling yards, he decided almost indifferently, and took a long hard puff on the cigar.

Chapter XIX - Close Call

The Year of the Dragon would soon give way to the Year of the Snake though no one aboard the *Field* was likely to take any notice. Of far more concern was the weather this bitter cold January as an impartial Mother Nature assailed the task force with continuous sub-zero temperatures, razor-sharp williwaws, and tons of ice that caked itself around guns and superstructures, creating bizarre sculptures that would rival any seen on the Murmansk run during World War II.

Back less than a week now, the *Field* had already been busily engaged carrying out a series of fire missions directed against rail trackage and trestles in the Susong area. Collaborating in the endeavor were destroyers *Kidd* and *Colohan*, which like *DD-505*, drew heavy return fire from North Korean shore batteries. Fortunately, the C.O.'s of all three vessels managed to outguess the communist gun layers except in one instance when the *Field* was showered with shrapnel from an air burst. Miraculously, none of the deadly metal fragments managed to hit any of the many exposed topside personnel manning the numerous open gun mounts and directors.

Now enjoying a few days respite from the enemy's coastal guns, the *Field* was back in the carrier screen climbing up and over dark gray mountains of water as she moved north with Task Force 77 to attack industrial targets above the 42nd parallel.

Lieutenant Stockwell scratched the back of his head as he stared at the surface-status board dimly visible in the faint light that reflected up from the plotting table. "I see we're operating without any carriers in the task force this morning, heh, Mister Coates?" he grunted priggishly.

"We've got three carriers today, Sir, as usual," the junior officer answered in a puzzled tone, not perceiving the barbed nature of his department head's remark.

"If that's the case, then why aren't they listed up there? If Mister Cobb walks in and sees that status-board, every one in here will be fried alive and you'll find yourself back in hack for another week," Stockwell advised.

"Hey, Gardiner! Get your ass out of that coffee mess and get that status-board up to date," Murray barked from his stool by the DRT. "I told you about that over an hour ago. You don't even have the *Missouri* up there, and Jocko Clark's riding her today as Sopa!"

"Okay, okay," Gardiner mumbled as he emerged clutching a vat-like mug of steaming black coffee. "What birdfarms we got running with us today, Nugey?"

"The 'Queer Barge,' 'Risky Whore,' and 'Happy Valley'," Nugent said, without lifting his gaze from the surface scope.

"The what?" gasped Stockwell.

"*Kearsarge, Oriskany* and *Valley Forge,* Sir," Nugent replied in a calm patronizing tone.

"Okay, Gardiner, put the coffee down and get those names up there right away, and be sure to list their call names while you're at it!" instructed the lieutenant.

"Yes, Sir, that's Trust Fund, Childplay and Cherry Tree," replied Gardiner, scribbling the call names on the Plexiglas with a yellow grease pencil. "You didn't ask about the *Missouri.* Her call name's Battleaxe."

"I thought you were told about memorizing call names? Wasn't that the reason you were given a captain's mast?"

"Negative, Sir. That was for memorizing signals from the General Signal Book," Gardiner answered with a hint of impudence which the Ops officer chose to ignore.

"There's another thing I want to say while I'm down here, and this seems the best time to do it, since Holiday's not around." The lieutenant pulled himself up to his full six-foot-two height. "Now, I'm only directing this to you and Nugent over there," Stockwell said looking straight at Gardiner. "That was a real dumb trick you two pulled, getting Holiday drunk and daring him to have a fly tattooed on his nose, especially when you know he plans to get married this summer."

"I don't know why you're blaming me, Sir," Nugent said in a tone of righteous indignation. "I wasn't even there. I was in the duty section that night. It was Gardiner here and Bacelli who went on liberty with him."

"Don't try to give me a snow job, Nugent. It's all over the ship that you cooked up the idea, and I also heard that you didn't waste any time claiming credit for it. As far as Bacelli's concerned, don't worry, he's not squirming off the hook either. All three of you can forget about taking that test for second-class in April. I just came from ship's office where I had your names taken off the exam list."

"That doesn't seem at all fair, Sir," Gardiner whined. "It was only a joke."

"Some joke," said Ensign Coates. "Don't you know the only way Holiday will be able to have that thing taken off his nose is by a skin graft? And that's pretty painful. Of course, he's got an alternative. He can always go through life wearing a Band-Aid," the C.I.C. officer added scornfully as Lieutenant Stockwell departed the radar shack. Then turning to the *Field's* senior radarman, Coates said, "Now to change the subject to something pleasant, I've been meaning to ask you, Murray, did you ever manage to get a call through to your wife last week?"

"Yes, Sir. Thanks to the old man...I mean Captain Royal. He was really great. He told me that he was going over to call his wife. He'd made arrangements for his call the last time we were in Yokosuka. He asked me if I'd like to come along with him. He was sure that he could fix things up for me since Mary Alice had just given birth."

"Did he have any trouble?"

"No, not really. He spoke to a couple of C.P.O.'s and some woman from the U.S.O. or Red Cross, I'm not sure which. Anyway, the next thing I know, I was standing there hearing Mary Alice's voice. Then I got to speak to my daughters...not Mary Kathleen, of course," the first-class laughed. "Mary Alice held her up to the phone and tried to get her to cry or make some kind of noise but I guess the baby wasn't in a cooperative mood. Anyway, being a short-timer, I'll be home soon and Mary Kathleen will probably be crying her head off twenty-four hours a day. I won't mind, though. It will be music to my ears," Murray said with a broad smile.

"Well, I'm glad you were successful," the ensign said. "How was the connection to Ohio?"

"Fine. I could hear Mary Alice and my girls just as clearly as if they were standing a foot away. I guess we really owe a lot to Don Ameche," he quipped, still smiling.

"How much did they charge you for the call?"

"I really don't know, Sir. Actually, that's something I wanted to talk to you or Mister Stockwell about."

"Why us?" the young officer looked totally puzzled.

"Well, I thought since you're an officer and you get to talk to the captain a lot, you might be able to find out how much he had to pay for my call."

"The captain paid for your call?"

"Yes. He insisted. I argued with him as much as I could, but he just laughed and said he was happy to do it. Anyway, I thought if you or Mister Stockwell could discreetly find out, maybe I could figure out a way to get the money back to him."

"Personally, Murray, I think you should just forget about it. I'm sure the captain enjoyed doing it for you. If you give him the money back, it's liable to hurt his feelings."

"Well, if you really think so," Murray shrugged. "You know, what I really feel bad about is that after the captain went to all that trouble to see that I got my call, he didn't get to talk to his own wife."

"How come?"

"They put the call through for him, but she wasn't in California. She'd gone to New York without telling her secretary where she could be reached."

"That's too bad," Coates frowned. "I remember that night back in San Diego when Mrs. Royal visited the ship. I had the quarterdeck watch. She certainly is an attractive woman."

"You can say that again," mumbled Gardiner from the surface-status board.

"What did you say?" Coates inquired irritably.

"Oh, I was just agreeing with you, Sir." Then looking over at Murray, Gardiner asked, "Has the captain changed your mind about the navy yet?"

"Not in the least. I thought from day-one that the captain was a good guy...a real gentleman. That's got nothing to do with my opinion of the navy."

"How can you say that?" Nugent called out from the Sugar-George. "If the navy's the great blue monster you say it is, then the captain couldn't be in it for all those years without turning into a monster himself. Look at Mister Cobb. He's been a civilian for most of his life and look what a monster he turned out to be."

"I'll make believe I didn't hear that last remark, Nugent!" Coates inserted with feigned annoyance.

Murray spun around on his stool to face in the direction of the surface scope. "All I know is the navy pulled a fast one on me when they tricked me into signing up for the inactive reserve. If I hadn't, I'd be home with my wife and kids right now instead of sitting here having to explain things to a meat-head like you."

"Come on, Murray. You know that nobody twisted your arm," Nugent retorted. "With all the combat you told us you had on those two flattops, you should have earned enough points to get out the second you hit the States."

"I wasn't the only one with a lot of points when the war ended, you know. Just about everybody at the receiving station that September had seen a heap of action. Some of them had been out there in the Pacific since before Midway."

"Well, you gambled that there wouldn't be another war and I guess you lost," Nugent said smugly.

"Maybe...but there's no way anybody's going to get me to trust the navy again. Hell! I'm still waiting for those steak and eggs they used to promise us at reveille. The navy couldn't even keep its word when it came to a little thing like that."

"What's the big deal about having steak and eggs for breakfast?" Gardiner asked. "Hell, you're always bringing that up. If you really want steak and eggs so bad, why don't you go over to the petty officers' club and order yourself up a batch next time we go into Yokosuka?"

Murray's jaw fell and he said, "You haven't understood one damn thing I've said, have you?"

"What's to understand about having steak and eggs unless maybe it's whether you want them fried or scrambled?" Gardiner replied with a blank expression.

"Fried or scrambled!" Murray's voice rose in total frustration. "Who cares if the eggs are fried or scrambled! You missed my point completely. Don't you see, the steak and eggs are only a symbol. They remind me of the days when I had complete faith and trust in the navy. The navy could do no wrong as far as I was concerned. Next to my religion and Mary Alice, it was the most important thing in my life," he said softly.

Nugent drummed his fingers on the glossy surface of the Sugar-George and asked with a sly smile, "If you loved the navy so much, how come you didn't just forget about the steak and eggs? You really didn't think the master-at-arms on your flattop was really serious, did you? Hell, even old Pheifer uses that steak and eggs routine to get us out of our racks every once and a while."

"You're just as dense as your buddy Gardiner here," Murray shrugged. "Can't you guys understand. It was never the steak and eggs. It's what they represent. I never thought anything about it until after the navy tricked me, and called me back to active duty."

Suddenly Ensign Coates gave a grunt that could only signify displeasure. "Somebody told me that you people were supposed to be standing a watch in here. I guess I was misinformed. Now knock off all this idle gab and get your minds back on your jobs."

Hardly had the ensign uttered his rebuke when a signal blared out of the TBS speaker sending the ships wheeling around to a new heading. As soon as the task force had steadied into the wind, the carriers, their flightdecks still dappled with great patches of snow, commenced hurling aircraft into the sky — their target, the recently repaired hydroelectric installations just south of the Yalu.

Swiveling slowly around on his stool, Andy Phelan, C.I.C. watch officer for the noon to four, took precise note of each new contact the instant Belton marked its position on the vertical air plot.

"Are you sure those contacts are all squawking friendly?" the Jaygee asked Holiday, who was hunched over the Sugar-Charlie.

"That's affirmative, Sir."

"Well, keep a sharp eye out for any tricks. There's nothing the Reds would like better than to slip a couple of Migs in with our returning aircraft."

"No sweat, Sir. They're all squawking Code-three."

"Think we lost many today?" asked Logan sitting at the master radar-console next to the C.I.C. watch officer.

"Probably. I hear the flak up near the Yalu's so thick, a pilot can step out of his plane and walk on it," Phelan said morosely. "Bacelli," he suddenly called out to the third-class on the SG, "what's your range to the guide?"

"Battleaxe bears two-two-zero, twenty-one hundred yards," came a quick reply.

"Very well. We'll be heading back into the wind any minute now. Let me know if the range to the *Missouri* opens or closes even the slightest." Turning back towards Logan, he said, "I certainly don't envy those airedales, having to set down on those pitching flightdecks in this kind of a sea."

"I know what you mean. I was watching the carriers from the signal bridge just before I came on watch. Big as they are, they're rolling every bit as much as we are. I watched one wave break up over the forward part of the *Valley Forge's* flightdeck. I'd be surprised if anybody was happy on the 'Happy Valley' today," Kevin grinned. "To make matters worse, that storm front we passed through an hour ago has probably dropped at least another three or four inches of fresh snow on those flightdecks. Can you imagine how those jets are going to come skidding in when they hit that wet wood," he shook his head. "I visited an old buddy on the *Oriskany* when we were in Yokosuka. He said they've been taking quite a few casualties from flightdeck accidents."

Then glancing back at the C.I.C. watch officer, Logan said with a smile, "Too bad my buddy hasn't been able to bring the 'Big-O' better luck. He was a plank owner on the second *Yorktown*...served on her right through V-J Day. I remember how back in Bridgeport he was always yapping about how lucky she was, and I guess he was right," Logan shrugged. "While all the other carriers out there were being clobbered almost on a daily basis, she got through the whole thing taking only a single bomb hit. I think he said it wiped out a gun tub. Funny thing though, he was really convinced that the only reason she made out so well was because of a red stripe painted right down the middle of her flightdeck. She was the only carrier in the Pacific marked that way, and he always said that the red stripe was the *Yorktown's* good luck charm."

"It wasn't very lucky for the guys in that gun tub," Holiday pondered aloud.

"Why doesn't your buddy paint a red stripe down the middle of the *Oriskany's* flightdeck?" snickered Bacelli, shifting in his chair.

Without responding, Logan turned towards Phelan. "Has Mister Ritter's replacement had much experience with the Mark-37?"

"Only what he got earlier this week when we were chewing up those railroad trestles at Susong," the Jaygee answered with a smile. "Ensign Keagan's only been out of O-C-S four or five months, but he did complete the fire-control course at Newport so he shouldn't have much trouble catching on. Speaking of the Mark-37, did I hear something about you being a former fire-controlman?" the watch officer asked.

"Yes, Sir. That was my rate during the war. I literally lived inside a Mark-37 when I was on the *Laffey*. We were at G-Q right around the clock at Iwo and Okinawa, to say nothing of the time we spent covering the Mindoro and Luzon landings."

"Are the enlisted replacements all reserves too?" Bacelli called back from the surface scope.

"I think so...all except the bo'sun who replaced Bites," Phelan answered. "He's already put in one Korean tour on the *Leyte*."

"Another flattop jockey," Holiday mumbled. "I wonder if he'll be in here grubbing all our coffee like old Bites used to do."

"Think they buried Sweetpea yet, Sir?" Belton asked sheepishly.

"You mean young Hopkins?"

"He ain't gonna' get any older," Bacelli said in a half whisper.

Phelan ignored the radarman's insensitivity and said, "I imagine his family has held the funeral by now. The captain saw to it that the body was transferred to a transport plane at Atsugi the morning we reached Yokosuka."

"Yeah, they carted Sweetpea off this bucket the same time they were carrying the mail aboard. Guess which got the most attention," Bacelli chuckled.

"Well, I know I'm happy Sweetpea made it home," Belton spoke up, "especially since I have to relieve Paulsen down on the mess deck in three more days. I certainly wouldn't feature having to climb over a body bag every time Turk sent me into the reefer to get a sack of spuds."

"How did you like the *Oriskany?*" Phelan asked, turning again towards Logan. "Did you get a chance to see much of the ship during your visit?"

"Yes, Sir. My buddy gave me the royal tour. She sure is big. Being accustomed to the tin can navy, I'm not certain I'd be able to get use to having all that space to walk around in. Until last week I never took Murray seriously when he'd tell me how, during his flattop days, it took him over a week just to figure out the shortest route between C.I.C. and his berthing compartment."

"Was the *Oriskany* carrying many planes?"

"Yes, she'd just about replaced all her lost or damaged birds by the time I came aboard." Logan hesitated for several seconds. "Remember those Migs that tangled with Task Force Seventy-Seven back in November?"

"Yes," answered Phelan.

"Well, I got to see the two Panthers that shot them down. While I was up on the flightdeck, I also managed to see the special elevator they use for their atomic bombs."

"Atomic bombs?" Bacelli yelled out as all heads turned towards Logan.

"Yes, she's got a slew of them aboard. They keep the bombs in a special magazine and refer to them only as special weapons."

"Come on, Logan," Holiday said, screwing up his nose and causing the already loose Band-Aid to slip off on to his shirt. "You've got to be pulling our jocks. You are, aren't you?" he quizzed nervously, the art work on his nose gleaming purple in the reflected light from the radar sweep.

Bacelli ran his tongue over his lips. "Logan's kidding about the *Oriskany* having A-bombs on board, isn't he, Mister Phelan?"

"No, I'm sure he isn't," the Jaygee murmured candidly. "The *Kearsarge* is probably carrying them too, since she's received the same modifications as the *Oriskany*. Of course, you all realize that none of this is for public consumption. Be sure to remember that when you're writing letters home."

"Sir, you mean that right now, right this very second, we're only fifteen hundred yards away from two ships loaded with atom bombs?" said Bacelli, suddenly clutching the Mickey Spillane paperback in his pocket as if it was the last thing he would ever possess on God's good earth.

"How big are those A-bombs?" Belton interrupted excitedly.

"Beats the hell out of me," Logan grinned.

"Didn't you get to see them?" asked Holiday.

"Of course not. The guy I was visiting has been on the ship for almost a year now and he's never seen one, and his berthing compartment's less than a hundred feet from where they're stored. I did get to see the passageway leading to the magazine, though. They had more jarheads posted down there than you'll find at Carney Gate on a Saturday night."

"I guess they've got special planes set aside just for lugging those A-bombs, heh?" asked Belton.

"No, from what they told me, they don't use any of their own aircraft. Every two weeks or so, a couple of A-J Savages fly out to the task force and land on board. They only stay overnight, but that gives the *Oriskany's* special-weapons people a chance to practice loading and handling the bombs." Logan drained his coffee and put the empty cup atop the glass cover over the DRT motor. "During the time the A-Js are on the flightdeck, the only people that can go anywhere near them are the special-weapons gang. They take turns parking each of the planes over the special bomb elevator. According to my buddy, they rig a canvas drop-cloth down both sides of the fuselage. That way, nobody but the special-weapons crew and the *Oriskany's* brass will know whether or not the planes will be taking off empty or with the eggs that are going to start World War Three."

"What's an A-J look like?" Holiday asked.

"They're twin-engine prop jobs," Phelan spoke up glibly. "They're quite large for carrier operations...even bigger than the Mitchell bombers the *Hornet* carried on Doolittle's Tokyo raid. But that's enough about A-bombs and A-Js. Remember what I said a few minutes ago about not mentioning this sort of thing in your letters," the Jaygee cautioned in a sharp tone of voice.

"What letters?" Holiday grunted. "They've been keeping us so busy lately with dawn and dusk alerts, and air-defense drills, we never get a chance to write any letters. Every time I start one to Toby, they sound G-Q or some other damn drill. Then the next thing I know, I'm back on watch in C.I.C."

"Yeah...dirty Band-Aid and all," said Bacelli with a smirk.

"I don't recall anyone asking for comments from the peanut gallery, so why don't you just keep your damn mouth shut!" Holiday growled.

"Knock it off you two!" Phelan instructed. "Get your eyes back on those scopes and keep your personal quarrels out of C.I.C. or you'll both be on report!"

"Yes, Sir," said Bacelli languidly, poking his head back towards the Sugar-George. "Sir, can I ask you just one question?" the third-class called back with sudden enthusiasm.

"Only if it pertains to C.I.C. business."

"Well, it does pertain to our operations."

"Okay, Bacelli. Ask your question, but don't drag it out like you usually do."

"Yes, Sir. Is there anything to the rumor that we're going back to the Formosa Strait in a few days, and that we might pull some liberty in Hong Kong?"

"That's the first I've heard anything about it."

"Really, Sir? That's been the scuttlebutt since we left Yokosuka. Afterall, the *Wayne*, *Ward* and *Morgan* managed to spend Christmas week in Hong Kong."

"Yes, and we spent most of the New Year's week in Japan, so what are you complaining about?" Phelan asked a bit irritably.

"I wish to hell I'd never spent it in Japan," Holiday cut in as he put his finger to the tip of his nose. Hey! What happened to my Band-Aid?"

"Last time I saw it," Logan said grinning, "it was dangling off your shirt pocket."

"Well, it's not there now."

"Here it is," Belton said, stooping to pick the small whiteish strip from the rubber deck matting.

Phelan looked startled. "You're not putting that thing back on your nose after its been on the deck, are you?"

"Why not? It's still clean," Holiday retorted, vainly trying to get the Band-Aid to stick to his nose.

"Come on, Holiday, give us a break and put a fresh one on," Logan prompted. "That Band-Aid you've been wearing looks like it's just about ready to get up and walk away."

"I don't have an endless supply of these things, you know," the radarman grunted sourly. "Who knows how long it's going to be before I can get ashore again and restock? I bought the last two boxes they had on the shelf in the P-X."

"Can't you get any from sick bay?" Phelan asked.

"No! Every time I ask those damn pill-pushers, they say they're only allowed to give out Band-Aids for cuts or burns, not for cosmetic purposes!"

"What makes you think things would have turned out differently if we had gone into Hong Kong?" asked Logan. "They've got tattoo parlors there too, you know."

Before Holiday could reply, the door from the passageway creaked open and Sammartino came bounding in. "Mister Phelan," the metalsmith called out, "can you sign this chit for me? I'd like to requisition a new vise and some toggle bolts. Coleman in supply is breaking balls again. He insists he needs a chit from you or Mister Kimmick before he can let me have anything."

"Okay, give it here," the Jaygee said, reaching out for the sheet of paper.

"Hey, Logan! How you doing?" Sammartino called out the instant he spotted Kevin. "Hey, when you gonna' go out on shore patrol with me again?"

"Never, I hope. The last time I went out with you I caught the chicken pox."

"Yeah, that sure was a tough break," the third-class said with an indifferent shrug. "Anyway, you should have been with me last week when I pulled shore patrol in Yokosuka. What a night. They assigned me to this dive called the Ichiban Cafe on 'Hunky-Dory' Street. You might know the joint. It's about two or three blocks from Womble Gate."

"Who'd they pair you up with? Anybody from the ship?" Bacelli asked.

"No, he was a motormack-third off an L-S-T. What a character he turned out to be." Sammartino laughed as he shook his head. "You guys have probably found out by now that those Jap broads can't drink to save their ass. Two or three drinks and they're out cold."

"I know a Wasp nurse with that kind of problem," Logan muttered with a broad smile. "Sorry to interrupt, get back to your story," Kevin coaxed.

"Well, by nine-thirty the place was getting pretty hairy. Most of the girls had slid under the tables by then and the guys were starting to fight over the few broads that were still on their feet and able to dance. It was just about this time that my partner, the motormack, decides to take the manager up on his earlier offer of a bottle of Old Grand-Dad. No sooner had he and the bourbon disappeared into the manager's office than this marine first-looey comes prancing in...not to check on what's going on, but to catch a shore patrol who's had a sip of booze or is maybe making it in the back room with some Jap dolly."

"I bumped into that guy back in July," Holiday volunteered. "They told us at shore patrol headquarters to watch out for him. Even the marines hate his guts. They said it was his hobby going around from bar to bar just hoping to find some S-P or M-P breaking the rules."

"That's him alright. Anyway, when he asked me where my partner was, I told him that the guy had gone to take a leak. I could see the bastard didn't believe me, and he was just starting to go look for himself when the motormack came walking out of the manager's office. First thing the lieutenant does is walk up to smell the guy's breath. Next thing I know, he's turning six shades of green and gagging all over the place. Seems the motormack was prepared for the little prick. He knew all about him from when he'd last pulled patrol in Yokosuka. This time he brought a big clove of garlic along. Not good Italian garlic but that wicked crap they grow over here with human fertilizer. When the lieutenant stepped up to smell the guy's breath, he got a full broadside smack in the kisser since the motor-mack was sucking on the full clove at the time."

"That and the bourbon must have proven a formidable combination even for a marine," Logan said with obvious satisfaction.

"Combat, bridge..." Came the captain's voice over the squawk-box.

"Combat, aye," Phelan replied.

"Andy, radio-central just sent up a crypto from Jehovah. We'll be detaching from the task force at fifteen-hundred. We'll be heading for the general area of Kansong. Get your C.I.C. team working on a course and speed that will put us four miles off the coast at a point midway between Kansong and Kosong by oh-seven-hundred. It looks like we're going to get a chance to show the army how good we can shoot," he said eagerly. "Mister Coates is on his way down to the radar shack. I've told him to round up all his people so they can brush up on what I hope they already know about C.I.C.'s role in gunfire support."

"Yes, Sir, I'll get on it right away." Phelan slowly released the talk-lever and looked around his murky watch station. Being the *Field's* assistant engineering officer, he hadn't spent very much time in the combat-information-center. He surveyed his shadowy surroundings and its ill-assorted inhabitants. With the possible exception of Logan, he decided, Messrs. Coates and Stockwell had his complete sympathy. Phelan was aware that carrying out gunfire support for ground troops was a whole different ballgame from popping away at railroad embankments and other targets in terrain far from friendly forces. He knew their upcoming assignment required precise shell placement. With your own troops in close proximity to the enemy, there was literally no room for the slightest error, he mused. Then the Jaygee's eyes focused on Holiday, now down on all fours hunting for a tiny strip of adhesive cloth that had mysteriously disappeared somewhere near the base of the air search radar. Phelan scratched the back of his neck, smiled nervously, and wondered what lamentable adventure the gods of sea and sky were now planning for the Charlie P.

At 14:25, the *Field*, with Owen Royal at the conn, scrambled over frenzied water to hold a ragged course parallel and perilously close to Jehovah's present flagship, the *Valley Forge*. Plowing headlong through mast-high waves that curled back from the flattop's charging prow, the destroyer pitched and shuddered as she completed the highline transfer from the gray colossus towering alongside.

Tucked safely within the sacks dispatched by Jehovah were maps and overlays of the coastal area above Chodo where communist troops faced the ROK I Corps now holding the all-important right anchor of the U.N. line. Included in the material sent over from the *Valley Forge* were intelligence profiles of enemy units present, details of the terrain topography, and a list of voice calls and frequencies to be employed.

By midnight, the sea had settled down to a simmer, prompting Logan to make the climb to the signal bridge. In spite of the near-freezing temperature, the crisp night air was a welcome tonic, especially after the claustrophobic atmosphere of C.I.C. Even the steady engine vibrations, usually quite irritating below decks, were now surprisingly soothing as the *Field* glided along under a bright brocade of stars.

Suddenly Logan found Candy intruding upon his thoughts. Maybe it was because of the way the stars were reaching down to touch the water, he reflected, remembering a summer night in forty-seven when he and Candy had taken a cruise on Long Island Sound. He could use that soft warm body against him now, he smiled.

Peering down at the silver water, he wondered how she was getting on with her husband. If he lived to be a hundred, he'd never be able to fathom why the ultra-ambitious Candy would tie herself down to an army officer...short of Eisenhower or MacArthur, he told himself with a chuckle.

His thoughts shifted to the ad agency...now a world away and as remote as Saturn or Mars. Yet, just a year ago he was sitting in an office on Madison Avenue cranking out copy for some imbecilic client's rep in Wilmington, Delaware. Now he was getting ready to let a bunch of gooks use him for target practice, he grimaced, then turned as he heard the scraping sound of someone coming up the ladder.

"That you, Logan?" a voice called loudly from the darkness.

"Yeah, Gordy," responded the radarman, catching sight of the *Field's* senior yeoman as the latter stepped into the star glow.

"You're 'bout as hard to find on this bucket as a piece of ass! Hell, I've been hunting you from one end of the ship to the other. I've been down in C.I.C. and your berthing compartment. I even checked the head. That's where I bumped into Holiday rubbing some kind of greenish glop on that damn fool tattoo of his. He told me he saw you heading up here."

"Okay, now that you've found me, what's up? Did the navy discover they went and activated the wrong Kevin Logan?" he quipped good naturedly.

"Don't you wish you could be that lucky...actually, I wanted to talk to you about Patterson."

"Patterson?"

"Yeah, your buddy Murray got Coates to tell me to drop his name off the list for the radarman-third exam. Cobb's got me helping out the personnelmen since our smart-ass exec just woke up to the fact that tomorrow's the deadline for getting the names off to BuPers. As exec, Cobb's ass would really be in a sling if that list went out late," Gordon snickered.

"Okay, but why are you coming to me? I've got nothing to do with whether or not Patterson takes the exam. Besides, I don't see how Murray or even Ensign Coates can take his name off the list at this late date. Patterson's quarterly performance grades are better than average, and I know he completed both his practical factors and correspondence course. Even more important, Lieutenant Stockwell recommended him for the exam."

"I know. That's why Coates asked me to delete his name but to make it look like a clerical foul-up."

"You can refuse to do it, can't you?"

"Ordinarily I'd love telling an officer that he can go screw himself when I know I'm on solid ground. Only in this case, it's kinda hard for me to do, at least as far as Coates is concerned. Back in Honolulu, he got me out of a really nasty mess. It would have cost me my crow for sure," Gordon shrugged. "I guess he's collecting on the favor. The problem is I don't feel too good about shafting Patterson. He never did anything to me. At least he's not a wise ass like those other three radar strikers you got."

"Yes, I agree, but I still don't see how I can do anything. Murray's the senior radarman. He's got a lot more influence with Coates than I have."

"Hell, all you've got to do is go to Coates and tell him you were passing ship's office, and you decided to check the exam list just in case there were any mistakes. After all, as a second-class petty officer, it's your duty to look out for the men under you. Tell Coates you noticed that Patterson's name wasn't on the list. Say you called it to my attention but I wouldn't put his name back on without a final okay from him. That will get me off the hook," Gordon smiled. "Coates won't turn you down. There's no way he can say he doesn't want the kid to take the exam just because he's on Murray's personal shit list. Since the radio-shack's got to send the names off before we go to G-Q in the morning, there won't be any time for Murray or Coates to play any more tricks."

"Anyone ever tell you you're a pretty decent guy for a hard-nosed thirty-year man?"

"No, and they better not, either! It's just that after spending almost half my life in the navy, I thought I could figure a guy out within a few minutes. Your buddy Murray fooled the hell out of me. I had him pegged as Mister straight-shooter all the way."

"He is. Except for this hang-up he's got about Patterson, he'd be a candidate for sainthood."

"What'd Patterson ever do to him?"

"Nothing. Murray's just miserable about the navy taking him away from his wife and kids and his job, and I guess being only human, he's got to take it out on somebody. Patterson's the perfect candidate. The kid's nuts about the navy, just the way Howie probably was when he was Patterson's age."

"You saying Murray sees himself in Patterson?"

"Exactly, of course he denies it whenever I tell him. As far as Coates is concerned, I don't think he's really down on the kid. He's just influenced by Murray's opinion. Hell, Coates isn't much older than Patterson, and here he is with limited experience running a destroyer's wartime combat-information-center. He's pretty nervous. He knows Cobb's just looking for an excuse to get on his ass. And to make things worse, he's discovered he's losing his hair...well, guess I'd better go find old Coatsie and see if I can get this thing squared-away. Thanks for letting me know."

"Good luck. Coates said something about going to the wardroom when he left the ship's office."

The wardroom was hot and dimly lit. Ensign Keagan was just leaving as Logan, hat in hand, knocked on the side of the open door. Coates was sipping a mug of coffee and studying the operational plan for the *Field's* upcoming fire support mission. He was alone except for a single steward who continuously shuttled between the wardroom and the pantry as if looking for some chore to keep him from dozing off.

"Take a seat, I'll be with you in a second," the ensign said, pointing to a chair. "We're really going to have our work cut out for us tomorrow. According to the Op-plan, we'll be supporting the Rok Fifteenth Division. This report says that they've only just been activated. General Van Fleet put them on the line last week to give the Rok Fifth Division a breather."

"With the Charlie P. furnishing their gun support, it sounds like the blind leading the blind," Logan said with a nervous smile.

"Luckily, they'll be a navy fire-control party over on the beach calling all the shots. In addition, we'll be operating with a division of veteran cans. I understand this is their fourth Korean tour. In fact, they were off the Korean coast the Sunday back in Fifty when the Reds launched their invasion. The captain said they and the *Juneau* fired the first American rounds of the war."

"What ships are they?"

"*Collett, Mansfield, Lyman K. Swenson* and *DeHaven*. Know them?"

"Yes, they sound familiar. I think I operated with them off Okinawa. They're *Sumner* class as I recall, same as the 'can' I was on."

"Well, I'm sure we'll get through tomorrow's mission without any hitches," said Coates cautiously. "After all, our job in C.I.C. is only back-up. Mister MacKinlay and his people in gun-plot and the gang up in the Mark Thirty-Seven are the ones who'll really be carrying the ball." The ensign glanced at his watch, shuffled the papers into a neat pile, and said, "It's getting pretty late. What brings you down here? Is something going on in C.I.C. that I should know about?"

"No, Sir. Murray's got the mid-watch. I'm sure everything's running smoothly. We do have a problem in ship's office though."

"Ship's office?"

"Yes, Sir. I remembered how my reserve training center screwed me up once when I was scheduled to take a rate advancement exam. I decided I'd better check the list they're putting together in ship's office, you know, just to make sure they don't foul it up and keep any of our eligible people from taking the test. It's a damn good thing I did. Can you believe those characters down there actually left Patterson's name off the list? Worse yet, when I called the mistake to Gordon's attention, he refused to put the kid's name back on the list. He said he couldn't do it unless I went and got an okay from you. Can you figure that guy out?" Logan asked in a tone of utter astonishment. "I reminded him that Lieutenant Stockwell had approved Patterson's taking the exam. That didn't seem to carry very much weight. I did consider going to see Lieutenant Stockwell but I heard he was in the sack so I didn't think it would be a good idea to disturb him, especially since I knew you could square things away."

"Yes, you're right. There's no sense bothering Mister Stockwell with something this trivial. I'm sure he's got a lot more on his mind tonight than whether or not Patterson goes up for third this time around."

"Yes, Sir. I know it's just a technicality since you've already recommended him for the test but I figure it wouldn't hurt to satisfy ship's office by getting another okay from you. I'm a firm believer in keeping on the good side of yeomen and P-Ns," Logan said, forcing a laugh. "Otherwise, I'm liable to wake up some morning and find that my pay records have been sent off to the Aleutians. Well, I don't want to take up any more of your time so if it's okay with you, I'll go straighten things out with Gordon," said the radarman edging toward the door.

"Wait a second, Logan." The young officer's face reddened in sudden discomfort. "About Patterson...I think it might be better if he didn't take the exam this time. He doesn't have one chance in ten of passing, and it won't look very good for the division's training program when he flunks."

"But, Sir, his quarterly grades are all qualifying, and he's been studying that *Radarman-third* training manual since we left Hawaii. He even takes it with him when he hits the sack."

"That doesn't mean anything. He hasn't attended Class-A school like our other three strikers. Besides, I've noticed he's not too sharp around the radar shack. He's made a couple stupid blunders recently...one just the other day in front of the exec."

"Farber, Paulsen and Belton make more than their share, Sir, to say nothing of our four third-class. I've screwed up quite a few times myself." Logan hesitated. "You know, Sir, this test is very important to Patterson. That's why he's been studying for it so hard."

"That's all very well," Coates answered nervously, "but it won't be the end of the world if he has to wait six more months to take it. That way he'll be much better prepared...besides, you know that pretty soon his turn at mess cooking will be coming around again. If by some quirk he should pass the exam and get his crow, we won't be able to send him back down to the mess decks."

"What about Farber, Paulsen and Belton?"

"There's not much likelihood that they're going to fail, not after nine months in radar school."

"As long as you're sure the odds are ten to one against Patterson's passing, what do you have to lose?"

"The questions are multiple choice. There's always an outside chance that he might guess enough of them to pass."

"Yes, I see your point," Logan said in a humble tone. "You know, Sir, when I first came in here, I was going to ask you to put his name back on the list as a personal favor to me. Remember back on New Year's Eve when I came up with those rhymes for you? I think I recall you did say something about owing me one."

Coates stared at him suspiciously.

"But now that you've explained things to me, I have to admit you're right about holding him back this time. I'm sure Gordon will be just as happy to leave him off the list. It'll certainly mean less paperwork for him. The only problem I can see is the captain."

"The captain?" Coates asked with a nervous squeak in his voice. "What's the captain got to do with this?"

"Well, I wasn't going to mention it. I've put enough time on active duty to know how delicate these things can be."

"I still don't understand."

"Well, only a day or so ago, the skipper asked me how Patterson was coming along."

"What'd you tell him?"

"I said that in my opinion, Patterson was a very competent watch-stander."

"Why would you do that?" Coates demanded angrily.

"It's the truth as far as my watch-section's concerned. I never had any trouble with him."

The ensign rubbed his chin. "Has the captain ever asked you about Patterson before?"

"Yes, Sir, quite a few times. You don't suppose Patterson could be related to Commander Royal, do you?"

There was a long silence as Coates suddenly remembered the time the captain had disapproved an earlier request to have Patterson transferred back to the deck force.

"All right, Logan. Go tell Gordon to put his name back on the list. After all, he has been studying. I guess it's only fair to let him have a crack at it. Shipboard politics can get sticky at times. I know you've tried to be tactful. I appreciate the fact that you told me about the captain's concern."

The ensign sweated profusely and scratched his bald spot as Logan hurried off in the direction of ship's office.

Daylight found the *Charles P. Field* steaming in a tight figure-eight pattern carefully calculated by Navigator Oetjens to bring the ship no closer than four miles from the Chodo coast. Far from the hellish reception Owen Royal had anticipated, a deceptive quiet hung languidly over the still gray water, lending itself to a scene that could just as easily have been set on a wintry Chesapeake or Narragansett Bay.

On the open bridge, the captain and Lieutenant Oetjens observed the huddle of two-stackers standing off to port. As Royal and the others watched, the closest of the destroyers pulled out of the pack and headed slowly towards the *Field*.

The captain focused his binoculars on the large white 730 on the approaching vessel's bow. "That's the *Collett* alright," he muttered dryly. "She's been paired off with us to form the northern support group. The *Mansfield*, *Swenson* and *DeHaven* will make up the southern group. They'll provide call fire for the Rok Twelfth Division just above Kansong."

"Aren't there any Americans on the lines these days?" Oetjens asked, lowering his binoculars.

"According to the sector maps Jehovah sent over, Van Fleet's got fifteen divisions facing the Reds along the M-L-R right now. Three are American with U.N. contingents, one's British Commonwealth, and the remaining eleven are South Korean. I imagine the general is trying to gradually turn the war over to the Roks. After all, we can't stay over here forever. The closest American outfits to where we are right now are the Fortieth and Forty-fifth Divisions. They're in the 'Punch Bowl' and 'Iron Triangle' well beyond the maximum range of our guns. They're both National Guard outfits, I understand," the captain explained, before turning towards the open door of the wheelhouse. "Mister Phelan," he called out. "Inform Don Coates and his radar gang that I'd like to know the minute the *Collett* has closed to within two-thousand yards."

"Aye, aye, Sir," the OD promptly acknowledged.

"What's *Collett's* call name?"

"Methodist, Sir," replied Phelan, glancing up at the wheelhouse status-board.

"Well then, call Methodist and tell her we will take up position directly astern for the run in to the firing area," Royal said a little stiffly, cognizant of the instructions in the day's Ops plan. Playing tail-end Charlie seemed to have become standard operating procedure for him lately, he commiserated, though in this instance he begrudgingly had to acknowledge that the reason was solely based on the fact that his consort's skipper was slightly senior in date of rank.

Below in the combat-information-center, a helmeted Aubrey Cobb was briefing Ensign Coates and the entire C.I.C. team. "To sum up," said Cobb glancing around the radar shack, "remember, your primary responsibility during this operation is to determine our exact position in relation to the land and any target we're ordered to take under fire. Be certain that Mister MacKinlay's people in gun-plot know precisely where the ship is every second. They won't be able to set up their computers unless you men provide an accurate range and bearing to the target." He suddenly turned towards Logan and said, "Since you're manning the D-R-T, you're the key to how well this team performs. Have you had any experience in close support fire?"

"Not on the D-R-T, but I'm thoroughly familiar with the drill."

"Well, this isn't a drill! This is the real thing and you'd better remember that! We'll be firing in close proximity to friendly troops. That means our shells will be landing as close as two hundred yards in front of our own lines. You'd better well know what you're doing. You're not out playing games with your weekend warriors, you know," said Cobb smugly.

"Yes, Sir. I've worked in support of ground forces before."

"You have? Where have **you** ever worked in support of ground forces?"

"Normandy, Cherbourg, Ormoc Bay, Mindoro, Luzon, Kerama Retto..."

Cobb's face reddened. "I don't remember asking you for your life story. Just make sure you don't screw up today," he sneered, then leaned over the DRT to peruse the chart with its grid overlay used to facilitate the location of friendly positions, front lines and targets.

By 09:30, the *Field* had thrown well over a hundred rounds of 5-inch "common" at the two 10,000-meter squares judiciously selected for destruction by the navy shore-fire control party. Designated box-number 6357 on the checkerboard-like grids in C.I.C. and in gun-plot, the first target area was the site of a well dug-in North Korean command post. The second square, box-number 6374, accommodated a trio of howitzers that had been intermittently shelling forward bunkers of the Rok Fifteenth Division.

Barely making headway so as to provide the South Koreans with the most accurate fire, *DD-505* moved sluggishly and in a sideward direction like a wary boxer jockeying for position while sizing up his opponent. A half-mile away, *Collett* was maneuvering in similar fashion, her six gray rifles belching out smoky salvos at the snow-covered hills beyond.

Far from the back-up role Coates had envisioned, the *Field's* combat-information-team was now shouldering a major portion of the work, a fact due largely to the nature of her assignment which called for indirect rather than direct fire; indirect fire being the term applied to engaging targets not in visual range of the ship or its gun director.

In contrast to the freezing temperature topside, C.I.C. was hot and sticky, its air acrid from fumes that seeped down from the over-worked forward 5-inch mounts. A sudden silence had fallen over the radar shack. Now that the guns had stopped, Murray could feel a ringing in his ears as he fidgeted with a pair of dividers and waited for word of the next target. Long moments passed. Logan looked up at the bulkhead clock, and Cobb angrily eyed Holiday who was manning the shore fire control spotting net, the radio-telephone circuit that linked C.I.C. and gun-plot with "Prodigal," the navy spotter team ashore.

"Are you certain you're still connected with that fire-control party?" snapped Cobb impatiently.

Holiday nervously jiggled the circuit switch on the radio-telephone, and was about to check the earphone level-control when his facial expression froze. "Fire mission!" he stammered, holding the handphone tightly to his ear. "Fire mission!" the third-class repeated excitedly, and all in C.I.C. knew that within seconds, the Charlie P. would again be hurling hot steel at the Communist enemy.

No sooner had the warning order from Prodigal been acknowledged, then designation of a new target, its bearing and location within the grid, the classification of fire, type of ammunition to be employed, and other pertinent data flew over the air waves in rapid order.

Holiday called out the azimuth given by the spotter so that Ensign Coates, working the grid-spot converter, could immediately pencil-in the all-important observer-target line which would serve as the principal line of reference in relation to the target's position.

"Prodigal reports that the target is infantry reinforcements transitting a gully. Location is grid number six-three-five-one...target deep! Prodigal requests one five-inch gun, one round! Prodigal will observe fall of shot and correct! Prodigal requests use of H-C ammo!" Holiday repeated in a breathless monotone.

Instantly, the spotter's request was passed on to Owen Royal on the bridge and to Lieutenant MacKinlay in gun-plot. The term "target deep" informed them that the infantry to be taken under fire was not within 600 yards of friendly forces. They also knew that by calling for HC, or "high capacity" shells, the shore party was seeking a maximum kill through use of high-velocity fragmentation ammunition which would scatter shrapnel over a wide area. Seconds later, the doomsday crack of a 5-inch projectile departing its muzzle told all in C.I.C. that the *Field* had responded to the spotter's request. In another minute, all five mounts in the main battery were spewing out H-C rounds at an unlucky platoon of Red infantry no one aboard *DD-505* could even see.

"Is the *Collett* firing at the same targets we are, Sir?" inquired Coates over the continuous cacophony of 5-inch.

"How the hell do I know?" the exec shot back, his face flushed and sweating. "I've got no way of telling what she's shooting at unless we call her on the C-I net, and right now, I'm a little too busy to worry about what's happening on some other ship." He wiped the back of his neck with a khaki handkerchief, then turning around, called to Nugent on the SG, "Where do you hold the *Collett* now?"

"Bearing zero-four-seven...two-thousand, one hundred yards, Sir," Nugent replied wearily before leaning towards Bacelli on the SC radar. "Why does that jerk keep asking me for ranges and bearings to the other can when he's got a perfectly good radar repeater right in front of him?"

"Probably because he doesn't know how to use it," Bacelli answered with a sneer.

"Well, how am I going to be able to keep feeding Logan ranges and bearings to the shore if Cobb keeps bugging me for information he can easily get himself?"

"Nugent! What the hell are you mumbling about back there?" the exec called out angrily. "In case you don't know it, you're at G-Q! And you!" he yelled, transferring his wrath to Bacelli. "You keep your damn eyes glued to that air-search scope! We're barely making five knots. Right now, we're meat on the table for any low-flying Mig jockey." Then, glaring at Coates, Cobb said, "I've already warned you about getting this C.I.C. squared away. From what I've seen in here this morning, Mister, you're doing a pretty piss-poor job of it!"

"Yes, Sir," the ensign answered in a subdued voice.

"Combat, bridge!" Royal's voice suddenly interrupted from the overhead speaker. "The *Collett's* being straddled. Tell Prodigal we're shifting from call-fire to counter battery. The engine room's lighting off all boilers so we can shag-ass out of here and get some room to maneuver. Let me know when we're exactly five miles off Point Tehju."

"Bridge, aye," Cobb answered nervously, his voice barely carrying over the din of the 5-inch which were now under direct control of Ensign Keagan in the Mark-37, and firing salvo after salvo at the gun flashes, sparkling like ragged rows of candles on a frosty white cake.

From the starboard wing, Owen Royal watched plumes of dirty-gray water dance high in the air close to the *Collett* which was now making heavy smoke and cutting a zigzag course toward the open sea.

"That last one almost got her," Royal muttered as he and Oetjens watched the destroyer dart through a cascading wall of water. Three distinct fires were visible along the shoreline and oily black smoke spiraled upward near the enemy guns. The captain focused his binoculars on the land again and wondered whether it had been his guns or those of the *Collett* that had caused the conflagration.

"*Collett* seems to be drawing all the fire," Oetjens exclaimed, "not that I'm complaining, mind you," he added with a grin as the *Field* spun around sharply.

"The *Collett's* got an unenviable reputation for drawing fire," Royal replied grimly. "I read that she took nine hits during the Inchon invasion."

Barroomp! Barromp!

Two giant black holes were suddenly torn out of the sea fifty feet in front of the *Field*. Water poured down upon the open wing thoroughly drenching Royal and Oetjens and a hapless lookout standing nearby.

"Guess I spoke a bit too soon," a soaking-wet Oetjens said, pulling himself back up to a standing position.

Already on his feet, the captain was issuing a deluge of orders to Daly and the others in the wheelhouse. "Hard left rudder! All engines ahead full!" Royal called out, and the destroyer lurched and quivered as she gathered way. Rolling on the turn as she came broadside to a string of mast-high shell splashes, she swung back on even keel before charging through a fresh mushroom of water that had suddenly erupted directly in front of her bow.

Within seconds, a third and fourth salvo was crashing all around, telling Royal that the North Koreans had successfully zeroed-in on him. Zigzagging now to throw off their aim, the captain relied mainly on his reflexes to weave the ship in and around the forest of shell splashes filled with flying steel.

Far off to starboard, *Collett* was barely visible running and ducking through her own watery gauntlet. The further away she stays the better, Royal told himself, aware that both ships would need maximum room to maneuver. The last thing he needed now was a collision, he grimaced, catching another quick glimpse of the *Collett* before she turned sharply to disappear once more amid a swirl of her own smoke.

It was then that Royal felt the ship shudder and heard the unmistakable clang of metal striking metal. The sound cut through the thunder of his own guns to tell him that worst of all news that his ship had been hit. Yet, there was no sign of an explosion, no smoke, no flame.

Ensign Daly was barely able to leap aside before his C.O. came barreling through the wheelhouse doorway. Royal reached for the squawk-box speaker and pulled the lever marked damage-control central.

"Mister Sternhagen!" he called. "I believe we've taken a hit but I'll be damned if I can figure out where."

"Yes, Sir. We felt it down here too, but so far nobody's reported anything. I've called main-engine-control. They seem to be okay, same with MacKinlay in gun-plot. I was just about to check with the exec in C.I.C. when you called, Sir."

"Well, wherever it is, we'd better find it mucho quick. Since there was no explosion, there's every chance it could be a dud. However, we can't ignore the possibility that it's a delayed-action shell with a time fuse that's ticking away right now ready to blow the lid off this bucket."

"Captain!" Ensign Daly called out excitedly as he placed the handphone back in its bracket on the bulkhead. "That call was from Beaumont. The shell...it passed clear through the wardroom."

"The wardroom?" Royal shook his head dubiously. "Was anyone hurt?"

"No, Sir. Beaumont says the shell passed right over the middle of the wardroom table, then went out the port side without touching anything."

"Thank God for that," Royal said with obvious relief. Then after ordering another evasive turn, he reached for the speaker button on the 21MC and called Lieutenant Sternhagen in damage-control-central. "Looks like we've just picked up two new port holes in the wardroom, Rolf. You'd better get some of your gang up there to see how extensive the damage is."

"Yes, Sir. They're already on their way."

A moment later, Coates notified the captain that the ship was exactly five miles off Point Tehju, and for the next hour, the *Field* joined the *Collett* in laying down a slow and very precise bombardment of the suspected gun positions. By 13:00, the enemy's return fire had completely slackened off and the two destroyers moved back to a point less than three miles from the Communist shoreline.

Reestablishing their communications with their respective spotting parties, the destroyers quickly resumed their fire support missions. Primary targets for the afternoon were North Korean entrenchments dug in on the reverse slopes of the small mountains and hills that lay in front of the ROK lines. These command posts, bunkers and ammo dumps, while sheltered from land-based artillery, were completely exposed to the guns of naval vessels, the latter being free to maneuver to points from where they could deliver deadly flanking or enfilading fire. Such tactics were executed to good advantage by the *Field* and *Collett* until late afternoon, when, with their magazines nearly depleted of 5-inch, both ships were withdrawn by the bombardment force commander.

After replenishing the following morning, the *Field* passed the rest of the day prowling the coastal area called "The Boulevard," otherwise known to Seventh Fleet sailors as the Hodo Pando-Hungnam-Cha-ho route.

Commander Royal had barely finished his evening letter to Candace when the executive officer tapped on the door to his cabin.

"Yes, Aub, come on in," beckoned Royal, buttoning the top two buttons on his shirt.

"Here's Sternhagen's report on yesterday's damage, Captain, late as usual," Cobb scowled, handing the C.O. a stapled set of papers. "Sternhagen feels that the canvas they rigged in the wardroom might not hold till we get back into port."

"That's a fair assumption," Royal nodded. "The temperature must have been close to freezing in there during dinner. I'm certainly not looking forward to eating all my meals in foul-weather gear."

"Yes, eh, well, Sternhagen would like to have his people weld steel plates over the holes. He'd like your permission to get them started on it right away so the stewards will have plenty of time to get things cleaned up in there before breakfast. Of course, it will mean canceling tonight's wardroom movie."

"That's the least of our problems. Tell him to get his gang hopping. I'd just about made up my mind to have the movie scratched anyway. While we're down here patrolling the Boulevard, we'll have to keep a maximum number of men on watch, especially mine-lookouts. That's why I had you cancel the crew's movie on the mess decks. With that in view, I don't think it would have been very fair to go ahead with a movie for the officers. Just out of curiosity, what did they have scheduled for tonight?"

"Something called '*Public Deb Number One*' with George Murphy and Brenda Joyce. It's one of the flicks the *Paricutin* sent over when she rearmed us this morning."

"Another golden Oldie?" Royal asked with a quizzical grin.

"I think the flyer that came with it said it was made in nineteen-forty."

"I guess they're still saving all the new ones for Commodore Price," the captain said dryly, motioning to the exec to take a seat. Then glancing swiftly at the report, Royal said angrily, "How come the starboard raft's salvageable but the port raft's a total write-off?"

"As you know, the shell was armor-piercing. It went through the first raft nice and clean like a hot knife going through butter. The hole it made in the raft's platform wasn't much bigger than its own diameter. By the way, from the size of the hole, Sternhagen figures it must have been at least a six-incher."

Royal nodded in agreement.

"Since the platform's only a lattice, Sternhagen says his boys can patch it up without too much trouble. Unfortunately, by the time the shell had passed through the two wardroom bulkheads, it came out the port side like a giant dumb-dumb bullet tearing the other raft all to hell...not just the platform but the float as well...split the damn thing right in half. It even busted the water kegs. Nothing was salvageable except the survival kit. I've already told Sternhagen to have his people deep-six what was left of it," Cobb said, scratching his bald spot.

"Looks like we've now got twenty-five men who'll have no way to get off this ship if we should meet a floating mine and come out second best," Royal said eyeing Cobb sharply. "You'd better get a message off to Birthrate informing him of our situation. Request that he make arrangements to get us a replacement raft as soon as possible, preferably at our next replenishment."

"Yes, Sir," Cobb smiled wanly.

"The water we took in after-steering," said Royal pointing to a section of the report, "how deep did it get this time before the D-C people were able to pump it out?"

"The usual four or five inches. That's no worse than what we get back there whenever we drop depth charges. The whole fantail area's nothing but a sieve. Those stern seams have been leaking ever since this tub came out of mothballs. That was one of the items the yard was supposed to take care of last April when we went into drydock."

"Apparently they didn't," said Royal, his voice strained. "Anyway, I guess we can be thankful we got off as lightly as we did yesterday. At least there were no personnel casualties." He handed the report back to Cobb. "By the way, has radio-central gotten any word yet on how we did yesterday?"

"No, I don't think so. I didn't see any mention of it in the Fox skeds when I glanced through them earlier."

"I'm sure it won't make much difference. The *Collett* will probably get all the credit anyway," said Royal with an amiable grin. "Well, I'd better not keep you any longer. I know you'll want to get some sleep before you go on watch. I see here on the P-O-D that you've got the mid-watch tonight."

"Yes, but that's okay, I wasn't planning to sack-in anyway. Actually, I did want to speak to you about Don Coates if you have a few minutes."

"Sure, Aub, what's the *Field's* own version of Ensign Pulver up to now? Is he still pestering you and Oetjens about getting a T.V. for the wardroom?"

"No, I'm afraid it's not that trivial. Now that I've been standing G-Q in the radar shack, I can see that there's no way he's ever going to make it as a C.I.C. officer."

"You mean that week in hack didn't do him any good? I figured he'd be an expert at the maneuvering-board after that."

"Oh, he's picked up on the maneuvering-board. Unfortunately, he hasn't learned how to control that smart-ass radar gang of his. Yesterday, right in the middle of our fire-support mission, I had to discipline two of his third-class for bullshitting while they were supposed to be looking at the scopes."

"Yes, I heard. I understand you disciplined Don Coates too, while you were at it."

Cobb compressed his lips. "I'm not quite sure I know what you mean, Captain."

"Well, the way I understand it, you told him he was doing a pretty piss-poor job."

"Did Coates tell you that?" Cobb's eyes flashed with anger.

"Of course not. He didn't have to. You should know a vessel this size is a small tight community. We hadn't secured from G-Q a full hour before it was all over the ship. I was up on the bridge-wing when I overheard a couple of our non-rated men laughing about it."

"Who were they, may I ask?"

"Come on, Aub, who they were is completely inconsequential. The fact is that by fourteen-hundred, just about everybody on board knew that you had reamed out Coates in front of his entire C.I.C. team. I don't think I have to tell you how it is with white hats. How they get their jollies at seeing one of their officers being chewed out, even if he is only an ensign," Royal added in a mordant tone.

"Well, he certainly had it coming to him."

"That's not the point. I don't enjoy having to lecture you about basic military etiquette, but I certainly shouldn't have to remind you that officers do not parade the short comings of their fellow officers in front of enlisted personnel. If, as you say, he had little control of his radar gang before you laid into him, how much control do you think he's going to have now? Was there any pressing reason why you couldn't have waited a little while and then called him to your cabin?"

Cobb stared vacantly for several seconds, his wire-frame glasses resting low on his nose. "Maybe I should have waited a bit. It's just that I have very little patience with inefficient people who can't perform their job properly. However, I do see your point. I assure you I'll try to curb such impulses in the future."

"Good," Royal said with a smile. "Now on a related subject, I don't think it would be a bad idea if you include something in the P-O-D every once in awhile about how well various divisions are doing. A little praise now and then can do a hell of a lot to boost the morale of a crew. In the ten months I've been aboard, I can't recall a single instance when you've complimented anyone on their job performance."

"Frankly Captain, I don't believe in patting people on the back just for doing what they're paid to do. I didn't have to do that in the merchant marine, so I certainly don't see any reason for doing it in the navy."

"I don't expect you to pat anyone on the back, Aub. However, I do expect you to do your damndest to help me boost the morale of this crew." Royal's face was flushed with anger. "Well, I don't want to detain you any longer. Thanks for bringing me Sternhagen's report. I'd better give it a closer reading."

Cobb disengaged himself tactfully, wished Royal a pleasant evening, then cursed his C.O. all the way back to his cabin.

Aubrey Cobb looked long and hard at the small black clock on the wheel-house bulkhead. It's fluorescent hands conveyed the disappointing news that only two hours had passed since he'd relieved Phelan as O.D. for the mid-to-four. The damn watch was really dragging, Cobb grumbled to himself, still furious with Royal for putting him on the carpet earlier. He mulled the details of the confrontation, recalling each word and nuance of the exchange. He'd fix that Annapolis son-of-a-bitch, he vowed, certain now that the captain was engaged in a determined effort to undermine his authority as executive officer.

Cobb hadn't seen the mine, nor had anyone else on board *DD-505* even though it had floated by less than 15 feet from the starboard side. Black as the sea and sky that concealed it, the lethal metal ball glided by with a charge of T.N.T. powerful enough to split a cruiser in half. It took a little more than 30 seconds for the mine to make its silent transit along the length of the hull before finally getting sucked up in the wake and drifting off still unnoticed into the vast void astern.

It was precisely at this time that Gardiner, struggling to keep awake, deposited another record on to the wobbly turntable of the shopworn 78-player which he, Nugent and Bacelli had acquired back in Yokosuka for three cartons of Lucky Strike, a humming yo-yo, and two tins of Spam. The disk, a product of Nippon-Columbia Co. Ltd., featured the talents of Frankie Laine and the Norman Luboff Choir in a collaboration that shared with all in C.I.C. the plaintive tale of an encounter with the hauntingly beautiful *"Girl in the Wood."*

The destroyer continued on through the night, a brisk wind from astern helping her on her way.

Chapter XX - Riding Shotgun

The *Field* climbed easily over the long, slow swells that rolled in towards the snow-crusted coast. For the past few days the ship had been assigned to the "Sweet Adeline" patrol guarding the approaches to the Yang-do's, an off-shore nest of islands just north of Songjin. This relatively quiet duty afforded the crew a welcome rest after the three days the ship had spent pounding the Songjin marshalling yards in company with destroyers *Boyd* and *McDermut*. That assignment had been followed by two nights of providing illumination fire for the 8-inch guns of cruiser *Rochester* in the Tanchon area.

Sharing the guard at Sweet Adeline was *H.M.C.S. Crusader*, a handsome one-stacker and a sister ship to *H.M.S. Charity* with which *DD-505* had briefly operated back in November. Always impressed with the trim lines of these British-built C-class ships, the captain slowly swept his binoculars fore and aft along the full length of the Canadian destroyer, taking special notice that his consort's hull number, 228, was displayed British fashion below the bridge rather than near the bow as was customary with American tin cans. Royal aimed his glasses now at *Crusader's* upperworks, focusing in on her gun-director which appeared much smaller than the *Field's* boxy Mark-37. His thoughts were interrupted by the sudden sound of squeaky shoes. He turned to see Ensign Keagan, clipboard in hand, approach from the wheelhouse.

"The messenger just brought this up from the crypto-shack, Captain," the young officer said as he saluted.

Extracting a small key from his pocket, Royal quickly unfastened the latch on the clipboard's metal cover and removed the decoded dispatch from Jehovah.

The ensign eyed his C.O., hoping to discern some hint of the message's content which he assumed was related to the ship's next assignment.

"It looks like we'll be dusting off that "*Slow Boat to China*" record again," said Royal smiling.

Keagan looked at him quizzically. "Record, Sir?" he asked, blank-faced.

"Yes, I forgot you weren't with us in December. The record is a little morale booster we use at reveille whenever we get the word to head over to the Formosa

Strait. I assume the men enjoy the humor although I know there's another record they'd much rather wake up to. It's tucked away in my bottom dresser drawer cushioned between two woolen sweaters. I'm not taking any chances that it might crack from the vibration of our guns. After all, we'll only be playing it one time."

"What record is that, Sir?"

"An old Jolson recording of "*California Here I Come*." I picked it up in San Diego just before we left the States. I plan to have it piped over the P-A system at reveille the day we officially detach from the Seventh Fleet and haul out for home." Royal folded the dispatch, slipping it inside his shirt pocket, and departed the bridge-wing in search of Cobb and Oetjens.

The third week of January found the *Field* in the China Sea forty miles off the port of Foochow. Responding to the dispatch from Jehovah, the destroyer, along with *John Morgan*, was bucking considerable wind and spray to keep well out in front of carrier *Oriskany* which had just completed a photo-reconnaissance launch. With the U-2 not yet on Lockheed's drawing boards, and spy satellites strictly the concern of Buck Rogers, *Oriskany's* modified photo-Banshees were considered state-of-the-art at this juncture of the Korean War.

By late afternoon, the specially trained pilots of Composite Squardon-61 had thoroughly photographed all harbors, estuaries, river traffic and anything else suspected of contributing to the barge build-up for the long awaited Communist thrust at Taiwan. Except for minor flak damage to one aircraft, all of the jets returned unscathed. Moments after the tail hook on the last Banshee had engaged the third rearmost of the carrier's fourteen arresting cables, the mini-task force reversed course; the *Field* and *Morgan* proceeding under orders to Sasebo; the *Oriskany* racing back to Korea to join *Kearsarge*, *Philippine Sea* and battleship *Missouri* in a maximum effort air and gun strike against Wonsan.

Like Yokosuka, Sasebo had been an important center of operations for the Emperor's Navy during World War II. Located on the Japanese home island of Kyushu, the port city was strategically perched on the edge of the Korean Strait just 165 nautical miles from Pusan. Also like Yokosuka, it was now a major base for Seventh Fleet units engaged in the war against North Korea.

It was midday when the *Field* and *Morgan* slid by the stone breakwater with its red toy-like lighthouse to enter the inner bay which was surrounded by hills blacker and even more foreboding in appearance than those at Yokosuka. The sky had turned dirty with patches of low gray cloud as the two destroyers threaded their way around the countless sampans and bumboats that kept criss-crossing the narrow channel.

"Don't these damn Japs know anything about rules of the road?" Gardiner exclaimed as he tried to make some sense out of the cluttered mass of blips that now obscured a good portion of the surface scope. "I've got contacts up the ass, Mister Coates. There's so many skunks showing up on this thing, I don't know how to designate them. I've already gone through the alphabet four times."

"Okay, Gardiner, don't worry about it. They're in too close for us to plot any-way," the ensign said stiffly. "Captain Royal's got the conn. I'm certain he can see them without any help from us. Just keep a sharp eye for any large contacts mov-ing down stream in our direction, and be ready to give Logan here any ranges and bearings he needs for the D-R-T."

"Mister Coates," Bacelli cut in from behind the surface-status board. "How much liberty do you think we'll get here in Sasebo, Sir?"

"As far as I know, you're not getting any liberty. For that matter, nobody is."

"No liberty?" exclaimed Nugent in high pitch.

"Boy, what a crock," Holiday chimed in. The fly on his nose seemed to move as he grimaced.

"What are you people complaining about?" Coates snapped. "You only left Yokosuka a couple of weeks ago."

"Well, if we're not gonna' get any liberty, how come we're pulling into this place?" said Bacelli in a markedly vexed tone.

"The captain had to go over to the flagship for a conference with Commodore Price. We'll take on stores and fuel overnight and be underway at sunrise. We'll also be getting a new raft to replace the one we lost off Chodo."

"I hope it floats," Gardiner said with a grunt. "You know, Sir, there's some bad scuttlebutt about the whaleboat we got to replace the one we lost with Bites and Mister Ritter. The word is it leaks."

"That's ridiculous," Coates said leaning across the plotting table. "That boat was thoroughly tested before we took it on board."

"Yeah, but didn't it come off one of those old frigates we saw rusting away at Yokosuka...the one's the Russian's gave back?"

Coates shook his head in a gesture of complete frustration. "What's that got to do with anything?"

"Well, how can we be sure the Reds didn't sabotage the equipment includ-ing the boats?" Gardiner persisted.

"You people really amaze me. You'd think you'd have enough things to keep you busy that you wouldn't have any time left over to start dreaming up problems that don't even exist."

"Yes, Sir, but I still don't see why we can't go ashore tonight," Holiday pouted.

"I suppose you think the ammo and fuel we need is going to load itself," Murray cut in.

"Well, what about after we get everything loaded?" asked Holiday disconsolately.

"I said there's no liberty and that's final. Now get your minds back on your jobs," Coates warned. "Remember, you're at special-sea-detail. It's a damn good thing the exec's topside with the captain or you'd all be written up and I'd be back in hack again."

"Yeah, Holly, Mister Coates is right," Bacelli said with a patronizing grin. "I don't know why you're so hot to go back over on the beach anyway. Do you want to get another tattoo?"

"Hey, that's a good idea," Nugent said. "Why don't you get a butterfly this time? You could have it tattooed on your..."

"I told you people to knock it off and I mean it!" the ensign cried out with fire in his voice. "One more wise crack and you're all on report! Now start giving Logan ranges and bearings to the anchorage off Kamashiro Point. Use the Okama jetty as a reference point. According to this track, it should bear just about zero-four-seven, three thousand yards," Coates advised, glancing at the projected course line Logan had penciled in on the harbor chart.

•   •   •

Six bells were being sounded aboard the flagship as the *Field's* motor whaleboat scraped against the bottom rung of the chain ladder that hung down loosely from *Abner Ward's* quarterdeck. The wardroom on the division leader was bustling as Owen Garrett Royal, followed closely by Cobb and Oetjens, entered. Exchanging the usual courtesies with Commodore Price and several other officers already gathered around the long green table, Royal found it hard to believe that almost a year had passed since the last time he had attended a captain's conference on board Gil Hedling's destroyer. Now he wondered what fateful assignment lay ahead to prompt another such gathering.

Owen glanced around the room. He recognized most of the officers from the *Field's* sister destroyers. The commander and lieutenant standing at the far end of the table talking to Price were unfamiliar; probably from the base, he assumed.

While Commander Royal was making small talk with Sandy Boland, a chief gunner's mate and a seaman shuffled in carrying a chart the size of a small movie screen which they quickly mounted on a steel easel.

Price turned towards the officers who were now all seated. He fidgeted with his blond beard which seemed to Royal to have lost much of its hue since San Diego. "Gentlemen," beckoned the commodore. "If you haven't all guessed it by now, I'd like to take this opportunity to inform you that our division has been chosen to participate in the siege of Wonsan. We'll weigh anchor tomorrow at seven and we should reach Wonsan sometime Thursday morning. Our tour inside the harbor will be approximately one month."

A month in Wonsan. Cobb wondered if he'd heard Price correctly. He closed his eyes and felt his heart flutter, opening them seconds later to see the commodore step over to the chart.

"Now I'd like to introduce you to Lieutenant-Commander Russell and Lieutenant Mercer here from Admiral Gingrich's staff. Both of these officers have had extensive experience in and around Wonsan. Commander..." Price gestured warmly to the three-striper who was standing next to the chart display.

Russell was a tall man, hard and lean with prematurely graying hair and eyes as black as cannon balls. He greeted his audience with a broad smile which seemed somewhat out of place when etched upon his rough features.

"Gentlemen," he said with a distinct hint of the Carolinas in his voice, "you are about to play an important role in what now qualifies as the longest siege in the history of the American navy. We began this siege way back in February of Fifty-One, and ah'm certain we will maintain it right up until the Reds decide they've had enough and put their Chong Hancocks on those armistice papers they've been stalling around with up at Panmunjom." "The commander paused allowing his audience to grasp the quip. "Ah assume," he added with a smile, "that you all know that Wonsan is the top dog among all North Korean ports. The harbor is quite large...approximately three hundred square miles, and the city is a strategic rail and highway center. In fact, it's the terminus of the cross-peninsular rail and road connections to the Commie capital, Pyongyang. It is also the pivotal hub of their north-south rail line, as it is for just about every major road they move troops and supplies over this side of Sonchon."

Owen leaned back in his seat. It creaked loudly, prompting a tepid look of disapproval from the commodore.

"In addition to it's importance as a transportation hub," Russell continued, "Wonsan has been a major industrial center for the North Koreans, especially during the last half century of Japanese occupation. During that period the city became a manufacturing center for everything from steel pipe to sake. Even more important, it's been the home of one of the biggest petroleum refineries in all of Asia. Until we started our blitz, it produced over two million barrels annually, catering mostly to Soviet tankers shuttling over from the Russian wells on Sakhalin Island."

Russell stepped closer to the chart. "Now ah'm sure ah don't have to emphasize the lethal reputation Wonsan's earned in the two years since we began the siege. You all have read the weekly battle reports and operational summaries so you know that the Reds have been able to clobber just about anything we send in. And ah'm not just talking about minesweeps, 'cans' and frigates. They've inflicted fatalities on our cruisers, and even on ships as big and well protected as the *New Jersey*. Since the harbor's almost landlocked, you'll be facing shore batteries on all four sides. Our photo interpreters recently determined that the Reds presently have over a thousand guns, seventy-five millimeter or larger, spotted around the harbor. Fortunately for us surface jocks," he grinned, "the majority are antiaircraft weapons. But don't start feeling complacent." His tone turned suddenly solemn. "At least a hundred-and-sixty of those guns, and that includes all the really big ones, are there for one specific purpose...to blow you and your people clear out of the water. And you're not going to have very much room to dodge what they throw at you," the briefing officer cautioned. "You're going to find that navigation inside the harbor is quite restricted, not only because of the mines but also because of the numerous islands and shoals."

The commander paused for a few seconds, then said, "On the subject of mines, the North Koreans have the nasty habit of continually sewing them all over the harbor faster than our sweepers can pluck 'em out. By the way, one of your primary duties will be riding shotgun for the minesweepers. And make sure you give them your best. Those little 'matchsticks' have it the roughest, having to work in really close to the shore. They're constantly under fire, not only from shore batteries, but from just about any gook who happens to come along with a rifle or machine gun. Lieutenant Mercer here will be talking to you about the minesweeping operations in a moment. He's already completed two Wonsan tours aboard the *Chatterer* and *Heron*. However, before ah turn the floor over to him, ah'd like to give you the benefit of my experience. Before ah got my half stripe, ah was gun-boss of the *Floyd Berry*, D-D five-twenty-three. She's a *Fletcher* too." The commander poured himself a glass of ice water. After taking a sip, he smiled and said, "You know, you people are actually getting off light, only pulling a month's tour. Last summer when we did the Wonsan waltz, we were in there for a full forty-two days. Most of the time, we were..."

"Now hear this..." suddenly blared out of the bulkhead speaker. "The movie for tonight in the crew's mess will be '*Don't Bother to Knock*,' starring Marilyn Monroe and Richard Widmark. The movie will commence immediately at twenty-hundred."

Price shot an annoyed glance at Gil Hedling. Within seconds, Hedling's exec, fire in his eyes, was off and running to the quarterdeck to soundly upbraid the O.D. and the petty-officer-of-the-watch for neglecting to disconnect the wardroom speaker from the general address system while the commodore's conference was still in progress.

"Ah hope you officers will bear with me for the next few minutes," said Russell with a good-natured grin. "Ah'm sure you all know, it's not easy standing up here and competing with Marilyn Monroe."

After a few seconds of moderate chuckling on the part of his audience, the lieutenant-commander resumed. "In addition to protecting the sweepers, you all will be responsible for the safety of our personnel occupying the seven largest islands inside Wonsan Harbor." Turning to face the mammoth chart, he extended his metal pointer, touching a gray irregular blob labeled Sin Do. "This was the first island we captured. As you can see, Sin Do is only four thousand yards from this finger of land." He moved the pointer to a small peninsular marked Kalmar Pando. "This is one of the hot spots you'll have to watch out for. It's been heavily fortified with shore batteries and it's also the site of an airfield which fortunately, we've been able to keep neutralized. Right out here at the tip...it's called Kalma Gak in their lingo, but you'll get to know it as 'Square Head'... Its got some really big guns, at least a few one-fifty-fives, we estimate. By the way, Kalma Pando has the unpleasant code name of 'Hairless Joe.' Sin Do, the island I mentioned a moment ago goes under the name of 'Curley Locks.' Now this island here...Tae Do...is even closer to the guns than Sin Do is."

Russell shifted the pointer. "For your information, Tae Do is called 'Slope Head.' Hwangto Do over here," he moved the pointer again, "has the code name 'Sad Sack.' Hwangto Do's really close...less than three thousand yards from the shore. Being so close, it's the best observation post we've got. Our people on Sad Sack really earn their shekels. They're constantly under fire from mortars as well as artillery. The island is garrisoned by a platoon of Rok marines plus a small party of our own leathernecks. All seven of the islands are occupied by South Korean marines with small contingents of our marines and navy personnel. Yo Do out here is the largest of the islands. You'll refer to it in your communications as 'Brass Hat.' It serves as our base island."

Sliding the pointer up from Yo Do, he stopped it on an island marked Ung Do. "This island's got an easy name to remember...'Slick Chick,'" he smiled. "The other islands which we're holding are these three here...Mo Do, Sa Do and Song Do. They're right under the guns of the Commies here at Hodo Pando which we call 'Orphan.' These batteries are about the meanest you'll ever come up against. They're manned by the North Korean Navy. All the other guns at Wonsan are army manned as far as we can learn. They're all good, but for accuracy, they can't match these Red Navy bastards on Hondo Pando. We also suspect the Hondo Pando guns are using radar, and there's a very good chance they're being direct-ed by Russian cadre. By the way, don't worry about memorizing all these names right now. At the conclusion of the conference, Chief Hunley here and Seaman Tully will be handing out packets that contain all this information including a complete list of code names. You'll note that just about everything in and around Wonsan has been given a code name, even the various stretches of water within the harbor that you'll be patrolling."

He touched the pointer to the chart once more. "This section of the inner bay we call the 'Hatchery.' Like the other areas penciled here in red, the Hatchery is routinely swept of mines." The commander moved the pointer in a counter-clockwise direction. "'Muffler,' 'Tin Pan Alley,' 'Gridiron,' 'Duckpin,'" he called out each time the tip of the pointer touched the chart. "Ah can't overstress the importance of staying within these designated areas. Stray just a hair and there's every likelihood you and your ship will experience an unfortunate event. And believe me Gentlemen, a collision with a mine can really do a lot to louse up your day. Now, ah'd like to turn this meeting over to Mister Mercer. When he gets through with his briefing, you'll have an opportunity to ask both of us any ques-tions you might have about your upcoming sojourn in beautiful Wonsan."

Thirtyish and red-haired, Lieutenant Mercer wore a slightly nervous smile as he strode up to the chart. Royal took instant notice of the speaker's Good Conduct ribbon, a clear indication the two-striper had served at least one hitch as an enlisted man prior to receiving his commission.

"Commodore Price...Captains...Gentlemen," the lieutenant said heartily, "if I can paraphrase Winston Churchill, I'd like to say that Wonsan has nothing to offer you but blood, sweat and very often boredom. Now I certainly don't want to lessen the dangers you are going to encounter, and Commander Russell in no way exaggerated the formidable nature of your opposition. It's just that some days you may find yourself just lolling around the harbor with the North Koreans taking little notice of you. Then a day or night later, all hell will break loose in exactly the same area where you'd been completely ignored," he smiled wryly. "For instance, when I was on *Heron*, every time we even got close to 'Broadway' or 'Lower Broadway,' we'd find ourselves getting blasted from three or four directions at once. Like some of the other North Korean harbors I assume you've already visited, you'll find that a good percentage of their guns are carefully hidden in caves and tunnels and very well camouflaged. A lot of those guns are also mounted on rails which makes it easy for the gooks to roll them in and out whenever they feel like it."

Mercer fidgeted with one of the gold buttons on his double-breasted dress blues. "Another thing they've got in Wonsan that's particularly annoying to the smaller sweeps like the two I served on are tanks. It's not at all uncommon for a T-thirty-four to come thomping down to the edge of the beach and start popping away at some little sweep with all her gear strung out. The long barreled eighty-fives on those 'caviar cans' can make a mighty big hole in a sweeper's wooden hull. I imagine they can also do a mean job on a destroyer if they hit you in the right place," he added with a frown.

Royal glanced up at the overhead, then across the table at Cobb and Oetjens. He saw the downcast look in their eyes and he considered for the first time the possibility that Wonsan might actually live up to its ominous billing. Owen tensed a bit, and he suddenly found it difficult to swallow. He remembered having that sensation only once before. It was on a June morning in forty-five when he'd gotten word that his destroyer, the *O'Bannon*, would be moving up to the picket slot off Sakashima Gunto known as "hell's half-acre." Well, Wonsan couldn't be compared to Okinawa and the Divine Wind, he reassured himself. Besides, the *Field* had been under fire from shore batteries now for the last three months, and except for a little impromptu cross ventilation in the wardroom, the Charlie P. had managed to dodge the best the Reds could deliver. Royal was confident that she'd continue to do so in Wonsan Harbor, Hungnam, or any other place Jehovah decided to send her.

Royal focused his mind back on the briefing in time to hear Mercer explain, "Sweeping mines inside Wonsan is a lot like trying to bail out the ocean with a thimble. The more mines you manage to destroy, the more they manage to lay. At first they were bringing the mines out in junks. Even a small junk could carry four or five. Their favorite tactic was to sneak out at night, dump their mines in one of our main patrol areas like Tin Pan Alley, or Muffler, then shag ass back to shore, hoping that their small size would permit them to slip by our radars. Sometimes it did, but almost as often it didn't. One thing's certain," the lieutenant snickered, "a direct hit on a junk crammed with mines is a sight you're not likely to forget in a hurry. Unfortunately, the Reds have come up with a new trick that's really got us by the short hairs. Now they're tying the mines to logs and floating them down the Namdae River."

He touched the chart with his pointer to show where the river emptied into Wonsan Harbor. "First they send some logs out without any mines attached. Using binoculars, they gauge the precise time it takes for the logs to float out into the areas and channels patrolled by our ships. Once they've worked out the time pattern in line with the existing winds and currents, they send out a second batch of logs. Each of these has a hefty contact mine lashed to it. The pelican hook holding the mine in place utilizes a soluble washer that's timed to dissolve and release the mine just about anywhere they want. Unfortunately, the system's pretty much foolproof. So much so, we've become reconciled to the unhappy fact that we can't stop them from laying the mines anymore. Of course that means we now have to be that more proficient at destroying the mines once they've been planted.

Mercer rubbed his palm across the back of his neck. "In regard to the mines themselves," the lieutenant said with a slight shrug, "you'll likely run into just about every type in the Russian inventory including some they captured from the Germans and Japs. You're certain to encounter both floaters and moored types, and you'll have to cope with magnetic and influence mines as well as contact. That's why it's impossible for me to pick out any one type as being typical. If I had to, I guess I'd say the eighteen-thousand pound magnetic mines are the most numerous. Of course, that's only my opinion based on my own experience in Wonsan. However, I've participated in the recovery of some that date back to before the Russo-Jap war of nineteen-oh-four."

Mercer glanced back at the chart and announced, "Recently, we've been encountering quite a lot of small anti-boat mines, the type you'd use against landing craft. They're about the size of a beach ball and each one packs a forty-four pound charge of T-N-T. Apparently, our siege strategy is working, at least as far as keeping the Reds on edge expecting a full-scale invasion. Well, gentlemen, I'm sure you have lots of questions for Commander Russell and myself, so just fire away and we'll do our best to answer them," he said with a broad smile.

Sandy Boland was first to speak up. "What about replenishment? How will we handle that?"

"No sweat, Commander," Russell said with a confident smile. "Since you will be operating with three other cans, we have strongly recommended to Commodore Price that he employ a rotation system with three ships in Wonsan on call at all times, and the fourth just outside the outer harbor where she can refuel and rearm as necessary. That way, each ship will be able to replenish every fourth day, pretty much as you do when you're running interference for the carriers."

"What speed do you recommend we use on our normal harbor patrol, Sir?" *Halsey Wayne's* exec asked.

"These days, fifteen knots," Russell replied. "At one time it was common practice to anchor right in the middle of the harbor in broad daylight. The Reds have gotten so accurate lately, our ships have even stopped dropping their hooks at night. Another thing, don't ever operate close to each other. Those Red gunners love to get two or more ships in the same area with little or no space to maneuver. There's nothing they'd like better than to force you out of the swept area right into the minefield, or cause you to run aground on one of the islands."

Russell hesitated for a second then said, "I hate to be all doom and gloom but I've got to report that they've not only quadrupled their volume of fire, they've been able to score a lot more hits with far fewer rounds. In addition, they seem to be using air bursts to a much greater extent so ah'd suggest you all keep a minimum number of personnel topside. Ah understand that one of your ships is still equipped with forty-millimeter guns," the two-and-a-half-stripper said, eliciting a frown from Owen Royal. "Since the forties are in open mounts, and since they're not likely to cause more than negligible damage when directed against shore fortifications, ah suggest that you keep them unmanned, even when you are engaged in counter-battery fire."

"Are there any specific areas we should try to avoid, Commander?" asked the navigator from the *John Morgan*.

"Ah don't want to sound facetious, but if ah was to answer your question with complete honesty, ah'd have to say you should try to avoid all of them. However, since we all know that that would be impractical, the best advice ah can offer is to tell you to stay away from the edges of the areas that have been swept clear of mines. Unfortunately, those yellow buoys our sweepers plant to delineate the border of a minefield also serve as made-to-order range markers for the Red gunners. They zero-in on them and then use them to correct their fall of shot. 'Ulcer Gulch' is a good example. That's our name for the inboard corner of the swept area just off Kalma Pando...ah mean Hairless Joe," he amended with a feigned tone of apology. "Ah'd also like to caution you all about what we call the Wonsan cocktail hour. It occurs late each afternoon when the sun is due west of the swept areas and in a position so that they can see you but you can't see them. Each day during that time you can expect to be on the receiving end of a heavy barrage from several of their biggest batteries."

Royal sipped some ice water, then asked, "When we're not actually engaged, what condition of readiness do you recommend we employ?"

"Naturally, as C.O., that decision will be up to you," said Russell. "However, the procedure most commonly used in Wonsan these days is to maintain a modified Condition-Three watch. That's what we did on the *Berry*. We usually kept two of our five-inch guns manned at all times. Of course, we also maintained Able setting below decks."

"Commander Russell," Sandy Boland spoke up again. "Discounting those times when we're engaged in counter-battery operations, will we be taking any specific shore targets under fire? I imagine after two years of continued sea and air bombardment, there's not much left to shoot at in Wonsan that's of any military value."

"On the contrary, Commander. In spite of all our efforts, Wonsan's managed to remain the busiest transportation complex the North Koreans have. While we've been able to cut their daylight rail and road movements to less than a trickle, we've had very little success in disrupting their supply runs at night. Our observers on the harbor islands constantly report that no matter how heavy a bombardment our ships lay down, the trains and trucks keep rolling southward. Aerial reconnaissance also confirms this. Our people on Sad Sack tell us that on a clear night they can count well over three hundred sets of headlights moving south. Intelligence estimates that there's probably at least four times that many trucks moving through the city with their lights off. On those nights when traffic's particularly heavy, you can bet the family jewels that the dogfaces and gyrenes on the M-L-R are going to take it on the chin two or three days later."

Russell looked around the wardroom, smiled mirthlessly and said, "There's another thing our intelligence people have told us, and that's that the Commie brass has issued a do-or-die order to the general running the show at Wonsan. He's to sink an American warship of at least destroyer size, and he's to do it mucho quick. They badly need something like that for propaganda purposes, and to show their bosses back in Moscow and Peking that all those rubles they've spent on elaborate shore defenses haven't been pissed away down the ole' rabbit hole. While Wonsan's probably the most heavily fortified harbor in Asia, after two years of siege, they've only managed to sink two minesweepers. And the *Pirate* and the *Pledge* were both victims of mines, not shore batteries. So far their comrade-gunners have managed to hit almost forty ships at Wonsan, but the important thing is, they haven't been able to sink a single one of them. Ah'm certain, as is Admiral Gingrich, that you gentlemen will see to it that the enemy's frustration continues for at least another month."

Aubrey Cobb wriggled slightly and asked, "Sir, with all the ships and aircraft we've committed to this operation,. and in view of the many personnel casualties we've taken in Wonsan, it seems to me that we're not getting much of a return on our investment?"

"That might be a valid contention if you consider it unimportant that our siege has forced the Reds to tie-down eighty thousand of their best troops in reserve just beyond the city to counter what they're certain is going to be an invasion. Ah'd also like to add that there's a hell of a lot of flyboys alive today that would have been pushing up daisies or rotting in a Commie P-O-W camp if we hadn't built an emergency landing strip on Yo Do Island. We've also permanently stationed an L-S-T equipped with rescue helicopters right inside the harbor. Her whirlybirds have fished out more pilots and air crew than ole' man Carter's got little liver pills. Besides, you have to consider what our Wonsan operations must be doing to the enemy psychologically. How do you think they must feel knowing that the Yankee devils...excuse the expression," he inserted with a loud chuckle, "have prevented them from using their most important harbor? Imagine how we'd have felt during the last war if the Germans had been able to shut down New York."

The remaining questions, all pertaining to the support requirements of the minesweepers, were fielded by Lieutenant Mercer. At the conclusion of the briefing, Lieutenant-Commander Russell happily announced, "For the next month, Captain Price here will be the commander of Task Unit Ninety-Five, point two, point one. As such, he will also hold the title 'Mayor of Wonsan.' It's purely honorary, of course, and ah'm certain it doesn't have the blessings of the North Koreans. Our present mayor, Captain Bull, will officially relinquish the title to Commodore Price when you people relieve him and his division on Thursday. Commodore Price will keep the title until next month when he and you are relieved by Captain Conwell and his destroyers. By the way, along with the title comes a symbolic 'Key to the City.' That's a large gilded wooden key that will be transferred over to the commodore the instant he officially takes charge of the harbor operations."

Fresh coffee and Danish were served after the meeting for those of the visitors choosing not to return immediately to their own vessels, all of which were moored within a short distance of *Abner Ward*. Royal, with Cobb and Oetjens, was just about to head for the flagship's quarterdeck when the commodore requested his presence in his stateroom for a brief chat.

"How are things coming along aboard the *Field*, Owen? Are you having any problems I should know about?" Price asked even before the captain had taken a seat on the small leather sofa opposite the commodore.

"No, Sir. I've made certain that you receive a status report at least once a week as you directed. Haven't they been satisfactory?"

The commodore's mouth tightened. "Yes, Owen, they've been quite satisfactory. I only wish the reports from my other three captains could be as detailed and complete. However, my question really wasn't aimed at the structural condition of the *Field* or her operational performance."

Royal looked at him quizzically.

"Tell me, Owen, and this is completely off the record if you like...how are you and your X-O getting along?"

"Why fine, Sir. May I ask what prompted your question?"

"Well, there's been rumors about some bad vibes between you and Lieutenant-Commander Cobb."

"Rumors, Commodore? I'm sorry but I don't understand. As far as I know, there's no problems between my exec and myself. Actually, he's a very conscientious officer...a workaholic in fact."

"Didn't he send a letter to the Bureau of Personnel complaining that he should have received a Purple Heart for that action you were engaged in off Songdo Gap?"

"Yes, Sir. In fact, it was routed through me in accordance with the rules governing chain-of-command. While I didn't endorse his request for the medal, I made certain it was promptly forwarded to BuPers."

"Yes, well I know for a fact that there's been at least one other letter," Price said with a frown.

"If so, Sir, I'm certainly not aware of it."

"No, but I am. I was the addressee. It came a few weeks ago, obviously without going through the command channel."

"Can you tell me its content?"

"Yes, your X-O seems to feel that morale among your ship's company is at an all-time low and threatening to hurt the *Field's* combat efficiency. He cites permissiveness on your part as the principal cause. According to him, you allow your white hats to do just about anything they want. He also stated that gross insubordination is the order-of-the-day aboard the *Field.* Frankly, Owen, you've got enough problems to worry about losing that Russian pilot and almost reporting to a combat assignment with two females on board. The very last thing you need right now is an exec out to cut your throat at the first opportunity. I suggest you get rid of him. If you'd like, I can have him transferred off the *Field* immediately. I'm certain we can locate an experienced replacement without too much trouble."

Royal was silent, and more surprised at the commodore's offer of assistance than at the discovery of his executive officer's perfidy.

"Thank you, but I don't think that will be necessary. Time-wise, we're over the hump as far as this tour is concerned. For the few months we've got left, I'd just as soon not have to break-in a new X-O. One thing about Aubrey Cobb, he's thoroughly familiar with the ship including all her eccentricities."

"Frankly, Owen, I think you're making a king-size mistake, but if that's your decision, so be it. One thing though, I won't condone another breach of the command channel. If Cobb ever tries skirting around it again, I'll personally see to it that he's transferred permanently to one of those little A-V-Ps working in the Persian Gulf...the one that's still without air-conditioning," added Price with a sly smile.

During the brief ride back to the *Field*, Royal was careful not to reveal his displeasure, or to give any hint of what had been discussed in the commodore's cabin. Having elected to retain Cobb, he saw little if any advantage in widening the obvious gap that now existed between him and his second-in-command.

The harbor breezes transported a pungent blend of tar and fish oil as the whaleboat seesawed noisily through the darkness.

• • •

It took all of Owen Royal's skill to guide his ship through this last gauntlet of water and steel being kicked up by the 155-millimeter guns on Kalma Pando, off to starboard. Although it had been only nine days since the commodore had led his destroyers into Wonsan Harbor, all of the ships had achieved the dubious honor of passing six of them under fire, thereby making each member of the division richer by 45 dollars.

Kalma Pando, alias "Hairless Joe," hadn't been half as hostile the day before, thought Royal as he watched more and more yellow flashes blossom along its shoreline. Long minutes passed as the *Field* zigged and zagged. Finally the North Korean batteries grew silent allowing the *Field* to terminate the engagement by drilling a final ten rounds into the enemy landscape.

Now prancing "Tin Pan Alley" like the proverbial cock-of-the-walk, the Charlie P. wheeled by "Ulcer Gulch" before heading south toward "Bunny Hug," the corner of the channel closest to Hwangto Do Island with its small but tenacious garrison of ROK marines. She hurried on past the guns near Um Do Island, attracting scant attention from the seemingly napping enemy. Cutting a course through "Gridiron," the destroyer slowed her engines to ten knots, then continued on as nonchalantly as if she was cruising the waters off Point Loma.

Soon it would be dark. If their luck held and the gooks cooperated, they might have an easy evening, the crew speculated hopefully. With no specific ops scheduled, there was even an outside chance that they might get to see a movie down in the messhall, providing the flyboys or the spotters on "Sad Sack" didn't report a truck convoy trying to sneak through downtown Wonsan.

Earlier in the day, the ship had replenished in the outer bay and had taken a small mountain of mail aboard, the first they'd gotten since departing Sasebo. The captain had received two letters from his wife, one from San Francisco, the other postmarked New York. Both letters were short, no more than five or six lines. Nevertheless, Owen was elated and carried them in his pocket even at GQ.

Below in the Ops Department berthing space, a stack of letters from Cindy Osbourne still lay unopened on top of Kevin Logan's bedding, as Howie Murray laid in wait to sandbag anyone passing through the compartment into viewing newly arrived snapshots of his baby's recent christening.

• • •

Ronald Paradise wasn't at all happy with his new job or the six thousand dollar cut in pay that went with it. Working for a two-bit ad agency in downtown Los Angeles after having risen to copy chief with the Rolls Royce of the industry was a real come-down, he brooded, glancing every few moments at the phone on his desk.

Margolis was supposed to have called from La Jolla an hour ago. So far all he'd gotten from that greasy bastard had been a pile of bills, including one for air fare and a plush hotel room in Acapulco. Well, he'd better come up with something tangible in the next week or so, Paradise sulked, painfully aware that his present salary could not support Margolis' high-living style of investigation for very much longer.

• • •

The "matchsticks" were in trouble off Kwansang-Ni. The mayday blared over the *Field's* bridge-speaker in plain language...*Jackbill*, *Reedfinch*, and *Redbreast* were being attacked by a train.

"Attacked by a train!" exclaimed Royal incredulously as his destroyer, patrolling "the Hatchery," and closest to the scene, received orders from the commodore to steam to the rescue. "I've heard about flak-cars shooting up low-flying planes but who ever heard of a donnybrook between three minesweepers and a train? Now I know what's meant by the inscrutable East," Royal scowled. "Mister Warden! Sound G.Q. We're off to the races again!"

The ensign pulled the handle controlling the general-alarm sending close to 300 bluejackets scampering to their battle stations. A dissonant belch erupted from the klaxon-horn, and the *Charles P. Field* swung around in a wide turn until her bow staff lined up with the three black specks maneuvering frantically among the forest of shell splashes in the distance. As the ship steadied up on her new heading, the noise of grinding gears informed all concerned that the Charlie P.'s midships and after gunhouses were swinging around as far forward as possible, their slender gray barrels reaching out towards the snow-splotched shoreline.

The destroyer charged on at full throttle. Soon Royal and the others on the open bridge were able to make out details of the minesweepers, including their bow numbers. Bearing stronger semblance to tuna clippers than to men-of-war, the wooden-hulled 136-footers appeared none the worse for their bizarre encounter. *Reedfinch* and *Redbreast* were still trailing their paravane gear. *Jackbill*, closer inshore, was making heavy smoke and firing her single-barreled popgun ardently if ineffectually at a cloud of soot and brown smoke rolling rapidly out of range to the north in the general area of a colossal smokestack. This had been the first time the *Field* had ever ventured into this sector of Wonsan Harbor, and the chimney was the tallest Royal or anyone else aboard the destroyer had ever seen. It towered scorched and unearthly above the gutted skeleton of what once had been the most prosperous sake brewery on the Korean coast.

"SHIFTLESS...THIS IS POLAND," the *Field's* bridge-speaker cackled loudly.

"Poland's the call name for the *Jackbill*, Sir," Ensign Daly volunteered, anticipating his C.O.'s question.

"SHIFTLESS, WE'VE GOT AN ARMORED TRAIN SHAGGING ASS TOWARD THE NORTH. THEY MUST HAVE SEEN YOU COMING! the message from the minesweeper continued in decidedly unregulation form. "HOPE YOU CAN HELP US OUT...OVER."

"WE'LL GIVE IT THE OLD COLLEGE TRY, POLAND...OUT," Royal answered. A flurry of bearings and ranges flooded the *Field's* gunnery circuits.

"Shoot!" cried Ensign Keagan in the director, and five of the *Field's* best bellowed from the muzzles to whine their high pitched song toward the enemy's coastline. A second, third, and fourth salvo followed in rapid order.

Black pillars of smoke swallowed up the train as 5-inch shells churned up clusters of rock and brick from the brewery rubble. Royal watched despairingly for a train axle or a locomotive boiler to come hurtling through the air with the other debris. He felt the *Field* shudder as her main battery continued to pummel the real estate near the demolished sake works. Suddenly, the chimney began to sway and teeter like a poorly stacked pile of books. Then in best Tower of Babel fashion, the huge cylinder came tumbling down with doomsday finality.

"Sooey pig!" exclaimed a goggle-eyed lookout standing nearby.

"Cease fire!" ordered Royal, his vision hampered by the enormous cloud of red dust.

The *Field* veered slightly as her engines were slowed. Royal was impatient as he waited for the smoke and dust to clear. Off the starboard quarter, *Jackbill* moved even closer inshore.

Royal hurried back into the wheelhouse where he joined Oetjens at the chart table. "I'd like to follow *Jackbill* in as close as our draft will allow. Maybe we can get a better look at the mess we just made over there. With all that dust, I still can't tell whether or not we got lucky and tagged that train." Royal hurriedly checked his ship's position and the fathom markings ahead. "I hope this damn thing's still accurate," he said with a frown, his eyes focusing on the legend at the lower left corner of the chart. It read: *From a Japanese survey of 1905 with additions to 1932.* Returning to the open bridge, Royal studied the *Jackbill's* probing maneuver. Decidedly tempting fate, he told himself as he watched the sweeper move in even closer.

"*Jackbill's* skipper must be off his rocker," Oetjens said, as he took his position at the C.O.'s side.

A flashing light came to life on the beach near where the train had last been seen. Royal aimed his glasses at the light in time to see a fiery stream of tracers chip a ragged line across the surface of the water just short of *Jackbill*, now swinging around to present as little a target as possible.

Puffs of white smoke and silver flashes suddenly blossomed from what looked to Royal like two stony mounds at the water's edge. The mark-37 was already on them, and at the captain's command, the *Field's* main battery got back into the fight. The first salvo was a straddle. So was the second. The third landed directly on target showering the sky with stones and sandbags. A plume of flame rocketed a hundred feet in the air, its peak crowned by the unmistakable outline of a tank turret.

The *Field's* gunners shifted their attention to the second target. Again their placement was right on the mark. When the smoke cleared, Royal could make out the burning chasis of a treadless T-34 which like its equally unfortunate mate had been salvaged and converted into a stationary pillbox. Jets of oily smoke seeped out of the tank's open hatch and from a hole near the base of its oversize turret. Then...before the *Field* could dispatch another 5-inch round, the T-34 disintegrated in a bubbling ball of orange that glimmered weirdly off the snow bank beyond.

Sweeping the shoreline with his binoculars, Owen Royal probed the thick smoke that drifted along the track bed behind the two tanks, both of which were blazing fiercely. He was well aware of the advice Tim Barrett had given him back in Pusan about the advantages of making it into the "Trainbusters Club." Right now he knew he could use any edge he could get, recalling dolefully how Commodore Price had recently made a point of reminding him that he was still in hot water over that dead Ruskie pilot and the two female stowaways.

"We've chopped up about a half mile of track but we missed that damn train," Royal grunted angrily at Oetjens. "Mister Warden!" he shouted in the direction of the wheelhouse doorway. "Have the radio shack dispatch a message to Jehovah...we estimate armored train moving north from Wonsan...request air strike."

Warden acknowledged and seconds later the message was speeding through the ether to the commander of Task Force 77. Carriers *Kearsarge, Philippine Sea* and *Valley Forge* swerved into the wind for the launch, and by noon, the locomotive and its six gun-cars lay in a smoldering heap two miles shy of Kowon.

Charles P. Field passed the remainder of the morning riding shotgun for *Reedfinch, Redbreast* and *Jackbill* as they completed their perilous chore. Several hours and six exploded contact mines later, the four gray ships took their leave of the "Hatchery" and cruised out to quieter waters on the windward side of Yo Do Island where *Jackbill* requested permission to lay alongside and exchange movies. While the *Field's* bluejackets were haggling over the exchange of "*Micheal Shayne Private Detective*" for "*Henry Aldrich Plays Cupid*," *Jackbill's* commanding officer came on board to present his respects to Commander Royal. Cobb traded courtesies with the visitor, a carrot-topped Jg. named Rooney who looked hardly passed his teens. In another minute the young officer was sharing coffee and slightly stale pound cake with Royal in the wardroom.

"How'd you people get yourselves in such a mess this morning?" Royal asked with a broad smile.

The Jaygee leaned forward and looked at Owen quizzically. "Oh, you mean the train. Come to think of it, I guess getting shot at by a train does seem a bit weird. Well, Sir, we were sweeping in about five hundred yards from shore. As usual, we beat both *Reedfinch* and *Redbreast* in stringing out our paravanes," he explained with the animated hand gesture of an overly-eager fighter pilot, "when my bow lookout spots this railroad construction party starting to work on some track. I was just getting ready to scatter them with a couple of air bursts from my three-inch when Kenny Hutton over on *Reedfinch* reports some white smoke rolling up from south of the city. In a couple of minutes, I'm able to make out this train puffing its way along in our direction with all the nonchalance of the Boston Merchant's Limited. Well, this is too good a chance to pass up so I cut loose my paravanes and start making speed to intercept at a point where the tracks come right down to the beach. *Reedfinch* and *Redbreast* have the same idea and they start moving in too," he said dunking his cake in his coffee cup. "We're still about five-hundred yards out, and my gun-gang's just shoving that first shell in the breach when this big clinker hauling six boxcars, grinds to a stop. It was damn disconcerting," the young officer said, "this Commie train just stopping like that when they can see, plain as hell, that we're sighting in on them."

"I imagine it was," said Royal, chuckling as he spoke.

"Well, the next thing we know, the sides come tumbling down and those boxcars aren't really boxcars at all...they're flatcars, and each is mounting what I figure's at least a four-inch gun. They sure surprised the hell out of me," he said, shaking his head. "You know, Sir, these little matchsticks the navy calls minesweepers weren't built to take on that kind of opposition."

"I don't know, Lieutenant. You people seem to have handled the situation pretty well this morning."

"Two parts evasion and eight parts luck," he answered with a grim smile. "We were sure glad to see this baby crashing the party. Now I know how those people in the covered wagons felt. The only thing missing was the cavalry bugle."

"Well, at least we were flying our cavalry flag." Royal grinned.

"Is that what the blue flag is? When I first picked it up with my binoculars, I figured it was some kind of a United Nations flag. Do you fly it all the time, Sir?"

"No, usually only when we're engaged. It's sort of an inside joke among the ships in our division. They all fly the Stars and Bars of the Confederacy."

"Well, one thing's certain. The gooks on that rail-hopping Q-boat aren't likely to forget that blue flag of yours. You sure sent them running with their caboose between their legs. They're probably all the way to Siberia by now."

"I hope not. We requested an air strike as soon as we discovered the train had moved out. I figure Jehovah's fly-boys should have caught it somewhere between here and Kowon."

"Hope so...speaking of Jehovah, Commander...how are you going to explain about clobbering 'Old Smokey'?"

"Old Smokey?"

"Yes, also known as the Sam-ho stovepipe. Sam-ho was the name of the sake works before the *Wisconsin* pounded it into sawdust last year."

"I still don't understand what you mean about the chimney. Why would we have to explain anything to Jehovah?" Royal's expression was now one of complete bewilderment.

"That stack's a sacred white cow with the airedales. It's...excuse me...I meant to say it was the tallest chimney on the entire coast and the only one still standing for two hundred miles in either direction. The pilots use it as a navigational beacon...sort of a reference point. I hear they're also superstitious about it. They consider it a good luck charm. There's been a standard ops order for two years now about not hurting Old Smokey. Just last month I heard that some jet jockey from the *Kearsarge* got himself grounded for just strafing the damn thing. There's also scuttlebutt that on the last day of the war just before a truce takes effect, the stack's going to be declared open game for the flyboys from several of the carrier squadrons. I heard they've formed an Old Smokey pool. The kitty would have gone to the first pilot able to bowl it over on his first pass using nothing larger than rockets or his wing cannons."

Commander Royal glanced up nervously. "Hopkins," he called to the steward who was approaching the table with a fresh pot of coffee. "Please inform Mister Stockwell that I'd like to see him as soon as possible. Excuse me, Lieutenant," said Owen politely as he rose from his chair and reached for the phone mounted on the bulkhead bracket. He dialed the two-digit number and heard...

"Radio Central, Chief Hamey speaking."

"This is the captain, Chief. Please bring any operational dispatches and advisories we've received from the commodore or Admiral Gingrich's people since February Second, the day we deployed here in Wonsan. I'm particularly interested in any that mention the Sam-ho sake works."

Owen returned to the table.

"I don't think they'll make a fuss about Old Smokey, Sir," Rooney interjected, acutely aware of the sudden tempest his remarks had stirred up. "It's not as though you went after the stack deliberately like that pilot from the 'Queer Barge'. You certainly had a good reason...the destruction of that train."

"Yes, but you've forgotten a very important fact. We didn't get the train."

"Maybe so, Sir, but you sure saved our bacon from frying when you knocked out those two caviar cans." Rooney, sensing his host's awkward position and wishing to disassociate himself from the impending wardroom confrontation, discretely suggested that he had better return to *Jackbill* to inventory his ship's lost sweeping gear.

Royal accompanied the Jaygee to the quarterdeck. When he returned, Lieutenant Stockwell and Chief Radioman Hamey were busily spreading operational dispatches from three clipboards across the wardroom table.

"Here's a copy of the one I think you want, Captain," Hamey snorted in his usual foghorn tone. "It's dated five February and informs all ships in Task Unit Ninety-five, point-two, point-one, that the Nine April dispatch is still in effect. It then goes on to say that all surface and air units are to avoid any action that might damage or destroy the smokestack at the Sam-ho sake brewery," he said, handing the paper to the *Field's* C.O.

"Why wasn't I informed of this when it was received?" demanded Royal as he read the dispatch. "You know I've issued a standing order that I'm to personally initial every dispatch received aboard this ship!"

"Yes, Sir," the chief replied. "I brought that one up to the bridge personally, Sir. I remember because it came through just a few minutes after we received this one with the call-names for the new Rok frigates," he said reaching for another dispatch which he handed to Royal. "I remember cause I brought them both up to the bridge together."

The captain studied the second paper. "Yes, I recall receiving and initialing this one about the Korean ships, but what happened to the other dispatch?"

"Well, Sir, you weren't on the bridge when I brought them up, but Mister Stockwell here was just coming off watch. He said he was going below to see you about something, and that he'd take the dispatches with him and give them to you."

Stockwell tensed as the captain glared at him.

"Alright, Chief. You'd better get back to the crypto-shack. Mister Stockwell and I can take it from here."

"Yes, Sir," Hamey said breathing heavily as he made a hasty exit from the wardroom.

"Okay, Don, what's the deal here? The chief says he gave you the original of this dispatch," Royal said, handing Stockwell the copy of the order from Jehovah.

"Yes, Sir, he did," the Ops Department head answered in a wobbly voice.

"Well...what the hell did you do with it?"

"I don't know, Sir...I...eh...I thought I had given you both dispatches. I don't know what could have happened to it."

"Well, think man! Were you carrying it in your hand? Perhaps you folded it and put it into your pocket."

"I had to be carrying it in my hand, Captain. I've a thing about never folding dispatches, the same way I'm always careful about never folding checks. I'd say I must have accidentally dropped it coming down the ladder, or maybe somewhere in the passageway near your cabin. I imagine one of the stewards or a compartment cleaner found it and probably tossed it over the side with the garbage."

"Our stewards aren't the brightest in the navy I'll admit, but I'm certain they know enough to recognize a dispatch from the radio shack. If they found it, they'd give it to one of the officers or at least take it back to Radio-Central. I suggest you go there right now and ask Hamey if there's any possibility that the dispatch might have been returned to one of his radiomen without him knowing it. There's always the chance the radioman just filed it away without checking it to see whether or not I'd initialed it."

Stockwell returned in less than five minutes, the elusive dispatch clutched tightly in his hand.

"You were right, Captain," he announced even before he'd reached the wardroom table. "One of the stewards...Ignaccio...found it and took it directly to Radio-Central. Buckley was the watch-P-O at the time. He assumed you'd seen it and filed it away without bothering to check for your initials."

"That doesn't explain how you could forget that you started out from the bridge with two dispatches in your hand."

"No, Sir. I have no excuse," the Ops officer answered in a half whisper.

"That's not good enough, Don. Ordinarily you're one of the most conscientious officers on this ship. Are you having any personal problems? Anyone sick at home or anything like that?"

"No captain. My family's not sick or anything like that."

"Well, something's been bothering you. I haven't seen you crack a smile since that morning we left Sasebo. And another thing, I've asked you three times in the past week for a list of the new electronics gear you want for C.I.C."

"I'll get working on it right away, Sir. You'll have it in the next hour." Stockwell paused, swallowed hard, and said, "Captain, about what happened this morning, it was entirely my fault. I'm damn sorry if it's going to cause you any embarrassment with the commodore."

"It's not only the commodore."

"Well, Sir. Admiral Gingrich's tour is up tomorrow. When Admiral Olsen relieves him, he'll probably bring in his own staff. There's a good chance the stack will get lost in the confusion that usually occurs during a transition period."

"That may be but there's still Jehovah and his airedales. That's where the order originated."

"Captain, with your permission, I'd like to submit a letter through channels to Jehovah explaining that I had lost the dispatch before you ever had a chance to see it."

"That won't be necessary," Royal said in a consolatory voice. "Destroying that stack might cause us some embarrassment, nothing more. Jehovah will judge our action within the context of the overall situation. I'm certain we'll get a fair shuffle."

Royal remained in the wardroom after Stockwell's departure. He studied the Ops order for the next assignment which called for a run into the swept area of the harbor known as "Duckpin." He knew this would be the first time the *Field* would come under the guns at Hodo Pando. He was well aware of their reputation but quickly decided there was little sense in worrying about them or what might happen tomorrow.

The Ops order fully digested, he left the wardroom and walked out through the thwartships passageway to the main deck. It was already dark and the winter moon seemed twice its normal size. It reminded him of the gaudy yellow lanterns strung along Hunky-dory Street. He watched the huge bulb, certain he could make out a ragged crack running down its center. Then the cold got to him and he decided to let someone else worry about the moon. He had enough to worry about just taking care of the *Field*, he smiled wryly.

He reentered the wardroom in time to hear the overhead speaker cackle out the word that, "the movie for tonight will be 'The Narrow Margin' starring Marie Windsor and Charles McGraw." At the same time a hundred miles away at Panmunjom, Communist negotiators were again obstructing the truce talks with fabricated charges that U.N. forces had bombarded the neutral zone.

Chapter XXI - "Tin Pan Alley"

"Straddle, Captain!" Ensign Warden reported superfluously as an avalanche of water crashed heavily upon the bridge roof and gun-director.

"They've got our range and we haven't even reached Duckpin yet," a helmeted Owen Royal growled. "Helmsman! Come left ten degrees!" the captain ordered as close to twenty white geysers walked across the water less than a hundred yards ahead of the racing destroyer. More water spouts danced off the port beam and now enemy shells were tearing up clumps of gray water uncomfortably close to the stern, making Royal painfully aware that he was under fire from three directions...Hodo Pando, Umi-do, and Kalma Gak. This was by far the most lethal fire the *Field* had yet encountered in "Tin Pan Alley" or any other part of Wonsan Harbor, Royal decided.

C.I.C. had just informed him that the ship had reached a point 18,000 yards from Hodo Pando, the maximum effective range for his 5-inch guns. "Come right five degrees!" bellowed Royal as a new mountain of water erupted close to the port bow, spraying the base of the bridge and forward gun houses with flying steel.

The *Field's* bow dipped abruptly as the ship ducked through and under the water. Now with all guns clawing out at Hodo Pando, she charged in to close the range.

Abner Ward and *Halsey Wayne*, zigzagging desperately a mile ahead, were undergoing an even more murderous ordeal. Luckless *Wayne* was already falling off to starboard, black smoke cloaking much of her bridge. From the *Field's* wheelhouse, Royal could see a fire spreading along the main deck from *Wayne's* afterdeckhouse. Another fire was raging in one of Sandy Boland's motor-whaleboats.

On *Abner Ward*, a twisted blob of scorched metal sat where her number-four 5-inch had been functioning only a moment before. As Royal watched, the flagship also veered off to starboard to disappear amid a new forest of shell splashes. The commodore's ship emerged seconds later hissing white steam from nearly thirty small holes along her port side.

More shells rained down around the *Field*. The destroyer dashed through the spray, her long gray rifles trading shell for shell as they spun about to bear on the enemy gun emplacements each time the destroyer swerved to a new heading. *Wayne* and *Ward* were well off the starboard beam now, and word had just been given to Royal that *John Morgan* had canceled her replenishment in the outer bay and was rushing towards Wonsan Harbor to join the fight. Even more reassuring was the message that forty strike aircraft were inbound from *Phil Sea* and *Valley Forge*.

The Charlie P.'s wheelhouse rattled with each crashing salvo. Royal studied the rocky face of Hodo Pando trying to spot his fall of shot, at the same time handling the ship, swinging her bow from left to right in a series of short sharp course changes.

A ragged line of explosions was now discernible on the enemy shore. Royal could see the black puffs erupting in a tight cluster near the concrete wall that housed Hodo Pando's main battery-control. Royal was reasonably certain it was his gunners' handiwork, although both *Wayne* and *Ward* were still firing sporadically.

It was almost thirty minutes now since the *Field* had been taken under fire, Royal reckoned, glancing at his watch. With *Ward* and *Wayne* now falling well astern, he wondered just how much longer his own ship's luck could possibly hold.

As if to answer, a loud scraping noise like heavy chains being dragged across corrugated steel suddenly pierced the din of the guns, followed an instant later by a thunderous explosion that lifted the *Field's* stern clear of the water sending officers and bluejackets reeling. By the time Royal and the others had regained a standing position, the first wing of Skyraiders from Task Force 77 were roaring overhead on their way to plaster Hodo Pando and the other Red hot spots around the harbor.

"Damage-Control says we've taken a direct hit in the after berthing space, Captain," exclaimed a slightly flustered bridge-talker. Hardly had the young sailor uttered the words when a message from Commodore Price blared over the TBS speaker ordering all of the destroyers to disengage and return immediately to the outer bay to assess battle damage.

Looking aft now over the signal bags, Royal and Oetjens grimly observed the black smoke funneling skyward through the jagged hole dead center between the two depth-charge racks which prudently had been emptied of ashcans the morning the division had taken up its Wonsan assignment.

"Damage-Control reports casualties in after-steering, Sir," the bridge-talker reported, trailing the extension cord from his headset as he followed the captain back to the signal bridge. "Damage-Control says they've also suffered three casualties among their after D-C party," the sailor added.

"Come hard right to zero-six-five, Helmsman," Royal directed, stepping back into the wheelhouse. The *Field* leaned abruptly to starboard as she wheeled around to narrowly slip in between two tall stalks of water that spired up from a fresh enemy salvo.

Swinging hard into the wind, *DD-505* passed through some of her own smoke. "Make turns for thirty knots!" instructed Royal as his destroyer whipped around to a course calculated to take her to the outer bay via the passage north of Ung-do Island. Ordering maximum smoke to mask his withdrawal, Royal released the speaker button seconds before a large caliber shell came whistling between the stacks to pass over the forward bank of torpedo tubes and skim by Don Stockwell and the others perched precariously on the open platform that served as secondary-conn.

Royal tensed as he reached up for the lever on the squawk-box. "Damage-Control Central...this is the captain. Is Mister Sternhagen there?"

"This is Lieutenant Sternhagen, Sir," came a quick reply.

"Rolf. What's the dope on our casualties? How bad is it?"

"Not too good, Sir. Just about everyone who was back there took some shrapnel. That includes Mike Daly and his two people in after-steering, and three of my people. They've all inhaled quite a bit of smoke, too. Larkin got it worst...lost an arm. I guess it could have been a lot worse, though. At least nobody bought the farm."

"Thank God for that," Royal grimaced.

"We've also got the fire out but there's still quite a bit of smoke."

"What's the extent of the structural damage?"

"We've lucked out there, Sir. There's hardly any as far as I can tell except for a king-size hole in the deck, of course. The hull and frame seem to be okay. There's some flooding near the stern plates but no more than we usually get when we drop our depth charges. However, the compartment's a royal mess. It's going to be quite some time before it's habitable again. There's racks and mattresses all over the place. Most of the lockers are smashed, too."

"What's the status of the wounded?"

"We've taken them to the battle dressing station in the messhall. Luckily, most of them were able to get there under their own power. Larkin is the only one we had trouble moving. Parish had a tough time stopping the bleeding, but he's got it under control now."

"Good. I'll be down there as soon as I'm certain we're out of this shooting gallery. Our planes are clobbering Hodo Pando right now so the worst should be over."

Royal walked back out onto the open wing. On shore, numerous fires were raging as puddles of napalm colored the rock a hellish orange.

By noon, the three wounded tin cans, squired by the *John Morgan*, were rounding the northern tip of Ung-do to enter the relatively tranquil waters of the outer bay. There, within the hour, the more seriously wounded would be transferred to the battleship *Missouri* and cruiser *Saint Paul*, both of which were equipped with extensive medical facilities.

•   •   •

Squatting on a foot locker in the Ops Department berthing space, Howie Murray fastidiously sealed the letter, the fifth he'd managed to write to Mary Alice and his girls in the week since the *Field* had reached Sasebo and nestled up alongside repair ship *Luzon.*

"Got a stamp I can borrow, Kev?" he called to Logan who was busily buffing his liberty shoes.

"Sure...in my locker. The door's open. The stamps are in the red box."

"Thanks. Say, did you hear Stockwell before when he was talking to Coates? He said the repairs to the First Division compartment are three days ahead of schedule. At that rate, we could be heading back to Wonsan sometime this coming weekend," the first class said glumly. "You know, we still had ten days left to do when they detached us."

"I don't think the navy's going to hold us to it, especially since we were officially relieved by DesDiv Seventy-two. Besides, the *Wayne* and *Ward* will be in the yard at Yokosuka for at least a month. From what Coates said, they really got themselves chewed up this time."

"Yeah, those guys on the *Wayne* must feel like citizens of Yokosuka by now," quipped Bacelli. "This is the second time they've gone in there for major repairs. Maybe the Nips will let them vote in the next election. One thing's for sure, they must have the inside track on all the best cat houses by now," said the third-class as he started up the ladder to the main deck. "Hey, Logan! If you're planning to make that liberty launch, you'd better shake your ass. It's leaving in about two minutes."

"That's okay, I'm in no great hurry. I'll catch the seven o'clock boat," Kevin casually replied as Bacelli departed on his way to join Gardiner and Nugent already waiting on the line at the *Luzon's* quarterdeck.

Cautiously, Howie glanced around the compartment. Except for him and Logan, and a couple of quartermaster-signalmen sacked out on their racks well out of earshot, the berthing space appeared deserted. "Tell me, Kev, and I want the straight scoop...what do you really think our chances are of making it back home in one piece?"

Logan stared hard at the first-class. "Come on, Howie, you're a short timer now. You're not starting to sweat this thing are you? After all the time you spent out in the Pacific, you should be able to coast through this one."

"Larkin, and all those guys we lost in the whaleboat won't be doing any more coasting. A shell made for a police action can make you just as dead as one made for a full-fledged war. As far as starting to sweat this tour, hell, I've been sweating it since that afternoon back in Dago Turk put out the scuttlebutt that the division was deploying to Korea. If you really want to know...I come damn near puking all over the maneuvering board every time we get within twenty miles of that Red coast. You must have noticed. You did, didn't you?"

"Hell no. You always look as cool as that proverbial cucumber."

"Don't try to snow me, Kev. It won't work."

"When did I ever try to give you a snow job? Now if you were talking about the exec, that would be a different matter," Logan said, standing erect to survey with satisfaction the glass-like shine on his shoes.

"Yeah, I guess Cobb sweats enough at G-Q to fill a bucket." The radarman's face brightened slightly. "Bet he's happy as a pig in shit that the old man booted his ass out of after-steering. It's just like that son-of-a-bitch to luck out though. Everybody on the ship figured he'd picked after-steering as his G-Q station 'cause he thought it was the safest spot on the ship."

"I learned at Okinawa that there's no such thing as a safe spot on a destroyer," answered Logan with a caustic laugh.

"I'm glad Daly wasn't hurt badly. He's not a bad Joe for an ensign. For that matter, all our ensigns are pretty good guys. That's probably because they're all reserves," Murray said with firm conviction. "I learned a long time ago that ensigns aren't really the pricks they're made out to be in books and movies. Of course, that's only because they don't know what the hell they're doing and they need all the help they can get from the chiefs and petty-officers. Unfortunately, as soon as they make J-G, they start thinking they know more than the captain. I've never known it to fail, even with ninety-day blunders. They get that extra half-stripe on their cuff and they turn into pricks over night."

"It wasn't that way with Mister MacKinlay. I'm sure he was always a prick," said Logan, adjusting the knot on his neckerchief so that both of the ends hung evenly. "Well, we should get to see if your theory's valid since all our ensigns will be getting their promotions to J-G pretty soon. All except Coatsie," Logan added.

"How did you find out Coates isn't making Jaygee?"

"From Gordon, who else? He typed up all the fitness reports. How come you look so surprised? You really didn't think the old man could possibly recommend Coates for a promotion after the way he screwed up any chance we had of getting that Russian pilot, did you?"

"Hell, that was back in November. Coates has sharpened up quite a bit since then," replied Murray in a frustrated tone.

"Maybe so, but when we missed fishing that Mig jockey out of the drink, it hurt the old man a lot more than it hurt Coates. Everybody on the ship knows that Coates isn't staying in the navy once his three years are up. Just last week he told me that he wasn't even planning to keep his commission in the reserve. Royal's spent most of his life in the navy, and now thanks to Coates, I doubt he'll ever see that fourth stripe. And in the navy, if an officer doesn't advance, he gets the boot," Logan added with a frown.

"You really believe Royal's going to get sacked just over one dead Russian?"

"One dead Russian? Don't you realize that the order to get that pilot must have come right from The White House, or at the very least, from the State Department. I'd hate to have to count all the admirals that are probably still running around the Pentagon red-faced because of one reserve ensign on the Charlie P. As C.O., Royal has to take full responsibility for the foul-up. You know that as well as I do."

"I suppose you're right," Murray said shaking his head. "It just doesn't seem fair. Coates has been doing a real good job lately. If anyone's been fouling up, it's been the All-American Boy."

"Lieutenant Stockwell?"

"Yeah. You haven't forgotten how he almost plowed our bow into the side of the *Luzon* last week, have you? He would have, too, if Royal hadn't grabbed the conn. Then just last night, Stockwell was checking the classified pubs in C.I.C. When he got through, he took off without putting them back into the safe. It's a good thing that I was the one who found them stacked up on the plotting table. If Cobb had seen them, Stockwell's head would have gone on the chopping block mucho fast."

"I have to admit, Stockwell has been acting strangely for the past few weeks."

"Maybe being up there on that open platform with all those shells whizzing around his head has finally gotten to him," said Murray.

"No, he's had that foggy look since the morning we pulled out of Sasebo and headed for Wonsan. I think he must have gotten some bad news in that mail we took on board just before we left. Maybe his father's sick again. He told me once that his father had to retire from his railroad job because of a bum ticker."

"That's too bad. I'll remember his father later tonight in my prayers."

"You mean you still say prayers at night?"

"When I can. Don't you?"

"You've got to be kidding," quipped Logan with a muffled laugh.

"Well, it certainly wouldn't do you any harm."

"Drop it, Howie. I thought we made an arrangement back in Yokosuka that you'd forget about playing chaplain and give up trying to save my immortal soul."

"Okay, Kev. It's your soul, not mine. What are you planning to do over on the beach?"

"Nothing special. I'll probably just have a few beers at the petty-officers' club. You're not in the duty section. Why don't you come along?"

"I would except that I want to see the movie over on the *Luzon* later. They're showing 'Blue Skies' with Bing Crosby and Fred Astaire. I remember taking Mary Alice to see it one night back in Warren. That was back in forty-six."

"Forty-six?"

"Yeah. That was the year we got married. Speaking of marriage, I've been meaning to ask you...how are things coming along with your nurse?"

"Okay, I guess. However, I wouldn't call her my nurse. In fact, next time we go into Yokosuka, I plan to break things off with her. All I'd need would be for her to start cramping my style when I get back to New York. She's got some wacky idea about putting in for a transfer to the naval hospital at St. Albans. I'll admit she's great looking and not a bad lay, but I've got to look at the big picture. I sure as hell don't want her bugging me about dates and things when I'm back at the agency. Besides, she's got some crazy idea that I'd make a good husband. Can you imagine? Me getting married?"

"Damn it, Kevin. Don't you have any conscience at all?"

"Of course I do. That's why I plan to see her the next time we're in Yokosuka so I can tell her in person. Otherwise, I'd just drop her a 'Dear John' or whatever the equivalent is for females," he said smiling. "Well, enjoy the movie. I'd better get over to the *Luzon* if I'm going to make the next liberty boat."

"Murray shook his head in frustration as Logan tramped hurriedly up the ladder.

•   •   •

Sasebo was heavily clouded over, a dull chilly morning with the sky the color of bad milk.

"Are you absolutely certain the captain said he wants to see me right now?" asked Lieutenant-Commander Cobb, standing on the foc'sle, one foot planted atop the starboard anchor chain.

"Yes, Sir, that's what he told me," Stephens, the duty-messenger replied with an indifferent shrug.

The exec paused. His lips twitched in a nervous smile as he glanced back and up at the 0-2 level and the regiment of quartermaster-strikers noisily hacking away at the base of the bridge with chipping hammers and wire brushes. A shower of sparks sprinkled down on the main deck as a lone welder turned his torch on the roof of the number-2 gunhouse.

"Have some people from the First Division rig some canvas over there," Cobb said to Ensign Coates who was officer-of-the-deck for the eight to noon. "Be certain they keep that area hosed down while that welding's going on." Turning his attention to the big repair ship alongside, and the pile of metal removed from the *Field's* after berthing space, the exec instructed, "Before that gang from the *Luzon* hauls any more scrap away, you'd better let Chief Lacey or one of his shipfitters take a look at what they're taking. There may be something we can salvage. If anything important develops in the next few minutes, I'll be in the captain's cabin," Cobb grunted as he strutted off, quickening his pace as he passed through the cascading sparks.

The door to the captain's cabin was open. Cobb tapped the steel bulkhead with his ring. The noise was barely audible against the din from the chipping hammers.

"Come in, Aub. Close the door, please. Maybe it will help drown out some of that noise. Coffee?" Royal asked, reaching for the fresh pot Chief DelRosario had brought in just moments before.

"No, thank you. I just had a cup in the wardroom." Cobb seated himself at the captain's invitation.

"I guess you know what I want to talk to you about," Royal said, pouring coffee into his own cup.

"To be perfectly honest, no, Sir, I don't."

"It's this request you made to have Parish court-martialed." Royal picked up a file of papers from his desk. "I've read your reasons over carefully. I have to tell you, I don't think you have a valid case. There's no way I'm going to proceed with this. If anything, I've been considering recommending a Commendation Medal for Parish."

"Captain, I assure you I am not being capricious in bringing these charges against this man. I gave the matter serious consideration for three days before I took action. I hope you don't think I get any personal satisfaction out of this. As hard as I tried, I just couldn't find a reasonable excuse for what Parish did. He had no justification in cutting off Larkin's arm like that."

"I've spoken to Rolf Sternhagen and Mike Daly. They both confirmed the fact that Larkin's arm was hanging by a single strand the size of a thread. It's Mister Sternhagen's opinion that there was nothing left of the arm to save."

"Yes, Sir, but Sternhagen's not an M.D. Besides, he wasn't present when Parish took it upon himself to go ahead and snip off the arm. I've requested a Special Court-Martial for Parish not because of what he did, but because of what he didn't do. Chief Claccum is the ship's senior medic and the person with the responsibility to make such decisions. It was up to Parish to obtain his permission before taking a serious step like that."

"I think you'll agree that Chief Claccum is not exactly a medical prodigy. Correct me if I'm wrong, but wasn't it you who once remarked that the chief was so dense, he needed explicit directions before he could use a roll of toilet paper?"

"Yes, but I was just a little ticked off at him that day."

"Are you sure you're not still ticked off at Parish? As I recall, you were pretty annoyed that afternoon off Songdo Gap when Parish insisted that the blood on your neck came from a fish."

"Captain, I'm much too professional to let something like that influence my judgment in a matter as important as this." Cobb gave an angry tug at the front of his collar. "As far as Claccum's concerned, with all due respect, I'd like to suggest that his competency or incompetency is not in question here."

"That's a point well taken, and I'm in full agreement. However, let's look at this thing from a practical viewpoint. When the alleged transgression took place, the chief was several compartments away in sickbay, completely occupied with three of the wounded. I questioned Parish a few minutes before you got here. He stated that Larkin's arm was pinning him under a stanchion that had collapsed from the explosion. Two of Sternhagen's D-C people have already backed him up on that. Parish is certain that if he hadn't cut the arm, Larkin would have bled to death before they could pull him out. I'm convinced that the corpsman's quick thinking was the only thing that saved that man's life."

"That may be true, but Parish is only a third-class P-O. He didn't have the authority to make that decision while there was senior medical personnel on board. It isn't as though he was in an isolated foxhole with no way of contacting a superior. Sickbay isn't that far away. Besides, he could have called Claccum on the sound-powered phones."

"That was the first thing I checked out," Royal retorted. "Parish did call Claccum for permission, but the chief wouldn't commit himself until he had a chance to personally inspect the situation. Unfortunately, he couldn't do that until he finished trying to save Aaker's leg, which as the base hospital informed us yesterday, Aaker's lost anyway."

"But the fact remains, the chief didn't give Parish permission."

"Granted, but he didn't refuse it either. Look, Aub. This thing isn't as cut and dry as it might appear to be in the rule books. Before we decide to nail Parish's ass to the bulkhead, there are some other factors to consider. Parish is a bright kid, and one of the most hard-working pharmacist mates I've met in my seventeen years in the navy. I've thoroughly reviewed his personal folder. When this mess started over here, he was in a pre-med class at N.Y.U. He could have easily obtained a college deferment if he'd wanted it. Next to engaging in panty raids, ducking the draft seems to be the number one priority of most of our collegians these days," Royal said in an irritated tone. "Parish not only volunteered for active duty, he specifically requested a tour in Korea. I know you're aware that he was flooding ship's office with requests for an assignment ashore with the marines until last month when he finally decided that we were in this war, too."

"That's very admirable, Sir, but you can't allow that to color your judgment. Parish's patriotism can't give Larkin back his arm."

"Of course not," countered Royal sharply. "However, I think you will agree that it gives a clear indication of his character."

Cobb's brow creased in a frown. He said nothing.

"You know damn well, Aub, in the case of a special court-martial or even a summary, the records are permanent. Even if Parish is acquitted, and I'm sure he would be, the mere fact that he was charged might be just enough to keep him from getting into medical school. I hear the competition is pretty stiff these days."

"I realize that. I just don't think it's a mitigating circumstance."

"Maybe not, but I've made my decision. I don't want any charges brought against Parish in this regard."

"Is that an order, Sir?"

"Yes, if you prefer it that way," Royal answered in a quiet voice.

A pained look crossed Cobb's face as the captain shifted the subject of the conversation to the progress of the work underway in the after-berthing space.

•   •   •

Clear of the *Luzon* now, the *Field* slid neatly out into mid-stream, thin wisps of gray smoke floating up from her forward funnel. Fully repaired, the destroyer had been ordered to Yokosuka for a one-day stopover, a period calculated sufficient for the fitting of a new decoding device in the crypto-shack.

During her stay, Commander Royal would be permitted to beach five of his ten torpedoes, a concession he relegated to the better-than-nothing category since he was convinced that in the type of war he was now fighting, his torpedoes were potentially more dangerous to himself and his crew than to the enemy. Nevertheless, Royal knew that there was little likelihood he would ever be allowed to dump his remaining tin fish. He was well aware that there were still senior officers in the Seventh Fleet who were expecting the Russians to enter the war and unleash their much vaunted *Sverdlov* class cruisers against the American carrier force.

It was early Wednesday morning when the *Field* approached the harbor master's station at Yokosuka and slipped passed the finger piers that jutted out into Truman Bay. As if by special arrangement, the sun began to knife its way through the low cloudshelf that overhung the harbor, igniting the usually somber hills beyond Yokosuka City with a sparkling dapple of rich greens and lusty browns. Even the sea moss that carpeted the knoll-like harbor islands came to life with an uncommon refulgence as the destroyer inched her way towards Berth 11 directly opposite Piedmont Pier, which now had carrier *Kearsarge* as its transient tenant. Having just completed a seven-month tour with Task Force 77, the big flattop was on her way home to North Island, San Diego.

Both the harbor and the base facilities were crammed with naval vessels of every type and size. Berthed directly ahead of *DD-505* at Pier 11 were destroyer-minesweepers *Endicott* and *Carmick* also now homeward-bound after particularly hectic duty along the Korean coast. Directly across the Pier at Berth 10, sat baby flattop *Bairoko*, in for R and R after operations in the Yellow Sea with Task Force 90. Beyond *Bairoko*, cruiser *Manchester* was easing away from Berth 8 to join Task Force 77 on the bombline off Hungnam. A few of the *Field's* line handlers, still lingering on the fantail, took time to watch the cruiser as she moved out into the open harbor, finally disappearing behind the towers and jumbled upperworks of battleship *Missouri*, which was swinging leisurely at anchor off Radford Point. To the left of the battlewagon, a gray smudge was slowly taking on the now all-too familiar shape of an *Essex* class carrier.

"*Boxer* is standing out, Sir," the quarterdeck messenger reported to Commander Royal, who had gathered all of his officers in the wardroom for a meeting.

"Very well," Owen acknowledged, and the young sailor departed.

"It's hard to believe, the *Boxer's* been back to the States, had her rest and over-haul, and is now back here for another tour," remarked Cobb, remembering that the carrier had rejoined Task Force 77 last summer shortly after the *Field's* arrival.

"This will be the fourth tour for the "*Battling Bee*" but she'll have to anchor out until the *Kearsarge* vacates Piedmont Pier on Friday," Royal said wearily. "Now for the business at hand. Since we're going to be in Yokosuka such a short time, I want liberty for the men restricted to a single section, and its to expire at midnight. And that means on-board, not at Carney gate," Royal said brusquely. "As far as you officers are concerned, you all know you've got plenty of work to do before we haul out for Korea tomorrow morning. I have no objection if any of you want to go over to the club for dinner and a drink or two, but please make sure you're back on board by twenty-one hundred. Remember, I expect a detailed report from each one of you on the operational readiness of your respective divisions. Mister MacKinlay..."

"Yes, Sir?"

"Have you made all the arrangements for the transfer of the torpedoes this afternoon?"

"Yes, Sir. I spoke to the people on the base the second we tied up. They promised to put a floating crane and ammo barge alongside at fourteen-hundred."

"Good. I want you and Mister Keagan to keep on top of it. Notify me as soon as they start to bring the ammo barge alongside. As soon as those fish are transferred to the barge, I'm going to make a quick run over to the hospital and see how Larkin is coming along. If any of you want to join me, you're welcome to."

"What about Aakers, Sir?" Ensign Warden asked.

"The word I got is that they flew him back to the States yesterday. Larkin is scheduled to leave tomorrow."

A loud knock on the wardroom door announced the second arrival of Gibson, the quarterdeck-messenger. "Captain, Chief Anderson sent me down here to tell you that there's a nurse standing on the pier over near the telephone booth. She's been standing there for over a half-hour. The chief says to tell you that she keeps looking at the gangway. He thinks she might be waiting for one of the officers to come ashore. He also says its pretty cold out there and she's starting to look like a Popsicle."

"Why didn't Chief Anderson ask her who she's waiting for?"

"I don't know, Captain. I guess since she's an officer he didn't want to say any-thing to her until he checked with you first."

"Is she pretty?" Phil Oetjens piped up with a broad smile.

"Yes, Sir, I'd say she's real pretty," the messenger answered sheepishly but with a sly smile.

"Well, Michael, I heard rumors that you were a dyed-in-the-wool Lothario, but this obviously confirms them," Royal said with a chuckle to Ensign Daly who was sitting at the far end of the table. "Even though you were only in the hospital for a brief stay, you certainly seem to have made an impression on at least one member of its nursing staff."

"Yeah, Mickey boy," Lieutenant Kimmick joined in. "You only reported back on the ship an hour ago. You mean she couldn't keep from running right after you? You must be quite a lover."

"Yeah, Mike. Tell us how you were able to perform so well with that right wing of yours in a sling," implored Sternhagen with a broad grin.

"I really don't know anything about this, Sir," an ashen-faced Daly pleaded. "If she's pretty like Gibson here says, then she's sure not the nurse who took care of me. My nurse was a fat and fortyish lieutenant-commander."

"What's her rank, Gibson?" the captain asked, still smiling.

"Lieutenant J-G, Sir."

"That's nobody I know, Captain. All the young ones were assigned to the enlisted wards," Daly said with a shrug.

"Tell Chief Anderson he'd better invite the lieutenant aboard before she freezes her tootsies off," Owen Royal instructed. "Tell him to ask her on my behalf if she'd care to join the officers of the *Field* for lunch in the wardroom."

"Yes, Sir," the messenger acknowledged, making a hasty retreat.

"I'm certain that none of you gentlemen object to my extending the hospitality of our wardroom to one of the navy's angels of mercy," Royal commented jovially.

"Not if she's young and pretty," Coates said, laughing aloud.

"Sir," Oetjens spoke up with exaggerated formality. "I'm sure I'm expressing the feelings of all at this table when I say that a little feminine pulchritude can't do anything but brighten things up around here, especially since the wardroom hasn't been graced by the presence of a comely young lady since Don brought his fiance aboard back in Hawaii."

"Say, how is Cassy Jean these days?" Kimmick asked. "You haven't mentioned her lately."

"Oh, she's fine. She's back in Alabama with her mother. College keeps her pretty busy," Stockwell replied matter-of-factly. Then turning towards the captain, the Ops officer asked, "Sir, could I be excused from lunch today? I've got some personal business with someone aboard the *Boxer*. This might be the only chance I'll have to go aboard her while we're over here. It won't take long. I'll be back in time to check out the new decoder before the people installing it take off."

"Okay, Don, as long as you give me your guarantee."

"Yes, Sir. You have it."

Stockwell's departure coincided with the reappearance of Gibson, the quarterdeck-messenger.

"Well, has the lieutenant accepted my invitation to join us for lunch?" Royal asked eagerly.

"No, Sir. She told Chief Anderson to tell you that she appreciated your kindness. She said she would very much have enjoyed having lunch with you and your officers, but she was already late for her next shift at the hospital."

"Did she mention who she was waiting for?" the captain probed.

"No, Sir. The chief didn't ask."

During the hour that followed, Ensign Daly attracted far more attention than did the baked ham and canned pineapple featured on the wardroom luncheon menu. And, although he professed complete innocence, he was clearly unable to convince his mess mates that he had not been the object of the nurse's mysterious visit.

Absent from the hazing, Don Stockwell nervously paced the fleet landing, waiting for his transportation to the *Boxer*. The boat inbound from the moored flattop had been in view for well over ten minutes now, yet to an impatient Stockwell, it appeared to be only slightly closer then when he'd first spotted it pulling away from the carrier. Recalling his mother's perennial counsel that a watched kettle never boils, he shifted his gaze to the *Missouri*, now catching the rays of the noonday sun on her mountainous upperworks.

Almost unconsciously, he reached into the pocket of his overcoat and extracted a pink envelope. He fidgeted with it not unlike one might fidget with a hot coal. Even so, this was the first time he'd been able to muster the will power to re-read the letter since that night he'd received it back in Sasebo.

The wind almost clutched the letter from his gloved hand as he started to read:

Dear Donald,

I am sorry I have taken so long to answer your last five letters, but so many terribly exciting things have happened to me lately that I simply do not know where to begin. As you know, I was Miss Cottonseed in the Rose Bowl parade on New Year's Day. Well, guess what happened afterward during the game. I bet you can't, so I will tell you. I met Harvey.

Harvey is fabulous. I am certain you will agree if you ever meet him. Everyone who knows him agrees that Harvey is really a fabulous person and so much fun to be with, and what a sense of humor. He is always doing something funny and unexpected. I guess that is what really attracted me to him. He isn't really handsome and nowhere near as good looking as you, but he keeps me laughing all the time.

Harvey is also in the navy. You know how I go for those navy uniforms. Here I am, going off in a dither again and forgetting to tell you the really big news. Last Saturday, Harvey and I were married. It was really wonderful. Mother cried all afternoon.

We could only have a five-day honeymoon, which we had to spend in San Diego. You see, Harvey's ship left for Korea. He is on the Boxer. That is an aircraft carrier but I guess you know that being in the navy and all.

I guess I had better end here for now. I just arrived home an hour ago and I have not completely unpacked, and besides, I can hear mother. She is in the next room. She is crying again. Write and take care of yourself.

Love and Kisses,
X   X   X   X   X   X   X
Cassy Jean

P.S.   The oriental dress you sent me was just fabulous. I wore it for Harvey on our honeymoon and he said he thought it was fab-

ulous also. Harvey thought the slits in the sides made my legs look real sexy. Thanks again.

Don Stockwell was breathing heavily as he slipped the letter back inside his pocket. His face wore a dazed look. Somehow, the content of the letter seemed even more incomprehensible now than it had the first time he'd read it.

The minutes crawled by. Finally, the launch, an open forty-footer, chugged alongside the landing to discharge a full load of liberty hungry white hats, and to take on board Lieutenant Stockwell and the small mix of officers and enlisted requiring passage out to the carrier. Approaching the boat, Stockwell's glance strayed for a second at the arrowed BOXER in black metal that adorned the wooden bow.

"How long before she shoves off again?" Stockwell asked the dispatcher, a warrant-boatswain.

"As soon as she unloads her liberty party which I reckon might take all of five seconds judging by the look of those eager beavers." His estimate was off by a hair as the mass of peajacketed sailors swept up and over the pier like a navy blue tidal wave.

Stockwell stood in the stern sheets as the boat spanked toward the big flat-top sitting solemnly out in the stream. The launch, befitting that belonging to a major man-of-war, was spotless and correct in every detail. Her brass fittings, polished and gleaming, could rival those found in an admiral's barge. Her engineer, bow and stern hook, stood at their stations trig and jaunty as tars on a World War I recruiting poster.

Only the coxswain, a gangling scarecrow in a frayed white cap, negated the setting. To Stockwell, he looked like something from a bad dream, standing clumsily up there at the tiller delivering an incredibly obscene though quite imaginative rendition of *"The Old Chisholm Trail."* A bony protuberance of wrist showed below the too-short sleeve of his washed-out blue jumper, and on the back of his hand, the words "Lover First-Class" were tattooed in a splendid Old English. Fixed upon the steersman's face was what appeared to be a perpetual giggle, and his spine-tingling "Ti-yi-yippee-yippee-yays," could not be drowned out even by the roar of the engine.

But Lieutenant Stockwell had weightier things to ponder than the eccentricities of other people's enlisted personnel, for his journey out to the *Boxer* was not one of pleasure. As the launch bobbed its way over the choppy water in the open channel, Stockwell wondered if his decision to visit the carrier had been a wise one. Suddenly he began to question whether or not his interest in meeting Harvey was completely unselfish, an act expected of any properly reared southern gentleman. All the while, another thought kept intruding, the idea that his motive was merely the satisfaction of an egotistical twitch...a desire to see for himself just who Cassy Jean could have possibly chosen over him.

The motor launch, with a loud clang of bells, made the officer's gangway, forward on the starboard side. Stockwell waited for the boat to rise from the deep swell and at the proper instant leaped for the square wooden grill that served as *Boxer's* landing platform. A swirl of salt water swept over the platform thoroughly drenching his shoes and the legs of his pants before he could reach the dryer rungs of the huge metal staircase which the navy insisted on calling a ladder.

An anxious tension gripped Stockwell as he made the long climb to the *Boxer's* quarterdeck. Saluting smartly, he requested permission to board ship.

Permission granted, Stockwell asked the officer-of-the-deck, a Jaygee, if he knew of a lieutenant or lieutenant-commander by the name of Harvey, and if so, was the officer aboard?

"First or last name?" the OOD asked politely.

Somehow Lieutenant Stockwell had never given any thought to that trifling consideration. His face knotted up in sudden confusion. The only Harvey he'd ever come across had been a fanciful rabbit in a college play. It wasn't likely that his former fiance would refer to her new spouse by his surname, or was it? he mused, keenly aware that Cassy Jean was usually "out to lunch" where logical action was concerned.

"Harvey is the last name," he blurted out.

The Jaygee extracted a brown folder from the highly polished wooden desk. The folder contained a complete list of all the officers presently assigned to the *Boxer.* Stockwell stepped aside, almost toppling one of the brightly painted dummy 5-inch shells used as stanchions to cordon off the quarterdeck, psychologically if not practically, from the ever-present turmoil of the hangar deck.

"We've got a Hailey, a Hanley, two Healeys and a Hurley, but no Harvey," the OOD exclaimed.

"No Harvey?"

"No Harvey."

"Have you checked the junior officers' roster? There's an outside chance he may be an ensign or J-G."

"Yes, Sir. I have."

"Maybe he's a pilot. Have you checked the air group listing?"

"Yes, Sir, I've checked that also."

"No luck?"

"No luck."

"Well, Harvey must be his first name."

"Don't you know this guy, Lieutenant?" the Jaygee quizzed, puff-cheeked and obviously annoyed.

"Not exactly. Anyway, it's kind of hard to explain. It is a bit involved."

"Involved! Sir, do you realize that including the air group, we presently have over six hundred officers embarked. There must be close to twenty-five names on this list that are preceded by the initial H."

"I understand," Stockwell sympathized. "Anyway, thanks for trying. Can you tell me when I can catch the next boat back to the fleet landing? I have to return to my ship as quickly as possible."

"The launch you came out on will be making another run in about eight minutes."

Hailey, Hanley, Healey and Hurley...sounds like the Irish mafia, Stockwell muttered to himself despairingly as he descended the ladder.

The same nautical phenomenon that had served as coxswain for the earlier transit tended the tiller for the return trip. Totally dejected, Stockwell sat on the after-most thwart, watching but not really seeing the busy harbor traffic around him. Even the shrill voice of the steersman now plodding through the fourteenth verse of "*The One-Eyed Riley's Daughter*," failed to pierce his melancholy.

In a short while, the launch coasted into the small inlet assigned to the Fleet Landing and the *Field's* Ops boss disembarked to trudge wearily back to Pier 11, and the mountainous backlog of confidential pubs that needed checking prior to the destroyer's impending departure.

"Cast off and return to your ship!" the duty-dispatcher ordered after a ten-minute respite, and the *Boxer's* launch raced away from the landing at a speed several knots above the prescribed limit, bouncing over the churning wake of inbound Danish hospital ship *Jutlandia*.

"Slow down, dammit!" the bow-hook shouted as a heavy vail of spray slapped him hard in the face and soaked several of the passengers in the forward part of the boat.

The coxswain's only reaction was to pull the bell cord for additional speed.

"Damn your scroungy hide! You gotta' be just about the most ornery loon ah have ever been unfortunate enough to encounter," the bow-hook twanged angrily, wiping fresh spray from his face. "You always think you're such a hoot. Well just wait till the old man spots you trying to play hot-rodder with his newest forty-footer. You'll find your ass back cleaning bilges mucho quick!"

Harvey flashed a toothy grin as he clanged the bell signaling the engineer to add on another knot.

·   ·   ·

"Come on, Logan," Holiday protested across the C.I.C. plotting-table. "Why the hell would I try to snow you?"

Kevin looked at the third-class sharply. "I don't know. You've got a pretty weird sense of humor. Who'd else have a fly tattooed on his nose?" Logan snickered as he tightened the screw-heads on a set of parallel rulers.

"The tattoo wasn't my idea. I was smashed. Anyway, that's got nothing to do with what I'm telling you now. I know it was her. I remember those snapshots you showed us. The ones you took in Tijuana. You don't think I could forget those legs do you?"

"How could you see her legs?" Logan scowled. "She must have been wearing an overcoat."

"Nah, she had a raincoat. Anyway, I got a good look at her face."

"How'd you manage to do that from up in the wheelhouse?"

"Ever hear of binoculars?"

"I still think it must have been another nurse. Cindy's too smart to come anywhere near the ship."

"Well, if you don't believe me, ask Nugent and Gardiner. They were looking her over, too."

"That must have been a pretty popular pair of binoculars."

"Okay, don't believe me. Hell, it's no skin off my teeth. Anyway, if I had a chance to make it with a piece as pretty as that, you wouldn't see me sitting down here in C.I.C., playing with parallel rulers."

"I'm not playing with them. I'm fixing them! You and those idiot friends of yours have been using these rulers for everything from scratching your backs to swatting flies, oops, sorry, Holly," he said mischievously.

"Very funny," the third-class scowled. "Look, Logan...do me a favor. Don't refer to Gardiner and Nugent as friends of mine. From now on, I consider them merely business associates. And that goes for Bacelli, too. You know, on account of those three, I'm gonna' have to have a slice of skin cut off my ass and grafted on my nose!"

"Maybe not," Logan chuckled. "Sometimes they take it off your thigh."

"Either way, I hear it hurts like hell. But that's not my only problem. I just got a letter from Toby. She'll be starting her summer vacation from college right around the time we head back to the States. She wrote that she's planning to fly out to San Diego so she can be waiting on the pier when we tie up. That's not gonna' give me any time to get this thing taken care of."

"I suggest you start stocking up on Band-Aids. Of course, you can always flash your U-N and Korean Campaign ribbons in her face. I'm sure she'll be so overwhelmed, she'll not notice the Band-Aid, or the fly for that matter." Logan had a difficult time keeping a straight face.

"Hmmm," Holiday mused aloud. "You really think so? You're not putting me on?"

"Hell no. When I came home in forty-five with all that 'fruit salad' on my chest, I scored with more girls than I could count," Kevin said with a broad grin.

"Come on, stop kidding," Holiday answered with a frown.

"Who's kidding. Females really flip over that hero stuff."

Holiday's face suddenly brightened. "Do you know we're also getting the China Service Medal for those patrols we made in the Formosa Strait? I read it in the P-O-D this morning."

"Yeah, I saw it. Don't forget, besides the glory bars you'll probably have a nice new second-class crow on your arm. That's bound to impress her."

"I'm not sure it will impress Toby, but I'm damn sure it's going to impress Nugent, Bacelli and Gardiner. I can't wait to see the expressions on their dumb faces when the results of the exams arrive. When they see my name on the promotion list, they'll go ape-shit. You know, they're really pissed that they weren't allowed to take the exam last week. They were sure Stockwell was going to change his mind."

"That should teach them not to be sure about anything in this life. How do you think our strikers did on their third-class exam?"

"I don't know. I suppose they had a good chance of passing...all except Patterson. He never attended Class-A school like the rest of them. Say...wouldn't it be a crock if Patterson managed to pass?" Holiday announced with an anxious grin. "Your buddy Murray would bust two guts. He's really got it in for that kid."

"That's Murray's problem. Right now, I'm more concerned about why Cindy took the chance of coming down to the ship. If it was Cindy, that is."

"Of course it was her."

"What was her rank?"

"Jaygee, just like your girlfriend. Say, you don't think you could have knocked her up the last time you two went to Tokyo, do you?" Holiday asked eagerly.

"Of course not. I don't make those kind of mistakes. Besides, she's a nurse. She wouldn't make them either."

"Maybe she didn't want to be too careful," the third-class said with much relish. "You know it wouldn't be the first time a broad used that little trick to get a guy to marry her. Although I don't know why anyone who looks as good as she does would have to trick anyone into marrying her. Hell, if I wasn't engaged to Toby, I'd be happy to take her off your hands."

"I'll bet you would."

"What's the matter, Logan? What happened to that big grin you were flashing a couple of minutes ago when I was telling you about my problems? Are you starting to get a little worried that I might be right about why she came trotting down to the ship?"

"No, I'm not worried about anything. Hell, I'm still not even sure it was her."

"Well, why don't you take a run over to the hospital and find out. It's not that much of a walk, and if you catch the shuttle bus, you can be there in a few minutes. Since we're gonna' be leaving for Korea tomorrow, this will be your only chance to find out what she wanted. Hell, you don't want to be worrying about that the whole time we're out there with the task force, do you?"

"Since when did you become so concerned about my mental state of health?"

"Well, we're shipmates, aren't we?"

"Yeah, that and a dime will get me a ride on a New York subway."

"Okay, suit yourself. I just think if you're gonna' become a father, it's always nice to know about it in advance. Hell, she's a nurse. I'm sure she could get some doctor friend of hers to get rid of it quietly," said Holiday with a sly grin.

"The hell she would!"

"Hey, calm down. I didn't think you gave a damn about something like that. I thought you told Murray you didn't practice your religion much anymore."

"Yeah, I guess I'm a piss-poor Catholic, but I still draw the line at abortion."

"You mean you'd marry her?"

"If it was a choice between that and an abortion."

"Since you feel so strongly about it, don't you think you'd better get your ass up to the hospital so you can find out."

"I don't know how I can. I'm in the duty-section."

"Where's Murray?"

"He's crapped out down in the compartment. He was supposed to help Stockwell check the pubs, but he was feeling sick. I told him I'd take care of it, but Stockwell's not back yet. He's over on the *Boxer*."

"No, he isn't. He just got back. I saw him coming aboard when I was coming down from the bridge a few minutes ago. He's probably in the crypto-shack watching them install that new gear. Why don't you go ask him if you can go visit Larkin in the hospital? A bunch of the guys are going over in the bus at sixteen-hundred."

"I don't even know Larkin. I don't think I ever said more than hello to the guy since the day I came aboard," Logan answered with a frown.

"Stockwell doesn't know that. Tell him you and Larkin are old buddies from the big war. Larkin is just about your age. Stockwell won't know you two never served together."

"What if Stockwell asks Larkin?"

"Larkin wasn't in the Ops department. I don't think Stockwell even knew him. Anyway, he won't have time to go over to the hospital. When he gets through in the crypto-shack, he'll be spending the rest of the day and night down here working on the pubs. And since Larkin is being flown back to the States in the morning, there's no way their paths are ever going to cross."

"Maybe it's worth a try. I'll go talk to Stockwell."

It was after 7 p.m. when Logan reached the reception area of the nurses' quarters. A female dental-technician striker was holding down the watch. Logan quickly slipped out of his peajacket so that the young lady could see the petty officer's rating on the sleeve of his dress blue jumper. Unimpressed, she continued to flip through the pages of a well worn issue of *Pageant*.

Hat in hand and peacoat slung over his right arm, Logan stepped up to the desk. "I'd like to see Lieutenant J-G Osbourne please," he asked forcefully.

"Is it important? She was in surgery most of the afternoon. She just came in a few minutes ago. She really looked beat. I'd guess she's in the sack by now."

"Yes, I understand, but it is very important. Could you tell her that her cousin Kevin is here?"

"Are you sure it can't wait?"

"It really can't. My ship's going back to Korea tomorrow morning."

"Okay, I'll tell her, only I hope she doesn't chew my head off for waking her up."

"I'm sure it will be alright."

"You say you're her cousin?" she asked with a disbelieving expression.

"That's right."

"Okay. Go take a seat over there in the lounge. I'll go tell her you're here."

416

Hardly had she disappeared down the hall when Logan heard the shuffle of slippered feet. He glanced up to see an obviously pleased and excited Cynthia Osbourne running towards him in her robe and pajamas.

"Kevin," she called out, her face beaming with anxiety as he rose from the chair.

Tears ran down her cheeks and choked her voice. The nurse clung to him passionately. "I was so worried. You can't imagine how I felt when they started flying the wounded in from your ship and from the *Ward* and *Wayne*. We'd heard some of the casualties were being sent to Yokosuka but I couldn't get a list of the names. Then when you didn't answer any of my letters..."

"Calm down, Cindy. I'm okay...not a scratch...honest."

Cynthia stiffened in his arms, and he found himself brushing strands of her rich brown hair back from her tear-stained cheeks.

"I told the young lady over there that we were cousins. What's she going to think," he said as she pressed herself tightly against him.

"If she says anything, I'll just explain that we're kissing cousins," the nurse said with a teasing smile. "Oh, Kevin, I wish there was some way I could sneak you into my room...even for a few minutes."

"I wish you could too, but I'm afraid if we get caught, we'd both spend the next ten years up in Portsmouth making little stones out of big ones. At least I would."

"Don't you think it would be worth it?"

Gently, Kevin placed his hands at the back of her waist pulling her in even more snugly. She felt soft and warm and smelled of jasmine scented soap. They kissed for a long carnal moment, both totally oblivious to the presence of the duty receptionist sitting at the desk outside the lounge.

Finally they broke for air.

"Cindy, I've only got a few minutes. I'm not even supposed to be here. I'm in the duty section. I had to snow my department head to get off the ship. He thinks I'm visiting a wounded buddy over in the hospital."

"You mean you can't stay...even for a little while?" Cynthia's eyes glazed.

"Well, maybe for just a few minutes. Can we sit down here and talk?"

"Yes, of course. You look so serious all of a sudden. Is something wrong?"

"No, I don't think so." Kevin smiled. After several seconds he asked, "Did you come down to the ship this morning?"

"Yes. How did you know?"

"Well, I really didn't. I just heard that a nurse...a Jaygee, was waiting on the pier."

"If you knew, why didn't you figure out a way to come ashore...even for a minute?" the nurse asked, her voice quavering. "I noticed several sailors from your ship carrying trash cans over to the dumper on the pier."

"You know, Cindy, I may not be a commissioned officer like you, but I am a P-O second. Maybe you're not aware of it but radarmen second-class usually don't get assigned to garbage details."

"I'm sorry, Kevin. I wasn't trying to put you down," she said reaching over from her chair. She took his hand, clasped it affectionately and said, "If you couldn't come to the pier, couldn't you have at least come up on deck. All I wanted to do was to see that you were alive and not hurt. I would have left as soon as I saw you were alright."

"I was working down in C.I.C. You were gone by the time I was told that a nurse had been on the pier watching the ship."

"Did you know that I was invited to have lunch on board?" she giggled.

"No, nobody said anything about that."

"Well, I was," she said with a teasing smile. "And the invitation came right from your captain, Commander Royal."

Kevin looked at the ceiling, then back at Cynthia. "As long as you were down there, why didn't you take him up on his offer? I've heard our wardroom sets a pretty good table," said Logan curtly.

"Now how could I do that? What kind of a reason could I give for being there? Besides...did you forget, I met your captain once back in San Diego? Remember, I told you how he came to the hospital to see you one night, but you were in quarantine and I couldn't let him come into the ward. I'm sure he would have remembered talking to me. I'm just as certain he would have connected you and I, and figured out why I was there."

"You're probably right," he shrugged. "Say, it must have been pretty cold standing out there all that time."

"Yes, I have to admit I was a bit numb by the time I left. I didn't get any feeling back in my hands or feet until I was in the operating room. It's a good thing I finally did, the afternoon was really hectic. We had two emergency operations."

"Wounded from Korea?"

"No, a bad fight in one of the bars. A bunch of sailors and marines tangled with each other. I guess they used everything from broken bottles to bar stools. Getting back to more pleasant subjects, when will I get to spend some time with you? Base-Ops told me this morning that your ship is heading right back to Korea tomorrow."

"Yeah, like they say in those old war movies, we sail with the tide."

"Will your next tour be a long one?"

"I don't know. Unfortunately, the brass doesn't confide in me. I imagine it will be at least a month or six weeks."

"Will you be dueling with shore guns again?" she asked in a nervous voice.

"I don't know...honestly. We never find that out until right before it happens. We've seen quite a bit of action lately. The *Ward* and the *Wayne*...that's half our division...took a real bad pounding. I'm pretty certain they won't be back in operation for at least another month, maybe two. By then we'll be heading back to San Diego. I've a strong feeling Jehovah will decide we've had our share of gore and glory and assign us to a permanent slot in the carrier screen."

"You really think so?"

"Sure, there's plenty of other cans off Korea. Besides, the navy's always rotating new ones from the States. We're even getting destroyer divisions from Norfolk and from Newport, Rhode Island. They make round-the-world cruises and put in four-month tours on the bombline. They're quite lucky, you know. They really get to see a big chunk of the world. They come over via the Panama Canal, do their stint with the task force, then head home by way of Suez. I guess the navy feels it's sharing the wealth," he chuckled, "by letting the guys in the Atlantic Fleet get a chance to pick up some ribbons, too." He paused, then said, "That's enough about the Atlantic Fleet. How are you feeling?"

"Oh, a little tired, but outside that, I'm in pretty good health."

"Are you sure?"

"Of course I am, darling, honest," she smiled affectionately. "I just had a physical two weeks ago. They said I was in great shape."

"That's a relief." His face brightened.

"Kevin, why are you suddenly so concerned about my health? You've never asked me questions like that before?" Cynthia asked in a puzzled tone.

"No particular reason. It's just that I know they're keeping you really busy over here with all the wounded coming in from Korea. You said yourself that this afternoon was pretty hectic. I just don't want to see you get sick from too much work, that's all."

"Oh, Kevin, you really are concerned about me, aren't you?" Her eyes sparkled.

"Of course I am. I shouldn't have to tell you that."

"You know, that really means a lot to me. Especially since I know what you have to face off Korea." She squeezed his hand. "Kevin, darling, I really love you so much. You know that don't you?"

"Yes," he answered in a half whisper. "Look, Cindy, I wish I could stay here a little longer, but if my division officer suspects I gave him a line and comes over to the hospital, you'll be addressing your next letter to me in care of the brig."

They walked through the small reception area and hurried on by the dental-technician who had put her magazine aside to observe Kevin's departure.

"You're really special, Cindy," he said with a smile, then kissed her gently on the brow.

The door opened and closed. She was alone.

．　．　．

It was dark now and Logan could feel a few flakes of snow in the air. Turning up the broad collar of his peajacket to shield his face from the night chill, he paid little attention to the lieutenant-commander walking about twenty feet ahead of him. In a few minutes, the officer crossed the street and entered the hospital. Logan continued on toward Pier 11 and the *Field*, much relieved that he would once again be spared the joys of fatherhood.

While Kevin Logan was congratulating himself, Aubrey Cobb was approaching the hospital's main reception area.

"May I help you, Commander?" petitioned a plump but pretty blonde nurse wearing the silver "railroad tracks" of a senior-grade lieutenant on her lapel.

"Yes, I'd like to visit one of the men from my ship. He's an amputee. His name's Larkin."

"Larkin, Andrew Wallace...damage-controlman second-class?" she quizzed, thumbing down the room roster. "He's in room two-twelve. His C.O. just brought him some books."

"Oh, yes...is Commander Royal in with him now?"

"No. I hope you aren't looking for him. He left over an hour ago."

"I'm Larkin's executive officer. I understand he's being flown back to the States tomorrow morning?" Cobb asked after a nervous pause.

"Yes, that's right. We're transferring him to the hospital in San Diego. He'll be able to get the very finest in therapy there," she said with a broad smile.

"Is anyone else from the ship in there with him now?"

"No, Sir. Several of the men were over for a visit but they left on the bus quite some time ago."

"I see, thank you, lieutenant. You say Larkin is in room two-twelve?"

"Yes, you can take the staircase over there, then turn left on the second floor. It's about five rooms down on the left side of the corridor."

"Thank you again." Aubrey Cobb peered back, slyly hoping to catch a revealing glimpse of the nurse's legs, but the side of the desk totally obscured his angle of sight. Can't win them all, he sighed, then tugging his collar away from his Adam's apple, walked briskly towards the staircase.

Back on the *Field*, Ben Cooper, petty-officer-of-the-watch for the eight to twelve, cleared his throat as he prepared to announce the evening's entertainment over the ship's P-A system. He flipped down the speaker-switch and drawled slowly, "Now the movie fo' tonight will be Henry the vee!"

"Henry the who?" squealed Ensign Warden, blank-faced as the words flew out of the wardroom speaker.

"The movie fo' tonight will be Henry the vee starring Lawrence Oliver!" boomed the speaker as if in reply.

Below decks, Vinnie Bacelli was busily unwrapping the package he'd received from his sister Josie earlier at mail call. It contained a can of cashew nuts, a nine-inch pepperoni, three tins of sardines, a jar of jellied tongue and Teresa Brewer's latest recording, "*Till I Waltz Again With You*."

Chapter XXII - Sayonara

Owen Royal's destroyer rejoined the carrier screen off Yonpo on a gray and gloomy Thursday, slipping into her assigned slot out in front of *Boxer*, *Oriskany* and *Valley Forge* just as radio receivers throughout the formation began belching out the news of Joseph Stalin's death. All in Task Force 77, from Jehovah and his staff on the Happy Valley to Turk and his mess cooks on the Charlie P. entertained a single thought...would Uncle Joe's demise bring about an immediate end to the Korean War or serve as the catalyst that would start World War III?

With less than four months remaining until his discharge date, the question was particularly perplexing to Howie Murray who was thoroughly convinced that even if the Russians didn't enter the war, the political climate would worsen, and the navy would have just the excuse it needed to extend all active duty tours, especially his.

But in spite of all the rumors and dire speculation, the afternoon still gave way to evening, and evening melted into night, and for Task Force 77, it was business as usual. The carriers launched their scheduled number of planes, and the tin cans raced, puffed and plodded through the same cold unfriendly sea.

At midnight, with a mirthless slash of his grease pencil, Murray deftly dispatched March 5th from his calendar. Taped next to the calendar on the locker door was a snapshot of his daughter Deirdre holding the baby. "Soon...very soon," he muttered softly. Then snapping off his pocket flashlight, he pulled himself up into his bunk. Five *Hail Mary's* and an *Our Father* later, Murray was ready to face March 6th.

March 6th arrived right on schedule, and the dawn alert for the task force passed without incident. Later in the morning, destroyers *Gurke* and *Gregory* detached to join *Los Angeles* for a gun-shoot near Cha-ho, necessitating a shift in screening stations for the *Charles P. Field*.

To Dick Warden, lolling on the signal bridge and casually watching a gaggle of fighter-bombers streaming back to the *Oriskany* after a noontime call at Wonsan, the day seemed pretty routine. With no watch scheduled until 18:00, the young officer had just decided to go below to finish lesson number 3 in the

"Naval Communications" correspondence course when he saw the sudden flash of an explosion near the afterpart of the *Oriskany's* flight deck. An earsplitting bang rolled across the water to be heard aboard every ship in the task force.

"*Oriskany's* on fire!" shouted an excited lookout as Warden took off for the wheelhouse where Rolf Sternhagen and Don Coates were anxiously staring at the TBS speaker, wondering if they would get an order to aid the wounded carrier.

"What happened to the *Oriskany?*" Royal called out from the wheelhouse stairway.

"I'm not sure, Captain," Sternhagen replied nervously. "We heard a loud bang, then saw all that smoke coming from her flight deck."

"It's starting to pour out her sides now, too," Coates added. "Her hangar deck must be on fire."

"Alright, Rolf. You'd better pass the word for all fire-and-rescue parties to man their stations. "We're the closest ship to her. I expect Jehovah or Birthrate will send us alongside to help with her fires." As Owen spoke, he remembered vividly how during the Leyte battle in '44, cruiser *Birmingham* had maneuvered alongside the first *Princeton* to help extinguish that flattop's fires and take off wounded. Tragically, the carrier exploded showering the *Birmingham* with steel and heavy debris, killing or seriously wounding almost 700 of the cruiser's good Samaritans including his former roommate at the Naval Academy. Ironically, *Birmingham's* casualties turned out to be far greater than those of the ill-fated flattop.

Royal stepped out on to the port wing and focused his binoculars on the burning ship. "She appears to be maintaining her speed and position in the formation. It looks like there's a plane burning just aft of her island."

"Yes, Sir," Warden spoke up. "She was landing Corsairs. One of them must have crashed into her deck, although from the flash I'd say it looked much more like a bomb exploding."

"It probably was a bomb. Those birdfarms are always bringing back planes with unexpended ordnance."

"Isn't that a bit dangerous, Sir?" Warden puzzled.

"Yes, I imagine so. Of course they only do it after the pilot's had a chance to jettison his bombs over the water. Occasionally, the bombs won't release due to flak damage or a malfunction. That's probably what happened with that F-4-U over there," said Royal, still focusing his glasses on the burning fighter-bomber.

"Sir," Sternhagen called out from the wheelhouse doorway. "Childplay just informed Jehovah that she expects to have her fires under control momentarily. She's asked permission to stay with the task force. She estimates that she'll be able to complete all repairs to both her flight deck and hangar deck by late tonight and she expects to be able to launch and land aircraft in time for tomorrow morning's strikes," the O.D. reported half out of breath.

"The Big O's a feisty old gal, I'll say that for her," Royal grunted, lowering his binoculars. "From the amount of smoke she's still giving off, I think her skipper, Captain Shands, is being a bit optimistic." Royal walked back inside the wheelhouse.

"Since Childplay doesn't need our help, should I secure the fire-and-rescue parties, Captain?" Sternhagen asked.

"No, we'd better wait a little longer. The *Oriskany's* still not out of trouble."

As if to confirm Royal's judgment, the cutting sound of several small explosions could be heard, the result of the flames reaching the plane's wing cannons. Royal turned his head just in time to see a large section of one wing soar high in the air, then float back down barely missing *Oriskany's* island as it pancaked into the sea.

To the carrier sailors fighting the fire, it seemed forever, but actually it was all over in a little more than an hour.

Relieved that *Oriskany's* C.O. had called it right on the mark, Owen secured his own personnel, and the *Field* resumed her normal screening routine.

It was late evening when Aubrey Cobb knocked on the half-open door of the captain's cabin. "Can I see you, Sir?" he asked politely.

"Sure, come on in. Take a seat. I'll be with you in a minute. I just want to finish this report the radio-shack sent down. I'm just reading the section on the *Oriskany's* damage. We'll be running close escort for her tonight while she completes her repairs. She'll be using welding torches so she's bound to give off some illumination. Make certain the people in sonar don't goof off. With the carrier looking like a neon sign in the dark, I wouldn't want to lock horns with a Red sub."

"How badly was she hurt?"

"According to this report, she's got a hole about the size of Howe's Cavern in her number-three elevator. She's also had seventeen personnel casualties. Even so, she was pretty lucky getting her fires out that fast. This report notes that shrapnel ripped open the tip tanks on several jets refueling on her hangar deck drenching it in av-fuel. A single spark from that fire on the flight deck and you could have scratched one flattop," said Owen grimly. "Now, why did you want to see me?"

"Can I speak plainly?"

"Have I ever suggested you speak otherwise?"

For a long moment their eyes interlocked. Then Cobb cleared his throat and said, "It's this collection of weekend warriors we've been saddled with."

"Are you referring to our enlisted weekend warriors or to our commissioned weekend warriors?" Royal asked with a broad smile.

"In this case, it's the officers, Captain, but I really don't see that there's anything humorous about their complete lack of respect for authority."

"I'm sorry, Aub. I was just amused by the term weekend warriors. Ours seem to be putting in a pretty long weekend."

"Well, that may be but that doesn't give them the right to use me as the butt of their dissatisfaction. I am the ship's executive officer, and I'm entitled to the respect that goes along with that position."

"Yes, Aub, you are. Now what have they done to get you so worked up?"

"They've done several things." Cobb's face reddened with rage. "This is their latest wise-ass trick." He handed the captain a small glass ashtray. "They were in such a hurry to get to their fire-and-rescue stations this afternoon, they forgot to hide this away before they shot out of the wardroom. I found it sitting there right in the middle of the wardroom table!"

The captain couldn't hold back his laughter. "You're not taking this seriously, are you, Aub?"

"Of course I am. This is flagrant disrespect for higher authority. If these people can get away with this kind of thing, what good is it for the navy to even have a command structure?"

"I think you're blowing this all out of proportion. Ten to one, there's another glass ashtray down there with my photograph glued to its underside."

"Well, I don't appreciate the prospect of some horse's ass like Kimmick or Coates grinding out his cigar or cigarette in my face."

"Come on, Aub. They don't mean anything by it. Back on the *Buffalo*, I found my picture pasted over the dart board in the machine shop."

"What did you do about it?"

"Nothing. I just ignored it. I recognize the fact that things like that go with the job."

"Well, I might expect this sort of screwball behavior from white hats, but I certainly don't expect it from commissioned officers." Cobb was obviously unpacified. "You know, Captain, this isn't the first time they've pulled something like this. I've found insulting poems tacked to the calendar in my state room, and one wise bastard went as far as to leave a box of ball bearings in my desk drawer."

Owen had to fake a cough to suppress the laughter he felt he could no longer control. "Well, Aub, what do you suggest I do, bring them up on charges?" The captain was suddenly embarrassed by his choice of words. He hadn't meant to be sarcastic. Sarcasm had always been something he detested in others. He couldn't tolerate it at all in himself. With the Parish affair still fresh in his mind, he was certain that to Cobb, his remark must have seemed like he was pouring vinegar in an open wound. The expression on Cobb's face quickly confirmed the captain's supposition.

"If you really feel so strongly about this, Aub, I'll bring it up at our next wardroom meeting. I won't mention specifics. I'll just point out that there's been a little too much clowning around lately on the part of officers and enlisted alike, and if it's not stopped, I'll see that future liberty in Japan is cut back."

"No, Captain. I wouldn't want to be the cause of something that drastic. I guess I was over-reacting. It's really not that important. If you'll excuse me now, I've got some work I'd like to get squared away in the chart-house before I turn in."

Cobb didn't go directly to the chart-house. Instead, he climbed up to the torpedo deck and walked aft until he found a deserted spot near the torpedo crane. Royal had been toying with him, of that he was certain. His humiliation was obviously a big joke to the captain, Cobb told himself, convinced now that Royal already knew about the ashtray and might even have instigated it. Well, the captain wouldn't have the last laugh, not if his recent visit to Larkin in the hospital pays off, and he had every reason to believe it would. He took solace in that thought as he made his way through the darkness to the bridge.

The *Field* remained with the carrier screen until the 16th when she and *John Morgan* were sent to hunt targets of opportunity in the Tanchon area. About the time that *DD-505* was entering inshore waters off Iwon, Candace Moffett Royal was alighting from a gleaming TWA Constellation at LaGuardia Airport.

Owen Royal was hoping he'd make it into the "Trainbusters Club" that morning, aware that the North Koreans had recently stepped up their rail activity in the area. Candace also had her priorities as she rode the taxi in from Queens. Her arguments for expanding the agency's West Coast operations were sound, she told herself as she reviewed the sales pitch which she would be delivering to the B.B.Y. and S. board of directors within the hour.

That evening, the *Field* destroyed a large mine-laying motor-junk which she had doggedly chased and finally cornered in a small inlet. Candace had a big evening too, celebrating her latest victory by accompanying Ham Barlow to the Empire Theater where Shirley Booth was racking up rave reviews for her performance in "*The Time of the Cuckoo.*"

•   •   •

With Commodore Price now riding *John Morgan*, the two destroyers sliced through the surface mist and ice floes off sprawling Tanchon. Hardly had the noon-hour bells been struck when word was received from a prowling PBM that a twelve-truck convoy was attempting a rare daylight run less than thirty miles upcoast. The observer in the patrol bomber was certain the trucks were troop carriers, probably hauling the better part of a North Korean or Chinese infantry regiment. He passed this estimation of the enemy force to the destroyers which were already lighting off all boilers to reach a suitable interception point along the snow covered coast.

"It should be a turkey shoot," said Oetjens eagerly as he and Royal perused the chart in the wheelhouse. "There's not a single tunnel for at least three miles in either direction if we can cut them off here," he said, pointing with his dividers.

Agreeing with his navigator, Royal quickly passed his recommendation on to the commodore. Concurring, Price advised, "They're handing us this one on a platter. Let's not blow it!"

"Thanks for the vote of confidence," Royal muttered under his breath as he released the speaker-lever on the TBS.

It was almost mid-afternoon when the line of dark green trucks rolled into view. An icy gust of wind whipped at Royal's face as he stood on the port wing and maneuvered his destroyer in toward shore, ever conscious of the shoals that had been haphazardly noted on his 30-year-old chart. They were less than a quarter of a mile away from land now. Up ahead, *John Morgan* was inching in even closer, the thin barrels of her gun-houses bristling like the raised hairs on an angry hound.

Oetjens aimed his glasses at the enemy vehicles now standing out prominently against the snowy backdrop. "Look at those crazy bastards! They haven't even bothered to camouflage their trucks," he cried out.

John Morgan was first to fire, getting off three fast broadsides before the *Field's* own 5-inch erupted. *DD-505's* bridge shuddered with each new salvo as the destroyer spun about bringing all guns to bear on the unfortunate road convoy. To Royal, the sound of his forward mounts seemed louder than ever before as fiery rings from the gun flashes floated up to encircle the entire bridge structure.

For the next half hour, Owen Royal had a ringside seat at a carnage even more terrible than any he had witnessed during three-and-a-half years of Pacific fighting. In accordance with the commodore's game plan, the *Field* had quickly dispatched the lead truck by hurling a 5-inch shell directly into its cab. At the same instant, Price's new flagship was making equally short work of the rear-most vehicle, thereby effectively sealing off any avenue of escape for the ten remaining trucks, each of which was crammed with up to 30 fully equipped CCF infantrymen.

In the ensuing moments, the two destroyers systematically cremated each of the remaining vehicles; the *Field* working from left to right, the *Morgan* blasting each of the troop carriers in a precise sequence starting from the opposite direction. Within minutes all twelve trucks were blazing against the snow. The almost uniform spacing between each distinct fireball made Royal think of footlights in a theater.

Sweeping his glasses along the snow bank beyond the burning trucks, he could make out what looked like hundreds of tiny ants trying to scamper away from the fire and the exploding gasoline. Only he knew they weren't ants. Switching from high-explosive to white phosphorous, the destroyers' gunners now showered the entire snow bank with the powder-like substance that burned through clothes and skin more lethally than the most powerful acid.

So far, everything had gone according to plan, a rare occurrence as far as *DD-505* was concerned. By 16:30, there was nothing left worth shooting at. Price issued the order to break off action, then signaled a "well done" to all hands. An hour later, the *Field* was trailing after *John Morgan* on a south-easterly heading that would bring about a morning meeting with the task force. Astern, the sky had taken on a blood-red glow.

For the next few weeks the *Charles P. Field* remained with the carriers as Task Force 77 shifted its attention from interdiction strikes and raids against industrial targets to increased support for United Nations ground forces holding the MLR. Only once during this period was *DD-505* detached from the carrier screen, and that was to lay down flak suppression fire for *Boxer's* warbirds attacking a Chinese bivouac north of Kosong.

On 8 April, Candace returned to her office in La Jolla quite pleased with all she had accomplished during her extended stay in New York. On this same morning, the *Field* paired off with destroyer-minesweeper *Thompson* to provide anti-submarine escort for carrier *Oriskany* during another reconnaissance patrol of the

North Formosa Strait. Scuttlebutt had it that the Charlie P's liberty port for Easter would be Hong Kong.

That evening, Logan entered the radar shack to the accompaniment of a loud and heated argument that centered around the relative prowess of Chinese and Japanese females during coitus. Carefully avoiding involvement, he poured himself a cup of coffee and took up his position at the plotting table. With neither Bacelli nor Gardiner willing to budge an inch, the great debate finally petered out to the strains of Richard Hayman's "*Ruby*" spinning soulfully on the phonograph in the adjacent coffee mess.

It was about this time that Donald Coates entered the combat-information-center. "Everything running smooth in here, Logan?" he asked.

"Smooth as a baby's ass, Sir. Any late word on those jet bombers that buzzed the task force this morning?" Gardiner asked.

"Yes, the captain got an update a little while ago. They were definitely I-L Twenty-Eights. There were two of them. Intelligence thinks they were Chinese."

"Is it true that our combat air patrol couldn't catch them?" Bacelli piped up.

"Yes, the skipper said those Panther pilots had their feet down to the floor boards but they couldn't close the range. Those I-L Twenty-Eights zoomed right over the entire task force. Intelligence thinks they were on a photo recon mission."

"Sounds to me like they're getting ready to launch a big one against Seventy-Seven," Gardiner added.

"Hope you noticed, they didn't fly those new jets over the task force until they knew we'd left the screen," Bacelli said with a good-natured grin.

"Yes, I'm certain they've heard about all those 'Deadeye Dicks' we've got in our gun gang," Gardiner cut in with a smirk.

"Hey, don't knock our gun gang!" Bacelli cried back indignantly. "That was some job they did on those trucks last week. Gordon told me that he heard we're going to get the South Korean Presidential Unit Citation from Syngman Rhee. Gordon says those troops we knocked out were being rushed south to attack the flank of some Rok outfit. Isn't that right, Mister Coates?"

"If Gordon says so, I'm sure it's gospel. He seems to have a direct line to Jehovah," Coates answered dryly.

"Say, Mister Coates," Gardiner called from his seat at the Sugar-George. "Any truth to the scuttlebutt that we're putting into Hong Kong for Easter?"

"What's the word from Gordon?"

"Oh, he says we're going there for sure."

"Then what can I add to that?" the young officer said with a sly smile as he glanced over at Logan before making a hasty exit.

• • •

"And the dawn came up like thunder out of China cross the bay," boomed Lieutenant Stockwell in a surprisingly rich baritone, signalmen staring at him queerly as he

sang his way up the outside ladder to the starboard wing. Stockwell hadn't felt this good in a long time. The sea breeze had the friendly kiss of spring, the sky was a kaleidoscope gone wild, and Cassy Jean was past history like that broken leg he'd gotten in the game against Tulane. The thought comforted him as he marched into the wheelhouse to assume the eight-to-noon.

"Below decks, a handbook was being distributed by ship's office to each member of the crew. Prepared by ComSeventhFleet staff, the book described Hong Kong and its customs. Gardiner grunted as he scanned the special note on security:

Hong Kong is a short boat ride from the Communist mainland, and it is abundantly supplied with spies, most of which are shapely, attractive females thoroughly trained and disciplined in Red China. They may appear only innocently curious about your work or how your ship operates, it's weapons, etc. These scraps of information may seem harmless, but they can serve as valuable intelligence to the Reds... So keep all mess-deck intelligence to yourself. The old cliche - 'a slip of the lip may sink a ship,' will not sound nearly so trite if it happens to be your lip that slips and your ship that is sunk.

By mid-morning, *Oriskany*, with the *Field* and *Thompson* trailing dutifully in her wake, shunted by the jutting nose of Communist Kwangtung Province to enter the wide estuary that served as Hong Kong's foyer. Plodding their way up the Pearl River, the big carrier and her two consorts were soon surrounded by an ill-assorted conglomeration of junks, bumboats, lorchas, sampans, and miscellaneous harbor craft far more numerous and noisier than any encountered thus far during the *Field's* Far East odyssey. One gaudy three-master, a Hangchow junk with countless patches on her bright red sails, took station abeam and dangerously close to the *Oriskany*. On her junk's ancient deck, an equally time-worn crone imperiously paraded her wares which consisted of eight fetching Chinese girls, all displaying a banner for the benefit of the sailors and marines lined up along the starboard edge of the *Oriskany's* flightdeck. Large black lettering on the banner proclaimed: WE WELCOME THE MEN OF THE U.S.S. KEARSARGE.

Focusing his binoculars on the banner and the junk's lively female deck gang, an amused Owen Royal found himself wondering if this seagoing house of ill-repute was merely a victim of faulty intelligence or a splendid example of Oriental frugality. Aware that the *Kearsarge* had called at Hong Kong the month before, and noting the junk's heavily patched sails and overall shoddy appearance, he quickly decided on the latter.

Up in the wheelhouse and below in C.I.C., ranges and bearings flew through the air in staccato tempo as quartermasters and radarmen pinpointed the ship's position in relation to places with bizarre names like Junk Island, Fat Tong Point, Jardines Lookout and Razor Hill. High above the busy activity on the open bridge, strings of brightly colored signal flags stood away from the ship as a resurgent harbor breeze plucked away at the halyards.

It was close to 14:00 when the *Field* reached the anchorage in Victoria Harbor, the mile-wide strait separating Hong Kong Island from the Kowloon Peninsula. Owen Royal's ship was ordered to moor directly astern of the *U.S.S. Doyle*, a destroyer-minesweeper which had arrived in the harbor the previous morning.

Aubrey Cobb had the conn as well as the nervous attention of all in the wheelhouse as he sloppily overshot the *Field's* assigned anchorage, finally having to reverse his engines to back awkwardly into the slot between the *Doyle* and *Thompson*, the latter already neatly anchored and now preparing to send her first liberty party off to their Hong Kong adventure.

With the *Field* finally swinging at anchor, Owen Royal came down from the bridge and gave the foc'sle a brief but thorough inspection. Satisfied that the proper amount of chain had been paid out, and that his anchor had taken a firm grip on "Victoria's bottom," he took a moment to glance around the storied harbor which had thus far eluded him during his long and traveled naval career.

Owen noticed that the two ships moored up ahead of him, the *Oriskany* and *Doyle*, bore the same number 34, and considering the hundreds of ships currently active in the navy, he speculated about the odds of such an occurrence. Not being a gambler, he quickly shifted his attention back to the busy harbor traffic.

Literally hundreds of junks and bumboats were swarming around the carrier now, even though the three smaller warships were being largely ignored. After a little thought, he concluded that Hong Kong's floating merchants preferred hawking their wares to the sailors on the flattop who were far too high above the water to get a discerning look at the merchandise offered for sale.

Royal returned to the open wing where he could enjoy a better view of his surroundings. Raising his binoculars, he perused Hong Kong Island, sweeping the shoreline slowly from right to left, stopping briefly to study the pier at the Star Ferry terminal which was to serve as the landing for the liberty boats. He wondered if the *Field's* mail had been delivered to the pier yet. A letter, even a postcard from Candace would be worth a million bucks to him right now, he mused, continuing his scrutiny of Hong Kong's Central District and its adjacent waterfront.

His attention focused on the two warships berthed along the wall of the tidal basin at H.M.S. Tamar, the British naval base. Both ships looked to be a very light blue in color, "crab fat" in Royal Naval lingo. The black lettering on the stern of the closest vessel, a frigate, told him that she was *H.M.S. Crane*. The destroyer sharing the berth was a big Aussie two-stacker which he speedily identified as *H.M.A.S. Warramunga*.

Below decks, frenzied activity was the order of the day as personnel in the liberty section queued up to shower and shave and generally take advantage of the unrestricted use of fresh water as was customary when a ship was in port.

"You look really hot to hit that beach, Murray," a freshly showered Gardiner said with a toothy grin as he stepped up to the aluminum sink next to the one

Murray was using. The first-class was busily lathering his face. "I'll bet you've got some little Chinese fortune cookie waiting over there for you. Right?" teased Gardiner.

"Wrong! And that's a pretty dumb question, even for you."

"What do you mean? Didn't you ever pull into this place when you were on those flattops?"

"How the hell could I? The Japs occupied Hong Kong throughout the entire war."

"They did?"

"Of course they did," Murray said in a depreciative tone as his safety razor cleared a wide swath through the shaving cream on his cheek. "Don't you know anything?"

"Well, I know we won the war."

"I guess that's a step in the right direction," Murray grunted.

Gardiner tightened the white bath towel he was wearing around his waist, then saturating his face with hot soapy water, he said, "You know, Howie, that bet you made about not putting even a foot inside a cat house counts for this place just as much as it does for Japan."

"That's alright by me," said the first-class smiling complacently. "I have no intention of going near any whores, here or anyplace else."

"Well, what are you going to do then...go sight-seeing?"

"Yes. I might even go to a movie, not that it's any of your business. I'm also going to find a church. I haven't received communion since we left Sasebo. Tomorrow's Easter you know. At least when I was serving on civilized ships like the *Franklin* and *Enterprise*, we had chaplains."

"Speaking of carriers, I heard Logan say he was going to meet that buddy of his from the *Oriskany*. Why don't you go over to the beach with them?"

"No thanks. His idea of a successful liberty is almost as bad as yours. Now stop bugging me. I've nicked my face twice since you started asking your dumb questions."

An announcement over the speaker system informed all aboard the *Field* that liberty for the men in sections 1 and 2 would commence sharply at 16:00.

The first five days of their week-long stay proved to be a restful interlude for the transient bluejackets and, with the exception of a minor donnybrook involving Her Majesty's Navy, their time ashore passed without incident. Even so, the presence of the Americans was duly noted, especially among the owners of the numerous clothing establishments along Gloucester Road and Wyndham Street, and within a matter of hours custom-tailored tweeds and cashmere sportswear crammed every storage locker aboard the visiting warships.

Owen Royal was fortunate in being able to snag accommodations at the luxurious Repulse Bay Hotel. Like many of his crewmen, the *Field*'s C.O. found himself staring in awe at the bizarre sculptures in the Tiger Balm Garden, gasping for breath as he climbed the exotic "ladder streets" of Wanchai, and savoring a "four-dish dinner" of carp, chicken, pork and vegetables aboard one of Aberdeen's count-less floating restaurants.

And while other members of the *Field's* company were trekking the well-worn tourist route or more likely, sampling Hong Kong's lubricious pleasures, a dogged Donald Coates was busily reconnoitering department stores and the few electrical appliance shops he could find, eventually returning to the destroyer with a lengthy list of "bargain prices." Even so, he was totally unsuccessful in per-suading Lieutenant Fickett, *DD-505's* mess treasurer, that there were ample funds available to acquire a T.V. for the wardroom.

On Thursday evening, Phil Oetjens joined the captain for dinner at the Repulse Bay's main dining room. The small string orchestra was plodding its way through a medley of songs from "*The King and I*," and the maitre d' was prepar-ing to extract the cork on a vintage port when a breathless Puchalski, wearing the bright yellow arm band of a shore patrolman, materialized, seemingly from nowhere. Saluting nervously, the machinist's mate-second stood at the side of the table and explained in a raspy voice, "Captain, I'm really very sorry about bustin' in on your dinner like this, but Mister MacKinlay and Mister Stockwell have been trying to get the word to you since this afternoon when you left the ship. They called the hotel from the pier, but the people at the desk didn't know where you had gone. Then a little while ago, Mister MacKinlay remembered that Mister Oetjens had mentioned he was meeting you here for dinner. That's why he sent me over."

"Okay, Puchalski," Royal said a bit impatiently, "do you know why they've been looking for me?"

"Yes, Sir. It's on account of Mister Cobb."

"Mister Cobb?"

"Yes, Sir. They wanted you to know about it right away."

"What'd he do, fall overboard?" Oetjens asked with a broad grin. His words had slipped out unintentionally.

"No, Sir," Puchalski said in a half-whisper. "He's been detached from the ship."

"Detached?" boomed the captain.

"Yes, Sir. He's already left...I think."

"Already left? What are you talking about?"

"Well, I saw him getting into a cab at the ferry landing about an hour ago. He had two of the seamen from the deck force with him, lugging his bags. I heard him tell the cab driver to take him out to the airport."

"Alright, Puchalski, thank you," the captain said after a long thoughtful pause. "You can return to your duties."

"Yes, Sir," the motor-mack replied as he saluted.

As soon as the petty officer was out of earshot, Oetjens turned towards Royal and said, "Maybe there's a death in his family. I've never heard of anyone leaving a ship that fast for any other reason."

"Puchalski distinctly said detached. Besides, if Aubrey was going on emergency leave, he wouldn't be taking all his gear with him."

"That's true, but I still find it hard to believe that the navy would suddenly take an executive officer off a ship that's still assigned to a combat area," said the navigator, shaking his head.

"The Lord and BuPers doth wonders to behold," Royal muttered.

"Where do you think they've sent him?"

"Almost anywhere, I imagine. He's not in a promotion zone for commander yet, but he is eligible to skipper a D-E or one of the larger sweepers. I heard they're looking for C.O.'s for those frigates they've been reactivating back in Yokosuka," Royal said tapping the wine glass with his fingers.

"Well, Captain, I'm sorry if I'm out of line, but I don't mind saying sayonara to that horse's ass one bit. And it's a safe bet nobody else aboard the ship is going to miss him either...except maybe Al MacKinlay."

"Oh, Aubrey had his good points."

"With all respect, Captain, can you name me one?" Oetjens said with a teasing smile.

Owen chose to ignore the challenge. "Right now my main concern is finding out how soon we're getting Aub's replacement," Royal advised. "We're already operating far below the recommended officer allowance for a *Fletcher* class D-D. You know, Phil, BuPers isn't famous for its dispatch." Royal rose from his chair. "You stay here and finish eating. I'm going up to my room to pack. There's still time to catch the nine o'clock boat back to the ship," he said, glancing at the wrist watch Candace had given him as a wedding present.

•   •   •

Aubrey Cobb's was not the only departure of note taking place on this particular Thursday evening. Approximately 1,650 miles northeast of the *Field's* anchorage in Victoria Harbor, a captured two-and-a-half-toner, its overpainted white star still discernable across its hood, had just delivered Major Mychenko to the Hapsu air strip.

The Russian's ride from Maksan had taken nine hours. It had rained part of the way and the canvas cover on the truck's cab was tattered in so many places as to make it almost useless. Alighting from the former "Amerikanski" troop carrier, a wet and rumpled Mychenko kicked the front tire with his heavy boot.

"Go easy with those bags, Comrade Monkey!" he barked in Russian. The driver, a Suiyuan Chinese, smiled blankly and continued to drop the major's luggage every few yards as the two made the muddy trek through the marshland to the firm patch of high ground beyond.

Within the hour, the twin-engined Douglas, a memento of America's generosity during the "Great Patriotic War," was skimming low over the gray landscape, a tactic not entirely to the major's liking as he peered nervously at the treetops below. They spiked up through the early evening haze uncomfortably close, he thought.

"Can't your plane fly any higher?" he grumbled to a crewman nearby.

"It's because of the Yankee night prowlers, Comrade Major," the Russian flight-sergeant replied as he adjusted the parachute harness on one of the three wooden crates that occupied most of the plane's cargo area. "The closer we hug the ground, the harder it is for their radar to detect us. Only last week, they destroyed a plane just like this one in this very area."

"You mean they destroyed a Russian aircraft?" Mychenko's face knotted in incredulity.

"Yes, Sir, one from the Fourth Transport Squadron. I knew the flight-engineer quite well," the sergeant said as he gave the harness buckle a final tug.

"Amerikanski gangsters!" exclaimed the major in an outraged tone. "Shooting down non-belligerents! One wonders what they will try next," he shrugged. "A few months back, they murdered my nephew Strogi."

The sergeant frowned in sympathy.

"Yes," Mychenko continued. "Who knows how much innocent Russian blood is being poured over this stink hole? And the way we are flying," he said worriedly, "I'm afraid our blood will be the next to flow."

"We will be climbing soon," the sergeant said surveying the rig on the crate. "We have a scheduled air-drop near Yongchon, and we will have to pick up altitude for the parachutes to open."

"What are you dropping?" asked Mychenko with keen interest.

"This box contains anti-tank rockets," he pointed. "The other two have heavy mortar components."

The plane was climbing now, and the major relaxed, his more than ample caudal area totally obscuring the small bucket seat and giving him the appearance, the sergeant thought, of a low-hung barrage balloon.

Leaving Maksan was like waking up to find you've suddenly been purged of the plague, Mychenko thought. And Tschanka, he laughed aloud, maybe the old cow really wasn't such a bad catch after all. Anyway, who of his associates could boast of a wife with such advantageous connections in the Kremlin. Maybe he would give her the pleasure of his company during the two weeks leave he was to spend in Moscow. There would be plenty of time for the sporting life at his next post, a dream assignment, he mused. He was certain Budapest would be far better than anything he had hoped for during those rainy nights back in Maksan.

There was an abrupt lurch as the plane leveled off from its bank toward Yongchon.

"We are approaching the drop zone now, Comrade Major," the flight-sergeant advised. "Pilot Zhorki requests that you sit forward of the engines for your own comfort during the operation."

"Very well," Mychenko grunted indifferently. Even his sinuses had stopped bothering him, the major noticed, as he shuffled his tonnage to the forward quarter of the aircraft. And now the din of engines was as welcome to his ears as his favorite movement from *Swan Lake*."

On the ground, less than a hundred miles south of the plane's present position, members of the Chinese People's Army general staff were busily planning a major spring offensive which they calculated would gain them a few more chips at the bargaining table in Panmunjon. Along the craggy real estate that made up the M-L-R, one hill held particular interest. Defended by only two platoons of the U.S. Seventh Division's 31st Regiment, it was expected to offer no more than token resistance to the massive artillery and infantry assault the communists were cooking up for that area. One of the Chinese generals was mildly amused by the name the Americans had given the hill because of its odd shape. The Americans, he was told, thought the hill looked very much like a pork chop.

Chapter XXIII - Short Timers

It was one of the rare times in his life that Owen Garrett Royal was quite happy to be wrong. BuPers, it turned out, had not dragged its feet. On the contrary, when the captain returned to the *Field* an anxious Don Stockwell greeted him at the quarterdeck with the welcome news that Aubrey Cobb's replacement had arrived within the hour and was waiting in the wardroom.

"What's his name?" asked Royal, obviously pleased.

"Bray, Sir...Stratton L," Stockwell replied, reading from where the name had been entered in the quarterdeck log. "He flew down from Atsugi in the same plane Mister Cobb was to take back."

"What kind of duty was Mister Cobb off to in such a hurry?"

"I don't know, Captain. I don't think he knew either. His orders just said to report to commanding officer, Yokosuka Naval Base, for further assignment as directed."

"Well, I still can't understand why they would just yank him off the ship without giving us advance notice," said Royal indignantly.

"The two messages came in only twenty minutes apart," Stockwell said wearily. "First we received the one detaching the exec. Then we got the message saying that a Lieutenant-Commander Bray would be reporting aboard this date to assume the duties of executive officer. The messages came in shortly after you left this afternoon. We tried to contact you at the Repulse Bay but the desk clerk said you hadn't arrived yet."

"Yes, I decided to hunt up a gift for my wife. Has Mister Bray settled in yet?"

"Yes, Sir, I think so. At least his bags have been brought down to Mister Cobb's old room. Mister MacKinlay told the stewards to make sure the room's all squared away with fresh towels and linen."

"Good. Well, I'd better go greet our new executive officer."

"Yes, Sir. I'll have Pedersen here take your luggage to your cabin," Stockwell said, glancing over at the messenger-of-the-watch as the commanding officer departed for the wardroom.

Lieutenant-Commander Bray had been sitting at the wardroom table, leafing through a two-month-old copy of *Look* when the captain entered. Almost toppling his coffee cup as he shoved the magazine aside, the newcomer rose from his chair and extended his hand which Royal firmly accepted.

Commanding in appearance, Stratton Leonard Bray was tall, well over six feet, with silver-gray temples that seemed decidedly out of place with his boyishly handsome features. His dress blue uniform looked new and contrasted markedly with the captain's dark brown sports jacket and tan slacks.

"Sit down, Commander," Royal invited cheerfully as he slid into his own chair at the head of the table. The captain instinctively took note of the ribbons the officer was wearing — World War II Victory, American Area Campaign Medal, Asiatic-Pacific Area Campaign, Navy Occupation Service and the National Defense and American Defense Service medals. The absence of battle stars on either of the two campaign ribbons was duly observed, as was the presence of the officer's Naval Academy ring.

The customary greetings exchanged, Owen took a few minutes to peruse the lieutenant-commander's orders and the voluminous service jacket Bray had handed him.

"Have we ever met?" Royal asked, glancing curiously at the new arrival. "I can't put my finger on it, but I could swear we've met somewhere before."

"Yes, Sir, we did," Bray said smiling. "It was during my plebe year. You were a first classman, and I'm afraid I incurred your wrath at the time."

"Really?" Royal looked genuinely puzzled. "What dastardly offense did you commit? I always thought I was pretty much of a soft touch when it came to dealing with fourth classmen," the captain said with a good-natured grin.

"Yes, Sir, as I recall you did have that reputation among my fellow plebes, only I guess I must have caught you on one of your off-days. You were making an inspection to see that we were all out of our beds at reveille. When you reached my room, I was sitting at the edge of my bed just getting into my slippers. You advised me that even though both my feet were touching the deck, my butt was still on the bed, so that meant I was technically in bed. You assigned me ten demerits and two hours marching. That night you came by at taps to make a bed check and you saw me sitting in exactly the same spot I had been in the morning, only this time I was just slipping out of my slippers. You then informed me that since my feet were touching the deck, I was technically not in bed, and you gave me another ten demerits and two more hours marching. The next morning I came to you with what I thought at the time was a pretty reasonable request. My contention was that it was illogical that I could be guilty of being in bed in the first instance, and also be guilty of being out of bed in the second, since I was sitting in precisely the same position both times. I asked you if under the circumstances, you could cancel out one of the two punishments."

"Did I?" Royal asked, highly amused.

"No, Sir. You gave me an additional fifteen and three for bothering you with a facetious comment."

"Damn, I must have been a real hardass," Royal laughed. "Well, Mister Bray, I hope you won't hold what happened almost twenty years ago against me. I'm sure you'll discover that I try to run a happy ship."

"Yes, Captain, I'm certain you do."

"I see here that you've already had a sea command." The *Field's* skipper smiled pleasantly as he scanned the papers in Bray's service jacket.

"Yes, when I was a Jaygee the last two years of the war. She was only a P-C-E."

"Where'd you operate?"

"Unfortunately we spent almost all our time training other P-C-E personnel in the waters around Key West. We made one escort run down to Rio de Janeiro and back, but if there were any U-boats lurking around, we never caught a sniff of them. We didn't even get the chance to raise some hell crossing the equator."

"How come?"

"I only had a little over a hundred men in my crew and none of them, including myself, were shellbacks, so when we crossed the line, there wasn't anybody to carry out the initiation. I'm afraid we all made the transition from polliwog to shellback quite painlessly."

"I see you're wearing the Pacific-Asiatic theater ribbon," Royal said, raising his glance from the folder.

"They sent us to Hawaii five months before V-J Day. We operated out of Pearl but our patrol area never extended more than a hundred miles beyond Oahu. Needless to say, that late in the war, we didn't get to see any action." Bray hesitated for an instant. Feeling a stir of embarrassment, he said, "I hope I don't sound gung-ho, Captain, but in all honesty, I'm looking quite forward to getting some combat experience under my belt. In my fourteen years active service, I've never heard a shot fired in anger. They told me back in Japan that the *Field* has really been in the thick of it for the last few months. You know, Sir, I've been requesting a combat assignment with the Seventh Fleet since that Sunday morning the Reds hopped over the thirty-eighth parallel. Until last week, BuPers had me salted away in the Fargo Building up in Boston doing an admin' job any Wave ensign fresh out of college could have handled. I'd just about given up hope of ever getting over here when I received orders to Yokosuka for cruiser duty."

"Cruiser duty?"

"Yes, when I flew out of Boston last Saturday, I was expecting to join the navigation department on the *Saint Paul*. At least that's what it said on my orders. Then when I checked in at Yokosuka, they told me my orders had been modified en route, and I'd be flying down to Hong Kong to report aboard the *Field* as her exec."

"Were you disappointed...not getting a cruiser?"

"Not at all. I've always had an affinity with the tin can navy, as you'll see in my records there," he said pointing to the folder. "After the war I served as gun boss on the *Steinaker*, and then I did a tour as navigator on the *Rich*. The *Field's* my first *Fletcher* though. I'm anxious to learn all her inner most secrets," he added with a chuckle.

"I'm afraid she doesn't have many. You'll find that except for a slight slug-gishness when she's coming around to port, she handles pretty easily. Of course, she's reputed to have a ghost."

"A ghost?"

"Yes, his, or should I say its, name is Wilbur Henderson. Naturally there's noth-ing to it. I tried to squash the story the first few weeks I was aboard. I thought it would be bad for morale. However," he laughed softly, "I soon discovered that the men seem to actually enjoy the idea of having a ghost on board. It gives the ship some added color, and gives them something to talk about when they go ashore."

"Who is Henderson supposed to be?"

"A chief torpedoman. He was the only fatality the ship suffered throughout all of World War Two. But I don't want to get into that right now. I'm sure you'll hear about old Willy adinfinitum from the crew. They love to bring the subject up every chance they get. As far as your seeing action over here, didn't they tell you in Yokosuka that our tour is almost up? We've only got another month left before we head back to San Diego, and I expect we'll spend most of it screening the carriers."

Bray stared at him open-mouthed. "They never said a word about the *Field* heading stateside. All they told me was that she'd been dueling with shore bat-teries, and that she'd taken a couple hits...and, oh yes, she'd been recommended by Rhee for the South Korean P-U-C." The pain in Bray's voice was mirrored by the expression on his face.

"Cheer up, Commander," Royal said, looking questioningly at his new exec-utive officer. "This is a crazy war. A lot of things can happen in a month. Now, I'd suggest you get your gear squared away. We've got a lot to do before we get under way tomorrow morning."

The arrival of Stratton Bray was not the only event of note to take place aboard the *Field* that Thursday. Prominently tacked to the bulletin board outside the personnel office was a white sheet of paper containing the long awaited list of names of those fortunate crewmen who had successfully passed the recent petty officer examination. Much to Holiday's disappointment his name was not on the list. Much to Howie Murray's frustration, Patterson's was.

It didn't take very long for Stratton Bray to settle in. Scanning the ship's organization chart given to him earlier by Don Stockwell, the new X.O. had lit-tle trouble discerning that the *Field* was woefully undermanned, especially in regard to her officer complement. Reaching toward the small, pull-out desk, he tapped his pipe against the ashtray. Satisfied that the pipe was empty, he leaned back and surveyed the stateroom, wondering what problems and tribulations his predecessor had contemplated within its modest confines.

The news about the *Field* heading home had been as unwelcome as it had been unexpected. He knew that as a two-and-a-half-striper, he had little chance of finding a billet on another Seventh Fleet combatant. The fact that the pro-motion board had recently selected him for commander was bound to lessen his chances still further.

It seemed insane that the navy would send him literally to the other side of the world just so he could sail right back. He wondered what his wife Susan and the kids would think, especially after the big send-off everyone had given him. And Susan's brother Steve...old "How I Won the War Stevie" with his three Air Medals and that Navy Cross he'd won at Bougainville. Good old Stevie, the pride of the flying marines...he'd never let him live this one down, of that he was certain.

Bray reached over and turned on the radio which had been tuned into a local station playing the latest American recordings. Maybe there was still a possibility of getting to the *Saint Paul*, he reasoned. Maybe if he got his request in right away and Royal endorsed it, he could transfer off the *Field* next month when she stopped in Yokosuka on her way home. Hell, her navigator could easily take over as acting X.O. for the run back to San Diego. The crew will probably spend most of their time laying around on the deck soaking up the sun anyway, he told himself confidently.

Patti Page was just asking "*How Much is That Doggie in the Window*" over the room's bulkhead speaker when Bray's thoughts were interrupted by a loud tapping on the doorframe.

"Good evening, Sir, I'm Jesse Fickett," announced the visitor as he grasped the exec's outstretched hand. "Welcome to the good ship Charlie P. The captain told me to drop off this copy of our Title B inventory for your inspection," the *Field's* supply officer said pleasantly.

For several minutes, the two officers discussed the condition of the *Field's* supplies, the capability of her galley and reefer spaces, the operation of the general mess and ship's store, and the status of the all-important stock records. Finally, Bray asked the question that had been on his mind since the second he'd crossed the *Field's* quarterdeck. "The officer I'm replacing...this Lieutenant-Commander Cobb...was there any reason he left the ship so suddenly?"

"No, Sir. Not that I know of," Fickett said haltingly.

"Where'd he go to?"

"Sorry, Sir, I don't know that either. Actually, I was ashore when he took off. I received the good news when I got back."

"Good news?"

Fickett wiggled a bit in his chair and looked uncomfortable. "Can I talk off the record, Sir?"

"Yes, of course, and forget the sir, it's Stratt."

"Well, Mister Cobb couldn't exactly be described as being beloved by the officers and crew of the *Charles P. Field*. He was dogmatic with the officers and he had an elitist attitude towards the enlisted. With Aubrey Cobb, you always knew there was only one answer to a question — his. And when he wasn't pontificating to the officers, he was running around the ship trying to write-up the white hats. If it wasn't for Captain Royal, I'm sure this ship would have racked up the all-time navy record for masts and summaries on a single cruise." Fickett frowned as he leaned back in his chair. "It's a sad thing to say, but Mister Cobb seemed to thrive on making other people miserable. I really don't think anyone's going to miss him."

"Tell you what, Jesse, if you ever catch me pontificating, let me know right away...okay?" said Bray with a friendly smile.

Fickett nodded sheepishly. "Yes, Sir, if you say so."

At the same time down in the Ops Department berthing space, a disgruntled Holiday had been doing his best to ignore the barbs of Nugent, Gardiner and Bacelli, all gloating over their former crony's unsuccessful attempt to achieve the noble status of petty-officer second-class.

"Hey, Murray! Who are you going to stick with mess cooking now that Patterson's got himself a crow?" Holiday called out, hoping to shift the focus of attention away from himself.

"Belton. He's next in the rotation," grumbled Murray from his bunk.

"Come on, Holiday, you shouldn't be bugging Murray while he's so pissed about Patterson making third," Gardiner spoke up.

"I'm not pissed! I'd just like to finish reading this magazine in peace," Murray said slowly turning the pages of the coverless *Colliers* he was holding.

"Yeah, you're not pissed...just like Lassie doesn't have fleas," said Nugent glibly.

"Hey, Howie," Bacelli called out, "when Patterson comes back from liberty tonight, are you going to have the pleasure of informing him that he made R-D-three?"

"Stuff it! As far as I'm concerned, he can find out for himself by checking the list outside ship's office just like anybody else."

"You know, Howie," Nugent cut in. "I think it would be real nice if we had some kind of party for Patterson now that he's a petty officer. What do you think?" Nugent asked with a nasty grin.

"I repeat my last transmission...stuff it!"

"Come on, Murray. Don't be such a sore head. If you don't want to have a party for Patterson, hell, let's have one to celebrate getting rid of Cobb," Bacelli volunteered. "That's gotta' be the best thing that's happened to this bucket since we left San Diego."

"Aren't you being a little premature?" Logan joined in from his bunk. "What makes you think the new X-O is going to be an improvement? Haven't you ever heard that old saying about the devil you know being better than the devil you don't know?" Kevin asked with a chuckle.

"Nobody could be as bad as Cobb," Bacelli said. "Besides, me and Gardiner just got the scoop on Bray from Gordon. He was just checking in his records up in ship's office."

"Ha," grunted Murray. "Hollywood's got Hedda Hopper, and we've got good old Gordon."

"Don't knock it, Howie," Gardiner said. "It's pretty handy having a direct pipeline to ship's office."

"Okay, Gardiner," Logan said quietly, not turning his head from the bunk. "Give us the run-down on Bray."

"Well, for one thing, Gordon says he's going to be our new skipper. That is, as soon as they shit-can Royal."

"How could Gordon know that?" asked Murray angrily.

"Easy. Gordon says Bray's records show that he's already been selected for commander. It's just a matter of weeks before his rank becomes effective. Since this bucket doesn't rate two three-stripers, why else would they send him to us?"

"Boy, what a kick in the ass this must be for the old man," Murray muttered in a disgusted tone. "If Gordon knows about Bray's third stripe, you can be damn sure the captain must know it too."

"Has Bray ever had a command at sea?" Logan spoke up.

"Yeah, according to Gordy, Bray was C.O. of something called the *P-C-E Eight-Sixty-One* during the war," Bacelli volunteered. "Say, what the hell is a P-C-E anyway?"

"A patrol-craft-escort...a glorified subchaser," Logan advised. "She looks like a destroyer-escort that somebody decided to chop in half," the second-class added with a snicker.

"Looks to me like the navy's decided to chop the old man in half," Murray growled, slapping the magazine hard against the steel rim of his bunk.

Nugent flashed a mirthless grin. "Take it easy, Howie. Stop getting all steamed up. Don't forget, you want to be all smiles when you give Patterson the big news about his crow."

"Damn it, Nugent! For the last time, knock it off about Patterson! The least I have to do with him, the better."

"Why do you hate him so much?" Bacelli asked.

"I don't hate him. I just don't like him. Hell, all you have to do is take a look at that kid and you can tell he's bad news. Now let's change the subject before I really get pissed."

There was a half-a-minute of silence, then Bacelli called out, "Hey, Logan. How'd that buddy of yours make out when that Corsair clobbered the *Oriskany* last month?"

"Okay. He was in C.I.C. at the time."

"You ought to tell him to paint a red stripe down the Big-O's flight deck. Maybe it will make her lucky like his old ship, the *Yorktown*," Nugent quipped sarcastically.

"He seems happy enough with the 'Risky' just the way she is," Logan said casually. "At least they have a lively sense of humor on the Big-O."

"Like how?" quizzed Gardiner.

"Well, last month they loaded an old kitchen sink on one of their planes, then dropped it on the North Koreans during an air strike. He says that way they'll be able to report when they get home that they dropped everything on the Reds including the kitchen sink." Logan leaned half way out of his bunk and looked over towards Murray. "And you'll be happy to know, Howie, that the *Oriskany's* crew just chipped in and bought some Salesian nuns a new building in Shizuoka that they needed for an orphanage. It's big enough to house a hundred kids."

"That seems only fair. They probably fathered half of them," Murray answered, not taking his eyes from the magazine.

"For a short-timer, Murray, you certainly are a cynic," observed Bacelli despairingly.

"Yeah, and I'm going to stay one right up until the morning me and my discharge papers board that Greyhound bus in San Diego."

"Scuttlebutt over on the *Oriskany* is that they're all going to be movie stars," Logan said with a chuckle.

"Movie stars?" piped up Gardiner.

"Yes, that new book Michener wrote...'The Bridges at Toko-ri.' Paramount's going to make a movie of it and the word's floating around the ship that the *Oriskany's* slated to play the lead."

"Hey," Holiday yelled out excitedly. "That's a coincidence. I was drinking with some of the pip jockeys from the *Thompson* last night and they told me that she's hauling ass back to Pearl Harbor next month so she can be used as the *Caine* in 'The Caine Mutiny'."

Logan smiled, recalling the line he'd fed Candy about working on the film script.

"Boy, what a crock!" Bacelli sneered. "How come those clowns on the *Oriskany* and the *Thompson* get to mug it up in the movies while we don't even make it into a lousy newsreel?"

"Hey, listen to the next 'Rudolph Vaselino' over there. The Charlie P.'s gift to the silver screen," said Nugent with a sadistic grin.

"Yeah, Vinnie, you giving up your Chinese egg rolls for Hollywood and Vine?"

"Blow it out your ear, Gardiner. This time next year when my egg rolls take off, I'll be able to buy Hollywood and Vine."

While the battle of the egg rolls droned on, a tired Owen Royal settled down in his cabin with a cold Coke and the small bundle of mail Valencia had just delivered to his cabin.

Disappointed at not finding a letter from Candace, Owen quickly leafed through the correspondence. Each envelope was of less interest than the one that preceded it, and the captain soon concluded that there must be someone back in the states anxiously committed to selling him anything from polish for his gold buttons to tires for an automobile he didn't possess.

Royal was about to chuck the entire pile of correspondence into the wastepaper basket, when he recognized familiar handwriting on one of the envelopes. With surging spirits, he extracted the letter and began to read.

3 April, 1953
San Francisco

Dear Owen,

Well, I've got the old girl nestled safely away in drydock here at Hunters Point. The Bureau had finally decided that it's high time she got her bottom scraped and her tanks cleaned. It's a shame you never had the pleasure of refueling from the Chicamauga. I was really looking forward to showing you how real pros handle a fleet replenishment.

The voyage home from Yokosuka was a real joy ride. Everyone picked up a tan and luckily, they gave us a full week at Pearl, most of which I spent at the Royal Hawaiian. Carolyn is flying out here to spend a little time with me. San Francisco's rather nice this time of year so I expect she'll find plenty of ways to enjoy herself during the days when I have to stay aboard. Joanne can't make it this time. She's still got six weeks to do before her college vacation begins. I'll see her in June when I go home on leave. Lee's in the Med flying off the F.D.R. He's in a Banshee squadron but he's been trying to work out a transfer to an air group operating with Task Force 77. I'm not too worried, though. I just read in the papers that the Reds have agreed to reconvene the truce talks on April 26th. They must be hurting from all that ordinance we've been dumping on them for three years.

I read about the Field taking a hit in after-steering and that you had some casualties. I hope the rest of your tour goes smoother. Since you've only got another month over there, try not to get in the way of any Commie Shells. I'm looking forward to seeing you and Candace when you get back. If Carolyn's still here, we'll try to fly down to San Diego so we can wave to you and that tin bucket of yours when you come steaming in.

I air-mailed you a little present. I wrapped it as best I could, but I hope it arrives without getting cracked or broken. I'm sure you and your crew will enjoy it.

A couple of Airedales in the O-club at Yokosuka told me about some can knocking over Jehovah's sacred smokestack. I did a little poking around and found out it was you. No, I'm not going to give you any more fatherly advice. Especially since I know you won't take it. Hope to see you soon.

All the best,
Tim

443

Three hundred and fifty miles south of the Hunters Point Naval Yard, Ronald Paradise was glancing uneasily at the small package Benny Margolis had just handed him.

"What's the matter? You think you're getting stiffed in this deal?" snorted Margolis belligerently.

"Well, I've paid you close to a thousand dollars, plus another six hundred in expenses. I certainly expected to get more than this...whatever it is," Paradise said, tearing the wax paper from the square cardboard box.

"Look," Margolis said throatily, "I wasn't too keen about taking this job. As it is, I broke my hump getting what's on that tape."

"Tape?"

"Yeah, now before you start bitchin' that I stole your dough, go get hold of a recorder and play it."

"You mean you don't have one here in your office?" Paradise asked, his eyes staring owlishly at the reel of chocolate colored audio tape.

"Hell, no. I rent the equipment as I need it. Besides, you work for an ad agency, you should be able to get your hands on one without too much sweat." Margolis handed him an envelope. "Here's a complete report of everything that's on that tape. There's dates, names of the hotels, identification of each guy this Moffett broad was shacked up with. I had to bug four hotel rooms and her flat in La Jolla to get what you're holding in your hand right now," he said pointing to the tape.

"Is her voice identifiable?"

"Hell, yes," Margolis retorted as if he'd been personally insulted. "That's the best quality tape you can buy. I guarantee that anybody who knows the bitch will be able to pick her voice out right away." He leaned back in the wooden chair. "I don't know what you've got against this babe, and I really don't care. One thing though, she's certainly a looker. I wouldn't mind knocking off a piece myself." He emphasized his comment with an obscene gesture.

"What did you find out about her husband?"

"That was the easy part. He's a navy officer. His name's Owen G. Royal. He's skipper of some destroyer over in Korea."

"Do you have the name of the ship and it's address?" Paradise asked eagerly.

"Yeah, it's all in the envelope. The address is the same for all navy ships in the Pacific. You just write to the ship in care of the Fleet Post Office in San Francisco. Uncle Sammy does the rest. Say, why are you so interested in her old man? You're not planning to send that tape to him, are you?"

"No, of course not. I'm just curious, that's all."

"Well, I don't know what kind of a sneaky deal you're hatchin' up, but I'd hate to think her husband's ever gonna' hear what's on that tape. Besides all the grunts and groans, there's a couple of conversations with her boss, a guy named Barlow..."

"Ham Barlow?" Paradise interrupted.

"Yeah, that's the guy. She tells him at least three times how she definitely plans to dump her old man as soon as his ship gets back from Korea."

"Has she been having sex with Barlow?"

"You've got to be kiddin'. If there was an Olympic record for time in the sack, those two would win it hands down," Margolis retorted with a leer.

Paradise nodded, a smile wreathed his thin face.

In another moment their business was concluded. Laughing to himself, the former B.B.Y. and S. copy chief strutted triumphantly out on to the sunlit street. San Diego never looked so good, he thought.

•   •   •

The morning in Hong Kong harbor blossomed to the tune of whistles, screeching jack-lines, and the hiss of hoses washing black mud from rising anchor chains. Special-sea-detail had been called away promptly at 07:30, and the *Doyle* and *Thompson* had already started forming up off Victoria as they prepared to lead *Oriskany* around the northwest tip of Hong Kong Island, then southward to the China Sea.

Aboard the *Field*, an uneasy Donald Coates surveyed the darkened radar shack counting heads as he wondered if the new executive officer would make an appearance or preferably remain topside on the bridge-wing as was Cobb's practice whenever the ship was entering or departing a foreign port.

"Are all stations manned and ready?" the ensign asked cheerfully.

"No, Sir, we seem to be missing our new third-class," answered Murray with a hint of delectation.

"Where's Patterson? Has anyone seen Patterson?"

"No, Sir," Logan volunteered. "Since the word was to muster on stations, there wasn't any way we could tell he was missing."

"Paulsen," Coates said sharply. "You went ashore with Patterson yesterday didn't you?"

"We were in the same liberty boat but I really didn't go ashore with him. Once we hit the beach, he took off by himself."

"He's a real loner, Mister Coates," Bacelli cut in. "He almost always goes off by himself."

"Yeah, just like Murray," Nugent muttered, catching a seething glance from the *Field's* leading radarman.

"Maybe he's still in his bunk," Coates said in a quiet, hopeful voice.

"No, Sir," Murray spoke up. "I checked the compartment right after reveille sounded. His bunk hadn't been slept in. I figured he missed the last liberty boat and would come back with the officers and chiefs this morning."

"I was on that boat," Coates scowled. "There wasn't any enlisted in it except the crew." The ensign reached for the lever on the squawk-box. "Bridge, combat," he nervously called into the speaker.

"Bridge, aye," came a quick response from the boatswain-of-the-watch. "This is Mister Coates. Is the captain on the bridge?"

"What is it, Don?" Royal answered before the petty officer could reply.

"One of my men is unaccounted for, Sir. It's Patterson. Nobody's seen him since he went on liberty yesterday."

"Didn't he just make third-class?"

"Yes, Sir."

"Well, unless he manages to swim out here in the next five minutes, he's going to miss ship. Call the radio-shack. Have them inform our consulate that we've got a man still on the beach somewhere. Maybe he had a run-in with the British shore patrol or Hong Kong police. And while you're at it, have the radio-shack check with the *Oriskany*. Their beach patrol was the last to leave the ferry landing. See if they know anything about Patterson."

"Yes, Sir," the ensign acknowledged.

"Looks like poor old Patterson's gonna' loose his crow before he even finds out that he got it," said Gardiner.

"Old?" Logan snickered. "The kid's only nineteen."

"Well, in a manner of speaking," Gardiner shrugged. "Besides, the way Murray's always pulling his chain, he's probably aged a few extra years."

"Bet you're really all broken up about Patterson screwing up just before he would have made third-class, heh, Howie?" Bacelli said smirking.

The first-class ignored the taunt as he helped Logan tape the corners of the chart to the plotting table.

"Murray probably jinxed him," Nugent cut in. "I haven't seen the king of the short-timers smiling so much since the day he got the word that he'd become a papa again."

"Yeah, tell me, Howie," Bacelli asked with exaggerated concern in his tone, "is there any truth to the scuttlebutt that you've got a voodoo doll of Patterson tucked away in your locker, and you stick pins in it whenever he gets you pissed?"

"In case you forgot, you're at special-sea-detail," said Coates, his eyes blazing. "Mister Bray's liable to walk in here any minute. Nugent...get that air-search radar fired up. The captain likes to see the antenna spinning around when we steam down the channel."

"It gives us a more business-like appearance, heh, Mister Coates?"

"Yes, Bacelli, I guess you could say that," the C.I.C. officer answered dispassionately.

Up on the bridge-wing, a messenger from the radio-shack had just handed the *Field's* C.O. a dispatch.

"Our missing radarman?" Stratton Bray asked in a cheerful tone.

"No," the captain muttered. "It's our acting division leader...the *John Morgan*." An expression of pain crossed his face. "She was searching for the crew of a downed Air Force bomber off Hungnam when she hit a mine."

"She go down?" a startled Phil Oetjens interjected.

"No, but she lost her bow and seventy-five feet of hull. According to this dispatch, everything forward of her superstructure, including her number-one five-inch mount, is now sitting at the bottom of the Sea of Japan."

"How bad were her casualties?" Bray asked.

"Six dead and twenty-three wounded," Royal said, handing the sheet of paper to his exec and navigator for their perusal.

"I wonder how the commodore and Captain Fenchurch made out," Oetjens mumbled aloud as he scanned the message.

"I don't know," Royal said worriedly. "There aren't any names mentioned."

Oetjens swallowed hard, then dragged deeply on his cigarette. "Well, knowing this crew, I'd give it about half-a-day before they start calling the ship Uncas."

"Uncas?" a puzzled Bray inquired.

"Yes, with the *Morgan* joining the *Ward* and *Wayne* in drydock, as far as the division's concerned, we're now the last of the Mohicans."

Conversation was terminated by the abrupt kick of the *Field's* screws. Soon the destroyer was passing down East Lamma Channel, moving abeam of Bluff Head Point, and on by Lo Chau and Po Toi Islands. By late afternoon, the *Field* was leaping over rolling gray water, her helmsman steadying on a course that would take *DD-505* and her consorts back to the Sea of Japan and the business of war.

On April 15th, the day the *Field* was passing through the Formosa Strait, the ship's newspaper reported that the Viet Minh had just invaded Laos with 40,000 troops. Nobody in the *Field's* wardroom knew much about Laos and even less about the Viet Minh. Joe Canavan thought they had some connection with the Mau Mau in Kenya, while Oscar Kimmick was reasonably certain the Viet Minh were Arabs, and that Laos was "one of those little sheikdoms up in the Persian Gulf." Owen Royal grabbed the wardroom gazetteer, dutifully informing his officers that Laos was "an associated state of the French Union of Indochina." Neither the gazetteer or the wardroom dictionary carried any mention of the Viet Minh. After a moment's discussion, the consensus in the wardroom was that Laos was too obscure a place ever to effect the United States or its national policy. Of more general interest was the newspaper's historical note that the day marked the 42nd anniversary of the sinking of the *Titanic*.

That evening, Royal found time to answer Captain Barrett's recent letter.

15 April, 1953

Dear Tim:

> *By the time you receive this, I imagine you will have gotten your land legs back and adjusted to that good life stateside. I'm glad you'll be able to spend some time with Carolyn. Please give her my very best regards. Let's definitely get together when I get back in June. I*

know Candace will be looking forward to seeing you and Carolyn again as much as I am.

It look's like my future career has gotten off to a roaring stop. I'm afraid my days as the Field's C.O. may be numbered. They've just sent me a new exec, an officer who has been selected for promotion to commander. His rank becomes effective one week after the date we're scheduled to hit San Diego. I'd like to think that they sent him aboard strictly as an expedient, and that his assignment is only temporary until they can dig up some junior two-and-a-half striper for me. However, I'm too much of a realist to really believe that. I imagine my goose was cooked even before we ever got to Korea. I guess you know we almost ran into the stern of the Crown Point during our O.R.I. off Hawaii. Wouldn't you know, with my luck, she'd have to be carrying a two-star at the time. Losing that Russian pilot off Chongjin didn't help my case any, either, I guess.

My new exec is Stratton Bray. He's academy, class of 1940. From what I've observed during the short time he's been aboard, he seems top-notch. By the way, I still haven't found out why they snatched my former X.O. off the ship without giving me advance notice. Seems like strange behavior even for our friends at BuPers.

Did you hear about the John Morgan hitting a mine off Hungnam? I understand she's in Yokosuka having a jury bow fitted so she can make it back to the states under her own power. We got the word this morning that Billy Price and Arnie Fenchurch were both hurt. Arnie's wounds were minor but the commodore is in the hospital at Yokosuka with a broken leg. When the division left San Diego last year for this tour, I never thought that the Field would be the only ship in the division to make it back in one piece. The fate's have been quite kind to us. Even our ghost, Chief Henderson, seems to have transferred to another ship, perhaps the Morgan.

I'm curious about the package you sent. It hasn't arrived yet but we're scheduled to refuel from the Kaskaskia in three more days. I expect she'll have some mail for us. Hopefully, your package will be included. Speaking of refueling, I'm really sorry we never had the opportunity to come alongside the Chickamauga. I'm certain we would have noticed the difference with you and your pros running the show.

I hope this letter hasn't painted too dark a picture of things. In spite of all the negatives, I am pleased to report that we've racked up a few positives also. For instance, the Field has been recommended for both the South Korean Presidential Unit Citation and the Navy Unit Citation. I'm fairly certain we'll spend the short time we've got *left over here escorting the carriers with Task Force 77. Short of a collision, I can't see how we can get into any more trouble. And who knows, maybe the navy will look at our overall performance and come up with that fourth stripe after all. The navy's been known to do less logical things, I'm sure you'll agree.*

 Until I see you and Carolyn in San Diego,

Have fun,
Owen

On the 18th of April, the same day the army's 17th Infantry was retaking bloody Pork Chop, the *Field* and *Oriskany* met and simultaneously refueled from oiler *Kaskaskia* off the northernmost tip of Honshu Island. This was a quiet period for those in ship's company not directly engaged in the refueling operation, thus Murray and Logan decided it would be ideal time to catch some sun up on the 0-3 level above the wheelhouse.

It was not at all hard for Howie Murray to forget for a few moments that he was still in the navy. Lying flat on his back, his head cushioned comfortably on a kapok life jacket, all he could see was sky as blue as sapphire...as blue as the sky he knew he'd soon be watching from the hammock in his yard back in Warren.

Logan, a few feet away, had slipped out of his T-shirt and was sitting with his back propped up against the cylindrical base of the gun director. Its recently painted surface felt warm and smooth in the morning sun.

"Does being a short-timer feel as good now as it did back in forty-five?" Logan asked, with a good-natured grin.

"Better, I've got a wife and three daughters to come home to this time. And you can be damn sure I'm going to look those discharge papers over with a magnifying glass before I sign them. They're not going to slip any reserve enlistment papers over on me again, that's for sure. From now on, as far as I'm concerned, U-S-N-R means un-submissive to navy recruiters." Murray scratched his stomach, then swallowed hard. "You know we'll be going into Yokosuka only one more time, don't you?" the first-class asked a bit stiffly.

Logan cast a side glance at him. "Yes, I imagine we'll stop off to refuel and take on water before we haul out for the States. Most of the ships stop in Yokosuka on their way home from Korea. So what?"

"Well, are you going to do what you said you would?"

"That depends on what I said I was going to do?" queried Logan.

"Stop fooling around, Kev. You know damn well what I'm talking about. You promised me that you'd go see your nurse and tell her that you're not going to marry her. That's the only decent thing to do, you know...that is unless you really do want to marry her," Murray added in a hopeful tone.

"Hell, no. What do I have to do to convince you that I'm not the marrying kind? Besides, I'll have to make up for a lot of lost time when I get back. I sure don't want Cindy popping into my office, all starry eyed in her neat little service dress blues and cramping my style."

"I hope you realize you've got absolutely no conscience whatsoever. I don't understand how you could take her up to Tokyo and have sex with her, and just think nothing of it."

"Hell, I gave it lots of thought. She's a damn good looking girl. In fact, I was just thinking about it a few minutes ago."

"That's not what I mean, and you know it!"

"Okay, get one thing straight. I never twisted her arm. She jumped into the sack under her own power, even that first time back in San Diego."

"Maybe, but from what you've said, she thinks you're going to marry her when you get deactivated. By the way, is she Catholic?"

"What's that got to do with anything?"

"A hell of a lot. You led her into mortal sin," Murray exclaimed angrily. "If you don't give a damn about what happens to your soul, as a Catholic you should at least care a little about hers. Supposed something happened to her while she was in a state of mortal sin?"

"Well, to answer your question, she happens to be a Wasp. Anyway, nothing's going to happen to her in Yokosuka," said Logan with an annoyed shrug. "You know, just for the record, Patterson's Catholic. How come I never noticed you taking any special interest in him, except to break his hump every chance you got?"

"I never went out of my way to hurt Patterson."

"You've sure got a convenient memory. Didn't you and Coates try to get his name dropped from the exam list?"

"Who told you that?"

"Let's say an unimpeachable source."

"Probably that big mouth Gordon. Sure, I tried to get his name taken off the list. He didn't deserve to take the test in the first place."

"That's funny, especially since he was the only one of our four strikers to pass it."

"Pure luck. The test was multiple choice. He must have been lucky and guessed right. Anyway, we weren't talking about Patterson. We were talking about your nurse. Now, I don't think it's too much to ask that you go see her and tell her that you've got no intention of marrying her. Suppose she resigns her commission so she can get to see you in New York, and then you go and tell her to get lost?"

"What do you care about her commission? You hate the navy."

"This has nothing to do with the navy. It has to do with a person's feelings."

"Come on, Howie. Commissioned officers don't have feelings. You've said so yourself," Logan answered in a teasing tone.

"Be serious, Kev. If you don't have the guts to tell her, I'm willing to go over to the hospital and do it for you."

"You're really serious about this, aren't you?"

"Of course I am. Look, I know it's going to be hard telling her, but don't you see, she'll be hurt a hell of a lot less this way."

"Alright. If it really means this much to you, I'll tell her as soon as we get to Yokosuka."

"You'll feel a lot better, believe me," Murray said with a smile.

"Okay, only one thing, this has to be a reciprocal deal."

"What do you mean?"

"Lay off Patterson when he gets back," Logan said in a serious tone. "It's going to be tough enough on the kid when he finds out that he was a petty officer for all of six hours."

"Losing his crow is going to be the least of his worries. You know, missing your ship when she's headed for an operational zone rates a general court martial. I doubt that the navy will send him back to the *Field*. It's much more likely they'll fly him up to Yokosuka and chuck him in the brig there. From what I've heard about the marines that guard that place, I wouldn't even wish that on Cobb."

"Speaking of Cobb," Logan said zestfully. "Nobody ever did find out why they yanked him off the ship so suddenly. You don't think he was dipping into the ship's funds, do you?"

"No, not a chance. If anything like that was going on, the supply officer would have to be in on it. You can bet the navy would have grabbed Fickett and Canavan along with Cobb. They didn't, so that can't be the reason. It's weird, though, even your buddy, the oracle in ship's office, doesn't have a clue to why Cobb left or where he went to…not that I really care. The important thing is we don't have to sweat him in C.I.C. anymore."

"Unfortunately, Mister MacKinlay didn't go with him," Logan said, shaking his head. "Did you hear what that ex-jarhead pulled this morning?"

"You mean about turning down Devlin's request for emergency leave?"

"Yes."

"I'm sure glad we didn't get stuck with him as our department head," Murray added. "Stockwell can be a real ball-buster sometimes, but overall he's a pretty good guy. I hope he makes it back home in one piece. That G-Q station he's got up there in secondary-conn certainly isn't conducive to good health, especially when the flak starts flying. Everyone knows that's why Cobb went and designated after-steering as the ship's secondary-conn."

"As it turned out, after-steering wasn't the inner-sanctum Cobb thought it would be," Logan said, laughing.

"Yeah, but it was just like Cobb to luck out anyway, getting booted out of after-steering just before it took a direct hit. You know, I'll bet that guy could fall in a pig sty and come up smelling as rosy as a French whorehouse."

"Come on, Howie," Logan chuckled. "How do you know what a French whorehouse smells like?"

"That's just an expression."

Logan smiled. "Tell me, just between you and I, have you ever been in a whorehouse?"

"No."

"You mean you never made the working girls on Hotel Street a little richer when the *Enterprise* was at Pearl?"

"Of course not."

"Not even once?"

"No, not even once. I had a lot better things to do with the little money the navy was paying me."

Logan nodded. "You know, maybe you'll win that bet after all."

"Of course I will. Why do you think I gave ten to one odds? I knew it was money in the bank."

"How many bets did you take?"

"Enough to get me four hundred dollars. That's going to be the easiest money I ever made. I can really use it right now, with the baby and all," Murray said smiling.

"You must be crazy. Do you realize you'll have to fork over four grand if you lose? Do you have that kind of money to spare?"

"No. I don't have that kind of money to spare, but there's no chance I'm going to lose. Actually, I feel a little guilty about taking their money on such a sure thing."

"Well, you'd better not lose. A buddy of mine once told me about a guy who was on his cruiser during the war. Seems this guy wasn't the world's greatest poker player and got himself in the hole for a few hundred bucks. Word got around that he'd started asking the people in ship's office about the possibilities of getting a transfer to another ship. Then one night he mysteriously disappeared. My buddy was pretty sure the people he owed money to decided he was trying to get out of paying and gave him the deep six. The captain of the cruiser thought so too, but since he couldn't prove it, and since nobody saw the guy go overboard, the captain had to put it down as an accident."

"I'm not worried about anything like that happening," Murray frowned. "There's no way anyone's going to get me into a cat house even if they put a gun to my head."

"I hope so for your sake." Logan stretched his arms and listened to the red baker flag sock the wind high above his head.

A deck below on the open bridge, Owen Royal kept careful measure on the *Kaskaskia* which was steaming parallel and approximately 100 feet to port. Beyond the oiler, the *Oriskany's* island and radar mast loomed like a gray skyscraper.

Stratton Bray had the conn, and it was obvious to the captain that his new executive officer was a prudent and highly skilled ship handler. By 14:30, the *Field's* tanks were bulging to capacity, a high line transfer had been carried out, and, almost as important, six sacks of mail had been received on deck.

Kaskaskia had barely disappeared over the horizon in the direction of Japan when Lieutenant Jg. MacKinlay entered the captain's cabin.

"You wanted to see me, Sir," MacKinlay asked, hat in hand.

"Yes, Allan. Sit down please. I'd like to discuss Devlin's request for emergency leave."

"Yes, Sir."

"You know, it's rather seldom that I countermand the recommendation of one of my department heads, but I saw no reason to stop this man from going home to see his family at this time. By the way, your people did a very nice job with the high line. I was happy to see that Devlin and his sea bag got over to the *Kaskaskia* without getting wet."

"Yes, Sir, thank you, Sir. Regarding Devlin. I hope you don't think I disapproved his emergency leave capriciously."

"That's exactly what I think."

A sudden chill gripped MacKinlay. "Captain, I turned down Devlin's chit because this ship and my department in particular, are grossly undermanned right now. Since we've only got less than a month left to do over here, knowing the navy, I'm sure they'd never bother to fly him back to us."

"The man's unrated, and you must have at least fifteen other gunner's-mate strikers in your division. I don't see that his presence, under the circumstances, will make any difference in the ship's performance."

"Well, Sir, as you know, the ship's been looking pretty cruddy lately. If my people are going to get the ship cleaned up and looking decent before we get back to San Diego, I'm going to need every man I've got."

"Are you telling me you decided to keep Devlin from attending his father's funeral just because the ship needs a little freshening up? Damn it, Mister! When are you going to learn that you can't be entirely dispassionate in dealing with your subordinates. You can't regard your people as pieces of machinery or potential paint brushes!"

MacKinlay's face turned a paler green. "But, Sir, the Red Cross telegram said that the funeral is scheduled for Wednesday. By the time the *Kaskaskia* reaches Sasebo and deposits Devlin, there's no chance he'll be able to make flight connections that will allow him to make the funeral. Therefore, I don't see that there's any rationale for granting him emergency leave."

"No, Mister, I truly believe that you don't. Now get your tail out of here," Royal snarled, glowering at the *Field's* first lieutenant.

Suddenly the captain was uncomfortable. It was rather late in his career to be dressing down junior officers, he told himself as he watched MacKinlay make a hasty exit. His gun-boss was a miserable bastard, Royal had little doubt of that, and he knew he really shouldn't waste any pity on him. After all, he'd often seen the jaygee reviling enlisted personnel for the most minor infractions. If anything, he was only getting a little bit of his own medicine. Even so, playing the martinet with his officers was a new and unpleasant experience, and he wondered why he'd let MacKinlay get to him like that. Was it really MacKinlay or a reluctant recognition that he'd soon be losing command of the *Field*, he asked himself. Not hearing from his wife the entire time they were in Hong Kong didn't help things either, he decided. Then, remembering the six sacks of mail that had come over from the *Kaskaskia,* he experienced a sudden surge of euphoria as he contemplated a backlog of letters from Candace.

Another hour passed before the mail was sorted in the *Field's* post office. Chief DelRosario, anticipating the captain's anxiety, lost little time in delivering the square-shaped package and the two letters addressed to his commanding officer. One of the letters was from Owen's brother in Idaho Falls, the other was from a former shipmate now serving aboard converted battleship *Mississippi* in the Atlantic. The package was the one promised by Tim Barrett. Inside the waterproof wrapping was a phonograph record well-protected by countless layers of cardboard. The note from Captain Barrett was brief. It read:

> *Hope you and your crew of short-timers enjoy this. I suggest you play it over your P.A. system. It did wonders to boost morale on the Chickamauga during the final weeks of our deployment.*

A dejected Owen Royal tried to muster up a smile as he read the label on the Guy Lombardo recording. Its title was *"When My Dreamboat Comes Home."*

Chapter XXIV - Coals to Newcastle

It was late April when the *Field* resumed her station in the destroyer screen, having squired the *Oriskany* back to the task force in ample time for her pilots to participate in the celebration of "Boy-san Day," a 24-hour period during which the navy birdmen were allowed to choose their own targets without direction or interference from higher authority.

Owen Royal's two-stacker passed the next two weeks performing the unglamorous but most vital of all destroyer functions, that of screening the vulnerable carriers which, in turn, were engaged in delivering an intensified series of "Cherokee Strikes," air attacks specifically aimed at destroying ammunition dumps, supply depots, and troop concentrations within relative proximity to the enemy lines but beyond the range of United Nations artillery.

The *Field* had just secured from the daily dawn alert, and the pungent smell of navy coffee was already pervading the air in the wheelhouse, reminding the captain that breakfast could now be had if he could spare the few minutes to go below. Hanging his helmet back on its bracket near the signal bridge, he briefly watched destroyer *Wiltsie* buck some big rollers as she maintained station a thousand yards to port. He glanced aft over the flag-bags, instinctively taking a quick inventory of the task force heavy-weights, carriers *Philippine Sea*, *Boxer* and *Oriskany*, and further back, battleship *New Jersey* which had relieved the *Missouri* as Seventh Fleet flagship.

"Message, Captain," Ensign Keagan announced, stepping out on to the open-bridge. "The messenger just brought it up from radio-central."

"Thank you." There was a silence, then the captain said almost inaudibly, "Please ask Mister Stockwell to come out here."

The J.O.D. departed. An instant later, the O.D. appeared. "You wanted to see me, Sir?" Stockwell asked in a shaky voice, wondering if his commanding officer had found something awry with the watch.

"Did you have a chance to read this, Don?"

"No, Sir. It was addressed to you so I had Mister Keagan bring it out to you the second it arrived."

"It's about Patterson," Royal muttered grimly. "He's dead."

"Dead?"

"Yes. You're his department head. Here, read it," the captain said handing the lieutenant the dispatch.

"Damn! The poor kid. What a lousy break. Do you want me to write the letter to his parents, Captain?"

"No, I'll take care of that," Royal said, clutching the cold rim of the splinter screen.

"It seems a bit ironic, doesn't it, Sir? We've been under direct fire over forty times since January, worked our way through a dozen minefields, been hit twice, and Patterson came through it all without a scratch. Then he goes ashore on liberty and drowns trying to save a mongrel dog some kids chased out on a ledge."

"I wonder how he was able to make it through boot camp without learning how to swim," Royal asked.

"He never went to boot camp. He was a reservist on a two-year active duty tour. Since he'd made seaman in the reserve before being activated, he was sent directly to a ship. I guess there's some irony in that too. If he'd only been a recruit or a seaman-deuce when called up, he'd have gotten the same three-month basic training as the regulars."

"I guess there's irony in almost anything if you look for it hard enough," Royal shrugged. "There's certainly more than a little in the fact that we suffered our first fatality because of a Coke machine, and now our last because of a good deed. Well, I'd better go below and write the letter," Royal said, shaking his head in obvious despair as he walked over to the ladder.

But for some minor grumbling from Belton when he learned that he'd been reassigned to mess-cooking, scant mention was made in C.I.C. of Patterson's passing. Half way through the evening watch, Vinnie Bacelli had been tempted to raise the touchy subject of voodoo dolls. Perceiving Murray's extraordinarily sullen mood, the third-class wisely dismissed the notion.

A little earlier, Ensign Coates had unceremoniously erased the young radar-striker's name from the division's watch-quarter-and-station-bill, and except for some not very well concealed feelings of guilt on the part of the Field's leading radarman, it was as if Thomas Spencer Patterson, Jr. had never existed.

The Field continued shepherding the carriers for the next two days during which time she managed to destroy a floating mine and rescue the pilot of a Phil Sea Panther that had lost power and pancaked on take-off. Then finally it was May 15th. Across the United States the date meant the long-awaited contest between Rocky Marciano and Jersey Joe Walcott for the heavyweight boxing championship of the world. Aboard the Charles P. Field, far out in screening station number-five, 43 miles northeast of Hongwan, May 15th meant only one thing — going home.

The sun exploded against the sky that morning with a special brilliance. The men of the Charlie P. were totally convinced of that, and scrambling to their various G.Q. stations for the dawn alert suddenly seemed like great fun. They were also in full agreement that no one in the history of the world could ever have sung as well as Jolson did at reveille when the speakers throughout the ship woke everyone up with "*California Here I Come*." By mid-afternoon the massive aggregation of warships known as Task Force 77 had disappeared to the north and the *Field* was suddenly alone...alone and heading south.

That night, deep within the great black void to starboard, tiny yellow flashes told the bridge-watch and lookouts that they were passing near the M.L.R. The artillery duel grew in intensity and the flashes came faster and faster like summer lightening. Once or twice, Stratton Bray thought he could make out the outline of a mountain ridge. The dogfaces must really be taking it but they were obviously dishing it out too, he decided, painfully aware that this was the closest he would ever get to seeing any action, that he was merely a spectator, and that another war was passing him by. A few feet away, Phil Oetjens was thinking how lucky he was after Normandy and Wonsan to finally be out of this bloody nonsense, to be cruising far beyond the range of the enemy's guns, to be headed for Japan, and then for home.

Yokosuka seemed strangely empty. Owen Royal found it hard to believe that this was the same port that just a relatively short time ago had been crammed end to end with fighting steel. Now, except for a few harbor craft, a solitary attack-transport, the *George Clymer*, swinging at anchor off Radford Point, and the former Soviet frigates still cloistered out in the boonies, it was as if the mighty Seventh Fleet had, like the Arabs, silently folded its tents and slipped away into the night.

A gray jeep manned by a sleepy-eyed journalist-third idled at Berth-8 as the *Field*, with cone-shaped fenders dangling awkwardly down her side, eased in gently alongside the quay. Before the destroyer's mooring lines had been made fast, the JO-3 dropped a bulky cardboard box on the concrete apron, then without a word or a wave, remounted the jeep and drove off.

Minutes later, the metal gangway was noisily slid out over the deck-edge and secured to the wharf. Word was passed to set the in-port watch, and the cardboard box, with "*DD-505*" scribbled atop its lid in black crayon, was quickly taken on board. Inside were several mimeographed sheets, a going-away present prepared by base staff for navy and marine corps personnel rotating stateside. Ensign Warden, O.D. for the morning watch, plucked a sheet from the box, stared at it dazedly, and then began to read:

MEMORANDUM

From: Yokosuka, Japan
To: Men Returning to the U.S.A.

1. Upon your arrival in America you will be amazed at the number of beautiful young girls with shoes on, but remember that San

Francisco is not Japan or Korea. Many of these girls have occupations such as stenographers or beauty operators. Therefore, do not approach them with, "How much." A proper approach is, "Isn't it a lovely day?" Then, "Are you on Television?" Then, say, "How much?"

2. When you are walking around the street you do not hit everyone in civilian clothes of draft age. He may have a Medical Discharge. Ask him for his credentials, and if he cannot produce, then hit him!

3. You no doubt go to the movies. Seats are provided, so you do not bring your helmet. Do not whistle at every female over eight and under eighty who appears on the screen. Don't say, "Gosh, wouldn't that be good!" Don't say, "Get the yellow bastards," every time a plane appears on the screen.

4. If visiting someone's home and spending the night, and you are awakened by a gentle tap on the door informing you that the household is arising, the proper answer is, "I'll be there," not "Blow it our your ass."

5. The first meal in the morning is breakfast. You will find a strange assortment of food, such as cantaloupe, fresh eggs, milk, etc. Don't be afraid as they are non-poisonous and palatable. If you wish more, turn to the person next to you and say, "Please pass the butter," not "Throw the damn grease!"

6. If, while in a group, you find the urge to excrete, don't grab a shovel in one hand and some paper in the other and head for the garden. Ninety percent of the houses have one room called the bathroom. For example, the room usually contains a tub, wash basin, medical cabinet and the toilet. The latter is used for such cases.

7. Several times a day you will have to urinate. Don't sneak around a car or tree to accomplish this. Toilets are provided for this purpose too. Use them, not the gutter.

8. When at dinner, you will be amazed to find items of food in separate dishes. In the navy you learned to eat such delicacies as corned beef patties, pudding or beans and peaches. Don't empty each item into your large dish to make it more palatable. Bear with this strange civilian custom and you will find that you enjoy the separate dish system.

458

9. *You are sure to be invited to someone's house. If when arriving you find that all the seats are occupied, don't squat in the corner Japanese fashion and say that you are perfectly comfortable! Have patience, your host will provide for you. Don't ask, "Where can I crap out?"*

10. *Never blow your soup to cool it unless you can whistle some popular tune of the day, such as "China Night."*

11. *Upon retiring you may find pajamas on the bed. (Pajamas are sleeping garments put on after other garments are removed, much the same as kimonos.) Upon seeing them, act as though you are accustomed to them. "My, what a delicate shade of blue," is adequate, not "How the hell can I sleep in that gear, we always sleep bare-assed!"*

12. *If you can't find your hat when you are ready to leave, it is probably in the closet. You say, "I don't seem to have my hat. Could you get it for me?" Do not say, "Don't anybody leave this room! Some son-of-a-bitch stole my hat!"*

13. *When visiting your parents and telling them of your travels and seeing your pictures, you will be very sleepy. Yawn several times and politely suggest that you be excused to retire. Don't say, "My ass is dragging! Let's hit the sack."*

14. *If a person makes a mistake, he is informed by his associates with a statement such as, "I believe you are mistaken," not, "You're all fricked up."*

15. *When you come home and greet your sweetheart, wife, or etc. your natural desire will probably be very hard to control, but you must restrain yourself and not be too hasty or enthusiastic. Put your gear down first, then say "Let's hit the rack, honey! It's been a long time..."*

From the *Field's* open bridge where barefooted quartermaster-strikers laggardly hosed down the salt stains of their ship's recent sojourn with Task Force 77, *John Morgan's* tripod mast and upper bridge structure were clearly discernible protruding up from Dry-Dock Number-4 at the foot of Perry Avenue. There was no sign of *Wayne* and *Ward* though, and it was assumed that they were most likely in one of the more distant repair basins over near King Street.

Commander Royal had been told that his ship would be in port for five full days, a period calculated to allow enough time to get the destroyer provisioned and in shape for the long Pacific crossing. It would also afford the men a final opportunity to do some sightseeing in Japan. Owen Royal found no fault with this idea and instructed Stratt Bray that maximum liberty be granted to all hands. Bray was determined to spend as much of this time over at Seventh Fleet headquarters as was necessary to persuade the brass that he was still needed aboard the *Saint Paul*.

The pharmacist-mate manning the main desk courteously informed Owen Royal that Commander Fenchurch and Captain Price had both been discharged from the hospital. Completely recovered from shrapnel wounds in his shoulder and left forearm, Arnie Fenchurch had returned to the *Morgan* to closely supervise the fitting of the temporary wooden bow that would enable the destroyer to reach the Hunter's Point yard at San Francisco under her own power. The commodore, who had only recently come out of traction, had vacated the hospital for the far more agreeable atmosphere of the nearby senior officer's B.O.Q.

Smiling broadly, Price greeted Owen in the B.O.Q.'s foyer. Except for the two crutches, the commodore looked surprisingly fit thought Royal as he watched the four-striper ease himself on to the rust colored sofa. Pleasantries exchanged, Price cheerfully announced that he was scheduled to be flown back to California at the end of the week. He also noted that *Halsey Wayne* and *Abner Ward* had completed their repairs and had departed for San Diego the previous Monday.

"Guess my navigator was right," Owen said. "It seems we really are the last of the Mohicans. Will the *Morgan* be able to leave soon?"

"Arnie Fenchurch is taking her out later this week to test her new bow. If all goes well, I imagine she'll be able to leave for Frisco next Monday. You know, Owen, you people are quite lucky."

"Lucky?"

"Yes, not being extended. The Communists have just launched an all-out ground offensive. They obviously expect the armistice to be signed soon and they want to grab as much land as they can before it goes into effect. Des-Div Three-eighty-five came in two days ago for what they expected would be a week's R and R. Instead, they were rearmed and refueled and sent right back to Task Force Seventy-Seven. They didn't even have a chance to get a good meal over at the O-club," Price said with a cynical smile. "There's even talk that Seventy-Seven's going to keep four carriers on the line instead of the usual two or three when the *Lake Champlain* joins up."

Royal's expression grew serious. "Guess that explains why the harbor's so empty. Maybe we'd better keep a low profile for the next five days."

"I'd say that's a wise course. I'd also advise you to keep your people away from the base admin' building. Maybe they won't notice you way over there at Berth-Eight."

Owen hesitated, then said, "Unfortunately, I think it's too late on that score. When my X-O left the ship an hour ago, he told me he was heading over there to see if he could get transferred back to the *Saint Paul* or to any other ship just starting a Korean tour."

"He sounds a bit gung-ho."

"Guess you could say that," Royal grinned. "Actually, I think it's that he feels deprived. You know, missing all the blood and thunder."

"Well, he's welcome to this damn leg of mine any time he wants it," Price scowled. "If I had a choice of going through this again," he patted his left leg, "or feeling deprived, I'd take deprived any day."

"Speaking of X-Os, Commodore, do you happen to know what ever happened to my former exec, Aubrey Cobb?"

"Hell, yes. Right about now I'd say he's just settling in at our weather station up in Adak. I passed through there once. It's got to be the most miserable duty in the navy. I'm certain it's even worse than the Persian Gulf," Price added in a tone of deep satisfaction.

"Adak?" Royal shook his head in complete bewilderment. "What could he have done to warrant getting shipped off to the Aleutians? I hear the Eskimos even go out of their way to avoid it."

"I told you back in Sasebo that I'd never let him get away with thumbing his nose at chain-of-command again. Well, that's exactly what the conniving bastard did. And if you think he had a bitch the first time, you should have seen this last letter. It's a damn good thing I've still got some friends on Jocko's staff. Otherwise, you could be in deep trouble," Price added grimly.

"What was his complaint?"

"Complaint? Hell! He had a lot more than a mere complaint. He was out for your head this time. He stated that you deliberately disobeyed a direct order from Jehovah during an operational situation."

Owen looked befuddled. "I'm sorry, Commodore, but I don't have the slightest idea of what he could have had in mind. Did he spell it out?"

"Yes. He said that back in November when you were operating off Kyongsong, and Jehovah ordered you to rejoin Task Force Seventy-Seven as quickly as possible, you requested permission to go into an inlet to shell some trucks you thought were hiding in a tunnel. According to him, Admiral Hickey's people flatly refused your request, but you went barreling into the inlet anyway with all guns blazing."

"That's quite a distortion of the facts, Sir."

"I'm certain it is. However, I'm not asking for an explanation, and I'm not putting you on the carpet. The important thing is there's no place for discord on the bridge of a destroyer. We both know that the C.O. and his X-O have to function like the well-honed parts in a watch. There isn't any rule that says they have to like each other, but they sure as hell have to work together as if they did. The slightest sniff of trouble in this area is ample justification for the immediate removal of an executive officer. And that's especially true right now with half the American public reading about this *Queeg* character and his X-O."

"Thanks for running interference for me."

"Forget it, Owen," said Price in a subdued tone. "I know you're the best C.O. I've got in my division. What I can't understand is how you can get yourself in so much trouble. You've gotten into more hot water in the last twelve months than any other naval officer I know could manage to do in twelve years. Unfortunately, Cobb's letter isn't the last of your problems," Price said morosely. "I'm afraid you've got an even bigger bombshell on your hands...one I can't help you with."

"What is it?" asked Royal, feeling the veins in his forehead tighten as he forced himself to mouth the question.

"You had a D-C-three named Larkin who was hurt when the *Field* took that hit in Wonsan."

"Yes. He's back in San Diego convalescing, I believe. He lost an arm."

"Well, right now he's raising holy hell about the way he lost that arm. Somehow, he's gotten it into his head that one of your corpsmen cut his arm off without justification or the proper authority, and that you've gone and covered for the corpsman's mistake. Larkin's parents have contacted their Congressman who's now screaming for an investigation, not only of this incident, but of the navy's entire program for the training of hospital corpsmen. You can just imagine how happy the Bureau of Personnel must feel about that."

"Well, I guess this is one thing I can't blame on Cobb," Royal said with a shrug. "It's funny though, Aubrey was quite concerned about Larkin having his arm amputated. He tried pretty hard to persuade me to court martial Parish. That's the corpsman who performed the amputation. Of course I didn't. If anything, Parish deserved a medal. I'm certain he kept that man from bleeding to death."

"I assume Larkin was here in the hospital for awhile. Maybe Cobb paid him a visit and put the bug in his ear."

"No, I'm certain I was the last person from the ship to see Larkin that night. The other people who visited him went over in a group earlier in the day. As far as I recall, Cobb didn't go with them. I remember thinking at the time that it seemed a little strange since he had been so concerned about Larkin."

"Did Larkin give any indication he was going to raise all this fuss?"

"No, quite the contrary. If anything, he was extremely grateful to Parish for saving his life. He told me that he knew Parish had no choice but to cut the arm."

"Do you think Cobb could have seen Larkin after you did?"

"I doubt it. They were flying Larkin back to San Diego the next morning."

"Well, whatever it was that made him change his mind, dragging a Congressman into the act isn't going to win you any points with BuPers."

"No, I don't imagine it will," Royal said, his expression now totally glum.

The commodore changed the subject to reminiscences of their days at the Naval Academy discretely avoiding mention of Owen's one-time interest in the present Mrs. Price.

Royal tried his best to appear cheerful but with this new cloud in the shape of Larkin's allegation hanging over his head, he was not very successful.

Aboard the *Field* in the Ops department berthing space, Murray and Logan were busily slipping into their best liberty blues to go ashore. Sitting on a foot-locker a few feet away, Holiday, down to his last Band-Aid, was carefully camou-flaging a grease-spot on his hat with a piece of white chalk.

"Why don't you try washing that thing once in awhile?" carped Murray.

"Hell, the rest of the hat's clean. Anyway, I'm only going over to the P-X. They'd better have a stock of Band-Aids this time," the third-class grunted petu-lantly as he scrambled up the ladder.

"Look, Kev, when you tell her, do it in a really nice way. You know, don't just come out with it matter-of-factly," Murray cautioned as his companion checked the position of the knot on his black neckerchief.

"Don't worry, Howie. I know how to handle it. Why do you think I asked her to meet me up in Tokyo instead of here in Yokosuka. I want the setting to be just right."

"Bullshit! You just want a chance to get into her pants one more time before you tell her!"

"Howie, you do me a great injustice," Logan smiled slyly. "Sleeping with Cindy is the last thing on my mind. Believe me."

"Well, I still think you could handle it a lot better if you just went over to the nurse's quarters and told her right off."

"No, by spending two full days with her, I'll have plenty of time to show her that I'm not really the person she'd want to spend the rest of her life with. Besides, that way I'll be able to pick exactly the right time to tell her. You know, Cindy's a creature of moods. The right timing can make all the difference in the world. Anyway, going up to Tokyo for the next two days was her idea, not mine. When I spoke to her on the telephone, she said she'd made arrangements to get today and tomorrow off as soon as she heard we were coming in."

"Hey, Logan! You still down here?" Holiday called from the top of the ladder.

"Yeah, what's up?"

"Mister Daly says to get your ass up here on the double. You've got a visitor."

"A visitor?" Murray said, looking as puzzled as Logan. "Who could be visit-ing you?"

"Beats the hell out of me unless Cindy decided she couldn't wait until tonight," Kevin retorted, grabbing his white cap and heading for the ladder.

"I never knew you were a personal friend of the Emperor," said Ensign Daly with a crafty smile as the radarman approached the quarterdeck.

"Excuse me, Sir?" quizzed Logan, raising his hand in salute.

"Your carriage awaits, my lord," Daly laughed, pointing to a steel-gray Rolls-Royce parked up near the bow. "The chauffer in that car left this for you," the young officer said, handing Logan a business card.

Kevin's face lit up. "Can I go over to the car for a minute and see what this is all about?"

"Certainly. I wouldn't want to keep the Emperor waiting," retorted Daly, still laughing.

Minutes later, an obviously pleased Logan was back on board. "Sir, I know liberty's not scheduled to be called away for another hour, but do you think there's a chance I could get away a little early...like right now?"

"Are you in the liberty section?"

"Yes, Sir. I've got a seventy-two hour pass. I've also got an out-of-bounds pass. The gentlemen whose name is on this card sent his chauffer all the way from Tokyo to pick me up. It's really very important."

"Judging by the looks of that car, I imagine it must be. This Japanese friend of yours must have a lot of clout to be able to get a civilian car on to the base."

"Yes, I guess he has. Back in New York he mentioned that he worked very closely with General MacArthur during the occupation."

"You knew him back in New York?"

"Yes, I gave him and a couple of his staff the grand tour. The ad agency I was working for picked up the tab, of course."

"Well, if the exec says you can leave early, it's okay by me. He's in the wardroom if you want to go and ask him."

Logan had no trouble in getting his request approved by Stratton Bray. His next stop was the telephone booth at the foot of the pier.

"What are you doing back here?" asked Daly as the radarman reappeared at the gangway. "I thought you were anxious to get going?"

"I am. I just have to go below and tell Murray something before I leave," Logan explained before heading for the hatch that led to the Ops berthing space.

"I can't believe you could do something like this," said Murray, trying to control his temper.

"Hell, it's not my fault that she's not at the hospital or at the nurse's quarters. I just lost five valuable minutes in the telephone booth trying to get hold of her. When I finally got through to her roommate, she told me that Cindy left early so she could stop at a going-away party for some doctor."

"Why didn't you call the party?"

"How could I? Her roommate said the party was being held on a house-boat up in Yokohama, and she didn't have the telephone number."

"Well, the solution's obvious. You'll just have to go out to the pier and tell that Jap chauffer to take off."

"I can't do that! Do you realize that I've got an invitation to the most luxurious, most prestigious geisha house in all Japan. According to the chauffer, it's the place that Tojo always went to when he wanted to unwind."

"Yeah...well, look what happened to him. Anyway, I don't see that you've got any choice. You certainly can't let her show up in Tokyo expecting to meet you, while you're off getting your jollies in some geisha house."

"I realize that. That's why I came back here. You've got to go up to Tokyo and stay with her until I can get there."

"Are you crazy? I'm not going anywhere but to the petty-officers club for a good meal and then maybe the base movie."

"Come on, Howie. Weren't you the guy who was willing to go over to the hospital to tell Cindy that I had no intention of marrying her?"

"I didn't say I'd go to Tokyo to tell her!"

"You don't have to tell her. I'll take care of that just like I promised. All you have to do is be there when she arrives. Tell her that I got stuck with some extra duty, and I'd be getting a late start. You can say I asked you to meet her since I wasn't able to get through to her on the phone."

"Forget it. I've got no desire to go up to Tokyo. Besides, that costs money, and I'm broke. I just sent a money order home to Mary Alice."

"The money's no problem. Here, take this. There's over eighty dollars worth of script in that wad," Logan said, handing the first-class a small roll of paper money. "And here's my railroad ticket. I won't need it since I'll be going up in the Rolls."

"I told you to forget it, Kev. There's no way I'm going anywhere near Tokyo."

"Okay, Howie. Don't blame me if something happens to her. After all, you never can tell what's going to happen when a pretty girl shows up at a bar all by herself, and then has to wait around for an hour or two."

"You're not meeting her at a bar, are you? I thought you said you always met her at the Shimbashi Station."

"I did. Only last time the M.P.s patrolling the waiting room were checking the identification of anyone who looked even slightly American. All they'd have to do is discover that she's a commissioned officer. You know that rule about fraternizing with enlisted personnel. That's why we decided to meet this time at the Nameko Cafe."

"Nameko?"

"Yes. It means slippery mushroom in Japanese. It's just three blocks north of Shimbashi Station."

"I don't care where it is. I'm not going up to Tokyo under any circumstances. And that's final!"

"Alright, I'm not going to high pressure you. I'm sure a nice young Catholic girl like Cynthia will know how to keep out of trouble while she's waiting all by herself in a strange Japanese bar. I have just as much confidence in her as I'd have in someone...say, like your wife, Mary Alice."

"Mary Alice would never go into a bar by herself. And don't think you can get me to change my mind by pulling that nice young Catholic girl routine. I could swear that you once told me that Lieutenant Osbourne was a Wasp."

"She is. She's a white-Anglo-Saxon-papist," quipped Logan with a broad grin. "Now how about helping me out?"

"Alright," Murray answered after a long pause. "Only I'm not doing this for you. I'm doing it for me. There's no way I could ever forgive myself if something really did happen to her."

"Great. I knew you wouldn't let me down. She'll be in civies so you shouldn't have any problems with rank. Now here's all you have to do..."

• • •

If Commander Royal had been depressed before his session with the commodore, the news about Larkin really sent his spirits plummeting. As he walked down the path from the Senior Officer's B.O.Q., he wondered how long it would take for word to get back to Price about the mess two of his radarmen had gotten themselves into the night before. Hitting a commissioned officer wasn't exactly a venial sin in the navy, the *Field's* skipper mused, as he headed for the base brig to learn the details of the incident, and to see if maybe a deal could be worked out.

By mid-afternoon, Howie Murray's train was chugging fitfully through the coastal countryside passing by an exaggerated patchwork of rice paddies, thatched huts and idyllic mountain ranges reminiscent of a *Kano* print. The coach, pride of the Yokosuka-Yokohama-Tokyo loop, was of pre-war vintage, possibly, pre-World War I, thought Murray as the wooden car, bulging at its hinges with Americans, swayed and rattled its way along the gleaming rails that led to the Japanese capital.

Murray had gotten the word about Nugent and Bacelli just as he was leaving the ship. Even those two lunk-heads couldn't be stupid enough to take a poke at an officer, the first-class reasoned as the gravity of the offense and its consequences slowly began to register. Well, they could both kiss their crows goodbye, that's for sure, he told himself aware that being broken back to seaman was the very least of the penalties they could expect. Five years on the Portsmouth rockpile was just as likely a possibility.

Reaching beneath his blue jumper, Murray carefully extracted a somewhat rumpled copy of the ship's newspaper which he had saved to read on the train.

The day's news roundup wasn't exactly world-shaking, he decided, noting that the lead story was about American aviatrix Jacqueline Cochran becoming the first woman to fly faster than the speed of sound. Hell, most women he knew could talk faster than that, he snickered, flipping the mimeographed sheet over to the "ship's news" side. Occupying a major portion of the page was a poem authored by an anonymous member of ship's company. Wondering if Kevin Logan might have been the mysterious contributor, Murray began to read:

> *Land of rice and pink pagodas,*
> *Backless shoes and green tea sodas,*
> *Girls in flowered gowns so bright,*
> *Lilting tunes like "China Night."*

> *Geisha ladies, Ginza joys,*
> *Nippon Beer and sailor boys,*
> *Rickshaws, fans, exotic spices,*
> *Darkened doors with special prices.*

Old Mount Fuji tipped with snow,
"What you pay young G.I. Joe?"
Silk-clad belles so ichiban,
Mail from home addressed Dear John.

Combat boots, black market yen,
Stunted trees and little men,
Perfumed maids with almond eyes,
Sushi, sake, commie spies.

Wac's and wine and fleeting smiles,
Ping-pong bouts at "Ernie Pyles's,"
Narrow streets and crowded bars,
Memories of my R and R's.

•　　•　　•

Back in New York on another business trip, Candace was finding Cole Porter's "Can Can" to be every bit as entertaining as the critics had reported. Sharing sixth-row center seats with her, a beaming Hampton Barlow was less than modest when it came to recounting what it took to acquire such choice seats for the week-old musical which was likely to play to standing-room audiences for the next two years.

It was during intermission, while returning from the powder room, that Candace thought she saw him. She'd only gotten a second's glance of his profile before he turned to enter the men's room, but there was no doubt in her mind that the man was Kevin Logan. What was he doing back in New York, Candace pondered, anxious and excited at the unexpected prospect of seeing him again.

She could see Ham waiting up near the staircase. It was incredible that he hadn't seen or recognized Kevin, Candace thought, especially since Logan would have to have walked right passed him. As hard as she tried, she couldn't think of a plausible excuse to offer for wanting to station herself outside the gentlemen's rest room for the next five minutes, knowing, that to Barlow, the mere mention of Kevin Logan's name was like waving a red flag in front of a charging bull.

It was impossible for Candace to concentrate on the final act, and Barlow was quick to notice that his companion seemed far more interested in the audience than in what was taking place up on the stage. Candace was just as distant and disorientated during the cab ride back to the hotel, and by the time the cocktails arrived at their table in the Carlton House lounge, the B.B.Y. and S. chairman was doing a slow burn.

"Something's definitely bothering you, Candace. You haven't spoken five words in the last hour," said Barlow, his hand nervously fidgeting with the lapel of his dinner jacket.

"I'm sorry," Candace said quietly, stubbing her cigarette out. "I guess I'm just a little pooped. The flight in today was quite bumpy. I think our pilot made a point of hitting every air pocket he could find between here and California."

"I can't help thinking it's a bit more than that. When we started out this evening, you were as cheerful as a teenager going off to her senior prom. Then all of a sudden you looked like the world had caved in on you. You know, it's not as if I'd taken you to see *Death of a Salesman*."

"I really am sorry," she said coyly. "The play was wonderful, and you've been wonderful, and I've had an absolutely wonderful evening...really."

"Are you telling me the truth?"

"Yes, of course I am. Now, can we please change the subject. You know I have to be back in La Jolla by tomorrow night, and you still haven't told me what you think of my idea about targeting the accounts of promising new companies instead of concentrating all our major efforts on established houses."

"I don't know, Candace, I'm inclined not to go along with you on this one." Barlow's tone was dryer than the vermouth in his Manhattan. "We didn't get to the top of the stack by going after speculative accounts. It takes a pile of money and a lot of time to mount a viable campaign. I don't have to tell you that. What happens if we do take on one of these so-called promising accounts and they go belly-up after the first year? You know you can't get rich in this business if your client goes bankrupt. At least you know an established company is likely to pay its bills."

"Yes, but I believe if we do our homework thoroughly before we choose our fledgling, the risk is minimal in comparison to the long-term profits we can realize by getting in on the ground floor. I assure you, Ham, the companies that I have in mind have real potential for going all the way. I hope you had a chance to read the company profiles I left with your secretary this afternoon, especially the one on Litton Industries."

"That's that little electronics outfit in San Diego...right?"

"Well, it's in San Carlos, and they make micro-wave tubes."

"Yes, I did read that one, and that's exactly the reason I'm dubious about this proposal of yours. You know, with the war winding down over there in Korea, this outfit is typical of the type of company that's bound to fold up before it ever gets off the ground. I'd bet my left foot they'll never last long enough to celebrate their first anniversary."

"I wouldn't be too sure of that, Ham. If you read my report carefully, you should have seen that note about Lehman Brothers underwriting a one-point-five million dollar stock offering in the company."

"It doesn't mean a thing. Mark my words, Candace, as soon as this Korean thing ends, defense purchasing will drop just like it did right after V-J Day. Two years from now, nobody but some very sorry ex-stockholders will remember that Litton Industries ever existed."

"Well, I hope you'll give it some serious consideration. Incidentally, did you find time to look at any of the other three profiles?"

"Yes, I looked at that new fresh food chain, the one with the Irish name."

"You mean McDonalds, and it's called fast food." Candace smiled for the first time since leaving the Shubert. "Actually, the company's not new. However, my research people tell me that the McDonald Brothers are getting ready to expand nationwide. For one thing, they've just placed a record-size order for milkshake mixers."

"That may be, but there's no way they'll ever compete with established chains like the Howard Johnson empire. And you certainly don't think they'll ever make inroads into the large metropolitan areas, do you?" Barlow chortled. "Hell, Candace, they'll never be able to take on chains here in New York like Nedicks or Chock-Full-o'-Nuts. And then where would we be? Out in the cold, that's where. No, you'll have to come up with some really sound arguments before I could give you the green light on this idea of yours."

The remainder of the evening passed quickly. When it came time to retire, Candace begged off from any lovemaking, noting mendaciously that the time of the month was inopportune.

Now in bed, listening to the occasional honk of a passing auto below on Madison Avenue, Candace was thinking only of Kevin Logan, and wondering if that really had been him, why hadn't he contacted her. It was months since she'd received that card from Tokyo. And then there was the mystery about what he was up to, the contradictions concerning his working for Columbia Pictures.

One thing she now knew though...she'd never get Kevin completely out of her system. Candace was finally willing to accept this sad fact as she tried unsuccessfully to ignore the loud snoring of the man in bed next to her.

•   •   •

Owen Garrett Royal's visit to the Yokosuka brig was a brief one. After signing the necessary papers, the two radarmen were released and sent directly back to the *Field*. An hour later, when the captain returned, Stratt Bray was waiting at the quarterdeck to greet him.

"Bacelli and Nugent get back okay?" Royal asked.

"Yes, Sir. A marine jeep brought them over. I sent them down to C.I.C. Coates has them working on pubs right now."

"Good. I want you to schedule a captain's mast for first thing tomorrow morning. Make it right after first muster," Royal instructed as he followed his X.O. down the passageway where coffee and a tray of buttered toast awaited them.

"You know, Stratt, it's days like this that I think I've chosen the wrong profession," Royal said as he sipped his coffee. "Every time I think I've got things running smoothly, another problem pops up out of nowhere."

"About Nugent and Bacelli...aren't you letting them off rather lightly? Hitting a commissioned officer usually rates a lot more than a captain's mast, doesn't it?"

"Yes, but there were some mitigating circumstances. The J-G they hit was in civilian clothes at the time, and the fight took place in a bar only frequented by enlisted personnel. Nugent and Bacelli both swear that the guy was a little smashed and threw the first punch. Bacelli said he never even hit the officer. He was just standing near Nugent when the fight started. Of course, Nugent swears it wasn't him either, but some big motor-mack from the *Manchester*. I'm certain they're both lying, but unfortunately the shore patrol didn't get any statements from witnesses. I managed to track the J-G down after I left the brig. He's a supply type over in the commissary office building. He was more than happy to drop the charges. He knows damn well that he shouldn't have been in that dive in the first place. I reminded him rather strongly that it showed a remarkable lack of judgment on his part. Naturally, the fight started over a bar girl. But don't worry, I have no intention of letting Nugent and Bacelli slip out of this one. Unless they can come up with a mighty convincing story at mast tomorrow morning, they'll both be seaman-strikers by the time they eat their lunch. By the way, Stratt, how did you make out this morning?"

"Not too well, I'm afraid. That slot I was originally slated for on the *Saint Paul* has already been filled, and none of the other ships operating with Task Force Seventy-Seven are presently in need of a lieutenant-commander. One officer, a two-striper in operations, did make a rather ambiguous comment, though."

"What'd he say?"

"He said something about me just sitting tight and I'd probably get to see a little action. I tried to get him to elaborate on his remark but just when he was going to say something, his boss, a Commander McAvoy, walked in and he shut right up. Of course, what he said doesn't make any sense. By the time we get back to San Diego the war will be almost over. Even if I am able to work out a transfer to a ship coming back, by the time I reach Korea again, I'm sure the armistice will be in effect."

"Cheer up, Stratt. The way things are going with the Russians and the Chinese, I'm certain you'll eventually find that war you want so badly. Right now, I'd settle for a letter or two from my wife. I know her job keeps her busy but I haven't heard from her for over a month now."

"We did get a little mail today, Captain. It was distributed about an hour ago."

"Good. Excuse me, I'd better go check my cabin. Maybe there'll be a letter this time," he muttered, smiling as he rose from his chair. His smile was short-lived. The only mail on his desk was the latest issue of *U.S. Naval Institute Proceedings* and a form letter inviting him to renew his membership in the "Navy League."

·   ·   ·

A frantic Howie Murray glanced at his watch. It was well past 7 o'clock and Logan was already two hours late. Sitting across the table from him at the

Slippery Mushroom, Cynthia Osbourne was sobbing uncontrollably, her make-up running in long shiny streaks down her face.

"Please Lieutenant, please, you've got to stop crying. Everybody's looking at us. I never would have said anything about Kevin if I knew you were going to take it this hard. Listen, Miss Osbourne, please. You're crying so hard, you're going to make yourself sick, and besides, it's sort of unmilitary, you being in uniform...which you weren't supposed to be wearing in the first place," the radarman added cryptically. "How about a drink? Maybe it will calm you down a little."

The nurse continued crying and refused to answer.

Excusing himself, he hurried over to the far side of the room and grabbed a passing waiter by the sleeve.

"Look, Boy-san, you bring drink to navy lady at my table." Murray glanced back and saw that Cynthia was even more hysterical now then when he'd left the table. "You'd better make that a strong drink," Murray advised. "Do you have a drink here called a Zombie?"

"Ah so, Zombie, yes, me bring."

"Good, and bring me another beer."

"Ah so." The waiter scurried over to the bar.

Looking around the room as he returned to the table, Murray was relieved to see that there was still nobody in the place but Japanese. His biggest worry was that some American officers would come in and see him sitting there with the Jaygee. If she'd only stop crying, things wouldn't be too bad. After all, they were sitting in a fairly dark corner of the room, and they were both in navy blue, he consoled himself.

The drinks reached the table almost as fast as Howie did.

"Here, Lieutenant, take a sip. It will help you stop crying," Murray said handing Cynthia the tall frosted glass.

The nurse said nothing. She put down her handkerchief and proceeded to drain the glass dry.

"Hey, Lieutenant, that's pretty potent stuff. You shouldn't really drink it so fast like that."

Suddenly, she stopped crying, much to Murray's relief. "I'm sorry about getting so upset. What you told me about Kevin is probably true. You're not the first person to tell me that Kevin's only been using me."

"Well, I didn't put it exactly that way."

"No, but that's what you meant, wasn't it?"

"Yes, I guess you could say that."

"I think I'd like to have another drink," Cynthia said, wiping her eyes with her handkerchief.

"Why don't you have a Coke or a ginger ale this time?"

"No, after what you told me about Kevin, I'd like something a little stronger than a Coke. That purplish fruit drink I just had was pretty good even if it did have a kind of funny taste. I'd like another one."

"No, I don't think you really want to try another one of those."

"Of course I do. Besides, I've got quite a reputation as a drinker. It goes all the way back to my days in student nursing. You mean Kevin never told you about my alcohol capacity? Why I'm a legend in my own time."

"No, he never mentioned it."

"I'm really surprised. He seems to have told you everything else about me. By the way, are you married?"

"I'll say."

"That's nice. Any children?"

"Yeah, I've got three daughters. The youngest was born a few months ago. I haven't seen her yet but I will in about three weeks."

"I'd like to get married some day. Only I doubt that I ever will. I'm not the Marilyn Monroe type," she said, glancing down at her bosom. "Besides, you know that old expression, the one that says lads don't make passes at lasses who wear glasses."

"Don't be silly, Lieutenant. If you don't mind me saying so, I think you're one of the prettiest young ladies I've ever seen. If you really want to know, I think Logan must be completely off his rocker."

"That's very nice of you to say, but can I have that drink now?"

"Why don't you wait until later when you get to your hotel?"

"I'd like it now."

"You know, I was expecting you to show up in civilian clothes. I was really surprised when I saw you come in here in uniform."

"I have civilian clothes in my bag," she said in an annoyed tone, glancing at the green suitcase next to the table. "I would have changed back in Yokosuka but I had to leave in a hurry if I was going to catch a ride up to Yokohama. I had to make an appearance at a party for one of our doctors. I thought I could use the bedroom on his houseboat to change, but my host had other ideas. Actually, as I think back, I guess I was lucky getting out of that party with my uniform still on. Now please stop changing the subject and order me that drink."

"Excuse me for saying so but I think you've got a death wish. Maybe, because of what I said about you and Kevin?"

"Don't be absurd. Now order me that drink or I'll just have to order it myself!"

"Alright, Lieutenant. I just hope you know what you're doing."

Two hours and three Zombies later, Howie Murray unhappily concluded that she didn't.

"See Kevin," she proclaimed loudly as she turned the glass upside down, "iss' all gone. Now you drink your drink and we can see if you're as good a drinker as I am."

"I'm Howie. Kevin's not here," answered Murray impatiently.

"Dun' be silly. Of course you're Kevvy...Kevvy, Kevvy, Kevvy," she bantered, reaching across the table in a vain attempt to twitch the radarman's nose. "Wass' the matter?" she demanded, her tone suddenly hostile. "Come on Kevvy. Les' go dass'. I wanna' dass'."

She was glassy-eyed and began to sway back and forth in her seat. The gold buttons on her jacket sparkled as they reflected the revolving lights from the dance floor.

Maybe dancing wasn't such a bad idea, Murray thought, hoping that if he could keep her moving, the effect of the booze might wear off. At least it was worth a try, he decided, grabbing her under the shoulders and pulling her out of the booth and on to the dance floor. At least his luck was holding in one respect, he told himself, taking note that he and his sottish companion were still the only Americans in the crowded cafe.

"I tol' you I dun wanna dass," the lieutenant shouted in his ear.

"No you didn't. You were the one who wanted to dance. Don't you remember?"

"Did I wanna dass? Oh, okay, les dass' then," Cynthia said with a happy grin.

For a fleeting moment Murray thought the strategy might work, but then he realized it was a losing battle.

Her eyes closed and she began to mumble. "I'm sleepy, Kevin, I wanna' sit down, sleepy, sleep..."

Murray gently slapped her face but there was no response. Her head bobbed back and forth like the tired pendulum on an old metronome. She started to sag, then her legs buckled and Murray had a difficult time holding her up. They looked like the final contestants in a Thirty's dance marathon and were beginning to attract quite a bit of attention from the many Japanese couples shuffling around the dance floor to the latest hit from the States, "*The Song from Moulin Rouge.*"

Murray realized that there was nothing to do but drag the totally flaccid nurse back to the table. He tried motioning a waiter that he needed assistance but couldn't catch his eye. The first-class finally reached the booth and with much difficulty slid Miss Osbourne on to the seat. She sighed once, then slumped back against the wall, dead to the world, her glasses sliding off her nose and landing on her lap. Murray caught hold of a passing waiter and asked him if they had anything in the kitchen like smelling salts or at least ammonia. The waiter seemed not to comprehend. Instead, he just stared down at the unfortunate young woman with the stern expression one might use to discipline an unruly child. If so, it was wasted on the now completely comatose Jaygee.

It was well past 10:30 and Murray couldn't believe that he had let himself get into such a predicament. If things had gone the way Logan had promised, he should just about be getting off the train back in Yokosuka, he reflected, shaking his head in total consternation. He sure hadn't planned on staying in Tokyo anywhere near this late, certainly not overnight. Hell, he didn't even have a toothbrush or a change of underwear with him. He looked over at the zonked-out nurse and realized that a toothbrush and clean skivvies had to be the least of his worries.

He had seen numerous drunks in his life, both male and female, but he'd never seen anyone as totally gone as this. He looked at her face. Her mouth was open but she wasn't snoring nor making any kind of breathing noises. He'd better check her pulse right away, he decided, frantically reaching out for her left arm. Gold cuff stripes never appeared so radiant or intimidating before. Then Murray's face brightened. He had done this enough times during first-aid drills to recognize that her pulse was strong and regular. Surprisingly so, he thought, after the hefty volume of rum and brandy she'd just put away. He let go of her wrist and the arm fell limply back to her side.

Glancing at his watch, he knew he had better quickly decide what he was going to do. With approximately 22 days left until his discharge date, logic dictated that he depart the Slippery Mushroom posthaste and let Lieutenant Osbourne fend for herself. Murray was also painfully aware of the strictly enforced Cinderella curfew that required all U.S. military personnel to be off the streets of Tokyo by midnight which didn't afford him an abundance of time to make it past the M.P.s that patrolled the streets around Shimbashi Station. His other option was to somehow transport the unconscious young woman to a hotel where hopefully she could sleep it off. That, however, was far easier said than done. Not at all familiar with Tokyo, he hadn't the slightest idea where or if he could find a hotel with two rooms available at this late hour. One thing was certain, he knew he couldn't stop and ask the military police for directions. And he had no doubt that if the M.P.s or shore patrol found him with a female officer, especially one in Lieutenant Osbourne's condition, he'd be lucky to get out of the brig in time to see his youngest daughter make her Confirmation.

He watched the lights from the dance floor play skippingly across the nurse's face, and he noticed that without her glasses, she was almost a dead ringer for movie starlet Barbara Bates, to Howie Murray, the personification of the all-American girl. But even if she had looked like the bearded lady in the circus, Howie knew that he really had no option. There was no way his upbringing and personal ethics would allow him to just take off and leave her there.

It was well past midnight when the waiter approached the table and grinningly informed the radarman of the establishment's owner, Kimmonoga-san's firm request that the "navy lady" be carried out to the street via the less observable kitchen route so as not to give his customers an unfavorable impression of the Slippery Mushroom.

"Now or never," muttered Murray aloud as he pushed himself up from his chair and stared down at the hapless Miss Osbourne who by now had slid halfway under the table. Tipping the waiter to carry Cynthia's suitcase, he tucked her purse under his jumper. "Upsy daisy, Cindy girl," he said, stooping slightly to haul her up to a semi-standing position. Mustering all his strength into a single effort, he slung the totally limp body up and over his right shoulder, shifting her weight to achieve a precise balance, legs and buttocks forward, upper trunk, head and arms dangling down behind. Following the waiter through the kitchen and then down a long dark alley that wound its way around to the street, it took him only half-a-minute to learn just how heavy 115 deadweight pounds can be.

The situation wasn't helped any by the irritation from her brass buttons pressing down on his shoulder.

In spite of all the alcohol she'd consumed, Cynthia smelled like soap and perfume, and the sensual combination was not lost on Murray, nor was the feel of warm female skin through smooth nylon stockings. It had been over a year now since he'd been close to anything female, the last time being when he had flown back to Warren to spend a long weekend with Mary Alice, the weekend Mary Kathleen had been conceived.

He was puffing for breath by the time he finally reached the 1937 Nissan and deposited his burden upon the back seat. The taxi's oval-faced driver, highly amused by the plight of the two Americans, steadfastly maintained that it was not possible to find a hotel anywhere in Tokyo that would still be open at such a late hour. The issue was settled when Murray produced a fistful of military script, prompting the cabby to suddenly remember that there was possibly one place he could take them to that was still willing to offer its rooms and hospitality to a pair of weary travelers.

After dropping the suitcase on the floor next to the driver, the first-class stepped around to the passenger compartment where the Jaygee lay sprawled across the back seat, her skirt hiked just high enough to reveal the dark brown tops of her nylons. "Come on now, Miss Osbourne, let's try to remember you're an officer and a gentleman," prated Murray, maneuvering the young woman back up to a sitting posture, while tugging her hem down to a less provocative position closer to her knees.

The Nissan pulled away from the curb and turned up darkened Showa-dori Street before heading towards the Asakusa District, then beyond to Yoshiwara. Slumped peacefully against the corner of the cab, Lieutenant Osbourne let the radarman know she was alive by an occasional whistling sound, not quite a snore, each time the taxi made a sharp turn and her mouth fell open.

The ride was extremely bumpy, and Murray didn't need mechanical training to recognize that the veteran vehicle, a Japanese copy of a Graham-Paige sedan, was in dire need of new shock absorbers. Probably still original issue, thought the petty-officer as the taxi went bouncing its way along Tokyo's deserted thoroughfares. It was almost a full hour before the Nissan squeaked to an abrupt stop.

The night was blacker than the inside of the *Field's* funnels, Murray decided, peering through the window at what looked like the faint outline of a building hidden away behind several tall pine trees. If it hadn't been for a brief bit of moon glow that managed to break through the low cloud cover, he would have never noticed the building at all. It wasn't very large, two stories at most, he reckoned as he stepped out of the cab.

"Are you sure this place is open?" Murray asked in a dubious tone.

"Yes. Is open. Very good rooms. You see," the driver replied with a throaty giggle.

"It sure looks like it's closed to me. I don't see any lights. You better not be pulling a fast one."

"Hotel open. You like very much, I sure. Now, you pay me."

"Hell, no. Not until I find out if they've got a couple of rooms for us."

"No. You pay first," the driver insisted angrily.

Murray was aware that the cabby had him over the proverbial barrel. The building was a good 200-feet away, and Lieutenant Osbourne was, as far as he could tell, out for the full count. He knew that once he had gotten far enough from the cab there was nothing to prevent the driver from simply taking off with the Jaygee all cuddled up neatly on his back seat. Hell, maybe she'd wake up to find herself the star attraction in some oriental version of a harem, Murray thought, certain that he'd read somewhere that white slavery was making a comeback in this part of the world. Concluding that he had no choice but to take the nurse with him, he hoped the hotel had two vacant rooms, knowing that otherwise he'd have to lug her all the way back to the cab, a chore he didn't welcome since his muscles were still throbbing from carrying her out of the Slippery Mushroom.

He paid the driver the full amount agreed upon but the cabby wasn't satisfied, insisting that the American sailor give him a generous tip. Murray flatly refused, then made another try at reviving Miss Osbourne. It took less than 30 seconds of face slapping and wrist rubbing to determine that his efforts were futile. Hoisting her up once more, he started out for the darkened structure beyond the trees. Crossing over a small wooden bridge, he finally reached what looked like a door. Knocking with his free hand, he fired off a quick prayer that someone would appear at the door and provide suitable accommodations for him and the young woman draped limply across his right shoulder. It was then that he noticed the lieutenant was missing a shoe. He hadn't heard it drop along the cobble walkway nor on the bridge, so he assumed it must be on the floor of the cab. It probably slipped off while he was half-lifting, half-dragging her out of the Nissan, he concluded, noting that he'd have to retrieve it when he went back for her suitcase. He wondered if her bag contained an extra toothbrush. The nurse was starting to get heavy, and he was in the process of shifting her weight when the door rattled open.

A small, jolly looking woman with eyes like dark red plums greeted him. "*Kohn-bahn-wa*, Sairor Boy," she said in a voice as squeaky as the hinges on the door she had just opened. "You rike nice crean girr?" she asked as Howie entered.

"I'm sorry but I don't understand." The radarman looked around the small foyer for some kind of a chair or couch where he could unload the Jaygee. He saw none, so he gently lowered her on to one of the large straw mats that carpeted the teak floor. Cynthia seemed to be snoozing quite peacefully, although her badly wrinkled uniform, soiled white collar, and runny hose would never pass an inspection, Murray snickered to himself.

"You 'rike nice crean girr?" his diminutive hostess persisted.

"Maybe, if you tell me what a crean gear is?" Murray wondered why a place like this would be peddling machine parts.

"Girr...girr!" the old woman cried out, pointing down at the supine Miss Osbourne. Just then, two very pretty Japanese girls clad in bright kimonos came shuffling down the staircase. The woman turned and pointed at the girls who were in their late teens. "Girrs...girrs," she repeated impatiently.

"Girrs? Oh, damn it. You mean girls, don't you?" Murray asked with a nervous grin, suddenly realizing just what type of hotel the cabby had taken him to.

"This Chikako. This Yukiko," the hostess announced proudly, as the two stood by, obviously puzzled by the young American woman on the floor and her unfortunate situation.

"I'm sorry, Mamma-san," Murray pleaded softly. "There seems to be a mistake. All I wanted was two clean rooms. If you don't mind, I think I'll take sleeping beauty here back to the taxi. It's waiting for us outside." He started to reach for the nurse.

"Oh no. Taxi go way," one of the girls, the one called Yukiko, volunteered.

"It couldn't go away. The cab driver still has the young lady's suitcase."

"Taxi go way. I see from window," Yukiko insisted.

Chikako, who spoke little English, chimed in in Japanese, obviously agreeing with her friend.

Murray opened the door and ran outside. He was back in a moment to sadly confirm the girls' report.

Mamma-san handed him a pair of backless slippers, then stood by patiently as the radarman stepped out of his shoes. At the same time, Yukiko removed the shoe from Cynthia's foot and placed it along with Murray's in a small wooden rack just outside the door.

The radarman hoisted the nurse over his shoulder one more time, then followed mamma-san and the two girls up the staircase to the second floor where he was informed that there was only one room still vacant. Giggling like a couple of schoolgirls, Chikako and Yukiko were highly amused by the fact that the American sailor insisted on waiting outside the room while the two dutifully undressed the sleeping "navy lady."

Almost twenty minutes passed before Yukiko emerged from the room. "You go in now," she announced with a proud smile. "'Merican lady all put to bed. Very nice. You see."

The Jaygee was neatly decked out in a red, white and green flower-patterned *nemaki*, or sleeping robe. Conscientious to a fault, the girls had taken the time to wash her face, remove her lipstick, and carefully comb her hair back away from her face.

"Thanks for taking such good care of the lieutenant, here," said Murray glancing uneasily first at the dormant figure on the bed, then at the stockings and pink unmentionables heaped atop the blue uniform folded neatly on the chair. "There's one thing though, I'm going to need something to sleep on. The young lady's not my wife."

Yukiko quickly translated the radarman's misgivings about the sleeping arrangements to Chikako and both girls broke out in a fresh fit of giggles.

Soon mamma-san reappeared on the scene. "Bed very big. Much room for you and 'rady friend," she exclaimed, obviously not fully appreciative of the radarman's dilemma.

"No. I don't think you understand. The young lady is not my wife."

"Ah so," said mamma-san, although she was still obviously befuddled.

Reaching into his pocket, Murray extracted a small booklet with an orange cover. He flipped to the section covering Japanese equivalents of English words and expressions that began with the letter W. The word meaning wife wasn't listed, nor could he find the Japanese word for woman. He did notice, however, that the War Department personnel responsible for the preparation of *Japanese Language Guide TM 30-341* had, in their infinite wisdom, remembered to include the Japanese words for "white radish."

Mamma-san, convinced that she was dealing with a total loon, finally agreed to have some pillows and blankets brought in and placed on the floor.

In spite of his fatigue, Murray didn't get much sleep lying there on a tatami mat listening to Lieutenant Osbourne's breathing. She was making that same whistling noise he had heard in the cab, and he wondered what caused it since her teeth were nice and straight, almost like a model's. He contrasted Cynthia's teeth with his daughter Deirdre's. He didn't like to think about Deirdre's pronounced overbite even though he knew that he and Mary Alice would soon have to decide about taking her to an orthodontist. He doubted that he'd be able to afford it, and there was also little Jenny to consider. In another couple of years she'd probably be needing braces too, he mused, aware that if he hadn't been activated, he would have gotten that promotion and the big boost in pay that went along with it.

He thought about the job he'd be going back to in just a few weeks, and he wondered if he'd still be covering his regular sales territory. Maybe old man Gibbons would decide to assign him to a new territory...make him start from scratch just like he'd had to do back in '46. Howie's thoughts continued to ramble from problem to problem. He listened to the night noises, and he began to perspire even though there was a noticeable chill in the room.

Having dozed off shortly before the first glimmer of dawn, Howie came drowsily awake in time to hear a nearby factory whistle announce that it was 8 a.m. The radarman could tell from the sounds the nurse was emitting that she was still in a deep sleep. Even so, he was nervous and highly embarrassed as he washed and dressed in her presence.

He found a small bottle of Listerine in her purse and swished some of it around in his mouth before deciding to make one final try at reviving her. He had no more success than he had had the night before. Pulling back an eyelid, he knew immediately that she'd be out for far longer than he could afford to stick around Yoshiwara. Making certain that he had kept enough money aside to pay for the room and his transportation back to Yokosuka, Murray stuffed the rest of Logan's eighty dollars under Cynthia's hat band where she couldn't miss finding it.

Waiting for Howie at the foot of the stairs, mamma-san grinningly informed him that he must also pay for the services of one of her young ladies even though he had not utilized said services. Morally opposed to supporting this type of enterprise, the radarman nevertheless paid the extra eleven dollars rather than stir up a donnybrook that might attract the attention of some roving M.P.s.

Howie's train was rumbling through the rice paddies beyond Kamakura when he realized that Cynthia's glasses were still in the breast pocket of his jumper. It was well past noon, and he wondered if the nurse had yet rejoined the world of the living. He hated to think of what her first thoughts might be when she woke up to find herself in a Japanese house of dubious virtue with a hangover the size of the *Queen Mary*. Assuming she could get through the day without her suitcase and a fresh change of skivvies, he wondered how badly she needed her glasses. Worse yet, how would she manage to make it all the way back to Yokosuka with one shoe? He knew he could drop her glasses off at the nurses' quarters but there was nothing he could do about the missing shoe. She sure was going to look weird reporting back to the base in dress blues and cork sandals, he thought, grinning as he reflected on the image. Well, if nothing else, the lieutenant's little misadventure should cure her of any lingering affection for Logan, Murray decided, convinced now more than ever that the nuns hadn't been snowing him when they said that the Lord works in strange and mysterious ways.

And, as the train rolled noisily on towards Yokosuka, Murray couldn't help but wonder which of the two girls he had paid for. After giving the matter a little thought, he smiled lustfully and hoped it had been Chikako.

Back aboard the *Field*, Ensign Coates, officer-of-the-deck for the noon-to-four, had just taken a telephone message from the yeoman who was calling for a commander named McAvoy. With only one day left before the *Field* was to depart for California, the young officer wondered why a three-striper, whoever he was, would want to set up a meeting on the base with the old man and the X.O. Coates looked perplexed as he dispatched the quarterdeck messenger to the wardroom.

Chapter XXV - "Where the Bullets Fly"

Owen Royal was afraid he had detected a drop of rain as he and his X.O. climbed out of the jeep in front of the grayish-white structure that housed ComSeventhFleet Operations. The captain hoped the rain would hold off at least until after the awards ceremony which he planned for pierside later that afternoon.

A Jaygee greeted the two officers and quickly led them down the well-waxed corridor past a marine sentry to the small conference room where Commander McAvoy and two lieutenants on his staff were waiting. Present also was an ensign from the ROK Navy.

Taking note of the assemblage as well as of the charts of the Korean coast that adorned the four walls, Owen knew immediately that his premonition about the meeting had unfortunately proven accurate. Obviously the *Field's* tour was being extended. The only question in his mind now was the length of the extension.

He glanced over at Bray. From the broad smile etched on the exec's face, it was a safe bet that he had also grasped the reason for the meeting. Bray was probably the only member of the *Field's* company who would welcome a chance to make a curtain call in Korean waters, reflected Royal, still wondering just how he was going to break the news to the rest of his crew.

"Commander Royal," McAvoy said with a faint smile. "I imagine you've already figured out why we've asked you and Commander Bray to come over here."

"Well, I assume it wasn't to give us a bon voyage party," Owen answered a bit briskly.

"No, I'm afraid not. Unfortunately we've been obliged to modify your departure date for the states just a little."

"A little? Isn't ComSeventhFleet aware that we've already been over here three months longer than most Des-Pac cans assigned this tour?"

"Yes, but this job we've got for you won't take very long. I promise you'll be back here and on your way home within two weeks. Unfortunately, every other ship this side of Hawaii has already been committed to either screening the carriers or interdiction. The word from our people in Panmunjon is that the prisoner exchange problem has finally been settled so now there's no major obstacle holding up the signing of an armistice. The Chinese know that as well as we do. That's the reason they've thrown everything they've got into what's shaping up to be the biggest ground offensive since they crossed the Yalu. It's obvious that they want to grab as much real estate as they can before the armistice goes into effect. Of course, it's up to us and the Air Force to provide maximum support for the troops dug in along the M-L-R."

"Yes, I understand that, but why bother to extend our tour by fourteen days? If you subtract the transit time to and from Korea, that doesn't allow us very much time on the bombline."

"Oh, we're not sending you to the bombline, Commander. You'll be operating independently." He stared coldly at Royal for an instant, then walked over to the closest chart. "We'd like you to carry out a little recon mission for us," he said touching the chart with the tip of his pointer. "The place we'd like you to take a look at is here. It's a fishing village just inside a little inlet. It's called Maksan. I believe you've spent some time patrolling that stretch of coast."

"Yes, we have. I remember chasing after a truck convoy in that general area. That coastline is pretty rocky. How close to shore do you suggest we go?"

"We'd like you to go right inside the inlet and put a scouting party ashore," McAvoy answered matter-of-factly. "Ensign Choi here from the South Korean Navy will lead it. I suggest you assign five or six of your enlisted to accompany him. I don't expect they'll meet any opposition. Of course, it's possible there may be a few North Korean militia policing the village, but that's all the better, providing your people allow them to get away and make their report."

"Get away?" Stratt Bray asked in a puzzled tone.

"Yes, we'd like the reds to think we're cooking up a plan to land troops on the flank of their main thrust."

"Like the feint we made at Kojo?" asked Royal.

"Exactly. Only this time we can't spare the ships or the men to make it quite so elaborate. The sudden appearance of an American destroyer, and a landing party of blue-jackets sniffing around a heretofore neglected fishing village should really shake them up back in Pyongyang. If the presence of your ship can induce the Chinese to pull even a single regiment out of the line to guard against a possible amphibious threat, it will be a handsome return on our investment. Of course, it's not inconceivable that they might shift the better part of a division," McAvoy announced cheerfully. "By the way, the request for this operation comes directly from Eighth Army headquarters. As a member of Jocko's staff, I think I can accurately state that the admiral is keenly interested in the success of this mission. He also views it as a tangible example of existing Army-Navy cooperation to counter the pressure from the faction back in Washington pushing for complete unification of the three services."

"I get the point, Commander," Royal said coolly. "Will you be able to supply me with up-to-date charts?"

"The Japanese conducted a hydrographic survey back in Thirty-Seven that includes the approaches to Maksan and its inlet. It's surprisingly detailed. It seems there are several large caves near the waters' edge that the Japs considered enlarging so they could serve as submarine pens. The idea never got beyond the drawing-board stage, but at least they did produce the charts."

"Why did they abandon the plan?" Royal asked.

"There were no decent rail connections to Maksan. Because of the particularly rocky nature of that area, the coastal railroad skirts well inland. The closest rails are thirty miles away. That's undoubtedly the reason the North Koreans have also ignored the place. There is a coastal road that touches Maksan, however," McAvoy said, tapping the chart with the pointer. "That's probably the same road your elusive truck convoy was using."

"How deep is the inlet?" Stratton Bray asked.

"Quite deep, at least in the center where the bottom's a good forty fathoms. There's also a small beach about a thousand yards from the village. I'd suggest you put your people ashore there. Ensign Choi comes from a very similar village down the coast. I'm certain he'll be able to placate any of the locals your men might encounter. He'll make a point of asking questions that hint at a possible U-N invasion. Of course, they'll be quite subtle. We don't want to give the intent of the mission away. We realize the enemy's not stupid."

"Do you want my people to gather any specific information?" Royal asked.

"Only what a scouting party might be looking for if we were planning an actual invasion. The inlet and village have no real military value as far as this war's concerned. Naturally, none of your men are to have the slightest idea that they're not carrying out an actual recon assignment. That way, if they should be captured, there's no chance that they'll be able to disclose the true nature of their mission. As you know, the reds are pretty adept at getting information out of prisoners. Besides, if your people think they're really on a recon mission, they'll perform like they are, and that will add a little authenticity to the operation."

"What about Ensign Choi, here?" asked Bray, glancing over at the young Korean.

"That situation's been thoroughly discussed with the ensign. He knows what to do if it looks like he may fall into enemy hands," McAvoy replied in a subdued tone. "Besides, there's very little chance of something like that happening," he added, with a faint smile showing once again. "Well, Commander Royal. What do you think? Can do?"

"Yes. The operation seems pretty straight forward, providing we don't get inside the inlet and discover its been mined and fortified." Royal looked around unhappily at his exec and the others in the room.

"There's little chance of that, Sir," a lieutenant named Wincott spoke up. "The South Koreans periodically send patrol boats snooping around those waters. I'm sure if anything was going on, they'd have spotted it by now."

"I hope you're right," Royal said. "I learned in the Solomons that it was always the supposed milk runs that gave us the most trouble...and usually the most casualties," he added half under his breath. "Right now, my main concern is figuring out how I'm going to drop this little bomb on my crew. You know, they all think they're sailing for home tomorrow morning. Most of them are reserves...short timers. I feel like a first-class heel having to do this to them. They're good men. They've served the navy and the country well. They certainly don't deserve this."

"It's only two weeks. It won't inconvenience them that much," said McAvoy, the amused twinkle in his eyes now gone. "Are any of your men scheduled for discharge in the immediate future?"

Royal looked over at Bray.

"No, Commander," the *Field's* exec spoke up eagerly. "I was just checking into that yesterday. Our personnelman informed me that our senior radarman, a first-class, is getting out in exactly three weeks. By coincidence, his discharge date is the very day we're scheduled...I mean, we were scheduled to pull into San Diego. Fortunately, we won't be losing anyone else until the third week of August when four of our men, all reservists, are scheduled for deactivation."

"Well, that shouldn't be a problem. You'll be home long before then. As far as your radarman is concerned, we should be able to take care of that too. You can tell him that when you get back here in two weeks, they'll be a seat reserved for him on one of our transport planes. He'll be home in plenty of time to make his scheduled discharge date."

"On the subject of radarmen," Stratt Bray said. "I don't know if you're aware of it, but the *Field* is woefully short of experienced R-Ds. According to the Des-Pac organization chart for a *Fletcher*-class D-D, we should have at least four more rated operators."

"How many rated R-Ds do you have?"

"We've got a first-class, a second, and two third-class. The captain busted our other two third-class back to seaman yesterday at mast. In addition we have three strikers. We recently lost a man in a drowning accident in Hong Kong which also hurt us," Bray added in a saddened tone.

"Can your two former third-class continue to stand watch in C.I.C.?" McAvoy asked.

"Yes, I suppose so, although I think a few weeks of manual labor in the deck force might serve as a good object lesson for them. However, even if I do keep them in C.I.C., we're still going to be operating way under our allowance."

"Well, I can't promise you anything, but I will have my people check with the petty-officer pool here on the base just in case they have some spare radarmen awaiting assignment. Naturally, you'll only get them on a T-A-D basis for this one mission. When you get back here in two weeks, you'll immediately detach them."

"Yes, Sir. Thank you, Sir," Bray replied with a broad smile, then said, "I'm certain that our men can handle this little foray behind the enemy lines, but isn't a job like that more suited to the marines or a ranger unit from the Army?"

"I understand you're a newcomer to our little police action," McAvoy said sharply.

"Yes, Sir. I reported aboard the *Field* just a few weeks ago."

"Well, if you'd been over here any length of time, you would have known that it's been standard operating procedure for destroyers and D-Es to put landing parties ashore in North Korea. When I was C.O. of the *Blackmoor* last year, I sent my people into red territory at least nine or ten times. Their missions ranged from scouting the location of gun emplacements and cutting up fishing nets, to laying demo charges and taking prisoners for our intelligence people to interrogate. Lieutenant Demarest did a tour aboard the *Hollister* last year," the commander said, glancing over at the young officer sitting in the back of the room. "On at least one occasion, his C.O. sent a party ashore to check the condition of the railroad tracks. If the rails were rusty, it meant the trains had stopped rolling in that area. If they were clean, then it was obvious that the reds were still sneaking their supply trains through after dark."

McAvoy and his staff went on to describe the known characteristics of Maksan including the last recorded tidal information for the inlet. The meeting concluded shortly before noon and Royal and his X.O. were back aboard the *Field* in time to participate in the awards ceremony slated for 13:30. During this event, the captain presented Purple Hearts to the men who had been wounded in Wonsan Harbor. Ensign Warden received a Bronze Star for his Christmas Eve encounter with the armed junk off Chuuronjang, while the men with him in the whaleboat that night were each awarded the Navy Commendation Medal with the Combat "V". Similar recognition went to McAlleney and the other survivors of Ensign Ritter's boat.

The announcement that *DD-505* would carry out one final assignment before heading home was greeted with the expectant number of groans and catcalls. Even so, most of the men took the news far better than Royal had anticipated, their main concern being whether or not they would have time to notify their families that the *Field*'s ETA in San Diego had been modified. In this regard, the captain obtained assurances from Commander McAvoy that the telegraph office would remain open an extra two hours that evening. The base post office would also cooperate, affording any mail from the *Charles P. Field* the very highest priority.

And, as a concession to the shortest of the ship's short timers, Howie Murray was summoned to the captain's cabin and informed that at the conclusion of the upcoming operation, he would be flown to California in ample time for his scheduled discharge.

Mail call was held aboard the *Field* shortly after the evening meal. Again there was no correspondence from Candace among the small bundle of letters delivered to the captain. Worried and depressed, Owen was heading for his sea cabin located up in the bridge behind the wheelhouse and sonar room, when Gosbecki, a ship's serviceman-third, caught up to him. Saluting smartly, the *Field*'s duty-mailman handed his C.O. a small package.

"Sorry, I didn't get this to you with the rest of your mail, Captain," Gosbecki panted. "I meant to give it to the steward but he took off too fast."

"That's alright, Gosbecki. No harm done. Thank you for bringing it to me."

Owen stopped in the wheelhouse and placed the package on the chart table, elated as he observed the San Diego postmark. The address on the label was type-written, and Owen wondered if Candace had typed it herself, or perhaps had had her secretary do it.

"Package from home, Sir?" asked Lieutenant Stockwell who was checking the most recent entries in the bridge-log.

"Yes, Don. There's no return address on it but I'm sure it's from my wife." The captain was smiling broadly as he extracted the small metal cylinder from its cardboard box. "Looks like she sent me a tape recording. This will make up for all those letters I haven't been getting for the past five weeks," he said, still grinning. Owen felt around inside of the box for a note or letter. There was none. Maybe it's inside the cylinder, he thought, as he pried open the aluminum container which he quickly discovered held only a reel of audio tape the color of rich milk chocolate. "Now all I have to do is get hold of a machine to play it on," Royal snickered, staring at the tape.

"I'll check the radio shack, Sir," Stockwell said cheerfully, "and send one of the radiomen up with a tape recorder. I'm certain you'd prefer to listen to it in the privacy of your sea cabin."

"Yes, Don, thank you."

In a few minutes, a lanky blond sailor named Wilfred appeared at the entrance to the wheelhouse. "Sorry, Captain. We don't have any equipment on board that will play a small non-commercial tape like the one you've got there," the sailor stammered, nervously eyeing the shiny brown disk in the captain's hand. Observing Royal's crestfallen expression, the radioman quickly added, "I've got a buddy in the radio gang over on the *Morgan* who owns his own tape recorder. It's a Wollensack, and I know it will play the type of tape you've got. I'm sure he'll loan it to me if I promise to get it back to him later tonight. I'd be happy to go over to the *Morgan* and get the recorder for you. Only thing," he shrugged. "The *Morgan's* all the way over on the other side of the base in drydock number four, and that Wollensack's pretty heavy...at least twenty-five pounds, I figure."

"Do you have a navy driver's license?"

"Yes, Sir."

"Very well, then, take the jeep. Tell the officer-of-the-deck that you have my permission. He'll give you the keys. I'll be down below in my stateroom. That way you won't have to lug the recorder all the way up to my sea cabin."

"Yes, Sir. Thank you, Sir. I should be back within the hour."

Owen's face was beaming as he made his way down the ladder, eager to hear Candace's voice and all the good things she must have been saving up to tell him.

Down in the Ops berthing space, Nugent leaned over his foot-locker, staring down at the rolled cotton towels that neatly camouflaged the two bottles of J&B

he had smuggled aboard the ship back in Hong Kong. As much as he dreaded the thought, he knew he'd have to deep-six the Scotch the second it got dark outside. In his mind's eye he could see Mister MacKinlay poking around through his gear, discovering the booze, and racking him up with a general court martial for breaching that most sacrosanct of all the navy's shipboard regulations.

He'd heard from the deck apes that MacKinlay was in the habit of making impromptu locker inspections. Hell, in all the time he'd spent in the Ops Department, neither Stockwell nor Coates had ever bothered to nose around anybody's personal gear, he told himself as he glanced over at Bacelli who had just started cleaning out his own locker for the imminent move to the First Division compartment. Losing his crow was bad enough, but getting transferred to the deck force, that had to be the ultimate indignity, Nugent decided.

"You're the big-time operator with all the bright ideas," grumbled Bacelli as he stuffed a handful of black socks into his sea bag. "What smart-ass scheme do you have to get us out of this one?"

"I don't know yet, but don't worry, I'll work out something. Right now I want to dump this Scotch before that frustrated jarhead MacKinlay spots it. If you've got any brains, you'll get rid of the bottle you brought aboard."

"Shit. I had a bitch of a time getting it passed the quarterdeck watch. I hope you know that all this mess is your fault! Why didn't you let that damn Jaygee buy the broad a drink. She wasn't that good looking. Besides, her girlfriend Kumiko told me she had the clap."

"Ever stop to think that Kumiko might have been trying to cut down on her competition? Anyway, it was a matter of pride. I couldn't let that guy horn in after I'd already spent almost three bucks on her. Besides, I didn't know he was an officer when I hit him. I figured he was base personnel. They're allowed to wear civies, you know," said Nugent with a frown.

"Speaking of hitting somebody, did you hear about Murray taking a poke at Logan this morning?"

"You're kidding, aren't you?"

"Hell, no. I saw the whole thing. Logan was standing by the plotting table when Murray threw the punch."

"Did he do much damage to the great profile?" Nugent's face brightened.

"No, unfortunately Logan's pretty fast on his feet. He managed to sidestep the punch. Then Holiday and Gardiner grabbed Murray and held him. Boy, I never saw him so pissed."

"Did Logan take a swing?"

"No. I don't think he was even mad. Murray was the one who was all steamed up."

"How come? Those two reserves have always been as thick as thieves."

"Beats the hell out of me," Bacelli shrugged. "It had something to do with Logan's nurse."

"What's Murray got to do with Logan's nurse?"

"I came in on the tail-end of the argument, but I heard Murray yelling something about the nurse passing out cold on him, and how he had to leave her all alone in some whorehouse up in Tokyo."

"What? Where'd he leave her?"

"She passed out and he took her to a whorehouse," Bacelli replied in a matter-of-fact tone. "Seems old Murray couldn't find a hotel with a vacant room so he left her in some cathouse where she could sleep it off."

"Bingo!" Nugent yelled.

"Bingo?" puzzled Bacelli.

"Yeah, Bingo. At ten to one odds, our pain-in-the-ass radar honcho now owes me a crisp one-hundred-and-fifty bucks. I'll bet he's the only guy in the world who ever went to a cathouse and brought along his own broad," Nugent laughed aloud. "It's probably an all-time first. It reminds me of that old expression about carrying coals to Newcastle. But, how'd Murray wind up in Tokyo with Logan's nurse?"

"I don't know. I didn't hear that part."

"Well, that's not important. The important thing is the hundred-and-fifty bucks he owes me."

"How do you figure that? Murray didn't go there to get laid. He went there to unload the nurse."

"That may be, but he still owes me the dough. When he made that bet, he said he'd never as much as set foot in a cathouse. Just tell me how he could carry her into the place without setting foot inside?" Nugent asked with a sly smile.

"Hey, you're right. That means he owes me a hundred bucks. I put up ten at the same ten-to-one odds."

"Poor old Murray. He bet half the ship that day. Hell, he'll have to sell his house to pay off those bets."

"Yeah," Bacelli laughed. "Maybe he'll even have to toss in Mary Alice."

"Forget it. I saw those snapshots of Mary Alice. He'd better just stick to selling his house," Nugent said pensively as he reached into the locker for the J&B.

In his stateroom, Owen Royal kicked off his shoes, leaned comfortably back in his chair, and completed his review of the provisions list. He was about to reach for the fuel log the ship's "oil king" had just dropped off, when Stratt Bray came by with a rough draft of the next day's plan-of-the-day.

"Royal looked up inquiringly as he reached for the P.O.D. "Has Ensign Choi settled in yet?"

"Yes, Sir. He's bunking with Daly and Canavan. Luckily, he speaks excellent English. He just finished six months training at the San Diego destroyer base."

"Good, that should make things a little easier, especially since no one on the *Field* speaks Korean."

Bray slid down onto the leather armchair. "Thought you'd like to know, Sir, the base is really giving us the red carpet treatment."

"Oh, you mean the food. I imagine Commander McAvoy feels he owes us."

"Well, whoever's responsible, they won't get any complaints from me. Fresh eggs, steaks, lamb chops, fresh vegetables...hell, I haven't had that kind of chow aboard ship since my second summer at the academy when I cruised on a pig-boat," the exec announced cheerfully. "Even the movies the base sent over are all new...well, no older than a year or two."

"That's a welcome change. They must have gotten us mixed up with one of the carriers. What did they send us?"

"I don't remember all the titles, but there's 'An American in Paris,' 'Soldiers Three,' 'Skirts Ahoy' with Esther Williams...I guess that's about the Waves."

"Let's hope so," said Royal with a good-natured grin.

"They've even sent us a Marilyn Monroe flick. 'We're Not Married,' I think it's called."

"I'm sure that one will be well attended."

"By the way, Sir, I noticed the jeep's not on the pier. I thought we didn't have to turn it back in until tomorrow morning?"

"One of the radiomen, Wilfred, has it. I sent him over to the *Morgan* on an errand. He's going to borrow a recorder that can play this tape I got in the mail." He held up the small brown disk. "It's from my wife."

Glancing towards the desk, Bray said, "Looking at her photograph, I can well understand your eagerness. If you don't mind my saying so, she's a knockout. Is she a photographer's model?"

"No, a V-P in an advertising agency. I don't think she ever modeled, but she was runner-up in the 'Miss Connecticut' contest for Miss America," Owen announced with a restrained tone of pride. "I have to admit though, I wish Wilfred would get back here with that recorder. It's been a hell of a long time since I've heard her voice. Every time I've managed to get a call through to her office, she's been off somewhere on business. I'm not ashamed to confess that this extension hits me as hard as any man on this ship."

"I'm sure the time will pass quickly."

"Not quick enough for me. I never knew I could miss anyone this much," he said, looking over at the picture. "We've been married almost four years now, but I still feel like a newly wed. Probably because I've seen so little of her," he said disconsolately. "One thing though, I've finally come to a decision. Something I should have done a long time ago. When my tour as C.O. of the *Field* is up, I'm requesting shore duty in the San Diego area. I'll take anything they give me just as long as it's near my wife. I'm aware that shore duty is the kiss of death in the eyes of the selection board, but I can't do much about that. I'm not even sure I'm suited for a desk job. The one thing I do know is that my wife is the most important thing in my life, so I guess I'd better start doing something to prove it to her."

Refocusing his attention on the P.O.D., Royal advised, "I'd move special-sea-detail up a half-hour. After a week in Japan, I'm sure the men are going to be a bit sluggish getting back into the swing of things. Besides, we've got three new radar operators aboard. I'd like to make sure Coates has a little time to work them into the right slots down in C.I.C. I imagine they can use the extra few minutes to get acclimated to their new surroundings. I understand all three of them are slated for carrier duty."

"Yes, Sir. They were flown over here to join the *Lake Champlain* when she arrives. It seems they just missed catching her at Pearl by a matter of hours."

"Look's like the *Lake Champlain's* temporary loss is our temporary gain." Royal's voice sharpened. "Anyway, a week or two standing watch in a destroyer's crammed radar shack should make them appreciate their big birdfarm when they get to her." The captain paused, then said, "While we're on the subject of C.I.C., are you really certain you want to transfer two experienced radar operators like Nugent and Bacelli to the deck force?"

"Yes, Sir. Even if they didn't know that supply type was an officer when they hit him...which I personally doubt, I still feel a little time chipping paint is definitely in order."

Royal shrugged his shoulders. "You're the exec, Stratt. I won't interfere in how you handle your personnel. Especially since I'm certain you'll keep in mind the fact they're both trained in a critical rate. I just don't want them losing any of their C.I.C. skills."

"Nor do I, I assure you. I've no intention of keeping them in the deck force after this Maksan operation is over. However, I want them to think the transfer is permanent. If they suspect otherwise, they'll just spend the next couple of weeks goldbricking. As long as I'm assigning them to Mister MacKinlay, he might just as well get a little work out of them."

A knock on the door announced the return of Wilfred.

"Sorry, Captain. I didn't have any luck getting the recorder. My buddy on the *Morgan* traded it off to a quartermaster on the *Halsey Wayne*, and I guess the *Halsey Wayne's* almost to Hawaii by now." The radioman breathed heavily. "If we weren't leaving at eight tomorrow morning, I could run over to the base exchange and pick one up for you. Unfortunately, the exchange doesn't open until ten."

"That's alright, Wilfred. Thanks for trying."

"That's a tough break, Sir," Bray said, as the sailor made a hasty exit.

Royal looked totally frustrated. "Hope you're right about that time passing quickly," he said, placing the tape back in its container and carefully tucking it away in his dresser drawer. Then the two officers shifted their consideration back to the plan-of-the-day and the final preparations for the *Field's* less than enthusiastic return to the Land of the Morning Calm.

. . .

The Sea of Japan was showing its temper as the *Field's* bow sliced its way through high breaking blue water. Propelled by a strong stern wind, Owen Royal's destroyer sped along within sight of the enemy shoreline, her decks awash and glistening in the late May sun.

Two days had slipped by since they'd passed north of the M-L-R, moving closer and closer to an obscure fishing village on a speculative mission they were sardonically referring to as a "freebee" for the navy.

Royal was in the wheelhouse watching Donald Coates' fumbling try at standing an O.D. watch when the executive officer approached.

"Are you ready for this one, Captain?"

"Royal shrugged impatiently. "I'm ready for just about anything these days, Stratt. Go ahead and fire away."

"Seems we're suspected of illegally possessing a training film on personal hygiene for female military personnel."

"I thought I was ready for anything, but you'd better hit me with that one again." Royal's expression was one of utter incredulity.

"That's the way I felt when I first read the message," Bray said, forcing back a smile. "Seems that on the last day the *Field* was at Pearl Harbor, several movies were signed out to her."

"Sure, and when we reached Japan, they were all turned in to the people at Yokosuka. But what's this got to do with a training film about...what did you say... feminine hygiene?"

"Yes, Sir. The film disappeared the morning one of our people was over on the base picking up movies."

"And somebody back at Pearl thinks our man lifted it?"

"Well, from the way the dispatch is worded, I gather they're not certain. They've apparently been checking with every ship and shore facility that sent somebody over there that day to pick up movies."

"And it's taken them nine months to get around to us!" the captain snapped.

"Guess so." Bray shrugged.

"Well, I've got a little too much on my mind right now to even dignify that stupid dispatch with an acknowledgement. Let's discuss it after this Maksan thing is over. With this two-week extension they've dumped on us, I'm just thanking God that we don't have a full-scale mutiny on our hands. Initiating a search for some film about female hygienic practices rates pretty far down on my list of priorities."

"Yes, Sir."

Royal glanced briefly at Coates, then turned back to the X.O. "Stratt, please have all the officers not on watch assemble in the wardroom in fifteen minutes. It's time I told them that we've been sent to reconnoiter Maksan. That's all they'll have to know about the purpose of our mission, but I'd like you to help me fill them in on the details of the inlet and the other information McAvoy's people gave us."

"About Maksan, Captain," said Bray in a half whisper, "if it's okay with you, I'd like to accompany the landing party when they go ashore."

"Forget it, Stratt. That's completely out of the question. McAvoy was quite specific when he said he only wanted white hats going along with Ensign Choi. Besides, I need you down in C.I.C. just in case Maksan doesn't turn out to be the sleepy little fishing village we've been told to expect."

"Yes, Sir. It's just that I thought the presence of a two-and-a-half-striper ashore might add a little more credence to our mission from the enemy's perspective."

"Nice try, but I'm certain McAvoy and his staff gave it plenty of thought before they decided on handing Choi the job. Just to bring you up to date, I intend to enter the inlet at approximately seven-thirty tomorrow morning. The tide will be up and we should have more than enough light. The landing party will go in at eight-fifteen. We'll pick them up forty-five minutes later. That should give them plenty of time to be seen and reported. If all goes according to plan and we don't encounter any real opposition, we'll be heading back to Yokosuka by ten-thirty the latest. Now let's go clue our junior management in on the general details."

Nothing was working out right. Murray was sure of that as he looked around the coffee mess for a can opener so he could use the evaporated milk. The sugar cubes he'd deposited in his coffee mug a full minute before seemed determined not to dissolve. Even stirring them did little good.

"Looking for this?" asked Logan, stepping through the doorway from the radar shack.

Murray ignored the can opener in Logan's hand and continued to rummage through the box of utensils under the coffee table.

"You know you're acting like a damn fool, don't you?"

Murray didn't answer. Emptying his coffee back into the pot, he started for the door.

"Damn it, Howie. I use to think the Irish were stubborn, but you Scots win the trophy for pigheadedness hands down."

"Look, from now on, the only time I talk to you is over the plotting board in there," Murray said, pointing to the door leading to C.I.C. "Comprende?"

"Okay, if that's the way you want it, but you can at least take the money. It was my fault you wound up in that place. Besides, I've got more dough in the bank than I know what to do with. I can have the money transferred to a bank in San Diego for you. Then you can send money orders to whoever you owe the dough to."

"I told you yesterday. You can take your four thousand bucks and shove it!"

"I admire your cavalier attitude, Howie, but how the hell are you going to cough up that kind of money? You know, some of those anthropoids holding your markers can get pretty nasty. I told you what happened to that guy on the cruiser for just a fraction of what you're in the hole for."

"Don't sweat it! If I have to, I'll take out a loan on my house. Anyway, I wouldn't take a cent from you if my life depended on it!"

"Let's hope it won't. I sure hope you know how to swim," Logan muttered under his breath as Murray left the coffee mess, slamming the door behind him.

•   •   •

Bacelli looked up from the torpedo tubes he had been half-heartedly wire-brushing. "You've been out in the sun to long, Nugent. I think you've gone completely ape shit!"

"Come on, Vinnie. Put your brain in gear for a minute. It's the perfect plan. It's bound to make points with Bray and get us transferred back to the Ops Department."

"Forget it! I ain't volunteering for any fuckin' landing party. I saw all those British commando movies when I was a kid. That shit's really dangerous. Besides, if I wanted to serve in the infantry, I would have joined the army."

"Hey, you don't really think I've got any intensions of actually setting foot on any red real estate do you?" A malicious gleam came into his eyes. "With all the eager beaver gunner's mates running around this bucket, there's no chance Bray's ever going to pick a couple of radarmen for a job like that."

"You mean former radarmen, don't you?" said Bacelli dejectedly.

"I'm telling you, there's no way the exec's going to let us go over on that beach."

"Then why waste his time and ours by volunteering?"

"Damn but you're dumb. Don't you want to get back to Ops?"

"Of course I do, but it sure isn't worth getting a bayonet stuck up my ass in the process. Besides, I still don't see how volunteering to play commando is going to get us transferred back to Operations."

Nugent shook his head disdainfully. "Look, there's only one way we're ever going to get off Bray's shit list, and that's to show him we're just as gung ho as he is. If we handle it right and don't overdo it, he'll be so impressed with our *esprit de corps*, he's bound to change his mind about keeping us in the deck force."

"Famous last words."

"Okay smart-ass. You got a better idea?"

"Yeah. I think we should just sit tight until we get back to Yokosuka. Once those three T-A-Ds take off for the *Lake Champlain*, C.I.C. is gonna' be short-handed again and the exec will have to transfer us back."

"Forget it. Gordon says those three third-class are staying put. He said Royal and Bray raised holy hell with the ComSeventhFleet people back in Yokosuka about this bucket operating way below her authorized strength. He said Royal was told he could keep any radarmen the base sent over."

"Then why are they still listed on our organization chart as T-A-D?"

"Bray told Gordon to keep them listed that way until their transfers become official. And he says that's just a matter of days."

"That doesn't make much sense. We're going back to the States. The *Lake Champlain's* just joining up with the task force. The way I figure it, she needs radarmen a hell of a lot more than we do."

"That flattop's got at least sixty R-Ds aboard, plus a slew of air-controlmen who are qualified to stand C.I.C. watches if they have to. I don't see that three more scope jockeys are going to make any difference."

"Boy, you've got an answer for everything," Bacelli said, putting down his wire-brush. "All I know is, you'd better be right this time."

"Don't worry so much. I know what I'm doing. Now let's go see the exec."

The sky began to cloud over as evening came. Up in the charthouse, Oetjens studied the known features of the Maksan inlet in preparation for the next morning's incursion, while on the open wing, Owen Royal watched a jet trace a white vapor trail across the only clear patch of sky.

The plane was squawking friendly, and the captain was reasonably certain it was one of the new Douglas Skyknights. He'd seen photos and drawings of the sophisticated night-fighter, but this was the first time he'd ever seen one in the flesh. It looked surprisingly big and unwieldy, yet from all the reports he'd read, the marines were finding it quite effective against night hecklers, and as close escort for B-29s raiding up near the Yalu. In a little while, the F3D disappeared among a low hanging cloud bank. Ten minutes later, C.I.C. informed the bridge that the plane had completely faded from the radars. On its way north to rendezvous with the Air Force, Owen reckoned, his attention now focused on the swirling spindle-tops of gray water the late-afternoon wind had started whipping up.

Below on the main deck, the chow line was already forming for the evening meal. On many American destroyers, first-class petty officers enjoyed the prerogative of going directly to the front of the line. Aubrey Cobb had steadfastly refused to grant this privilege to the *Field's* senior noncoms, and in the short time Stratt Bray had taken over as X.O., no one had bothered to bring the matter to his attention. Thus, in true democratic fashion, Howie Murray found himself trapped at the end of the line when Holiday and Gardiner queued up.

"Old Turk's dishin' out real shippin' over chow these days, heh, Howie?" Gardiner crowed excitedly.

"It's alright. I've had lots better back home."

"Scuttlebutt has it that we're gonna' get steak and eggs tomorrow for breakfast," Holiday gleamed.

"Yeah, I guess now you'll have to stop bitchin' about the navy never keeping a promise," Gardiner piped up.

"I'll believe it when I see it."

"Damn it, Howie," Holiday said, shaking his head. "Lighten up. Hell, you're going to be home with your family in two weeks. I can't figure out what you're so pissed about. The old man's got it all arranged to fly you to California, and as far as that four grand's concerned, most of the guys are letting you off the hook on a technicality. The rest of us have accepted your I-O-Us. You are going to pay up, aren't you?"

"Of course I am. Don't sweat it. You'll all get your dough...every lousy cent!"

"Personally, I think you should have let Logan pay it like he wanted to," Gardiner said. "Hell, those advertising guys are ass-deep in dough."

"I wouldn't take a bloody penny from Logan."

"Yeah, but if you let him fork out the money, we'll get it that much faster," Gardiner retorted wryly.

"I told you not to sweat it. You'll all get paid."

"Why are you so sore at Logan? I thought you two were buddies," Holiday said, as he adjusted the Band-Aid on his nose. "Hell, I've even forgiven Gardiner for suckering me into getting this damn tattoo."

"That's your business. I guess I'm not as charitable as you are."

"Charitable. Hell, you've turned into a first-class prick these last couple of days," Gardiner blurted out. "You've even started jumping all over our T-A-Ds. You're beginning to remind me of Cobb."

"I think Howie's just a little itchy about going into that North Korean harbor tomorrow morning. Is that it?" Holiday asked in a taunting tone.

"That's ridiculous! Why would I sweat some lousy little fishing village? From what Stockwell said this afternoon, we'll be in and out of there before the reds even know what's up. Besides, it's not even a harbor. Stockwell called it an inlet."

"Well, something's obviously bothering you," said Holiday, reaching for a food tray.

"That's just your imagination."

"I know what's buggin' Howie," Gardiner spoke up, grinning wildly. "Murray loves us all so much, he's just pissed that he won't have the fun of sailing home with us."

"Yeah, and since he's already lost the bet, there'd be nothing to stop him from coming along with us to the Hibiscus Club. I'd even fix him up with Myra. Boy, would she get him in shape for Mary Alice," Holiday quipped.

"Forget it. I'm still not interested in whores. All I care about is getting home to my family. Then you guys will just be part of a bad dream."

"You know, flying back to Hawaii might be a blast after all," Holiday commented with a shrug. "I heard you can look down and see the whole outline of the *Arizona* sitting on the bottom next to Ford Island."

Murray's face suddenly brightened. "Flying to Hawaii!" he blurted out cheerfully. "Flying to Hawaii. That's not the same as sailing passed Diamond Head into Pearl Harbor, is it?"

"Of course it isn't. You crackin' up or something?" asked Gardiner with a puzzled expression. "A plane's not a ship!"

"Do you still have that copy of *'From Here to Eternity'*?" Murray inquired eagerly.

"I think Sammartino's got it."

"Well, do me a favor and get it back for me. I want to check something in it."

"If you're looking for the name of that whorehouse, I'm sure it was fictitious," Gardiner answered dogmatically.

"Don't you have anything on your mind but whorehouses? I assure you I want to check something else. Try to get it for me right after chow. It's really important."

"Okay, if it means that much to you. Speaking of chow, I see they've got baked Virginia ham tonight," Gardiner announced. "Smells good, heh?"

"Yes. It smells good. Just don't forget to get me that book!"

Sammartino had been on watch, and it was almost nine when Gardiner finally delivered the well-worn paperback. Murray remembered that the specific passage he wanted was near the back. He found it on page 851.

He read the sentence slowly, muttering the words to himself in a half-whisper. It told him how if you threw a lei overboard as you passed Diamond Head, it would tell you whether or not you would ever come back to Honolulu. Murray read the words a second time, beaming as he quickly decided that the lei he had tossed in the water off Oahu only indicated that he would not be returning to Hawaii aboard a ship. Returning to Hawaii in a plane was a whole different ball game, he rationalized with a deep sigh of relief. Hell, the whole thing was silly, anyway, he told himself, now feeling guilty that he had ever given the old legend any credence. He glanced at his watch and smiled, knowing he still had enough time before lights out to write a letter to Mary Alice.

Commander Royal passed much of the evening studying the Japanese charts of Maksan Inlet with Bray and Oetjens. The narrow entrance was of particular concern. It was obvious that if the reds did have guns in the area, they would certainly position them there, and the *Field* or any other ship forcing passage would be a sitting duck, reflected Royal with a nervous frown.

He looked at the wheelhouse clock. Everything was right on schedule. They would reach the waters off Maksan shortly after midnight. All department heads had been thoroughly briefed on the upcoming operation, and except for those on watch, there was little to do now but get some sleep, yet sleep was the last thing on the captain's mind as he slowly made his way aft along the torpedo deck, inspecting the 40-millimeter guns and the other G.Q. stations now awash in a silvery moonglow.

Owen could feel his heart thumping. He wondered why he should be so uneasy about what even he had started jokingly calling the navy's freebee. He knew he hadn't been half this jittery the night before Wonsan. He guessed it was the idea of an extra mission just coming out of left field. Then the captain remembered the wisecrack he'd made to McAvoy about milkruns, a remark that unfortunately contained much more truth than flippancy. Anyone who had been with him at Tassafaronga could testify to that.

His thoughts rambled back to Candace and the tape in his cabin. He shook his head, thinking that if it had come just one mail call earlier, he would have had ample time to locate a recorder. Right now, he'd give a month's pay to hear Candace's voice...two month's pay, he quickly amended, glancing up disdainfully at the big white ball of a moon. He thought it strange that Candace hadn't included a note.

Owen could hear noise coming from the area of the after-deckhouse. Approaching the darkened structure, he discerned the sound of guitar music. As he got closer, he determined that it was coming from much further aft, back on the fantail.

It was the *Field's* resident troubadour, Culpepper, vigorously rendering his favorite ballad, the time-honored "*Trail to Mexico*". Thanks to the Korean winter and a late spring, it had been many months since Culpepper had had the opportunity to entertain his shipmates.

In the past, Owen had never been able to make out all the words, especially those of the closing verses. Now the elements were cooperating. Each syllable resounded loud and clear.

> "*When I started back to my once loved home,*
> *Inquired for the girl I called my own,*
> *They said she married a richer life,*
> *Therefore wild cowboy, find another wife.*
>
> *Oh curse your gold and silver too,*
> *God pity the girl who won't be true,*
> *I'll travel west where the bullets fly,*
> *I'll stay on the trail till the day I die.*"

Bacelli was still in shock. Nugent, looking like he'd just been given a double overdose of Novocain, stared blankly ahead with his mouth open. Neither of them could quite comprehend that within a matter of hours, the terra firma beneath their feet would be the property of the Democratic People's Republic of Korea.

The captain was in his cabin checking over the final list of volunteers for the landing party when the executive officer came by.

"How many men did you say volunteered?" Owen asked.

"Forty-five, Sir. That's not including officers."

"How many officers wanted to go?"

"Well, all our ensigns volunteered...guess I should say all our new Jaygees plus Ensign Coates. Don Stockwell and Andy Phelan tried to make the list too."

"You mean our ex-marine didn't want to hit the beach?"

"Not exactly. However, Mister MacKinlay did make a point of telling me he'd like to join the landing party but he realized that as gun-boss, his primary duties were here aboard the *Field*."

"Alan's absolutely right, so we should give him the benefit of the doubt."

"Yes, Sir," Bray answered with a sly grin.

"Did any of our C-P-Os volunteer?"

"No. That surprised me a little."

"I can't say it surprises me. Our chiefs have too much sense. I'm sure they had all the adventure they needed in the last war," the captain said with a cynical smile. "I am sorry about Don Coates not making Jaygee along with the others. After the screw-up he pulled back in November, there was no way I could in good conscience recommend him for promotion. When the promotion list came in today, how did he take it?"

"Quite well. I doubt he ever expected to get that half stripe. Actually, I don't think it makes much difference in his case. He's made it well known around the wardroom that he has no intention of reenlisting when his reserve commitment's up next year. Seems he wants to go into advertising. Just this morning I heard him telling Daly that one of our radarmen promised to get him a job with an advertising agency back in New York."

"One of our radarmen?" quizzed Royal.

"Yes, Sir. Logan, our R-D-two. I understand he's got quite an important job in one of the big agencies on Madison Avenue. He's a copy chief or senior copy writer or something like that. I assumed you knew."

"No, I didn't," Royal mused aloud. "I know several of our enlisted reserves have college degrees. I heard that a couple of them even have M-As, but I never really took the time to ask any of the men about their civilian employment. I suppose I should have taken a little more interest in them than I have." He shook his head forlornly. "Do you happen to know what agency Logan was with?"

"Yes. Coates mentioned it was Brice and Gwin. I think that's one of the biggest."

Royal paused. "I was hoping he might have been with B.B.Y. and S. That's my wife's agency."

"Perhaps he knows her."

"I doubt it. I imagine asking a person if he knows somebody in the advertising business is a lot like asking a navy vet if he knows somebody's relative who was in the navy." Royal glanced down at the list on his desk. "I see you've accepted our two delinquent R-Ds for the landing party. How come? I assumed you were only going to choose gunner's mates or gunner's-mate strikers?"

"The other four volunteers are all G-Ms," Bray said, pointing to the paper. "Actually, it was my intention only to pick G-Ms until I spoke to Nugent and Bacelli. When I realized how badly they wanted to go, it would have been pretty tough to refuse them. I hate to admit it, but I was really quite moved by their enthusiasm." He smiled proudly. "It's ironic too, because at first, I figured they were bluffing. I was sure they were only trying to con me into transferring them back to Ops."

"Are you certain that really wasn't their motive?"

"Absolutely. I'm sure they were sincere. I'd stake my life on it. My only reservation about letting them go was the fact that as former radarmen, they both have been privy to classified information. However, since we don't have anything aboard this ship that we haven't already given the Russians, I didn't think that was a serious obstacle. As far as the new I-F-F interrogator's concerned, they don't know anything about its technical make-up. If they had been electronic technicians, naturally, I wouldn't have approved their request," Bray added with a tone of conviction.

"What do they know about small arms? Have they fired an M-one or a carbine since they left boot camp?"

497

"That was the first question I asked. They assured me that they were thoroughly familiar with both pieces. Nugent said that he grew up in the Mohawk Valley and constantly went on hunting trips with his father."

"Not for Mohawks, let's hope. Anyway, I hope you made the right decision in picking those two."

"I'm certain I have. Today, most fellows in their age bracket are more interested in panty raids than in raiding the enemies of their country. I found their patriotism quite refreshing. I'm even inclined to believe they really didn't know that Jaygee they slugged was an officer."

There was a loud knock on the door. The visitor was Ensign Daly.

"Sorry to disturb you, Captain...you too, Sir," he said nervously, his hat clutched tightly in his hand.

"That's alright, Mike. Congratulations on your promotion. It was well deserved," the captain said with a warm smile.

"That's ditto for me," Stratt Bray quickly added.

"Thank you, Captain...Commander," the young officer answered, glancing first at Royal and then at the X.O.

"What's keeping you up this late? It's almost midnight. Don't you have the four-to-eight watch? You should be getting some sack time."

"Yes, Sir. It's just that I think we've got a problem."

"What else is new?" Owen shook his head.

There were several seconds of silence.

"Alright, let's have the bad news."

"Captain, I..."

"Come on, Mike. What's this big problem that brings you down here this late?" The captain's tone was suddenly impatient.

"Sir, I'm sorry, I just don't know how to explain this without both of you thinking I'm completely crazy."

"Well, do the best you can. I promise I won't think you're playing with half a deck."

"Yes, Sir, I guess I should start at the beginning."

"That's usually the best place to start. Now go ahead," the captain said in a less sympathetic tone.

"Well, about ten minutes ago, Mister Choi came running into the cabin he's sharing with me and Joe Canavan. He was really fuming. He'd gone topside to inspect the motor-whaleboat that he'll be using tomorrow morning, and he found one of our chiefs leaning up against the boat. He says he tried to strike up a friendly conversation with the C-P-O but this chief just snarled at him...said he wouldn't talk to, excuse the expression...a fucking Jap."

"Ensign Choi is Korean," Bray cut in. "Everyone aboard ship must know that by now."

"Yes, Sir."

"Go on, Michael," the captain said calmly.

"Well, according to Ensign Choi, the chief then spit at him."

"That doesn't sound like any of our chiefs."

"No, Sir. That's exactly what I told Choi. Anyway, I figured I'd better go up to the boat deck and see what Choi was so upset about." Daly bit his lower lip, then took a deep breath.

"Well, come on," said Bray irritably. "Was the chief still up there?"

"No, Sir."

"Do you have any clue as to his identity?" Royal asked.

"Yes, Sir. I mean no, Sir."

"Well, which is it, yes or no?"

"It's kind of hard to say since I didn't actually see him. The only clue I have, if you can call it a clue, is the way Choi described him."

"Okay, then based on Mister Choi's description, who do you think it was?"

"Really, Captain, I'd only be guessing," pleaded a distraught Daly.

"Come on, Mike. I appreciate the fact that you don't want to get this chief, whoever he is, in trouble. However, I think you'll agree that we can't have our senior petty officers going around spitting and cursing at our allies. Now, can we?"

"No, Sir, I guess not."

"Okay, now that we're in agreement on that fine point of naval etiquette, who was it?"

"Chief Henderson!"

"Who!"

"Chief Henderson," the officer repeated in a deliberate tone.

"Isn't Henderson the name of your resident ghost?" asked Bray with a puzzled look.

"Yes, Sir. I told you you'd think I was crazy."

"What makes you so certain it was Henderson? You've never seen him," Royal said sternly.

"No, Sir, but I've heard descriptions of what he's supposed to look like, and they sure match the description Choi gave, especially his height. Choi said this C-P-O was very tall. Our chiefs are all on the short side. And another thing, whenever anybody ever talks about Henderson, they always mention his beat-up chief's cap. According to Choi, the cap this guy was wearing looked like it had been run over by a Sherman tank."

"Nobody in this crew ever served with Henderson. I wouldn't put much stock in any description they might give."

"Yes, Sir, but I'm over six-two, and I know for a fact that there's not a chief on the ship anywhere near that tall. So how do you explain Choi's description? He said the chief was at least an inch or two taller than I am."

"I'd say that Choi's not a very good judge of height," Royal said, struggling hard to muster a smile as Daly stood by, still fidgeting with his hat. "Well, Michael, if there's nothing else, I suggest you just forget about this ghost nonsense and go get some sleep. I don't want you dozing off in the wheelhouse later."

"Yes, Sir."

"Oh, one more thing. Have you said anything to Choi or anyone else about Henderson?"

"No, Sir. I came right down here from the boat deck."

"Good. Make sure you don't. I'm sure you can appreciate what kind of trouble a story like that could cause if it circulated among the crew."

The young officer nodded sheepishly. "But what should I tell Mister Choi?"

"Just tell him the truth…that none of our chiefs fit the description he gave you. Tell him that the man he encountered will be thoroughly punished if he can identify him for us."

"Yes, Sir," Daly said, taking leave of his C.O.'s presence.

Daly and Bray stared blankly at each other.

"Do you think there is anything to Daly's theory?" the exec asked, breaking the silence.

"No, of course not. Besides, with all the whacky problems I've run into since I assumed command of this ship, I have neither the time nor the inclination to take on a ghost…especially one that spits," Royal added in an attempt to lighten the situation.

Bray laughed softly, completed his business with the captain and then departed. Outside the door, he hesitated for a second, contemplating the advisability of taking a stroll back to the darkened fantail. Dismissing the notion, he headed for his stateroom and hopefully, he thought, a little sleep, aware that reveille would be sounded an hour earlier than usual.

Chapter XXVI - Steak and Eggs

The smell of stale coffee in the combat-information-center seemed more irritating than usual to Howie Murray as he strained to read the plan-of-the-day in the dim light of the plotting table. Even worse, the watch was really dragging. Murray always hated the four-to-eight. It was far worse than the midwatch, he reasoned. At least with the mid, you could catch a couple hours of sleep before reveille, and if you opted to skip breakfast you could stay in the sack an extra half-hour, a privilege only granted to midwatch standers. But with the four-to-eight, you were up for the rest of the day, he reflected discontentedly.

Logan and the rest of the relief watch had better show up early, he decided, knowing that otherwise he'd never make the chow line before the mess deck was secured. According to the P.O.D., the ship would be going to general quarters at 06:00. Ducking his head to avoid hitting the overhead light, Murray slid down from the stool and walked over to the surface scope where Krueger, one of the transient third-class from the *Lake Champlain*, was adjusting the fine-tuning. Peering over Krueger's shoulder, he sensed something distinctly foreboding about the ragged outline of the coast. The range rings on the Sugar-George showed it to be less than twenty miles away. He could see the gap that indicated the entrance to Maksan Inlet.

Holiday was sitting at the air-search radar humming an indefinable tune, possible "*China Night*", Murray thought. Holiday had obviously run out of clean Band-Aids, and the yellow-green glow from the radar scope was illuminating the "horse fly" on his nose, giving it a remarkably lifelike appearance.

At the far side of the plotting table, a thoroughly frustrated Ensign Warden scratched the back of his neck and dug the points of his dividers into the maneuvering board paper as he struggled to complete a particularly complex torpedo problem in his "C.I.C. Watch Officer" correspondence course. The sour smell from the nearby coffee mess was getting to him too.

Gardiner was the first of the oncoming watch standers to make an appearance. He was followed moments later by Logan, Belton and Farber. Then Hill, another of the T.A.D.s from the *Lake Champlain* wobbled in.

"It's about time you all arrived," Holiday croaked with a good-natured grin. "Old Murray here can't wait to sink his choppers into those steaks and eggs. Right, Murray?"

"If Murray's gonna' sink his choppers into any steak and eggs, he ain't gonna' do it on this bucket, at least not this morning," Gardiner shot back.

"What are you talking about?" demanded Murray in a sizzling tone. "I saw steak and eggs for today on the menu hanging outside ship's office!"

"That may be, but take my word for it. There's no steak and eggs this morning. I ought to know, I just came from the mess deck."

"Okay, there's no steak and eggs. Then it's just like I've been telling you right along...you can't trust the navy! Boy, I'm glad I've only got two weeks left to serve in this misbegotten outfit!"

"Simmer down, Howie," Farber interjected. You can't blame the navy for this one. Turk was all set to dish up steak and eggs this morning until he cracked open a couple of the eggs and they stunk out the entire galley. The mess-cooks are busy deep-sixing them off the fantail right now."

"Yeah, the reefer where the eggs were being stored crapped out," Belton cut in. "Turk didn't discover it till about an hour ago."

"That doesn't surprise me," Murray replied. "This whole ship's as fouled up as a Chinese fire-drill."

"The steaks are all okay," Gardiner cheerfully retorted. "Turk said he didn't want to serve them for breakfast without the eggs, so we're gonna' get them with spuds and vegetables today for lunch."

"What'd he substitute for breakfast?" Murray asked in a calmer voice.

"S-O-S."

S-O-S! Dammit!" roared Murray as he grabbed his hat from atop the pub cabinet and headed for the door.

"Are you going to breakfast?" Gardiner asked.

"Hell no! I'm going back to the fantail. Maybe I can pass the time doing something really meaningful like watching the mess cooks throw eggs overboard!" Murray shook his head in total disgust and disappeared down the passageway.

"What's with him?" asked Hill acidly.

"Howie's just a little superstitious, although he'll never admit it," Logan said smiling. "Whenever we get S-O-S, he skips breakfast and goes back to the fantail."

"Yeah," Gardiner piped up. "It's become sort of a tradition with him. It goes back to when he was on the *Franklin*."

"Murray was on the *Franklin*?" Hill's eyes lit up.

"Yeah, but don't get him started on that," Gardiner implored. "If you do, we'll all have to listen to how the only reason he's alive today is because he didn't eat S-O-S that morning the Japs hit the carrier. We must have heard that story a hundred times by now."

"Why were you surprised that Murray was on the *Franklin?*" Logan asked, as he taped a fresh tissue to the glass over the D.R.T.

"Oh, it didn't really have anything to do with Murray," Hill said. "It's just that from where I live in Staten Island, you can look across the Kill van Kull and see the *Franklin* just sitting there at the Bayonne Naval Base like a big gray coffin." Hill stared blankly for a few seconds, then muttered aloud, "I wonder if Murray knew Tommy Bursey."

"Tommy Bursey?" quizzed Gardiner.

"Yeah, he was on the *Franklin,* too. He was killed that day. His father still lives in the house next door. It's kind of sad, you know. Tommy was his only kid. I was twelve-years-old when it happened, but I still remember how bad the old man took it. He didn't even say hello to anyone for a year or so afterward." Hill shrugged. "I wonder how he likes looking out his window every morning with the *Franklin* sitting there to remind him."

"I'm sure it's not very pleasant," Logan said. "At least with the army nobody can wrap up Bataan or the Kasserine Pass and drop it in front of your doorstep."

"Sure makes you think, don't it?" Gardiner declared somberly.

"Thinking causes ulcers," Logan retorted with a sardonic smile.

• • •

It was the fifth day of June but there was little hint of spring in a dawn that brought with it slate-gray clouds and a sea the color of gun metal. The crew had been at general quarters for the better part of an hour when word was finally passed to proceed to Maksan. Over went the helm and the *Field* swung around in a slow easy circle until her jackstaff pointed like a gunsight at the dark crust of rock barely visible along the horizon.

Bracing himself against the splinter screen that girded the open bridge, a helmeted Owen Royal could feel the breeze increase as each additional knot was laid on. High above his head, the now faded banner of the Grand Army of the Republic beat the wind with a ferocious rapidity as if competing with the loud drum of the turbines for the captain's attention.

Combat had advised him that the range to the shore had now closed to 12,000 yards (6 nautical miles) when the messenger from the crypto-shack approached.

"This just arrived from Com-Seventh-Fleet, Sir," the sailor said, saluting.

Royal read the dispatch. "On your way back to radio-central, stop off at C.I.C. and tell the X-O I'd like to see him up here on the bridge."

The messenger departed and within minutes, Bray was standing beside the captain reading the decoded dispatch.

The body of the message read: SOUTH KOREAN INTELLIGENCE REPORTS INORDINATE AMOUNT OF ACTIVITY IN GENERAL VICINITY OF MAKSAN — [BREAK] — WHILE AERIAL RECONNAISSANCE

HAS NOT BEEN ABLE TO CONFIRM AN ENEMY PRESENCE IN FORCE, MONITORING STATIONS REPORT A MARKED INCREASE IN RADIO TRANSMISSIONS ORIGINATING IN SUBJECT AREA — [BREAK] — SUBSEQUENTLY, YOU ARE ADVISED NOT TO ENTER MAKSAN INLET — [BREAK] — YOUR GENERAL MISSION WILL PROCEED AS ORDERED — OUT.

Bray tugged at his belt buckle. "Mother dear, may I go in for a swim, yes my darling daughter. Hang your clothes on a hickory limb, but don't go near the water," he murmured aloud.

"I have to plead guilty to recalling that same rhyme when I first read it." Royal folded the paper and tucked it into his shirt pocket. "Apparently, they want the landing party to go ashore as scheduled while we stay just outside. I'll make it plain to Choi that if things don't look kosher, he's to get that boat turned around and back to us pronto. I've no intention of losing him and nine of my men to the reds...certainly not this late in the game." Royal glanced toward Maksan, then turned back to Bray. "How are things down in C.I.C.? Are our three transients from the *Lake Champlain* pulling their weight?"

"Yes, Sir," Bray said. "Don Coates worked them right into the routine. Each one of them is manning a station."

"Good, well, you'd better get back down there. I've a funny feeling we're going to need all the help we can get from you and your radar gang before this morning's over."

"You really think we'll see some action?" the exec asked eagerly.

"Yes, I'd say there's an outside chance you might get your wish," Royal replied, sending the X.O. off with a broad smile.

Because the *Field* would not be entering the inlet, H-hour for Ensign Choi, his six volunteers, and the three-man boatcrew came a full half-hour earlier than originally planned.

Looking down from the starboard wing, Royal and Oetjens watched uneasily as the motor-whaleboat rose and fell with the tossing sea, then went wallowing down into a seemingly bottomless trough before finally pulling clear of the ship to buck headlong into an unwelcome Force-5 wind. Even from as far away as the open bridge, it was obvious that McAlleney, who had recently been elevated from bow-hook to coxswain, due to Bites demise, was having considerable difficulty in bringing the whaleboat around to the proper heading. Finally, the 26-footer steadied up on the specified course to chug noisily off in the direction of Maksan. In a little while the boat passed from view beyond the tar-black rocks that guarded the inlet.

By this time the *Field* had worked her speed back up to 14 knots. At Royal's order, the destroyer commenced a series of figure-eights, each carefully calculated to clear the closest point of land by at least two miles.

The captain swept his binoculars across the somber seascape till his focus rested on the cliffside beyond. He studied the rocks for several minutes, then lowering his glasses, peered back at the shore despondently.

Oetjens sensed his C.O.'s apprehension. "Is something wrong, Sir?" the navigator asked.

Owen shook his head. "No, not really." His tone was unconvincing.

"Excuse me if I'm out of line, Captain, but something seems to be bothering you. Are you sure you didn't spot anything over there?"

"The only thing that's bothering me is that I can't spot anything...not even a single cave. Don't you think that's a little strange?"

"Yes, now that you mention it. As I recall from the last few times we worked this general area, there were caves all over the place. I remember one morning counting at least ten within a half-mile stretch of that coast. Do you think they've camouflaged the caves since then?"

"That's exactly what I think," Royal said as he resumed probing the crag with his binoculars. "And we both know there's only one logical reason for camouflaging caves," he answered sharply.

Royal re-entered the wheelhouse, nudging Warden, the O.D., out of the way so he could reach the lever on the overhead squawk-box. "Combat...this is the captain. I'd like to talk to the X-O please."

"Bray here, Sir." The exec's voice flew back seconds later.

"Stratt, I hope your people are manning the S-P-R-Two."

"Affirmative, Captain. I've got Allingham on it."

"Allingham?"

"Yes, Sir. He's one of the R-Ds from the *Champlain*."

"Is he thoroughly familiar with the gear?"

"Yes, the S-P-R-Two was his G-Q station on his last ship."

"Good. Tell him to be especially alert for radar signals coming from the beach. If the reds do have guns over there, it's a fair bet they'll have radar-fire-control directors, too. The first second they start pulsing, I want to know about it. Make sure he checks all the known frequencies for Russian-made radars."

"Yes, Sir. He's doing that right now."

Back on the open bridge, Royal resumed his visual examination of the enemy coast which, due to the *Field's* reversal of course, was now broad off the port beam. "Damn it, Phil, I'm really worried about our people in the boat. They should have radioed long before this."

Oetjens glanced at his watch. "They're probably ashore by now. I wouldn't worry though...it's most likely the radio. I've never had much faith in those portable jobs. I remember the set we had at Normandy crapped out on us too. Same model as the one the shore party has, come to think of it," the navigator added with a faint smile.

The captain returned to the wheelhouse where Little Gillie informed him via the squawk-box that radio-central was having no success in raising the landing party on any of the prescribed frequencies. Little Gillie also suggested that the radio was most likely at fault, noting that it had been "liberated" from the army during the *Field's* sojourn in Pusan.

"I wish we'd been allowed to enter that inlet," Royal grumbled. "At least that way we'd have been able to maintain visual contact with Choi and his people. Without any communications, God only knows what's happening to them now."

Bacelli, his dungarees dripping wet from wading ashore, made no secret of his displeasure as he and Nugent woefully surveyed the ten-foot wide strip of gravel, manure and dead fish loosely described back in McAvoy's office as a "small beach." Choi and the four gunner's-mates had departed on their quarter-mile trek to the village, leaving the two defrocked radarmen behind to guard the landing site. Now the two RDs' only link to the *Field* and to home seemed to be the sputter and chug of a Fairbanks-Morse diesel as the motor-whaleboat, well out near the center of the inlet, circled around and around under a sky streaked and blotched like a poorly erased blackboard.

"I still say I saw that big rock flutter just as we were passing through the harbor entrance," Bacelli persisted.

"And I still say you're nuts! How the hell can rocks flutter?" barked Nugent.

"That's exactly my point! They can't! Not unless they're fake. You know what Stockwell told us during the Songjin briefing about how the reds like to cover their gun positions with canvas that's been camouflaged to look exactly like the terrain."

"Come on, Vinnie. That doesn't make any sense. If the reds did have any guns in those cliffs, they'd have blasted away at the ship long before this. Hell, she was a sitting duck when she slowed down to put the whaleboat over the side."

"Maybe they didn't want to disclose their positions. Maybe they were waiting to see if the *Field* was going to enter the inlet," Bacelli retorted, resting the butt of his carbine in the soft gravel. "The reds probably figured if they laid low and let the ship come inside, they'd be able to cripple her enough so she couldn't make it back out again. Can you imagine what a piece of propaganda that would be...capturing an American tin can and her crew inside one of their harbors?"

Nugent shook his head. "You ought to forget about peddling midget egg rolls when you get out. With your imagination, you should become a writer. You could write that science-fiction junk the movies are all going ape shit for."

"I see you're still handing out advise," Bacelli grunted. "As I recall the last advice you gave me is what got me over here. And another thing, how come you've got an M-two carbine while they handed me this old M-one model?"

"How the hell do I know? Anyway, I don't see much difference. They both look pretty much the same to me."

"Well, they might look the same, but the one you've got is fully automatic. I heard Gargan tell you it can get off seven-hundred-and-fifty rounds a minute."

"Yeah, well what good is that when the magazine that comes with it only holds thirty rounds?" Nugent snickered.

"Thirty-rounds is twice as many as the magazine in this M-one holds."

"You're always bitching about something, Vinnie. You're starting to get as bad as Murray. Anyway, there's nothing to shoot at around here so why worry about who's got a better piece."

"What's that noise?" Bacelli snapped.

A shattering clamor suddenly came from the direction of the village.

It was followed closely by the crackling sound of rifle fire. Ours or theirs, the radarmen thought in unison. Then as Nugent tightened the chin strap on his helmet, and Bacelli fingered the magazine to see that it was securely locked into the trigger housing, the thumping rattle of a machine gun erupted from a rocky ledge behind them.

"Head for those rocks!" gasped Nugent and the two scampered away from the beach just as searing beads of steel began criss-crossing in every direction.

Near the middle of the inlet, a flare was soaring skyward from the whaleboat, to burst seconds later in a thousand red and yellow streamers.

Still running towards the rocks, his carbine set on automatic fire, Nugent spotted a heavy machine gun being set up on his flank. Wheeling, he let fly a two-second burst from the M-2. The North Korean gunner and his ammo feeder reeled backwards in grotesque somersaults. Nugent couldn't believe wiping out a machine gun nest could be so easy. He'd hardly aimed the carbine, yet he'd bowled them over with less trouble than they do in the movies, he thought, as he leaped up and over a large black boulder.

A few feet behind him, Bacelli stopped suddenly to exchange fire with four North Koreans who were racing across the beach in hot pursuit. He managed to get off five quick rounds, one of which passed through the throat of the closest red infantryman. The soldier stopped like he'd hit a brick wall, then dropped like a sack. Bacelli started to squeeze off a sixth round when a fresh rain of bullets brought him down in a rolling flailing heap.

Nugent was still scrambling over the rocks, leaping blindly for the haven he hoped awaited him on the other side. Finally, his feet hit solid ground. It was then he saw the thicket just yards ahead. He looked around for Bacelli. There was no sign of him. Vinnie must be ahead somewhere, Nugent decided, working his way through the tall grass that bordered the thicket.

He was completely out of breath now, and his mouth was sour from vomit although he couldn't remember throwing up. He spit, wiped his lips with the sleeve of his foul-weather jacket, then felt around the dirt for his carbine which he suddenly discovered was missing. He tried to remember where he had dropped it, certain that he'd had it when he began pushing his way through the brush. He felt around the ground for a full minute without any success. Maybe he'd dropped it back by the rocks, he thought. The hell with it...that two second burst he'd unloaded at those machine gunners would have used up all thirty rounds anyway, he told himself, hunched down and moving cautiously through the brambles and small trees. Where the hell was Vinnie, he wondered. He remembered that they had been running towards the rocks, and Vinnie had almost been trampling his back. The bullets were zipping all around them then, one round bouncing off a rock inches from his face. He felt his cheek, expecting to find blood but was surprised to discover none. He wondered why his cheek was still stinging so badly. Maybe that was when he dropped the carbine, he thought.

A sudden shrill of whistle pierced the copse. The sensation was far worse than the earlier gun fire. He was quaking as he dropped to the ground, constricting his legs to make himself as small a target as possible. Maybe they hadn't seen him after all, he thought. Maybe the whistle was just some red officer trying to call his men together. A burst of fire from a "banjo-gun" rattled through the thicket splitting several of the small trees around him. The fire was coming from the left, or maybe behind him. He wasn't sure. The only thing he knew was he had to get out of there. Now he was running again. Suddenly he was out of the thicket and racing across an open field, bullets kicking little jets of dirt where his feet had been only seconds before.

He stopped running. Directly ahead were soldiers, twelve or fifteen, he figured, his eyes focusing in on their bulky uniforms. They looked different than the reds that had chased him and Vinnie across the beach. Maybe they were Chinese, he reasoned, as he raised his hands over his head. He wondered if the commie prison camps were really as bad as he'd heard. Then a soldier walked up to him. His jacket was cut a little neater than the others Nugent noticed. Probably an officer, he concluded as he prepared to sing out the standard name, rank and serial number which he knew he was required to reveal.

The red officer was only five or six feet away from him now. Nugent was still wondering if his captor was North Korean or Chinese when the officer extended the Tokarev pistol at arms length, braced his wrist with the other hand and pulled the trigger. The first slug caught Nugent in the jaw. The second and third tore great ragged holes in his chest. The soldiers left the body where it had fallen.

Having expended all emergency flares, McAlleney, Gibbs the engineer, and bow-hook Coleman were now racing towards the beach, moving with a fast running surf and bucking a wind that came from shore cold and strong. His eyes smarting from the salt spray, McAlleney couldn't be certain from 200 yards out if the figures running along the sand were Choi's shore party or a squad of red infantry. The matter was clarified within seconds when a barrage of mortar shells looped up from the high ground beyond the beach to come raining down with lethal thunder ahead, astern and on both sides of the boat, heeling her far to starboard, then just as far back to port. Hardly had the water, kelp and shredded sea life settled down upon the three crewmen when a second volley of mortar shells arched out from the black rocks. Twelve new spouts danced along the surface of the water, this time forming an almost perfect circle around the launch.

McAlleney pulled hard on the tiller, struggling to bring the boat around until a near miss sent the craft spinning. Another close shot lifted the launch several feet out of the water, hurling Coleman back towards the center of the boat where he crashed against Gibbs, breaking the engineer's arm. Gibbs never had a chance to cry out. At that instant, an 82-millimeter mortar shell soared down at an almost vertical angle splitting the thwart directly behind the engine housing and detonating against the deck planking. A blinding flash of light shot out through the bilge strake and the boat disintegrated, showering the surface of the water with chunks of wood and body parts for a hundred yards in any direction.

Still following the prescribed pattern of figure-eights, the *Field* was making a slow turn to seaward when McAlleney's three emergency flares rocketed up from the inlet.

"Combat, bridge!" Royal called into the bridge speaker.

"Combat, aye," responded Ensign Coates.

"Put Mister Bray on the horn, please."

"Bray here, Captain."

"Looks like you're getting your wish, Stratt. We're going in."

To Bray, the words were electric.

"I expect we'll be taking fire any minute now, so keep the bridge and gun-plot up to date on the range to the beach. The land to the left of the entrance is designated Point-Able. The land to the right will be Point-Baker."

Royal rejoined Oetjens on the open wing. The ship was almost steadied up on a base course of 282-degrees true, which would point her directly at the center of the half-mile wide entrance to Maksan Inlet.

The navigator lowered his binoculars and turned to face the captain.

"Sir, don't misunderstand me. I'm all for going in there after our people, but what about Com-Seventh-Fleet? The last message they sent instructed us to keep the ship out of the inlet."

"Not quite, Phil. That dispatch advised us to keep the ship outside. The way I interpret the word advise, I'd say they were giving me a distinct option, wouldn't you?"

"Well, knowing the navy, I'd say if everything works out okay, then the dispatch could be interpreted as giving you the option. If it doesn't, I wouldn't even want to think of the consequences."

"Consequences or not, there's no way I'm going to leave Choi and nine of my people in there," the captain said crisply. Surveying the port and starboard wing as well as the narrow walkway in front of the wheelhouse, Royal soon satisfied himself that all his lookouts had taken cover, even though he was cognizant that cover aboard a destroyer was a nonentity since quarter inch steel afforded protection against nothing more formidable than wind, rain or the occasional swirl of sea spray.

Almost to the wheelhouse doorway, Royal and Oetjens were confronted by Ensign Warden. "Combat reports they've intercepted electronic signals coming from Point Able. The signals bear two-nine-seven," the O.D. announced, glancing down at the small pad he was holding. "Frequency, pulse repetition and beam width all indicate fire-control radar...probably Russian type-twelve or fourteen."

Before Owen could fully digest the unwelcome news, he became conscious of someone yelling over the clatter and clang of the forward gunhouses, now being rotated from side to side in preparation for their possible employment. The voice was coming from above. Turning, the captain looked up to see Korvin, one of the fire-controlmen, protruding half-way out of the open observation hatch atop the Mark-37 gun-director. "Guns, Captain! There's guns all over those rocks!" the sailor shouted, forgetting in his excitement to use the sound-powered telephone that dangled loosely around his neck.

Royal spun around, pinching his binoculars hard against his eye sockets, searching the shadowy rock section by section.

"I count four...no, five!" Oetjens corrected. "There's two more over there on Baker. Hell's bells, Captain, it's Normandy all over again!" The navigator's features were stretching in disbelief.

A stab of flame belched from the blackest cave on Point Able and a puff of grayish smoke floated lazily along the face of the cliff. Two yellow blotches bloomed among the crag on Baker. Three more flashed in rapid succession on Point Able.

"I have the conn, Mister Warden! Port ten degrees!" cried Royal as he and Oetjens reached the confines of the wheelhouse. A quartermaster secured the steel door tightly behind them.

'Crumppppppph'...the far-off rumbling sound rolled angrily across the water as six black specks creased the sky directly overhead to tumble down a hundred yards astern. Columns of water spiraled upward, neatly dissecting the ship's wake. A ranging salvo, Royal was certain, grateful to the Almighty that the red gunners had overshot their target by such a generous margin. Unfortunately, the bearing they had chosen was right on the money.

"Come back to course two-eight-two!" Royal ordered loudly as he peered through the glass port. The *Field* lurched steeply, then rolled back to even keel. "Mister Warden. Pass the word for all hands topside except secondary-conn to take cover."

"Does that include the forty-millimeter gun crews, Captain?"

"Yes. They won't be very effective against what the reds have over there. I'd rather not risk exposing them to shrapnel. Our main battery will have to do the job. Pass the word to Mister MacKinlay to commence fire."

'Barroomp!' roared the two forward mounts in immediate affirmation.

Royal leaned toward the closest porthole, straining to spot his fall of shot through the smoke and cordite fumes now swirling back from the muzzles of the 5-inch guns.

"Come left five degrees! Steady up on two-seven-seven," Royal instructed, initiating a zigzag he hoped would baffle the enemy battery commander although he knew that a base course of two-eight-two would have to be maintained during the zigzag if the *Field* was to enter the inlet. His opposition had to be just as aware of that fact, Royal sadly concluded.

The two forward mounts were shooting steadily now, concentrating their fire on the battery at Point Able, which, if the report from C.I.C. was accurate, also housed the enemy's radar and principal fire-control system. So far, Royal had been unable to bring his midships or his two after guns into play. To do so, he would have to swing the ship almost broadside to the shore, an action that would deter him from his primary mission, that of rescue.

A purple column of water climbed steeple-high as a large caliber shell chipped the surface of the sea directly ahead of the charging destroyer.

"Hard right rudder! Steady up on two-eight-six!" barked Royal. The ship twisted, then shuddered as her screws cleared the water, throwing Oetjens and the boatswain-of-the-watch hard against the bulkhead. Grabbing for the binnacle post, the captain braced himself just before another purple plume danced high in the air, this time no more than thirty yards off the port bow. Astern, yellow, green and crimson-red geysers were hopping off the water, a spectacle worthy of an old Esther Williams movie.

"They're using shells loaded with dye to range in on us," Royal observed.

"Yes, Sir, and those bastards with the purple dye seem to have done just that," a sweating Chief Anderson replied just as another purple water spout erupted close off the port beam.

At that moment, a considerable amount of sweat was also being expended down below in the combat-information-center as Bray, Coates and ten not-too-happy radarmen busily cranked out a continuous stream of ranges and bearings for the bridge and gun-plot.

The clock on the C.I.C bulkhead read 09:14 when the radar gang felt a sudden lurch and heard a noise like hailstones. Then, for a split second, the surface scope lost its picture. Except for that, the air burst that had just showered shrapnel upon the Mark-37 director and the bridge would not have been noticed down below in the combat-information-center.

"Combat, bridge!" came Royal's voice from the overhead speaker.

"Combat, aye!" replied Bray, looking up from the plotting table.

"The reds just peppered the Mark-Thirty-Seven. The director's okay but one of the fire-control-men, Gilmore, took a mean hunk of shrapnel. We've brought him down to the wheelhouse. Parish is tending him now. The only problem is, we're now short one man in the director. I understand your second-class, Logan, is a former fire-controlman with Mark-Thirty-Seven experience. Can you spare him?"

"Yes, Sir...I believe we can."

"Good...let me speak to him."

"Logan here, Captain."

"Logan, do you still remember how to handle a Mark-Thirty-Seven?"

"Yes, Sir. I think so. I spent over a year in one aboard the *Laffey*."

"What position did you man?"

"Just about all of them except the fire-control officer's. They liked to rotate us through the other positions, but I guess I spent most of my time as either the pointer or trainer."

"Good. It's the trainer position we need you in. You'd better get up there on the double, and wear your helmet, at least while you're climbing up that outside ladder."

"Yes, Sir." Logan released the speaker-lever, then glanced over at Murray. "Well, Howie, fight the good fight," he said with a warm smile.

Murray hesitated, then looked away without answering.

For the first time in the 13 months since he'd reported aboard, Logan was not cockily sure of himself nor of his survival. He turned dejectedly and headed for the door. "Good luck," rang out from several voices. Logan listened carefully for Murray's but it was not among them.

The clock now read 09:17. Still dashing towards the opening to the inlet, the *Field* was continually straddled and near missed by a deluge of shells. Even so, they didn't seem to be coming quite as close as they did just minutes before, Bray noticed, concluding that the enemy's fire-control radars must be in need of calibration to cope with close-in targets. He knew that within a matter of minutes the *Field* would reach the entrance and start passing between the two jagged fingers of rock. At that point there would be no more than 500 yards clearance on either side of the ship. Bray wondered if the reds would have guns positioned to cover the relatively short channel that led into the inlet. It seemed unlikely, he decided, since such an arrangement could result in the battery on Point Able firing directly into the Point Baker guns and vice versa. Also to the *Field's* advantage, she would be able to utilize all five of her 5-inch, something she'd not been able to do during the charge in.

Bray looked down at the chart that was taped tightly across the plotting table. He wondered if the shore around the inlet was fortified. Even if there were more guns inside, he had no doubt that the *Field* could handle them in good order, especially since the inlet appeared wide and deep enough to permit a modest degree of maneuvering. Mines could make it a whole new ball game though, he reckoned, but so far there was no sign of any. If the reds hadn't bothered to place them in the most logical place, just outside the entrance to the inlet, there was every likelihood they hadn't taken the trouble to sow them inside either.

While Bray was puzzling about mines and speculating about how his gyrene brother-in-law was going to like sharing the family limelight with another combat vet, Gardiner was hunched over the surface scope calling out the latest range and bearing while, moving the cursor on the scope over to the greenish-yellow smudge that indicated Point Able. The combat-information-center was boiling and Gardiner was relieved that Bray hadn't insisted that they wear helmets below decks like Cobb always had. Gardiner suddenly wondered what Cobb was doing up in Adak about now...freezing his ass off, the radarman fervidly hoped as he called out a new range and bearing to Point Able.

In the wheelhouse the captain was relieved to see a string of water spouts appear far off the starboard quarter.

"Their fire-control system must be fouled up," Oetjens said in a sudden relaxed tone as three more geysers erupted astern ever further off the mark.

512

The captain pulled the speaker-switch linking him to the Mark-37. "Mister Keagan, has Logan gotten up there yet?"

"Yes, Sir. He's all tucked in. Can we resume rotating the director?"

"Affirmative. Get on Point Baker. Most of their fire's coming from there. I'm turning hard right in about thirty seconds. I'll hold a course of two-nine-zero long enough for you to unmask your after mounts. Make sure you get in at least four good broadsides before we come back to base course." Royal turned to Shubrick, the helmsman, and ordered the change of course. The destroyer swung around smartly, and within seconds all five of her gray rifles were spewing out a steel-jacketed mix of black powder and T.N.T. at the enemy coast. Royal's pulse quickened as he counted seven salvos thunder from the muzzles of the *Field's* main battery. The ship was close enough now so that he didn't need binoculars to observe his shells striking home in the area where most of the enemy guns seem to have been concentrated. A large fireball erupted among the rocks as one of his 5-inch detonated deep inside a cave being used to store ammunition.

A unanimous cheer echoed among the sailors in the wheelhouse as they watched a series of violent explosions tear black boulders from the cliffside and toss two enormous guns into the air along with the steel rails they had been mounted on just seconds before.

Now back on course two-eight-two, the destroyer went bounding ahead, seemingly immune to anything the enemy might throw at her.

Three hundred yards...two hundred yards...one hundred yards. Still unscathed except for a ragged hole in the gun-director, the *Field* continued her charge, her flags flying and her forward battery belching flame.

'Whoomph'...the air burst went off with a deafening blast just ten feet above the jackstaff. To Royal and the others in the wheelhouse, it was as if the sky had split apart to produce a hellish orange ball. The air in front of the wheelhouse was suddenly pocked with blue-black specks.

Royal wasn't certain how many moments had passed before he was able to pick himself up from the pile of moaning bodies. There was a terrible buzzing in his ears and when he looked up he could see more than two square-feet of daylight where overhead plating should have been.

Suddenly he realized that the wheel was spinning wildly. He coughed as acrid fumes swirled in through small holes in the face of the wheelhouse.

Ensign Warden was the first to scramble up from the mass of shattered glass and debris. He leaped for the wheel and in spite of two straddles, finally managed to pull the *Field* back around to an offensive heading.

The men were all to their feet now...all except Shubrick who was slumped over the engine-telegraph with the top of his head missing as if he'd been scalped, his dead eyes staring down at the black decking matting and the widening red puddle that was slowly forming at his feet.

"Bridge...Main-Battery-Control!" Ensign Keagan's voice blared from the battered squawk-box. "The director's a mess, Captain. We've picked up some new cross ventilation and I'm not sure about the antenna."

"Anyone hurt?"

"No, Sir. Are you people all right down there?"

"Well, we're not likely to win any awards from "*Good Housekeeping*" but we're still functioning," Royal said, as he glanced at the quartermaster who had just relieved Warden at the helm.

The ship was easing by the rocky entrance to the inlet now as Royal peered ahead looking for any sign of the whaleboat. Something was burning on the surface of the water over towards shore. He couldn't tell if it was the whaleboat or some hapless fishing boat that managed to be in the wrong place at the wrong time.

Royal swept the area with his binoculars. The distance and the weaving course the *Field* was following made positive identification of the burning debris impossible, but the captain could make out pieces of gray planking and something orange floating in the water. He was painfully aware that the crew of the whale-boat had been wearing orange life jackets.

The water inside Maksan Inlet was smooth with a moderate ground swell. The *Field's* speed now reduced to a cautious twelve knots, the destroyer had ceased fire upon entering the inlet, though considerable smoke was still eddy-ing up from her red hot gun barrels. Royal and Oetjens began combing the shoreline with their glasses, hoping to see some sign of the shore party. Suddenly, a string of bright flashes blossomed along a stretch of beach to the right. Almost simultaneously, the hilly area at the far corner of the inlet sparkled with gun fire.

Even before this new storm of shells flew over at nearly masthead level, Royal knew there was no chance of saving anyone in the shore party. To height-en his sense of frustration, he'd just gotten word from Parish that Gilmore had expired. Now his only option was to break out to open sea. Looking around at the shambles within the wheelhouse, Royal vowed that the *Field* would not go gen-tly. Confirming his pledge, long sheets of flame spewed out from each of the 5-inch guns at three-second intervals.

Freeing MacKinlay in gun-plot and Keagan in the Mark-37 to choose their own targets without waiting for direction from the bridge, Royal had barely ordered the helmsman to apply "Right full rudder!" when another torrent of steel crashed down on all sides of the destroyer. Enormous columns of dirty brown water shot high into the air thoroughly soaking Don Stockwell and his men on the exposed platform that served as secondary conn.

Wheeling around, the *Field* pivoted on her screws until her bow was finally pointing at the opening in the rock and at the Sea of Japan beyond. Royal could feel the ship quiver as if she might fall apart from the strain of her pounding engines. Neverthe-less, she quickly picked up speed and within minutes was slic-ing her way through the faster running channel water. Royal and the others in the wheelhouse could feel the hot blast each time the two forward mounts lashed out at the exposed side of Point Able. The midships and two after mounts were matching them shot for shot as was evidenced by the many fires raging along the far rim of the inlet.

The *Field* was midway through the channel when an enormous explosion erupted from an area close to the village. It was followed in rapid order by three more deafening explosions and a mushroom cloud resembling a miniature atomic blast. Speculation was rampant as to its cause, Royal and the others in the wheelhouse having no way of knowing that a stray round from mount-4 had landed dead center in a field being used as a temporary marshalling yard for over 200 newly arrived submarine torpedoes. It would be several months before United Nations intelligence would learn of the torpedoes or that they were to have been transferred to specially prepared magazines on the afternoon of the *Field's* unexpected visit.

In the Mark-37, Kevin Logan was still trying to wipe Gilmore's blood off the various cranks and handwheels within his reach. He felt a dampness at the seat of his dungarees, and he hoped that the liquid he was sitting in was merely salt water.

The destroyer was emerging from the channel now and Logan, his brow pressed firmly against the rubber eyepiece of his telescope, knew that within minutes the ship would again be under the guns of Able and Baker. On Keagan's orders, he had rotated the Mark-37 around as far aft as it would face without its target acquisition capabilities being compromised by the mast and funnel tops. With all the action now astern, Logan was uncomfortably aware that the two forward mounts could no longer be brought to bear on the enemy batteries, thus reducing the *Field's* firepower by a crucial 40 percent.

As he maneuvered the crosshairs in his telescope, Logan wondered how Howie was making out now that he had to take his place at the D.R.T. The D.R.T. was never Murray's forte, Kevin reflected, hoping that the first-class wouldn't screw up and embarrass himself in front of Bray and those three hot shots from the *Lake Champlain*.

Hardly had the thought cleared his brain when he heard Ensign Keagan bark the order to "Shoot!" A bone-breaking crack rang out from the midship's mount. Two more followed in rapid succession as the stern guns joined in, and the first of the *Field's* abbreviated salvos was off and running.

Through his telescope, Logan could see bright ripples of flame appear along the high ground on Baker. Able came alive next. Within seconds, enemy shells were whining through the rigging, falling ahead, astern, and off the port beam of the destroyer.

Kevin had no way of knowing which of the enemy batteries had hurled the shell, or that it had been fired by a random field piece not even hooked into the enemy's fire-control system. Perhaps it would never have hit the *Field* had the captain chosen to come hard left just a few seconds earlier. This is something no one will ever know...not Royal... not Logan...not Mary Kathleen Murray who would from that day on grow up without ever having known her father.

The howitzer shell that would change so many lives had spun in almost vertically like a falling bomb. Missing the roof of number-2 gun by a matter of inches, it penetrated the 0-2 level at the base of the bridge, then plunged down through the captain's stateroom, finally exploding in the combat-information-center. In one terrible blazing instant, Commander Bray, Ensign Coates, and nine radarmen would cease to exist.

With countless air bursts ripping the sky all around him, Logan barely noticed the muffled explosion. Somewhat disoriented by the constant rotation of the gun-director, Kevin was certain that the shell had hit somewhere aft of the bridge, probably in the vicinity of the torpedo deck, he decided, wondering if Mister Stockwell and the others up in secondary-conn were still alright.

In the wheelhouse, Owen Royal was getting the bad news from Lieutenant Sternhagen.

"C.I.C.'s completely wiped out, Sir. I'm afraid your stateroom went with it. The fire must have shot back through the hole the shell made. Everything in your room's burnt to a cinder."

"The hell with my room, Rolf! How many men did your people get out of C.I.C.?"

"None, Sir."

"None!"

"I'm sorry, Captain. There was no way we could save Mister Bray or Don Coates or anybody else in there. The place was a total inferno. Right now, my people have got all they can do just keeping the fire confined to the radar shack."

"The C.O.'s exchange with his damage-control officer was cut short by a fresh forest of shell splashes leaping skyward off the port bow."

Swinging the ship hard starboard, the captain barely missed passing through the shrapnel-packed fountains of water that the Point Baker battery had just strewn across his path. Royal was ordering a 15-degree turn back to port when an explosion jolted everyone in the wheelhouse. The shock wave that followed buckled deck plates and made stanchions quiver the entire length of the ship.

The hit was somewhere aft, Royal was certain. Without waiting for a report, he charged out on to the wing and rushed back to the signal bridge.

Aft of the second stack, his ship was now a gutted bleeding wreck. Looking over the flag-bags, the captain could see that the after deckhouse had been transformed into a jumble of twisted, smoldering metal. Mount-3, the midships 5-inch, was out of action, its drooping barrel split and hissing white smoke. Royal's only relief came in the realization that his two stern guns were still socking round after round into the communist positions. If the number and size of the fires now raging on Able and Baker could serve as an accurate measuring rod, both guns were giving a first-rate account of themselves, Royal decided.

"Captain!" the bridge-talker called out, jerking at the extension cord that snaked behind him. "Mister Sternhagen reports they've now got the fire completely under control in the radar spaces, but the fire-main aft of the stack has ruptured, and they still haven't extinguished the fire in the crew's head."

Royal reentered the wheelhouse and pulled the lever on the squawk-box that linked him to damage-control-central.

"Rolf, this is the captain. What's the story on the fire aft?"

"We've lost pressure on the hoses aft of the engine room, but Daly and his gang have gone after it with C-O-two He just reported that they've got it pretty much under control."

"Pretty much doesn't count," said Royal sharply. "What about casualties?"

"No dead as far as we can tell, but we've got six wounded. Since the head's been knocked out, we've taken them to the forward dressing station."

"What about the sprinkler system in the handling room under mount-three. Did it kick in okay?"

"Yes, Sir. The sprinklers wet down everything, even the wounded."

"Just make sure Daly smothers that fire before the temperature gets high enough to activate the sprinklers in mount-four's handling room. If the number-four gun stops firing, we'll have only one gun that can bear on those red batteries."

Daly's damage-control party managed to extinguish the fire, and the *Field* swerved and twisted and zigged and zagged through barrage after barrage for another twenty minutes by which time she had finally slipped beyond the range of the largest of the enemy's guns.

"Captain, if you ever hear me using the word freebee again," Oetjens said, "please do me a favor and kick me square in the rump."

Faking a smile, Royal transferred the conn back to Ensign Warden, then went below to visit the wounded.

It wasn't until the closing moments of the engagement that Logan learned about C.I.C. and the fate he'd so narrowly escaped. The grim word came from Korvin who in turn had gotten it from Ensign Keagan.

Several more moments would pass before the gravity of the news would fully register. The Mark-37 was still facing aft, and Logan could see Maksan's hilly outline gradually receding astern. Almost unconsciously, he began focusing in on the tallest of the peaks that loomed up from a distant mountain ridge.

Clutching the crucifix he had earlier attached to the chain that held his dog tags, he remembered the time he and Howie had gone ashore in Pusan, and the young girl who had told them the story of the Arirang hill. Staring into the eyepiece, he wondered if the peak he was watching by some strange coincidence might be legendary Arirang. His eyes began to water as he suddenly thought about two little girls in Ohio waiting anxiously to greet their father.

He moved the focus control and the peak sharpened. He could see another peak beyond and still another beyond that.

Korea, Logan reflected, a place where people sing silly little songs about a flower covered hill they will never see.

Licking her wounds, the *Field* limped slowly towards Japan.

Epilogue

After ongoing extensive repairs at Yokosuka, the *Charles P. Field* finally reached San Diego on August 15th. On August 21st Commander Royal was awarded the Silver Star "for gallantry in action." A day later, he was relieved of command of DD-505 and transferred ashore spending the next three years at the San Diego Naval Base carrying out humdrum staff assignments for Commander Cruiser-Destroyer Forces Pacific. Passed over repeatedly for promotion to captain, Owen was permitted to remain on active duty just long enough to qualify for his pension. He left the navy in 1956, two years after his divorce from Candace who soon after married her ad agency's top honcho, Ham Barlow.

Logan, Candace and Royal would never learn of their respective "relationship" nor would they ever have any future contact.

In October of 1956, while visiting his favorite "house of ill repute" in downtown Budapest, Major Mychenko would suffer the dubious distinction of becoming the first Russian fatality of the Hungarian Revolution.

In 1964 on a Sunday afternoon in Saigon, Lt. Comdr. Cynthia Osbourne was killed by a Viet Cong bomb. She along with several other U.S. personnel had been viewing the film *"The List of Adrian Messenger"* in a local theater.

The *Charles P. Field* received further repairs and a modest amount of new equipment during the fall of 1953, and by the New Year was ready to resume her duties as a training vessel for naval reservists. In 1957, her home port was shifted from San Diego to Long Beach. Continuing her assignment, DD-505 carried out a series of 14-day training cruises calling at various liberty ports from Mexico to British Columbia.

Ironically, the *Field*, which had been created to destroy Japan's Imperial Navy in 1943, would in 1959, be chosen to play a major role in its rebirth. Transferred to Japan's Maritime Self-Defense Force along with sister ships *Heywood L. Edwards* and *Richard P. Leary* , she would trade her name for that of a former enemy destroyer sunk off Formosa. For the next five years as *Minekaze ("Wind form the Mountain Peak")*, she would fly the blood red rising sun from her gaff as she patrolled the once-unfriendly waters off Honshu and Shikoku. In 1974, she would go to the ship breakers in Nagoya without as much as a passing note in either the American or Japanese press.

Note: At this writing, the author has been unable to determine if a strange looking American C.P.O. had ever been encountered aboard the *Minekaze*.

Glossary of Terms*

Able - letter A in the phonetic alphabet.

Absentee pennant - flown when the commanding officer of a US Naval vessel is not on board.

AD Skyraider - single-engined (prop.) attack bomber built by Douglas Aircraft Corporation. AD-3 and AD-4 were most numerous of this type used in Korea. AD-3E carried submarine detection equipment. AD-4N was specially fitted for night operations. AD-3W carried early-warning radar.

Admin' - short for administration in Navy jargon.

Affirmative - word for "yes" during radio-telephone transmission.

After-steering - a secondary area aboard ship equipped to takeover steering function should the wheelhouse lose steering control due to power failure or enemy action.

"Airedale" (also "airdale") - slang for naval aviation personnel.

AJ Savage - built by North American, this twin-engined (prop.) bomber was specifically designed to give US Navy carriers a nuclear-strike capability.

"All Hands" - a magazine published by the US Navy Bureau of Personnel to keep its men and women abreast of news pertinent to their professional performance and general interest. Each copy of this magazine was to be passed on to at least 10 readers.

Anemometer - instrument used aboard ship to measure wind velocity.

Angels - code word for altitude of friendly aircraft in 1,000s of feet. Used in C.I.C. during air-control and air-plotting operations. For example, "angels one-five" means 15,000 feet in altitude, "angels six" means 6,000 feet, etc.

AO - Navy designation for fleet oiler.

APA - Navy designation for attack transport.

Arresting cable - arranged at 90 degrees axis of aircraft carrier's flight deck; designed to stop aircraft during landing by engaging the plane's tailhook.

A-scope - a type of radar screen used to determine a more accurate range to target than was usually obtainable when using the PPI-scope. However, the A-scope does not show a target's bearing.

Ash can - slang for barrel-shaped depth charge commonly used during the two world wars. This type of weapon was usually rolled off stern or fired from "K" - or "Y" - guns.

ASP - (or "Asp") - stands for anti-submarine patrol. Usually applied to aircraft such as the AD-3E when assigned to sub searching duties with a carrier task force.

ASW - designation applied to aircraft, weapons, operations, etc. directed against enemy submarines; stands for anti-submarine warfare.

Athwartships - at right angles to the centerline of a ship. An athwartships passageway is one running from the port side to the starboard side of a ship or vice versa.

A-26 - the Douglas A-26 Invader was a twin-engined (prop.) attack bomber used by US Army Air Corps during closing stages of World War II and by US Air Force for tactical intruder missions during the Korean War. Although redesignated B-26 in 1948, this aircraft was still commonly referred to as the A-26, proving again that old habits are hard to break. Several of these planes served the USN as target tugs under the designation JD-1.

AVP - Navy designation for a small seaplane tender.

Azimuth - the bearing of a place or object from the observer measured as an angle clockwise from true north.

Baker - letter B in the phonetic alphabet.

Baker flag - small red flag flown aboard USN vessels when fuel or ammunition is being handled such as during replenishment or general quarters.

"Bam" - service slang for a female member of the Marines Corps. The letters B-A-M stand for "broad-ass marine." Term was applied because there was no official acronym for women serving in the Marines in contrast to the Navy (WAVE), Coast Guard (SPAR), Army (WAC) and Air Force (WAF).

Banshee - name given McDonnell's F2H series of carrier-based jet fighters. Model used in Korea was the F2H-2. A long-nose photo-reconnaissance version also operated from Task Force 77 flight decks as the F2H-2P.

"Banjo-gun" - nickname given to the PPSh-41 submachine-gun by G.I.s who thought the Russian-made weapon with its large circular magazine (71 rounds) resembled a banjo. Used by both Chinese and North Korean infantry.

B.A.R. - (also "Bar") - stands for Browning Automatic Rifle. Although this 30 cal. machine gun was developed during World War I for US Army, it was still standard equipment for Navy landing parties throughout Ko-War period.

"Battle-axe" - call name for USS Missouri, BB-63 during Korean War.

"Battleship row" - name given to mooring area off Ford Island. It was here where battleships and other large vessels moored when the US Pacific Fleet came into Pearl Harbor.

Battle stars - worn on campaign ribbons. Awarded to crew members of vessels that engaged enemy forces in combat. Except for Inchon Invasion, battle stars awarded to US Navy personnel during Ko-War were given for extended combat periods. For example, a star was awarded for "Fall-Winter 1952 Offensive," another for the "Winter 1952-Spring 1953 Offensive."

Battlewagon - slang for battleship.

Beam - the width of a vessel.

Beaufort scale - is used for rating velocity of winds.

Beaufort scale 5 - when winds are 17-21 knots in velocity with moderate size waves.

"Big Ben" - nickname for USS Franklin, CV-13.

"Big E" - nickname for USS Enterprise, CV-6.

"Big O" - nickname for USS Oriskany, CVA-34.

"Birdbath" - call name for Commodore Price as Commander of Destroyer Division 291. Used during radio-telephone transmissions.

"Birthrate" - call name for Task Force 77 screen commander.

"Bitch-Box" - (also "Squawk-box") - slang for the 21MC. Internal communications system providing two-way transmission between the bridge and key control stations aboard a US Navy warship. It is officially known as the "Captain's Command Announcing System."

"Black gang" - slang for engine-room personnel. Name stems from time when ships used coal for fuel and stokers were covered with black soot.

"Black shoe navy" - the surface and submarine personnel (see "brown shoe navy").

Blinker - used for sending flashing light messages.

Boatswain's mate - petty officer in charge of deck hands.

"Bogey" - unidentified air contact assumed to be hostile.

"Bonnie Dick" - nickname for USS Bon Homme Richard, CVA-31.

"Boonies" - (also boondocks) - slang for any remote area of no importance.

Bore - the inside of a gun barrel.

B.O.Q. - Bachelor officers' quarters. For officers not accompanied by their wives.

Bow - forward section of a vessel.

Bowhook - sailor stationed in the bow of a small boat (launch) who mans the boathook and bow line and serves as the boat's lookout.

"Bought the farm" - service slang for getting killed.

"Brown shoe navy" - naval aviators. Name stems from time when aviators were the only US Naval Officers permitted to wear brown shoes. Such shoes were worn with "forestry green" uniform, unique to officers in the Navy's air arm.

Bulkhead - the "walls" of a ship, the vertical structures enclosing a ship's compartments.

Bull nose - a closed chock at the tip of the bow near the jackstaff. The mooring line for the bow is passed through this chock or bull nose.

Bumboat - a small boat used to sell merchandise to personnel aboard ships moored in a harbor.

BuPers - The Bureau of Naval Personnel - a division of the Navy Department directly responsible to the Chief of Naval Operations.

BuShips - The Bureau of Ships - a division of the Navy Department directly under the C.N.O.

Call name - used to conceal actual name of a vessel during radio-telephone transmissions. Call names are changed periodically.

Camel - large raft-like float used to keep the side of a vessel away from a pier or from scraping the hull of another vessel nested alongside. Camel is often made up of one or more logs.

"Can" - slang for destroyer (see "tin can").

Capricorn - collective call name for Destroyer Division 291. This call name is used when a radio-transmission is being sent simultaneously to all four destroyers in the division.

C.A.P. - (also "Cap") - stands for Combat Air Patrol. Term is applied to fighter aircraft protecting a carrier task force or other naval force.

Captain's mast - hearing conducted by the captain of a US Naval vessel or shore facility during which an enlisted man is tried for a minor offense. The commanding officer has authority to acquit the offender or give him punishments as prescribed by the Uniform Code of Military Justice.

"Captain Shands - reference to Captain Courtney Shands, USN, commanding officer of the USS Oriskany during her Ko-War tour with Task Force 77.

Charlie - the letter C in the phonetic alphabet.

Chuichi Nagumo - Rear Admiral, Imperial Japanese Navy, who commanded the task force that attacked Pearl Harbor.

Chock - steel deck fitting through which mooring lines are passed.

C.I. Net - radio net in a ship's combat-information-center. It is used for reporting air raids, and for exchanging information between ships.

"Claude" - allied code name for Mitsubishi A5M4, a single-seat, single-engined Japanese Navy fighter distinguished by its open cockpit and fixed landing gear. Obsolete for first-line duties, it was phrased into the *Kamikaze* role in closing months of the Pacific War.

C.O. - stands for commanding officer, the captain of a ship or station.

C.N.O. - stands for Chief of Naval Operations, the senior military officer of the Department of the Navy. He takes precedence above all other US Navy officers except one who may be serving as the Chairman of the Joint Chiefs of Staff.

ComAirPac - Commander Naval Air Forces Pacific.

ComCruDesPac - Commander Cruiser-Destroyer Forces Pacific. Also unofficially referred to as ComDesPac, DesPac, etc.

Common - a type of ammunition. The common projectile carries a larger explosive charge than the armor piercing projectile, but has considerably less penetrating power.

Compartment - a "room" aboard a ship.

C.P.O. - a chief petty officer.

Condition Watches - the state of a ship's readiness for combat - (see below).

Condition Three - attack is not probable. Crew is on a normal watch schedule with normal steaming routine.

Condition Two - a surprise attack may occur at any time. Half the crew is on watch rather than the normal third as in Condition Three.

Condition One - the same as general quarters. Battle stations are fully manned and the ship is buttoned up for maximum watertight integrity.

Corsair - the Vought F4U was a single-engine single-seat fighter developed for carrier operations during World War II. Type most commonly used by Navy and Marine Corps in Ko-War were the F4U-4, F4U-5 and F4U-5N (a night fighter version).

Coxswain - the enlisted man in charge of a small boat (launch). He is usually the man at the tiller.

Crow - slang for the eagle insignia on the sleeve of a petty officer's uniform.

Crypto - short for cryptograph. Basically a device aboard ship for encoding and decoding radio messages.

CVA - Navy designation for an attack carrier. These ships were originally designated CV. All carriers operating with Task Force 77 during Ko-War became CVAs as of October 1, 1952.

CVE - Navy designation for an escort carrier. Small and slow and built on merchantship type hulls, they were not suited for operations with a fast carrier task force. Even so, CVEs like *USS Bairoko, USS Sicily* and *USS Badoeng Strait* proved highly effective against the communists in direct support of UN ground forces. Other CVEs were used extensively to ferry aircraft from the US to Korea and Japan.

CVL - Navy designation for a light carrier. Larger than a CVE but smaller than a CVA, light carriers were built on cruiser hulls. While capable of high-speed operations, only one CVL, the *USS Bataan*, was actively engaged during the Ko-War, operating primarily off Korea's west coast.

"Dago" - Navy slang for San Diego.

DD - Navy designation for a destroyer.

"Deck apes" - slang for members of the deck force such as boatswain mates.

D.C. - a damage controlman.

DE - Navy designation for a destroyer escort.

DesDiv - a destroyer division. During the Korean War, a typical division was made up of four destroyers.

DesPac - (see ComCruDesPac)

DesRon - a destroyer squadron. During Ko-War, typical US destroyer squadron was made up of three divisions (twelve DDs).

Divine Wind - translation from the Japanese *kamikaze*. Term is used for Japan's suicide offensive.

D.R. - stands for dead reckoning, the estimate of a ship's position from the course steered and the distance the ship has steamed.

"Drink" - to refuel, to take on oil from a tanker at sea.

D.R.T. - the dead reckoning tracer, working in conjunction with other dead reckoning equipment in C.I.C. It is used to maintain a continuous, up-to-the-minute, geographic plot of own ship and all surface contacts within radar range.

"Duckpin" - code name for a specific area within Wonsan Harbor.

Douglas JD-1 - (see A-26).

Easy - letter E in the phonetic alphabet.

"E" boat - the Allies' designation for German motor torpedo boats. The term E-boat was a misnomer since they were actually "S"-boats, the S for the German *Schnellboote* (fast boat).

"E" division - the ship's engineering division. Those personnel concerned with the operation and upkeep of a ship's power plant and related propulsion machinery.

E.M. club - enlisted men's club.

Enfilading fire - firing a gun or guns in a sweeping motion as if to wipe out a column of troops.

Engine-order telegraph - apparatus for transmitting speed and direction orders from the wheelhouse to the engine room. Also called an annunciator.

Ensign - the national flag.

Ensign - lowest ranking commissioned officer in the US Navy and Coast Guard. Rank is the equivalent of a second lieutenant in the Army, Air Force and Marine

Corps.

E.T. - an electronics technician. An enlisted man responsible for maintaining a ship's electronics system in proper working order.

E.T.A. - estimated-time-of-arrival.

Fantail - the after portion of the main deck. The area near the stern.

Fender - something lowered over a ship's side to protect it from chafing when alongside another ship or pier. It is usually made of canvas or tightly-bound bundles of rope. On smaller ships, rubber tires are commonly used as fenders.

F.C. - a fire-controlman. Men in this enlisted rate are concerned with the aiming of a ship's weapons.

Fire control - shipboard system of directing and controlling gunfire or the launching of torpedoes.

First lieutenant - a ship's officer in charge of the deck force and responsible for the cleanliness and general upkeep of the hull and ship's boats. In the Navy, this is a title and not a rank.

"Fish" - (also "tin fish") - Navy slang for torpedoes.

Foc-sle - (corruption of forecastle) - the section of the main deck near the bow. This area contains the anchor chains and related gear.

Flag bags - large box-like containers, mounted on the port and starboard sides of the signal bridge. They are used for stowage of signal flags and pennants.

Flat hat - Navy blue pancake-shaped woolen hat worn with the enlisted man's winter uniform. It is no longer worn in the US Navy.

Flank speed - faster than full speed, but less than emergency full speed.

Fletcher class - the most numerous class of destroyers built for USN during World War II. The first of the 175 *Fletchers* to commission was the *USS Nicholas, DD-449* (4 June 1942). The last *Fletcher* to receive a commissioning pennant was the *USS Rooks, DD-804* (2 Sept. 1944). Of the 71 American destroyers lost during World War II, 19 were of this class.

Flush deck - a continuous deck running on the same plane from bow to stern.

"Four-pipers" - slang for American destroyers built during the First World War. All such DDs had four smokestacks.

"Four-stripers" - a naval officer holding the rank of captain. Equivalent in rank to a colonel in the Army, Air Force and Marines.

Foremast - the forward mast (usually near the bridge) of a two-masted ship.

Fox - the letter F in the phonetic alphabet.

Fox skeds - log sheets on which all dispatches sent to USN ships at sea are copied by radio operators and kept in the radio shack for a specified time period. Messages pertinent to their own ship are immediately delivered to the communications officer and the C.O.

Friendlies - aircraft positively identified as non-enemy.

Frigates - convoy escorts built during World War II to a British design. Not mounting torpedo tubes or heavy deck armament, they were primarily used in the anti-sub role. Designated PF, the USS Tacoma was class ship for this type.

Gaff - small spar abaft mainmast from which the national ensign is flown when a USN ship is underway.

Galley - a ship's kitchen.

G.A.R. - Grand Army of the Republic - the Union forces in the Civil War.

"Gator navy" - slang for the Navy's amphibious forces.

George - the letter G in the phonetic alphabet.

"Gitmo" - Navy slang for Guantanamo Bay, Cuba.

"Glory bars" - slang for service ribbons (also called "fruit salad").

G.M. - gunner's mate.

"Goldbricking" - service slang for "goofing off", trying to avoid work.

G.Q. - stands for general quarters, that condition aboard ship when all hands are at their battle stations - (see Condition Three).

"Gridiron" - code name for a sector of Wonsan Harbor.

Gun boss - Navy slang for the gunnery officer aboard ship.

Grumman Avenger - a torpedo bomber of World War II vintage. Those built by General Motors were designated TBM. During Ko-War, they served in a variety of roles including that of "hack", ferrying V.I.P. passengers to and from 7th Fleet aircraft carriers.

Gun director - (also fire-control tower) - mounted above the wheelhouse, the director located the target (usually with the help of C.I.C.) The computer, linked to the director, automatically solves the fire-control problem and transmits electrical signals to aim the guns. The gyroscopic stable element provides corrections for the pitch and role of the ship.

Gun plot - located deep down in the ship, gun plot receives range and line-of-sight data transmitted electrically from the gun director. This data is then plotted along with such factors as the ship's course and speed, probable speed of the target, target angle, ballistics, weather conditions, etc.

Gyrene - slang for marine.

Halyard - line used for hoisting signal pennants and other flags.

"Happy Valley" - nickname for USS *Valley Forge*, CVA-45.

Hash mark - slang for service stripe worn on an enlisted man's sleeve (including C.P.O.s). Each stripe signifies 4 years of service.

Handling room - compartment directly below a gun mount or gun turret. It is used to feed ammunition directly to the gun or guns above.

HC ammunition - stands for high capacity. This type of projectile is made with an extremely thin wall and a maximum explosive charge. Designed primarily for bombarding shore positions, its destructive power lies chiefly in fragmentation.

Heckler strikes - air attacks intended to annoy the enemy, harm his morale, and generally keep him off-balance. Most heckler strikes take place at night and are aimed at denying the enemy the chance to rest his troops.

Hedgehog - a box-like apparatus with four rows of spike-like spigots (24 total). Used against submerged submarines, the hedgehog could hurl a projectile from each of these spigots well out in front of the attacking ship. These projectiles, which exploded on contact with the enemy sub, could be fired in a cluster. Although hedgehogs were widely used during World War II aboard destroyer-escorts and frigates, they were not fitted to US destroyers until the late 1940s and the early 50s.

High line - a line stretched between two moving ships. It is used to transfer passengers, mail or supplies from one ship to the other. Such transfers are often made during a replenishment operation.

Holystone - bricks, sand stones or soft sand-rock used for scrubbing the wooden decks of a ship.

Homeward bound pennant - flag flown by a US warship returning to US after being overseas for nine months or more. The flag flies from the time she starts for home until sunset of her first day in a US port. The flag bears a star for the first nine months, and an additional star for each six months. It is one foot long for each man on board, but never longer than the length of the ship.

"Honey barge" - sailor's slang for a garbage lighter.

How - the letter H in the phonetic alphabet.

H.M.C.S. - Her Majesty's Canadian Ship.

H.M.S. - Her Majesty's Ship.

I.F.F. - stands for "identification-friend or foe." It is method of identifying a friendly airplane or ship through a special electronic signal that appears on a radar scope next to the target echo.

"In hack" - a non-judicial punishment imposed upon an officer by his C.O. It calls for the officer to be restricted to specified limits aboard ship, namely his cabin, the head, and the wardroom (at time of meals). While in hack, he is usually suspended from his stipboard duties including watch standing.

Interdiction strikes - those attacks aimed at cutting off an enemy's supplies and reinforcements. Rails, roads and other arteries of transport are the primary targets.

Island - the superstructure of an aircraft carrier.

Item - the letter I in the phonetic alphabet.

Interog - (also interrogatory) - this word is used when you do not understand the meaning of a radio-telephone message or a flag hoist which you have received. It is a request for clarification.

IL-28 - the Ilyshin IL-28 was a twin-jet light bomber which would form the mainstay of the Soviet Bloc's tactical air striking forces during the 1950's.

Jackstaff - the small staff at the bow of a USN ship from which the jack is flown. The jack contained 48 white stars on a field of blue signifying the Union.

"Jarhead" - Navy slang for a marine.

Jaygee (also Jg.) - a lieutenant junior-grade. This is the equivalent of a first lieutenant in the Army, Air Force and Marine Corps.

"Jehovah" - call name used during the Ko-War for the admiral in command of Task Force 77.

Jig - the letter J in the phonetic alphabet.

"Jill" - Allied code name for the Nakajima B6N. Japanese carrier based torpedo bomber used extensively during the last 12 months of World War II.

J.O.D. - the junior-officer-of-the-deck. He assists the officer-of-the-deck in the running of the ship during his watch assignment in the wheelhouse.

"Joe" - Navy slang for coffee.

"Judy" - Allied code for the Yokosuka D4Y, a Japanese Navy dive bomber in service from 1942-45.

Kakuichi Takahashi - a lieutenant commander assigned to the Japanese carrier *Shokaku* during the Pearl Harbor attack. He led the dive bombers against the ships in the harbor. He was killed five months later at the Battle of the Coral Sea.

Kido Butai - Japanese name for the carrier striking force sent against Pearl Harbor.

Kikusui - (means "Floating Chrysanthemum") - the suicide operation launched against US warships off Okinawa. The plan called for a series of coordinated attacks by both Japanese Navy and Army aircraft.

King - the letter K in the phonetic alphabet.

Knot - a measure of speed used for ships and aircraft. A knot equals one nautical mile per hour (about 1.15 statute miles per hour).

KPA - (Korean People's Army) - the North Korean ground forces.

LCM - Landing craft medium.

LCVP - Landing craft vehicle personnel.

Lee - the direction away from the wind.

Lee helmsman - a relief steersman. He often mans the engine-order-telegraph while not at the wheel.

Liberty - authorized absence from ship or station not to exceed 48 hours, however, during the Korean War, this period was often extended by C.O. to 72 hours, especially when personnel were being granted R and R.

"Little Beavers" - nickname given to DesRon 23, which won particular fame for its combat proficiency under the command of Arleigh Burke during the Solomons campaign.

Lifelines - lines stretched fore and aft along the edge of the ship's weather decks to prevent personnel from being lost over the side. They are the "railings" of a ship.

L.O.D. - means "line of departure" during an amphibious operation. Landing craft must be formed up in their respective assault wave prior to reaching the L.O.D. It is during the run in from the L.O.D. that the landing craft and their personnel are most likely to come under fire from shore guns.

"Long lance" - name applied to the highly efficient torpedo carried by Japanese cruisers and destroyers during World War II. This 24-inch torpedo (30 feet long) could far outrange its American counterpart. It also boasted a 1,210-pound explosive charge, compared to the 415 pounds of explosive carried by US Navy torpedoes. It was propelled by oxygen instead of compressed air.

Love - the letter L in the phonetic alphabet.

LST - the Navy designation for a landing ship tank. Personnel aboard these vessels often stated their belief that the letters actually meant "large slow target."

Mariner - name applied to the Martin PBM series of flying boats. These twin-engined, gull-wing patrol bombers first entered squadron service in 1940.

Mast - (see captain's mast).

Mast - the upright spar ("pole") supporting the signal yard and radar antennas on a naval vessel.

Master-at-arms - is usually a chief petty officer assigned to "police" the ship by the executive officer. Master-at-arms is often a collateral duty, especially aboard smaller warships.

Mayday - a distress signal, a call for help.

"Med" - slang for the Mediterranean Sea.

Mess - the area aboard ship where her personnel eat their meals.

Mig - during the Ko-War, this name most often applied to the Russian Mig-15. A single-seat jet fighter with a speed of 683 mph, some 18,000 of this type were built. Migs engaged during Ko-War were flown by Chinese, North Korean and Russian Pilots, the latter primarily serving as formation leaders.

Mike - the letter M in the phonetic alphabet.

"Milk run" - an easy mission, one without enemy opposition.

M.L.R. - stands for "main line of resistance," a static defensive line that stretched 155 miles across Korea from the Sea of Japan to the Yellow Sea. It came into being in November 1951 when General James Van Fleet was forbidden to mount an attack of greater than battalion size without the express permission of higher authority. Thus, a bloody World War I type of warfare, with no appreciable gain in real estate, was forced upon UN ground forces until the Korean armistice was finally signed on 27 July 1953.

Mothball fleet - term applied to vessels deactivated and put into a state of preservation after World War II.

M.P. - military police.

Musashi - she and her sister ship *Yamato* were the two largest and most powerful battleships ever built. Both were sunk by US Navy aircraft.

Nan - the letter N in the phonetic alphabet.

Nautical mile - for purposes of radar plotting, a nautical mile is considered to be 2,000 yards.

Negative - (also "negat") - means "no" in radio-telephone parlance.

Neptune - name applied to the Lockhead P2V, a USN twin-engined land based patrol bomber.

N.R.O.T.C. - Naval Reserve Officer Training Corps.

Oboe - the letter O in the phonetic alphabet.

Officers' country - that portion of the ship set aside for the officers' berthing and messing areas.

O-club - officers' club.

O.O.D. - (also O.D.) - stands for officer-of-the-deck. The officer on watch in charge of the ship. While on watch, he serves as the direct representative of the commanding officer.

Oil king - name applied to the petty officer aboard ship in charge of fuel oil storage.

O.N.I. - the Office of Naval Intelligence..

"On the beach" - Navy slang for being ashore. Beach in this case means land, sandy or otherwise.

Ops - short for "operations".

Oscar - Allied code name for the Nakajima Ki. 43, a single seat Japanese Army fighter used extensively throughout World War II.

Panther - Grumman F9F series of single-seat jet fighters. The most widely used Navy jet of the Ko-War, the Panther was often equipped with bombs and/or rockets and used in the fighter-bomber role. From June 1950 until July of 1953, Navy and Marine Corps Panthers flew more than 78,000 combat missions against the communists.

Paravanes - torpedo-shaped devices streamed out on either side of the ship's bow to cut the cables holding moored mines in place.

Pay out - to increase the amount or length of anchor cable, to ease off or slack a line.

PBM - (see Mariner).

PC - Navy designation for a large class of steel-hulled sub chasers (174' long) also used as escort vessels.

PCE - Navy designation for a patrol craft escort. These 185-foot-long vessels performed a variety of escort duties for the USN in World War II and Korea.

Peter - the letter P in the phonetic alphabet.

Petty officer - the term for a non-commissioned officer in the Navy.

"Pig boat" - Navy slang for a submarine.

"Ping Jockey" - slang for a sonarman.

P.I.O. - Public Information Office or Officer.

Pip-target echo on a radar scope - (see blip).

Piping - the three thin white stripes on the collar and cuffs of a Navy enlisted man's dress blue uniform.

"Pip jockey" - slang for radarman.

P.O.D. - the plan of the day. This is the schedule of the day's routine as ordered by the executive officer with the C.O.'s approval. It is posted prominently throughout the ship.

Pointer - member of a gun crew who controls the elevation of the gun (see trainer). When guns are being aimed remotely from the gun director, the pointer inside the director performs this function.

Pitlog - indicates the speed in knots of a vessel moving through the water. The shipboard equivalent of a "speedometer".

Plank owner - a member of a ship's crew at the time of her first commissioning.

Posit - short for the word position. Often used in navigation.

"Pouncer" - term applied to destroyers stationed between the outer screen of escorts and the main formation of heavy ships. Their function is to attack any submarine which may have managed to slip under the outer screen.

P.P.I. - standard radar scope in use aboard US Navy ships during World War II and the Korean War. P.P.I., which stands for Plan-Position-Indicator, presents the view you would have if you were looking down on your own ship which would be located directly at the center of the scope. The sweep radiating out from the center continuously moves 360 degrees in a clockwise direction.

Prow - the part of the bow above the water.

PT - Navy designation for a motor torpedo boat.

PN - a navy personnel man. He is responsible for general administrative work related to the classification, training, personal benefits and rate advancement of enlisted personnel.

P.U.C. - Presidential Unit Citation - awarded to the crew of a US Naval vessel for outstanding performance in combat.

P.X. - means post exchange. A facility on a military base roughly equivalent to a civilian department store. In the Navy it is often referred to as "Ship's Store" even though it is located on a shore establishment.

Quarterdeck - that area of the ship (usually a portion of the main deck) set aside as the station for the officer-of-the-deck while a ship is in port.

Queen - the letter Q in the phonetic alphabet.

R.C.M. - radar countermeasures - later changed to E.C.M. (electronic countermeasures). Includes the interception and analysis of enemy radar signals, and the jamming of such signals so as to make the enemy's electronic systems ineffective.

RD - Navy designation for a radarman.

Ready deck - term used in radio-telephone transmissions to indicate that a carrier's flight deck is clear and capable of receiving aircraft.

Reefer - a refrigerator aboard ship for storing perishables.

"Regs" - slang for Navy regulations.

Rengo Kantai - Japanese for "Combined Fleer", the name applied to the collective fighting force of warships that made up the Japanese Imperial Navy in World War II.

"Riding Shotgun" - running interference for lesser armed ships such as a destroyer protecting a small minesweeper.

Roger - the letter R in the phonetic alphabet. During radio-telephone transmissions, it means "I have received your message and understand." As a flag hoist, it signifies that the ship is ready for immediate action, or that the ship is ready to put to sea on an instant notice for an emergency.

R.O.K. - Republic of Korea (South Korea).

"Roks" - members of the South Korean armed forces.

R.P.M. - revolutions per minute- refers to how fast a ship's screws (propellers) are rotating, which determines the speed of the ship.

Sabre - the North American F-86. This single-seat Air Force jet fighter established supremacy over the vaunted Mig-15 by the second half of the Korean War when sufficient numbers of the "F"-model entered squadron service.

"Sack" - slang for the thin mattress that served as a sailor's bunk. "His sleep area."

SC - the Sugar Charlie air-search radar. Earliest models of this radar were installed on US warships just prior to the Pearl Harbor attack. The SC-2, the model carried aboard the *Field*, came into service during 1943. It could detect a bomber 80 nautical miles away, a fighter at about half that range.

Scuttlebutt - a drinking fountain aboard ship. It also means a rumor because most rumors aboard ship originated in this area where sailors often congregated. The term goes back to the days of the sailing ship when sailors gathered around the water cask.

Screws - a ship's propellers.

"Seaman deuce" - slang term for a seaman-apprentice. The word deuce stems from the two small stripes worn by a seaman-apprentice or SA.

Sea return - false echoes that clutter up a radar scope and make it difficult to detect a true target. This generally occurs when the sea is rough and causes the radar beam to bounce off the crests of waves.

Secondary conn - an area aboard ship that serves as an auxiliary control area should the wheelhouse be knocked out.

Service jacket - the packet that contains a Navy man's service history, as well as his medical and pay records. It is kept in ship's office and is given to the man to take with him when he reports to another ship or station for a new duty assignment.

SG - the Sugar-George surface radar. Entered USN service in 1942. The model carried by the *Field* was the SG-1 which became operational in 1943. It could detect a very large vessel at 22 nautical miles.

Shadow - indicates a message is being sent in code.

Ship's company - personnel permanently assigned to a ship.

"Shit city" - Navy slang for Norfolk during Ko-War years.

Single up - to reduce the number of lines ("ropes") holding a ship to a pier in preparation to getting underway. This leaves only one easily cast off line in each place along the pier where lines had been doubled up to give the ship a firmer, more secure mooring.

Skyraider - (see AD Skyraider).

Skunk - term used in radar plotting and radio transmissions for an unidentified surface contact.

Skyknight - the Douglas F3D series were the Navy's first jet-propelled night fighters. They carried a pilot and radar operator. Skyknights operating in Korea were assigned to Marine squadrons and did not operate from carriers.

Small boys - term used in radio-telephone transmissions to indicate the smaller ships in a task force, that is the destroyers in the protective screen.

Snipe - Navy slang for the members of a ship's engineering department (see "Black gang).

SNJ - one of the most successful training planes ever built (16,000 constructed in the US, hundreds more overseas) between 1935 and 1945. Various models of the SNJ served the Navy under the name "Texan" as primary, basic and instrument trainers. Some Air Force "Texans" saw combat action as artillery spotting aircraft.

Sonar - is an acronym for Sound-Navigation-and-Ranging, applied to a device used for detecting submerged submarines by emitting vibrations similar to sound waves, and then measuring how long it takes for these vibrations to reach a submerged object and bounce back.

S.O.P.A. - (Senior Officer Present Afloat) - when two or more naval vessels are operating together, it is customary that the senior line officer have overall charge of the combined force. He is referred to as "Sopa".

S.P. - stands for shore patrol, the Navy equivalent of military police.

Spaces - areas aboard ship for certain functions, engine-room, berthing spaces, etc.

Spank - to move briskly or spiritedly.

Spring line - a mooring line leading to the pier at an angle of 45 degrees off the centerline of a vessel. Springs leading forward or aft prevent a vessel from moving aft or forward respectively.

SPR-2 - radar intercept equipment which went into fleet service in 1944. It was basically a receiver unit used in conjunction with a DMB radar direction finder. Such equipment could detect the presence of an enemy ship or plane by picking up the foe's radar signal. This often occurred before the skunk or bogey had been detected on the conventional radar scopes.

Square away - get things in order, settle down.

Squawking friendly - giving off a signal on I.F.F. that shows that the plane or ship is a US or allied unit.

Stern - the after part or rear of a ship.

Stern sheets - the space in a boat or launch abaft the after thwart.

Stern hook - duties similar to those of the bow hook except that he is stationed at the stern of a small boat or launch.

Stow - to put gear away in its proper place.

Striker - an enlisted man or woman below the grade of petty officer. As a designated striker, he or she is allowed to train for a particular naval specialty such as radarman, gunner's mate, boilerman, yeoman, pipe fitter, dental technician, etc.

Sugar - the letter S in the phonetic alphabet.

Sugar Charlie - (see SC).

Sugar George - (see SG).

Summary Court-Martial - if a commanding officer decides an offense deserves a punishment more severe than he is authorized to assign, he may convene a summary court-martial. This court consists of one officer. A summary can give harsher punishments than the C.O. can give at captain's mast. The offender may object to a summary, and thereby obtain a special or general court-martial, depending on what the convening authority deems appropriate.

Sunderland - the Short Sunderland was a 4-engined flying boat used by the Royal Air Force in the Korean War. These patrol bombers performed valuable service in World War II protecting allied convoys from Axis submarines. Sunderlands were the R.A.F.'s principal contribution to the Korean War.

"Swabby - (also "swab jockey") - Marine Corps slang for sailors. Swabs were mops in nautical lingo, and a great deal of a sailor's day in peacetime was devoted to "swabbing" or mopping the decks of his ship.

"Sweet Adelaide" - code name applied to the UN naval patrol that guarded the Yang-do group of coastal islands from communist raiding parties.

"Sweet-P" - nickname for the USS Princeton, CVA-37.

T.A.D. - means temporary additional duty. Term is applied to naval personnel attached to a ship or station for a special purpose. T.A.D.s are usually assigned to a host command for a short duration.

Tare - the letter T in the phonetic alphabet.

TBM - (see Grumman Avenger).

TBS - means talk-between-ships. This World War II term was gradually replaced by the term radio-telephone during Ko-War years. It served as the name for the short-range radio used by ships operating together for the exchange of voice messages. The limited range was advantageous because it prevented interception by enemy radio receivers.

"Tenacious Tanaka" - nickname given Japan's Admiral Raizo Tanaka by US forces engaged in the Solomons campaign. One of the foremost destroyer tacticians in

World War II, Tanaka was acknowledged for his skills and daring by friend and foe alike. In a struggle where American flag officers were not noted for praising their Japanese opponents, Pacific Fleet Commander Admiral Chester W. Nimitz, stated: "Only Admiral Tanaka's skill in keeping his plans disguised, and his bold celerity in carrying them out, enabled the Japanese to withdraw the remnants of their Guadalcanal garrison."

Three striper - The rank of Commander, the Navy's equivalent of a Lieutenant Colonel in the Army, Air Force and Marines.

Uncle - the letter U in the phonetic alphabet.

Victor - the letter V in the phonetic alphabet.

William - the letter W in the phonetic alphabet.

Xray - the letter X in the phonetic alphabet.

Yoke - the letter Y in the phonetic alphabet.

Zebra - the letter Z in the phonetic alphabet.